A TEXT BOOK OF

TRIBOLOGY

(ELECTIVE – I)

FOR
SEMESTER – I

FINAL YEAR (B.E.) DEGREE COURSE IN
MECHANICAL & PRODUCTION ENGINEERING

As Per the New Revised Syllabus of
Savitribai Phule Pune University
(2012 Pattern)

R. R. GHORPADE
M.E. (Mech.), Design Engg.
Assistant Professor,
Mech. Engineering Deptt.,
Maharashtra Institute of Technology,
Kothrud, Pune.

H. G. PHAKATKAR
M.E. (Mech.), Design Engg.
Professor & Head,
Mech. Engineering Deptt.,
Vishwakarma Institute of Technology,
Pune.

N3694

Tribology (B.E. Mech. SEM. I PU) ISBN 978-93-5164-696-9

| First Edition | : | July 2015 |
| © | : | Authors |

Published By :
NIRALI PRAKASHAN
Abhyudaya Pragati, 1312, Shivaji Nagar,
Off J.M. Road, PUNE – 411005
Tel - (020) 25512336/37/39, Fax - (020) 25511379
Email : niralipune@pragationline.com

☞ **DISTRIBUTION BRANCHES**

PUNE

Nirali Prakashan : 119, Budhwar Peth, Jogeshwari Mandir Lane, Pune 411002, Maharashtra
Tel : (020) 2445 2044, 66022708, Fax : (020) 2445 1538
Email : bookorder@pragationline.com, niralilocal@pragationline.com

Nirali Prakashan : S. No. 28/27, Dhyari, Near Pari Company, Pune 411041
Tel : (020) 24690204 Fax : (020) 24690316
Email : dhyari@pragationline.com, bookorder@pragationline.com

MUMBAI

Nirali Prakashan : 385, S.V.P. Road, Rasdhara Co-op. Hsg. Society Ltd.,
Girgaum, Mumbai 400004, Maharashtra
Tel : (022) 2385 6339 / 2386 9976, Fax : (022) 2386 9976
Email : niralimumbai@pragationline.com

☞ **DISTRIBUTION BRANCHES**

JALGAON

Nirali Prakashan : 34, V. V. Golani Market, Navi Peth, Jalgaon 425001,
Maharashtra, Tel : (0257) 222 0395, Mob : 94234 91860

KOLHAPUR

Nirali Prakashan : New Mahadvar Road, Kedar Plaza, 1st Floor Opp. IDBI Bank
Kolhapur 416 012, Maharashtra. Mob : 9850046155

NAGPUR

Pratibha Book Distributors : Above Maratha Mandir, Shop No. 3, First Floor,
Rani Jhanshi Square, Sitabuldi, Nagpur 440012, Maharashtra
Tel : (0712) 254 7129

DELHI

Nirali Prakashan : 4593/21, Basement, Aggarwal Lane 15, Ansari Road, Daryaganj
Near Times of India Building, New Delhi 110002
Mob : 08505972553

BENGALURU

Pragati Book House : House No. 1, Sanjeevappa Lane, Avenue Road Cross,
Opp. Rice Church, Bengaluru – 560002.
Tel : (080) 64513344, 64513355,Mob : 9880582331, 9845021552
Email:bharatsavla@yahoo.com

CHENNAI

Pragati Books : 9/1, Montieth Road, Behind Taas Mahal, Egmore,
Chennai 600008 Tamil Nadu, Tel : (044) 6518 3535,
Mob : 94440 01782 / 98450 21552 / 98805 82331,
Email : bharatsavla@yahoo.com

niralipune@pragationline.com | www.pragationline.com
Also find us on www.facebook.com/niralibooks

PREFACE

It gives us great pleasure in presenting the book on **"Tribology"**, which is strictly written as per New Revised Syllabus (2012 course) of Savitribai Phule Pune University's and in most concised form. The book will also be very useful for the students preparing for Engineering Service Examination and AMIE Examination.

The subject matter is presented in simple and easy form so as to enable the students to understand the subject easily. Sufficient care is taken to present the subject matter in the point wise form in most of the chapters.

It consists of eight chapters, which cover all the syllabus.

This book has been written to satisfy the needs of undergraduate syllabus of the Mechanical and Production Engineering Courses in most of out Universities. The book Comprehensively covers the various aspects of Tribology such as Lubrication and Lubricants, Hydrostatic Squeeze Film and Gas Lubrication, Hydrodynamic Thrust Bearing, Elastohydrodynamic Lubrication, Bearings, Oil Seals, Shields and Gaskets. We are quite sure that this book will serve its purpose very well for all Engineering Students.

Special features of this book are lucid theory, solved examples including examples from University of Pune engineering papers.

We are sincerely thankful to **Shri Dineshbhai K. Furia, Shri. Jignesh C. Furia, Mrs. Nirali Verma, Shri. M. P. Munde** and the entire team of Nirali Prakashan who really have taken keen interest and untiring efforts in publishing this text. We are also thankful to Mrs. Deepali Lachake (Co-ordinator) Mrs. Ulka Chavan, Miss. Rani Zinjade, and Miss. Rajashri Jadhav for their kind co-operation throughout the work.

Also, it is important to mention invaluable moral support of our beloved family members, who consistently encouraged us for better work.

Despite the best efforts taken by authors, it is possible that some unintentional errors might have taken place. Authors would gratefully acknowledge if any of these is pointed out.

Suggestions and comments for further improvement of this book will be gratefully received and acknowledged from the students, teachers and others. Feel free to write to ratnakar.ghorpade@mitpune.edu.in.

Pune

Authors

15th July 2015

SYLLABUS

Unit I : Introduction (8Hrs)

1. Tribology definition.
2. Tribology in design- bearing material its properties and construction Tribological design of oil seals and gasket.
3. Tribology in industry (Maintenance).
4. Lubrication-Definition, basic modes of lubrication, properties of lubricants, additives, EP lubricants, Recycling of used oil, oil conservation, oil emulsion.
5. Bearing Terminology-Types of Sliding contact, rolling contact bearings.
6. Comparison between sliding and rolling contact bearing. (Theoretical treatment only)

Unit II : Friction and Wear (8Hrs)

1. Friction- Introduction, laws of friction, Friction classification, causes of friction.
2. Theories of dry friction.
3. Friction measurement.
4. Stick-slip motion and friction instabilities.
5. Wear-classification, wear between solids, wear between solid and liquids, factors affecting wear.
6. Theories of wear.
7. Wear measurement.
8. Approaches to friction control and wear prevention. (Numerical)

Unit III : Hydrodynamic Lubrication (10Hrs)

1. Theory of hydrodynamic lubrication, mechanism of pressure development in oil film.
2. Two dimensional Reynold's equation and its limitations, Petroff's equation.
3. Infinitely long journal bearing, infinitely short journal bearing and finite bearing, designing journal bearing using Raimondi and Boyd approach.
4. Hydrodynamic thrust bearing-Introduction, types.
5. Flat plate thrust bearing-Pressure equation, load, centre of pressure, frictional force equation.
6. Tilting pad thrust bearing- bearing-Pressure equation, load, centre of pressure, frictional force equation. (Numericals on Raimondi and Boyd approach and thrust bearing only)

Unit IV : Hydrostatic Lubrication (8Hrs)

1. Hydrostatic lubrication-Basic concept, advantages, limitations, viscous flow through rectangular slot, load carrying capacity, flow requirement of hydrostatic step bearing, energy losses, optimum design of stepped bearing, compensators and their actions.
2. Squeeze film lubrication- Basic concept, circular and rectangular plate approaching a plane (Numericals on hydrostatic bearing, Squeeze film lubrication).

Unit V : Elasto-Hydrodynamic Lubrication and Gas (Air) Lubrication (8Hrs)

1. Elasto-hydrodynamic lubrication-Principle and applications, pressure viscosity term in Reynold's equation, Hertz theory, Ertel-Grubin equation, lubrication of spheres.
2. Gas(air) lubricated bearings-Introduction, advantages, disadvantages, applications of tilting pad bearing, hydrostatic and hydrodynamic bearing with air lubrication, Active and passive magnetic bearings(working principle, types and advantages over conventional bearing). (Theoretical treatment only)

Unit VI : Tribological Aspects (10Hrs)

1. Lubrication in rolling, forging, drawing and extrusion.
2. Mechanics of tyre road interaction, road grip, wheel on rail road.
3. Surface engineering for wear and corrosion resistance-diffusion, plating and coating methods, selection of coatings, properties and parameters of coatings.
4. Other bearings-porous bearing, foil bearing, Lobe, hybrid bearing. (Theoretical treatment only)

CONTENTS

Unit - I

Unit - III

Unit - IV

Unit - VI

✠ ✠ ✠

Chapter 1

INTRODUCTION TO TRIBOLOGY

1.1 INTRODUCTION

'Tribology' has been defined as the science and practice of interacting surfaces in relative motion and the practices related there to.

Elements of Tribology :

(a)   Friction.

(b)   Wear

(c)   Lubrication.

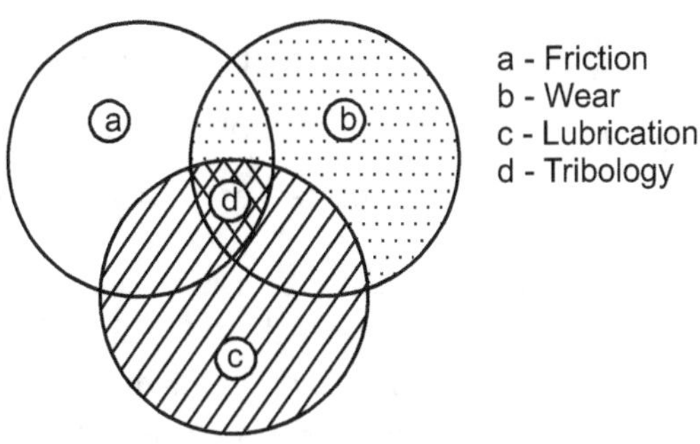

Fig. 1.1 : Elements of tribology

The subject **'Tribology'** generally deals with the technology of **lubrication, friction control** and **wear prevention** of surfaces having relative motion under load. **Friction** is usually classified as a branch of Physics or Mechanical Engineering. **Wear** is often considered to be a part of Metallurgy or Mechanical Engineering. **Lubrication** and Lubricants, which affect friction and wear are considered to be a part of chemistry. However, the surface interaction phenomena are closely related to all the above disciplines. This makes the study of tribology a multi-disciplinary concept. Thus, **tribology is truely an interdisciplinary science and is very useful for its practitioners**. It involves, principally, Mechanical Engineering, Production Engineering, Fluid Dynamics, Chemistry and Chemical Engineering, Material Science and other related topics.

1.2 HISTORY OF TRIBOLOGY

	Principal Investigator	Theory/Laws
(i)	Leonardo da Vinci (1452-1519)	– Deducted a scientific approach to friction. He postulated laws governing the motion of a rectangular block bearing over a flat surface. This work remained unpublished for a long time.
(ii)	Guillaume Amontons	– He rediscovered the laws based on Leonardo da Vinci's Hypothesis. **First** The friction force resisting the sliding at the interface is directly proportional to the normal loads. **Second** The friction force does not depend on the apparent area of contact.
(iii)	Charles-Augustin Coulomb	– Verified Amontons laws and added a third law. **Third** The friction force is independent of velocity once the motion starts.
(iv)	Newton	– Postulated essential laws of viscous flow.
(v)	Robert Hooke	– Suggested the use of contamination of steel shafts and bell-metal bushes as preferable to wood shod with iron for wheel bearings.
(vi)	N. P. Petroff	– Made theoretical interpretations of principles of hydrodynamic lubrication.
(vii)	Beauchamp Tower	– Made experimental studies of principles of hydrodynamic lubrication.
(viii)	Osborne Reynolds	– Studied principles of hydrodynamic lubrication.

1.3 TRIBOLOGY IN DESIGN

Tribology, the collective name given to the science and technology of interacting surfaces in relative motion, is indeed one of the most basic concepts of engineering, especially of engineering design. Successful design of machine elements depends essentially on the understanding of tribological principles. During contact of two nominally flat surfaces, contact occurs at discrete spots due to surface roughness and adhesion occurs due to intimate contact. When one solid body moves over another, it experiences the resistance to motion called **friction.** The surface damage or material removal that take place in a moving contact is termed as **wear.** Surface coatings and treatments are provided to monitor friction and to control wear. The most effective way of friction and wear control is by using proper **lubricants** which can be either **liquid, solid** or **gas.** Thus, **tribodesign** is considered as a branch of machine design concerning all machine elements where friction, lubrication and wear play a significant part.

- **Plain Sliding Bearings :**

When a journal bearing operates in hydrodynamic regime of lubrication, a hydrodynamic film develops. Under these conditions, conformal surfaces are fully separated and a flow of lubricant is provided to prevent overheating. This is the ideal situation (which is not always achieved) where there is a complete separation of two elements having relative motion and hence mechanical wear does not take place.

Sometimes misalignment, may cause metal to metal contact. Moreover, contact may occur at the instant of starting (before the hydrodynamic film has had the opportunity to develop fully), the bearing may be overloaded from time to time and foreign particles may enter the film space.

- **Rolling Contact Bearings :**

In ball bearings and roller bearings, although contact is basically a rolling one, in most cases an element of sliding involved. As in most engineering applications, lubrication of a rolling Hertz contact is undertaken for two reasons – to control the friction forces and to minimise the probability of the contact's failure. The failure control is the most important purpose of rolling contact lubrication.

- **Piston, Piston Rings and Cylinder Liners :**

A piston within a cylinder arrangement is found mainly in engines, pumps, hydraulic motors, gas compressors and vacuum exhausters.

Pistons are normally lubricated although in some cases, notably in the chemical industry, specially formulated piston rings are provided to function without lubrication. Materials based on polymers, having intrinsic self-lubricating properties are frequently used.

A very effective lubrication of the piston assembly (i.e. thick oil film, low friction and no blow-by) could lead to high oil consumption in a internal combustion engine. On the other hand, most of the wear takes place in the vicinity of the top-dead-centre where the combination of pressure, velocity and temperature are least favourable to the operation of a hydrodynamic film.

- **Cam and Cam Followers :**

Although elastohydrodynamic lubrication theory can now help us to understand how cam-follower contact behaves, from the point of view of its lubrication, it is not yet provided an effective design criterion. The cam with the thicker film operates satisfactorily in service whereas the cam with the thinner film fails prematurely.

- **Friction Drives :**

Friction drives, which are being increasingly used in infinitely variable gears, two smooth machine elements should roll together without sliding, while being able to transmit a peripheral force from one to the other. Friction drives normally work in elastohydrodynamic lubrication regime.

- **Involute Gears :**

In really compact designs, which require a high degree of reliability at high operating stresses, speeds or temperatures, the lubricant truely becomes an engineering material. Two concepts of defining adequate lubrication have received some popularity in recent years. One is the minimum film thickness concept and the other is the critical temperature criteria. Involute gears normally work in elastohydrodynamic regime.

- **Hypoid Gears :**

Hypoid gears are normally used in right-angle drives associated with the axles of automobiles. Tooth actions combine the rolling action characteristic of spiral-bevel gears with a degree of sliding which makes this type of gear critical from the point of view of surface loading. Successful operating of a hypoid gear is dependent on the provision of the so-called **extreme pressure oils** i.e. oils containing additives which form surface protective layers at elevated temperatures.

- **Worm Gears :**

Worm gears represent a fairly critical situation in view of the very high degree of relative sliding. From the wear point of view, the only suitable combination of materials is phosphor-bronze with hardened steel. Also essential is a good surface finish and accurate, rigid positioning. Lubricants used to lubricate a worm gear usually contain surface active additives and the prevailing mode of lubrication is mixed or boundary lubrication. Therefore, the wear is mild and probably corrosive as a result of the action of boundary lubricants.

Thus, from all above discussions, it clearly follows that the engineer responsible for the tribological aspect of design must be expected to be able to analyze the situation with which he is confronted and bring to bear the approximate knowledge for its solution.

1.4 BEARING MATERIALS

1.4.1 Introduction

There would be no problem in the selection of a bearing material if the operating conditions in a bearing were ideal. If the rubbing surfaces of a bearing were always separated by a film of lubricant, if there were no elastic or thermal distortions, no roughness of surfaces and no grit or other abrasive particles in the lubricant, in that case almost anything would serve as a bearing material. Therefore, the only consideration would be to select a material of sufficient strength. Sometimes, the conditions of operation may be such that complete fluid films are not developed to separate the rubbing surfaces. Some bearings must be operated under conditions that prevent the formation of fluid films. Some important properties need to be taken into account while selecting a suitable material for a particular application of bearing.

These properties are a measure of mechanical, metallurgical and chemical characteristics of bearing materials that have been found essential.

1.4.2 Desirable Properties of Bearing Materials

Following standard requirements are taken into account while selecting a suitable bearing material for a particular application. These are considered as desirable properties of bearing materials.

- Score resistance.

- Mutual solid solubility.

- Compressive strength.

- Fatigue strength.

- Deformability :

  (a) Conformability

  (b) Embeddability

  (c) Bondability

- Corrosion resistance

- Structure

- Thermal properties :

  (a) Thermal conductivity

  (b) Thermal expansion

- Cost and availability.

- **Score Resistance :**

Bearing material should not damage the journal surface when operating under the condition of boundary lubrication. Some materials have a tendency to adhere or weld to the shaft if the fluid-film conditions break down. Thus, bearing materials which operate with low friction, display low score resistance.

'Score resistance is defined as the antiweld or antiseizure characteristics of a bearing material and not the action of cutting or grooving of a bearing material by dirt or foreign matter'.

Table 1.1 shows score resistance of some metals.

Table 1.1 : Score Resistance of Some Metals

Score Resistance	Metals
Good	Silver, Cadmium, Tin, Lead
Fair	Carbon, Copper, Selenium
Poor	Magnesium, Aluminium, Copper, Zinc, Barium, Tungsten
Very poor	Beryllium, Silicon, Calcium, Titanium, Chromium, Iron, Cobalt, Nickel, Gold, etc.

- The bearing may score or wipe on the shaft surface if the score resistance is not sufficiently high.

- When score resistance is a primary requirement, white metals are used which includes both the tin-base and lead-base alloys.

- Improved resistance to scoring is obtained at the expense of hardness and strength.

- Sometimes, special bearing materials are used as score resisting materials e.g. silver, trimetal types, gridded bearings, aluminium bronzes.

- **Mutual Solid Solubility :**

Mutual solid solubility promotes adhesion, surface welding and consequently wear and high friction.

- Copper, zinc and gold have poor score-resistance against steel and are in the B-subgroup of metals. They have relatively high solubility.

- Magnesium, calcium and barium have low solubility and have poor score-resistance and are in the A-subgroup.

- **Compressive Strength :**

It is the ability of the bearing material to carry the imposed load without extrusion or disintegration.

The bearing material should have high compressive strength to withstand the maximum pressure (which is much greater than the average pressure i.e. load per unit projected area) and to prevent this extrusion or disintegration of the bearing.

- **Fatigue Strength :**

Sometimes, the load is variable either in magnitude or direction or both the corresponding variables. Stresses imposed upon the bearing material introduces the condition of fatigue. Thus, in certain applications like automotive and stationary engines, bearings are subjected to high fluctuating loads. The bearing materials in that case should possess sufficient endurance strength to avoid the fatigue failure.

e.g. Fatigue strength of bronze without a steel backing is high.

Table 1.2 shows order fatigue strength of typical bearing metals.

Table 1.2 : Order Fatigue Strength of Typical Bearing Metals

Metals	Order of Fatigue Strength
Bronzes	1
Copper lead with tin or silver	2
Thin-babbitt	3
Aluminium alloys	4
Copper-lead	5
Cadmium alloys	6
Lead and tin-base babbitts	7

- **Deformability :**

Some of the operating conditions which have more influence on the imposition of fluctuating load that leads to deformation and in turn total failure are –

- Time.

- Temperature : High operating temperatures sharply reduce the strength of many bearing materials.

- Design of bearing housing.

- The amount of flexibility in both the shaft and bearing backing : Relatively soft bearing materials when used in thin layers over stronger backing materials, result in increased strength.

Order of deformability is exactly opposite to that of the order of fatigue strength as given in Table 1.1.

It can be explained with the following three properties.

- **Conformability :** It is the ability of a bearing material to yield to deformation while operating, without causing failure. Thus conformability is the ability of the bearing material to yield and adjust itself or adopt its shape to that of the journal. When loads are applied to the structure the bearings and journals deflect, often leading to edge contact. If the bearing material is conformable, it will adjust itself by wearing or wiping without causing a serious high temperature condition to develop.

   e.g. Tin-base babbitt develops superfacial softening at the points of high friction, wipes locally, relieves itself and settles down to an extended period.

- **Embeddability :** 'It is the ability of the bearing material to embed small dust, dirt, hard-metal particles and other foreign material without scoring the journal'.

When dirt enters the clearance space, it must embed itself in the relatively soft bearing material or jam itself into the clearance space between a hard bearing material and the shaft and cut or gauge a groove in the bearing and shaft. The bearing material should be soft and should have high embeddability characteristics to allow these foreign particles to get embedded in the lining.

- **Bondability :** 'It is the ability of the bearing material to form strong bonds with the mating material'.

  For high capacity applications, bearings are made by bonding one or more thin layers of bearing material to a high strength steel shell. Thus, the bondability of the bearing material is an important consideration while selecting suitable bearing material for such type of construction.

- **Corrosion Resistance :**

At high operating temperatures oxidation of lubricating oil takes place, thereby deteriorating the surface of the bearing and resulting in the formation of acid. This acid attacks vigorously with disastrous results. This deterioration is termed as corrosion. Hence, the bearing material should have sufficient resistance against such kinds of failure due to corrosion.

The danger of bearing corrosion can be greatly diminished by inhibited oils which resist the formation of corrosive acids.

e.g. In applications like engine bearings.

Table 1.3 shows corrosion resistance for different bearing metals.

Table 1.3 : Corrosion Resistance for Metals

Corrosion Resistance	Metals
Non-corrodible	Al-alloys, Tin-base babbitt, lead-base babbitt, cadmium-indium alloys, bronze (low lead).
Intermediate	Bronzes (high lead), copper-lead, Alkali-hardened lead, silver.
Corrodible	Cadmium alloys.

- **Structure :**

Structure is of great importance. Since a particular structure for each type of bearing material gives the best performance. A good bearing material should possess a duplex structure with hard particles supported in a soft matrix. e.g. in a tin-base babbitt where hard crystals of tin, copper and antimony are supported in a soft, tin-rich matrix.

The hard particles in the duplex structure of the babbitt contribute very little to the load-supporting capacity of the material. With white metal-alloys, the basic frictional properties are determined essentially by the softer matrix material itself and the hard particles have little influence.

● **Thermal Properties :**

The bearing material should possess good thermal properties as given below.

(a)   Thermal Conductivity : The bearing material should possess high thermal conductivity so as to dissipate heat developed in the bearing rapidly.

(b)   Thermal Expansion : For bearing operating under wide range of temperatures, the bearing material should have low coefficient of thermal expansion. There is no undue change in clearance.

● **Cost and Availability :**

The selection of a proper bearing material may be influenced by the cost and by the availability of the material. Therefore, the bearing material should have reasonable cost and should be easily available. Table 1.4 gives some of the commercial bearing metals with the approximate order of increasing cost.

Here, it is difficult to find all the above stated properties to a reasonable level in any single bearing material. Therefore, the bearing material should be selected from the various bearing materials available, depending upon the requirements of the actual service conditions.

Table 1.4 : The Approximate Order of Increasing Cost of Commercial Bearing Metals

Metals	Order of Cost
Bronze bushing	1
Lead-base babbitt	2
Tin-base babbitt	3
Sintered copper-nickel with lead babbitt	4
Aluminium alloys (solid)	5
Cadmium alloys	6
Copper-lead	7
Copper-lead with thin overlay	8
Aluminium-alloy with thin overlay	9
Silver with thin overlay	10

1.5 TYPES OF BEARING MATERIALS

For successful operation of a bearing system, it is necessary to select proper material for a particular application. Following are the important bearing materials which are commonly used.

1.5.1 Bearing Materials : Metallic Group

1.   Babbitts (white metals)

(i)   Lead-base babbitt

(ii)   Tin-base babbitt

2. Bronze

3. Copper-lead alloys

4. Aluminium alloys

5. Silver

6. Cast-iron

7. Porous Metal Bearings (Sintered Metal Bearings)

8. Hard materials

1. Babbitts (White Metals)

These prove to be excellent bearing materials. They have a silvery appearance and are generally called 'white' metals or babbitt metals. Babbitts are used where score resistance is a primary requirement. Babbitts can be classified into two categories :

- Lead-base babbitt and

- Tin-base babbitt.

Table 1.5 shows the typical composition of these two categories.

Table 1.5 : Composition of Babbitts

Constituent Elements	Types of Babbitts	
	Lead-Base Babbitt	Tin-Base Babbitt
Lead	74	0.5
Tin	9.25 – 10.75	86.0
Antimony	14 – 16	6.0 – 7.5
Copper	0.5	5 – 6.5
Others (Iron, Arsenic, Bismuth, Zinc, Aluminium)	1.0	0.5

(i)   The babbitts are to a large extent the standard of desirability for bearing materials in many applications as discussed earlier.

(ii) The babbitts possess excellent bondability, embeddability and comformability but relatively weak fatigue strength, especially at temperature above 121°C.

(iii) Tin-base babbitt is able to wipe locally, relieve any high spots or areas of metallic contact and then reform its contour so as to reestablish fluid-film condition.

(iv) Tin and lead-base babbitts are non-corrodible as tin-base babbitt is one of the most resistant of all the possible bearing materials.

(v) Effects of Lining Thickness on Fatigue Life :

- They are bonded as a thin layer or many thin layers over backing material; like bronze or steel. This results in increased strength with softer bearing material.

- Fig. 1.2 shows a comparison of the life of a bearing under a mean load of 13.79 MPa against varying thickness of white-metal bearing alloys. A graph is plotted from the test results run under accelerated laboratory conditions.

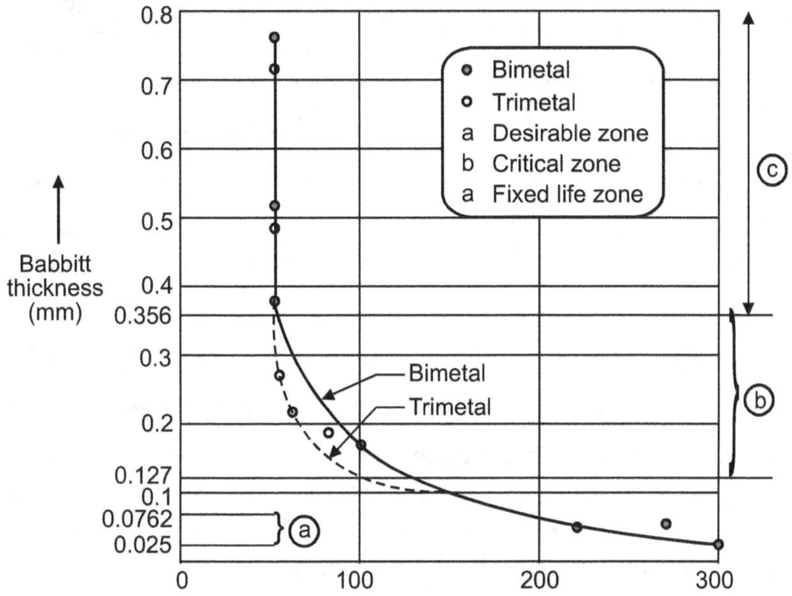

Fig. 1.2 : Bearing life vs. babbitt thickness

- **Fixed-Life Zone :** It is clear that in the thickness range (0.813 mm to 0.356 mm), variation in lining thickness has no effect on the bearing life. It is found to be upto 55 hours.

- **Critical Zone :** The thickness ranging from (0.356 mm to 0.127 mm) there is a very noticeable increase in bearing life. This is called a critical zone. The ultimate gain is reached in the region where the thickness varies from 0.127 mm to 0.0254 mm.

- **Desirable Zone :** For the thickness variation from (0.0762 mm to 0.025 mm) there is ultimate gain in bearing life called as desirable zone.

(vi) Effect of Temperature on Strength and Hardness of Babbitt : High operating temperature sharply reduces the strength of babbitts. Hardness reduces by 50% as temperature rises to 121°C especially in automotive work.

2.   Bronzes :

These are most common types of bearings and used where service conditions in terms of load, speed and temperature are moderate. Bronze is an alloy of copper and tin. It is used as machined bush pressed into a shell. The bush may be in one piece or split.

Table 1.6 shows composition of two variables of bronzes, which are commonly used as bearing materials.

Table 1.6 : Composition of Bronzes

Constituent Elements	Composition %	
	Gun Metal	Phosphor Bronze
Copper	87-88	89-90
Tin	10	9-10
Lead	0.3	–
Zinc	2.0	–
Nickel	1.0	–
Phosphorus	–	0.3

Advantages :

- Due to their adequate bearing properties, they are used for most of the applications.

- They have great strength and are helpful if the speeds and temperatures are not so high.

- They can be easily and economically fabricated in special flanged designs as well as in the simple cylindrical forms. Thus they have excellent casting and machining characteristics. They can be made as a single, solid unit with no bond to fail and no lining to wear through. Thus they are highly reliable.

- The thick walls of bronze provide an adequate reserve for wear which is the basic consideration for industrial machinery exposed to abrasive or contaminating condition.

Disadvantages :

- It has a tendency to adhere to the shaft surface at higher temperatures. When the temperature increases as a result of heavy load, high rubbing speeds and poor lubricating conditions, steel journals get overheated until they turn blue and the bronze gets scored and adheres to the shaft. Therefore, bronze bushings are used for milder applications where mildness is measured in terms of moderate speeds, loads and temperature.

- Compared with babbitts, it has poor conformability and embeddability.

Applications :

They are used in applications like bushings, gears, pump impellers, guides, cams and wire drawing dies where strength is combined with good friction and wear characteristics.

3.   Copper-Lead :

These materials are made from a mixture of copper and lead and often with small amounts of other elements like tin, nickel, zinc, iron, etc.

Table 1.7 gives the composition of copper and lead.

Table 1.7

Constituent	Composition %
Copper	55-75%
Lead	25-45%

- They are used where loads are higher than that which can be carried by babbitts.
- They are produced by casting or by sintering the powdered metals, which result in a continuous phase of copper with unalloyed lead dispersed through it.
- They are bonded in thin layers to a backing of steel.

Advantages :

- They have high compressive strength combined with high fatigue strength.
- They are used in heavy duty applications at high temperatures.

Disadvantages :

The conformability of the copper-lead bearing is lower than that of the babbitts. Also, they possess average embeddability. Therefore, they are used for applications with rigid shafts where deflection and end rubbing are less of a problem. The conformability characteristics can be improved by using 'Trimetal construction'.

Trimetal Bearings :

The construction of a bearing obtained by depositing a thin overlay of lead-base babbitt on the copper-lead which improves conformability characteristics of bearing is called as 'Trimetal bearing'. The constructional features of trimetal bearings can be explained with the following figure.

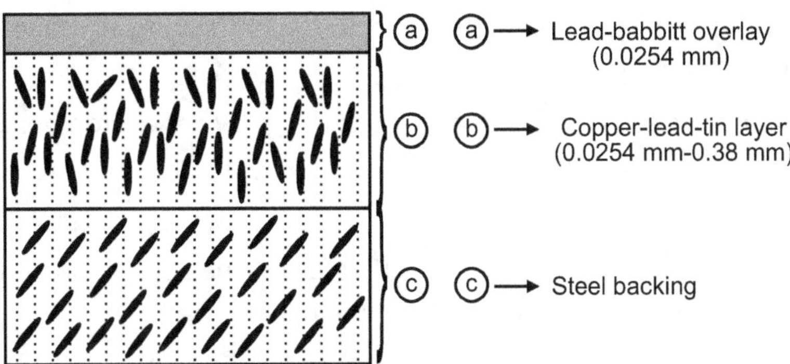

Fig. 1.3 : Trimetal bearing material

- In trimetal bearings, a layer of copper-lead whose thickness varies from 0.254 mm to 0.38 mm is bonded to a thick steel backing.

- Then an overlay of lead babbitt about 0.0254 mm thick is precision plated on the copper-lead.

- The resulting construction produces one of the highest load-carrying plain bearing.

- For thin babbitt overlays, the load varies from limits 13.8 MPa to 27.6 MPa.

  e.g. Moraine - 100 Bearing.

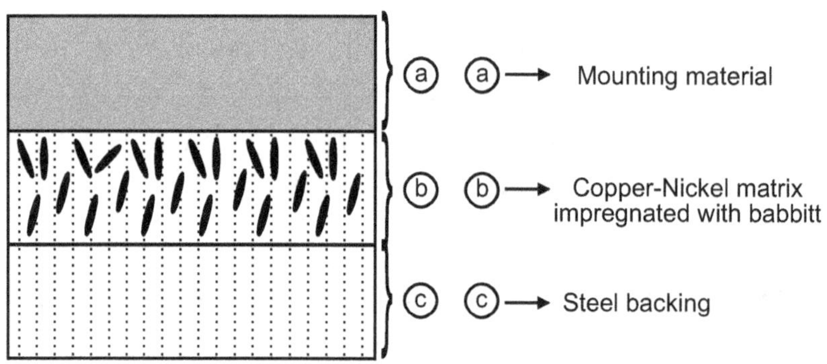

Fig. 1.4 : Moraine - 100 trimetal bearing

- It is manufactured by Moraine Products Division of General Motors.

- A mechanical mixture of pure copper and nickel powder is applied to a steel backing. Then this combination is passed through a furnace. As the copper melts in the reducing atmosphere of the furnace, it brazes the powder to the steel.

- The alloying of the copper and nickel continues till the layer of powder develops a fine porous texture.

- Matrix of copper and nickel is formed on the steel backing and is consequently given a precision rolling.

- Then, it is allowed to pass through a vacuum impregnating machine which fills the pores of the matrix with babbitt.

- The matrix supports the babbitt on its surface and provides a large bond area for both chemical and mechanical bonding.

Application :

This bearing has proved to be an excellent bearing for engine applications where it provides high strength with good conformability and embeddability.

4.   Aluminium Alloy :

Aluminium when alloyed with small amounts of tin, nickel, copper, silicon or cadmium performs very well (Refer composition of type 750). Table 1.8 shows the percentage composition of the three typical aluminium alloys.

Table 1.8 : Percentage Composition of Three Typical Al-alloys

Constituents	Composition % of Types of Al-Alloys		
Al	91.5	89.5	95
Sn	6.5	6.5	0
Ni	1	0.5	0
Cu	1	1	0
Si	0	2.5	4
Cd	0	0	1.0

Advantages :

- **Good Fatigue Strength :** They possess good fatigue strength and yield strength when solid or backed by steel.

- **High Thermal Conductivity :** It has good thermal conductivity which is highly advantageous in conducting heat away from the bearing surface, the source of heat being to friction. This is specifically important for bearings that are not supplied with a sufficient amount of lubricant for cooling purposes. Generally, the bearing operating with mixed or boundary lubrication fall into this category.

- **e.g. Al-Alloy - GM 3889 M :** It is backed by steel and carries a lead-tin copper overlay of about 0.0254 mm thickness.

  - The layer of lead-tin-copper reduces the possibility of corrosion and improves ductility and score resistance.

  - The copper gives the overlay higher load-carrying capacity.

  - It provides excellent service life in engine bearings with unit loads upto 27.5 MPa, average pressure.

Disadvantages :

- **Poor Embeddability :** Al-alloyed bearings have poor embeddability characteristics as compared to that of babbitt.

- **High Thermal Stressing :** For high temperature applications, the expansion of the aluminium alloy may cause high thermal stresses exceeding the elastic limit in compression of the material and resulting in permanent plastic deformation on cooling. The aluminium alloy shrinks and may cause tensile failure cracks. Therefore, Al-alloys should not be used for temperature between 107 to 149°C.

- **Limited Use on Rail Road Axles :** Al-alloyed bearings are being used to a limited extent for rail road axle bearing specially on Italian rail roads.

5.   Silver :

They are commonly used in aircraft applications. Pure silver has certain disadvantages.

Disadvantages :

- The performance of silver as a bearing material is not considered to be satisfactory and found to be quite erratic.
- Pure silver has poor score resistance and a low degree of embeddability.
- They have relatively low conformability.
- Cost of silver is high.

To overcome the above problems, the following remedy is suggested.

Overlay of Lead or Lead-Indium on Steel Backing, Improves Embeddability : Performance of silver bearing can be improved by giving an overlay of a soft material such as lead or lead-indium. This makes it more reliable. Most silver bearings are electroplated on a steel backing, annealed and after final machining the bearing surface is given a thin coating of lead or lead-indium of approximately 0.0254 mm thickness. The surface overlays greatly improves the embeddability properties.

Advantages :

- **Increase in Fatigue Resistance :** Under repeated stresses, silver bearings are superior to all other standard materials. Thus, bearing material have high fatigue resistance and they have replaced copper-lead bearings in certain aircraft engine master connecting rod applications with considerable increase in fatigue life.
- **High Thermal Conductivity :** Silver bearings possess excellent thermal conductivity.

6.   Cast-Iron :

- It is one of the oldest bearing materials. It is used for relatively light-duty applications.
- It has been suggested that clearances on cast-iron bearings should be a little larger than usual so that if hard particles are torn loose from the cast-iron, they will not tend to jam the clearance space.
- Steel journals have run successfully against cast-iron if the hardness of the journal is in the range from 150 to 250 Brinell.
- The hardness of cast-iron restricts its use to the applications where edge rubbing or shaft deflections are held to a minimum, i.e. the applied load must be light and the alignment between shaft and bearing can be carefully maintained.

7.   Porous Metal Bearings (Sintered Metal Bearings) :

- These bearings are used when plain metal bearings are impracticable because of lack of space or inaccessibility for lubrication.

- They are made of powdered metals which are pressed in dies. After compression, they are sintered at a high temperature in a reducing atmosphere. The sintering operation causes the powdered metal bearings to fuse into a strong compact.

- After the sintering process is over, the bearings are submerged in oil for impregnation and finish-sized in a punch press to close tolerances.

The flow diagram of sintering process is given below.

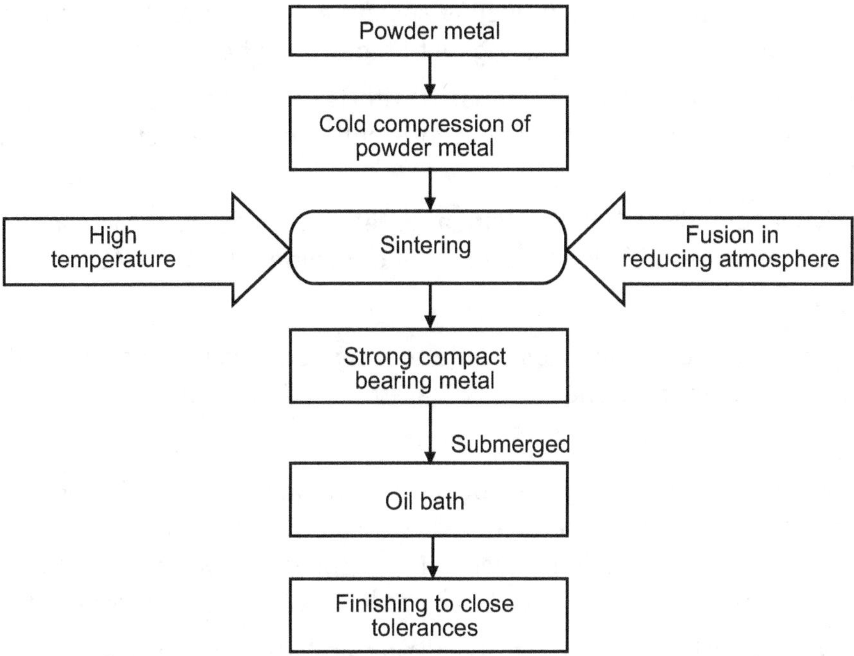

Fig. 1.5

- Following are the varieties of sintered bearings :
  - Iron-base sintered bearings
  - Copper-base sintered bearings

- Sintering temperature for two different powder metals are given below.

Powder Metals	Sintering Temperature
Bronze powder	815°C
Iron (plus copper) powder	1093°C

- Porous bearing is strong and contains voids into which the non-gumming lubricant (which is strongly resistant to oxidation) is drawn. These voids may vary from 16% to 36% of the volume of the bearing.

- For Bronze bearings, lubricant with viscosities 250 to 350 SUS are recommended, and impregnated with graphite, molybdenum disulphide, grease or wax, with 85.5°C maximum suggested temperature. Lubricant may be supplied by wicks or drop-feed oilers to the outside of the bearing housing and by capillary action.

- These bearings are suitable for light loads and moderate speeds. These bearings will tend to build up a thinner hydrodynamic fluid-film than a solid bearing because of the porosity of the material.

- The principle applications for porous metal bearings are probably limited to less than 140 kPa average pressure and moderate speeds, as heating of these bearings is always a problem since there is no circulating oil to remove the heat.

  - Teflon - porous metals impregnated with teflon at light loads and speeds, show that coefficient of friction is 0.05 consistently upto temperatures of approximately 250°C.

  - Molybdenum disulphide – With a sintered copper porous bearing containing molybdenum disulphide, the coefficient of friction is 0.13 to 0.15 upto 300°C.

Applications :

Pedal bushings, water pump bearings, guide bearings on small generators and distributor shafts, vacuum cleaner motors. They are also called less-oil bearings.

8.   Hard Materials :

In certain applications, with a high temperature and with the use of lubricants with low viscosity and little natural oiliness perhaps with operations where no lubricant are present. Hard materials are used as bearing material. If the speed is low and wear is an important factor, then both surfaces should be hard. The harder the material, the lesser is the wear.

Minimum total wear takes place when the sliding and stationary surfaces have the same degree of hardness.

e.g.

- Refractory materials and ceramics.

- In case, where there is shortage of high grade cast-iron, surface plates are made of glass, granite and ceramics, or fine grains of crystalline fused alumina bonded with a glass-type bond and containing 10-15% of very fine pores. Also, surface plates are made of glass bonded silicon carbide grains called as 'Crystolon'.

1.5.2 Bearing Materials : Non-metallic Group

1.   Carbon-graphite
2.   Ceramics and cermets
3.   Plastics
4.   Rubber
5.   Wood

1.   Carbon - Graphite :

- These bearings have self-lubricating qualities, they are chemically inert and can tolerate wide range of temperatures in air as well as in inert atmosphere.

- These bearings are available in simple or complex sleeve or split type, and can be pressed fit, shrink fit or mechanically fitted to shaft housing. They can be soft-metal plated for anchoring to cast or may be rubbed coated for self-alignment.

Applications :

- Graphite is combined with carbon or impregnated with metals such as babbitt to produce bearings, machine-elements and seals in a wide variety of shapes and sizes.

- As graphite can tolerate temperatures of 370°C to 400°C in air and upto 650°C in inert atmosphere, they are extensively used in ovens, driers, strokers and conveyors where temperatures are high to allow the use of ordinary lubricated bearings.

- Since graphite is chemically inert, it is suitable for acidic environment and in process fluids, which would otherwise corrode ordinary bearing materials.

- Carbon-graphite bearings are used in pump handling molten salt at 650°C, piston, piston rings, pump blades, seal rings, valve parts.

- Graphite bearings are also found in water pumps, gasoline pumps, fuel oil pumps, meters, mixers and rotary filters.

2.   Ceramics and Cermets :

- These materials have superior wear resistance.

- They are bonded with metals using cobalt as a binder to improve the ability to handle impact and shock loading.

- One major disadvantage associated with ceramics is that they have relatively high friction which may be a problem in gyroscopes instrument. The electric motor drive is small and light and has low starting torque. Unless the friction of the bearing material is low enough, the motor will not start and will stall.

By introduction of some form of boundary lubrication, the friction in ceramic bearing can be reduced to great extent.

e.g. Experimental study shows that if the final grinding of the ceramics is done in a bath of a boundary lubricant, a modification in surface is achieved which provides lower friction. Table 1.9 gives two typical ceramics with bath of boundary lubricants used.

Table 1.9 : Ceramic with Particular Bath of Boundary Lubricant

Type of Ceramic	Type of Boundary Lubricant Used
• Silicon nitride	Octadecanoic armide
• Glass ceramics (e.g. Pyroceram)	Dioctedecyl disulphide

3.   Plastics :

It is one of the important non-metallic bearing materials incorporated in bearings of industrial machinery. It provides better overall performance, and has the following advantages.

- It has lower coefficient of friction and less wear characteristics.

- It provides good resistance to impact and vibration.

- Plastic performs well with water as a lubricant, so that for these applications copious sprays of water can be used for both lubrication and cooling.

- Cost of plastic bearing is quite low.

Plastic has some disadvantages which are listed below.

- On contact with liquids it swells. Thus the volumetric stability of a particular plastic is a matter of consideration. This can be reduced to some extent by enlarging the initial clearance of the bearing.

- Plastics can operate satisfactorily for a temperature below 93.5°C. Softening of the plastic and its adherence to shaft occurs above this temperature limit.

- Plastic has poor thermal conductivity. Therefore special attention must be given to carry away heat that is generated by friction at plastic bearing surface and journal interface.

e.g.

Telfon :

It is the most well-known plastic. The term polytetrafluroethylene (PTFE) is known as Teflon. The structure is quite similar to polyethylene except that the hydrogen atoms are replaced by fluorine atoms.

Advantages :

- It has excellent low-friction characteristics, due to its low adhesion tendency with the other materials. Therefore, it has been used as a surface coating on skiis in place of wax.

- Telfon can be incorporated into the surface of porous metals such as sintered bronze or porous chrome, or filling teflon with a matrix such as fibre-glass. Thus, the resulting material has mechanical and thermal properties of a metal or the filler and the surface properties of teflon.

- A bronze-sintered bearing impregnated with teflon shows a coefficient of friction as low as 0.05, resulting in great influence on wear rate.

Disadvantages :

- It is not mechanically strong.

- It is a poor conductor of heat.

- It has a high coefficient of thermal expansion.

These difficulties are almost overcome to large extent.

4.   Rubber :

Rubber is a good bearing material, under circumstances where abrasive material may be present in the lubricant. Generally, water is used as a lubricant and it also serves as coolant. It finds wide applications in the stern tube bearings of ships, on a number of centrifugal pumps, and for shafting bearings on deep-well pumps. Fluted bearings are most common. Constructional features of it show a number of parallel surfaces to support the shaft in line with the axis of the shaft. The faces are separated by longitudinal grooves for the passage of the lubricant. The faces of the ribs are rounded so as to prevent no wiping edge to remove the hydrodynamic water film as it is built up. It is shown in Fig. 1.6.

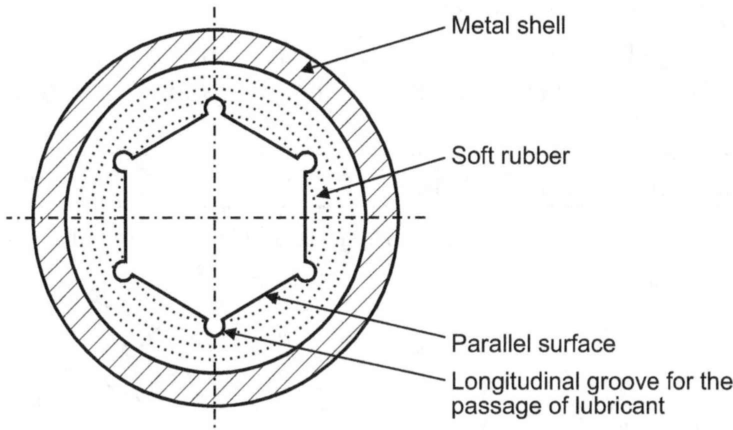

Fig. 1.6 : Fluted rubber bearing

Advantages :

- The bearing is immune to the action of sand and grit.

- It has good resilience in yield to the sand grain or abrasive particles.

- Plain cylindrical rubber bearings have coefficient of friction as low as 0.001 with minimum value of $\left(\dfrac{\mu N}{P}\right)$ of about 25.

- Rubber bearings are most effective at speeds above 500 r.p.m. and with loads limited to 1.4 MPa based on the projected area.

- Rubber bearings effectively reduce vibration and noise and compensate for misalignment, which is useful for high speed operation.

- They have high degree of comformability and embeddability characteristics.

5.   Wood :

It has varieties of applications as mentioned below.

Light-duty machinery and apparatus employ small impregnated hard maple wooden bearings.

Heavy-duty operations employ lignum vitae, which have the following properties :

- It is hardest self-lubricating and most dense of all woods.
- It will not float in water as the grain is very closely interwoven, giving the material high resistance to wear and compression and thus difficult to split.
- It is also non-contaminating so that it can be used for machine parts and bearings in chemical process and food industries.
- It is used successfully in contact with salty water, mild acids and alkalies, oils and bleaching compounds, liquid phosphorus and many food and drug and cosmetic compounds.

1.6 BEARING CONSTRUCTIONS

Two basic types of bearing constructions are generally in use, as solid bushing and lined bushing.

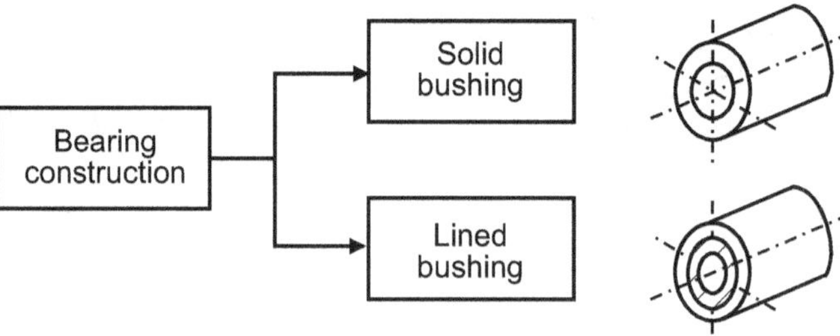

Fig. 1.7

(i)   Solid Bushing :

It can be manufactured from a round bar or can be produced by casting process as a single cylindrical unit with central bore and finally, finished to required size by grinding and reaming operations.

Fig. 1.8 shows the solid bushing.

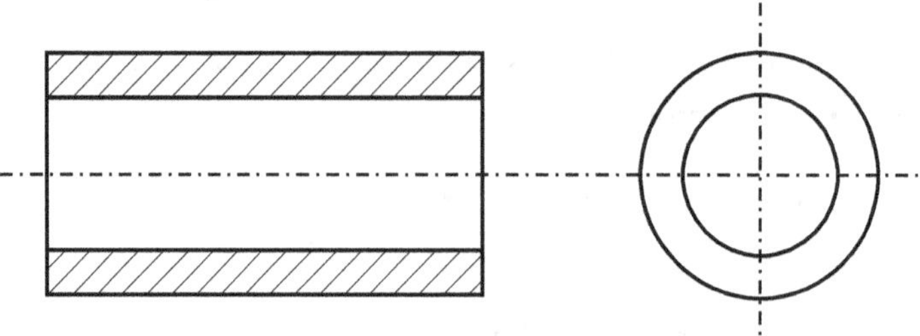

Fig. 1.8 : Solid bushing

e.g. Bronze bearing is a particular example of this type of bushing. When worn out, it can be replaced as a whole element.

(ii)   Lined Bushing :

It is similar to solid bushing but has an additional ring inside, generally of babbitt (white metal) material. The outer ring is made up of steel. Thus, babbitt is backed by outer steel bush. Therefore, it is called as lined bushing or simply liners in automotive.

Fig. 1.9 shows the lined bushing.

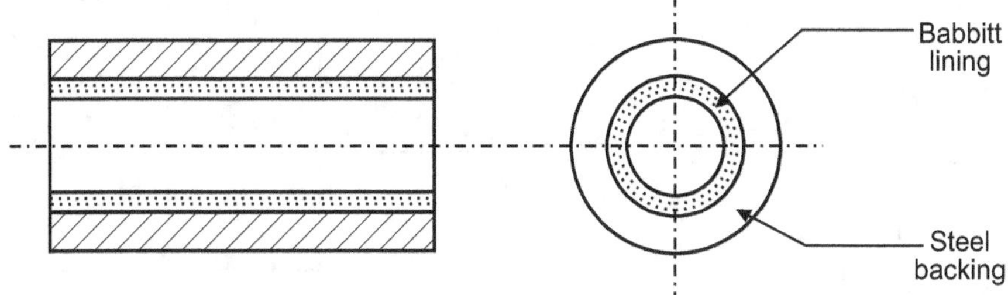

Fig. 1.9 : Lined bushing

Usually, lined bushing is split into two halves and is provided with a locking element which prevents the axial as well as rotational movement of the bearing with respect to the bushing.

Types of Patterns of Oil Grooves :

Suitable positioning and locating an oil groove in the bearing is very much essential to have better performance of the bearing. There are various patterns of oil grooves in the bearings to serve this purpose. Groove have often been placed in bearings with the result that they scrap off the oil and interrupt the film.

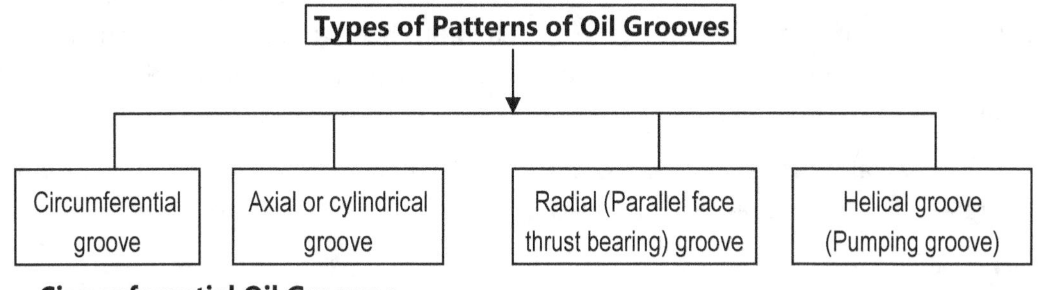

•   Circumferential Oil Groove :

It distributes lubricant around the shaft at the oil hole when placed at the ends of a bearing. They act as collector rings and salvage the lubricant that is ordinarily forced out at the ends of the bearing.

This is shown in Fig. 1.10.

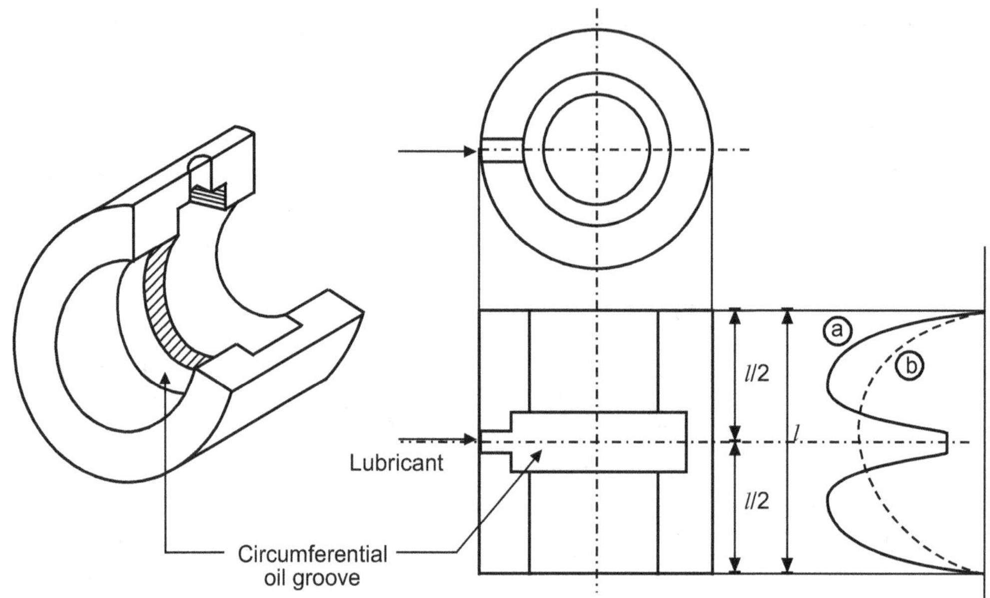

(a) Bearing with groove, (b) Bearing without groove

Fig. 1.10 : Circumferential oil groove

It divides the bearing into two small bearings each of length $\left(\dfrac{l}{2}\right)$, where l is total length of the bearing. In this type of construction of oil groove pattern, the pressure developed in the bearing along the axis is reduced due to the groove pattern which affects the load-carrying capacity. Thus the load-carrying capacity decreases. But in general, the flow through a journal bearing with a circumferential groove will be greater than the flow through a bearing fed with oil under pressure from a single hole. Approximately, the flow may be four times greater. But sometimes, the centrifugal force acting on the oil in the circumferential groove may build pressure higher than the supply pressure, which may restrict the flow of the lubricant.

Some experimental results show the effect of groove width, location and edge radius on the oil flow rate, such that oil flow rate increases by providing edge radius to a square groove.

Application :

These types of bearings are most widely used for the crank shaft and connecting rod of automotive engines.

- **Axial Groove or Cylindrical Groove :**

These groove patterns are as shown in Fig. 1.11.

Axial grooves distribute lubricant lengthwise in the bearing or along the axis of the bearing. This type of bearing has an axial or cylindrical groove almost along the total length of the bearing.

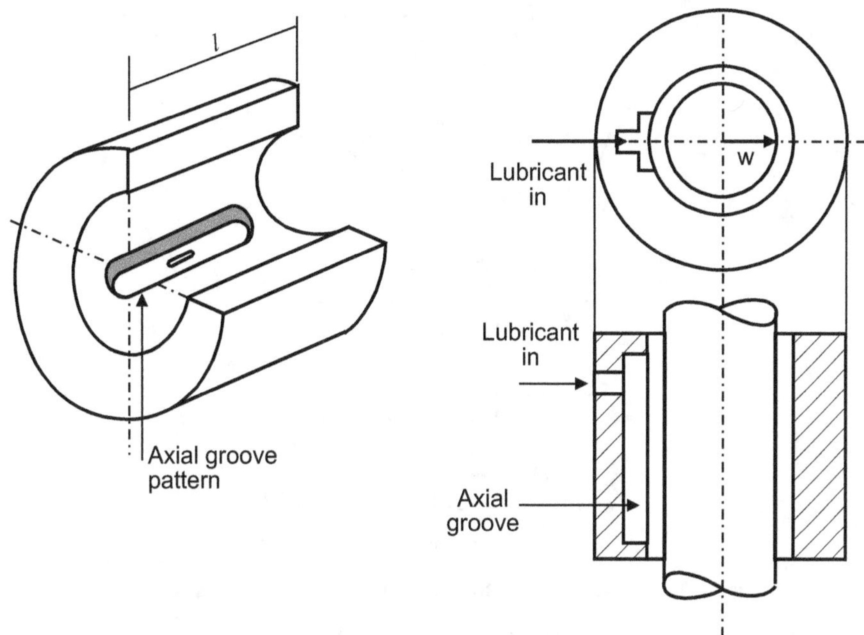

Fig. 1.11

As compared to the circumferential groove bearings, the axial groove bearing has higher load-carrying capacity. But such types of bearings are very much prone to shocks and vibrations during operation. Number of similar patterns are obtained by combining axial groove pattern with circumferential groove pattern.

Application :

These types of grooves in bearings are used for gear boxes and high-speed applications.

- **Radial Oil Groove :**

Sometimes, radial grooves cut in the thrust plate give better results. A parallel face thrust plate as shown in Fig. 1.12 will make a very satisfactory bearing if a radial groove with well rounded or bevelled edges are placed in the faces.

Experimental investigation for a flat steel thrust plate of 60 mm outer diameter and 42 mm inner diameter, with a unit load of about 690 kPa gives the values of coefficient of friction for flat plate thrust bearing and for flat plate with radial grooves. (Table 1.10)

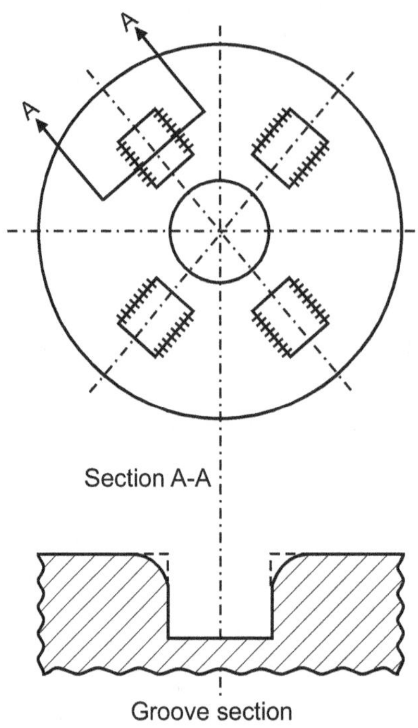

Fig. 1.12 : Parallel face thrust plate with groove section

Table 1.10 : Flat Plate Thrust Bearing with Radial Groove

Speed r.p.m. (N)	Coefficient of Friction for Flat Plate Thrust Bearing	Coefficient of Friction for Flat Plate with Radial Grooves
260	0.011	0.0065
520	0.0099	0.0067
900	0.015	0.0067

(iv)   Helical Groove Pattern :

It is as shown in Fig. 1.13 where a helical groove is cut inside the bearing. It has a lubricant inside and it flows helically.

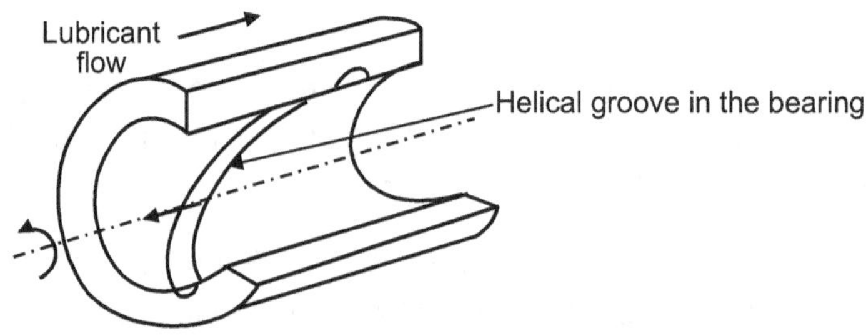

Fig. 1.13 : Helical groove in bearing

As the lubricant flows through the helical groove, the groove provides pumping action for the lubricant to flow. It is used for some of the special applications.

1.7 TRIBOLOGICAL DESIGN OF OIL SEALS AND GASKETS

All bearings function in association with some form of sealing device.

Seals are mechanical elements used to –

- Prevent leakage of oils through the clearance between the moving and stationary parts.
- Seal out dirt, foreign matter and fluids.
- Maintain controlled atmosphere within a sealed volume.
- Maintain specific applied pressure or vacuum across it.

Seals are broadly classified into two main classes :

- Static seals
- Dynamic seals

Classification :

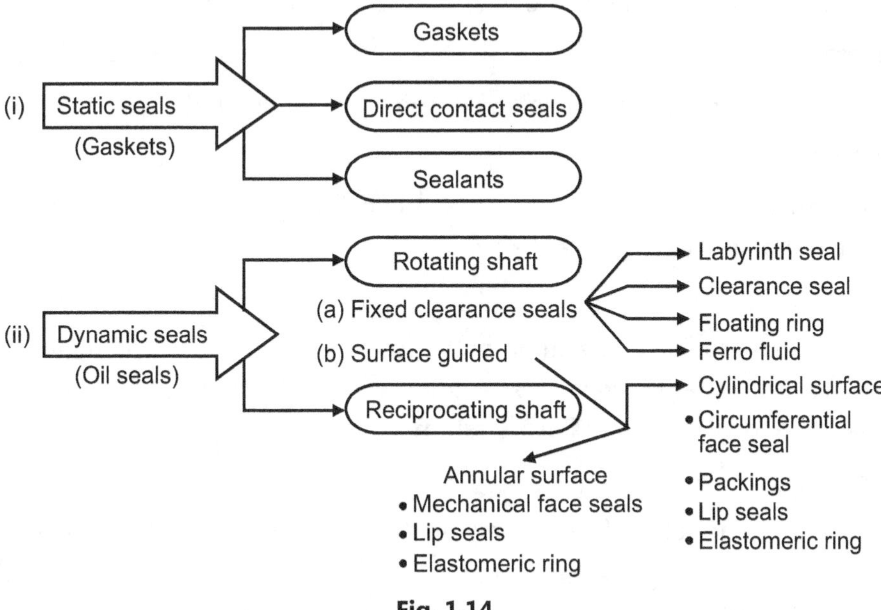

Fig. 1.14

1.7.1 Essential Properties of Seals

In order to perform their function effectively, the seals should have the following properties or characteristics.

- **Tensile Strength :**

Tensile strength gives an indication of other properties e.g.

- Wear and tear resistance.

- Resilience.
- Cut resistance.
- Stress relaxation.
- Creep.

These properties correlate with tensile strength. For elastomeric seals, tensile strength is less than 200 kg/cm^2.

Those materials with tensile strength less than 70 kg/cm^2 may not be suitable for dynamic seals.

- **Abrasion Resistance :**

It is an essentially important property for dynamic seals. Abrasion resistance can be improved by increasing hardness and by compounding.

- **Tear Resistance :**

Tear resistance is a measure of stress required to continue failure of sheet of elastomer with an initiated cut. High tear resistance provides low possibility of seal failure.

- **Elongation :**

It is the maximum possible extension of an elastomer at the point of rupture.

- **Resilience :**

It is an ability of an elastomer to regain its original shape when a compression load is removed. A seal should have good resilience.

- **Squeeze :**

Excessive squeeze can cause undue stress on the seal material, causing premature aging and thus high friction for dynamic seals. A 32% compression is recommended for nitrile rubber and it can be more for silicone and fluro-elastomers.

- **Hardness :**

It is a measure of an elastomer to resist deformation and it can be modified by compounding. Less hardness leads to better sealing and conform better with surface roughness but are more susceptible to wear, abrasion and extrusion. For most of the seal materials, hardness lies between 40 to 90 shore 'A', with hardness of 70 ± 5 shore 'A'.

1.7.2 Oil Seals (Dynamic Seals)

These are mechanical elements, also called as dynamic seals. Dynamic seal is used to prevent the leakage of any fluid across the sealing surfaces which are in relative motion. Thus, dynamic sealing is the relationship between the rotating shaft and the seal and is handled by the sealing element.

Following factors are taken into account while selecting a particular type of oil seal :

- Type of lubrication system used.
- Shaft speed.
- Shaft arrangement.
- Space requirement.
- Temperature, pressure and corrosive atmosphere.
- Material of seal.

Following are the basic types of oil seals.

(a)   Radial seals for rotating shafts

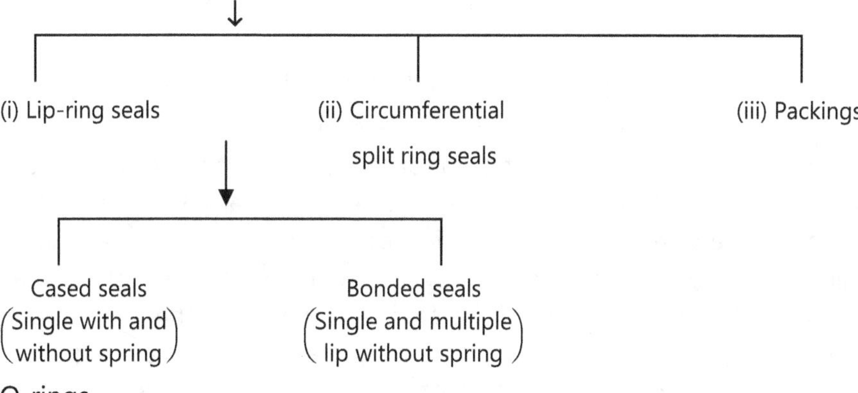

(b)   O-rings

(c)   Labyrinth seal

(d)   Felt seal

(a)   Radial Seals for Rotating Shafts :

- **Lip-Ring Seals :**

These are elastomeric seals encountering interfacial flow. These are used to retain oil and other lubricants in equipment operating with rotating shaft. They are relatively more insensitive to moderate shaft misalignment, dynamic shaft run out and even variation in rotational shaft speeds. These are used for high speed and continuous duty and for excluding dirt, abrasive particles or liquids from the container to be sealed and sealing off vapours at low pressure. In this type of seal, the sealing effect is due to the interference fit between the flexible element and the shaft.

Constructional Details of Lip Seal :

Lip seal consists of :

- Sealing element or sealing lip.
- The metal case.
- The spring (Garter spring).

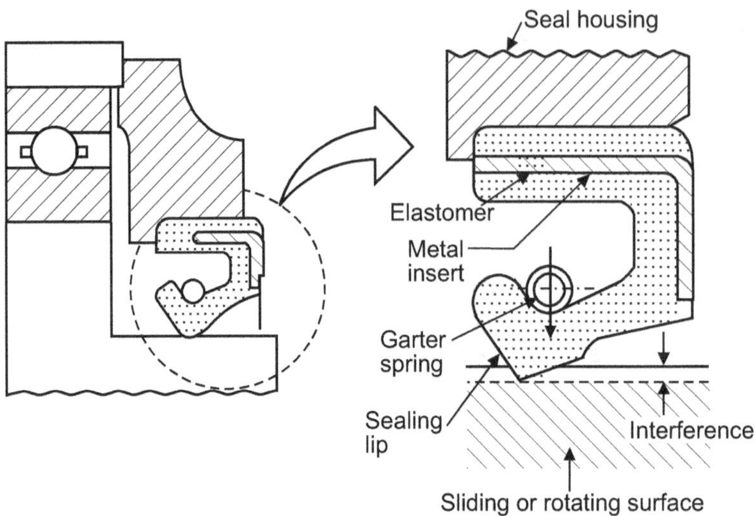

Fig. 1.15 : Commercial lip seal

The sealing lip is pressed against the contact point on the surface of the shaft. Garter spring exerts a radial pressure on the sealing lip and keep the sealing lip always in contact with the rotating shaft. Also the service pressure helps in sealing. Thus, it provides interference between the sealing lip and the contact point for which the inner diameter of the sealing lip must be slightly smaller than the diameter of the shaft and maintains the joint leakage free. The metal case will give rigidity and strength to the seal while it is being held in the bore. For better performance of the lip seal, the contact pressure between the sealing lip and the rotating shaft surface is an important parameter. If contact pressure exerted, which is a combination of service pressure and the spring pressure force becomes too large, there is excessive friction and rapid wear of the sealing lip. If the contact pressure is low, there is possibility of leakage of the lubricating oil. To avoid leakage the best oil film thickness between the rotating shaft and flexible sealing lip is 0.0025 mm, which results in effective sealing, reduced friction and long life of the seal.

Sometimes lip seals can be made in two forms.

- **Cased Seals :** In this the sealing element is retained in a precision-manufactured metal casing by means of the case-construction. This type of seal is available with either a leather or a synthetic elastomeric element.

- **Bonded Seals :** These are generally made only with the synthetic sealing elements permanently bonded to the metal case structure. Spring loaded configurations are most commonly used lip-seal devices and can retain oils or grease at all kinds of rotational shaft speeds. These seals can be used for pressures upto 3.5 MPa.

Characteristics of Lip Seals :

- Positive sealing ability and have low initial cost.
- Occupy small space and are easy to install.

- It is simple in design and it has high degree of reliability.
- It can be replaced easily and gives excellent performance characteristics.

Materials for the sealing elements can be given in the following Table 1.11 with their abrasion resistance and temperature ranges.

Table 1.11 : Material with Temperature Ranges for Sealing Lip

Material for Sealing Lip	Abrasion Resistance	Temperature Range
Nitrile	Excellent	0°C to 80°C
Polyacrylate	Fair	0°C to 175°C
Leather	Excellent	– 15°C to 90°C
Silicone	Good	– 20°C to 220°C

- **Circumferential Split Ring Seals :**

These are used for systems handling gases, e.g. air, carbon dioxide, hydrogen, helium, nitrogen, etc. These are also known as expansion split rings. These can be produced in two types.

- Paralleling piston ring seals (with one, two, three ring configurations).
- Segmental ring seal which is shown in Fig. 1.16.

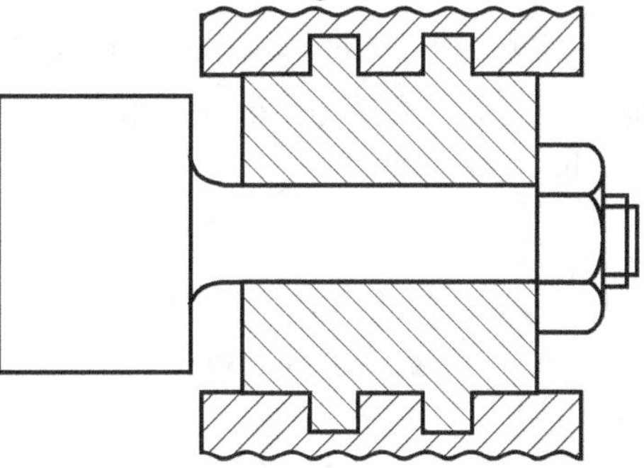

Fig. 1.16 : Segmental ring seal

(b)   O-Rings :

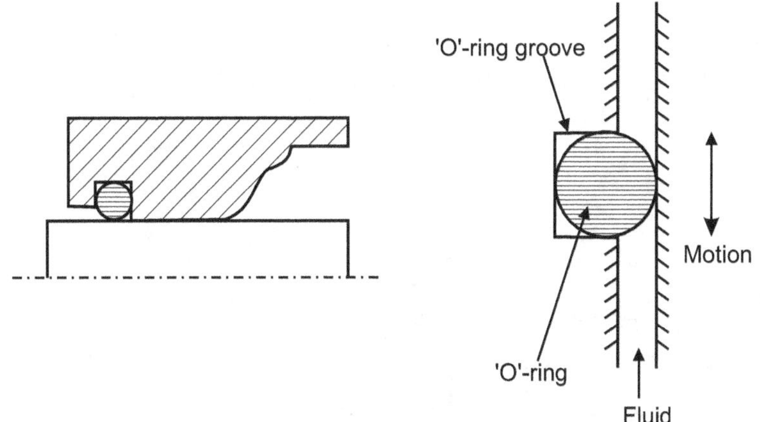

Fig. 1.17 : O-rings

It is commonly used squeeze type of packing. These types of seals possess the following characteristics :

- They are inexpensive and easy to install.
- They are generally reliable in service.

Requirements :

- For satisfactory performance it is important that the groove in which the ring sits should be of correct dimensions, i.e. the depth of the seal groove should be such so as to impose a compression of about 10-20 percent of its cross-section on the ring. Over-compression can cause damage and permanent set to the ring or even cause it to extrude out of the groove, while too little squeeze may allow leakage.

- The sealing surfaces have approximate surface finishes. For dynamic situations, the surface finish of the sliding surface should be no more than 0.4 microns Ra.

- The material out of which the ring is made does not react adversely with the sealed fluid.

Applications :

- O-rings are most widely used for hydraulic and pneumatic sealing applications.

- Simple 'O'-rings can be used for reciprocating seals or slow-speed rotation through rings of other more specialized sections.

(c)   Labyrinth Seal :

These are also known as clearance seals, and used to limit the leakage by closely controlling the annular clearance between a rotary shaft and the stationary housing under the conditions where the temperature, pressure and shaft speed prevent the use of positive contact seals. Fig. 1.18 shows labyrinth seal effective for high-speed installation. The clearance may vary from 0.25 to 1.0 mm.

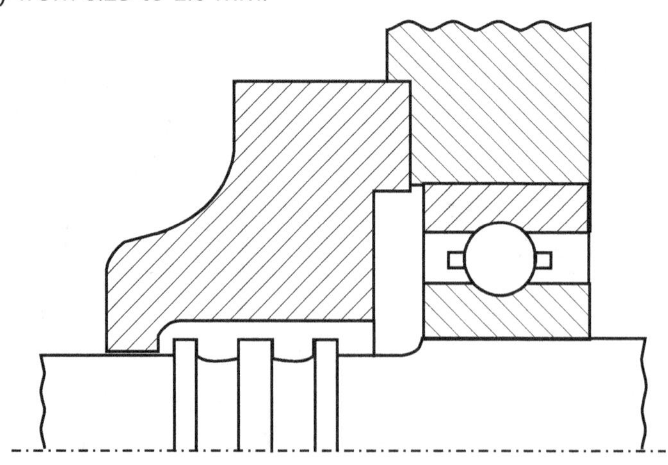

Fig. 1.18 : Labyrinth seal

The fluid throttling is achieved in steps, using a series of small chambers, where a sudden irreversible acceleration with subsequent deceleration of the leaking fluid takes place. It is suited for sealing shafts operating at high rotational speeds. It requires neither lubrication nor maintenance. These seals can be produced in wide variety as given below.

- Non-interlocking seal.

- Interlocking seal.

- Staggered seals.

- Seal with axial clearance.

- Seal with radial clearance.

- Seal with combination of axial and radial clearance.

Application :

Labyrinth seals are used in centrifugal compressors and steam turbines.

(d)   Felt Seals :

These seals may be used with grease lubrication when speeds are low. Fig. 1.19 shows arrangement of felt seal.

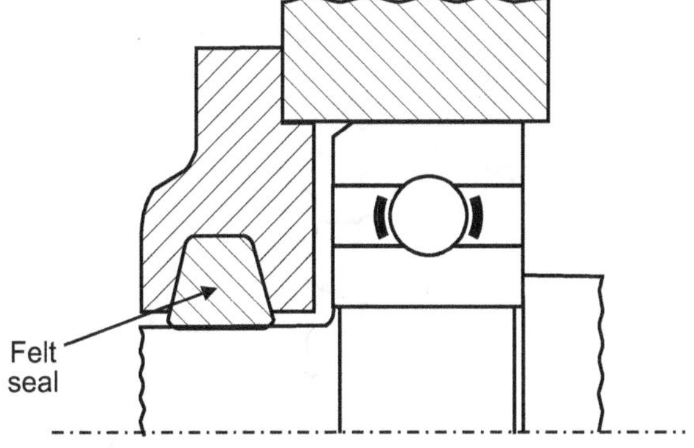

Fig. 1.19 : Felt seal

The rubbing surfaces should have a high polish. These seals should be protected from dirt by placing them in machined grooves or by using metal stampings as shields.

1.7.3 Gaskets (Static Seals)

Static seal is a mechanical element used to prevent leakage of fluid between the mating members. Gasket is a static sealing device, made up of a relatively plastic and soft material so that it gets deformed and fills the surface irregularities of the member between which it is placed to provide sealing. It is used to maintain a barrier against flow of fluids across the stationary mating surfaces of a mechanical assembly. e.g. between cylinder head and cylinder block of an engine. It is used in static joints such as pressure vessels. The mating surfaces need not be given a smooth finish. There are two types of gaskets :

    (i)   Metallic gaskets.

    (ii)   Non-metallic gaskets.

(i)   Metallic Gaskets :

Lead, copper, aluminium are used as gasket materials for high temperature and high pressure applications. Lead gaskets can withstand temperature upto 70°C, copper can withstand upto 250°C, while aluminium can withstand upto 420°C. They can have plane, corrugated, round or metal jacketed constructions. The metallic gaskets are permanently set when compressed during the assembly and will not recover to its original shape and size even after separation of contacting surfaces. Chemical atmosphere may attack metallic gaskets.

Fig. 1.20 shows different metallic gaskets.

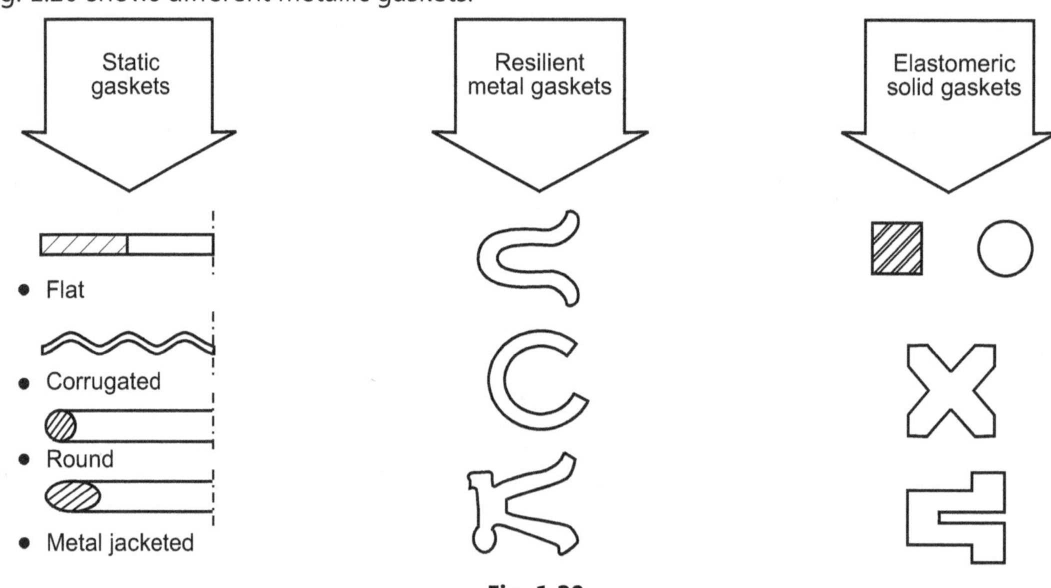

Fig. 1.20

- **Non-Metallic Gaskets :**

They are made of asbestos, cork, rubber or plastics.

Material	Temperature Limit
Asbestos	265°C
Rubber, Cork	75°C

They have good corrosion resistance. Rubber gaskets have an ability to flow into joint imperfections when compressed. They cannot withstand higher temperature limits.

Properties of Gasket Materials :

- Softness.

- Deformability.

- High degree of elasticity and flexibility with hardening and fatigue.
- Provision of self-energizing effect; that utilizes the internal pressure to increase the contact pressure with rising hydrostatic internal pressure without increasing the tightening force in the closure system.

Choice of the Gasket Material for any Application Depends Upon :

- Operating conditions.
- Mechanical features of the flanged assembly.
- Gasket characteristics.

Figs. 1.21, 1.22, 1.23 show three basic gasket configurations.

- **Unconfined Gasket :**

  It is subjected to the full compressive load between the members.

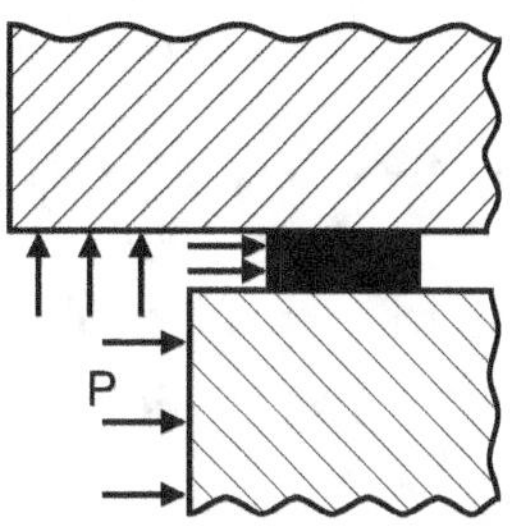

Fig. 1.21 : Unconfined gasket

- Confined gasket in which sealing is achieved by pressure P.

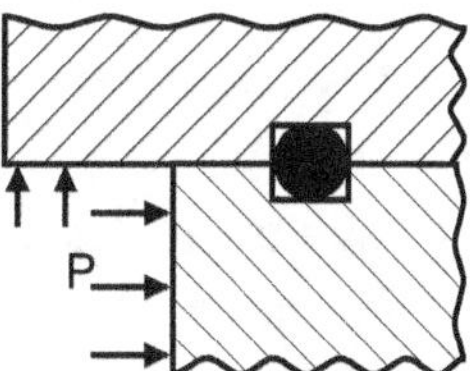

Fig. 1.22 : Confined gasket

- Confined gasket in which sealing is achieved by compressing the gasket.

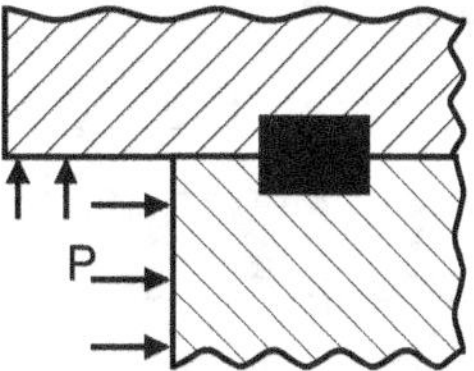

Fig. 1.23 : Confined gasket

1.8 TRIBOLOGY IN INDUSTRY

All mechanisms, machines and equipments are affected by the tribological factors. It is estimated that about 70% of failures in mechanical components are due to tribological aspects. Also, about one third of the world's energy resources appear as friction in one form or the other and most of these result in waste. This shows the importance of tribological study and tribological treatment in industries result in considerable savings.

Following are the considerations :

- **Energy Losses :**

Tribology is vital to modern machinery involving sliding and rolling surfaces. Brakes, clutches, bolts, nuts, driving wheels on automobiles etc., use friction in a productive manner. Writing with a pencil, polishing, machining and shaving, etc., use wear in a productive manner. Unproductive friction and wear take place in engines, gears, cams, bearings and seals, etc. Friction and wear usually cost money in the form of energy loss and material loss, can decrease national productivity, can affect national security and quality of life.

- **Wear :**

Wear can also cause accidents. Thus, knowledge of tribology can lead to various substantial and significant savings without deployment of large capital investment. Research in tribology leads to increased plant efficiency, fewer breakdowns, better performance and, above all, significant savings.

- **Control :**

Some amount of minor design defects are corrected at the manufacturing stage and some manufacturing defects are corrected at the installation and commissioning stage by use of tribology.

- **Operation and Maintenance :**

Operation and maintenance are probably the most important stages for use of tribology as the equipments have been designed, manufactured and installed and are supposed to work and produce as intended. Maintenance personnel have to use tribology in order to take necessary actions on equipments to reduce chances of friction, wear and damages and other consequent defects/failures so that equipments can work for their intended functions, trouble-free at desired effectiveness and reliability.

- **Environment :**

  Tribological aspects are very important in following industrial environment :

  (a)   Sheet metal refractories.

  (b)   Shaping processes of iron and steel.

  (c)   Mining industries.

  (d)   Paper and pulp industries.

  (e)   Glass fibre industry.

  (f)   Transport sector.

  (g)   Metal working processes like rolling, drawing, extrusion, forging, metal cutting/removing, etc.

- **Friction Devices :**

In many situations, friction is a prior requirement for the functioning of the device. e.g. brakes and clutches where heat release and rate of wear are important design considerations.

1.9 ECONOMIC ASPECTS IN TRIBOLOGY

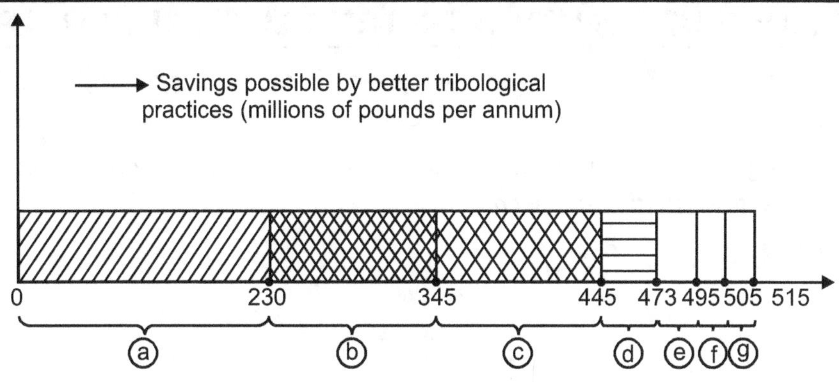

Fig. 1.24 : The jost report

(a)	–	Less maintenance and replacement
(b)	–	Fewer breakdowns
(c)	–	Longer life of machines
(d)	–	Less frictional dissipation
(e)	–	Investment savings
(f)	–	Lubricant savings
(g)	–	Manpower savings

- **Reduce Friction :**

It is important to reduce friction wherever required in order to save energy in some form. As we see from the reports, one-half of the world's energy production is used to overcome friction in some form, and affects the overall economy.

- **Savings Based on Better Tribological Designs :**

Therefore, savings by better tribological design could have considerable significance in terms of the total conservation which in turn concerns the whole future of mankind.

- **The Jost Report :** (Lubrication Education and Research D.E.S. Report 1966).

e.g. In Britain, the Jost Report suggested that this country could save no less than £ 515 million per annum by better tribological designs. This amount arises from the constituent savings as indicated in Fig. 1.24. Such costs include the loss of production etc. due to tribological failures in modern industry.

These savings do not need new way of research but they can be well balanced by the application of the current knowledge.

(iv) Optimum Balance of Various Losses and Savings :

It is necessary to strike an optimum balance of losses and savings made in order to apply better tribological practices.

1.10 METHODS OF SOLUTION OF TRIBOLOGICAL PROBLEMS

To introduce a problem-oriented view of any system, is the most predominant effect of the introduction of the word 'tribology'.

Following section gives *'the best possible solution to the problem of carrying load across the interface with acceptable friction and wear'*.

- **Dry Contact :**

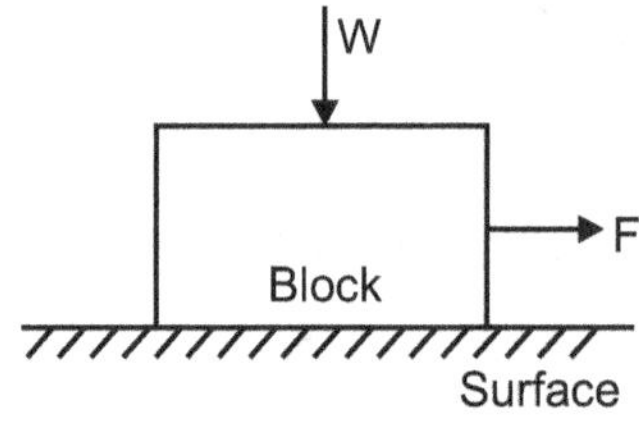

Fig. 1.25 : Dry contact

- Selecting suitable in-contact materials having low friction and wear characteristics, may have lower load-carrying capacities (when plastic materials are used).

- In most of the cases, the materials as surface layers supported on substrates that fulfil the basic structural requirements of the particular component. e.g. This method is used in bearing shells of automotive engines.

- **Chemical Films :**

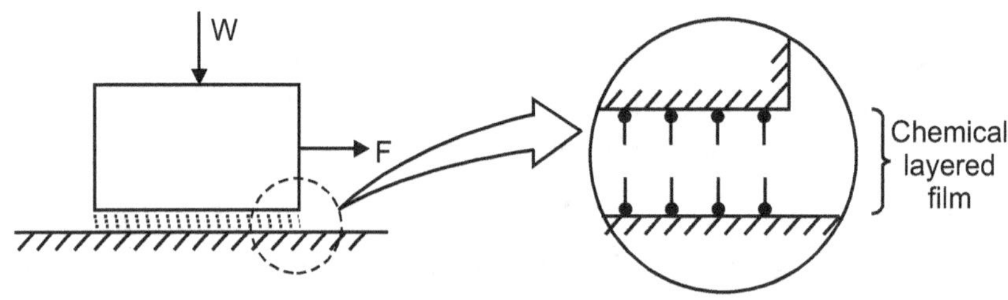

Fig. 1.26 : Chemical films

- Chemical films protect the surface and it reduce the intimate contact of the base materials.

- During sliding, an important aspect of the chemical films is their thermal stability due to the high local temperatures created at the points of intimate contact.

- **Lamellar Solids :**

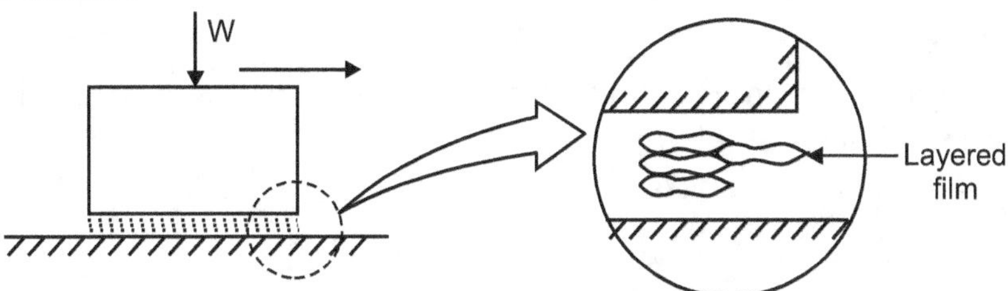

Fig. 1.27 : Lamellar solids

- Solid surface coatings are employed as they possess low resistance to transverse shear e.g. graphite and molybdenum disulphide.
- These lamellar materials have a layered structure with strength to carry normal load and weakness along planes at right angles to facilitate sliding action.

- **Pressurised Lubricant Films :**

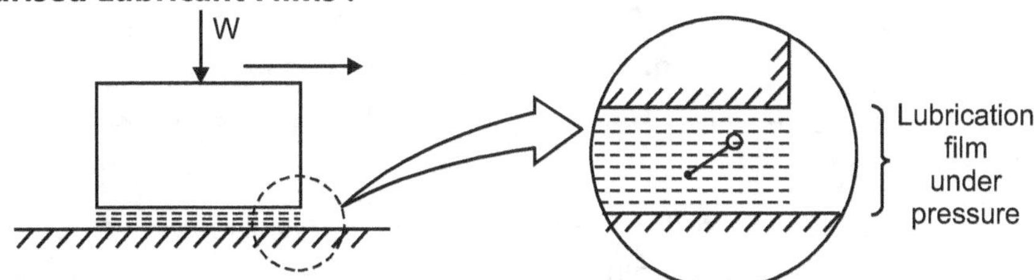

Fig. 1.28 : Pressurised lubricant films

- Two surfaces may be separated by a continuous film of either a liquid, a vapour or a gas. In this case, the fluid film must have a built-in pressure to withstand the effects of the applied normal load.
- Pressure may be developed by two mechanisms :
    - The first is to supply the fluid at a pressure generated by an external pumping system e.g. the hydrostatic or aerostatic bearings.
    - The second is to generate pressure by the motion of the surfaces themselves as they tend to drag the fluid into a converging gap. e.g. hydrodynamic bearing.
- Fluids used for these two mechanisms are water, oil, air and liquid metals in nuclear reactors.

- **Elastometers :**

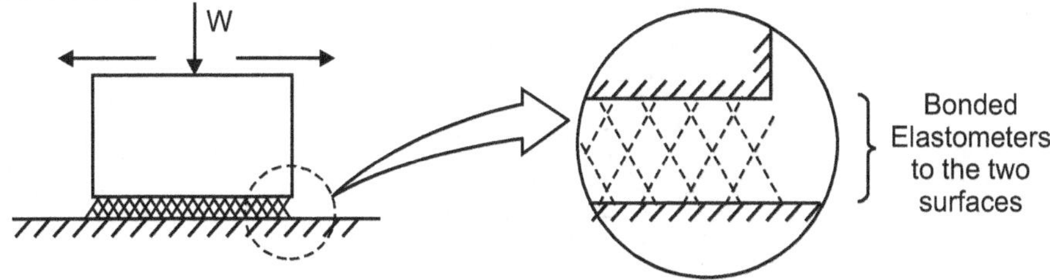

Fig. 1.29 : Elastometers

- In this case, the surfaces may be separated by elastometers bonded to the two surfaces.

- The degree of transverse displacement is of small amplitude. This offers an excellent tribological solution.

- **Flexible Strips :**

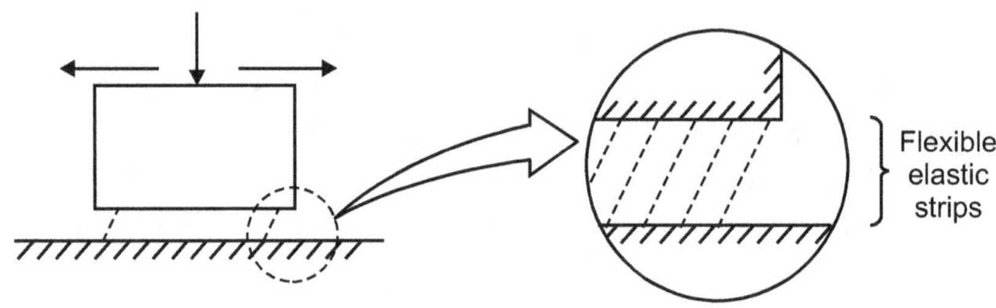

Fig. 1.30 : Flexible strips

- The two surfaces may be separated by flexible elastic strips bonded to the two surfaces.

- The degree of transverse displacement in this case is also of small amplitude, thus giving a better tribological solution.

- **Rolling Elements :**

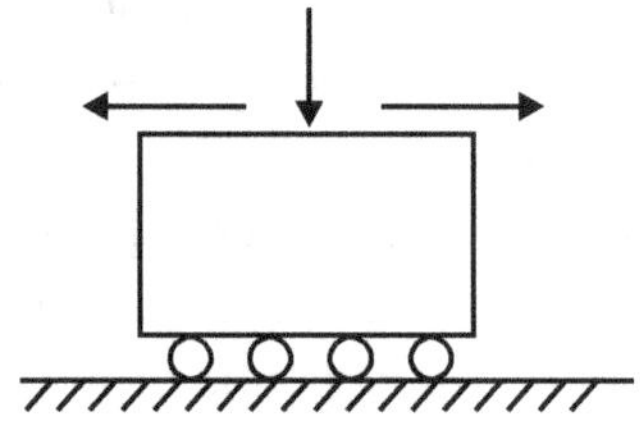

Fig. 1.31

- The two surfaces may be separated by rolling elements such as balls, cylinders, etc.
- This is widely used as a tribological solution.

  e.g. Rolling contact bearings.

- **Magnetic Fields :**

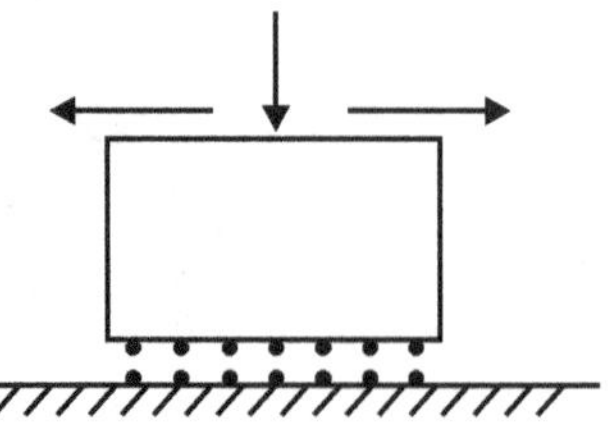

Fig. 1.32 : Magnetic fields

- The two surfaces may be separated by creating magnetic field between them. Thus, load can be carried without mechanical contact. e.g. such kind of bearings are found in the domestic electricity-supply meter.

Selecting a Particular Solution to a Tribological Problem Depends on the Following Factors :

- The load to be carried,
- The speed,
- The nature of environment and
- Any limitations on friction and wear.

1.11 LUBRICATION

Lubrication is the most important component of tribology as it takes care of friction and wear, in addition to performing other functions.

In moving parts of machines, friction is undesirable. It causes loss of energy which is converted in the form of heat energy. Due to friction, an additional force is required to cause the motion of a body. To improve upon the efficiency of working machines, the frictional force is reduced to the minimum possible. The act of doing so is called as **lubrication** and the substance used for lubrication is called a **lubricant.**

Laws of dry friction are not applicable to film friction.

When the two surfaces in contact are completely separated by a film of lubricant, the friction occurs due to resistance of relative motion between the lubricant and surfaces in contact. This is known as **film friction, fluid friction** or **viscous friction.**

It is thus obvious that the film friction is not due to the surfaces in contact but it is due to **viscosity** and **oiliness** of the lubricant.

Thus, lubrication is the science of reducing friction by application of suitable substance called lubricant between the rubbing surfaces of bodies having relative motion.

1.11.1 Purpose of Lubrication

Though lubrication is important in reducing friction, it also performs multiple functions as listed below :

- To reduce friction (primary function) between surfaces in contact where the relative motion exists.
- To dissipate heat, which is generated due to frictional loss of power in machines.
- To take away foreign particles.
- To reduce or prevent wear in between surfaces in contact where the relative motion exists.

- To protect the surfaces against corrosion.

- To reduce the electrical and mechanical power consumption (again by reducing friction).

- To reduce noise, vibration and shock between gear teeth and other components.

1.11.2 Basic Modes of Lubrication

For performing various functions during lubrication, the basic modes of lubrication are classified as follows :

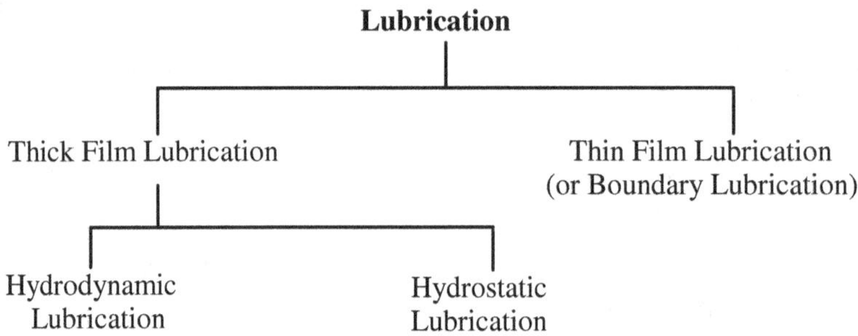

Thick Film Lubrication describes a condition of lubrication where two surfaces of the bearing in relative motion are completely separated by a film of fluid. Film fluid (oil film) always remains in between the two components. Since there is no contact between the surfaces, least wear takes place between these components. The performance of the bearing is affected by the viscosity of the lubricant. Hydrodynamic lubrication and hydrostatic lubrication are considered as Thick Film Lubrication.

Thin Film Lubrication describes a condition of lubrication where the lubricant film is relatively thin and there is partial metal to metal contact. Boundary lubrication is considered as Thin Film Lubrication.

1.11.2.1 Hydrodynamic Lubrication

In heavily loaded bearings such as thrust bearings and horizontal journal bearings, the fluid viscosity alone is not sufficient to maintain a film between the moving surfaces. In these bearings, higher fluid pressures are required to support the load until the fluid film is established. If this pressure is supplied by an outside source, it is called hydrostatic lubrication. If the pressure is generated internally, that is, within the bearing by dynamic action, it is referred to as hydrodynamic lubrication.

In hydrodynamic lubrication, a fluid wedge is formed by the relative surface motion of the journals or the thrust runners over their respective bearing surfaces.

The principle of hydrodynamic lubrication in journal bearing is shown in Fig. 1.33. In hydrodynamic lubrication, the load supporting fluid film is created by the shape and relative motion of the sliding surfaces.

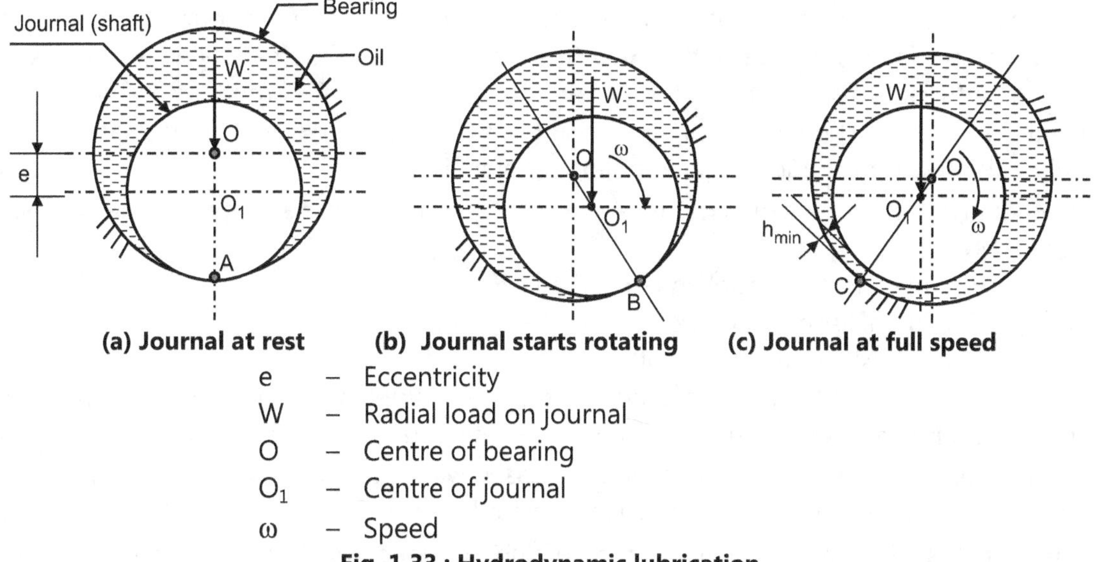

(a) Journal at rest   **(b) Journal starts rotating**   **(c) Journal at full speed**

$$
\begin{aligned}
e &\quad - \quad \text{Eccentricity} \\
W &\quad - \quad \text{Radial load on journal} \\
O &\quad - \quad \text{Centre of bearing} \\
O_1 &\quad - \quad \text{Centre of journal} \\
\omega &\quad - \quad \text{Speed}
\end{aligned}
$$

Fig. 1.33 : Hydrodynamic lubrication

As shown in Fig. 1.33 (a), initially, the journal (shaft) is at rest and it rests at the bottom of the bearing A, under the action of load W. Metal to metal contact is established at A. This point of contact is called as **seat of pressure.**

The journal now starts to rotate in the clockwise direction, inside the bearing as shown in Fig. 1.33 (b). Due to friction between the two rubbing surfaces, the friction starts opposing the motion. The seat of pressure or point of contact between the two surfaces then climbs up the bearing in a direction opposite to that of rotation. The point of contact shifts from A to B. As the speed of journal is further increased, it will force the fluid into the wedge-shaped regions as shown in Fig. 1.33 (c). Since more and more fluids is forced into the wedge-shaped clearance space, sufficient pressure is generated within the system to carry the load. The pressure distribution around the periphery of the journal is shown in Fig. 1.34.

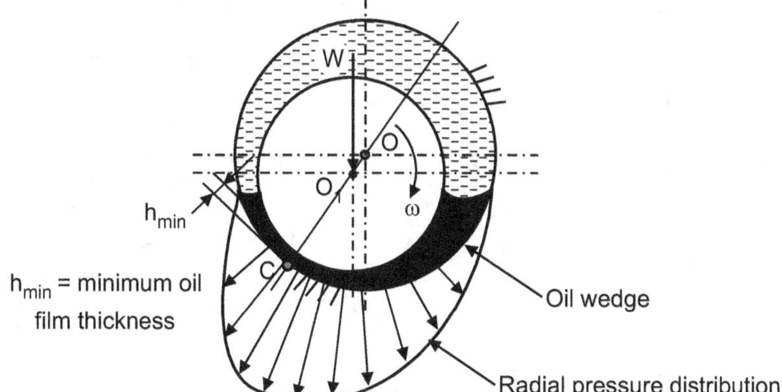

Fig. 1.34 : Radial pressure distribution in hydrodynamic lubrication

Since the pressure is created within the system due to rotation of the journal, this type of bearing is also known as **self-acting bearing.** At a particular journal speed, the pressure becomes sufficient to support the load (W) and the journal is shifted to the other side [i.e. to left side as shown in Fig. 1.33 (c)] of vertical. In this situation, there is minimum clearance and oil film thickness is minimum (h_{min}) at point C. [Refer Fig. 1.33 (c)].

The amount of rotation of the line of centres of the journal and bearing from the load-line depends on :

- The magnitude of applied radial load (W).
- The journal speed (ω), and
- The viscosity of the lubricant.

Thus, in hydrodynamic bearings, it is not necessary to supply the lubricant under pressure. The only requirement is to ensure sufficient and continuous supply of the lubricant.

The minimum thickness of the fluid film increases with an increase in fluid viscosity and surface speed and decreases with an increase in load.

Examples : Main bearings, connecting rod bearings, gudgeon pin bearings, etc. mounted on engines. Also the applications of these bearings are seen in centrifugal pumps, compressors, etc.

Hydrodynamic bearings are simple in construction, easy to maintain, initial and maintenance cost is less as compared to hydrostatic bearings.

In hydrodynamic bearings, the journal always runs eccentric in the bearing and there is a wear at the start-up and stopping of rotation of the journal.

1.11.2.2 Hydrostatic Lubrication

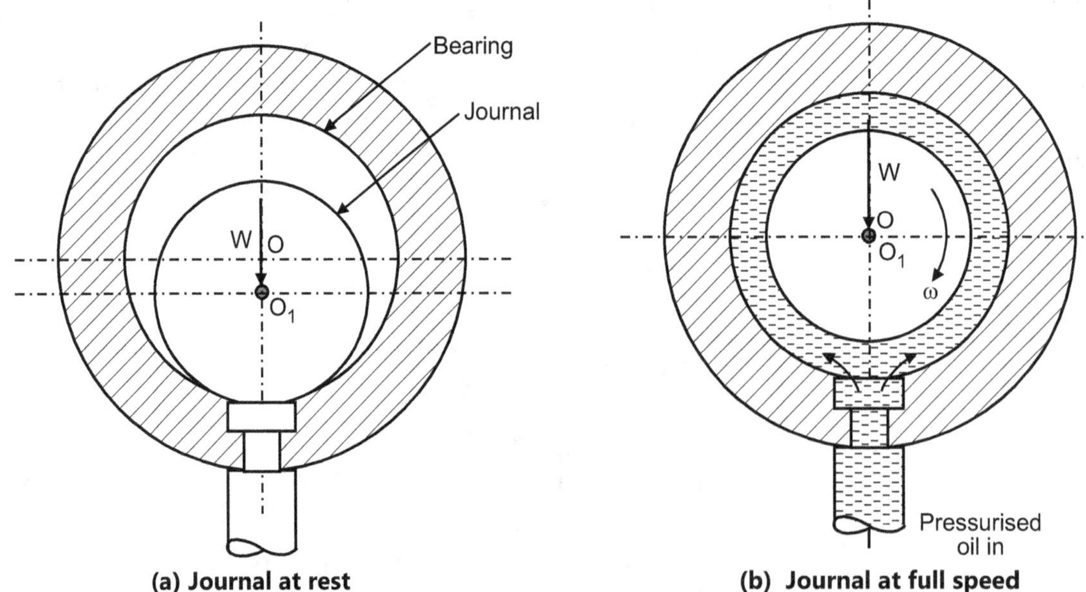

(a) Journal at rest   **(b) Journal at full speed**

Fig. 1.35 : Hydrostatic lubrication

In hydrostatic lubrication, the load supporting fluid film, separating the two surfaces is created by an external source like a pump, supplying sufficient fluid under pressure as shown in Fig. 1.35.

Since the lubricant is supplied under pressure, this type of bearing is also called as **externally pressurised bearing.**

Fig. 1.35 shows the principle of hydrostatic lubrication in journal bearing. As shown in Fig. 1.35 (a), initially the journal rests on a bearing surface under the radial load W. As the pump starts, high pressure lubricant is admitted in the clearance space forcing the surfaces of the bearing and the journal to separate out as shown in Fig. 1.35 (b).

Examples :

- Vertical turbo generators, centrifuges, ball mills, etc.

Hydrostatic bearings are costly as compared to hydrodynamic bearings. However, it offers the following advantages :

- High load carrying capacity even at low speeds.

- No starting friction.

- There is no rubbing action at any speed and load, hence wear and tear is less in hydrostatic bearings as compared to hydrodynamic bearings.

1.11.2.3 Boundary Lubrication

When a complete fluid film does not develop between potentially rubbing surfaces, the film thickness may be reduced to permit momentary dry contact between the wear surface high points or asperities. This condition is the characteristic of boundary lubrication. Boundary lubrication occurs whenever any of the essential factors that influence formation of a full fluid film are missing. The most common example of boundary lubrication includes bearings, which normally operate with fluid-film lubrication but experience boundary lubricating conditions during routing, starting and stopping of equipment. Other examples include door hinges, machine tool slides and guideways, etc.

Thus, in boundary lubrication, the lubricant film is relatively thin and there is partial metal to metal contact. Various causes of boundary lubrication are as follows :

- Excessive load

- Insufficient oil supply

- Low speed

- Misalignment

1.11.2.4 Elasto-Hydrodynamic Lubrication (EHL)

The lubrication principles applied to rolling bodies, such as ball or roller bearings, gears, cams, etc., is known as elasto-hydrodynamic lubrication (EHL).

Although lubrication of rolling objects operates on a considerably different principle than sliding objects, the principles of hydrodynamic lubrication can be applied, within limits, to explain the lubrication of rolling elements. An oil wedge, similar to that which occurs in hydrodynamic lubrication exists at the lower leading edge of bearing. Adhesion of oil to the sliding element and the supporting surface increases the pressure and creates a film between the two bodies. Because the area of contact is extremely small in a roller and ball bearing, the force per unit area, or **load pressure is extremely high.** Under these pressures, it would appear that the oil would be entirely squeezed from between the wearing surfaces. *However, the viscosity increase that occurs under extremely high pressure, prevents the oil from being entirely squeezed out. Consequently, a thin film of oil is maintained. The surfaces which carry this load are likely to deform. A very thin lubricant film actually supports the load. Thus, elastohydrodynamic lubrication (EHL) deals with the lubrication of elastic contacts.*

All the assumptions used in the classical theory of hydrodynamic lubrication cannot be used especially because the variation of viscosity with pressure must be considered here. In addition to this, a heavy load which causes elastic deformation of solids changes the geometry of the lubricating film. Thus, *in the problems of elastohydrodynamic lubrication, it is necessary to solve simultaneously the hydrodynamic as well as elasticity equations concerned with the contact, since the shape of oil film largely controls pressure distribution.*

1.11.2.5 Extreme Pressure (EP) Lubrication

Extreme Pressure (EP) Lubrication is applicable to extreme boundary cases where high contact pressure and intense sliding combine to generate high localised temperature. EP additives are added to lubricants to allow chemical reactions leading to the formation of organometallic components of low shear strength. During motion, shearing takes place between the organometallic layers, thus reducing friction and wear. The shearing and regeneration of reaction products is a continuous process. As the melting points of the EP additives are high, they remain on the rubbing surfaces and work effectively at higher temperatures.

1.12 LUBRICANTS

Lubrication is the use of a substance to provide smoothness to the movement of the surfaces of machine elements, which move relative to each other. The substance used to achieve this purpose, is termed as **lubricant.**

1.12.1 Types of Lubricants

A large number of lubricants are used in industries; some are general purpose and some are tailor made, but all can be grouped into the following four categories.

- Lubricating oils
- Greases
- Solids
- Gases

The primary function of all the above lubricants is to reduce friction and wear. In addition to this, they perform several other important functions such as – they act as a coolant, protect surfaces against corrosion, flush away contaminants, provide damping effects, reduce noise and act as a sealent.

1.12.1.1 Lubricating Oils

Any liquid having some amount of viscosity can be regarded as a lubricant. At the same time, it should be as mobile as possible to remove heat and to avoid power loss due to viscous drag. It should be stable under thermal and oxidation stresses, have low volatility, good mechanical stability, non-toxic or harmless etc. The bulk of lubricating oils today are made from crude petroleum. Lubricants are liquids varying in appearance from light yellow to black.

Lubricating oils include **natural organics** like animal fat, whale oil, shark oil, vegetable oils, mineral oils, etc.

The most commonly used lubricants are **mineral oils**. The refining of petroleum produces mineral oils. These are the crude oils or mixtures of hydrocarbons blended with chemicals to cater to various lubrication requirements for a specific application called additives. The chemical compounds making up mineral oils are mainly hydrocarbons of three types :

- Paraffins – Open chain hydrocarbons.
- Napthenes – Closed ring hydrocarbons.
- Aromatics – Hydrocarbons based on benzene rings.

Oil is termed as a paraffinic oil or napthenic oil depending on the majority percentage of paraffins or napthenes in it. The aromatical, though present in a small percentage, play a vital role in the boundary lubrication. Mineral oils can be used upto a maximum temperature of 200°C whereas animal and vegetables can be used upto a maximum temperature of 120°C.

Lubricating oils also include **synthetic organics** like synthetic hydrocarbons, diesters, chlorofluorocarbon, fatty acid esters, polyglycoether, fluoroester, phosphate ester, silicate ester, polyether, etc. Synthetic hydrocarbons are prepared by the polymerisation of specific olefin monomers and these can be prepared to optimize their viscosity-temperature, stability and volatility properties. Synthetic organics have evolved as a result of the requirement of lubricants to be used at extreme temperatures, pressure, humidity, etc. These can be used upto a maximum temperature of 400°C.

Functionally, Lubricating Oils are Classified into the Following Categories :

- Automobile lubricating oils (including aviation oils).
- Industrial lubricating oils.
- Metal working oils.
- Industrial speciality oils.
- Marine lubricating oils.

Following Types of Lubricating Oils are Commonly Used in Automotive Equipments :

- Crank case oil (engine oil).
- Gear oils.
- Transmission oils.
- Universal tractor oils.
- Two stroke engine oils.
- Preservatives and running-in oils.
- Special oils (brake oil, shock absorber oil, calibration fluid, etc.)

For standardization and variety reduction of these oils, for the ease of consumers and to maintain quality, grading of these oils are generally governed by SAE, API and BIS specifications, etc.

Industrial lubricating oils have to cater to the needs of today's modern machineries, operating at high speed, heavy loads or extreme temperatures and occasionally under tight schedules in automatic production lines. Because of the variety of applications, the industrial lubricating oil can be further classified as –

Turbine oils, circulating and hydraulic oils, industrial gear oils, spindle oils, machine tool-way oils, general purpose machinery oils, steam cylinder oils, refrigeration compressor oils, etc.

Many of above oils are graded by ISO, BIS, BS, DIN, AGMA specification etc.

Metal working oils serve the dual purpose of lubrication in cutting zones and also cooling of workpiece in machines. Cutting fluids, hot and cold rolling oils, wire drawing and deep drawing oils, etc. come under this category.

Industrial speciality oils are primarily not used for lubrication but for other functions such as heat transfer, heat treatment and other finishing operations in order to improve the quality and serviceability of the product as well as to improve its sales appeal. Quenching oils, heat transfer fluids, electrical oils, rubber process oils and rust preventives etc. come in this category.

Marine lubricating oils are modified versions of automotive oils to make the oil sea-worthy.

1.12.1.2 Greases

Greases are oils that are thickened with solids to form semi-fluid products. The type of thickener determines the characteristics of the grease. Greases are preferred to liquid lubricants in cases where :

- The application of continuous supply of lubricant is not needed or
- The enclosure is not tight enough to retain a liquid lubricant.

- Greases have a great advantage that they remain in the bearing system. Hence the lubricating arrangements are extremely simplified. Due to this advantage, greases are common lubricants in rolling-element bearings.

- In the above case, grease acts as a seal against dirt as well as a lubricant. But the use of grease is limited as they do not flow easily and cannot carry away the heat generated at high-speed operations. Grease consists basically of the following components :

- Fluid (about 85-90% by volume) which can be selected from mineral oils, polyglycols or other synthetics or a combination of such fluids.

- Fatty materials (vegetable, animal or fish), about 3 to 15% of the total usually called fatty acids.

- Thickeners (in the form of base or alkali), about 1 to 4% of the total, these are mainly metallic soaps of calcium, aluminium, sodium, barium and lithium components, etc.

- Additives and modifiers – Very small quantity as per desired properties, graphite, MoS_2, fluorocarbon powders, zinc oxides, etc. are used to increase tackiness, low temperature performance, water resistance, oxidation resistance, EP and anti-wear properties, etc.

One of the most important properties of a grease lubricant is its **drop point**, a temperature at which the grease melts under certain operating conditions. If a grease is used at a temperature above the drop point, it loses any advantage it has over an oil lubricant.

Most lubricant greases used in industry have petroleum oils as their liquid base. The petroleum oil-based greases can be used upto 175°C depending on their thickener. The synthetic oil-based greases can be used at a higher temperature. However, they are more costly.

1.12.1.3 Solid Lubricants

Lubrication with liquids and greases has some technological and economic limitations. e.g. for hot working of steel, no suitable additive is available for liquid lubricants and the liquid evaporates due to the low volatility of hydrocarbons. Also, in some cases, liquid lubricants may be too expensive as they require pumps and seals, etc. and any leakage may be very costly. All these led to the development of solid lubricants. The requirement of the solid lubricant was, it should be able to completely separate two sliding surfaces even under very high load and adverse conditions, while allowing the surface to slide.

Graphite and molybdenum disulphide (MoS_2) are the two best known solid lubricants in the industry. A solid lubricant is a thin film composed of a single solid or a combination of solids introduced between two rubbing surfaces for the purpose of modifying friction and wear. Solid lubricants are solely used in chiples metal working such as drawing, rolling, stamping, extrusing and spinning. In the machining operation where chips are formed, these solid lubricants are used with fluids or oils as base.

Polymers and polymer-based materials have most of the advantages of other solid lubricants plus they have following additional advantages :

- They absorb vibration and are generally noiseless.
- Their conformability is better and they absorb minor dimensional in-accuracy better.
- Polymer components can be easily formed by machining or moulding etc.

Of the wide range of commercially available polymers, PTFE, polyacetal, polyethylene, nylon and polyamide are commonly used in tribology and PTFE is the most outstanding amongst all. However, many reinforcements and fillers are to be incorporated in these materials at PTFE and other polymers have poor creep resistance and mechanical stability.

Coefficient of friction of PTFE, sliding on itself, can be as slow as 0.04 but, for other polymers, coefficient of friction varies from 0.15 to 0.4. However, the use of polymers is limited by temperature.

The main requirements for solid lubricants are :

- Thermal stability
- Low shear strength
- Surface protection and
- Good bonding properties

1.12.1.4 Gases

The principle of operation of a hydrodynamic or hydrostatic bearing using gas as a lubricant is basically same as that of an oil-lubricated bearing. In general, gases have extremely low coefficient of absolute viscosity as compared to oils. Consequently, viscous resistance is very less. In gas lubrication, the film thickness is thinner than oil-lubricated bearings. **Air** is used as one of the main lubricants and hence the bearings are called as **aerodynamic bearings** or **aerostatic bearings**. To operate an aerodynamic bearing successfully, the following points should be kept in mind.

- The surfaces of the journal and bearing should be finished with high accuracy.
- The alignment between the journal and bearing must be very good.
- The dimensions and clearances must be accurate.
- The speed must be high.
- The load should be relatively low.

One of the exclusive advantages of gas bearings is that these can be operated over extremely wide ranges of temperature. Due to this gas bearings can be used at temperatures upto 500°C for prolonged periods. One more important advantage of gas bearings is its low frictional characteristics. For this reason, these bearings are being used in near-static apparatus, such as dynamometers, wind-tunnel balances and other sophisticated mechanical instruments. Low frictional characteristics of externally pressurised gas bearings can be exploited in machine tool slideways. Gas bearings can also be used effectively where it is necessary to keep the environment free from contamination by liquid lubricants, such as in high-purity gas handling plants. However, gas bearings are prone to instability. Therefore, a designer, or a user of gas bearings should be conversant with the characteristics for successful operations.

1.12.2 Properties of Lubricants

The physical and chemical properties of mineral oils affect lubrication. A few properties may have both physical and chemical effects. Recognition of these properties is useful for designing lubrication systems, choosing lubricating oils, diagnosing lubrication, friction and wear problems, and selecting the appropriate testing method.

1.12.2.1 Viscosity

The most important single property of a lubricant is its **viscosity.**

 'Viscosity' is defined as the internal frictional resistance offered by a fluid to change its shape or relative motion of its parts. Sir Isaac Newton was the first person to propose that a force is necessary to shear a fluid film. This force is a measure of internal friction of a fluid and it resembles friction between two solid surfaces.

In fluid-film lubrication, load-carrying capacity depends on the viscosity of the lubricant. A lubricant with extremely low viscosity cannot form a layer of fluid film between two sliding surfaces. Again, if the viscosity of a lubricant increases, the frictional resistance and heat generation in the bearing increases. Thus, the choice of a lubricant with proper viscosity is an important consideration in bearing design.

An oil film of thickness h, placed between two parallel plates is shown in Fig. 1.36. The lower plate is stationary while the upper plate is moved with a velocity U by means of a force F.

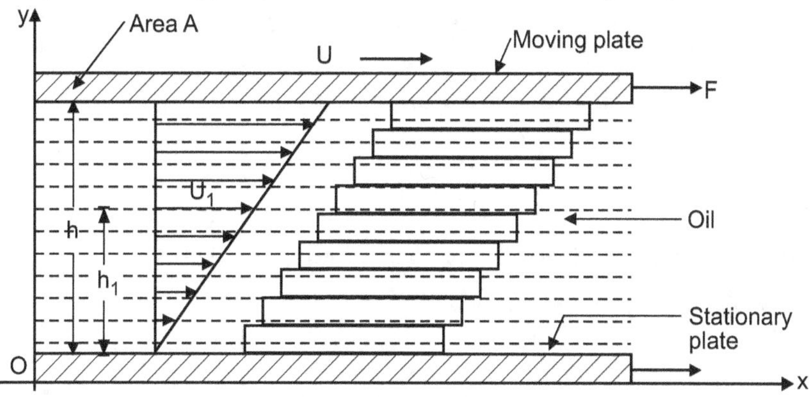

Fig. 1.36 : Newton's law of viscosity

The velocity of oil adhering to the top surface will have the velocity of top surface, whereas the oil particles adhering to the stationary surface (bottom surface) will have zero velocity.

Under this condition the velocity of oil at any point in the film is proportional to the distance of the point from the stationary surface. It may be considered that the flow is equivalent to a large number of thin layers of fluid sliding over each other. Therefore,

$$\frac{U}{h} = \frac{U_1}{h_1} = \frac{U_2}{h_2} \text{ etc.}$$

This type of orderly movement is called **streamline, laminar** or **viscous flow.**

The tangential force per unit area i.e. $\left(\dfrac{F}{A}\right)$ is shear stress, while the ratio $\left(\dfrac{U}{h}\right)$ is the rate of shear. According to Newton's law of viscosity, the shear stress is proportional to the rate of shear at any point in the fluid.

Therefore,

$$\frac{F}{A} \propto \frac{U}{h}$$

or

$$\frac{F}{A} = \mu \frac{U}{h} \qquad \text{... (1.1)}$$

The constant of proportionality μ in the above equation is called **absolute (dynamic) viscosity.**

The equation (1.1) can also be written as,

$$F = \mu A \frac{U}{h} \qquad \text{... (1.2)}$$

When the velocity distribution is non-linear with respect to h, the term $\left(\dfrac{U}{h}\right)$ in the above equation is replaced by $\left(\dfrac{dU}{dh}\right)$ and the equation is rewritten as,

$$F = \mu A \left(\frac{dU}{dh}\right) \qquad \text{... (1.3)}$$

Any lubricant which obeys the above law is a **Newtonian lubricant.**

The reciprocal of viscosity is called **fluidity.**

$$\frac{1}{\mu} = \frac{\dfrac{dU}{dh}}{\left(\dfrac{F}{A}\right)} \qquad \text{... (1.4)}$$

The **unit of absolute (dynamic) viscosity** is given by,

From equation (1.1), μ is given by,

$$\mu \;=\; \frac{Fh}{AU} \tag{1.5}$$

$\therefore$ Unit of absolute viscosity is,

$$\Rightarrow \frac{(N)\ (mm)}{(mm^2)\ (mm/s)}$$

$$\Rightarrow N\text{-}s/mm^2$$

In S.I. units, the absolute viscosity is **N-s/m² or Pa-s.**

In c.g.s. units, the absolute viscosity is dyne-s/cm². The popular unit of viscosity is **Poise**, which gives **absolute viscosity in dyne-s/cm².**

Also,

$$1\ P \;=\; 0.1\ Pa\text{-}s \tag{1.6}$$

Poise is a large unit and viscosities of most of the lubricating oils are given in terms of **centi-Poise (cP),** which is one-hundredth of a Poise. Therefore, two separate notations are used for viscosity, viz.,

$$\mu \;=\; \text{Viscosity in units of } (N\text{-}s/mm^2)$$

and

$$z \;=\; \text{Viscosity in units of } (cP)$$

The relationship between z and μ is as follows :

$$1\ cP \;=\; \frac{1}{10^2}\ \text{Poise}$$

$$=\; \frac{1}{10^2}\left(\frac{dyne\text{-}s}{cm^2}\right)$$

$$=\; \frac{1}{10^2}\times\left(\frac{N}{10^5}\right)\left[\frac{s}{(10^2\ mm^2)}\right]$$

$$=\; 10^{-9}\ N\text{-}s/mm^2 \text{ or MPa.s}$$

$\therefore$ $$1\ N\text{-}s/mm^2 \;=\; 10^9\ cP \tag{1.7}$$

Therefore, $$\mu \;=\; \frac{z}{10^9} \tag{1.8}$$

The viscosity of most lubricants lie in the range of **2 to 400 cP**. To give a quantitative idea of absolute or dynamic viscosity, the water has the viscosity of the order of 1 cP at room temperature, while air has a viscosity of 0.02 cP.

Another measure of viscosity is **kinematic viscosity (z_k) which equals z divided by density (ρ).**

$$z_k = \frac{z}{\rho} \qquad \qquad \text{... (1.9)}$$

where,

z_k = Kinematic viscosity

z = Absolute (dynamic) viscosity

ρ = Mass density of fluid in gm/cm^3

In c.g.s. units, the unit of kinematic viscosity is **Stoke (St).**

Also, $\qquad 1\,St = 1\,cm^2/s$ $\qquad\qquad$ ... (1.10)

Like poise the stoke is a large unit, so it is used as **Centistoke (cSt)** which is one-hundredth of a stoke.

In S.I. units, the kinematic viscosity is **m²/s.**

Measurement of Viscosity :

Instruments that are used to measure viscosity of a fluid are known as **viscometers.** Most viscometers do not measure the absolute viscosity directly but measure kinematic viscosity z_k.

In practice, it is difficult to carry out an experiment with two parallel plates for measurement of viscosity. The popular method of determining viscosity is to measure the time required for a given volume of oil to pass through a capillary tube of standard dimensions. The oil is kept in a reservoir which is immersed in a constant temperature bath. Based on this principle, there are three commercial viscometers named after Saybolt, Redwood and Engler.

The ASTM standard method recommends the use of a viscometer called the **Saybolt Universal Viscometer.** The method is based on noting the time of emptying a given quantity (60 ml) of the lubricant at a given temperature through a capillary tube of standard dimensions and the time is measured in seconds. The unit of viscosity is called **Saybolt Universal Seconds (SUS)**, which is related to kinematic viscosity by the following relationship.

$$z_k = \left[0.22\,t - \frac{180}{t}\right] \qquad\qquad \text{... (1.11)}$$

where, t is viscosity in Saybolt Universal Seconds (SUS) and z_k is the kinematic viscosity in centistokes (cSt). The Saybolt Universal viscometer is widely used in U.S.A.

In SI units, kinematic viscosity $z_k = \left(0.22\,t - \frac{180}{t}\right) \times 10^{-6}\,m^2 s$

In SI units, dynamic (absolute) viscosity $z = \rho \cdot z_k$ N-s m^2 where ρ-kg/m^3 is the density of the lubricant.

In Redwood viscometer, 50 ml of lubricating oil is passed through a capillary tube of specific dimensions and the time is measured in terms of **Redwood seconds**. The Redwood viscometer is widely used in U.K.

1.12.2.2 Effect of Temperature on Viscosity

The viscous resistance of a lubricating oil is due to intermolecular forces. As the temperature increases, the oil expands and the molecules move farther apart and the intermolecular forces decrease, as a result of which the viscosity decreases. Thus, *viscosity of a lubricating oil decreases with increasing temperature.* The change of viscosity due to a change in temperature is different for different oils. Therefore, the two oils having the same viscosity at some temperature may have different viscosities at another temperature. There is no unique way to represent the variation of viscosity with temperature. A simple equation which gives reasonable accuracy for liquid lubricants is,

$$\log_e \mu \;=\; A + \frac{B}{T} \dots \tag{1.12}$$

where, A and B are constants and T is the absolute temperature. The rate of change of viscosity with respect to temperature is indicated by a number called **viscosity index. (V.I.).** To find the V.I. of an oil, its temperature-viscosity relationship must be considered with two standard oils. This is shown graphically in Fig. 1.37.

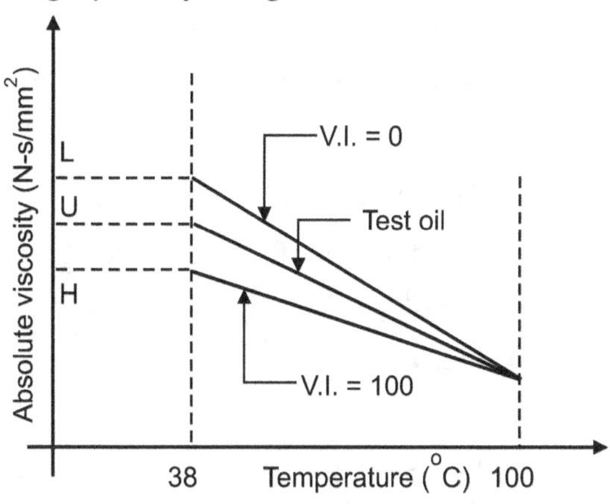

Fig. 1.37

The V.I. can be calculated from the following equation :

$$\text{V.I.} \;=\; \frac{L - U}{L - H} \times 100 \tag{1.13}$$

where,

U = Viscosity at 38°C of the test oil whose viscosity index is to be calculated

L = Viscosity at 38°C of an oil with V.I. = 0 having same viscosity at 100°C as the test oil whose viscosity index is to be calculated

H = Viscosity at 38°C of an oil with V.I. = 100, having same viscosity at 100°C as the test oil whose viscosity index is to be calculated

In this system, two groups of mineral oils were used for comparison. These are **Pennsylvania** and **Gulf Coast Oils.** The Pennsylvania oils were considered to be a superior group and were given V.I. = 100 (least change in viscosity with respect to temperature). The other group, that is Gulf Coast oils were rated V.I. = 0 (maximum change in viscosity with respect to temperature). A V.I. of 90 indicates that the oil with this value thins out less rapidly than oil with a V.I. of 50.

1.12.2.3 Effect of Pressure on Viscosity

As the pressure of lubricating oil is increased, the molecules are forced to come closer thereby, decreasing the intermolecular forces. This increases the viscosity.

The viscosity of lubricating oils increases with pressure relatively slowly at low pressure, but the influence of pressure on viscosity at higher pressure is significant. As the pressure is further increased, the rate of change of viscosity increases, until at high pressure the oils become plastic solids. The variation of viscosity with pressure is very important in the case of elastohydrodynamic line and point contacts, such as in cams, gears and rolling-element bearings.

For most mineral oils the following equations give reasonable accuracy.

$$\mu = \mu_o \exp(\alpha p) \qquad \qquad \dots (1.14)$$

where,

μ_o = Absolute viscosity at atmospheric pressure

α = Pressure coefficient of viscosity

μ = Absolute viscosity at pressure p

p = Normal pressure

1.12.2.4 Oiliness

The oiliness is the property by virtue of which the lubricant remains attached with the surface. Oiliness is that property of a lubricant that produces low friction under conditions of boundary lubrication. The lower the friction, the greater the oiliness.

1.12.2.5 Pour Point

It is defined as the temperature at which the oil just ceases to flow freely under the specified conditions. Thus, it imposes a lower limit on the oil working temperature and determines the suitability of lubricants for low-temperature installations.

1.12.2.6 Flash Point

It is defined as the lowest temperature at which the vapour given off by oil, when heated in a standard apparatus, ignites momentarily on the application of a flame. It is the measure of the fire hazard. The knowledge of flash point of oils is particularly important when used in high pressure systems of aircraft or in forging process where oil, leaking from a pipe, may come into contact with a hot metal leading to fire hazards.

1.12.2.7 Fire Point

It is the temperature at which the lubricating oil gives off sufficient vapour to burn it continuously, when ignited.

1.12.2.8 Oxidation Stability

At room temperatures, the oxidation rate of mineral oils is fairly low but it is greatly accelerated at temperature above 90°C. The oxidation products vary but in general they consist of acidic compounds, sludge and lacquers. The insoluble products may clog oil holes, pipelines, filters and other elements. The soluble products may cause the oil to become corrosive and to increase in viscosity. Thus, oxidation has an influence on the life of oil as well as the lubricating system.

1.12.2.9 Foaming

Foaming is defined as the production and coalescence of gas bubbles on a lubricant surface. Excessive foaming of oil due to churning may lead to inadequate lubrication and related problems. This is especially true for hydrostatic bearings where the pump used in the hydraulic line cannot deal efficiently with a frothy mixture. Excessive foam can starve bearings and pumps of liquid lubricant (pump cavitation) causing failure, and cause poor performance in hydraulic systems.

1.12.2.10 Thermal Conductivity

Thermal conductivity is the rate of transfer of heat for a given temperature gradient through a material. The rate of transfer of heat from a hot spot to a cooler area in a bearing is a factor in controlling overheating. Therefore, an oil with a high thermal conductivity would be expected to lower the temperature of a bearing. Thermal conductivity of a lubricating oil is used in equations to calculate heat transfer in bearings. Most mineral oils have approximately the same thermal conductivity. Thermal conductivity does not change appreciably with the change in temperature.

1.12.2.11 Demulsibility

This property is usually desired in oils, which may come into contact with water by leakage or by condensation. Demulsibility is the ability of a oil that is insoluble in water to separate from the water with which it may be mixed in the form of an emulsion. The demulsibility number of an oil can be found from a standard test which determines the time in seconds required for a known volume of oil to separate from an equal volume of condensed steam. Emulsifiable oils are used in metal cutting processes where the function of the emulsion is to cool the system rather than to lubricate it.

1.12.2.12 Acidity and Alkalinity

Traces of weak organic acids present in lubricating oils do not cause any harm. But acids formed by combustion or oxidation and introduced by contamination may cause harm. Acidity of oil is expressed in terms of **neutralisation number,** which is defined as the weight of potassium hydroxide (KOH) in milligrams required to neutralize one gram of oil.

In some specialised applications, alkalinity is introduced in the lubricants. For example, engine oils are alkaline for the purpose of neutralizing fuel combustion products.

1.12.2.13 Specific Gravity or Relative Density

It is the ratio of density of lubricant to density of water at the same temperature and pressure.

Most mineral oils have relative densities in the range of 0.85 to 0.95.

1.12.3 Types of Additives

In order to have improved characteristics, most modern lubricating oils contain chemical compounds as additives. Thus, additive is a compound that enhances some property, or imparts some new property to the base fluid. In some hydraulic fluid formulations, the additive volume may constitute as much as 20% of the final composition. The most important types of additives include anti-oxidants, anti-wear additives, corrosion inhibitors, viscosity index improvers, and foam suppressants.

Viscosity index improvers (V.I. improvers) are added to an oil to reduce the rate of change of viscosity with temperature and these are usually high-molecular weight polymers.

Oiliness Additives : Number of vegetable, animal and fish oils have a much greater oiliness than mineral oils. To have the benefits of thermal stability and at the same time to retain the benefits of oiliness, the above mentioned oils are added to mineral oils.

Pour-Point Depressants are used to delay the formation of rigid structure from waxy crystals precipitated from cooled mineral oils and this is done by forming a coating on the waxy crystals. Complex polymers are generally used for this purpose.

Oxidation Inhibitors reduce the rate of formation of oxidation products.

Detergents or Dispersants are used mainly in engine oils to keep the engine clear by holding insoluble material in suspension and preventing the formation of sludge or deposits. Polymer compounds are mostly used as detergents for low-temperature conditions, while for high-temperature conditions, organometallic salts are the usual type of additives.

Extreme Pressure Additives (E.P. additives) allow a mineral oil to operate satisfactorily under conditions of extremely high pressures and temperatures. The most common extreme pressure additives are compounds of sulphur, phosphorous and chlorine. These react with the metal surfaces to form coatings, which exhibit plastic flow and have low-shear resistance.

Corrosion Inhibitors : Alcohols, esters, organic acids, amines or soaps are used as corrosion inhibitors, which are absorbed on or react with the metal surfaces to form protective films.

Anti-Foam Additives : Silicon-based compounds are used as antifoam additives which minimize foaming in situations where this might cause problems.

Emulsifiers : Metallic soaps and petroleum sulphonates are used as emulsifiers to stabilize oil-water emulsions and are particularly used for metal cutting oils, fire resistant hydraulic fluids, etc.

Anti-Friction Additives : Anti-friction, sometimes called lubricity, is defined as the ability of a lubricant to reduce friction, other than by its purely viscous properties. Anti-friction additives reduce friction below that of the base oil alone under conditions of boundary lubrication. The additives are absorbed on, or react with the metal surface or its oxide to form monolayers of low shear strength material. The compounds are long chain (greater than 12 carbon atoms), alcohols, amines, and fatty acids. A classic example is oleic acid reacting with iron oxide to form a film of the iron oleate soap. The low shear strength of the soap film causes the low friction.

Anti-Wear Additives : Anti-wear additives are those which reduce or control wear. They form organic, metallo-organic, or metal salt films on the surface. Sliding or rolling occurs on top of, or within the films, thus reducing metal-to-metal contact. Anti-wear additives only reduce the rate of wear.

Anti-Scuff Additives : Anti-scuff additives are those that prevent scuffing. **Scuffing** is defined as damage caused by solid-phase welding between sliding surfaces. Anti-scuff additives reduce scuffing by forming thick films of high melting point metal salts on the surface which prevent metal to metal contact which, when extensive, may cause scuffing.

There is some overlapping of anti-wear and anti-scuff performance. That is, some additives have good anti-wear properties and can prevent scuffing to a limited degree.

1.13 LUBRICATING OILS

A Lubricating Oil should have Certain Desirable Properties as Listed Below.

- The oil should be available in a wide range of viscosity.
- It should be able to dissipate frictional heat efficiently.
- It should be stable under thermal stresses i.e. the change in viscosity with respect to temperature should be minimum.
- It should be stable under oxidation stresses. i.e. it should be chemically stable and not react with the bearing materials.
- It should have low volatility i.e. it should have a good fire resistance.
- It should have good mechanical stability.
- It should be economical.
- It should have a long life.

The two major categories of lubricating oils are – (i) mineral oils and (ii) natural oils (vegetable or animal oils). The availability, good performance, variety and cheapness of mineral oils have made them the first choice in almost 90% of the applications. These oils are classified by the **Society of Automotive Engineers (SAE)** in terms of grades as discussed below.

1.13.1 SAE Classification

Commonly used viscosity grade have been standardised as **SAE (Society of Automotive Engineers) viscosity grades.** Each lubricating oil is designated by a SAE grade or number which is indicative of the viscosity, though it does not directly represent the viscosity. Table 1.12 gives the SAE grades and their viscosity range.

Table 1.12 : SAE Grades and their Viscosities

SAE Grade	Viscosity Range	
	at 0°F (–18°C)	at 210°F (99°C)
	in SUS	in SUS
Motor Oils		
SAE 5 W	Less than 6000	–
SAE 10 W	6000 – 12000	–
SAE 20 W	12000 – 48000	–
SAE 20	–	45 – 58
SAE 30	–	58 – 70
SAE 40	–	70 – 85
SAE 50	–	85 – 110
Gear Oils		
SAE 75 W	Less than 15000	–
SAE 80 W	15000 – 100000	–
SAE 90	–	75 – 120
SAE 140	–	120 – 200
SAE 250	–	200 and above

The viscosities of oils are measured at 210°F (99°C) and viscosities of oils with W suffix are measured at 0°F (–18°C). The W suffix indicates the winter grading of the oils. When SAE number is more, it indicates more viscous oil. e.g. "5W" signifies the oil viscosity when the oil is cold.

Some oils, with polymers added to them have high viscosity indices, and are called **multigrade oils.** This is because they are in **one** grade at 0°F and in a **higher** grade at 210°F. As an example **10W/30** oil may have a viscosity of 8000 SUS at 0°F and 65 SUS at 210°F. It falls into the 10 W range at 0°F and SAE 30 at 210°F. For this reason, it is called **10 W/30**.

1.13.2 Recycling of Used Oils and Oil Conservation

We can make a difference by recycling the used motor oil from our car, truck, motorcycle, boat, recreational vehicle or lawnmover, etc. This can prevent pollution and conserve energy for a safer and healthier tomorrow.

Benefits of Recycling :

Many individuals who are unfamiliar with the importance of recycling used oil are unconsciously harming the environment by throwing it away with their normal garbage or emptying their used oil into storm drains. Such actions, especially emptying used oil into storm drains, can cause real harm to the environment. To put into perspective, just one gallon of used oil can contaminate 1 million gallons of water.

Recycling used motor oils keeps it out of our rivers, lakes, streams and even the ground water. In many cases, that means keeping it out of our drinking water, off our beaches, and away from our wild life. We all share the responsibility of protecting our environment and keeping our water safe. Recycling used oils allows us to continue to enjoy what many of us take for granted everyday - clean water.

What happens to Used Oil ?

There are many practical uses of used motor oil. A primary use is to re-refine it into a base stock for lubricating oil. This process is very similar to refining of crude oil. The result is that the re-refined oil is of as high a quality as the virgin oil product. In fact, re-refining used oil takes 50 to 85 percent less energy than refining crude oil.

A secondary use of the used oil is to burn it for energy. Large industrial boilers can effectively burn the used oil with minimum pollution. As a result some used oil is sent to power plants or cement kilns to be burned as fuel. On a smaller scale, small quantities of used oil is burned in a specially designed heater to provide space heating for small businesses.

Uses of Recycled Motor Oil :

Recycling used motor oil keeps oil out of land fills and ensures that this oil is available for re-use, reconditioning, reprocessing or re-refining. *Currently, used motor oil can be reused or recycled in one of three ways – reconditioning, reprocessing or re-refining.*

(a)   **Re-Refining :** Proper, modern re-refining with careful feed and product quality control, as well as sophisticated processes can successfully treat used motor oil to remove impurities so that it can be used as base stock for new lubricating oil. In other words, with good design and process management the used oil can be re-refined into "new" oil giving it a second life so it can be used for vehicle motor oil again.

Currently, 14% of used motor oil is re-refined and the consumer demand for this product has not made re-refining economically efficient for oil manufactures. The result is that in some cases re-refined motor oil may be more expensive than virgin motor oil. When purchasing re-refined motor oil make sure that the oil specifications for the product meet those required by your vehicle manufacturer.

(b)   Reconditioning : In some industries, oil is filtered through a commercial filtration system or otherwise cleaned. This process helps to remove insoluble impurities so the oil potentially can be used again and again. Although the cleaning process does not always bring the oil back to its original quality, such cleaning, when combined with replenishment of key additives, does extend the oil's life and use.

(c)   Re-Use and Reprocessing : Both lubricants, such as motor oil, and fuels, such as heating oil, and petroleum products.

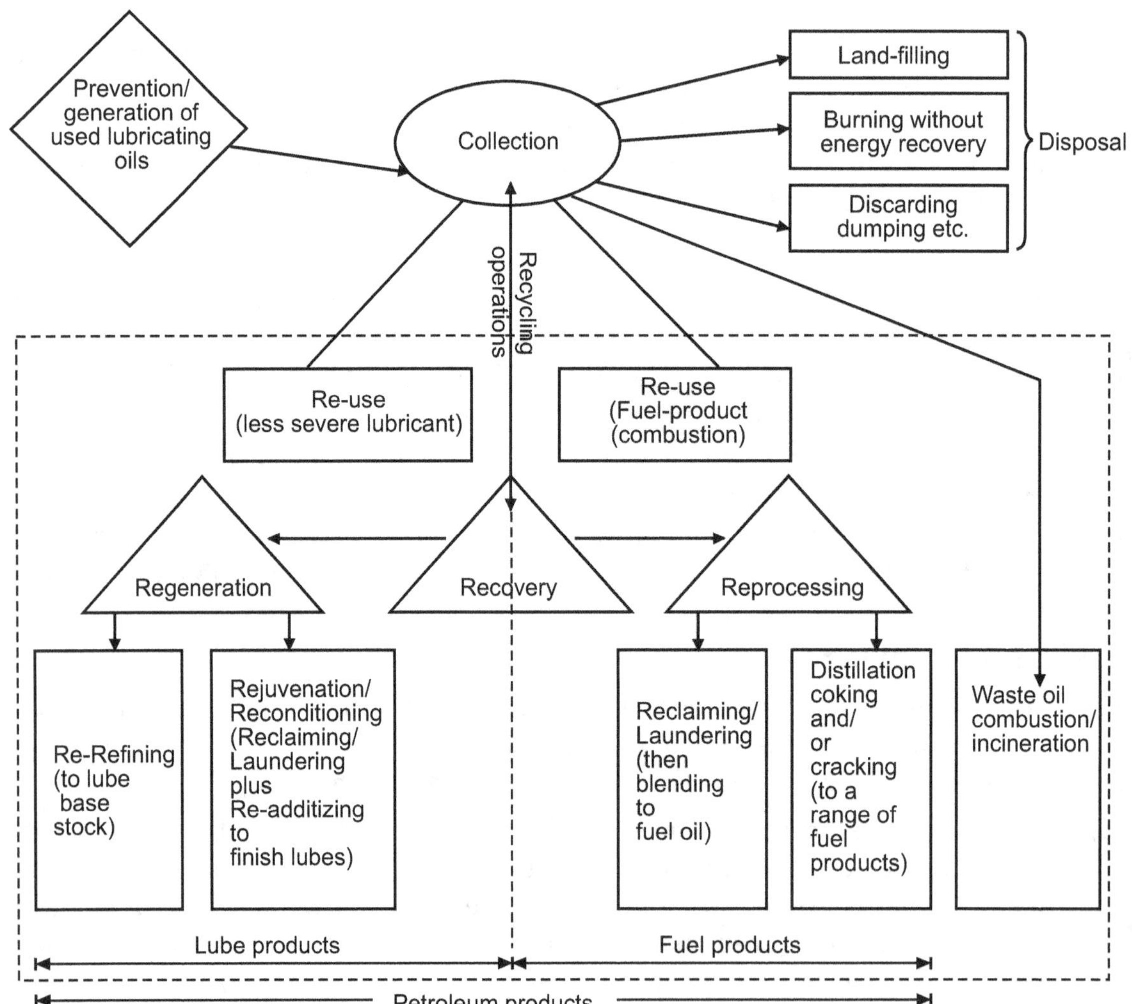

Fig. 1.38 : Used oil management diagram

When an oil can no longer perform its original lubrication job, it may be perfectly suitable for re-use and second life as a fuel petroleum product in, say, a power plant with little or no treatment. If some treatment is needed, reprocessing of used motor oil removes some water and particles so that the oil can be burned and used as fuel to generate heat or electricity for commercial applications. 74% of all oil re-use/recycling in the United States is burning in turbines, incinerators, power plants, cement kilns and manufacturing facilities (asphalt, steel, etc.). An additional 11% of the used motor oil is burned in specifically designed industrial space heaters. This creates a valuable form of energy, which helps the nation's economy by avoiding the need to refine new commercial heating oil from imported crude oil.

Fig. 1.38 shows the used oil management diagram.

It is important to know that, if we recycle just two gallons of used oil, it can generate enough electricity to run the average household for almost 24 hours. *Recycled used motor oil not only conserves a valuable resource, it keeps our surface waters and ground water supplies safe from potential contamination from improperly disposed oil.*

1.13.3 Disposal of Scrap Oil

During normal use of oil, impurities such as dirt, metal scrapings, water or chemicals, can get mixed in with the oil, so that in time, the oil no longer performs well. Eventually, this used oil must be replaced with virgin or re-refined oil to do the job correctly.

Currently, used motor oil can be re-used or recycled one of three ways – re-refining, re-conditioning or reprocessing. In **re-refining**, (the process is similar to refining of crude oil) the used oil is successfully treated to remove impurities so that it can be used as bask stock for new lubricating oil. In **re-conditioning**, the used oil is filtered through a commercial filtration system, to remove insoluble impurities so the oil potentially can be used again and again. In **reprocessing**, the used oil is suitable to burn it for energy (as a burning fuel) in large industrial boilers and used to generate heat or electricity for commercial applications.

When all above recycling processes of used oil are not possible, then the oil is considered as **scrap oil**.

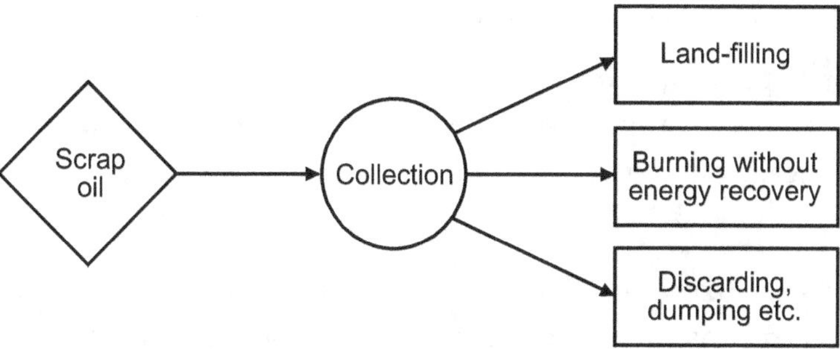

Fig. 1.39 : Disposal of scrap oil

Fig. 1.39 shows the various processes of disposal such as, disposal of scrap oils - by land-filling, by burning without energy recovery or by discarding/dumping of it.

During Disposal the Following is Prohibited :

- Any discharge into inland surface water, ground water, territorial sea water and drainage systems.

- Any deposit and/or discharge harmful to the soil and any uncontrolled discharge of residues resulting from the processing of waste oils.

- Any processing causing air pollution which exceeds the level prescribed by existing provisions.

All these disposals must be subject to registration and national supervision, possibly including a system of permits, from the competitive authority.

1.13.4 Oil Emulsion

An **emulsion** is a dispersion of minute drops of one liquid in another where an emulsion incorporates small amount of disperse phase. It resembles a lyophobe solution including exhibition of Brownian movement. (e.g. colloidal dispersions have the distinguishing characteristics of maintaining continuous random motion called as Brownian movement and the particles are submicroscopic, the system of which is called as disperse system) and precipitation by electrolysis. Stable emulsions of two or more pure liquids require the addition of an emulsifier (i.e. emulsifying agent). For convenience, emulsions sometimes are classified as :

- **Oil-water types** (oil or other immiscible material dispersed in water i.e. water is the continuous phase).

- **Water-oil types** (where water is the discontinuous phase).

Emulsion is a intimate mixture of oil and water, generally of a milky or cloudy appearance.

The first type i.e. oil-water type of emulsion is more common. Emulsions are particularly important in mining processes and in food, drug and cosmetic manufacture.

Breaking-up an emulsion is termed as de-emulsification.

The properties of disperse systems essentially arise from the large surface of the dispersed phase. The surface effects of a material which may be negligible in macro-dimension may become very significant when so magnified.

Application :

Emulsifiers may be included in defoamers. (It is a formulation of surface active materials used at low concentrations to prevent the formation of foam or to destroy foam which has formed) formulations to accelerate the dispersion of the defoamer throughout the foaming system. Such formulations are added to the foaming system neat or diluted with water.

Common type of defoamer consists of a dispersion in hydrocarbon oils of fine particles of silica coated with silicone; the silicone surface of the particles causes them to be hydrophobic. Hydrophobic particles can act as an emulsifying agent where the defoamer oil constitutes the continuous phase and the foam constitutes the dispersed phase.

A particle must be wetted to some extent by the dispersed phase in order to function as an emulsifier.

1.14 TYPES OF SLIDING CONTACT BEARINGS

The bearings in which the relative motion between the contacting surfaces is of sliding type are known as **sliding contact bearings.**

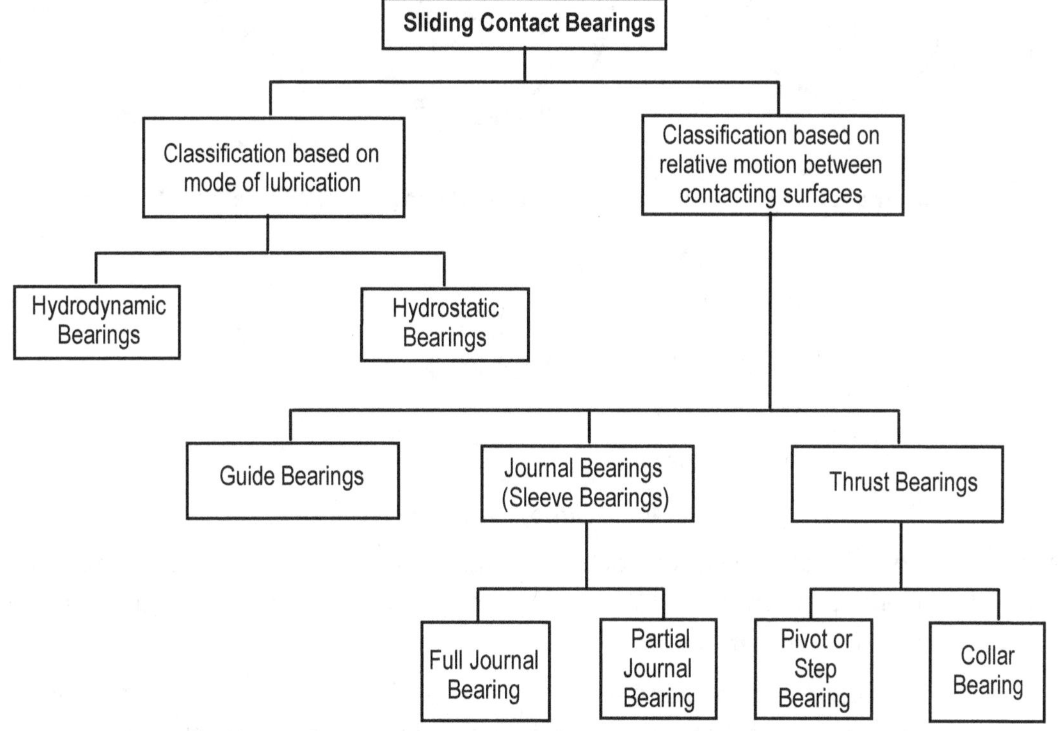

1.14.1 Classification Based on the Mode of Lubrication

1.14.1.1 Hydrodynamic Lubrication

In heavily loaded bearings such as thrust bearings and horizontal journal bearings, the fluids viscosity alone is not sufficient to maintain a film between the moving surfaces. In these bearings, higher fluid pressures are required to support the load until the fluid film is established. If this pressure is supplied by an outside source, it is called hydrostatic lubrication. If the pressure is generated internally, that is, within the bearing by dynamic action, it is referred to as hydrodynamic lubrication.

In hydrodynamic lubrication, a fluid wedge is formed by the relative surface motion of the journals or the thrust runners over their respective bearing surfaces.

The principle of hydrodynamic lubrication in journal bearing is shown in Fig. 1.40. In hydrodynamic lubrication, the load supporting fluid film is created by the shape and relative motion of the sliding surfaces.

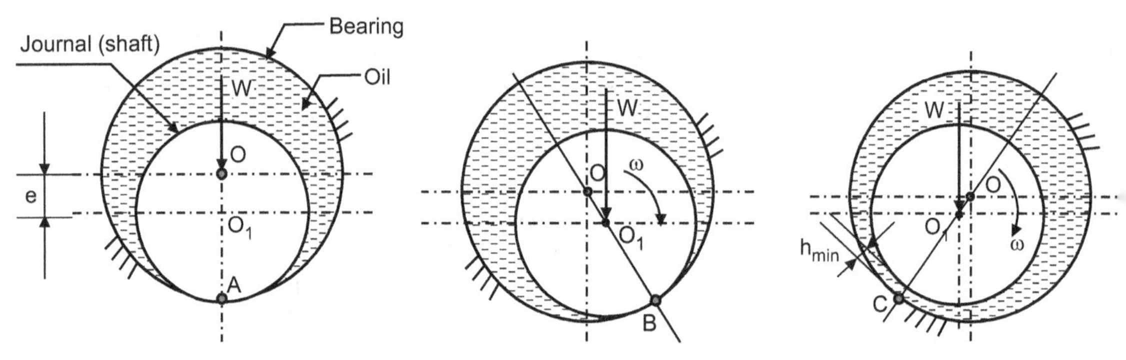

(a) Journal at rest   **(b) Journal starts rotating**   **(c) Journal at full speed**

e   –   Eccentricity

W   –   Radial load on journal

O   –   Centre of bearing

O_1 –   Centre of journal

ω   –   Speed

Fig. 1.40 : Hydrodynamic lubrication

As shown in Fig. 1.40 (a), initially, the journal (shaft) is at rest and it rests at the bottom of the bearing A, under the action of load W. Metal to metal contact is established at A. This point of contact is called as **seat of pressure.**

The journal now just starts to rotate in clockwise direction, inside the bearing as shown in Fig. 1.40 (b). Due to friction between two rubbing surfaces, the friction starts opposing the motion. The seat of pressure or point of contact between two surfaces then climbs up the bearing in a direction opposite to that of rotation. The point of contact shifts from A to B.

As the speed of journal is further increased, it will force the fluid into the wedge-shaped regions as shown in Fig. 1.40 (c). Since more and more fluids is forced into the wedge-shaped clearance space, sufficient pressure is generated within the system to carry the load. The pressure distribution around the periphery of the journal is shown in Fig. 1.41.

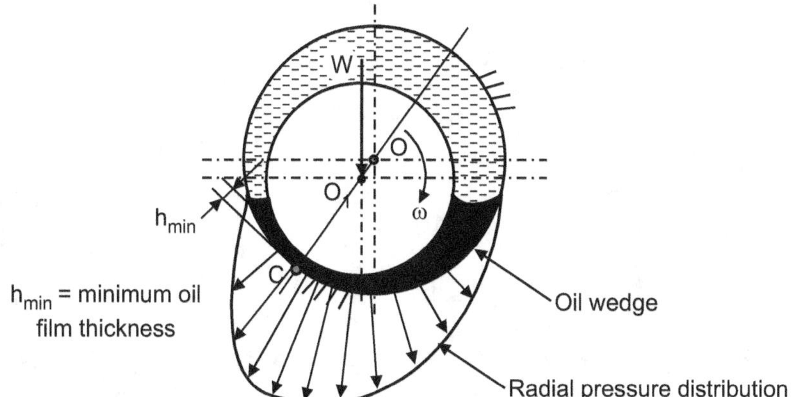

Fig. 1.41 : Radial pressure distribution in hydrodynamic lubrication

Since the pressure is created within the system due to rotation of journal, this type of bearing is also known as **self-acting bearing.** At particular journal speed, the pressure becomes sufficient to support the load (W) and the journal is shifted to other side [i.e. to left side as shown in Fig. 1.40 (c)] of vertical. In this situation, there is minimum clearance and oil-film thickness is minimum (h_{min}) at point C. [Refer Fig. 1.40 (c)].

The amount of rotation of the line of centres of journal and bearing from the load-line depends on :

- The magnitude of applied radial load (W).
- The journal speed (ω), and
- The viscosity of the lubricant.

Thus, in hydrodynamic bearings, it is not necessary to supply the lubricant under pressure. The only requirement is to ensure sufficient and continuous supply of the lubricant.

The minimum thickness of the fluid film increases with an increase in fluid viscosity and surface speed and decreases with an increase in load.

Examples : Main bearings, connecting rod bearings, gudgeon pin bearings, etc. mounted on engines. Also the applications of these bearings are seen in centrifugal pumps, compressors, etc.

Hydrodynamic bearings are simple in construction, easy to maintain, initial and maintenance cost is less as compared to hydrostatic bearings.

In hydrodynamic bearings, the journal always runs eccentric in the bearing and there is a wear at the start-up and stopping of rotation of the journal.

1.14.1.2 Hydrostatic Lubrication

In hydrostatic lubrication, load supporting fluid film, separating the two surfaces is created by an external source like a pump, supplying sufficient fluid under pressure as shown in Fig. 1.42.

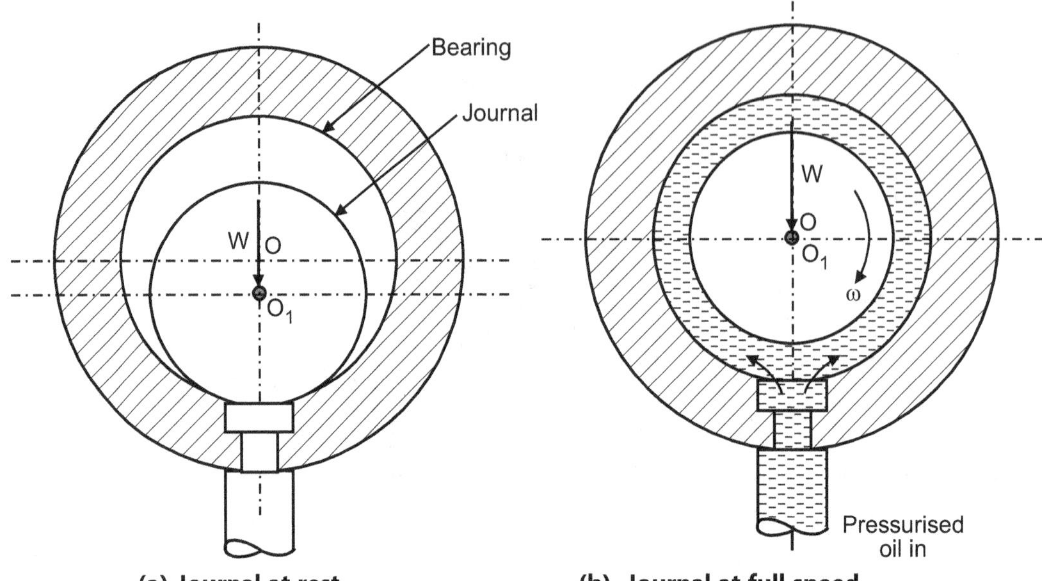

(a) Journal at rest   **(b) Journal at full speed**
Fig. 1.42 : Hydrostatic lubrication

Since the lubricant is supplied under pressure, this type of bearing is also called as **externally pressurised bearing.**

Fig. 1.42 shows the principle of hydrostatic lubrication in journal bearing. As shown in Fig. 1.42 (a), initially the journal rests on bearing surface under the radial load W. As the pump starts, high pressure lubricant is admitted in the clearance space, forcing the surfaces of bearing and journal to separate out as shown in Fig. 1.42 (b).

Examples :

- Vertical turbo generators, centrifuges, ball mills, etc.

Hydrostatic bearings are costly as compared to hydrodynamic bearings, however, it offers the following advantages :

- High load-carrying capacity even at low speeds.
- No starting friction.
- No rubbing action at any speed and load, hence wear and tear is less in hydrostatic bearings as compared to hydrodynamic bearings.

1.14.2 Classification based on Relative Motion between Contact Surfaces

1.14.2.1 Guide Bearings

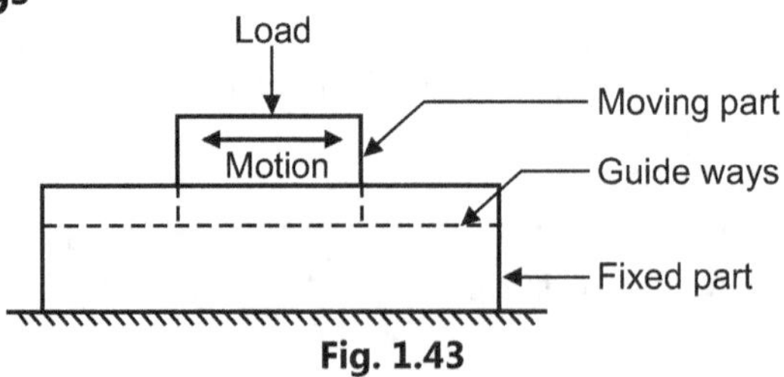

Fig. 1.43

In guide bearings, as shown in Fig. 1.43, the relative motion between two parts is linear. Examples of guide bearings are – guide-ways of machine tools, piston-cylinder, cross-head of steam engine, etc.

1.14.2.2 Journal (Sleeve) Bearings

If the relative motion between the two parts is of rotation and the pressure on the bearing is perpendicular to the axis of the shaft, the bearing is known as journal or sleeve bearing. The part which is enclosed is called the **journal** and the part which encloses the journal is called the **bearing.** Normally, the journal rotates in the fixed bearing. e.g. crankshaft rotating in main bearing. However, in some cases either the bearing rotates on the fixed-journal as in the hoisting drum, or both the journal and bearing rotate, as in crank-pin bearing.

The journal bearing may be a full journal bearing (as shown in Fig. 1.44) or a partial journal bearing (as shown in Fig. 1.45).

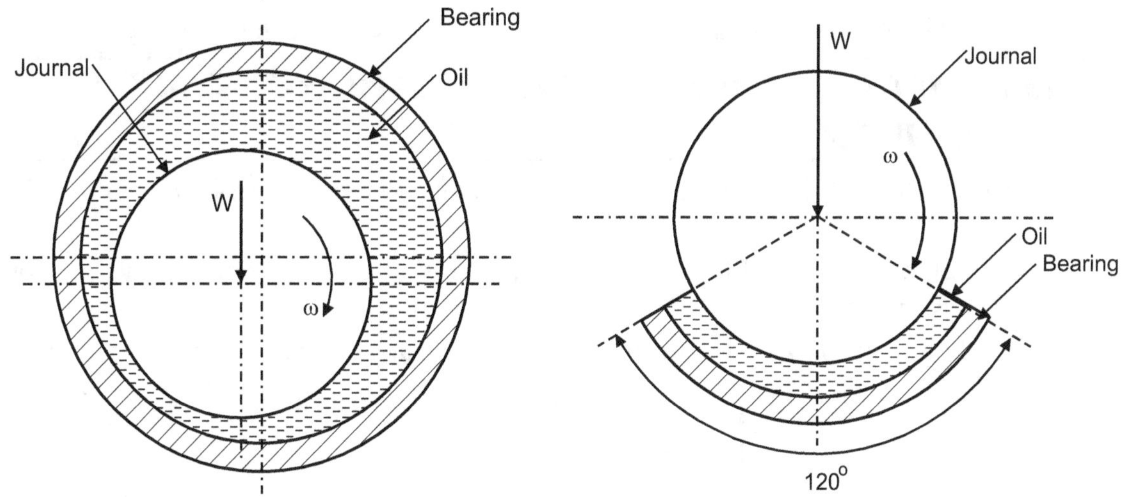

Fig. 1.44 : Full journal bearing   **Fig. 1.45 : Partial journal bearing**

1.14.2.3 Thrust Bearings

If the relative sliding motion between the two parts is of rotation and the pressure on the bearing is parallel to the axis of the shaft, the bearing is called thrust bearing.

In the thrust bearing, if the shaft terminates at the bearing surface, as shown in Fig. 1.46, then it is called **pivot bearing**, whereas if the shaft extends through and beyond the bearing, as shown in Fig. 1.47, then it is called **collar bearing.**

Pivot bearings are further classified as flat-pivot bearing or conical-pivot bearing. Similarly, collar bearings are further classified as single collar bearing or multi-collered bearing.

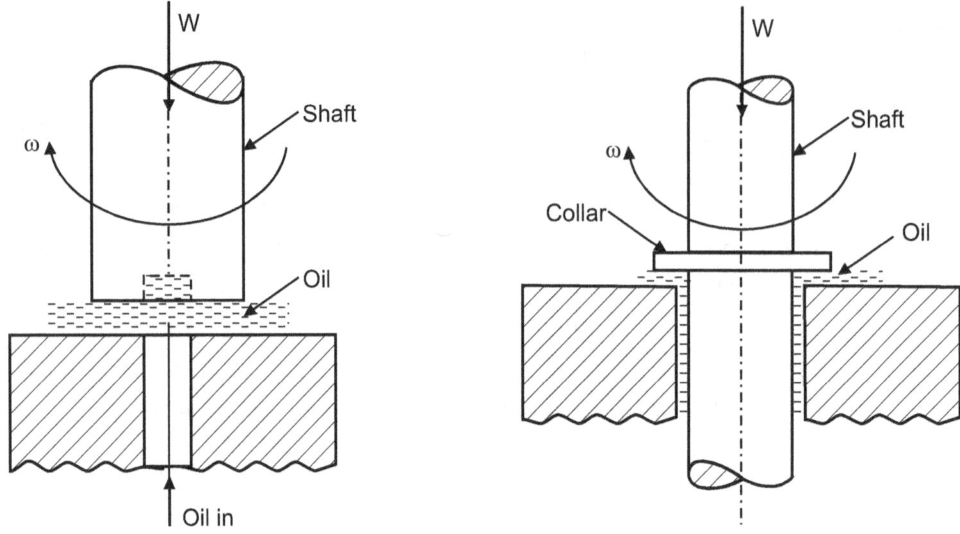

Fig. 1.46 : Pivot bearing   **Fig. 1.47 : Collar bearing**

1.15 COMPARISON OF SLIDING AND ROLLING CONTACT BEARINGS

The various factors which influence the selection between the two basic types of bearings are :

Magnitude of load, nature of load, speed, life, frictional loss, space requirement, positional accuracy, noise and cost.

Fig. 1.48 shows the plot of load-carrying capacity against speed for different types of bearings.

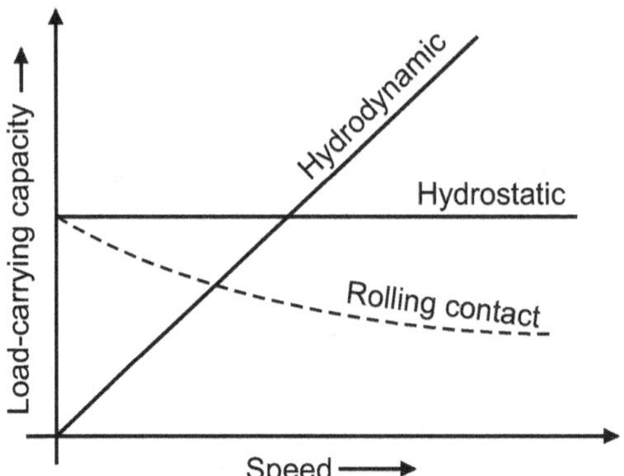

Fig. 1.48 : Load characteristics of bearings

1.   Magnitude of Load :

The sliding contact bearings are more suitable for large loads as compared to rolling contact bearings.

2.   Nature of Load :

The rolling contact bearings are vulnerable to shock loads due to poor damping. Because of the metal-to-metal contact, the rolling elements and races are subjected to plastic deformation under shock and fluctuating loads, which lead to the fatigue failure.

The sliding contact bearings with full-oil film are capable of taking shock and fluctuating loads. The oil film separating the journal and bearing surfaces absorb the shock. Therefore, the sliding contact bearings are used in heavy I.C. engines as main and connecting rod bearings.

3.   Speed :

Because of the centrifugal forces acting on the rolling elements, the rolling contact bearings are not suitable for high speed applications. As shown in Fig. 1.48, the load carrying capacity of the rolling contact bearings, reduces marginally with the speed.

On the other hand, the load-carrying capacity of the hydrodynamic bearings is directly proportional to the speed. As the speed increases, the oil-film thickness as well as the pressure increases. In hydrostatic bearings, the load-carrying capacity is independent of the speed. Therefore, the sliding contact bearings are more suitable for high speed applications.

4.   Life :

Due to fluctuating loads, the rolling contact bearings have very limited life as compared to sliding contact bearings.

5.   Frictional Loss :

The rolling contact bearings have lower starting friction compared to hydrodynamic bearings. In hydrodynamic bearings, during starting metal-to-metal contact in the boundary lubrication region results in a higher starting friction. However, under running conditions, because of the full oil-film the hydrodynamic bearings have lower frictional losses compared to rolling contact bearings. Therefore, the rolling contact bearings are suitable where there are frequent starts and stoppages. On the other hand, the hydrodynamic bearings are suitable where there is comparatively light load at the start and the load gradually increases with speed.

6.   Space Requirement :

Rolling contact bearings require more radial space, while sliding contact bearings require more axial space. In addition, sliding contact bearings require auxiliary equipments like pump, filter, sump, pipings, etc.

7.   Positional Accuracy :

The rolling contact bearings give better positional accuracy than the sliding contact bearings. In rolling contact bearings, the relative position of the inner race with respect to the outer race is independent of the operating parameters. On the other hand, in sliding contact bearings, the position of the journal with respect to the bearing varies with the operating parameters.

8.   Noise :

Rolling contact bearings generate more noise compared to sliding contact bearings due to metal-to-metal contact.

9.   Cost :

The cost of the sliding contact bearings is much higher compared to the rolling contact bearings due to auxiliary equipments like pump, filter, sump, pipings, etc. In addition, maintenance cost of sliding contact bearings is also more.

SOLVED EXAMPLES

Example 1.1 : Determine the viscosity of the lubricant in centipoise having viscosity 160 SUS and specific gravity 0.86.

Solution :

We have the equation for viscosity of lubricant,

$$z = \rho \cdot z_k$$

$$= \rho \left[0.22\, t - \frac{180}{t} \right]$$

where, ρ = Mass density of lubricant (kg/m^3)

$\qquad\qquad$ = 860 kg/m^3 $\qquad\qquad$ (as specific gravity = 0.86)

$\qquad\quad$ t = Viscosity in SUS

$\qquad\qquad$ = 160

$\therefore \qquad z = 860 \left[0.22 \times 160 - \frac{180}{160} \right] \times 10^{-6}$

$\qquad\quad z = 0.0293045$ N-s/m^2

$\qquad\quad z = 29.3045 \times 10^{-3}$ N-s/m^2

$\qquad\quad z = 29.3045 \times 10^{-3} \times 10^{-6}$ N-s/mm^2

$\qquad\quad z = 29.3045 \times 10^{-9}$ N-s/mm^2

$\qquad$ (1 cP $= 10^{-9}$ N-s/mm^2)

$\therefore \qquad z = 29.3045$ cP

Example 1.2 : Determine the viscosity of lubricant in centi-poise and centi-stokes, having viscosity 200 SUS and specific gravity 0.8. **[P.U. Dec. 2009, 4 Marks]**

Solution :

Viscosity of lubricant

$$z = \rho \cdot z_k$$

$$= \rho \left[0.22\, t - \frac{180}{t} \right]$$

Here, ρ = $0.8 \times 1000 = 800$ kg/m^3

$$t = \text{Viscosity in SUS} = 200$$

$$\therefore \quad z = 800\left[0.22 \times 200 - \frac{180}{200}\right] \times 10^{-6}$$

$$z = 0.034480 \ \text{N-s/m}^2$$

$$z = 34.48 \times 10^{-3} \ \text{N-s/m}^2$$

$$z = 34.48 \times 10^{-3} \times 10^{-6} \ \text{N-s/mm}^2$$

$$z = 34.48 \times 10^{-9} \ \text{N-s/mm}^2$$

$$(1 \ \text{cP} = 10^{-9} \ \text{N-s/mm}^2)$$

$$\therefore \quad z = 34.48 \ \text{cP}$$

Viscosity in centi-stokes (cSt) :

$$z_k = \left[0.22 \ t - \frac{180}{t}\right]$$

$$= \left[0.22 \times 200 - \frac{180}{200}\right]$$

$$z_k = 43.1 \ \text{cSt}$$

Example 1.3 : A rectangular plate of 250 mm width and 500 mm length is placed over a plane stationary surface. The two surfaces are separated by an oil-film of thickness 0.15 mm. The viscosity of oil is 40.5 cP. Determine the force required to pull the plate at a speed of 1.5 m/s.

Solution : Given :

$$b = 250 \ \text{mm}$$

$$l = 500 \ \text{mm}$$

$$h = 0.15 \ \text{mm}$$

$$\mu = 40.5 \ \text{cP}$$

$$= 40.5 \times 10^{-9} \ \text{N-s/mm}^2$$

$$U = 1.5 \ \text{m/s}$$

$$= 1500 \ \text{m/s}$$

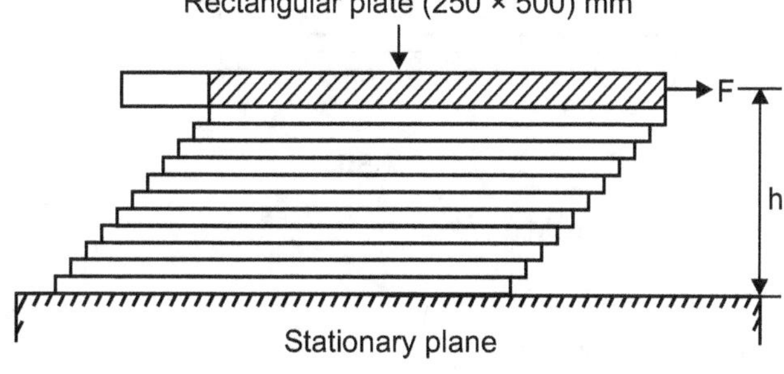

Fig. 1.49

- **Surface area of rectangular plate = A**

  i.e. $\qquad A = b \cdot l$

  $\qquad\qquad = 250 \times 500$

  $\qquad A = 125000 \text{ mm}^2$

- **Force required to pull the plate (F) :**

  $$F = \mu A \cdot \frac{dU}{dh}$$

  $$= \mu A \cdot \frac{U}{h}$$

  $$= 40.5 \times 10^{-9} \times 125000 \times \frac{1500}{0.15}$$

  $$F = 50.625 \text{ N}$$

Example 1.4 : A square plate of 400 × 400 mm is placed over a plane stationary surface. The two are separated by oil-film of thickness 0.1 mm. The viscosity of oil is 50 cP.

Determine the force required to pull the square plate at a speed of 2 m/s.

(P.U. Dec. 06, 4 marks)

Solution : Given : $\qquad b = 400 \text{ mm}$

$\qquad\qquad l = 400 \text{ mm}$

$\qquad\qquad h = 0.1 \text{ mm}$

$\qquad\qquad \mu = 50 \text{ cP} = 50 \times 10^{-9} \text{ N-s/mm}^2$

$\qquad\qquad U = 2 \text{ m/s} = 2000 \text{ mm/s}$

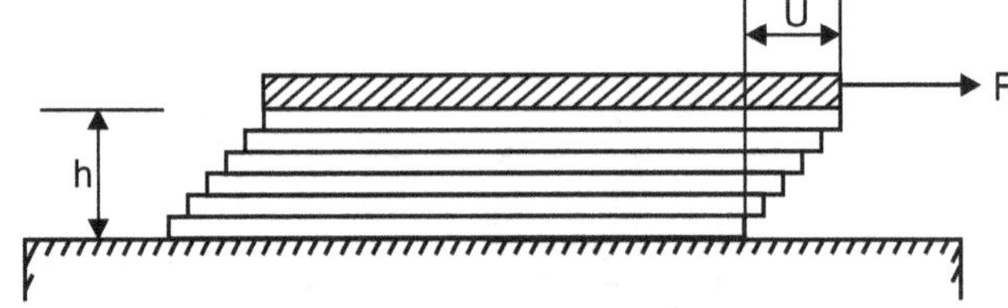

Fig. 1.50

- **Surface area of the square plate :**

  $\qquad A = b \times l$

  $\qquad\qquad = 400 \times 400$

  $\qquad A = 160000 \text{ mm}^2$

- **Force required to pull the plate :**

$$F = \mu \cdot A \cdot \frac{dU}{dh}$$

$$= \mu \cdot A \cdot \frac{U}{h}$$

$$= 50 \times 10^{-9} \times 160000 \times \frac{2000}{0.1}$$

$$F = 160 \text{ N}$$

Example 1.5 : A fluid coupling is used to transmit power from a diesel engine to a gear box. It consists of two identical hollow discs of inner diameter 150 mm and outer diameter 400 mm. One of the discs is mounted on the engine shaft running at 3600 r.p.m, while the other disc is mounted on the gear box shaft running at 3200 r.p.m. The two discs are separated by a fluid-film of 0.15 mm thickness. If the viscosity of fluid is 90 cP, derive the equation necessary for it and evaluate :

(i)   Power at gear box.

(ii)   Power supplied (i.e. power input) and

(iii)   The power lost in fluid coupling.

Solution : Given :

$$R_o = \frac{400}{2} = 200 \text{ mm}$$

$$R_i = \frac{150}{2} = 75 \text{ mm}$$

$$N_i = 3600 \text{ r.p.m.}$$

$$N_o = 3200 \text{ r.p.m.}$$

$$h = 0.15 \text{ mm}$$

$$\mu = 90 \text{ cP} = 90 \times 10^{-9} \text{ N-s/mm}^2$$

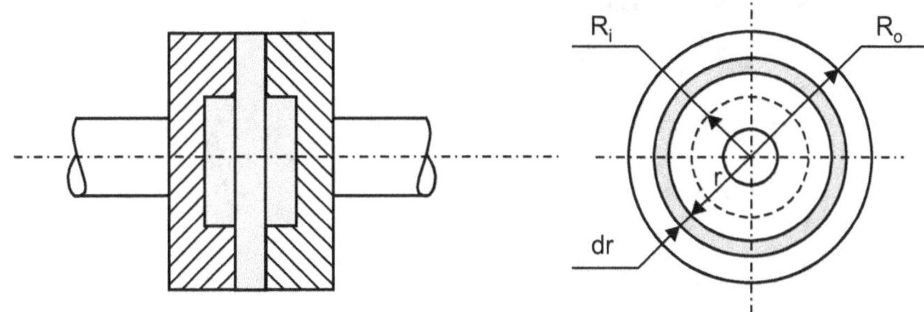

Fig. 1.51

Derivation :

- Difference between r.p.m. of disc on engine shaft and disc on gear box is,

$$N_R = N_i - N_o$$
$$= 3600 - 3200$$
$$= 400 \text{ r.p.m.}$$

- **Torque transmission :**

Torque is transmitted from the disc on the engine shaft to the disc on the gear box shaft due to viscous friction between the two. Thus, we need to find the viscous force causing the viscous friction.

Consider an elemental ring of radius 'r' and radial thickness 'dr' on the two discs.

- **Elemental area :**

$$dA = (\text{Circumference at radius r}) \times (\text{Radial thickness of ring})$$
$$dA = (2\pi r)(dr)$$

- **Relative velocity between two discs :**

$$U = \frac{2\pi r \cdot N_R}{60}$$

From Newton's law of viscosity, the viscous force on elemental ring is,

$$dF = \mu \cdot dA \cdot \frac{dU}{dh}$$
$$= \mu \cdot dA \cdot \frac{U}{h}$$
$$= \mu \cdot (2\pi r \cdot dr) \frac{\left(\dfrac{2\pi r \cdot N_R}{60}\right)}{h}$$
$$dF = \frac{4\pi^2 \cdot \mu \cdot N_R \cdot r^2 \cdot dr}{60 \cdot h}$$

- **Viscous torque on elemental ring :**

$$dT = r \cdot dF$$
$$dT = \frac{4\pi^2 \cdot \mu \cdot N_R \cdot r^3 \cdot dr}{60 \cdot h}$$

- Total viscous torque between two discs is,

$$T = \int_{R_i}^{R_o} dT$$

$$= \int_{R_i}^{R_o} \frac{4\pi^2 \cdot \mu \cdot N_R \cdot r^3 \cdot dr}{60 \cdot h}$$

$$= \frac{4\pi^2 \cdot \mu \cdot N_R}{60 \cdot h} \int_{R_i}^{R_o} r^3 \cdot dr$$

$$= \frac{4\pi^2 \cdot \mu \cdot N_R}{60 \cdot h} \left[\frac{R_o^4 - R_i^4}{4} \right]$$

$$T = \frac{\pi^2 \cdot \mu \cdot N_R (R_o^4 - R_i^4)}{60 \cdot h}$$

which is an equation for total viscous torque between the two discs.

(i)   Power at the gear box :

$$P_G = \frac{2\pi \cdot N_o \cdot T}{60 \times 1000}$$

$$= \frac{2\pi \cdot N_o}{60 \times 1000} \left[\frac{\pi^2 \cdot \mu \cdot N_R (R_o^4 - R_i^4)}{60 \cdot h} \right]$$

$$= \frac{2\pi \times 3200}{60 \times 1000} \left[\frac{\pi^2 \times 90 \times 10^{-9} \times 400 \, (200^4 - 75^4)}{60 \times 0.15} \right]$$

$$= \frac{2\pi \times 3200}{60 \times 1000} [61916.3464]$$

$$P_G = 20748.367 \text{ W}$$

$$\therefore \quad P_G = 20.748 \text{ kW}$$

(ii)   Power input :

$$P_i = \frac{2\pi \cdot N_i \cdot T}{60 \times 1000}$$

$$= \frac{2\pi \times 3600 \times 61916.3464}{60 \times 1000} = 23341.913 \text{ W}$$

$$P_i = 23.342 \text{ kW}$$

(iii)   The power lost in fluid coupling :

$$P_L = \frac{2\pi \cdot N_R \cdot T}{60 \times 1000} = \frac{2\pi \times 400 \times 61916.3464}{60 \times 1000}$$

$$P_L \ = \ 2593.546 \text{ W}$$

$$\therefore \qquad P_L \ = \ 2.5935 \text{ kW}$$

Example 1.6 : An oil of viscosity of 62 cP and relative density of 0.75 is used for lubrication. Convert the viscosity into centistokes, SUS and Pascal second units.   **(P.U. June 07)**

Solution : Given : $\qquad z \ = \ 62 \text{ cP}$

$$\text{Specific gravity} = \text{Relative density} = 0.75$$

$$\therefore \qquad \rho \ = \ \text{Mass density of lubricant}$$

$$\rho_w \ = \ \text{Density of water}$$

$$\text{Relative density} \ = \ \frac{\rho}{\rho_w}$$

$$\therefore \qquad \rho \ = \ \rho_w \ (\text{Relative density})$$

$$= \ 1000 \ (0.75)$$

$$\rho \ = \ \textbf{750 kg/m}^3$$

We know the relationship :

Viscosity in cP, $\qquad z \ = \ \rho \cdot z_k$

Absolute (dynamic) viscosity $= \ \rho \cdot (\text{Kinematic viscosity})$

$$z \ = \ \rho \cdot \left[0.22 \, t - \frac{180}{t} \right] \times 10^{-6}$$

$$10^{-3} \times 62 \ = \ 750 \left[0.22 \, t - \frac{180}{t} \right] \times 10^{-6}$$

$$= \ 750 \left[\frac{0.22 \, t^2 - 180}{t} \right]$$

$$0.22 \, t^2 - 180 \ = \ \frac{62 \times 10^{-3}}{750} \times 10^6$$

$$0.22 \, t^2 - 86.667 \, t - 180 \ = \ 0$$

$$t_{1,2} \ = \ \frac{-b \pm \sqrt{b^2 - 4ac}}{2a}$$

$$= \ \frac{[82.667 \pm \sqrt{(-82.667)^2 - 4 \times 0.22 \times -180}}{2 \times 0.22}$$

$$t \ = \ 377.923 \text{ SUS}$$

Viscosity in centistokes (cSt) :

$$z_k = \left[0.22\,t - \frac{180}{t}\right]$$

$$= 0.22 \times 377.923 - \frac{180}{377.923}$$

$$z_k = 82.666 \text{ cSt}$$

Viscosity in Pascal second units [Pa · s] :

$$z = 62 \text{ cP}$$

$$\mu = \frac{z}{10^9} = 62 \times 10^{-9} \text{ N-s/mm}^2$$

$$= \frac{62 \times 10^{-9}}{10^{-6}} \text{ N-s/m}^2$$

$$= 62 \times 10^{-3} \text{ Pa} \cdot \text{s}$$

$$\mu = 0.062 \text{ Pa} \cdot \text{s}$$

Example 1.7 : An oil of viscosity of 70 cP and relative density of 0.7 is used for lubrication. Convert the viscosity into centistokes and SUS. **(P.U. Dec. 2011, 4 marks)**

Solution :

Given :

$$z = 70 \text{ cP}$$

$$\text{Relative density} = 0.70$$

$$\rho = \text{Mass density of lubricant}$$

$$\rho_w = \text{Density of water}$$

$$\text{Relative density} = \frac{\rho}{\rho_w}$$

$$\rho = (\text{Relative density})\,\rho_w$$

$$= 1000\,(0.70)$$

$$= 700 \text{ kg/m}^3$$

Viscosity in cP :

$$z = \rho \cdot z_k$$

$$\text{Absolute (dynamic) viscosity} = \rho \cdot (\text{Kinematic viscosity})$$

$$z = \rho\left[0.22\,t - \frac{180}{t}\right] \times 10^{-6}$$

$$70 \times 10^{-3} = 700 \left[\frac{0.22\, t^2 - 180}{t} \right] \times 10^{-6}$$

$$0.22\, t^2 - 180 - 100\, t = 0$$

$$\therefore \quad t_{1,2} = \frac{100 \pm \sqrt{(-100)^2 - 4 \times 0.22 \times (-180)}}{2 \times 0.22}$$

$$= \frac{100 \pm 100.788}{0.44}$$

$$\mathbf{t_{1,2} = 456.33\ SUS}$$

Viscosity in centistokes (cSt) :

$$z_k = \left[0.22\, t - \frac{180}{t} \right]$$

$$= 0.22 \times 456.33 - \frac{180}{456.33}$$

$$z_k = 100.3944 - 0.394444$$

$$\mathbf{z_k = 100\ cSt}$$

Example 1.8 : An oil of relative density 0.8 has a viscosity of 0.4 Pascal-second at a given temperature. Convert it into centistokes, SUS and cP.   **(P.U. Dec. 07)**

Solution :

Given : Relative density or Specific gravity

$$= \frac{\rho}{\rho_w}$$

$$0.8 = \frac{\rho}{\rho_w}$$

$$\therefore \quad \rho = 0.8 \times \rho_w = 0.8 \times 1000$$

$$\mathbf{\rho = 800\ kg/m^3}$$

Viscosity in cP :

$$1\ cP = 10^{-3}\ Pa \cdot s \text{ or } N\text{-}s/m^2$$

$$\therefore \quad 1\ Pa \cdot s = 10^3\ cP$$

$$\therefore \quad 0.4\ Pa \cdot s = 0.4 \times 10^3\ cP$$

$$\therefore \quad \mu = 400\ cP$$

Viscosity in SUS :

$$z = \rho \left[0.22\, t - \frac{180}{t} \right] \times 10^{-6}$$

$$0.22\, t^2 - 180 = \frac{z}{\rho} \cdot t$$

$$0.22\ t^2 - \frac{0.400}{800}\ t - 180 \ = \ 0$$

$$0.22\ t^2 - 500\ t - 180 \ = \ 0$$

$$t \ = \ \frac{-b \pm \sqrt{b^2 - 4ac}}{2a}$$

$$= \ \frac{500 \pm \sqrt{(-500)^2 - 4 \times 0.22 \times -180}}{2 \times 0.22}$$

$$t \ = \ \frac{500 \pm 12.5956}{0.44}$$

$$t \ = \ 2273.087 \ \text{SUS}$$

Viscosity in centistokes (cSt) :

$$z_k \ = \ \left[0.22\ t - \frac{180}{t} \right]$$

$$= \ 0.22 \times 2273.087 - \frac{180}{2273.087}$$

$$z_k \ = \ 500 \ \text{cSt}$$

Example 1.9 : A rectangular plate of 500×400 mm is placed over a plane stationary surface. The two are separated by oil-film of thickness 0.25 mm. The viscosity of oil is 80 cP. Determine the force required to push the plate at a speed of 5 m/s. **(P.U. June 07)**

Solution :

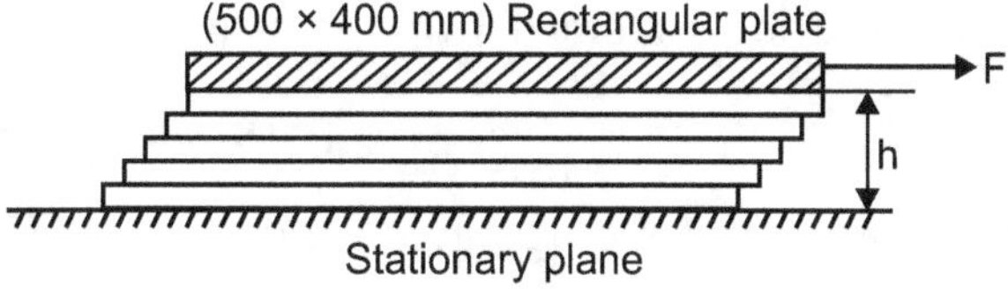

Fig. 1.52

Given :

$$b \ = \ 500 \ \text{mm}$$

$$l \ = \ 400 \ \text{mm}$$

$$h \ = \ 0.25 \ \text{mm}$$

$$\mu \ = \ 80 \ \text{cP} \ = \ 80 \times 10^{-9} \ \text{N-s/mm}^2$$

$$U = 5 \text{ m/s} = 1500 \text{ mm/s}$$

Surface area of rectangular plate :

$$A = bl$$
$$= 500 \times 400$$
$$= 200000 \text{ mm}^2$$

Force required to push the plate :

$$F = \mu \cdot A \cdot \frac{dU}{dh}$$
$$= \mu \cdot A \cdot \frac{U}{h}$$
$$= 80 \times 10^{-9} \times 200000 \times \frac{1500}{0.25}$$
$$F = 96 \text{ N}$$

EXERCISE

1. Explain "Tribology is an interdisciplinary science". **[P.U. June 2009, 4 Marks]**

2. Explain the importance of 'Tribology' in the design of machine elements.

   [P.U. June 2010, 8 Marks]

3. Define the following terms :

   (i) Tribo surfaces, (ii) Tribo system, (iii) Tribology, (iv) Antifriction bearings.

   [P.U. May 2006, Dec. 2008, 4 Marks]

4. Explain the importance of 'Tribology' in industries. **[P.U. June 2010, 6 Marks]**

5. Explain the economic aspects of tribology. **[P.U. June 2010, 6 Marks]**

6. Explain the purpose of lubrication.

7. What do you understand by 'Thick-Film Lubrication' and 'Thin-Film Lubrication ?

8. Explain the basic modes of thick-film lubrication.

9. Explain the following terms :

   (i)   Hydrodynamic lubrication   (ii)   Hydrostatic lubrication

    (iii)   Boundary lubrication   (iv)   Elasto-hydrodynamic lubrication

    (v)   Extreme pressure lubrication

10. Explain with neat sketch 'Hydrodynamic lubrication'.   **[P.U. June 2011, 4 Marks]**

11. Explain different types of lubricants.

12. Explain the various lubricating oils which are classified according to their functions.

13. State the operating conditions where grease is preferred over mineral oils as a lubricant. State different types of greases along with their applications.

14. Explain the following types of lubricants :

    (i)   Lubricating oils   (ii) Greases

    (iii)   Solid lubricants   (iv) Gases

15. Write short notes on :

    (i)   Types and uses of greases   **[P.U. Dec. 2010, 8 Marks]**

    (ii)   Factors influencing the selection of lubricant.

16. State the desirable properties of lubricants.   **[P.U. Dec. 2010, 6 Marks]**

17. Explain the effect of temperature and pressure on the viscosity of lubricating oil.

                                                   [P.U. Dec. 2008, 6 Marks]

18. Explain the following properties of lubricants :

    (i)   Viscosity **[P.U. June 2011, 2 Marks]** (ii)   Effect of temperature on viscosity

    (iii)   Effect of pressure on viscosity   (iv) Oiliness

    (v)   Pour point **[P.U. June 2011, 2 Marks]**(vi) Flash point **[P.U. June 2011, 2 Marks]**

    (vii) Oxidation stability   (viii) Foaming

    (ix) Thermal conductivity   (x)   Demulsibility

    (xi) Acidity and alkalinity

19. Explain the following terms of lubrication :

    (i)   SUS   (ii) Viscosity index **[P.U. June 2011, 2 Marks]**

    (iii) Fluidity   (iv) Absolute viscosity

    (v)   Kinematic viscosity

20. Explain the various units of absolute viscosity and kinematic viscosity and show the relation between the two viscosities.   **[P.U. Dec. 2010, 2 Marks]**

21. Explain in detail why viscosity is generally measured in kinematic units rather than absolute units.   **[P.U. Dec. 2008, 4 Marks]**

22. Write a short note on :

    Measurement of viscosity.

23. What is viscosity index ? Explain the method to find the VI of a test oil.

    [P.U. Dec. 2009,6 Marks; June 2010, 6 Marks]

24. What are additives ? Explain the different types of additives used in lubricating oils.   **[P.U. Dec. 2010, 6 Marks; June 2011, 4 Marks]**

25. Explain the use of following additives :

    (i)   V.I. improvers   **[P.U. June 2011, 2 Marks]**

    (ii)   Oiliness additives

    (iii) Pour-point depressants   **[P.U. Dec. 2009, 3 Marks; June 2011, 3 Marks]**

    (iv)   Oxidation inhibitors   **[P.U. Dec. 2009, 3 Marks]**

    (v)   Detergents or dispersants

    (vi)   E.P. additives

    (vii) Corrosion inhibitors

    (viii) Anti-foam additives

    (ix)   Emulsifiers

    (x)   Anti-friction additives

    (xi)   Anti-wear additives   **[P.U. June 2009]**

    (xii) Anti-scuff additives   **[P.U. June 2009]**

26. What is the role of additives in lubrication ?

27. State the desirable properties of lubricating oils.   **[P.U. Dec. 2009, 4 Marks]**

28. Explain 'SAE classification' of lubricating oils.

29. What do you understand by 10 W/30 motor oil ?   **[P.U. Dec. 2010, 2 Marks]**

30. Write short notes on the following :

    (i)   Recycling of used oils and oil conservation   **[P.U. June 2010, 4 Marks]**

    (ii)   Disposal of scrap oil

    (iii) Oil emulsion

31. Explain 'Used Oil Management Diagram'.

32. Explain the importance of recycling of used oils. Explain the different ways of disposal of used oil.   **[P.U. Dec. 2008, 6 Marks]**

33. Explain the 'oil conservation' by recycling of used oils.   **[P.U. Dec. 2009, 6 Marks]**

34. Explain the following terms related to used motor oil :

    (i)   Re-refining   (ii) Reconditioning   (iii) Reprocessing

35. Explain the benefits of recycling of used oils.   **[P.U. June 2009, 4 Marks]**

36. Explain different types of sliding contact bearings.

37. Explain the classification of sliding contact bearings based on relative motion between contacting surfaces.

38. Explain the classification of sliding contact bearings based on mode of lubrication.

39. Compare sliding contact bearings with rolling contact bearings.

                                                    [P.U. Dec. 2008, 6 Marks]

40. Give a comparison of sliding and rolling contact bearings with reference to the following points :   **[P.U. June 2011, 8 Marks]**

    (i)   Magnitude of load   **[P.U. June 2010, 4 Marks]**

    (ii)   Nature of load

    (iii) Speed   **[P.U. June 2011, 4 Marks]**

    (iv)   Life

    (v)   Frictional loss

    (vi)   Space requirement   **[P.U. June 2010, 4 Marks]**

    (vii) Positional accuracy   **[P.U. June 2010, 4 Marks]**

    (viii) Noise   **[P.U. June 2010, 4 Marks]**

    (ix)   Cost

41. Explain the plot of load-carrying capacity against speed for different types of bearings.

42. State the reasons where the following lubricants are used.

    (i)   Straight mineral oils   (ii)   Mineral oils with additives

    (iii) Greases   (iv)   Solid lubricants

43. State desirable properties of bearing materials. List few suitable bearing materials.

    [P.U. Dec. 2010, 6 Marks]

44. Write short notes on :

    (i)   Score resistance   (ii)   Deformability

    (iii) Structure   (iv)   Corrosive resistance

45. List various bearing materials.

46. Explain various materials for bearings with their advantages, disadvantages and give atleast two applications of each material.

47. Explain bearing constructions with different oil groove patterns.

48. Give brief classification of seals.

49. Explain static seals and dynamic seals.   **[P.U. June 2009, 8 Marks]**

50. Discuss requirements of oil seals.

51. Explain oil seals used in lubrication practice.

52. Explain in brief :

    (i)   Lip seals   (ii)   Circumferential split-ring seals

    (iii) O-rings   (iv)   Labyrinth seal

    (v)   Felt seals

53. Explain different types of gaskets in brief.

NUMERICALS ASKED IN VARIOUS UNIVERSITY EXAMINATIONS

1. Determine the viscosity of the lubricant in centipoise having viscosity 160 SUS and specific gravity 0.86.

Solution :

Refer Example 1.1 on page 1.72.

2.   A rectangular plate of 250 mm width and 500 mm length is placed over a plane stationary surface. The two surfaces are separated by an oil-film of thickness 0.15 mm. The viscosity of oil is 40.5 cP. Determine the force required to pull the plate at a speed of 1.5 m/s.

Solution :

Refer Example 1.3 on page 1.73.

3.   A square plate of 400 × 400 mm is placed over a plane stationary surface. The two are separated by oil-film of thickness 0.1 mm. The viscosity of oil is 50 cP.

Determine the force required to pull the square plate at a speed of 2 m/s.

Solution :   **(P.U. Dec. 06, 4 marks)**

Refer Example 1.4 on page 1.74.

4.   A fluid coupling is used to transmit power from a diesel engine to a gear box. It consists of two identical hollow discs of inner diameter 150 mm and outer diameter 400 mm. One of the discs is mounted on engine shaft running at 3600 r.p.m, while the other disc is mounted on gear box shaft running at 3200 r.p.m. The two discs are separated by a fluid-film of 0.15 mm thickness. If the viscosity of fluid is 90 cP, derive the equation necessary for it and evaluate :

(i)   Power at gear box.

(ii)   Power supplied (i.e. power input) and

(iii) The power lost in fluid coupling.

Solution :   **(P.U. Dec. 06, 4 marks)**

Refer Example 1.5 on page 1.75.

5.   An oil of viscosity of 62 cP and relative density of 0.75 is used for lubrication. Convert the viscosity into centistokes, SUS and Pascal second units. **(P.U. June 07)**

Solution :

Refer Example 1.6 on page 1.78.

6.   An oil of relative density 0.8 has a viscosity of 0.4 Pascal-second at a given temperature. Convert it into centistokes, SUS and cP.   **(P.U. Dec. 07)**

Solution :

Refer Example 1.8 on page 1.80.

7. A rectangular plate of 500 × 400 mm is placed over a plane stationary surface. The two are separated by oil-film of thickness 0.25 mm. The viscosity of oil is 80 cP. Determine the force required to push the plate at a speed of 5 m/s.**(P.U. June 07)**

Solution :

Refer Example 1.9 on page 1.81.

✠ ✠ ✠

UNIT II

Chapter 2
FRICTION AND WEAR

FRICTION

2.1 INTRODUCTION TO FRICTION

Whenever two surfaces of different bodies undergo sliding or rolling under load, friction and wear processes are inevitable, wherein friction is a cause of energy dissipation and wear is the main cause of material wastage. It is our first aim to keep the frictional forces as small as possible to have the most efficient system e.g. in machining processes, heavy duty worm gear box, planetary gear boxes, etc. The exception to this is in some cases where friction is desirable e.g. friction in brakes and clutches, automobile tyres on a roadway, variable speed transmission systems, nuts and bolts, etc.

Definition:

Whenever there is relative motion between the surfaces of two bodies in contact, it has been observed that a resistance to motion is set up due to the nature of the surfaces in contact. This resistance to the relative motion of contacting bodies is termed as 'friction' or 'frictional resistance'.

Illustration:

There are two kinds of relative motion in general practice:

- Sliding motion and
- Rolling motion

During sliding motion, sliding friction is experienced and during rolling motion, rolling friction is experienced.

Coefficient of Friction: It can be defined as the degree of friction which is the ratio of the force required to initialize relative motion to the normal reaction i.e.

$$f = \frac{F}{N} \qquad \qquad \qquad \text{... (2.1)}$$

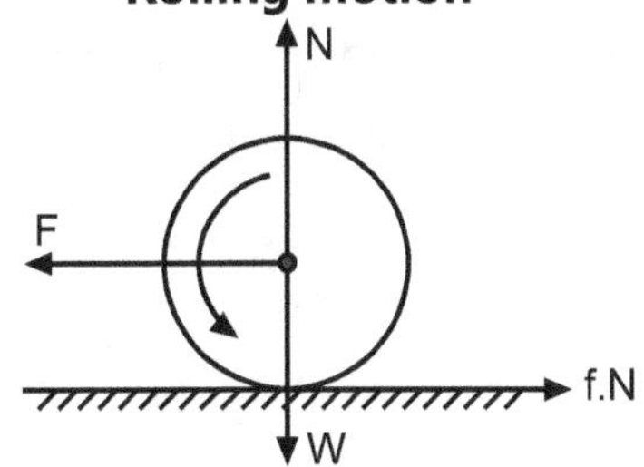

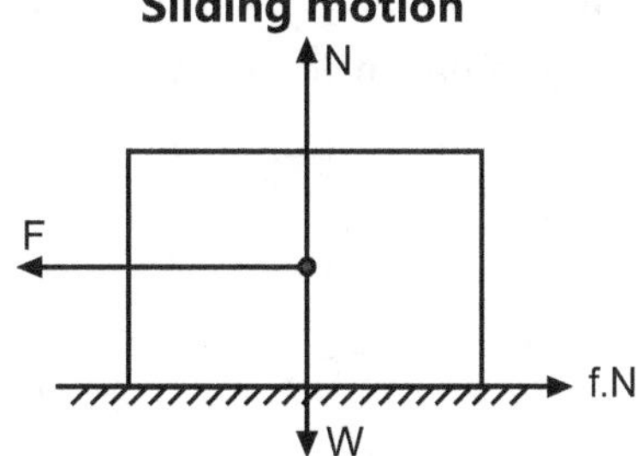

Fig. 2.1

---

where,   F – Tangential force required to move the upper body over the stationary counter face

N – Normal reaction

W – Weight of the body

f – Coefficient of friction

2.2 LAWS OF FRICTION

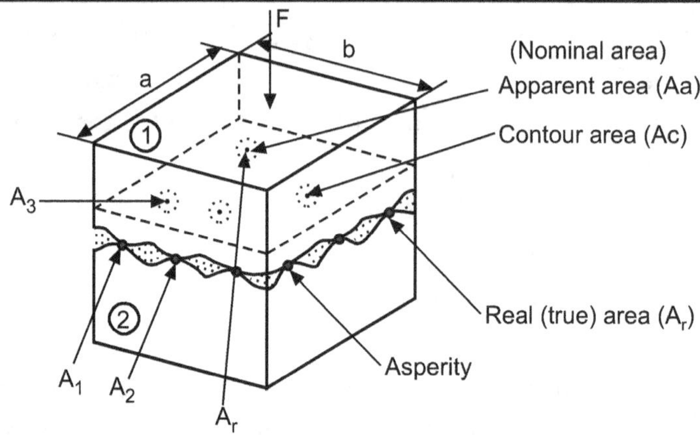

Fig. 2.2

Consider simple model showing two bodies [body (1) and body (2)] in contact with each other depicting three kinds of areas.

*   **Apparent Area or Nominal Area of Contact:** It is the overall noticeable area of the body in contact with other body. It is denoted by 'A_a'.

$$A_a = a \times b$$

*   **Contour Area of Contact:** It is the total area of outer edges of the asperities on the body. It is denoted by 'A_c'.

*   **Real Area or True Area of Contact:** When two surfaces come in contact with each other, they actually touch at number of contact spots of the asperities. When normal load is applied, local welding occurs at the tips of the major asperities of the surfaces till the total pressure on the area of contact approaches the applied load. This area formed by summation of individual contact spots is termed as the real area or true area of contact. It is denoted by 'A_r',

where, $A_r = \sum\limits_{i=1}^{n} A_i$

n – Number of contacting tips of asperities

$$A_r < A_c < A_a$$

The first two laws of friction were investigated by Leonardo da Vinci (1452-1519), who put forward a very basic concept of friction of the rectangular block sliding over a plane surface, and deducted certain laws from his experimentation. French Engineer Amontons in 1699 rediscovered these laws. Later on the observations of different experiments were verified by Coulomb in 1781.

Leonardo-da-Vinci's Hypothesis:

According to his experimentation results, he wrote "the friction made by the same weight will be of equal resistance at the beginning of the movement, although the contact may be of different breadths or lengths".

He also deducted that, "friction produces double the amount of effort if the weight be doubled".

Amontons Laws of Friction:

Rediscovery of these laws by Amontons, led to the formulation of two laws called 'Laws of Sliding Friction', stated as follows.

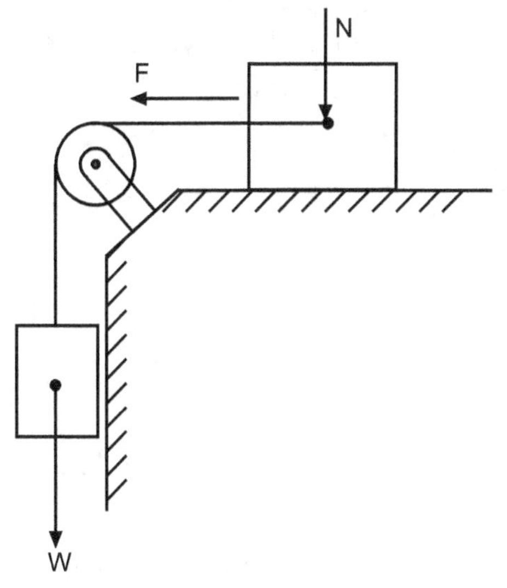

Fig. 2.3

Statement 1:

"Friction force is directly proportional to the normal load".

$$F \propto N$$

Illustration:

Amontons evaluated the frictional force between a solid and the surface. This law provides the constant of proportionality between F and W universally known as coefficient of friction (f). The value of f largely depends on the nature of both the solid surfaces.

$$f = \frac{F}{N}$$

Statement 2:

"Friction force is independent of the gross area or apparent area of the contacting surfaces". The magnitude of the maximum static frictional force is independent of the area of contact provided that the normal pressure is not very low or great enough to deform the contacting surfaces of the bodies.

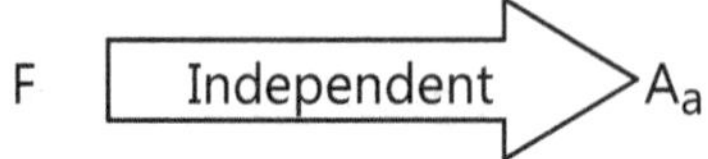

Statement 3:

"Friction force depends upon the nature of the sliding surfaces".

Static Friction Force: It is the force required to initiate sliding and denoted by F_s. The ratio of static friction force to normal reaction F_N is termed as starting or static coefficient of friction (f_s).

Kinetic or Dynamic Friction Force: It is the force necessary to maintain the relative motion (sliding) and denoted by F_k. The ratio of kinetic friction force to the normal reaction (F_N) is termed as kinetic or dynamic coefficient of friction (f_d).

"As $F_k < F_s$, coefficient of static friction (f_s) is greater than coefficient of dynamic friction (f_d)".

$$f_s > f_d$$

Coulomb's Laws of Friction:

Statement 4:

It states that, "the kinetic friction force is independent of the sliding speed".

Once sliding is achieved, f_d is found to be nearly independent of sliding velocity over quite a wide range, although at high sliding speeds, f_d falls with increasing velocity.

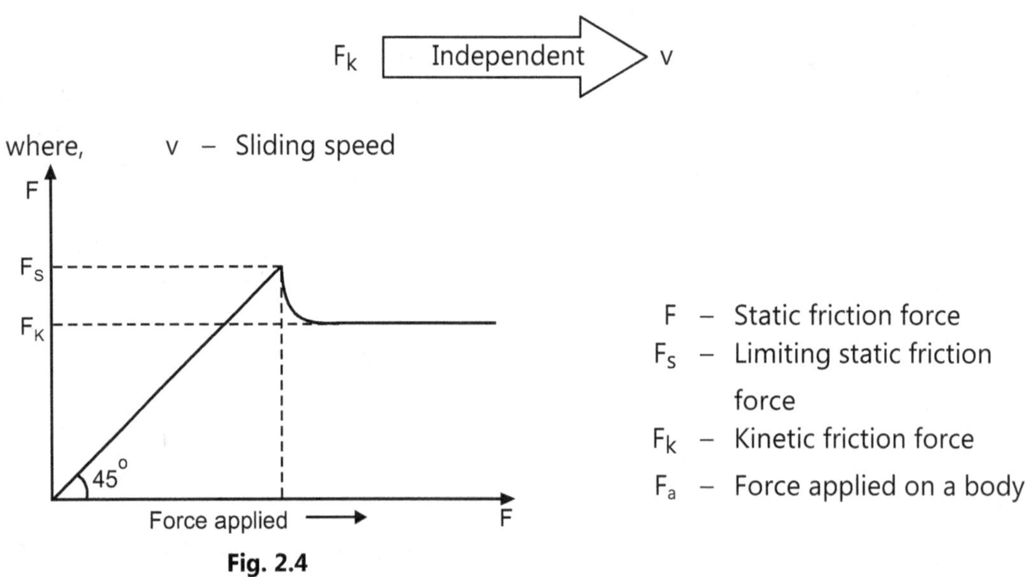

Fig. 2.4

The magnitude of the maximum static frictional force is generally greater than the magnitude of kinetic frictional force for any two surfaces of contact. But if one body is moving with a very low velocity over the surface of another,

$$F_k = F_s$$

Statement 5:

For a single asperity of equal height (e.g. a spherical asperity of constant radius and height), elastic behaviour of the asperity is given by the relation,

$$A \propto (W)^{2/3}$$

where, A – is the total real area of contact

and W – is the total load (e.g. πa^2) where, a – radius of sphere

For perfectly plastic behaviour of the asperity,

$$A \propto W$$

In case of real surfaces comprising of uniform asperities of a single radius and height, as load on a real surface is increased, more asperities will come into contact and start to carry some load. Under this situation, if the average area of contact for each contacting asperity remains constant, then even for purely elastic contact the total area will be directly proportional to the load.

2.3 KINDS OF FRICTION

There are various kinds of friction depending on the presence and absence of a lubricating film between contacting surfaces.

    (I)   Dry friction.

    (II)   Boundary friction.

    (III) Fluid friction.

    (IV) Mixed or Semifluid friction.

(I) Dry Friction:

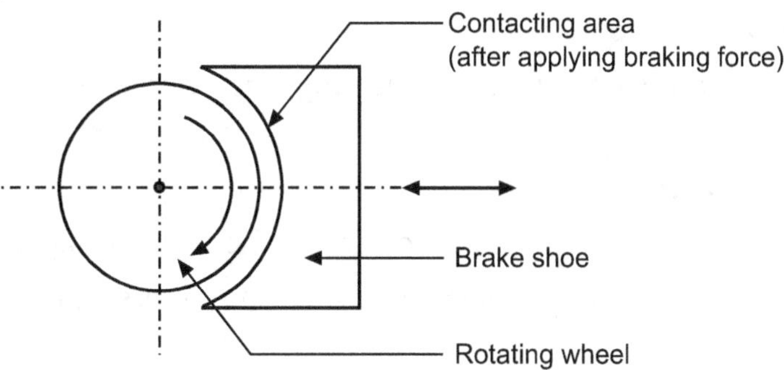

Fig. 2.5

Dry friction is the type of friction wherein the contacting surfaces are free of oxide, moisture or other kinds of contaminating (lubricating) films.

Amontons and Coulomb were the proponent of the laws of dry friction which we have discussed earlier.

Dry friction is of two kinds:

- Static
- Kinetic

where the static friction is a measure of the force necessary to initiate motion or start sliding and kinetic friction is a measure of the force necessary to maintain the motion.

Examples of Dry Friction:

- Brake shoes applied on a rotating train wheel or on a locomotive wheel.
- Friction between grinding wheel and metallic workpiece.

(II) Boundary Friction:

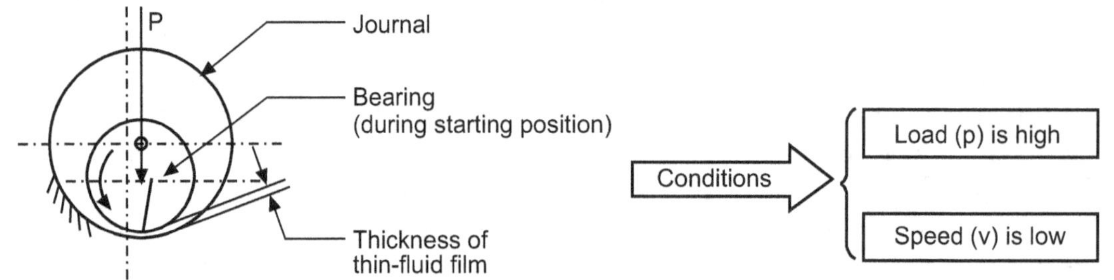

Fig. 2.6

Boundary friction is an extension of dry friction wherein the contacting surfaces are not in intimate solid contact but are separated by one or more molecular layers of lubricant.

This kind of friction results from heavy loads or slow sliding speeds. Boundary lubrication depends on the strong adhesion of the lubricant to the material of the contacting surfaces.

Variables of Boundary Friction:

Friction force depends on temperature, surface roughness, vibration, chemical composition of lubricants, etc.

Examples of Boundary Friction:

- The starting, stopping or reversing period in case of journal bearing.
- Rubbing surfaces in case of pistons and piston rings, cross-heads and machine tool guide.
- Friction in between gear teeth; especially hyploid gears (hypoid gears are offset bevel gears).
- Friction in power screws, wire drawing dies, cutting tool and workpiece.

The design engineer, production engineer and lubrication engineer must consider the boundary friction condition.

(III) Fluid Friction:

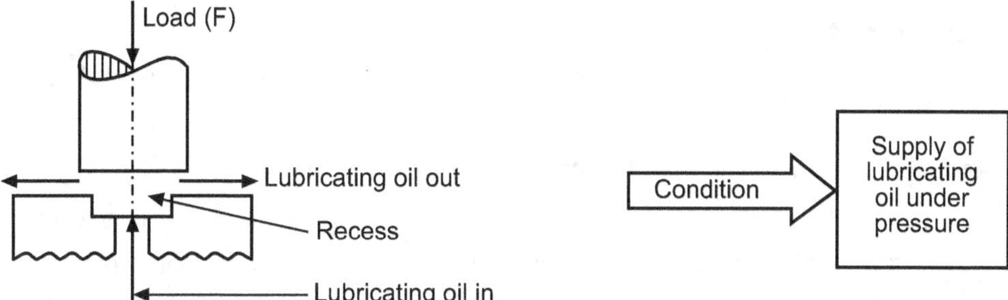

Fig. 2.7

Fluid friction is the type of friction wherein the solid contacting surfaces are separated by a fluid film.

This type of friction is found in Hydrostatic bearing in which lubricating oil is supplied in the recess and clearance which supports the bearing shaft.

Examples of Fluid Friction:

- Hydrostatic and Hydrodynamic lubrication in journal bearing and thrust bearing.
- Ship at sea is propelled by the oil-film pressure in it's thrust bearings.

(IV) Mixed or Semifluid Friction:

Mixed or Semi-fluid friction is the type of friction wherein the contacting surfaces are separated by incomplete or partial fluid films.

This kind of friction is an intermediate state between fluid and boundary lubrication. This condition exists whenever bearings do not have an ample supply of oil.

Examples of Semifluid Friction:

- Oil-starved bearings in which the rubbing surfaces are separated partly by viscous films and partly by areas of boundary lubrication.
- Bearings with drop-feed lubricators, wick-feed oilers.

2.4 CAUSES OF FRICTION

2.4.1 Case of Sliding Friction

As the contacting surfaces move relative to one another, work is done by the forces causing the motion and there is a possible energy loss at the contacting surfaces. Following factors and their combined effects cause sliding friction.

- **Surface Interactions:**
(a) Contact of two bodies under load.
(b) Adhesion between the flat surfaces.
(c) In absence of adhesion, material displacement or macro displacement occur, comprising of three stages:
    - Asperity interlocking.
    - Asperity deformation.
    - Ploughing by wear and hard surface asperity.

The above points are discussed in detail below.

(I) Surface Interactions:

Surface interaction is one of the major causes of friction and occurs in the following situations.

(a) Contact of Two Bodies under Load:

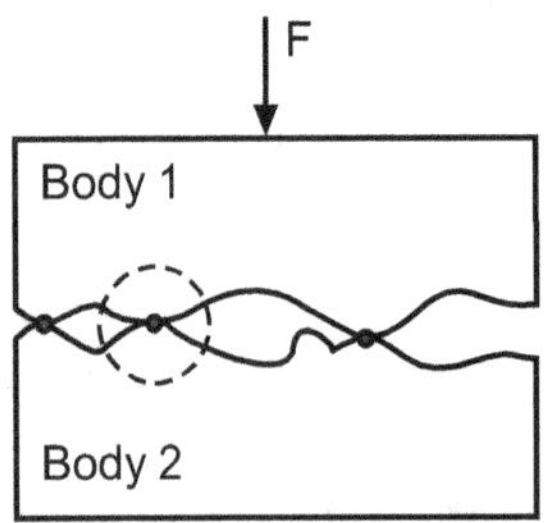

Fig. 2.8

When surfaces of two bodies, body 1 and body 2 are loaded together, adhesion takes place over some part of the contact. This leads to friction.

(b) Adhesion between Surface Asperities:

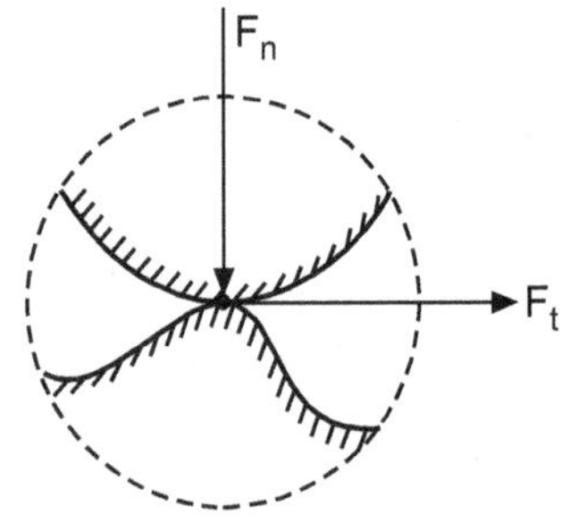

Fig. 2.9

Due to the applied load, two surfaces of bodies adhere over some part of the contact. There are interfacial adhesive bonds formed between the surface asperities in loaded condition. Friction starts with the rupture of these interfacial adhesive bonds. Thus, we can define the adhesion component of friction as the ratio of the interfacial shear strength of the adhesive junctions to the yield strength of the asperity material.

$$f_a \; = \; \frac{F_a}{W} \approx \frac{\tau}{F_y}$$

(c) In absence of adhesion, material displacement or macro displacement is the cause of friction. In case of no adhesion, one needs to consider only two interactions for this condition.

(i) Asperity Interlocking:

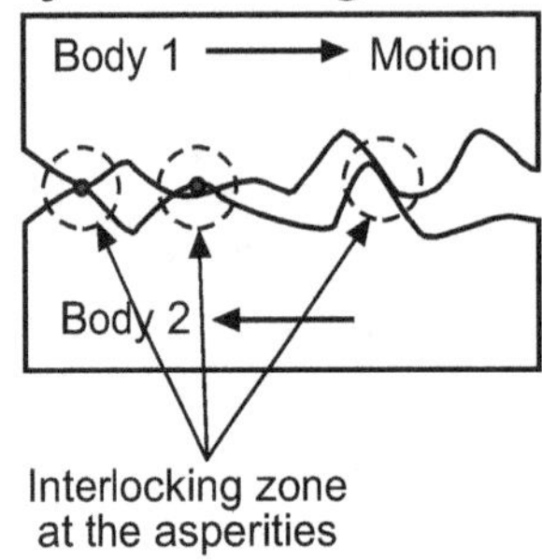

Interlocking zone
at the asperities

Fig. 2.10

Whenever two surfaces are loaded together, then in no adhesion condition, micro asperities interlock with each other causing no motion or displacement. This situation is called asperity interlocking.

In this situation, motion is not possible without deformation of the asperities. It is shown in Fig. 2.10.

(ii) Asperity Deformation:

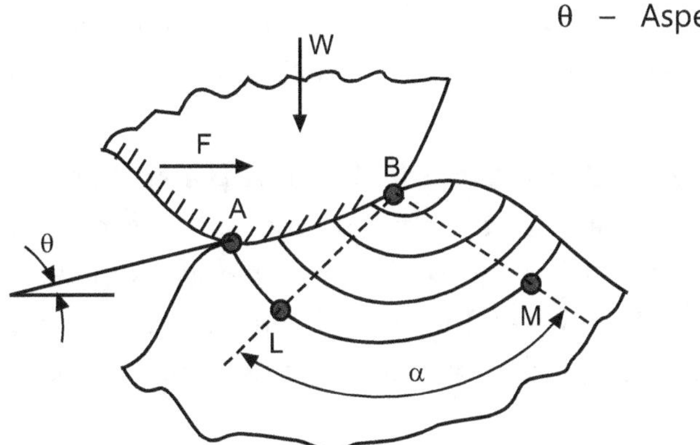

Fig. 2.11: A slip-line deformation model of friction

For a single surface asperity, the general method used to analyse the deformation is the slip-line field theory. According to this theory,

$$\left\{ \begin{array}{l} \text{for } \theta = 45° \quad \Rightarrow \\ \left[\begin{array}{l} \text{For completely plastic} \\ \text{asperity contact} \end{array} \right] \end{array} \quad \begin{array}{l} \text{Coefficient of friction} \\ f = 1.0 \end{array} \right\}$$

$$\left\{ \begin{array}{l} \text{for } \theta = 45° \text{ to } 0° \qquad \Rightarrow f = 0.55 \\ \text{i.e. asperity slope approaching zero} \end{array} \right\}$$

According to the energy-based plastic deformation approach,

$$\Rightarrow \quad \text{Frictional work performed} = \text{Work of plastic deformation during steady- state sliding}$$

(iii) Ploughing by Wear and Hard Surface Asperity: Consider two sliding surfaces out of which one surface is softer and the other contacting surface is harder. Then the asperities of the harder surface may penetrate and produce grooves on it. This is called as ploughing. This ploughing resistance is added to the friction force for tangential motion. Fig. 2.12 shows two cases of ploughing.

- Ploughing by hard conical asperity.
- Ploughing by hard wear particles present in the contact zone.

(i)   **(ii)**

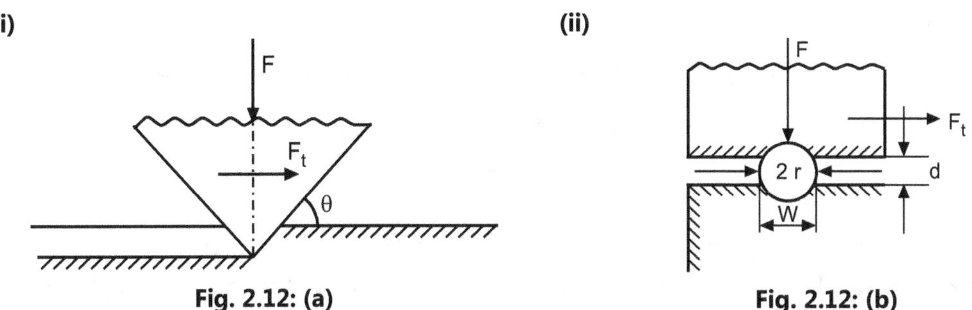

Fig. 2.12: (a)   **Fig. 2.12: (b)**

(II) Dissipation of Energy During Friction (Energy Losses):

In most of the practical problems, friction is always associated with energy loss. Three mechanisms which can cause major loss of energy at the interacting surfaces are depicted below.

- **Energy Loss During Elastic Deformation of Asperity:** As relative motion takes place in initial stage, the material at the contacting surfaces of the bodies gets deformed elastically constituting less part of the total energy dissipated at the interface. Most of this energy can be recovered. The loss of energy due to elastic deformation is negligible compared with energy losses during plastic deformation i.e. rate of energy dissipation are much lower.

- **Energy Loss During Plastic Deformation of Asperity:** Plastic deformation of asperity is characterized by high rates of energy dissipation i.e. it constitutes major part of the energy loss of the total energy loss between the interacting surfaces.

- **Energy Loss in Fracture of Asperity:** Fracture is the result of relative motion of interlocking asperities. Fracture can be realized by the wear debris formed on the sliding surface. Energy losses during fracture are small in comparison with those due to plastic deformation.

(III) Elastic Hysteresis Loss:

In case of a rigid hemisphere rolling on a flat sheet of well-lubricated rubber, the friction is due to the elastic hysteresis rather than the force required to deform the material plastically.

2.4.2 Case of Rolling Friction

Rolling friction is a complex phenomenon and much smaller than sliding friction. It depends on the:

- Varying amount of sliding called as 'slip' and
- Energy losses during mixed elastic and plastic deformations.

Rolling friction can be classified into:

- A kind of friction in which large tangential forces are transmitted e.g. traction drives and driving wheels of locomotive and
- A kind of friction in which small tangential forces are transmitted called free rolling.

Following factors mainly contribute to the friction in rolling contact.

(a) Adhesion: The adhesion component of friction may be only a small portion of the friction resistance.

(b) Microslip: Consider a sphere in contact with a flat surface in which the condition of pure rolling prevails. Forward and backward slip occur during rolling of the sphere as shown in Fig. 2.13 and Fig. 2.14.

Rolling of sphere on a flat surface

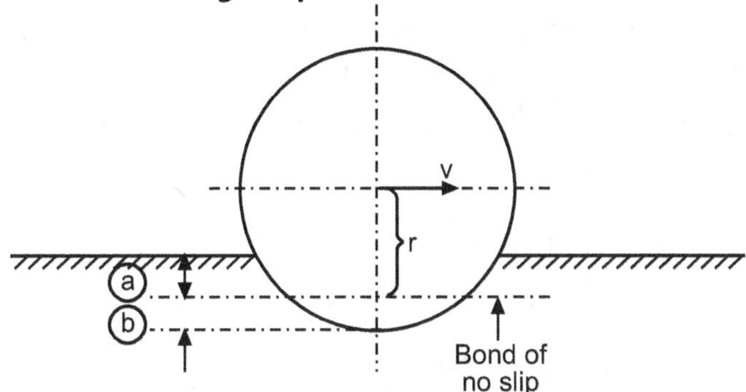

(a) – Zone of forward slip during rolling
(b) – Zone of backward slip during rolling
r – Rolling radius

Fig. 2.13

Rolling of two rollers

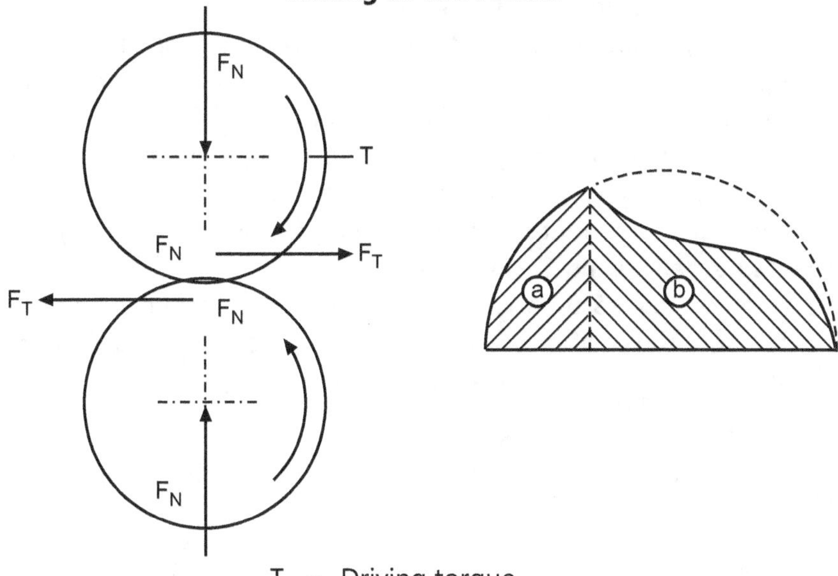

T – Driving torque
a – Region of slip
b – Region of No-slip

Fig. 2.14

(c) Elastic Hysteresis: The elastic hysteresis losses of a material are related to damping and relaxation properties of the material and are more predominant for viscoelastic material than for metals.

(d) Plastic Deformation: In case of a ball rolling over a plane, rolling resistance is due to the plastic deformation in front of the rolling ball, i.e. plastically deformed rolling track is formed.

Mechanism of Rolling Friction:

- It is found to occur between a roller and a flat surface. Let a force F_r be applied on a cylinder or a roller to make it start rolling on a flat surface.
- The ratio of the rolling force F_r to the normal load W is called coefficient of rolling friction.

$$f_r \;=\; \frac{F_r}{W}$$

- For steel roller on steel surface,

$$\mathbf{f_r \;=\; 0.001}$$

2.5 FRICTION MEASUREMENT

It is an important task for an engineer to measure the amount of friction between two surfaces in contact.

Essential Features of Friction Measuring Device:

Any device designed for measuring friction must be –

- capable of supplying relative motion between the two test specimens,
- capable of applying a known normal load between the two test surfaces, and
- capable of measuring the tangential load to motion.

There are a wide variety of methods available for friction measurement and the final selection will depend upon the exact nature of the surfaces in contact.

Following are some of the important friction measuring methods.

(I)   Friction Measurement Using Tilting Plane:

It is the simplest method to measure friction. In this method, a specimen block is placed on a flat surface. To measure the friction between the block and the flat surface, the surface is gradually tilted until the block starts sliding on the plane.

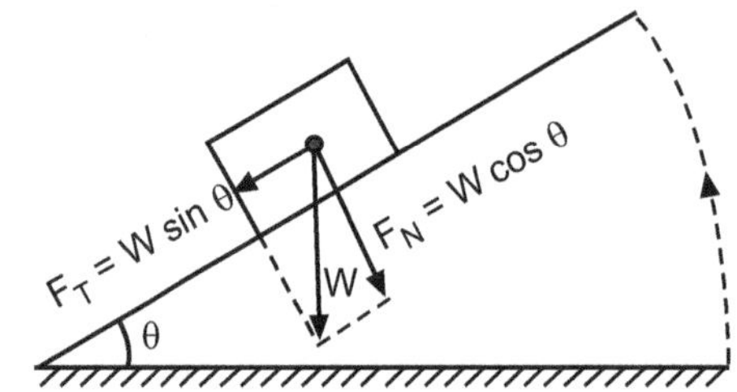

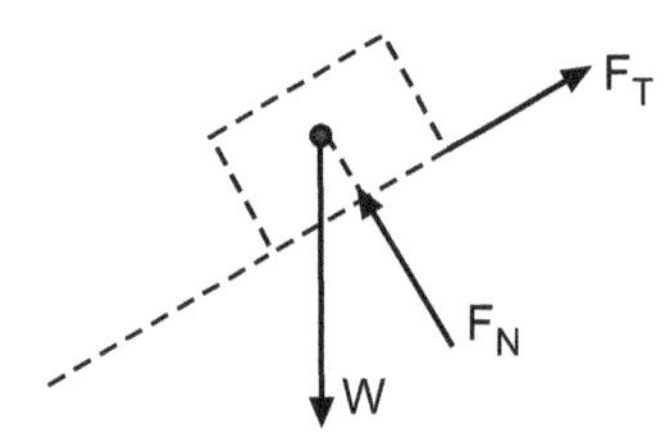

θ – Inclination for which the block starts sliding   Free body diagram

Fig. 2.15

$$\text{Coefficient of friction, } f \;=\; \frac{F_T}{F_N} = \frac{W \sin \theta}{W \cos \theta} = \tan \theta \qquad\qquad \text{... (2.2)}$$

Limitation:

This method is not suitable for continuous friction measurement over longer time.

(II) Arrangement of Pin-on-Disc Machine:

It is the most common form of friction measuring rig in tribology laboratories used during the development of materials for tribological applications. In this test apparatus, the pin is held stationary and the disc rotates or oscillates continuously.

The pin may be –

- A non-rotating ball.
- A hemispherically tipped rider.
- A flat ended cylinder.
- A rectangular parallelopiped.

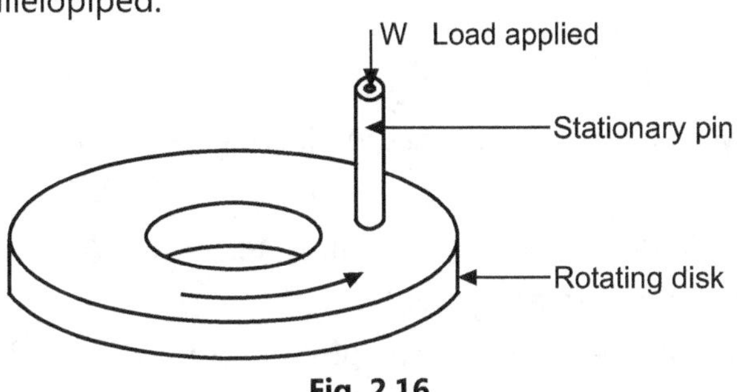

Fig. 2.16

(III) Pin-on-Flat:

In this arrangement, load is applied on a stationary pin while the flat plate reciprocates. e.g. Bowden Leben Apparatus.

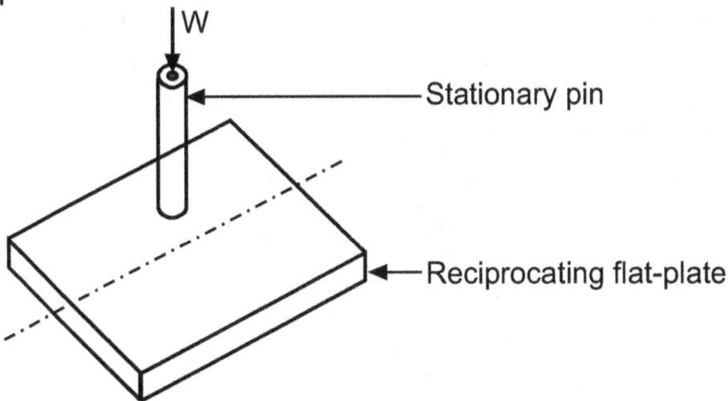

Fig. 2.17

(IV) Pin-on-Cylinder:

It is the simplest arrangement and similar to the pin-on-disk test rig, except that loading of the pin is perpendicular to the axis of rotation or oscillation.

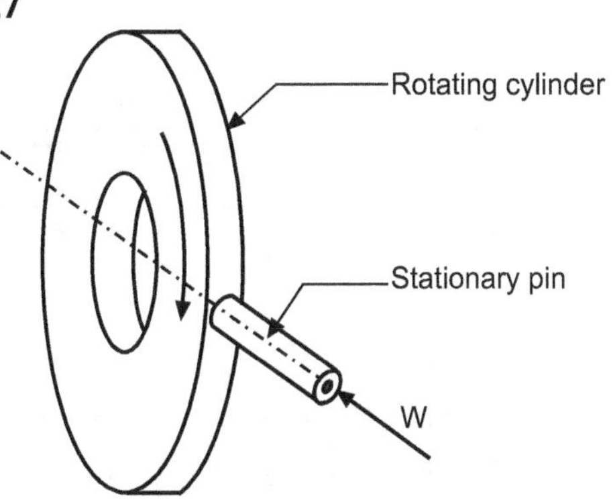

Fig. 2.18

(V) Rectangular Flats on a Rotating Cylinder:

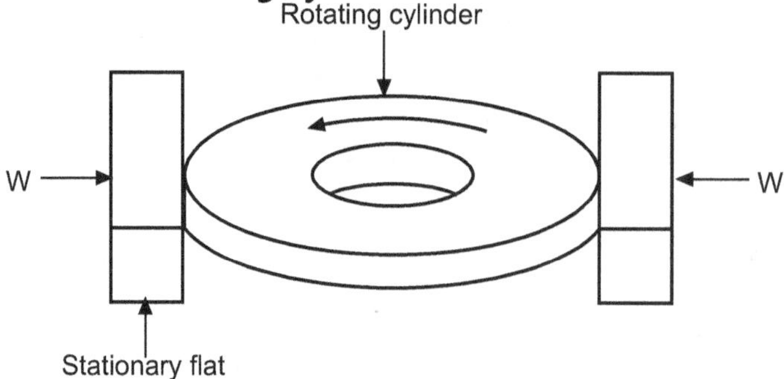

Fig. 2.19

In this arrangement, two rectangular flats are loaded perpendicular to the axis of rotation of the disk.

e.g. Hohman A-6 tester, Alpha Model LFW-1, Timken tester and Almon-Wieland tester.

(VI) Simple Crossed Cylinder Arrangement:

- It is very simple and convenient method of measuring friction. In this case, loading of stationary specimen can be done by simple dead weight or by hydrostatic or magnetic type of loading.

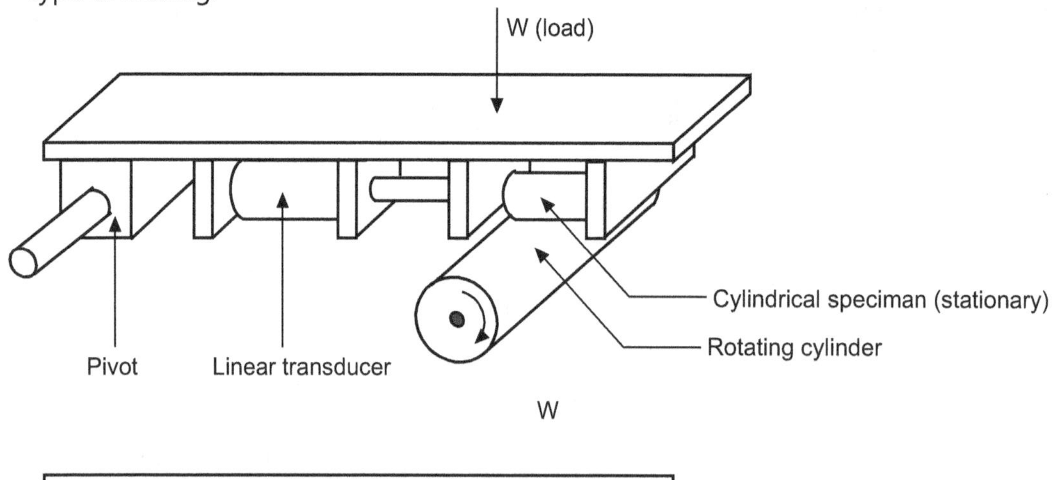

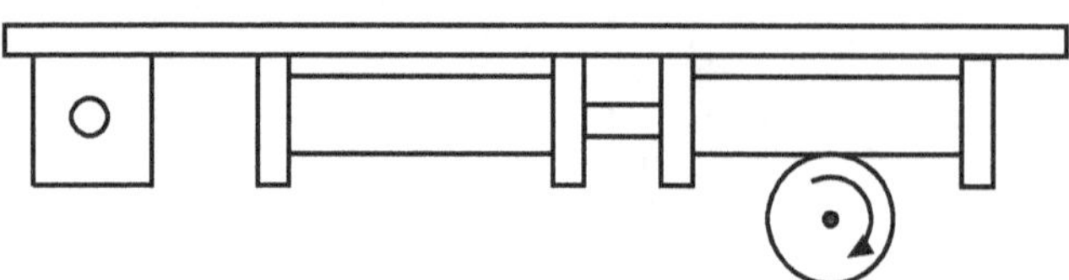

Fig. 2.20

- For continuous friction measurement over a period of time, one specimen (i.e. cylinder) is driven continuously, while the second specimen which is nominally stationary is loaded against it.

- The specimen is mounted on leaf spring which allows a small movement in the direction of the friction force. This very small tangential movement is proportional to the frictional force.
- The movement can be calibrated to give the frictional force and is measured by capacitance or inductance method while being recorded continuously.
- e.g. **Reichert tester.**

2.6 THEORIES OF FRICTION

There are various friction theories suggested by workers in different fields.

2.6.1 Simple Adhesion Theory of Friction (Bowden-Tabor Theory)

This theory is also called as Single Asperity Adhesion Theory or Theory of Welding, Shearing and Ploughing.

This theory have been suggested by Bowden and Tabor which takes into account 'cold-weld' phenomenon.

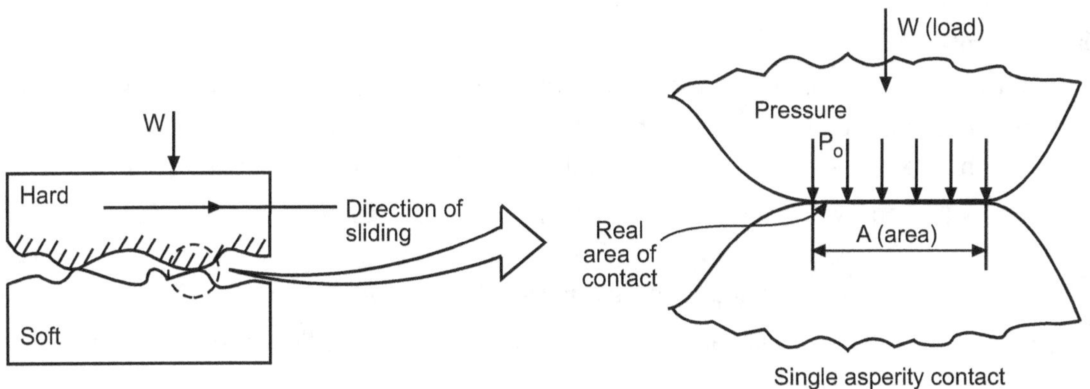

Fig. 2.21

This theory can be explained in three major stages.

(a)   Formation of cold-weld junction.

(b)   Shearing of junction.

(c)   Ploughing of hard asperity.

(a)   Formation of Cold-Weld Junction:

- When two bodies are pressed together, they adhere to each other over some part of the contacting surface and result in intimate metal to metal contact. This strong adhered junction is termed as 'cold-weld'.
- When two metal surfaces are loaded against each other, they make contact only at the tips of the asperities. Three mechanisms are involved which can cause loss of energy during friction contact –

- Elastic deformation - which can be small.
- Plastic deformation - accounts for a major part of frictional loss.
- Fracture of asperities.

- Since the real area of contact is small and the pressure over the asperities is assumed high enough to cause them to deform plastically, this plastic flow over the contacting asperities causes an increase in the area of contact until the real area of contact is just sufficient to support the load.

- For these conditions, the elastic-plastic behaviour of material follows the relation:

$$W = A \cdot P_0$$

i.e. $$A = \frac{W}{P_0} \qquad \qquad \dots (2.3)$$

where, W – Normal load

A – Real area of contact

P_0 – The yield pressure of the metal

(b) Shearing of Junction:

- At the regions of intimate metal to metal contact, strong adhesion takes place and results in cold-welding.

- If the hard surface is given a sliding motion by applying force F_s, the relative motion will be possible only when the cold-welded junctions are sheared.

$$\therefore \qquad F_s = A \cdot S \qquad \qquad \dots (2.4)$$

where, F_s – Friction force due to adhesion component

and S – Shear stress required to cause plastic flow and final fracture

(c) Ploughing of Hard Asperity:

- Even after shearing the junction, the surfaces are still not be able to slide, because some more force is required to plough the harder sheared junction (asperities) through the softer surface. The force required to plough is F_p.

$$\therefore \qquad F_p = P_e \qquad \qquad \dots (2.5)$$

Under this situation,

Total friction force required due to adhesion and deformation components =

$$\begin{bmatrix} \text{Force required to shear the} \\ \text{cold-weld junction} \end{bmatrix} + \begin{bmatrix} \text{Force required for ploughing action of the} \\ \text{hard asperities through a softer surface} \end{bmatrix}$$

i.e. $$F = F_s + F_p$$

$$\therefore \qquad F = A \cdot S + P_e \qquad \qquad \dots (2.6)$$

For most of the unlubricated metals,

$$P_e << (A \cdot S)$$

$\therefore$ Neglecting P_e from above equation, we have,

$$F = AS = \left(\frac{W}{P_0}\right) \cdot S$$

and $$\frac{F}{W} = \frac{S}{P_0} = \text{constant} = f \qquad \qquad ... (2.7)$$

Conclusions of Simple Adhesion Theory of Friction:

(a) This theory gives the explanation of the two laws of friction.

- Friction is independent of the apparent area of contact.
- Frictional force is proportional to the load.

(b) In current analysis, effects of work hardening are neglected.

∴   We may consider,

Shear stress = Critical shear stress

i.e. $S = S_0$

∴ $$f = \frac{S_0}{P_0} \qquad \qquad ... (2.8)$$

This ratio is constant for most of the metals.

(c) Yield pressure for most of the metals,

$$S_0 \approx \frac{1}{5} \cdot P_0$$

∴ $f \approx 0.2$

But for many metal combinations in air,

$$f > 0.5$$

(d) In case of two metals in rubbing contact, we have the following three possibilities for area of contact, shear stress and yield stress.

Parameters ↓	For hard on soft surface	For hard on hard surface	For soft on soft surface
	Fig. 2.22	Fig. 2.23	Fig. 2.24
S_0	Low	High	Low
A	High	Low	High
P_0	Low	High	Low

(e)   One can obtain lower values of coefficient of friction by depositing a thin layer of soft metal on to a hard metal substrate.

Limitations:

*   This theory does not provide a more realistic description of the friction based on adhesion.

*   This theory does not consider the following two phenomena –
    (a)   Junction growth and
    (b)   Work-hardening.

2.6.2 Modified Adhesion Theory of Friction

2.6.2.1 Modified Adhesion Theory of Friction without Contaminant Film

*   Under high vacuum conditions for metals, very high values of adhesion friction coefficients have been recorded. In simple theory, the assumption was made based on the true area A, yield pressure of softer metal (P_0), and normal load (W) for static contact.

$$A \cdot P_0 = W$$

*   In case of friction where tangential force is applied, yielding is accompanied by combination of normal stress and shear stress.

*   For yielding to occur for two-dimensional system,

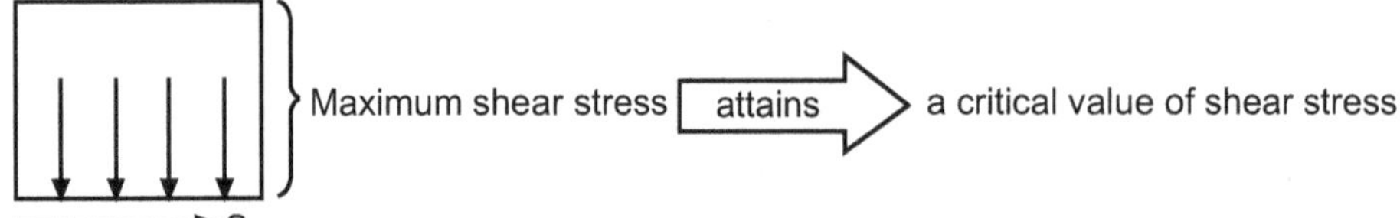

Fig. 2.25

*   Let us consider Mohr's circle to find maximum shear stress in a system.

$\therefore$ Maximum shear stress = R = Radius of Mohr's circle

$$R_2 = \left(\frac{P}{2}\right)^2 + S^2$$

When R reaches a critical shear stress, yielding takes place.

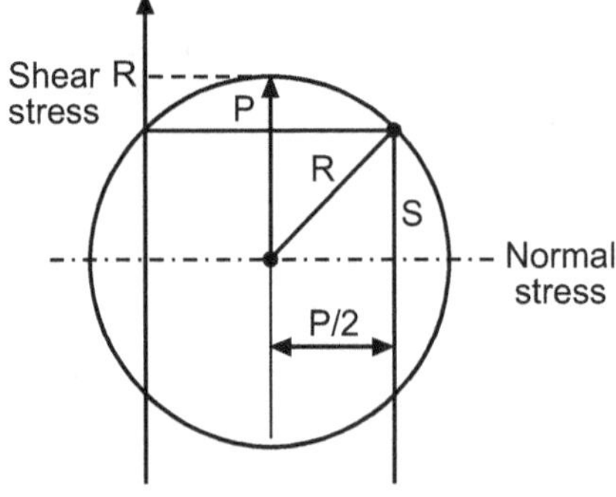

Fig. 2.26

Therefore, yielding depends on the combined action of normal stress and shear stress.

- This theory can be well elaborated with the help of two phenomenas –
    - (a)   Junction growth phenomenon.
    - (b)   Work-hardening phenomenon.

(a) Junction Growth Phenomenon:

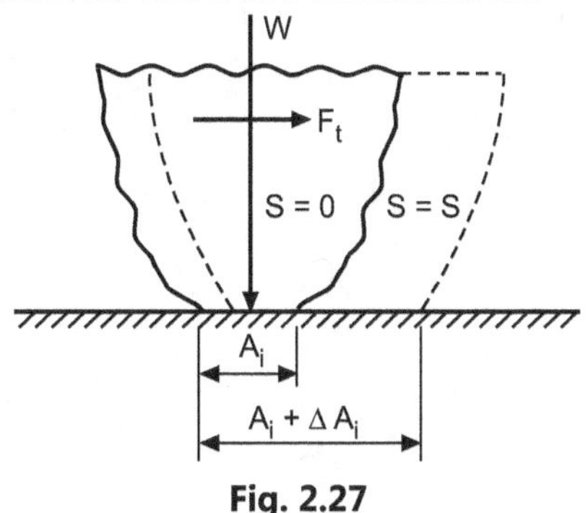

Fig. 2.27

Let us consider a single asperity contact where normal load W is applied.

Area of contact,

$$A = \frac{W}{P_0}$$

Area of contact at any location,

$$A_i = \frac{W_i}{P_0}$$

- If the tangential load is now gradually applied upto a value F_i, P_0 will tend to approach the elastic pressure P_i and further plastic flow will take place, causing an increase in contact area from (A_i) to $(A_i + \Delta A_i)$.

Thus, we can write,

$$A_i + \Delta A_i = \frac{W_i}{P_i}$$

- This phenomenon of increase in the real area of contact due to the superposition of the shear stress on the normal stress is termed as 'junction growth'.

A junction growth parameter is thus defined as the ratio of the true or real area of contact to the total area of contact for friction force to be zero.

i.e. $F = 0$

$$A_0 = \sum_{i=1}^{n} A_i \quad \text{and} \quad A = \sum_{i=1}^{n} A_i + \Delta A_i$$

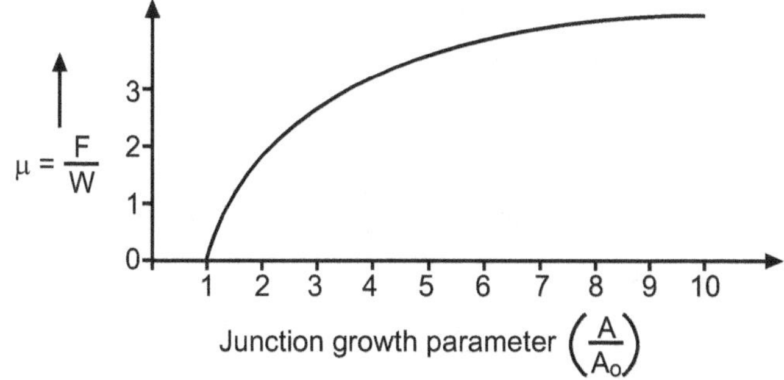

Fig. 2.28

$$\therefore \qquad \text{Junction growth parameter} = \frac{A}{A_0}$$

Following plot shows variation of $\left(f = \dfrac{F}{W}\right)$ with respect to junction growth parameter.

- As the area increases further, the junction growth continues till the combined stresses obey a relationship for a 3-dimensional system as,

$$P^2 + \alpha S^2 = K^2 \qquad \qquad \text{... (2.9)}$$

where, α and K are constants and need to be evaluated.

$$\text{Now, } P = \frac{W}{A} \quad \text{and } S = \frac{F}{A}$$

where,

$\qquad$ P – Normal stress (normal pressure)

$\qquad$ S – Shear stress

Substituting P and S in above relation for combined stresses,

$$\left(\frac{W}{A}\right)^2 + \alpha\left(\frac{F}{A}\right)^2 = K^2$$

- When tangential force $F = 0$, $S = \dfrac{F}{A} = 0$

Therefore, pressure over the junction P must be equal to P_0.

i.e. when $F = 0$, $S = 0$ and $P = P_0$

Thus, from the relation for combined stresses,

$$P^2 + \alpha S^2 = K^2$$
$$P_0^2 + 0 = K^2 \implies K = P_0$$

Substitution of above condition in given equation yields

$$P^2 + \alpha S^2 = P_0^2 \qquad \qquad \text{... (2.10)}$$

- Junction growth stops when P drops below P_0. If F increases to a very large value then

$$P = \frac{W}{A} \text{ tends to zero, but junction growth continues till } \left(\frac{W}{A}\right) \text{ is small compared with } \left(\frac{F}{A}\right)$$

for which we have,

$$\alpha S^2 \approx P_0^2$$

$$\text{In case} \qquad S \approx S_0^2 \implies \alpha \cdot S_0^2 = P_0^2$$

$$\therefore \qquad \alpha = \frac{P_0^2}{S_0^2} \qquad \qquad \text{... (2.11)}$$

- For most of the metals,

$$\text{Critical shear stress } S_0 = \frac{1}{5} \cdot \text{Yield pressure}$$

$$S_0 = \frac{1}{5} \cdot P_0$$

$$\therefore \quad \alpha = \frac{P_0^2}{S_0^2} = \frac{P_0^2}{\frac{1}{25} \cdot P_0^2} = 25 \Rightarrow \alpha = 25$$

Experimentally, $\alpha < 25$.

Bowden and Tabor assumed $\alpha = 9$

i.e.
$$S_0 = \frac{1}{3} \cdot P_0$$

$$P_0 = 3 \cdot S_0$$

$\therefore$ We have,

$$A^2 = \left(\frac{W}{P_0}\right)^2 + \alpha \left(\frac{F}{P_0}\right)^2 \Rightarrow A^2 = A_r^2 + \alpha \left(\frac{F}{P_0}\right)^2 \qquad \ldots (2.12)$$

where, $\left(\dfrac{W}{P_0}\right)$ = is the real area of contact based on simple theory which considers the effect of only the normal load

$\left(\dfrac{F}{P_0}\right)$ = is the additional area of contact based on shear or friction force

- Junction growth is a function of surface contamination also, for which we consider the surface contamination factor or cleanliness factor $K = \dfrac{S}{S_0}$.

When $f = 0 \Rightarrow$ Junction growth is zero.

For $f = 1$ and $K = 0.95 \Rightarrow$ Contact area increases by three times.

(b) Work-Hardening Phenomenon:

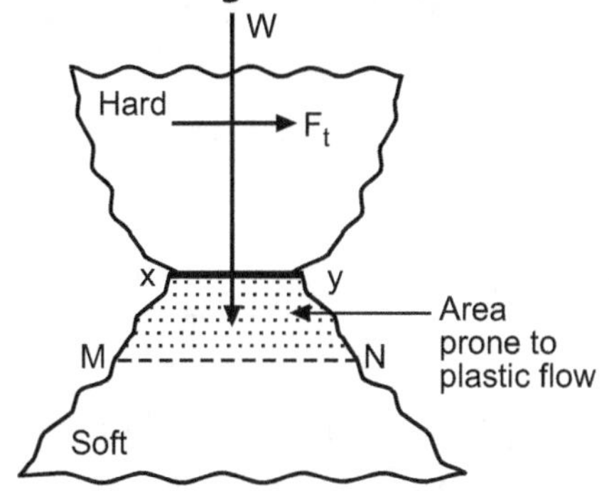

Single asperity contact during plastic flow

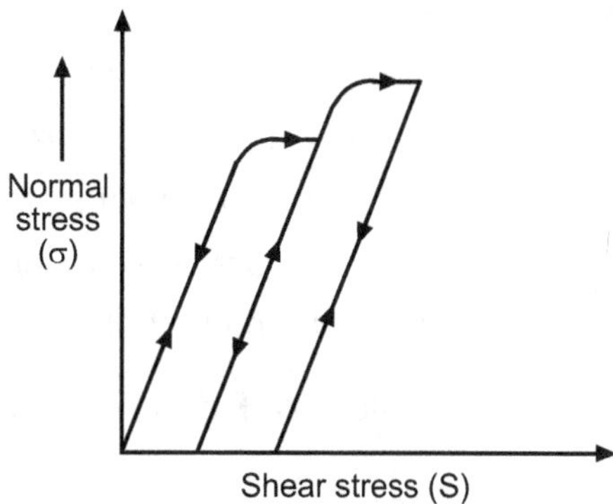

Fig. 2.29

- Whenever there is plastic flow, a phenomenon called as work hardening occurs and the resulting welded junction will have larger strength than the soft metal. In this process, the shearing plane shifts from xy to MN.
- Due to work hardening, pressure P increases by ΔP.

  i.e. $$P = P_i + \Delta P_i$$

  and critical shear stress is increased by ΔS_0 given by,

  $$\Delta S_0 = 0.18\ P_0 \text{ to } 0.22\ P_0$$

- For work hardening effect,

$$f = \frac{F}{W} = \frac{S}{P_0} = \frac{S_0}{P_0} = \frac{\text{Critical shear stress}}{\text{Yield stress in tension}}$$

Therefore, the effect of work hardening on the value of coefficient of friction is small compared with the effect of junction growth.

2.6.2.2 Modified Adhesion Theory of Friction with Contaminant Film

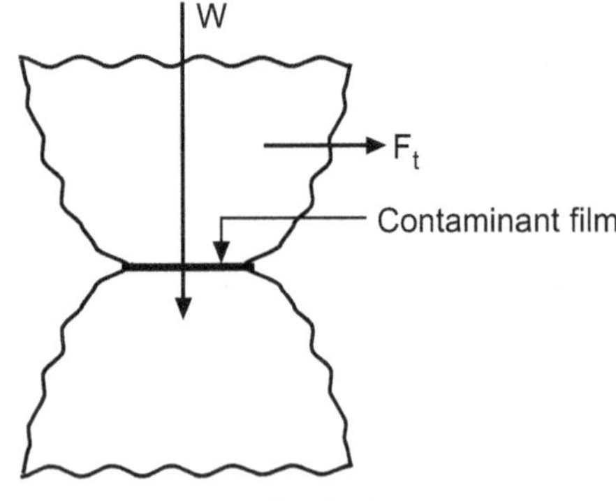

Fig. 2.30

Consider single asperity contact between two surfaces with a thin contaminant film between them.

W = Normal load

F_t = Gradually increasing shear load (tangential load)

- For single asperity junction, we assume that there is a thin contaminant film having critical shear stress S_f

  and $$S_f = C \cdot S_0 \qquad \qquad \text{... (2.13)}$$

  where, S_f – Critical shear stress of the contaminant film

  S_0 – Critical shear stress of the material

  C – A factor ranging from 0 to 1.

$C = 1 \Rightarrow$ absence of contaminant film and presence of vacuum.

Here, $C < 1$ and values of F and A are such that $\left(\dfrac{F}{A}\right) < S_f$ for a normal junction growth phenomenon to occur.

i.e. $\dfrac{F}{A} < S_f \Rightarrow$ Junction growth continues.

When $\dfrac{F}{A} = S_f \Rightarrow$ The junction breaks.

i.e. the contaminating film will shear, junction growth will come to end and pure sliding will occur.

Thus, we can write the condition for gross sliding.

$$P^2 + \alpha\, S_f^2 = P_0^2 \qquad \qquad \text{... (2.14)}$$

But, we have,
$$P_0^2 = \alpha\, S_0^2$$

Using this relation in above equation,

$$P^2 + \alpha\, S_f^2 = \alpha\left(\dfrac{S_f^2}{C^2}\right) \qquad\qquad \left(\begin{array}{l} \because \quad S_f = C \cdot S_0 \\[2mm] \quad S_0 = \dfrac{S_f}{C} \end{array}\right)$$

$$P^2 = \dfrac{\alpha}{C^2}\, S_f^2 - \alpha \cdot S_f^2$$

$$P^2 = \alpha \cdot S_f^2\left[\dfrac{1}{C^2} - 1\right]$$

$$\dfrac{S_f^2}{P^2} = \dfrac{1}{\alpha\left[\dfrac{1}{C^2} - 1\right]}$$

$$\dfrac{S_f^2}{P^2} = \dfrac{C^2}{\alpha(1 - C^2)} \qquad\qquad \dfrac{S_f}{P} = \dfrac{C}{\sqrt{\alpha(1 - C^2)}}$$

$$\therefore \quad \text{Coefficient of friction, } f = \dfrac{F}{W} = \dfrac{S_f \cdot A}{P \cdot A} = \dfrac{S_f}{P}$$

$$\therefore \qquad f = \dfrac{C}{\sqrt{\alpha(1 - C^2)}} \qquad\qquad \text{... (2.15)}$$

As $C \to 1,\ f \to \infty$

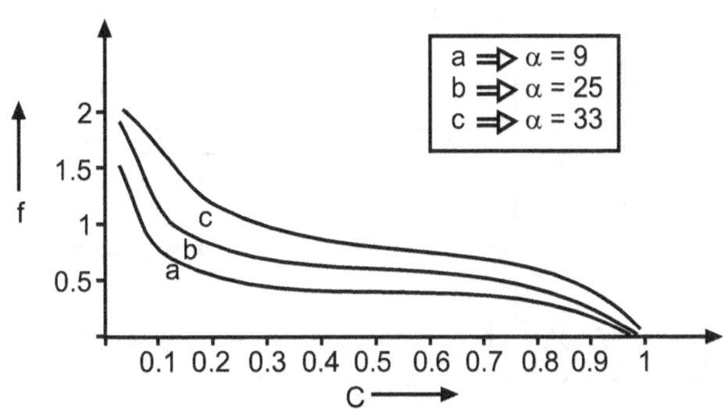

Fig. 2.31: Variation of f with C for different values of a

$$f = \frac{C}{\sqrt{\alpha}} \qquad \text{... (for small values of C)}$$

$$f = \frac{C}{\sqrt{\dfrac{P_0^2}{S_0^2}}} = C \cdot \frac{S_0}{P_0}$$

$$f = \frac{S_f}{P_0} \qquad \text{... (2.16)}$$

$$f = \frac{\text{Critical shear stress of the interface}}{\text{Yield pressure of the bulk material}}$$

Conclusions of Adhesion Theory with Contaminant Film:

- Plastic deformation is used to define the real area of contact.
- Shear strength of the film between two rubbing surfaces can vary from low values upto the bulk shear stress of the substrate material, and
- Friction force is the force required to shear the separating film.

2.6.3 Abrasive Theory of Friction

It is the theory of 'A Hard Conical Shaped Single Asperity'. Sometimes, it is called as 'Ploughing Effect' by Conical Asperity. This theory is also called as Deformation Theory of friction.

Ploughing is the major component of friction during an abrasion process. Asperities on a hard metal surface penetrate into a softer surface of metal and plough out a groove by plastic deformation in the softer metal.

Consider a conical asperity as shown in Fig. 2.32.

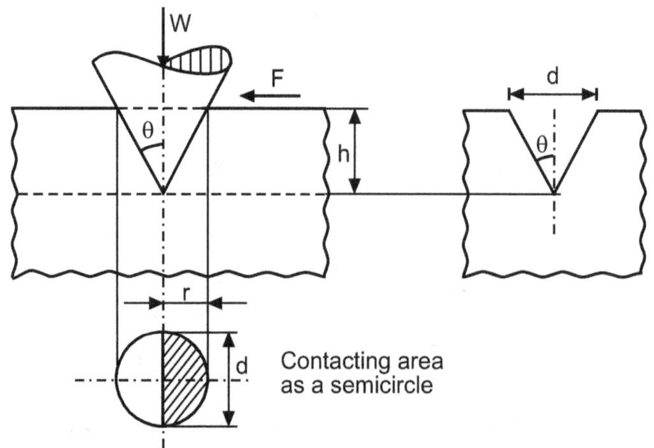

Fig. 2.32

Let
$$\theta \; - \; \text{The semicone angle}$$
$$W \; - \; \text{Normal load on conical asperity in contact}$$
$$h \; - \; \text{Vertical depth of plough}$$
$$r \; - \; \text{Radius of conical asperity at contact zone}$$

Now, during sliding, only the half portion of asperity is in contact with the softer material.

Vertical projected area of contact

$$= \frac{\pi r^2}{2} \qquad \qquad \text{... (for single asperity)}$$

$$A_V \; = \; n \cdot \left(\frac{\pi r^2}{2}\right) \qquad \qquad \text{... (for 'n' number of asperities)}$$

$\therefore$ Vertical load applied,

$$W \; = \; A_V \cdot P_0$$

$$= \; n \cdot \left(\frac{\pi r^2}{2}\right) \cdot P_0$$

For calculating friction force F, the total projected area of material which is being displaced by the plastic flow is considered.

$\therefore$

$$F \; = \; (\text{Area projected in the direction of travel}) \cdot P_0$$

$$F \; = \; A_H \cdot P_0$$

$$= \; \left(\frac{1}{2} \cdot d \cdot h\right) \cdot P_0$$

$$F \; = \; \frac{1}{2} \cdot 2r \cdot h \cdot P_0 \qquad \qquad \text{... (for single asperity)}$$

$$F \; = \; n \cdot r \cdot h \cdot P_0 \qquad \qquad \text{... (for 'n' number of asperities)}$$

Coefficient of friction,

$$f \; = \; \frac{F}{W} \; = \; \frac{n \cdot r \cdot h \cdot P_0}{n \cdot \left(\frac{\pi r^2}{2}\right) \cdot P_0} \; = \; \frac{2h}{\pi r}$$

But we have $\dfrac{r}{h} = \tan \theta$ and therefore f becomes,

$$f \; = \; \frac{2}{\pi \cdot \tan \theta} = \frac{2}{\pi} \cdot \cot \theta \qquad \qquad \text{... (2.17)}$$

Thus,
$$f \; = \; \frac{1}{2} \left[\frac{\text{Vertical projected area}}{\text{Horizontal projected area}}\right]$$

$$f \; = \; \frac{1}{2} \cdot \frac{A_V}{A_H} \qquad \qquad \text{... (2.18)}$$

Bowden and Tabor states the following relation for which the tangential resistance to sliding for a single asperity is made up of a shear term and ploughing term.

i.e. $$F = A_V \cdot S_0 + A_H \cdot P_0 \qquad \qquad \text{... (2.19)}$$

where, A_V and A_H are the vertical and horizontal projected areas respectively.

2.6.4 Amonton's Mechanical Interlocking Theory

Amontons suggested that friction is due to mechanical interlocking of asperities; which can provide possible explanation about the existence of friction. This theory does not take into account energy dissipation. The sliding of one surface over the other mating surface involves no energy dissipation. This theory doesn't give proper justification of all the aspects of friction.

2.6.5 Tomlinson's and Hardy Theory of Molecular Attraction

This theory provides sufficient explanation about the friction and energy dissipation. This theory was developed based on a molecular concept. According to this theory, dry friction is the result of molecular interaction between the contacting surfaces.

Tomlinson's Hypothesis:

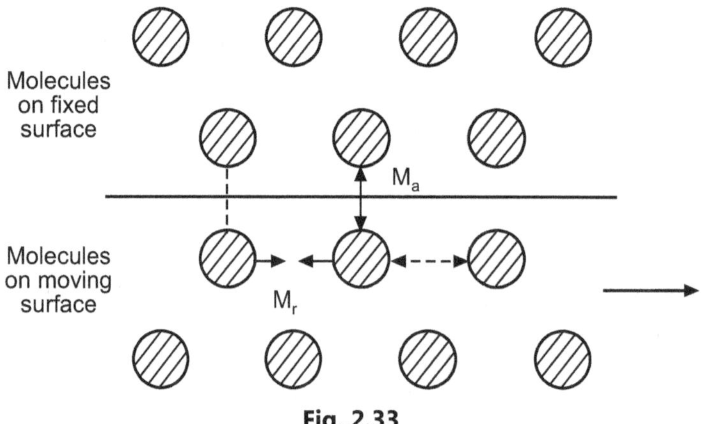

Fig. 2.33

According to Tomlinson,

- A solid consists of tiny molecules which are locked under the action of attractive and repulsive type of electrostatic forces.

- The field of molecular attraction extends a distance of several diameters from the centre of the molecule and the field of repulsive force extends to a much shorter distance.

- When two bodies collide but do not penetrate each other, i.e. when molecules come into this repulsive field and then separate, Tomlinson assumes that there is a loss of energy which is the basis of the friction. Hence, when molecules pass other molecules, either kind may be pulled out of equilibrium position and cause heat.

- This theory also gives explanation about the relation of coefficient of friction with the elastic constants of the materials involved. Tomlinson obtained an equation for coefficient of friction in terms of modulus of elasticity in tension and shear for each of the sliding materials.

$$f = 1.07 \times 10^4 \left[\frac{3E_1 + 4G_1}{G_1(3E_1 + G_1)} + \frac{3E_2 + 4G_2}{G_2(3E_2 + G_2)} \right]^{2/3} \quad ... (2.20)$$

where, E_1 and E_2 are modulus of elasticity in tension for two materials.

G_1 and G_2 are modulus of rigidity in shear for two materials.

Explanation:

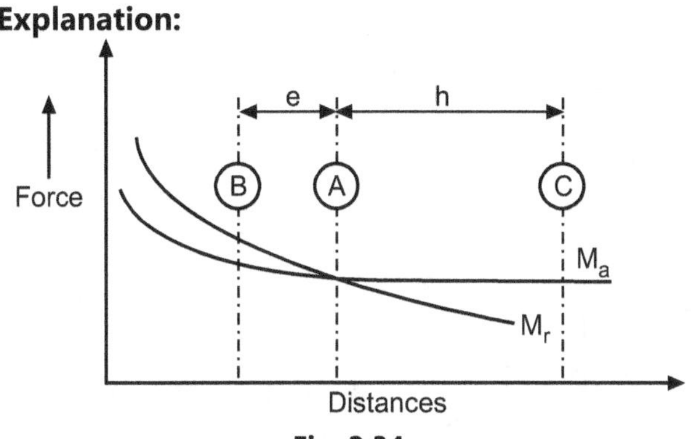

Fig. 2.34

Consider the molecule A. When repulsive forces and attractive forces reach equilibrium, molecule D is then in equilibrium with its neighbouring molecule B. Molecule A then will be located at distance 'e' from B. For molecule C; when it moves past A, if 'h' is the distance between A and C which is large enough compared with 'e', the effect of their mutual attraction is negligible.

If molecules pass by each other within the range of the attractive and repulsive forces, energy is absorbed as the molecule is attracted to C and snaps back. This interaction causes vibration and heating, which results in a temperature rise. The vibration of attraction and repulsion absorbs energy.

Limitations:

- According to this theory, friction varies as the area of contact.
- Coefficients of friction as computed by the relation suggested by Tomlinson are lower than that for clean bodies.
- This theory doesn't provide a clear explanation of friction and stiction and also the variation of f with sliding speed.
- This theory cannot explain the relationship between friction and contact pressure, and also between wear and contact pressure.

2.6.6 Stick-Slip Phenomenon

At velocities that fluctuate widely, a sliding phenomenon of one body over another body occurs under a steady pulling force. If the friction force or sliding velocity varies as a function of distance or time and produces a form of oscillations, it is called a 'stick-slip phenomenon.

Illustration:

Consider a completely generalised frictional system.

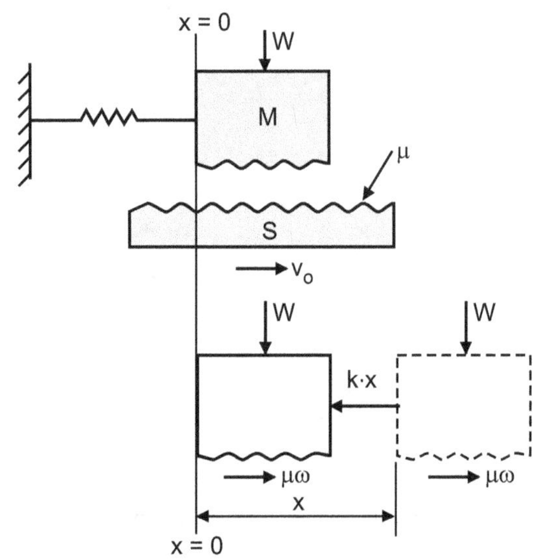

Fig. 2.35: Generalised frictional system

$$M \ = \ \text{An element of mass}$$
$$S \ = \ \text{Surface which can move at velocity } v_o$$
$$k \ = \ \text{Spring stiffness of system}$$
$$W \ = \ \text{Load on element of mass}$$
$$\mu \ = \ \text{Coefficient of friction between the element and the surface}$$

When the system starts to move, the system is relaxed as $x = 0$.

If the mass is displaced by a distance, x as shown in Fig. 2.35, there will be a spring force $(-k \cdot x)$.

$$\therefore \qquad \text{Spring force, } F_s \ = \ -k \cdot x$$

Force of mass M due to sliding is $(+\mu \cdot W)$

$$\therefore \qquad \text{Force on mass M, } F_m \ = \ +\mu \cdot W$$

These two forces will cause the system to accelerate,

$$F_M + F_s = M \ddot{x}$$

$$\therefore \quad \mu W + (-kx) = M \cdot \ddot{x}$$

$$\mu \cdot W - k \cdot x = M \cdot \ddot{x}$$

If μ = constant $\Rightarrow$ The system would be stable when

$$\mu W = k \cdot x$$

$$x = \frac{\mu W}{k} \qquad \qquad \dots (2.21)$$

A. J. Morin suggested that there were two coefficients of friction:

- Static coefficient of friction (μ_s) and

- Dynamic coefficient of friction (μ_d)

A sliding system with these characteristics can oscillate and this behaviour of this sliding system results in a 'stick-slip' action.

When the system starts to move with velocity (v_o), spring force is zero, mass (M) moves with (v_o), till displacement is $\left(\mu_s \cdot \dfrac{W}{k} \right)$.

i.e. spring force 'kx' just equals static friction force $\mu_s \cdot \mathbf{W}$.

At this point 'P', the components start to slide and as soon as this happens, the lower dynamic friction (μ_d) takes over from (μ_s).

$$k_x > \mu_s \cdot W$$

So (M) will accelerate until (k_x) reduces to ($\mu_d \cdot W$), i.e. point 'P$_2$' in Fig. 2.36.

'M' continues to move under its stored kinetic energy till it comes to rest at 'P$_3$' when the higher static friction takes over and the whole cycle is repeated.

It was found that, stick-slip process occurs as a result of one or both of the following two features:

- The coefficient of static friction is greater than the coefficient of dynamic friction.

  i.e. $\qquad \qquad (\mu_s) > (\mu_d)$

- The rate of change of coefficient of dynamic friction as a function of velocity at the sliding velocity is negative.

- The stick-slip process may be prevented or minimised by the following means:

- The mechanical system may be so designed that the amplitude of the stick-slip oscillations would be small.

- The friction pair may be selected so that the difference between (μ_s) and (μ_d) is small. It is possible by the use of boundary lubricant film.

- A friction pair may also be selected so that a positive ($\mu_d - v$) characteristic at the sliding velocity is exhibited. It is done with a soft metallic coating and polymers.

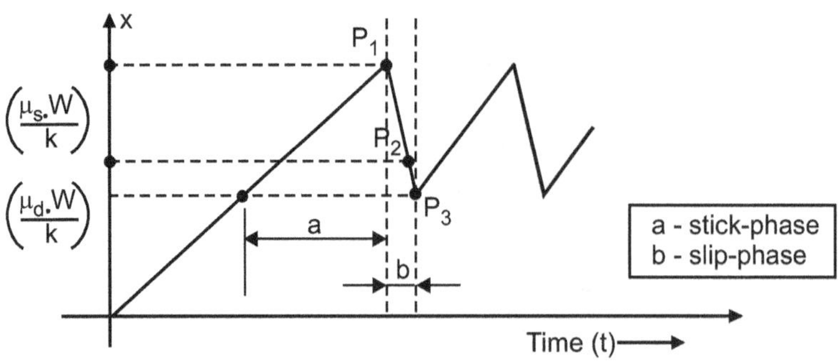

Fig. 2.36

2.7 INTRODUCTION TO WEAR

- **Wear:** It is defined as the process of removal of material from one or both of the two solid surfaces in solid-state contact.
- A committee of the Institution of Mechanical Engineers defines wear as "the progressive loss of substance from the surface of a body brought about by mechanical action".
- Kragelskii defines wear as "the destruction of material produced as a result of repeated disturbances of the frictional bonds".
- Wear is a characteristic of the Engineering systems which depend on load, speed, temperature, hardness, surface finish, environmental conditions, etc.

The wear behaviour of a material is a very complicated phenomenon involving various mechanisms and factors.

2.8 TYPES OF WEAR

Following are the various types of wear processes based on the type of wearing contacts.

(i) Single-Phase Wear: In this, a solid, liquid or gas moving relative to a sliding surface causes material to be removed from the surface. The relative motion for wear to occur may be sliding or rolling.

(ii) Multi-Phase Wear: In this wear, the solid, liquid or gas moving across a surface, acts as a carrier for the second phase that actually produce the wear.

Common Types of Wear Mechanisms are Listed Below:

- Adhesive wear (or Galling or scuffing).
- Abrasive wear and cutting.
- Wear due to surface fatigue.
- Corrosive wear (or tribo-chemical wear).
- Minor wear.
    - (a)   Erosion:
        - By solid particles and fluids
        - Fluid erosion

- Erosion by cavitation (i.e. wear between solids and liquids)

(b)   Fretting wear.

2.8.1 Major Types of Wear

2.8.1.1 Adhesive Wear (Galling or Scuffing)

Initiation of adhesive wear is due to the presence of interfacial adhesive junctions that form if solid materials are in contact on an atomic scale. The local pressure at the asperities become extremely high as a normal load is applied. The asperities deform plastically as the yield point stress is exceeded, until the real contact area has increased sufficiently to support the applied load.

In this case, the surface would adhere together in the absence of surface films. The relative tangential motion at the interface acts to disperse the contaminant films at the point of contact and results in a cold-weld junction. Further sliding causes the cold-weld junction to be sheared and a new junction to be formed.

The amount of wear depends on the position at which the junction is sheared.

- If the junction is sheared at the position of the interface then wear is negligible or zero.

- If the junction is sheared away from the interface, then metal is transferred from one surface to the other.

Adhesive Wear Processes and Generation of Wear Particle:

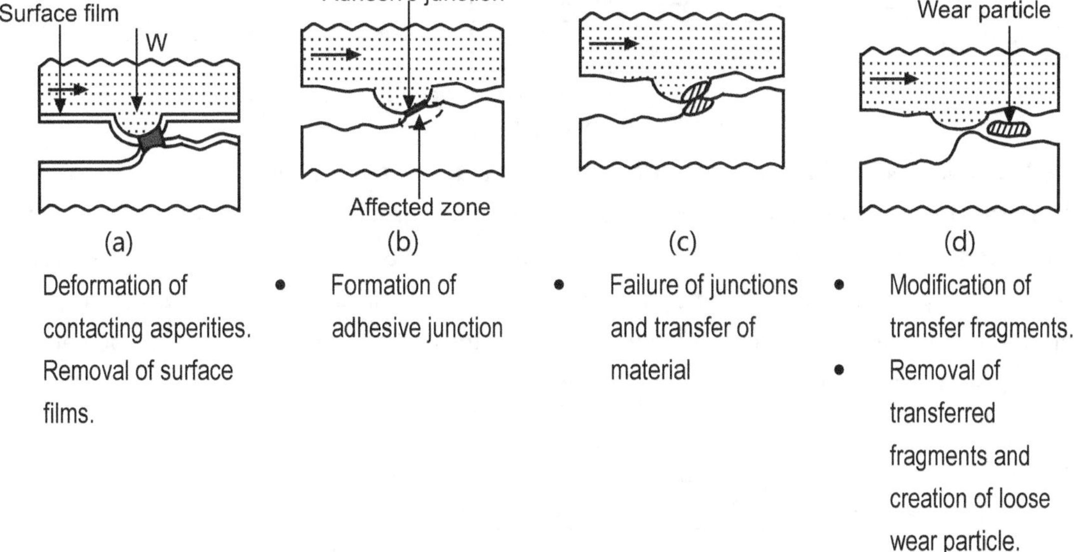

• Deformation of contacting asperities. • Removal of surface films.	• Formation of adhesive junction	• Failure of junctions and transfer of material	• Modification of transfer fragments. • Removal of transferred fragments and creation of loose wear particle.

Fig. 2.37

Typical wear behaviour over a life of component is shown in Fig. 2.38.

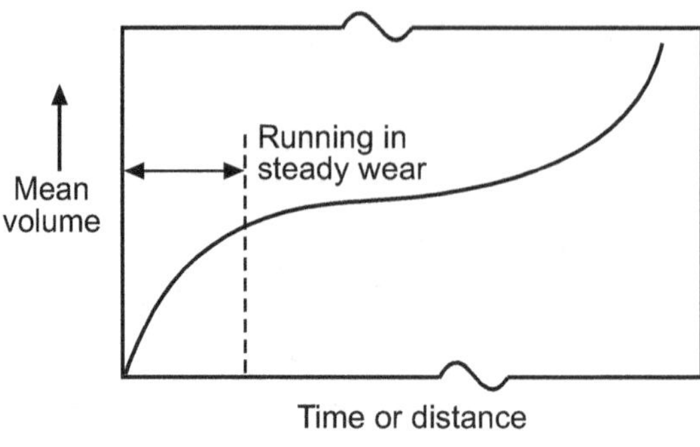

Fig. 2.38

2.8.1.2 Abrasive Wear

Abrasive wear is simply the process of damage to a surface by a harder material. In the abrasive wear process, asperities of the harder surface press into the softer surface causing plastic flow of the softer surface around the asperities from the harder surface. When a tangential load is applied onto the surface, the harder surface removes the softer material by combined effect of microploughing, microcutting and microcracking.

Abrasive wear comprises of two general situations.

(i)   Two-Body Abrasion: In this situation, one of the surfaces must be harder and rough and here the wear is caused by hard protuberances on the counterface. This type of wear occurs under low stress conditions.

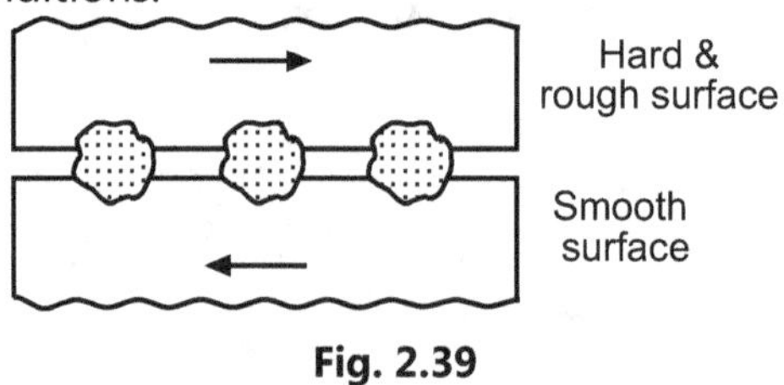

Fig. 2.39

e.g. Mechanical operations such as grinding, cutting, machining, drilling, etc.

(ii)   Three-Body Abrasion: In this situation, a small particle of grit or abrasive, i.e. hard surface acts as a third body i.e. contaminant between the two surfaces in relative motion. The third body should be sufficiently harder than the two surfaces to cause abrasion. Loss of material in this case depends not only on the hardness of the wearing surface but also on the counterface and the contaminant. This type of wear results in high stresses.

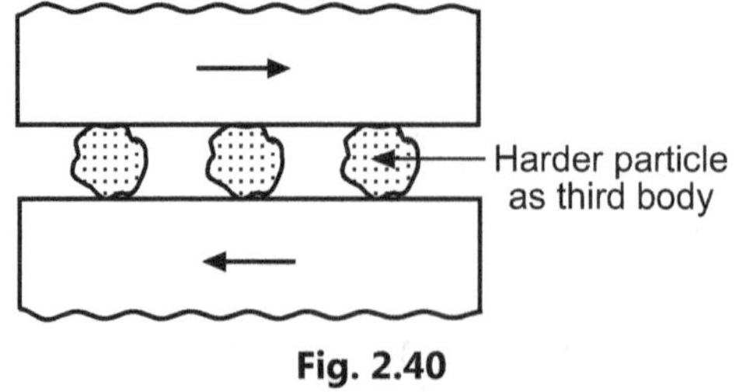

Fig. 2.40

e.g. Metal finishing operations like lapping, polishing, etc.

Depending on the degree of severity of damage to the surfaces, abrasive wear can be classified into:

(i) Gouging Abrasive Wear: It is caused by impact and results in micro-deformation of the surface. It is normally measured as the rate of metal removal normal to the surface of the material and expressed in terms of 'miles per hour'.

(ii) Grinding Abrasive Wear: In this type of abrasive wear, whenever two surfaces rub together with force to crush the abrasive grains entrapped between them, the stresses on individual grain are very high.

(iii) Erosion Abrasive Wear: It is caused by impact of particles at high velocity on the component surface and largely depends on the hard and normally sharp particles. It is usually described by specific weight loss (W_S).

$$W_S = C \times v^n \qquad \qquad ... (2.22)$$

where, C – Constant

v – Velocity of a stream of abrasive particles blasting against the target specimen (5 – 500 m/s)

n – Index depending on the target material

e.g. Impact of dust particles on the blades of turbo machinery operation of fluid-bed combuster.

2.8.1.3 Fatigue Wear

Fatigue wear phenomenon can be explained with two kinds of contacts:

* Case of rolling contact.
* Case of sliding contact.

* **Case of Rolling Contact:**

Wear at the surface due to fatigue is generally quite common in rolling contacts. The rolling elements subjected to repetitive cycle of Hertz-type contact stresses lead to development of subsurface cracks causes gradual spalling failure.

Nature of stresses in this case show that the maximum compressive stresses occur at the surface, and the maximum shear stresses occur some distance below the surface. As rolling proceeds, the directions of the shear stresses for any element change sign. The failure is attributed to multiple reversals of the contact stress field. Therefore, this type of failure is classified as fatigue failure.

For the perfect material subjected to rolling contact, the position of failure will be given by the position of maximum reversed shear stress. But materials are rarely perfect and the exact position of ultimate failure will be affected by inclusions, porosity, micro cracks, etc.

For rolling contact, the useful life in terms of numbers of revolutions or time at a given speed is of prime importance than the amount of material removed by fatigue failure. A test conducted on large number of bearings has shown that the life N is inversely proportional to the cube of the applied load W.

$$W^3 \times N = \text{Constant} \qquad \qquad \text{... (2.23)}$$

The position of maximum shear stress in pure rolling is proportional to $(WR)^{1/3}$ for a ball and proportional to $(WR)^{1/2}$ for cylinder.

- **Case of Sliding Contact:**

Surface fatigue is the result of the cyclic contact loads at relatively mild stress. In sliding contacts, the asperities are also subjected to cyclic stressing which leads to stress concentration effects and finally the crack generation and propagation.

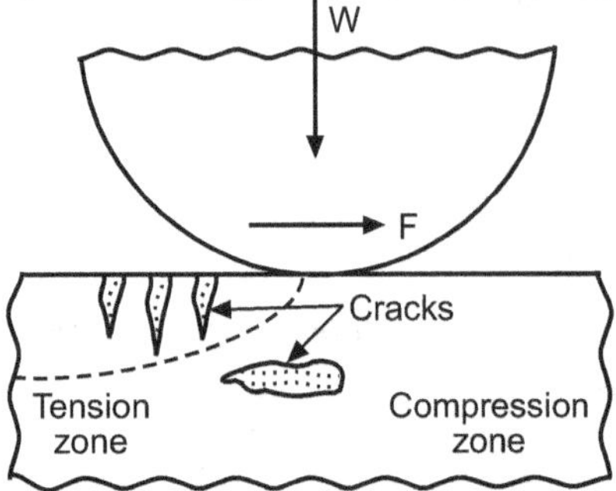

Fig. 2.41: Fatigue wear due to formation of surface and subsurface crack

In analysis of elastic-plastic stress fields in the subsurface regions of sliding asperity contacts, the following events are detailed out.

- Whenever two sliding surfaces come into contact; asperities on the softer surface are deformed by repetitive loading which results in relatively smooth surface and finally softer surface experiences cyclic loading as the asperities of the harder surface plough through it.
- Plastic shear deformation of softer surface with repeated loading occurs.
- Due to continual subsurface deformation, cracks are nucleated below the surface.
- Further loading causes the cracks to propagate parallel to the surface.
- Finally the cracks intercept the surface resulting in long, thin, wear sheets delaminate, and producing platelike particles.

For sliding contacts, the amount of material removed due to fatigue can be estimated with the help of relation,

$$v_f = C \frac{\eta \cdot \gamma}{\varepsilon_1^2 H} W \cdot L \qquad \qquad \text{... (2.24)}$$

　　　where,　　　η　–　the distribution of asperity heights

　　　　　　　　　γ　–　the particle size constant

　　　　　　　　　ε_1　–　the strain failure in one loading cycle

　　　and　　　　H　–　the hardness

2.8.1.4 Corrosive Wear

In corrosive wear phenomenon, the dynamic interaction between environment and mating material surfaces plays a major role. In this case, rubbing of two surfaces takes place in a corrosive environment which may be gaseous or liquid, then surface reaction occurs that deposits the reaction product on one or both surfaces. These reaction products adhere poorly to the surfaces and due to further rubbing they are removed. Repetition of this process leads to corrosive failure of the mating surfaces.

Further, the process of rubbing leads to increase in temperature resulting in an increase in the reactivity of the asperities. Finally, the whole process results in change of the mechanical properties of asperities.

Corrosive Wear Depends on –

- The reaction products, that further depend upon the exact composition of the environment. Therefore for the study of mechanism of tribo-chemical wear, greater understanding of the chemistry of the reaction product formation is required.
- Relative electropotential of rubbing metals.

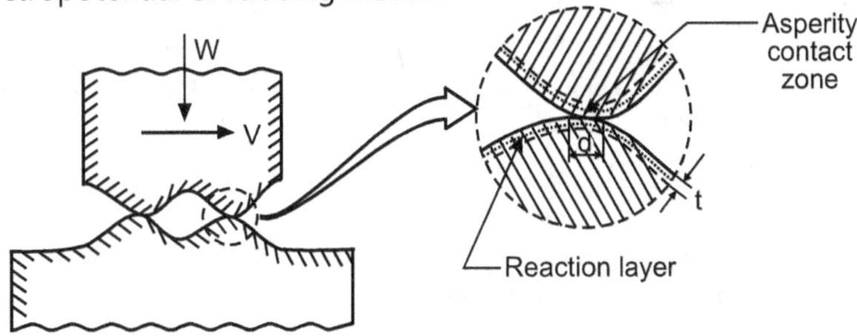

Fig. 2.42

A simple model of chemical wear is shown in Fig. 2.42 above. It gives a relation to estimate the material loss from surface due to corrosion (v_c).

$$v_v = \frac{k_v d}{\xi^2 t^2 \cdot H \cdot v} \cdot W L \qquad \qquad \dots (2.25)$$

where, k_v – the velocity factor of oxidation
    d – the diameter of asperity contact
    t – the thickness of the reaction layer
    ξ – the critical thickness of the reaction layer and
    H – the hardness
    v – the sliding velocity

2.8.2 Minor Types of Wear

2.8.2.1 Erosive Wear

It is the process of removal of material by the impingement of particles at high velocity on component surfaces. Erosion is more prominent for materials with high strength to density ratios, together with high operating speed of the mechanisms. Erosion wear can be explained with three subcategories:

- Erosion by solid particles and fluids.
- Fluid erosion.
- Erosive wear by cavitation (wear between solids and liquids).

- **Erosion by Solid Particles and Fluids:**

The solid particle erosion takes place when discrete solid particles strike a surface. In erosion process, forces of different origins may act on a particle in contact with a solid surface. In addition to this, the neighbouring particles may exert contact forces and the flowing fluid will cause drag.

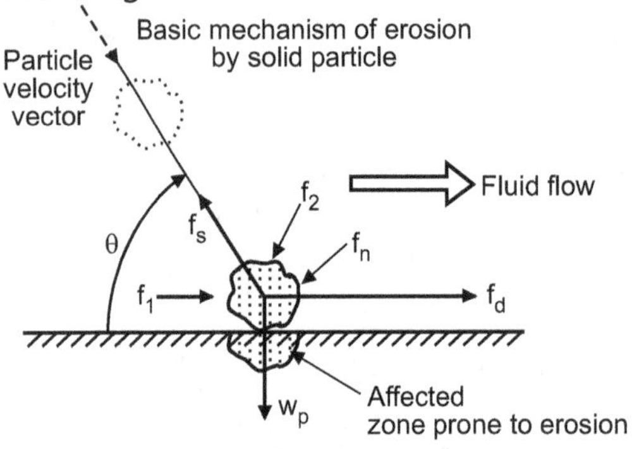

$f_1, f_2, ... f_n$ = Inter particle contact forces

f_s = Surface contact force

f_d = Drag force due to flowing fluid

W = Weight of the particle

θ = Impingement angle

Fig. 2.43

In this case, wear rate depends on

- Class of material.
- Environmental parameters such as impact velocity, impact angle, particle type and size.

The features of erosion on ductile and brittle materials as a function of impact angle are as given below.

(a) Soft ductile metal
(b) Brittle solid (glass)
(c) Elastomer
(d) Cast iron

Fig. 2.44: Dependence of solid particle erosion rate on impact angle for ductile and brittle materials

Observations:

- For ductile material, the maximum erosion occurs at an impingement angle of 20°. The volume V_e removed from the surface by a mass M of eroding particle was predicted as,

$$V_e \;=\; \frac{M \cdot v_p^2 \cdot f(\theta)}{P_h} \qquad\qquad \text{... (2.26)}$$

where, V_e — Volume of material eroded from the surface

v_p — Particle velocity

$f(\theta)$ — Function of angle measured from the plane of the surface to the particle velocity vector

P_h — Horizontal component of flow pressure between particle and surface

(ii) Erosion by Fluid:

When small drops of liquids are made to impinge on the surface of a solid at high speeds (i.e. 1000 m/s), very high pressures are experienced, which exceeds the yield strength of most materials. Thus, fluid erosion causes plastic deformation or fracture from single impact.

(iii) Erosive Wear by Cavitation (Wear between Solids and Liquids):

It arises when a solid and a fluid are in relative motion. This causes formation of bubbles that become unstable and implode against the solid surface.

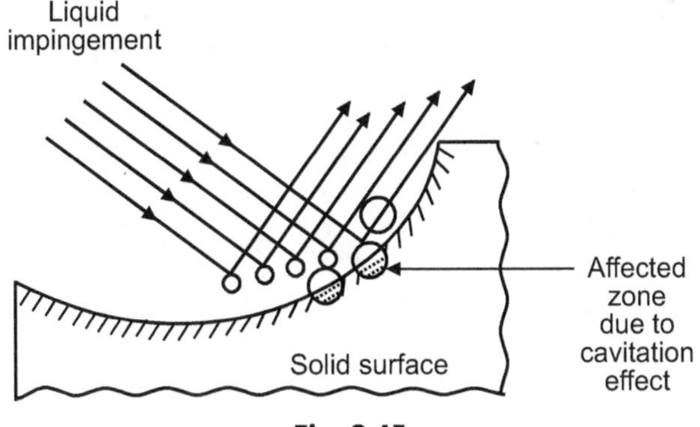

Fig. 2.45

Mechanism:

- The formed bubbles due to the relative motion of solid and fluid implode onto the solid surface.
- The impingement liquid brings the gaseous bubbles to the surface at relatively high velocities.
- The bubbles strike the solid surface and collapse on impact. Thus, due to collapse, it imposes shock waves on the solid surface resulting in the liberation of material from the surface.

Examples of Cavitation Erosion:

In fluid handling machines as marine propellers, hydro foils, dam slipways, gates, all hydraulic turbines.

2.8.2.2 Fretting Wear

It occurs between two metal surfaces loaded together when subjected to a low amplitude oscillatory motion (or vibratory motion).

- Fretting wear frequently occurs between components that are not intended to move e.g. press fit.

- Surfaces subjected to fretting have a characteristic appearance with red-brown patches on ferrous metals and adjacent areas that are highly polished.

- Fretting wear largely depends on environmental conditions as the amount of fretting wear in moist atmosphere is higher than that in dry atmosphere.

Examples of Fretting Wear:

- In many practical situations in which fretting can be troublesome i.e. many static joints - as flanges, couplings, keyways which are subjected to vibration.

- It can take place between the undersides of screw or bolt heads and the components being joined and can lead to the loosening of such joints resulting in an increased vibration and thus an acceleration. Finally, wear takes place due to fretting.

2.9 FACTORS AFFECTING WEAR

There are number of factors which lead to considerable variation in the wear rates between rubbing surfaces.

Following are some of the important factors affecting wear:

1. Surface films
   - Wear under vacuum
   - Oxide films
   - Boundary lubrication
   - Solid lubricants
   - Other surface layers
2. Temperature
3. Load
4. Compatibility (mutual solubility)
5. Crystal structure

We will discuss effects of the above factors in more details.

(1) Surface Films:

- As friction and wear both are surface phenomena resulting from surface interaction, the presence of surface film and the properties of the surface films have a prominent effect on wear. We can categorize wear under no vacuum condition (i.e. in absence of surface film) and in presence of contaminants.

(a) Wear Under Vacuum:

Due to the action of normal and tangential loads, junction growth occurs and welds are made over larger areas of contact resulting in high friction coefficient. Further, these welded bonds must be broken. Thus, wear depends on the exact position of the fracture relative to the junction. The larger the area of the junction, the larger the wear rate. Hence, for most of the practical tribological problems, possible solutions are the use of low shear strength metal films, plastics or solid lubricants.

(b) Oxide Films:

*   *Effects of oxide films on adhesive wear:* Normally, all metals are covered by an oxide film. When asperities make metallic contact, localised welding takes place and the oxide film between the surfaces prevents the junction growth thus reducing both the friction and wear rate.

In mild wear zone, which occurs at lower loads, the contact resistance is high. The wear debris is fine and consists of metal oxides and the rubbed surfaces become polished. In severe wear zones, which occur at higher loads, the contact resistance is low and wear debris includes coarse metallic particles and the rubbed surfaces are rough.

The properties of the oxide films are also important e.g. the hard brittle oxide formed on aluminium provides poor protection against heavy wear.

*   *Effect of oxide films on abrasive wear:* Many oxides are hard and when present in the form of wear, debris act as abrasive particles. Thus, oxide films have large influence on abrasive wear.

(c) Boundary Lubrication:

The presence of oil film of insufficient thickness to prevent asperity contact through the film leads to boundary lubrication. It does not prevent metallic contact at asperities and inhibits junction growth. It can be shown that the effectiveness of boundary lubrication is increased in those cases where a solid metallic soap film is formed over the metal surface.

(d) Solid Lubricants:

These are used to reduce wear in the situations where a conventional lubricant cannot be used. e.g. in high vacuum or at higher temperature solid lubricant is added to the oil in a motor car engine. It acts to reduce the number of metallic contacts and inhibits junction growth, thus providing a low shear strength interface.

(e) Other Surface Layers:

A coating of metal having higher wear resistance is provided on the substrate metal, thus reducing wear between metals e.g.

*   Electroplating of Rhodium or Chromium on substrate metals of cylinder liners, crankshafts.

- Coatings of cobalt, chromium and iron using spraying and fusing technique, which have good hot-hardness properties and are also highly corrosion resistant.
- Increase in wear resistance of substrate metal is obtained by chemically treating the surface e.g. phosphating and sulfurizing process for steels, nitriding and carburising to harden ferrous surfaces.

(2) Temperature:

The effect of temperature on wear of rubbing surfaces is prominent and it can change –

- the properties of rubbing materials
- the form of surface contaminant
- the properties of lubricant

(a) Effect of Temperature on Properties of Bearing Materials:

- Temperature affects the hardness of a metal, the higher the temperature, the lower the hardness. As hardness decreases, wear rate increases. Therefore, for bearing materials operating at higher temperatures, it is necessary to use metals with high hot-hardness e.g. tool steels, alloys with base composition of cobalt, chromium and molybdenum.
- Sometimes, properties of bearing materials change drastically due to the temperature induced phase change. Variation of coefficient of friction and wear rate at different temperatures, for cobalt on cobalt in vacuum can be shown with the help of following figure. It shows that the wear rate at 350°C is one hundred times greater than that at 280°C. (Pressure 10^{-7} N/m^2, sliding speed 2 m/s, load 9.81 N).

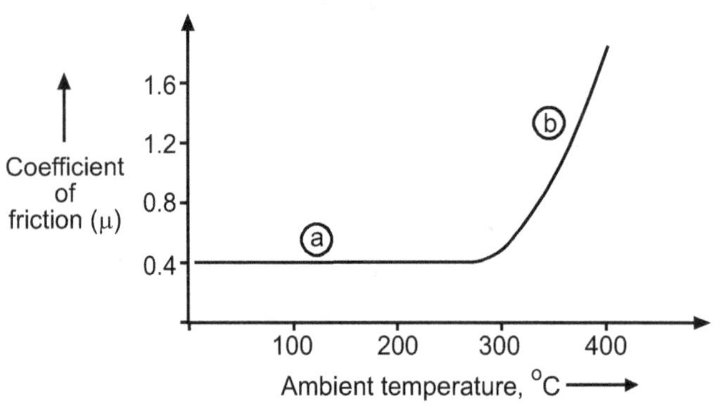

(a)   Wear rate
      3.73×10^{-9} mm^3/mm

(b)   Wear rate
      3.5×10^{-7} mm^3/m

Fig. 2.46: Variation of f and wear rate at different temperatures for cobalt on cobalt in vacuum

(b) Effect of Temperature on the Form of Contaminant:

Most metals are covered by an oxide film in normal atmospheres. The exact form and thickness of the film is dependent on the temperature of formation.

(c) Effect of Temperature on the Properties of Lubricant:

Due to rise in temperature of operation of a bearing lubricated by an oil, deterioration is caused. It is due to first by oxidation of the oil and then by thermal degradation. Oxidation and thermal degradation cause irreversible changes in the lubricating properties of an oil e.g. A fatty acid lubricating reactive metal surfaces will provide good wear resistance beyond its melting point due to the formation of the metallic soap.

(3) Load:

- As the load increases, the frictional force goes on increasing which in turn increases the temperature at the contacting asperities.

  We have discussed earlier the effect of temperature.

- An increase of load can result a transition from mild wear to severe wear. This change takes place at the condition when

Nominal contact pressure $\dfrac{W}{A_a} = \dfrac{H}{3}$

As $\qquad \dfrac{W}{A_a} > \dfrac{H}{3} \Rightarrow$ Transition from mild wear to severe wear occurs for many metals

where, $\qquad$ W $\ -$ Normal load on surfaces in contact

$\qquad$ A_a $\ -$ Apparent area of contact

$\qquad$ H $\ -$ Hardness

- *Effect of relatively low loads:* Under relatively lower loads, mild wear occurs wherein there is no interaction between the plastic zones beneath the contacting asperities.

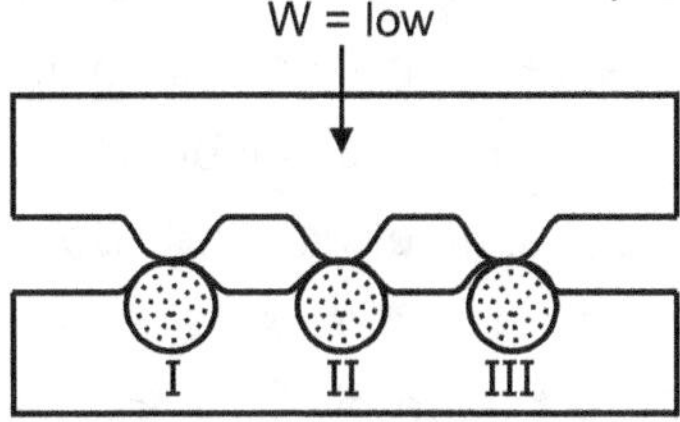

Mild Wear:

I, II and III $-$ Plastic zones under relatively lower loads.

Fig. 2.47

As per Archard's hypothesis, 'Mild wear rate' $\propto (W)^{4/5}$.

- *Effect of high loads:* As the load is increased further, severe wear occurs, wherein the plastic zones interact and the substrate regions become entirely plastic. Amonton's law is no longer holds good beyond this point.

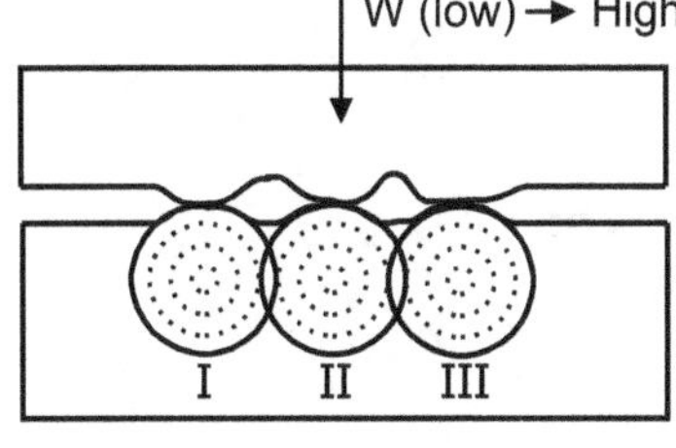

Severe Wear:

I, II and III $-$ Plastic zones interact under high loads.

Fig. 2.48

As per Archard's hypothesis, 'severe wear rate' $\propto$ W.

- To avoid the transition from mild to severe wear, it is desirable to choose materials which have a hardness several times greater than the apparent contact pressure.

(4) Compatibility:

- It has shown that the metal pairs with low metallurgical compatibility will exhibit low friction and low wear. Thus, metals showing high degree of mutual solubility are 'metallurgically compatible'. Metals exhibiting a high degree of mutual solubility will have poor tribological properties. One can obtain compatibility rating from the binary phase diagram.
- Robinowicz has shown zero correlation of mutual solubility with adhesion, a positive correlation with friction and a greater correlation with wear.
- The study suggested that –
  - Metal pairs for boundary lubricated or unlubricated sliding should be chosen to have low mutual solubilities.
  - Similar metals having 100 percent mutual solubility should be avoided.

(5) Crystal Structure:

- According to Bowden Tabor Theory, perfectly clean surfaces which are able to deform plastically will exhibit seizure before gross sliding can occur.
- There are some metals having hexagonal closed packed crystal structure which will give reasonable friction coefficient and low wear rates even when absolutely clean. These metals plastically deform by slip on a single slip plane (i.e. basal plane).
- Temperature-induced phase changes can have drastic effect on tribological properties i.e. Cobalt at 417°C changes from its low temperature hexagonal closed packed structure to a face centred cubic structure. Thus, the combined, ambient and frictional heating that transforms the interface material into the face centred cubic regime, enables junction growth due to the increased number of operative slip systems.

2.10 MEASUREMENT OF WEAR

There are various means of wear measurement given below.

(I) Commonly Used Techniques.

- Weight-loss technique.
- Stylus profiler or non-contact optical profiler.
- Vickers or Knoop microhardness indentation technique.

(II) Less Commonly Used Techniques.

- Radioactive decay.
- Scanning Electron Microscopy (SEM).
- Scanning Tunneling Microscopy (STM).

(III) Wear Debris Analysis Techniques.

Following are the commonly used techniques for 'wear debris analysis'.

(a)   Magnetic Plug.

(b)   Ferrography.

(c)   Spectroscopic Oil Analysis Process (SOA).

(I)   Commonly Used Techniques:

(a)   Weight-Loss Technique:

- This technique is preferable to measure large amounts of wear.
- It can be used only when the density of material remains constant and transfer of material does not occur during wear process.
- This technique is not effective in the case of thin wear-resistant coatings, where the amount of wear is very small.
- Resolution of this technique ranges from 10-100 µg.

Limitations:

- As wear is mainly related with the volume of material removed, such methods may give different results if materials to be compared differ in density.
- Weight-loss measurement does not take into account a wear by material displacement i.e. a specimen may gain weight by transfer.

(b)   Stylus Profiler or Non-Contact Optical Profiler:

- It is easy to use and commonly used to measure the depth of wear with a resolution of upto a fraction of a nanometer.
- With the help of fully automated profiler, three-dimensional worn surface profiles can be obtained.
- Stylus profiler has resolution ranging from 25-50 nm, while optical profiler has resolution ranging from 0.5-2 nm.
- Wear-track profile obtained with stylus profiler is as shown in Fig. 2.49 below.

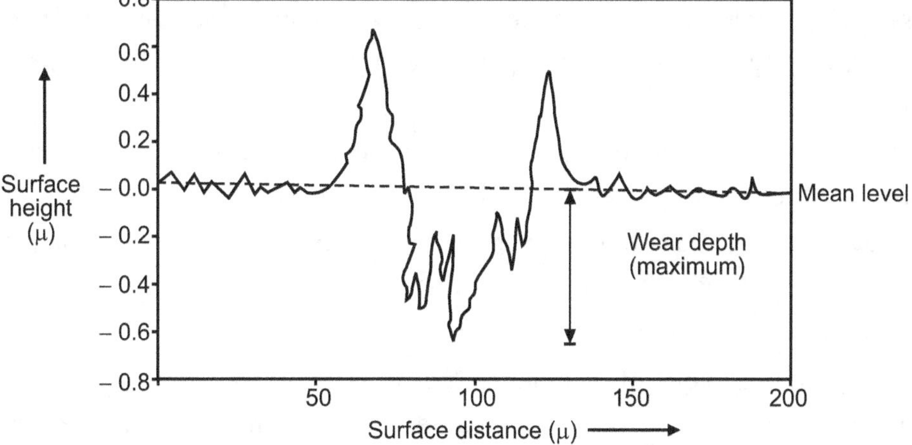

Fig. 2.49: Wear-track profile obtained by Stylus profiler

(c) Vickers or Knoop Microhardness Indentation Technique:

- It is easy to use and commonly used to measure the depth of wear with a resolution of upto a fraction of a nanometer.

- In this technique, Vickers and Knoop indentations are made on the wear surface. By measuring the width of the indentations before and after the wear test under a microscope, the depth of wear can be calculated.

- This technique has resolution ranging from 25-50 nm.

(II) Less Commonly Used Techniques:

(a) Radioactive Decay:

- It is used to measure small wear and is also called autoradiography.

- It is very sensitive but requires facilities to irradiate one of the members and measure the changes in radiation.

- This technique has resolution of approximately 1 pg.

(b) Scanning Electron Microscopy (SEM):

- Scanning electron microscopy of worn surfaces is commonly used to measure microscopic wear.

- This technique has resolution upto 0.1 nm.

(c) Scanning Tunneling Microscopy (STM):

- Scanning tunneling microscopy can be used to measure wear on an atomic scale.

- This technique has resolution ranging from 0.02 – 0.05 nm.

(1) Magnetic Plug:

- These are simple magnetic blocks positioned in the lubricating system for getting maximum wear debries.

- These are generally provided at the bottom of a sump, reservoir, bigger pump and compressor casings, in order for periodical removal along with collected metallic debries.

- The debries collected, can be quantified and examined visually by the electromagnetic debries tester or Scanning Electron Microscope (SEM).

- The magnetic blocks also help in partial cleaning of the lubricating oil in addition to collecting the metallic debries for monitoring.

(2) Ferrography:

- It is basically a technique of separation of wear particles from the used oil. This study is useful for analysing the nature, magnitude and the way of growth in wear rate by particle size distribution of wear debries.

- Ferrography works in two stages as
  - (a)   Direct Reading Ferrograph.
  - (b)   Analytical Ferrograph.

(a)   Direct Reading Ferrograph:

The 'direct reading ferrograph' instrument consists of the following elements:

- Glass Capillary Tube.
- Precipitator Tube.
- A Magnet.
- Lamp and Photodetectors.
- Digital Readout.

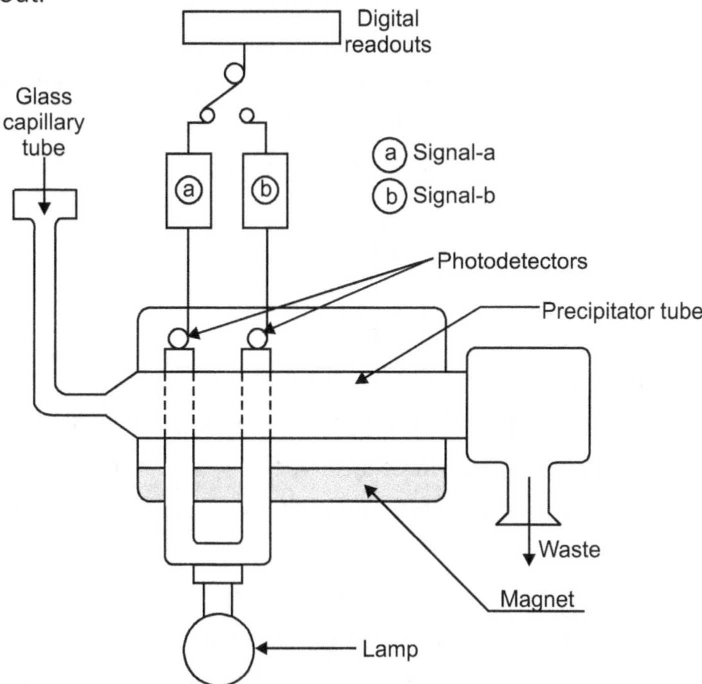

Fig. 2.50: Direct Reading Ferrograph - Schematic

The wear debries are arranged according to their particle size, in a glass capillary tube. The sample oil is heated in a furnace at 65°C to 70°C in order to get a homogeneous suspension of particles in the used oil. An oil of 1 ml along with a solvent carbon tetrachloride (1 ml), is shaked in a test-tube for reducing the viscosity of oil.

Now, this oil flows by capillary action through a precipitator tube. A magnet is placed below the glass tube. A powerful magnetic field aligns the particles according to size. Larger particles (about 5 micron and above) are deposited at the entry point of the tube, while smaller particles (about 0.5 to 5 microns) are concentrated away from the entry.

The magnetic force is directly proportional to the volume of wear particles and the viscous force resisting the motion is proportional to the particle area. The motion of wear particles downward through the glass tube is proportional to the effective particle diameter. Light source is used with two light beams passing through the precipitator tube. The first beam is located in the vicinity of the tube entry where large particles (P_L) are deposited. The second beam is positioned a small distance from the first one. It crosses the tube, where the smaller particles (P_S) are deposited. The device measures the total number of P_L and P_S by the attenuation of light from the light source. Then the light passed is detected by a photodetector which are photoelectric transducers producing 'signal-a' that 'signal-b' and finally give digital readouts.

An indicator of wear is the 'severity index' (S.I.), which is an important characterising parameter in ferrography study. It is given by

- $$\text{S.I.} = (P_L)^2 - (P_S)^2$$

   where,

$$P_L = \text{is the quantum of larger wear particles}$$

   and $\qquad P_S = \text{is the quantum of smaller wear particles}$

The following additional indicators are also calculated.

- **Total Wear:**

$$\text{T.W.} = P_L + P_S$$

- **Severity of Wear:**

$$\text{S.W.} = P_L - P_S$$

(b) Analytical Ferrograph:

- Failure mode analysis of some of the samples can be done with analytical ferrograph.
- In this device, lubricating oil is pumped at a very low and controlled rate across a glass slide, which is held at an angle (preferably small) above the poles of a very powerful magnet.
- The wear debries, deposits on the slide in a microscopic manner. After magnification through 100 to 1000 times, suitable visible ferrographs are photographed and printed.
- The shape, configuration and surface characteristics of these particles include the type of wear and the type or mode of failure.

(3) Spectroscopic Oil Analysis Process (SOA):

- In this technique, a small concentration of metallic wear products (about 1 to 2 ppm), suspended in used lubricating oil can be identified and analysed by a spectroscopic analyser.
- Spectroscope is an optical instrument which is designed to study the spectrum of light.
- It is used to identify the chemical elements and thus to determine the chemical composition of the wear particles by examination of spectral lines in the emitted or absorbed light. These spectral lines are the fundamental characteristics of the element

or metal present in the wear debris. The element absorbs or emits energy of only specified wavelength which is a characteristic of the atoms of that element.

- The intensity of the energy emitted or energy absorbed at specified wavelength, is taken to be a representative of the concentration of the corresponding element in the oil sample.

- SOA can also identify elements from oil seals, coolers and other components. By knowing the elements and their concentration, one can find the wearing out component in the machine and their rate of wear.

Following Table 2.1 gives the comparison of the three techniques of the wear debries analysis, SOA magnetic plug, ferrography and SOA.

Table 2.1 : Comparison of Magnetic Plug, Ferrography and SOA

Limiting Factor Type of Technique	Efficiency of each technique	Types of Debries			Warning time for gradual failure	Type of Surveillance	Possibility of Alarm
		Ferrous	Non-ferrous	Non-metallic			
Magnetic plug	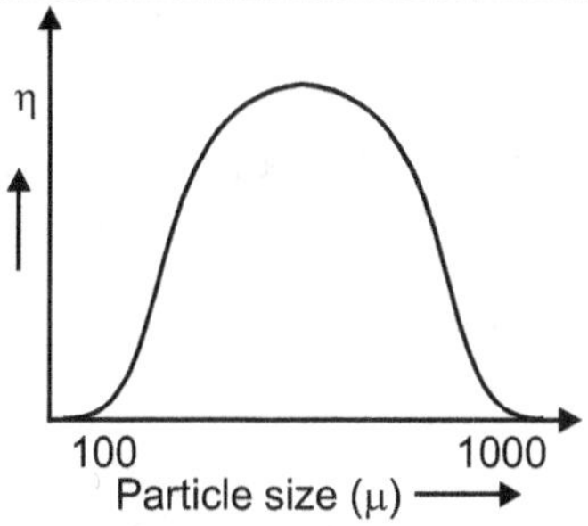	Suitable	Not suitable	Not suitable	Good	Continuous possible by online electronic chip detector	Possible
Ferrography	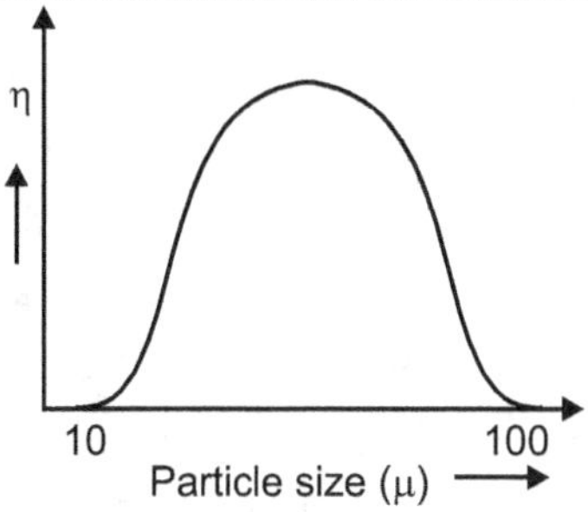	Suitable	Suitable for few	Suitable for few	Very good	Continuous possible by online DR ferrography	Possible
SOA (Spectroscopic Oil Analysis Process)	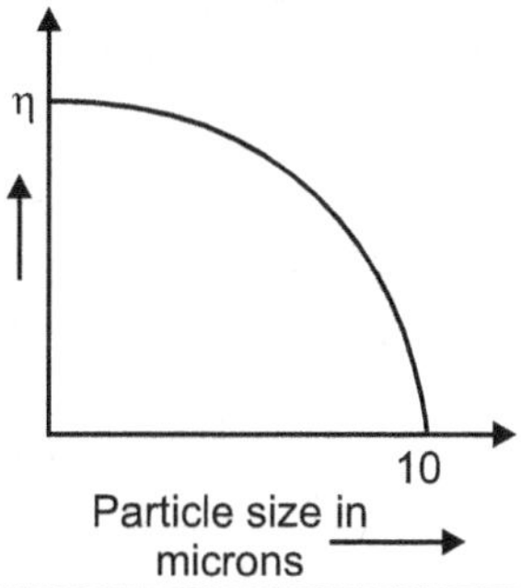	Suitable	Suitable	Suitable	Very good	Periodic, based on samples	Not possible

2.11 THEORIES OF WEAR

2.11.1 Theory of Adhesive Wear (Archard's Wear Theory)

- Wear takes place when two surfaces in contact slide over each other. It highlights the main variables which influence sliding wear and also determines the severity of wear by means of wear coefficient K.

- **Assumptions Made for Adhesive Theory (Archard's Hypothesis):**

(i) The contact between the two surfaces will occur where asperities touch and the true area of contact will be equal to the sum of the individual asperity contact areas. For a single asperity contact, we assume the area to be circular in plane view and of radius a (i.e. both the contacting surfaces have spherical asperities).

$$\therefore \quad \text{Area of each contact} = \pi a^2$$

$$\text{Total area, } A = \sum_{i=1}^{n} A_i$$

where, n – Number of asperities in contact.

(ii) This area is proportional to the normal load and under most conditions for metals, the local deformation of the asperities will be plastic.

$$\therefore \quad \text{Load supported by each contacting area of asperity,}$$

$$w = A \cdot P_0$$
$$= \pi a^2 \cdot P_0$$

Total load supported,

$$W = W \cdot n = P_0 \cdot \pi a^2 \cdot n \qquad \qquad \dots (2.27)$$

where, P_0 is the yield pressure.

(iii) During sliding, the surface will pass completely over each asperity in a sliding distance of L.

$$\text{where,} \qquad L = 2a$$

(iv) Continuous sliding causes continuous formation and destruction of individual asperity contacts. Wear is closely associated with the detachment of fragments of the material from the asperities. We assume that the wear fragment produced at each asperity is hemispherical in shape.

(v) The volume of the material removed by wear (δV) is proportional to the (i) square of the contact dimension for layer removal or (ii) cube of the contact dimension 'a' for lump removal which implies that the shape of the wear particle is independent of its size.

$$\therefore \quad \text{Volume of material removed}$$

$$\delta V = \frac{2}{3} \pi a^3 \qquad \dots \text{(Assuming hemispherical shape of asperity)} \qquad \dots (2.28)$$

(vi) All contacts are not responsible for the formation of wear particles, only a fraction 'K' of all asperity contacts are responsible for producing a wear particle.

Evolution of a single contact patch as two asperities move over each other:

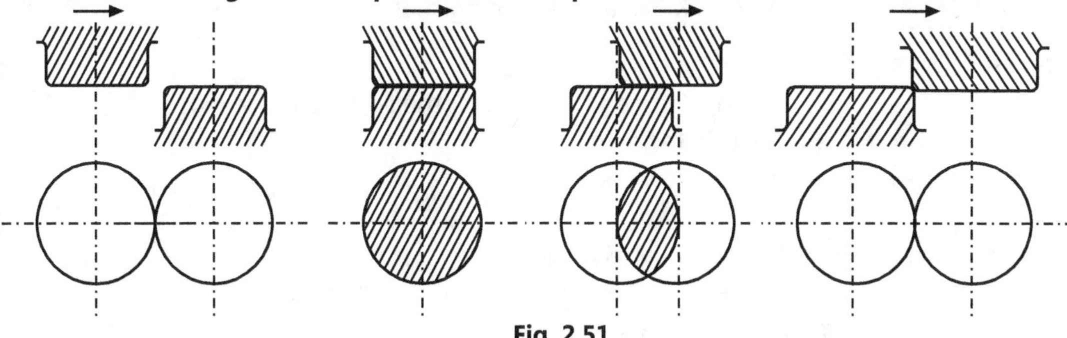

Fig. 2.51

(a)   Considering that all asperity contacts give rise to wear particles.

Average Wear Volume (δQ) per unit distance of sliding due to sliding of the one pair of asperities through a distance of L = 2a, is given by,

$$\delta Q = \frac{\delta V}{L} = \frac{2/3 \cdot \pi a^3}{2a} = \frac{1}{3} \cdot \pi a^2$$

$$\delta Q = \frac{1}{3} \pi a^2 \qquad\qquad \text{... (2.29)}$$

Total Wear Volume (Q):

$$Q = \sum \delta Q = \frac{1}{3} \sum \pi a^2$$

$$Q = \frac{n}{3} \cdot \pi a^2 \qquad\qquad \text{... (for 'n' number of contacts)}$$

$$\therefore \qquad n\pi a^2 = 3Q \qquad\qquad \text{... (a)}$$

But we have,

$$W = P_0 \cdot \pi a^2 \cdot n$$

$$\therefore \qquad n\pi a^2 = \frac{W}{P_0} \qquad\qquad \text{... (b)}$$

Equating equations (a) and (b), we can write,

$$3Q = \frac{W}{P_0} \text{ i.e. } Q = \frac{W}{3 \cdot P_0}$$

(b)   Considering that only a fraction 'K' of all asperity contacts produce wear particles, the above equation becomes,

$$Q = k\left(\frac{W}{3 \cdot P_0}\right) \qquad\qquad \text{... (2.30)}$$

where, k is the probability factor showing the probability of an asperity contact producing a wear particle. 'k' can be determined for different combinations of sliding materials and for different conditions of rubbing.

- In above equation, it is convenient to combine the factor of $\frac{1}{3}$ into the constant of proportionality by substituting $K = \frac{k}{3}$ and assuming that,

Yield pressure for plastically deforming asperity (P_0)

$$= \text{Indentation hardness of the softer surface (H)}$$

∴   We can rewrite the equation in the form,

$$Q = K \cdot \frac{W}{H} \qquad \qquad \text{... (2.31)}$$

This equation is called as 'Archard's wear equation'.

where,   Q – Wear rate or volume worn per unit sliding distance

W – Total normal load on surface

H – Indentation hardness of softer surface

$K = \dfrac{k}{3}$ – Wear coefficient or coefficient of wear is dimensionless and always less than unity. (i.e. K < 1).

This equation leads to three laws of wear called as "laws of adhesive wear".

- **Statements of Laws of Adhesive Wear:**
1. The volume of wear material is proportional to the distance of travel.
2. The volume of wear material is proportional to the load.
3. The volume of wear material is inversely proportional to the yield stress or hardness of the softer material.

- **Comment on Magnitude of Factor K (i.e. Adhesive Wear Coefficient):**

The adhesive wear coefficient $K = \dfrac{k}{3}$ and K < 1.

where, k is the fraction of all asperities encountered in producing wear particles.

This factor provides a valuable means of comparing the severity of wear processes in different systems.

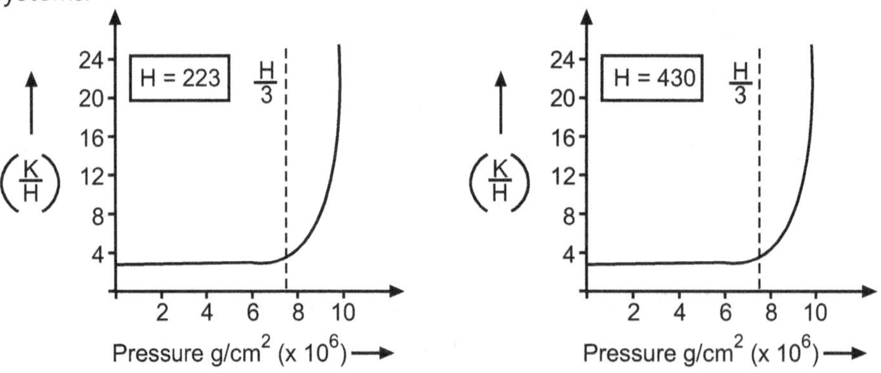

Fig. 2.52: The variation of wear coefficient with apparent pressure for steel

For steels of different hardness:

- K remains constant upto $P_0 = \dfrac{H}{3}$ and after this pressure it increases rapidly. At higher loadings large-scale welding and seizure occur.
- When tangential forces are present then the whole surface becomes plastic at a lower normal pressure than H/3.
- The values of wear coefficient vary over nearly five orders of magnitude (from $Ca \cdot 10^{-2}$ to $Ca \cdot 10^{-7}$). Some typical values of K, measured for dry sliding wear in pin-on-ring tests for a range of materials are listed in table below.

Table 2.2

Material	K (mm³/N · m)	Material	K (mm³/N · m)
Mild Steel (over M.S.)	7×10^{-3}	Cu-Beryllium	3.7×10^{-5}
α/β Brass	6×10^{-4}	Hard tool-steel	1.3×10^{-4}
PTFE	2.5×10^{-5}	Stellite-1	5.5×10^{-5}
α Brass	1.7×10^{-4}	Stainless steel (Ferritic)	1.7×10^{-5}
DMMA	7×10^{-6}	Polyethylene	1.3×10^{-7}

2.11.2 Rowe's Modified Adhesion Theory

- **Modification in Adhesion Theory:**

Rowe used the effect of surface films as modification in simple adhesion theory of wear. Basic Archard's equation for wear is given by,

Volume of material removed per unit sliding distance,

$$Q = k \cdot \frac{W}{3 \cdot P_0} \qquad \text{... (2.32)}$$

$$Q = K' \cdot A$$

where, K' is related to both the properties of lubricants and those of the sliding metals, in case of lubricated systems.

- **Volume of Adhesive Wear:**

$$Q = K_m \cdot A_m \quad \text{(for metal to metal contact)} \qquad \text{... (2.33)}$$

where, K_m is a constant for the sliding metals.

A parameter β called as the fractional surface film defect is introduced which depends on the lubricant properties or on surface films.

$$\beta = \frac{A_m}{A}$$

$$\therefore \qquad A_m = \beta \cdot A$$

Substituting this value in equation (2.33), we get

$$\therefore \qquad Q = K_m \cdot \beta \cdot A$$

$$\therefore \qquad Q = K_m \cdot \beta \cdot \frac{W}{P_0} \qquad \qquad \text{... (2.34)}$$

β is higher for poor lubricant which would allow more metal to metal contact. β is lower for a good lubricant. K_m is the characteristic of the sliding metal and β is the characteristic of the lubricant or contaminating film.

- Now the relation for the value of yield pressure which is obtained under combined shear and normal stresses is,

$$P_0^2 + \alpha S^2 = P_s^2$$

where, P_0 – Normal pressure (or flow pressure under combined stresses)

P_s – Flow pressure under static load case

S – Shear stress

α – Constant

From friction theory, we have,

$$S = \frac{F}{A} = f \cdot \frac{W}{A} = f \cdot P_0$$

where, F – Friction force

P_0 – Yield pressure

$$\therefore \qquad P_0^2 + \alpha(f \cdot P_0)^2 = P_s^2$$

$$P_0^2 (1 + \alpha f^2) = P_s^2$$

$$\therefore \qquad \text{Yield pressure, } P_0 = \frac{P_s}{\sqrt{1 + \alpha f^2}}$$

Using this in wear equation,

$$Q = K_m \cdot \beta \cdot \frac{W}{P_0}$$

$$= K_m \cdot \beta \cdot \frac{W}{\left(\dfrac{P_s}{\sqrt{1 + \alpha f^2}}\right)}$$

$$Q = K_m \cdot \sqrt{1 + \alpha f^2} \cdot \beta \cdot \frac{W}{P_s} \qquad \qquad \text{... (2.35)}$$

which is Rowe's equation for modified adhesion theory of friction.

2.11.3 Theory of Abrasive Wear (Rabinowicz's Quantitative Law)

- This theory gives a 'Simplified Model for Abrasive Wear'.
- The abrasive wear rate of the two-body contact has been obtained by Rabinowicz.
- Consider a hard conical asperity of a semi angle θ. The second surface is softer and flat. The asperity forms a groove in the material which is displaced by the particle from the groove.

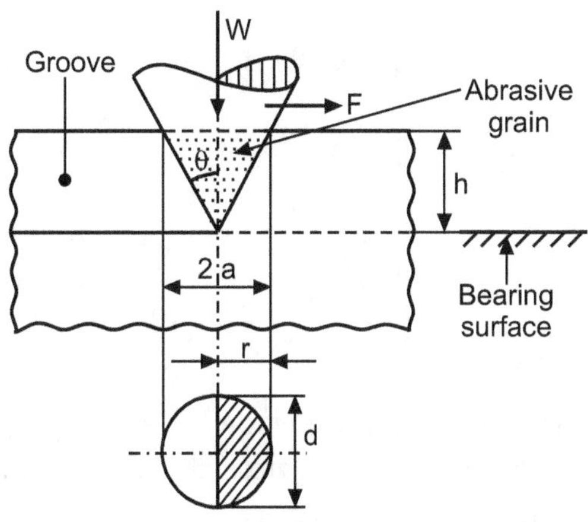

Fig. 2.53

- Volume displaced by the asperity in traversing unit distance,

$$\delta v = r \cdot h$$

$$= r \cdot (r \cdot \cot \theta) \qquad \left(\because \ h = \frac{r}{\tan \theta} = r \cot \theta \right)$$

$$\therefore \quad \delta v = r^2 \cdot \cot \theta$$

Assuming that the material has yielded under normal load.

$\therefore$ The asperity supports a load

$$W = A \cdot P_0$$

where, P_0 – Yield pressure

$$= \left(\frac{\pi r^2}{2} \right) \cdot P_0 \qquad \text{... (for single asperity contact)}$$

$$= n \cdot \left(\frac{\pi r^2}{2} \right) \cdot P_0 \qquad \text{... (for 'n' number of asperity contacts)}$$

$\therefore$ Total normal load,

$$W = \frac{n\pi r^2 P_0}{2} \Rightarrow r^2 = \frac{2W}{n\pi P_0}$$

and the total volume of the material displaced per unit distance for n asperity contacts,

$$Q = n \sum \delta v$$

$$= n \cdot r^2 \cot \theta$$

$$= n \left(\frac{2W}{n\pi \cdot P_0} \right) \cdot \cot \theta \qquad \text{...} \left(\text{using } r^2 = \frac{2W}{n\pi P_0} \right)$$

$$\therefore \quad Q = \frac{2W \cdot \cot \theta}{\pi \cdot P_0} \qquad \text{... (2.36)}$$

which is of similar form to that of adhesive wear equation.

$$Q = \left(\frac{2}{\pi} \cdot \cot\theta\right) \cdot \frac{W}{P_0}$$

$$Q = k_a \cdot \frac{W}{P_0}$$

$$Q = k_a \cdot \frac{W}{H} \qquad \cdots \left(\begin{array}{l}\text{Substituting } P_0 = H \\ = \text{Indentation hardness}\end{array}\right) \qquad \cdots (2.37)$$

where,
$$k_a = \frac{2}{\pi} \cdot \cot\theta$$

where,

W – the total applied normal load

k_a – Constant (i.e. dimensionless abrasive wear coefficient

H – Hardness of softer material

Comment on factor k_a (i.e. dimensionless abrasive wear coefficient):

- It depends on the number of asperity contacts and on the geometry of the abrasive particle.
- It can be effectively used as a measure of the severity of wear.
- In the two-body abrasive wear, k_a lies between

   $\sim 5 \times 10^{-3}$ to $\sim 50 \times 10^{-3}$

- In the three-body abrasive wear, K_a lies between

   0.5×10^{-3} to 5×10^{-3}

Sometimes, the specific energy U_a for material removal is used to express the severity of abrasive wear.

$$U_a = f \cdot \frac{W}{Q} \qquad \cdots (2.38)$$

where,

f – Coefficient of friction

W – Total normal load

Q – Total volume removed per unit sliding distance

Importance of Hardness Parameter in Abrasive Wear:

- Kruschov showed that there is linear relationship between the resistance to wear and hardness for a range of annealed pure metals. It revealed that during abrasion a metal surface work-hardens to a maximum value and this value of hardness is appropriate while considering abrasion resistance.
- Richardson has shown that the abrasion wear depends on two factors:

   H_a – i.e. Hardness of abrasive and

   H_m – i.e. Hardness of metal.

He considered the ratio (H_m/H_a).

Variation of wear resistance	Region	Value of $\left(\dfrac{H_m}{H_a}\right)$
Wear resistance increases rapidly	Soft abrasive wear	$\dfrac{H_m}{H_a} > 0.8$
Wear resistance decreases	Hard abrasive wear	$\dfrac{H_m}{H_a} < 0.8$

- Thus, $H_m > 1.3\, H_a$ is used as criterion for low-wear abrasive rate.

  $H_m = H_a$ is used as criterion for abrasive wear to be negligible.

2.11.4 Delamination Theory of Wear

The delamination theory of wear was put forward by Suh N. P. in 1973. As the name implies, this theory involves a detailed analysis of the surface, sub-surface cracks and void formation, and finally joining of cracks by shear deformation.

Prediction of the Theory:

The wear particle produced by shear deformation is a thin flake shaped sheet and surface layer undergoes a large plastic deformation.

Representation:

A circular wear track produced in pin-on-disc type of wear test is considered. Fig. 2.54 shows schematic representation of the metal removal layer by layer.

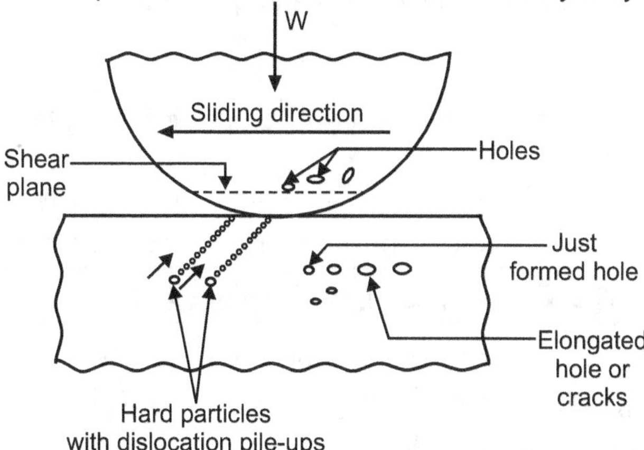

Fig. 2.54: Wear Model – Delamination Theory of Wear

Steps of Formation of Thin Wear Sheets:

- When two sliding surfaces (one is harder and other is softer) interact with each other, the asperities on the softer surface get flattened and fractured out by repeated loading, leading to small wear particles. The formed wear particles (hard particles) are removed at slow rates. Thus, a smooth surface is generated due to formation of these asperities.

- The harder asperities formed exert the surface traction at the contact points which result in induction of incremental plastic deformation for every cycle of loading. This accumulates with repeated loading.
- Further the sub-surface deformation continues, and results in nucleation of cracks under the surface.
- Nucleation of cracks cannot take place very near to the surface due to triaxial state of compressive loading that exists just below the contact region.
- Further loading causes deformation of the cracks and results in extension and propagation of cracks. Thus, it also joins the neighbouring cracks.
- The long joined crack now tends to propagate parallel to the surface at a depth which is governed by the properties of the material and the state of loading.
- Finally, the surface gets sheared off due to propagation of the long crack and thin, long wear sheets delaminate from the surface.
- The thickness of the wear sheet is evaluated by the location of the sub-surface crack growth which is governed by the normal and tangential loads at the surface.
- The wear rate is controlled by the crack nucleation rate or the crack propagation rate, whichever is slower.

Conclusions:
- This theory can explain many phenomena and give insight into the microscopic causes of wear.
- Metal wears layer by layer.
- The number of wear sheets per layer is proportional to the average number of asperities in contact.
- The wear rate decreases if shear deformation of the surface layer is prevented.
- The wear rate increases due to uncontrolled inclusions of hard particles in metals.

2.12 METHODS OF CONTROLLING WEAR

In many practical situations, it becomes much necessary to reduce wear rate. The following discussion reveals information about reducing various types of wear.

2.12.1 Controlling Adhesive Wear

Following factors are significant in reducing adhesive wear phenomenon.

- **Hardness of Mating Members:** Hardness of the mating pair should be comparable in an unlubricated contact. For low wear, hardness of mating members should be high and should be comparable with each other.
- **Minimum Tendency of Sliding Metal Pair to form Solid Solution:** For preventing adhesive wear, the sliding metal pairs should be selected to have a low tendency to

form solid solutions and it is possible by choosing metals having different crystal structures and chemical properties.

- **Role of Microstructure:** Role of microstructure is much important in reducing wear. Microstructure affects bulk properties and microstructural features become effective as discrete components and their individual properties assume increasing importance.
- **Interposition of Dissimilar Metal or Non-Metal Coatings:** Adhesive wear can be prevented by the interposition of dissimilar metal or non-metal coatings e.g. soft deposits of Pb or Ag, hard coatings of metals, alloys and ceramics.
- **Employing Surface Treatments:** Many surface treatments are employed to reduce adhesive wear. e.g. in severe wear (i.e. scuffing) conditions, short-life surface treatments such as phosphating and nitrocarburizing are used.

2.12.2 Controlling Abrasive Wear

Following factors contribute to the reduction in abrasive wear.

- **Presence of Hydrodynamic or Elastohydrodynamic Lubricant Film:** In order to reduce abrasive wear, by rough hard surface sliding against a softer surface, there should be presence of hydrodynamic or elastohydrodynamic lubricant films sufficiently thick to separate the surfaces.

  Also in case of abrasion by contaminant, for hard particles trapped between sliding surfaces, the presence of hydrodynamic or elastohydrodynamic lubricant films sufficiently thicker than the largest hard particles will greatly reduce friction.
- **Strength, Hardness and Toughness of Surface Layers:** For few metals, the surface layers should have enough strength and hardness to resist indentation from hard asperities. Also they should possess sufficient toughness to prevent fractures from surface imperfections or incipient fatigue crack.

  For pure materials like ceramics, plastics, metals, abrasive wear resistance is directly proportional to hardness.
- **Deposition of Hard Coatings:** High hardness and toughness can be achieved simultaneously by depositing hard coatings onto ductile metals or by using suitable surface treatment.
- **Hard-Facing Processes:** Hard-facing processes are widely used to provide abrasive wear resistant surfaces.

2.12.3 Controlling Fatigue-Wear

Following factors contribute for reducing fatigue wear.

- **Suppressing the Microcrack Formation:** As fatigue wear results from the repetitive types of stress on the surface of the body, usually at inclusions, formation of microcracks take place and these cracks are further transmitted throughout the surface. Fatigue wear can be reduced by suppressing the microcrack formation.

- **Selecting Optimized Combination of Hardness and Toughness for a Single Microstructure:** If hardness of material is increased it reduces the subsurface deformation and in turn the crack nucleation rate. If toughness of material is increased, it decreases the crack growth rate. Thus, for controlling wear effectively it is always necessary to design the microstructure of the materials with high hardness and toughness.

  But it is not always possible to achieve a combination of both high hardness and toughness with a single microstructure. Therefore, it is necessary to optimize this combination.

- **Providing Hard Coating on a Substrate or Using Suitable Surface Treatment:** It is possible to reduce wear by putting a very hard coating on a substrate or using a suitable surface treatment in such a way that plastic deformation cannot occur in the substrate. The depth of plastic zone has not been observed deeper than 200 μm. The coating provided must be coherent and free of microcracks as there is a possibility of crack propagation even in the absence of plastic deformation.

2.12.4 Controlling Erosive Wear

- **Ultimate Resilience of the Surface:** It is the energy that can be absorbed before deformation or cracking of material. Thus, high value of ultimate resilience should be preferred for most of the materials to withstand cavitation erosion.

- **Metal-Metal Bond Energy:** Whenever the atoms of a metal are held together strongly in the crystal lattice and do not leave the lattice easily in any attempt, it is said to have high metal-metal bond energy values. Thus, for better wear resistance, materials should have high values of metal-metal bond energy.

- **Melting Point of the Metal:** Hutching experimented erosive wear phenomenon and the results for erosive wear showed that erosive wear rates are inversely correlated with the product $\rho \cdot C_p \cdot \Delta T$.

  i.e.   Erosive wear rate $\propto \dfrac{1}{\rho \cdot C_p \cdot \Delta T}$

  where,

  ρ – the density of metal

  C_p – the specific heat

  ΔT – the difference between the temperature of the metal and its melting point

  High values of ΔT indicate low thermal softening. Thus, the above formula indicates that erosive wear resistance will be higher for materials possessing higher melting points.

- **Controlling Impingement Angle:** Erosive wear can be controlled by proper control of impingement angle. It is described in earlier section (2.7.5 a (i)).

EXERCISE

1. State laws of friction.   **[P.U. June 2011, 4 Marks]**
2. Explain the terms :
   (i)   Real area of contact, (ii)   Apparent area of contact.   **[P.U. Dec. 2008, 4 Marks]**
3. Explain how Coulomb's vision of friction explain these laws of friction. Also explain how Coulomb explained friction and stiction.
4. Write note on Tomlinson's theory of friction.
5. Write notes on Rolling friction and Rolling resistance.
6. Discuss 'Adhesion theory' of friction.
7. Explain the modified adhesion or junction growth theory of friction.
   [P.U. June 2009, 6 Marks]
8. Using modified junction growth theory, prove that the coefficient of friction is given as,

$$f = \frac{C}{\sqrt{\alpha\,(1 - C^2)}}$$

   with usual notations   **[P.U. June 2010, 8 Marks]**
9. Explain mechanism of rolling friction.
10. What are causes of friction ?   **[P.U. Dec. 2010, 2 Marks]**
11. Explain the method of friction measurement by pin-on-disk apparatus.
    [P.U. June 2009, 4 Marks]
12. What are the laws of dry friction ? What are the laws of boundary friction ?
13. Discuss various types of frictions.
14. Derive an expression to find coefficient of friction for conical asperity by using deformation theory.   **[P.U. June 2009, 6 Marks]**
15. Explain the following theories of friction:
    (i)   Coulomb's classical theory
    (ii)   Tomlinson's theory of molecular attraction
    (iii)   Bowden's theory of cold-welded junction
16. Explain how Coulomb's vision of friction explain these laws of friction.
17. How one can measure the amount of friction between two surfaces in contact?
18. Explain stick-slip friction.
    [P.U. June 2009, 6 Marks; June 2010, 4 Marks; Dec. 2010, 4 Marks]
19. Define wear.
20. Name and elaborate on different types of wear.
21. State assumptions made, prove Archard's equation of adhesive wear.

$$Q = k \cdot \frac{W}{3P_0}$$

   and comment about magnitude of factor 'k'.   **[P.U. June 2010, 8 Marks]**
   Comment on the range of values of cofactor 'k'.
22. Write a short note on 'Archard's theory of Adhesive wear.   **[P.U. June 2009, 6 Marks]**
23. What is wear ? What are the parameters which govern wear ?

24. Elaborate on surface fatigue wear. What is it ? Where it is seen ? How it operate or occur ? How it is controlled ? **[P.U. June 2009, 4 Marks]**

25. Explain in short Abrasive wear.

26. What is meant by Abrasive wear ? Deduce the equation for volume of abrasive wear per unit sliding distance with conical abrasive particles. **[P.U. June 2010, 6 Marks]**

27. Discuss laws of wear. **[P.U. June 2009, 6 Marks]**

28. Explain the term wear. Explain in detail different types of wear experienced in mechanical systems. Discuss the effect of temperature and load on wear.

[P.U. June 2010, 6 Marks]

29. Write short note on (i) Fretting wear, (ii) Percussion wear. **[P.U. June 2010, 6 Marks]**

30. Write short notes on :
    (i)   Two body and three body abrasive wear
    (ii) Erosive wear
    (iii) Surface fatigue wear
    (iv) Stick-slip phenomenon of friction **[P.U. June 2009, 8 Marks]**

31. Define wear and explain in brief the parameters which govern wear.

[P.U. Dec. 2008, 3 Marks; Dec. 2010, 4 Marks]

32. What precautions are taken to keep adhesive wear magnitude lower ?

33. What is fatigue wear ? Where does it occur ? How is it avoided ?

34. Derive a relationship between the coefficient of friction and the wear rate for two body abrasion.

35. State different techniques of wear debries analysis. **[P.U. June 2010, 2 Marks]**

36. Show that the adhesive wear rate is proportional to the load and inversely proportional to the hardness of the softer of the two rubbing materials. **[P.U. June 2009, 8 Marks]**

37. Discuss the effects of the following parameters on wear rate:
    (i)   Load   (ii) Temperature
    (iii) Surface films   (iv) Compatibility
    (v)   Crystal structure

38. What is Rowe's modified adhesion theory ? How it differ from simple adhesion theory ?

39. Name any four experimental methods of wear measurement. Explain any one of them.

[P.U. Dec. 2010, 6 Marks]

40. Explain Rabinowicz Quantitative Theory for abrasive wear.

41. Explain surface fatigue theory for various wear regime. Comment on 'zero wear' limit.

42. Explain Delamination theory of wear. State various assumptions.

43. Derive $Q = k \cdot W \cdot s$
    where,
    Q = Wear rate
    k = Wear factor that depends on surface topography
    s = Distance solid

44. Show that according to Delamination theory of wear, wear rate is proportional to the normal load and the sliding distance.

✠ ✠ ✠

Chapter 3

HYDRODYNAMIC LUBRICATION

3.1 PRINCIPLE OF HYDRODYNAMIC LUBRICATION

Mechanism of hydrodynamic lubrication is essential for the efficient functioning of most of the tribological problems of modern industry e.g. Motor vehicles, locomotives, machine tools, domestic appliances, gear boxes, pumps, all types of engines, etc. All these equipments are based on hydrodynamic films for their operation.

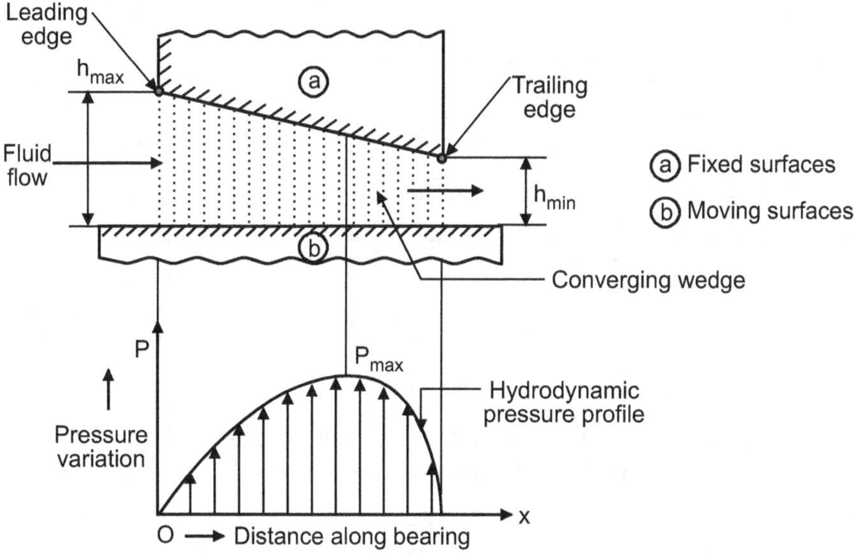

Fig. 3.1

With the help of above figure, generation of pressure due to hydrodynamic action can be explained. Characteristic geometric profile is a converging wedge type having maximum thickness at leading edge and minimum thickness at its trailing edge. From Fig. 3.1,

- Pressure is zero at leading stage and pressure remains low in the zone of leading edge, it increases towards trailing edge and maximum in the zone of trailing edge.
- The condition of hydrodynamic lubrication is governed by bulk physical properties of the lubricant e.g. viscosity, relative speed of the mating surfaces.

Fluid in the clearance between the shaft and bearing remain adhered to both the surfaces. In motion for the bearing of convergent shape, the fluid adhering to moving surfaces will be dragged into the rapidly narrowing clearance space converging in the direction of motion, thus building up a pressure sufficient to carry the load. This is the principle of hydrodynamic lubrication.

3.2 MECHANISM OF PRESSURE DEVELOPMENT IN OIL FILM

Reynold in 1886, reviewed the detailed experimental work of Beauchamp Tower and put up the following views about Hydrodynamic Lubrication.

- Lubrication of bearing depends to a large extent on hydrodynamic action.
- The viscous properties of oil significantly affect the hydrodynamic action.
- Hydrodynamic pressure built-up occurs which supports the applied load, this is due to the phenomenon of dragging the oil into the reduced converging space in the direction of the motion.

Following two cases clearly reveal the mechanism of pressure development.

3.2.1 Two Parallel Plates Separated by a Oil Film

Two parallel plates separated by a oil film of constant film thickness (h) as shown in following Fig. 3.2.

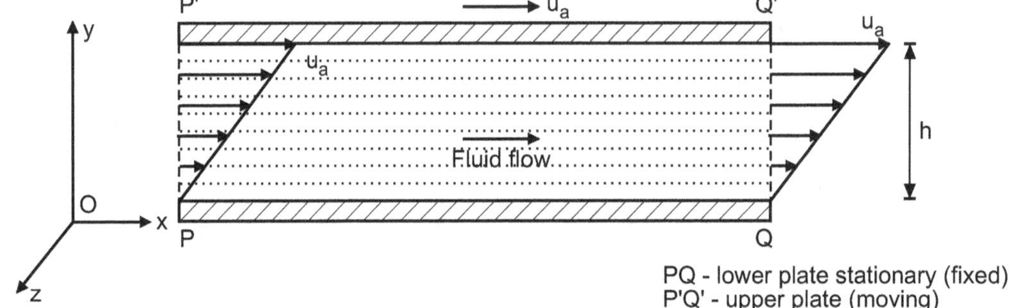

Fig. 3.2

The length of plate is very long in z-direction which will ensure the flow to take place only in one dimension. The upper plate P'Q' is moving with a constant velocity u_a parallel to lower plate. For no-slip condition, the velocity variation of fluid is as shown in Fig. 3.2. It is zero at surface PQ and increases gradually and becomes equal to that of velocity of upper plate (i.e. u_a). As the velocity distribution across the film at PP' and QQ' is identical,

(The volume flow rate at PP') = (Volume flow rate at QQ')

There is flow due to velocity gradient; and as these are equal the flow continuity is satisfied without pressure build-up.

3.2.2 Two Non-Parallel Plates Separated by an Oil Film

One plate is kept inclined with respect to other plate.

In this case, the top plate is kept inclined with respect to the lower plate. Due to this inclination, the converging oil film separates two plates which will cause different types of velocity distribution at different sections. The velocity variation at sections PP' and QQ' be assumed to vary linearly from the velocity u_a of moving plate to zero of the stationary plate. Considering this variation, the flow continuity is not satisfied.

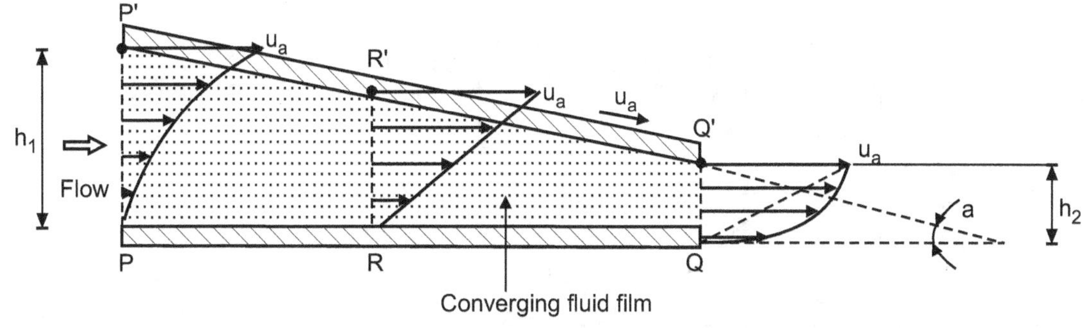

Fig. 3.3

Assuming that at particular section RR', the velocity be linear, and in order to satisfy the flow continuity, the velocity variation at sections PP' and QQ' are to be given by the solid lines. Pressure build up automatically as the flow will have both pressure induced term (Poiseuille) and velocity induced term (Couette). Such type of film is termed as convergent film. This film can produce positive pressure if there is relative velocity and the surfaces are separated by a viscous fluid film.

Poiseuille Flow : The velocity distribution for a fluid flowing under laminar conditions through a small clearance 'h' as a result of the pressure gradient, $\partial p/\partial z$ is termed as pressure induced flow or Poiseuille flow.

Couette Flow : The velocity distribution which results from the motion of the bearing surfaces alone, under constant pressure condition, is termed as velocity induced flow or couette flow.

3.3 LUBRICATION REGIMES

Various lubrication modes except hydrostatic can be done on the basis of the Stribeck curve which gives clear explanation about the frictional behaviour of different lubrication regimes.

Stribeck Curve :

It illustrates change in the coefficient of friction as a function of lubrication parameter $\dfrac{\mu \cdot v}{p}$.

where,

    μ – The lubricant viscosity

    v – The sliding velocity

    p – The pressure.

Thus, based on the geometry, the properties of lubricant and the operating conditions, three main lubrication modes can be given,

- Boundary Lubrication (BL)
- Mixed Lubrication (ML)
- Hydrodynamic Lubrication (HL) and Elastohydrodynamic Lubrication.

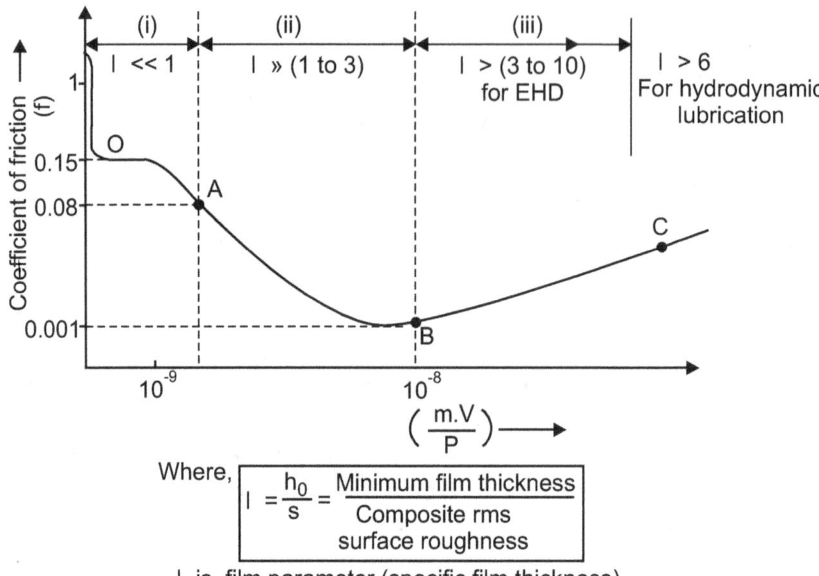

Fig. 3.4 : Stribeck curve

- **Boundary Lubrication :**

It is also called as thin-film lubrication. At low speed i.e. for low value of $\left(\dfrac{\mu \cdot v}{p}\right)$, fluid-film thickness is smaller [i.e. h << σ, where σ is composite rms surface roughness of the mating surfaces, and σ = $(\sigma_1^2 + \sigma_2^2)^{1/2}$]. Therefore, there is metal to metal contact with high friction. It describes the situation in which bearing surface physically contact and adhesive or abrasive wear may occur. In this region, coefficient of friction ranges between 0.08 at A to 0.15 at 'O'. And **film parameter** (i.e. specific film thickness)

$$\lambda = \frac{h_0}{\sigma} = \frac{h_0}{(\sigma_1^2 + \sigma_2^2)^{1/2}} << 1$$

i.e. λ << 1 for boundary lubrication.

Boundary lubrication occurs at the beginning and at the end of operation during which speeds are low.

- **Mixed Lubrication (ML) :**

As sliding velocity is further increased, the factor $\left(\dfrac{\mu v}{p}\right)$ increases, and the lubrication in between the zone A to B is mixed film lubrication, where the contacting surfaces are separated by a thin lubricant film, also asperity contact may take place. The total applied load is supposed to be carried partly by asperity contacts and partly by hydrodynamic action. Thus, total friction is due to the combination of asperity contacts and viscous friction of lubrication. Mixed lubrication mode exists for film parameter λ between 1 to 3. [i.e. λ ≈ (1 to 3)].

Thus coefficient of friction varies between 0.02 to 0.08 for mixed lubrication.

- **Hydrodynamic and Elastohydrodynamic Lubrication :**

(a) Hydrodynamic Lubrication :

It occurs beyond point 'B' where sliding velocity is high i.e. $\left(\dfrac{\mu v}{p}\right)$ is large and the surfaces are separated by thick-film of lubricant. Therefore, it is also called thick-film lubrication.

There is no metal to metal contact and the geometric profile is a converging wedge. The pressure is low at leading edge while maximum at the trailing edge of wedge. The hydrodynamic lubrication is governed by the bulk physical properties of the lubricant i.e. viscosity and relative speed of moving surfaces.

(b) Elastohydrodynamic Lubrication (EHD) :

It applies to hydrodynamic conditions where surface deformation is comparable with hydrodynamic film thickness and surface deformation affects the hydrodynamic behaviour of the interface. A plane contact zone is formed with a length in the sliding direction of on the order of 100 μm and a film thickness of on the order of 1 μm. e.g. EHD occurs in rolling contact bearings, gears, and cams.

Fig. 3.5 shows variation of 'f' with the film parameter λ.

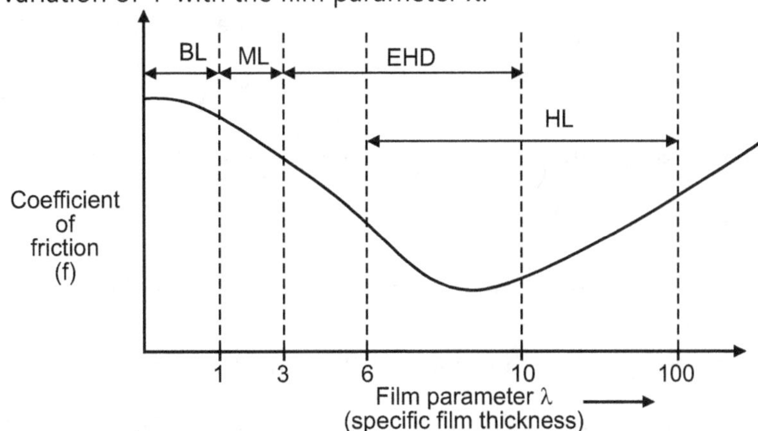

Fig. 3.5 : Coefficient of friction versus film parameter λ

Table 3.1 shows various lubricant film properties for different modes of lubrication.

Table 3.1

Mode of Lubrication	Lubricant Film Properties		
	Film Thickness (h_0) μm	Film Parameter (λ)	Coefficient of Friction (f)
BL	0.005 to 0.1	<< 1	0.08 to 0.15
ML	0.01 to 1	1 to 3	0.02 to 0.08
EHD	0.01 to 10	3 to 10	0.01 to 0.1
HL	1 to 100	6 to 100	0.001 to 0.01

3.4 REYNOLD'S EQUATION FOR HYDRODYNAMIC LUBRICATION

Need : Derivation of the classical Reynolds equation reflects insight into fluid behaviour in bearing lubricant films which then leads to the science of hydrodynamic lubrication. Solution of Reynolds equation can be used to determine the pressure distribution in a bearing with an arbitrary film shape. Once the pressure profile is evaluated, all other bearing performance parameters such as load-carrying capacity (W), friction force (F), flow rates (Q), etc. can easily be determined.

3.4.1 Assumptions in Reynold's Equation

For analysis of hydrodynamic bearing, following basic assumptions are necessary :

- The fluid is considered to be Newtonian (i.e. the shear stress is directly proportional to the rate of shear strain).

- The fluid flow is considered to be viscous and laminar (i.e. no vortices and no turbulence in the fluid flow).

- The fluid is incompressible (i.e. the volume of fluid flowing past any section in unit time will be constant).

- Inertia force $\left(\text{i.e. } F_I = \rho \dfrac{Du}{Dt}\right)$ due to acceleration of fluid and body forces (i.e. F_B) are small compared with the pressure and viscous force terms i.e. $F_I = 0$ and $F_B = 0$.

- Pressure variation across the film is negligibly small $\left(\text{i.e. } \dfrac{\partial p}{\partial z} = 0\right)$ but it varies along the length of film (i.e. $P = p(x, y)$).

- Velocity at any point in the fluid film is a function of both x and y. (Partial derivatives $\dfrac{\partial u}{\partial z}$ and $\dfrac{\partial v}{\partial z}$ are large compared with other velocity derivative components). It is due to the fact that u and v are usually greater than w, and z is much smaller dimension.

- Curvature effects are neglected and the thickness of the fluid film is much smaller as compared with length or width of the film.

- Usually, fluid-film thickness = h = 0.0254 mm

And $\qquad \dfrac{h}{l} = \dfrac{\text{Fluid-film thickness}}{\text{Fluid-film length}} = 10^{-3}$

- (viii) There is no slip at the bearing and the fluid-film interface (i.e. the velocity of the lubricant film is identical with the surface velocity at the bearing surface).

- The viscosity of the fluid remains constant as it flows through the bearing.

3.4.2 Reynold's Equation for Two-dimensional Flow

Reynold's equation for hydrodynamic lubrication can be derived in following two ways :

(i) By Direct Method : In which we consider equilibrium of forces acting on faces of fluid element, which is dragged into a rapidly narrowing clearance space, converging in the direction of motion.

(ii) From Navier-Stroke's Equations : For a Newtonian fluid, the equations of motions for a viscous fluid, called Navier-Stroke's equations are taken into account for deriving Reynold's equation.

3.4.2.1 Reynold's Equation for Two-Dimensional Flow by Direct Method

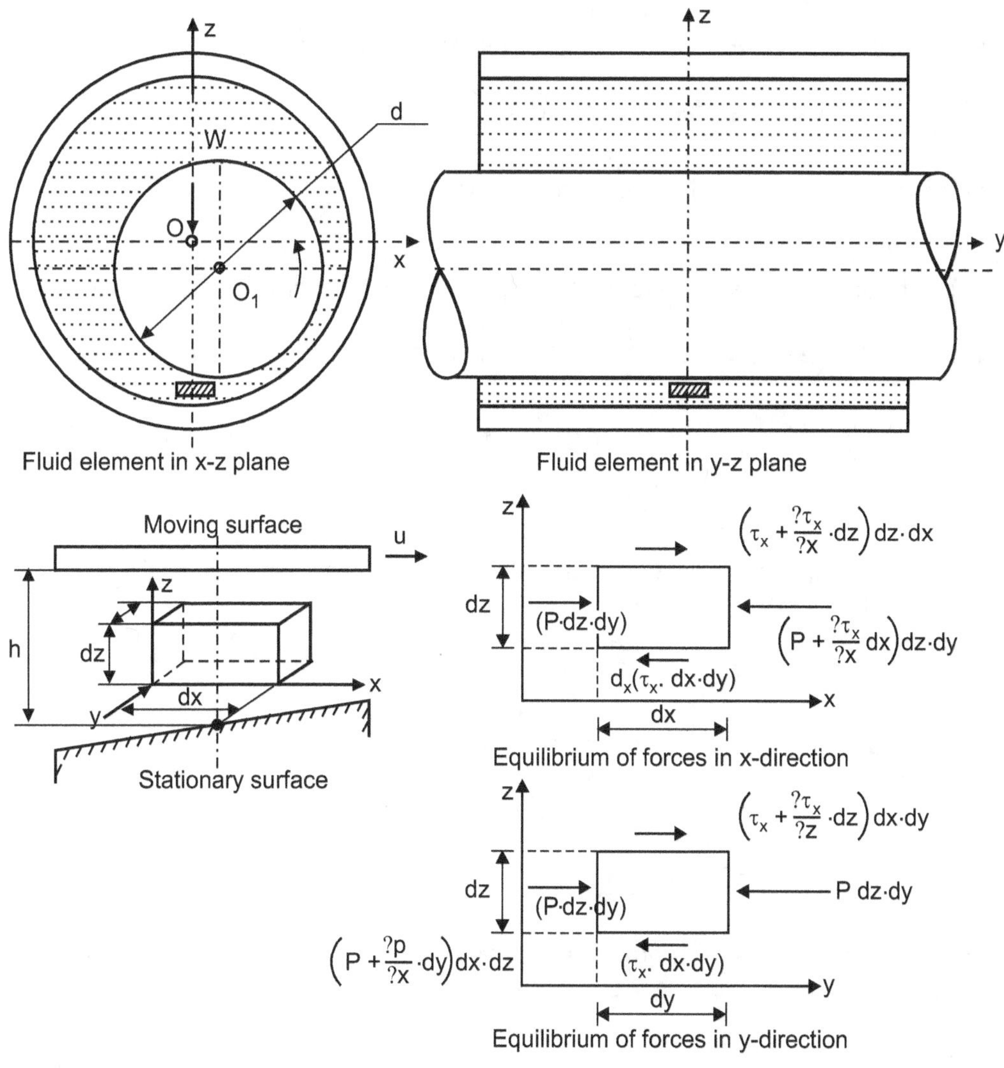

Fig. 3.6

Consider a journal rotating in a bearing with a constant surface velocity u_b. For analysis a fluid element having dimensions dx, dy, dz and x, y, and z directions respectively is taken into account; as shown in Fig. 3.6. Here 'x' axis represents direction of motion of fluid. 'y' axis is parallel to journal axis and 'z' axis is radial direction of journal.

Let u_b, v_b and w_b be the components of velocity of moving surface in X, Y, Z directions respectively.

Velocity Distribution :

Various forces acting on the faces of fluid element in horizontal (i.e. X-direction) are :

- Fluid pressure force ('P' dz dy) in positive x-direction.

- Fluid pressure force $\left(P + \dfrac{\partial P}{\partial x} dx\right) dy \cdot dz$ in negative x-direction.

- Shear force on bottom surface $(\tau_x \cdot dx \cdot dy)$.

- Shear force on top surface $\left(\tau_x + \dfrac{\partial \tau_x}{\partial z} \cdot dz\right) dx \cdot dy$.

For equilibrium of forces on fluid element (x-z plane) in X-direction, we have,

$$P \, dz \cdot dy - \left(P + \frac{\partial P}{\partial x} \cdot dx\right) dy \cdot dz + \left(\tau_x + \frac{\partial \tau_x}{\partial z} dz\right) dx \cdot dy - (\tau_x \cdot dx \, dy) = 0 \qquad \text{... (3.1)}$$

$$P \, dz \cdot dy - P \cdot dy \cdot dz - \frac{\partial P}{\partial x} \cdot dx \cdot dy \cdot dz + \tau_x \, dx \cdot dy + \frac{\partial \tau_x}{\partial z} \cdot dz \cdot dx \cdot dy - \tau_x \cdot dx \cdot dy = 0$$

$$\therefore \qquad \frac{\partial P}{\partial x} = \frac{\partial \tau_x}{\partial z}$$

Here, $dx \cdot dy \cdot dz \neq 0$ ... (which indicates volume of fluid element)

According to Newton's law of viscosity,

$$\tau_x = \mu \cdot \frac{\partial u}{\partial z}$$

Substituting above equation in equation for $\dfrac{\partial P}{\partial x}$, we get,

$$\therefore \qquad \frac{\partial P}{\partial x} = \frac{\partial}{\partial z}\left(\mu \cdot \frac{\partial u}{\partial z}\right)$$

$$\therefore \qquad \frac{\partial P}{\partial x} = \mu \frac{\partial^2 u}{\partial z^2} \qquad \text{... (3.2)}$$

Above equation gives pressure gradient in X-direction.

∴ Pressure gradient in Y-direction and Z-direction are,

$$\frac{\partial P}{\partial y} = \mu \frac{\partial^2 v}{\partial z^2}$$

$$\frac{\partial P}{\partial z} = 0 \dots \text{(As per assumption number v)}$$

Now, we have an equation

$$\frac{\partial P}{\partial x} = \mu \frac{\partial^2 u}{\partial z^2}$$

$$\frac{\partial^2 u}{\partial z^2} = \frac{1}{\mu} \frac{\partial P}{\partial x}$$

Integrating above equation twice with respect to z,

$$\frac{\partial u}{\partial z} = \frac{1}{\mu} \frac{\partial P}{\partial x} \cdot z + A$$

$$u = \frac{1}{2\mu} \frac{\partial P}{\partial x} \cdot z^2 + A \cdot z + B$$

where, A and B are constants of integration and can be evaluated by using the following boundary conditions.

Boundary Conditions :

At $z = 0$;　　$u = u_a = 0$

At $z = h$;　　$u = u_b$

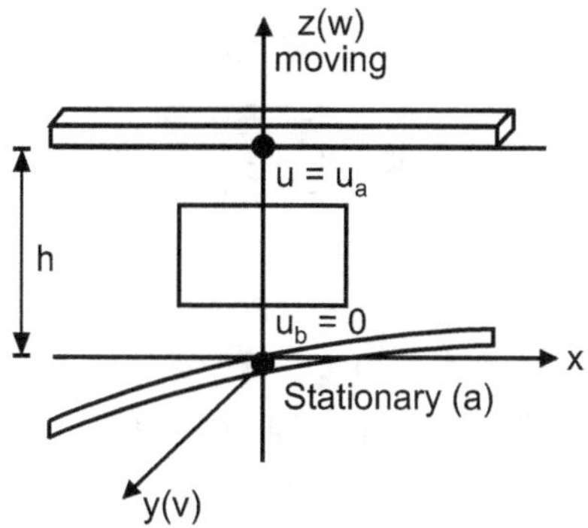

Fig. 3.7

Substituting in above equation for 'u',

$$0 = 0 + 0 + B \Rightarrow B = u_a = 0$$

$$u_b = \frac{1}{2\mu} \frac{\partial P}{\partial x} \cdot h^2 + A \cdot h + B$$

$$\therefore \quad u_b = \frac{1}{2\mu} \cdot \frac{\partial P}{\partial x} \cdot h^2 + A \cdot h + 0$$

$$A = \frac{u_b}{h} - \frac{h}{2\mu} \cdot \frac{\partial P}{\partial x}$$

and　　　　　　$B = 0$

Substituting values of constants A and B in equation for 'u'

$$\therefore \quad u = \frac{1}{2\mu}\frac{\partial P}{\partial x}\cdot z^2 + \left[\frac{u_b}{h} - \frac{h}{2\mu}\frac{\partial P}{\partial x}\right]z + 0$$

$$\therefore \quad u = \underbrace{\frac{1}{2\mu}\frac{\partial P}{\partial x}(z^2 - h\cdot z)}_{} \quad + \quad \underbrace{\frac{u_b\cdot z}{h}}_{} \qquad \dots (3.3)$$

'Poiseuille flow term' 'Couette flow term'   due to pressure(due to motion of

gradient $\dfrac{\partial P}{\partial x}$ surface b) also called   as shear term

Above equation gives velocity distribution of lubricant as a function of 'z' and pressure gradient $\dfrac{\partial P}{\partial x}$ (i.e. velocity variation along x-direction for the limits z = 0 to z = h).

Rate of Flow of Fluid :

Rate of flow of fluid (q_x) in x-direction per unit width in y-direction,

$$q_x = \int_0^h u \times 1 \times dz$$

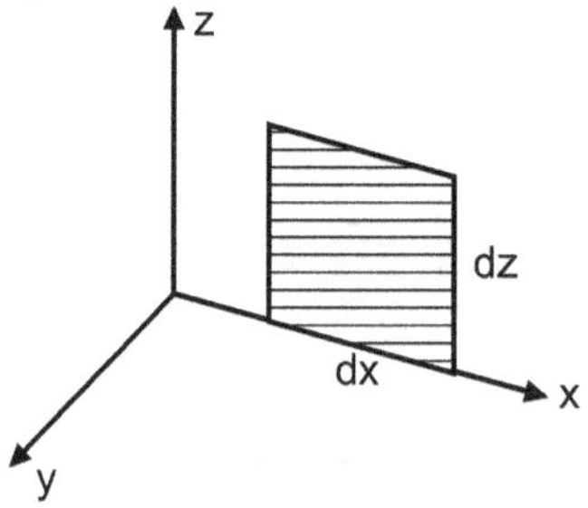

Fig. 3.8

Substituting value of u from equation in equation above,

$$q_x = \int_0^h \left[\frac{1}{2\mu}\frac{\partial P}{\partial x}(z^2 - h\cdot z) + \frac{u_b}{h}\cdot z\right]dz$$

$$= \left[\frac{1}{2\mu}\cdot\frac{\partial P}{\partial x}\left(\frac{z^3}{3} - h\frac{z^2}{2}\right) + \frac{u_b}{h}\cdot\frac{z^2}{2}\right]_0^h$$

$$= \frac{1}{2\mu}\frac{\partial P}{\partial x}\left(\frac{h^3}{3} - \frac{h^3}{2}\right) + \frac{u_b}{h}\cdot\frac{h^2}{2}$$

$$q_x = -\frac{h^3}{12\mu}\cdot\frac{\partial P}{\partial x} + \frac{u_b\cdot h}{2} \qquad \dots (3.4)$$

Similarly, the rate of flow of fluid in y-direction per unit width in x-direction is,

$$q_y = -\frac{h^3}{12\mu}\frac{\partial P}{\partial y} + \frac{v_b \cdot h}{2} \qquad \text{... (3.5)}$$

Consider continuity equation for incompressible flow,

$$\frac{\partial u}{\partial x} + \frac{\partial v}{\partial y} + \frac{\partial w}{\partial z} = 0$$

Now, $\qquad \dfrac{\partial w}{\partial z} = 0 \quad \cdots \left(\begin{array}{l}\text{As per assumption (vi) i.e. no flow} \\ \text{in z-direction}\end{array}\right)$

$$\therefore \qquad \frac{\partial u}{\partial x} + \frac{\partial v}{\partial y} = 0 \qquad \text{... (3.6)}$$

Integrating above equation w.r.t. z within the limits z = 0 to z = h,

$$\int_0^h \frac{\partial u}{\partial x}\cdot dz + \int_0^h \frac{\partial v}{\partial y}\cdot dz = 0$$

$$\therefore \quad \frac{\partial}{\partial x}\left[\int_0^h u\cdot dz\right] + \frac{\partial}{\partial y}\left[\int_0^h v\,dz\right] = 0$$

Bracketed quantities indicate the rate of flow of lubricant along x and y-directions respectively.

i.e. $\qquad q_x = \displaystyle\int_0^h u\cdot dz \quad$ and $\quad q_y = \displaystyle\int_0^h v\cdot dz$

Substituting values of q_x from equation (3.4) and q_y from equation (3.5), we get,

Above equation becomes

$$\frac{\partial}{\partial x}[q_x] + \frac{\partial}{\partial y}[q_y] = 0$$

$$\frac{\partial}{\partial x}\left[-\frac{h^3}{12\mu}\frac{\partial P}{\partial x} + \frac{u_b\cdot h}{2}\right] + \frac{\partial}{\partial y}\left[-\frac{h^3}{12\mu}\cdot\frac{\partial P}{\partial y} + \frac{v_b\cdot h}{2}\right] = 0$$

$$\therefore \quad \frac{\partial}{\partial x}\left[\frac{h^3}{12\mu}\frac{\partial P}{\partial x}\right] + \frac{\partial}{\partial y}\left[\frac{h^3}{12\mu}\cdot\frac{\partial P}{\partial y}\right] = \frac{\partial}{\partial x}\left(\frac{u_b\cdot h}{2}\right) + \frac{\partial}{\partial y}\left(\frac{v_b\cdot h}{2}\right)$$

$$\frac{\partial}{\partial x}\left[h^3\cdot\frac{\partial P}{\partial x}\right] + \frac{\partial}{\partial y}\left[h^3\frac{\partial P}{\partial y}\right] = 6\mu\left[\frac{\partial}{\partial x}(u_b\cdot h) + \frac{\partial}{\partial y}(v_b\cdot h)\right] \qquad \text{... (3.7)}$$

which is Reynold's equation for two-dimensional flow.

Simplifying the above equation,

i.e. for constant viscosity and $\dfrac{\partial h}{\partial y} = 0$

$$\frac{\partial}{\partial x}\left[h^3 \frac{\partial P}{\partial x}\right] + \frac{\partial}{\partial y}\left[h^3 \cdot \frac{\partial P}{\partial y}\right] = 6\mu\left[u_b \cdot \frac{\partial h}{\partial x} + 0\right]$$

i.e. $$\frac{\partial}{\partial x}\left[h^3 \frac{\partial P}{\partial x}\right] + \frac{\partial}{\partial y}\left[h^3 \frac{\partial P}{\partial y}\right] = 6\mu \cdot u_b \cdot \frac{\partial h}{\partial x} \qquad \text{... (3.8)}$$

- Reynold's equation cannot be solved directly. However, solution can be obtained by using numerical methods.

  For infinitely long bearing, as per assumption (vi), there is no flow in y-direction.

  i.e. $$\frac{\partial P}{\partial y} = 0$$

  Hence, above equation is further reduced to

  $$\frac{\partial}{\partial x}\left[h^3 \frac{\partial P}{\partial x}\right] = 6\mu \cdot u_b \cdot \frac{\partial h}{\partial x} \qquad \text{... (3.9)}$$

  which is Reynold's equation for one-dimensional flow.

  Exact solution is possible by considering bearing to be infinitely long, or very short.

3.4.2.2 Reynolds Equation for Two-dimensional Flow from Navier-Stroke's Equation

For the study of lubricant films, the equations of motions for a viscous fluid are basics which are normally referred as Navier-Stroke's equations for a Newtonian fluid and can be given as below.

(i) Inertia force per unit volume in x-direction :

$$\rho \frac{Du}{Dt} = \rho X - \frac{\partial p}{\partial x} - \frac{2}{3}\frac{\partial}{\partial x}(\mu \cdot \Delta) + 2\frac{\partial}{\partial x}\left(\mu \cdot \frac{\partial u}{\partial x}\right) +$$

$$\frac{\partial}{\partial y}\left[\mu\left(\frac{\partial u}{\partial y} + \frac{\partial v}{\partial x}\right)\right] + \frac{\partial}{\partial z}\left[\mu\left(\frac{\partial u}{\partial z} + \frac{\partial w}{\partial x}\right)\right] \qquad \text{... (3.10)}$$

(ii) Inertia force per unit volume in y-direction :

$$\rho \frac{Dv}{Dt} = \rho Y - \frac{\partial p}{\partial y} - \frac{2}{3}\frac{\partial}{\partial y}(\mu \cdot \Delta) + 2\frac{\partial}{\partial y}\left(\mu \cdot \frac{\partial v}{\partial y}\right) +$$

$$\frac{\partial}{\partial z}\left[\mu\left(\frac{\partial v}{\partial z} + \frac{\partial w}{\partial y}\right)\right] + \frac{\partial}{\partial x}\left[\mu\left(\frac{\partial v}{\partial x} + \frac{\partial u}{\partial y}\right)\right] \qquad \text{... (3.11)}$$

(iii) Inertia force per unit volume in z-direction :

$$\rho \frac{Dw}{Dt} = \rho Z - \frac{\partial p}{\partial z} - \frac{2}{3}\frac{\partial}{\partial z}(\mu \cdot \Delta) + 2\frac{\partial}{\partial z}\left(\mu \cdot \frac{\partial w}{\partial z}\right)$$

$$+ \frac{\partial}{\partial x}\left[\mu\left(\frac{\partial w}{\partial x} + \frac{\partial u}{\partial z}\right)\right] + \frac{\partial}{\partial y}\left[\mu\left(\frac{\partial w}{\partial y} + \frac{\partial v}{\partial z}\right)\right] \qquad \text{... (3.12)}$$

where, $\dfrac{Du}{Dt}$, $\dfrac{Dv}{Dt}$ and $\dfrac{Dw}{Dt}$ are the total derivatives of x, y and z components of velocities of fluid respectively. (OR component of acceleration of fluid along x, y and z directions respectively).

X, Y and Z are components of body forces per unit mass,

$$\Delta = \frac{\partial u}{\partial x} + \frac{\partial v}{\partial y} + \frac{\partial w}{\partial z} \text{ is pressure viscosity coefficient}$$

ρ is mass density.

u, v and w are velocity components of fluid in x, y and z directions respectively.

$\rho\,\dfrac{Du}{Dt}$ – Inertia force per unit volume in x-direction.

ρX – Body force per unit volume.

$\dfrac{\partial p}{\partial x}$, $\dfrac{\partial p}{\partial y}$ and $\dfrac{\partial p}{\partial z}$ – Pressure gradients in x, y and z directions respectively.

These equations are used to derive generalised Reynolds equation. Also the flow of lubricant must satisfy continuity requirements expressed by the continuity equations given below.

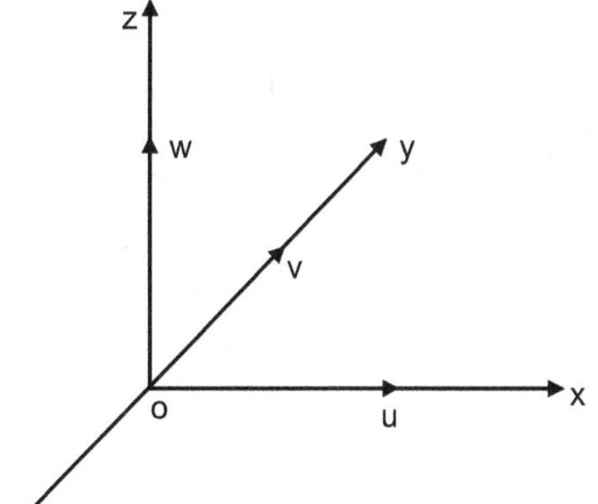

Fig. 3.9

In Cartesian co-ordinate system,

$$V \equiv v(x, y, z)$$

The continuity equation takes the following form :

$$\frac{\partial \rho}{\partial t} \equiv \frac{\partial}{\partial x}(\rho u) + \frac{\partial}{\partial y}(\rho v) + \frac{\partial}{\partial z}(\rho w) = 0$$

Total change of velocity in x-direction in time interval dt is,

$$Du = \frac{\partial u}{\partial x}\cdot dx + \frac{\partial u}{\partial y}\cdot dy + \frac{\partial u}{\partial z}\cdot dz + \frac{\partial u}{\partial t}\cdot dt$$

$$\therefore \quad \frac{Du}{dt} = \underbrace{\frac{\partial u}{\partial x}\cdot u + \frac{\partial u}{\partial y}\cdot v + \frac{\partial u}{\partial z}\cdot w}_{\text{Convective derivative}} + \underbrace{\frac{\partial u}{\partial t}}_{\text{Local Derivative}} \qquad \text{... (3.13)}$$

Based on assumptions made, reduced form of Navier-Stroke's equation is given by,

$$\frac{\partial p}{\partial x} = \mu\left(\frac{\partial^2 u}{\partial z^2}\right)$$

$$\text{and} \qquad \frac{\partial p}{\partial y} = \mu \left(\frac{\partial^2 v}{\partial z^2} \right) \qquad \qquad \dots (3.14)$$

As 'p' is a function of x and y, on integrating above equations with respect to z, the general expression for velocity gradients treating viscosity constant can be given as,

$$\int \frac{\partial p}{\partial x} \cdot dz = \int \mu \left(\frac{\partial^2 u}{\partial z^2} \right) dz$$

$$z \frac{\partial p}{\partial x} + A = \mu \frac{\partial u}{\partial z}$$

$$\frac{\partial u}{\partial z} = \frac{z}{\mu} \cdot \frac{\partial p}{\partial x} + \frac{A}{\mu} \qquad \qquad \dots (3.15)$$

Similarly,   where, A and C are constants of integration

$$\frac{\partial v}{\partial z} = \frac{z}{\mu} \frac{\partial p}{\partial y} + \frac{C}{\mu} \qquad \qquad \dots (3.16)$$

Once again integrating above equations w.r.t. z,

$$u = \frac{z^2}{2\mu} \cdot \frac{\partial p}{\partial x} + \frac{A \cdot z}{\mu} + B$$

where, B and D are additional integration constants to be determined using suitable boundary conditions.

$$\text{and} \quad v = \frac{z^2}{2\mu} \cdot \frac{\partial p}{\partial y} + \frac{C \cdot z}{\mu} + D$$

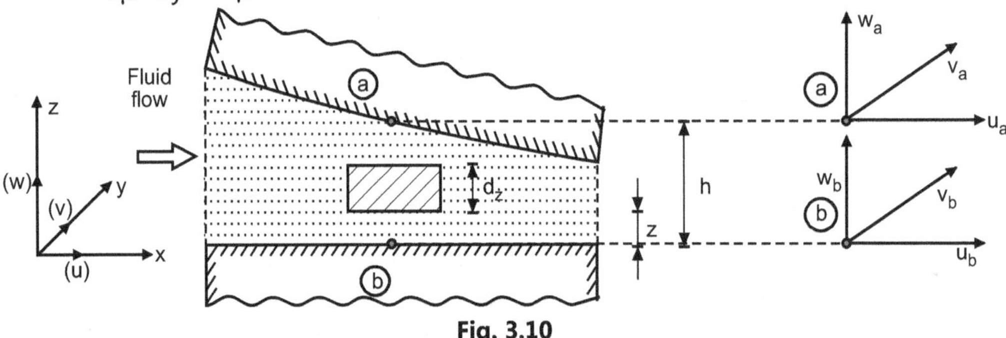

Fig. 3.10

where, u_a, v_a and w_a are velocity components of upper surface in x, y and z directions respectively. u_b, v_b and w_b are velocity components of lower surface in x, y and z directions respectively.

Boundary Conditions :

(i)   At z = 0 $\begin{cases} u = u_b \\ v = v_b \end{cases}$ (ii)   and at z = h $\begin{cases} u = u_a \\ v = v_a \end{cases}$

Using the boundary conditions in above equations for velocities u and v, we have,

(i) $u_b = \frac{0^2}{2\mu} \frac{\partial p}{\partial x} + \frac{A(0)}{\mu} + B \Rightarrow B = u_b$

$$v_b = \frac{0^2}{2\mu}\frac{\partial p}{\partial y} + \frac{C(0)}{\mu} + D \Rightarrow D = v_b$$

Substituting these constants in equations for u and v, we get,

$$u = \frac{z^2}{2\mu}\frac{\partial p}{\partial x} + \frac{A \cdot z}{\mu} + u_b$$

and

$$v = \frac{z^2}{2\mu}\frac{\partial p}{\partial y} + \frac{C \cdot z}{\mu} + v_b$$

(ii)

$$u_a = \frac{h^2}{2\mu}\frac{\partial p}{\partial x} + \frac{A \cdot h}{\mu} + u_b \Rightarrow A = \left[(u_a - u_b) - \frac{h^2}{2\mu}\frac{\partial p}{\partial x}\right]\frac{\mu}{h}$$

and

$$v_a = \frac{h^2}{2\mu}\frac{\partial p}{\partial y} + \frac{C \cdot h}{\mu} + v_b \Rightarrow C = \left[(v_a - v_b) - \frac{h^2}{2\mu}\frac{\partial p}{\partial y}\right]\frac{\mu}{h}$$

Substituting constants A and C in above equations for u and v, we get,

$$u = \frac{z^2}{2\mu}\frac{\partial p}{\partial x} + \left[(u_a - u_b) - \frac{h^2}{2\mu}\frac{\partial p}{\partial x}\right]\frac{z}{h} + u_b \qquad \text{... (3.17)}$$

$$= \frac{z^2}{2\mu}\frac{\partial p}{\partial x} - \frac{z \cdot h}{2\mu}\frac{\partial p}{\partial x} + \frac{z}{h} \cdot u_a - \frac{z}{h} u_b + u_b$$

i.e.

$$u = \frac{1}{2\mu}\frac{\partial p}{\partial x}[z^2 - zh] + \left(1 - \frac{z}{h}\right)u_b + \frac{z}{h} \cdot u_a \qquad \text{... (3.18)}$$

'Poiseuille flow term'   'Couette flow term'
(due to pressure   (due to motion of
gradient ∂p/∂x)   surfaces a and b)
pressure constant,   also called as 'shear term'

and

$$v = \frac{z^2}{2\mu}\frac{\partial p}{\partial y} + \left[(v_a - v_b) - \frac{h^2}{2\mu}\frac{\partial p}{\partial y}\right]\frac{z}{h} + v_b$$

Actual volumetric flow rates in direction of sliding per unit width.

Consider elemental fluid at a distance z from body b having thickness dz and unit width in y-direction.

In x-direction,

$$q_x' = \int_0^h (dz \times 1) \cdot u$$

$$= \int_0^h \left\{\frac{z^2}{2\mu}\frac{\partial p}{\partial x} + \left[(u_a - u_b) - \frac{h^2}{2\mu} \cdot \frac{\partial p}{\partial x}\right]\frac{z}{h} + u_b\right\} dz$$

$$= \left\{ \frac{z^3}{6\mu} \frac{\partial p}{\partial x} + \left[(u_a - u_b) - \frac{h^2}{2\mu} \frac{\partial p}{\partial x} \right] \frac{z^2}{2h} + z \cdot u_b \right\}_0^h$$

$$= \frac{h^3}{6\mu} \cdot \frac{\partial p}{\partial x} + \left[(u_a - u_b) - \frac{h^2}{2\mu} \frac{\partial p}{\partial x} \right] \frac{h^2}{2h} + u_b \cdot h$$

$$= \frac{\partial p}{\partial x} \left[\frac{h^3}{6\mu} - \frac{h^3}{4\mu} \right] + (u_a - u_b) \frac{h}{2} + h \cdot u_b$$

$$\therefore \quad q_x' = -\frac{h^3}{12\mu} \cdot \frac{\partial p}{\partial x} + \left(\frac{u_a + u_b}{2} \right) h \qquad \text{... (3.19)}$$

Couette velocity induced flow term

Poiseuille pressure induced flow term

Similarly, we can write volume flow rate in y-direction as,

$$q_y' = -\frac{h^3}{12\mu} \cdot \frac{\partial p}{\partial y} + \left(\frac{v_a + v_b}{2} \right) \cdot h \qquad \text{... (3.20)}$$

Now, consider continuity equation,

$$\frac{\partial \rho}{\partial t} + \frac{\partial}{\partial x} (\rho u) + \frac{\partial}{\partial y} (\rho v) + \frac{\partial}{\partial z} (\rho w) = 0 \qquad \text{... (3.21)}$$

Integrating above equation over the film thickness w.r.t. dz,

$$\int_0^h \left[\frac{\partial \rho}{\partial t} + \frac{\partial}{\partial x} (\rho u) + \frac{\partial}{\partial y} (\rho v) + \frac{\partial}{\partial z} (\rho w) \right] dz = 0$$

Let $\quad I = \int_0^h \frac{\partial \rho}{\partial t} dz = \frac{\partial \rho}{\partial t} \cdot h = h \cdot \frac{\partial \rho}{\partial t}$

$$II = \int_0^h \frac{\partial}{\partial x} (\rho u) \, dz$$

Using General form of Leibnitz's integration rule,

$$\int_0^h \frac{\partial}{\partial x} [F(x, y, z)] \, dz = -F(x, y, z) \frac{\partial h}{\partial x} + \frac{\partial}{\partial x} \int_0^h f(x, y, z) \, dz$$

Now, $\quad \text{II} = \displaystyle\int_0^h \frac{\partial}{\partial x}(\rho u)\, dz = -\rho u \frac{\partial h}{\partial x} + \frac{\partial}{\partial x}\int_0^h (\rho u)\, dz$

$$= -(\rho u_a)\frac{\partial h}{\partial x} + \frac{\partial}{\partial x}\left[\rho \int_0^h u\, dz\right]\Bigg\}\begin{array}{l}\text{at } z = h \\ u = u_a\end{array}$$

$$\text{III} = \int_0^h \frac{\partial}{\partial y}(\rho v)\, dz = -(\rho \cdot v_a)\frac{\partial h}{\partial y} + \frac{\partial}{\partial y}\left[\rho \int_0^h v \cdot dz\right]\Bigg\}\begin{array}{l}\text{at } z = h \\ v = v_a\end{array}$$

$$\text{IV} = \int_0^h \frac{\partial}{\partial z}(\rho w)\, dz = \rho \int_{w_b}^{w_a} \partial w = \rho(w_a - w_b)$$

Substituting I, II, III and IV in equation above,

$$\therefore\ h\frac{\partial \rho}{\partial t} - \rho\, u_a \frac{\partial h}{\partial x} + \frac{\partial}{\partial x}\left[\rho \int_0^h u\, dz\right] - \rho \cdot v_a \frac{\partial h}{\partial y} + \frac{\partial}{\partial y}\left[\rho \int_0^h v\, dz\right]$$

$$-\rho\, v_a \frac{\partial h}{\partial y} + \frac{\partial}{\partial y}\left[\rho\left(-\frac{h^3}{12\mu}\frac{\partial P}{\partial y} + \frac{v_a + v_b}{2}\cdot h\right)\right] + \rho(w_a - w_b) = 0$$

$$\therefore\ h\frac{\partial \rho}{\partial t} - \rho\, u_a \frac{\partial h}{\partial x} + \frac{\partial}{\partial x}\left[\rho\left(\frac{-h^3}{12\mu}\cdot\frac{\partial p}{\partial x} + \frac{u_a + u_b}{2}\cdot h\right)\right]\rho(w_a - w_b) = 0$$

$$\therefore\ \frac{\partial}{\partial x}\left[\frac{\rho h^3}{12\mu}\cdot\frac{\partial p}{\partial x}\right] + \frac{\partial}{\partial y}\left[\frac{\rho h^3}{12\mu}\cdot\frac{\partial p}{\partial y}\right] = \frac{\partial}{\partial x}\left[\frac{\rho h(u_a + u_b)}{2}\right] + \frac{\partial}{\partial y}\left[\frac{\rho h(v_a + v_b)}{2}\right] + \rho(w_a - w_b)$$

$$-\rho\, u_a \frac{\partial h}{\partial x} - \rho\, v_a \frac{\partial h}{\partial y} + h\frac{\partial \rho}{\partial t} \qquad \text{... (3.22)}$$

which is the Generalised Reynold's Equation.

- Left hand side terms describe flow rate due to pressure gradients known as 'Poiseuille pressure induced flow rate'.

- First two terms on right hand side describe flow rate due to motion of surfaces or shear known as 'Couette velocity induced flow rate'.

- Last four terms on right hand side describe the net flow rates due to squeeze motion and local compression.

Neglecting side leakage (i.e. pressure is constant in y-direction), Reynolds equation can be written as,

$$\frac{\partial}{\partial x}\left[\frac{\rho h^3}{12\mu}\cdot\frac{\partial p}{\partial x}\right] = \frac{\partial}{\partial x}\left[\frac{\rho h(u_a + u_b)}{2}\right] - \rho\, u_a\frac{\partial h}{\partial x} + \rho(w_a - w_b) + h\cdot\frac{\partial \rho}{\partial t} \quad \dots (3.23)$$

3.4.3 Terms involved in Reynold's Equation and their Physical Interpretation

Couette flow rate term in x-direction

$$\frac{\partial}{\partial x}\left[\frac{\rho h(u_a + u_b)}{2}\right]$$

Differentiating each term partially w.r.t. ∂x, we have,

- $\left.\dfrac{\rho h}{2}\cdot\dfrac{\partial}{\partial x}(u_a + u_b)\right\}$ called **'Physical Stretch'**.

- $\left.\dfrac{\rho(u_a + u_b)}{2}\cdot\dfrac{\partial h}{\partial x}\right\}$ called **'Physical Wedge'**.

- $\left.\dfrac{h(u_a + u_b)}{2}\cdot\dfrac{\partial \rho}{\partial x}\right\}$ called **'Density Wedge'**.

Also we have three more terms on R.H.S.

- $\left.-\rho\, u_a\dfrac{\partial h}{\partial x}\right\}$ called **'Geometric Squeeze'** or **'Translational Squeeze'**.

- $\rho(w_a - w_b)\}$ called **'Normal Squeeze'** term.

- $\left.h\dfrac{\partial \rho}{\partial t}\right\}$ called **'Local Expansion'** term.

Physical Interpretation of Each Term Involved in Reynold's Equation :

(i) Physical Stretch : It takes into account the variation in tangential velocities.

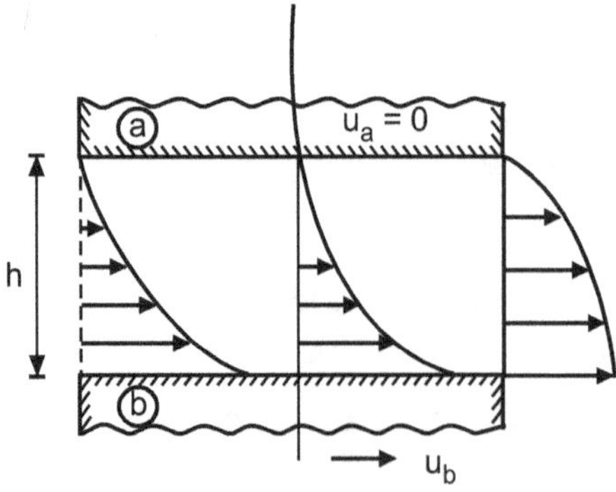

Fig. 3.11

$$\text{Physical stretch} \quad = \quad \frac{\rho h}{2} \cdot \frac{\partial}{\partial x}(u_a + u_b)$$

Assuming inelastic bearing surfaces,

$$\frac{\partial}{\partial x}(u_a + u_b) = 0$$

and
$$u_b = f[u_b(x)]$$

(ii) Physical Wedge :

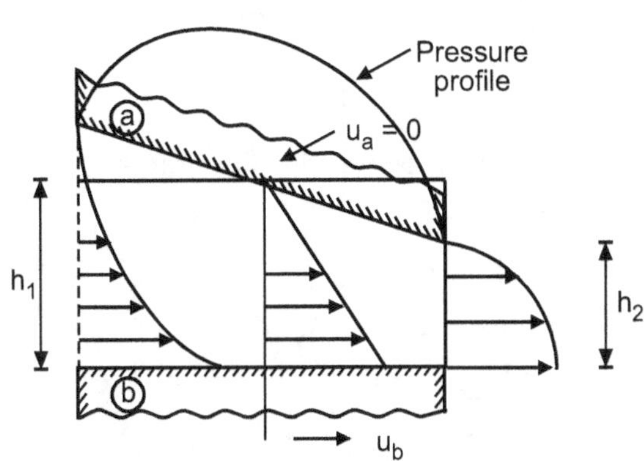

Fig. 3.12

- It is one of the most important terms responsible for pressure generation in hydrodynamic bearings.

- Physical wedge $= \dfrac{\rho(u_a + u_b)}{2} \cdot \dfrac{\partial h}{\partial x}$

- Here, $\dfrac{\partial h}{\partial x} < 0 \Rightarrow$ for positive load-carrying capacity, the surfaces should possess a convergent gap.

$\dfrac{\partial h}{\partial x}$ – rate of change of film thickness in the direction of motion

Mass flow rate :

$$a v \rho = \text{Constant}$$

$$(h \times 1)\, v \rho = \text{Constant}$$

As ρ remains constant,

$$h v = \text{Constant}$$

i.e.
$$h_1 v_1 = h_2 v_2$$

- For positive pressure generation, film thickness 'h' must decrease in the direction of motion.

(iii) Density Wedge :

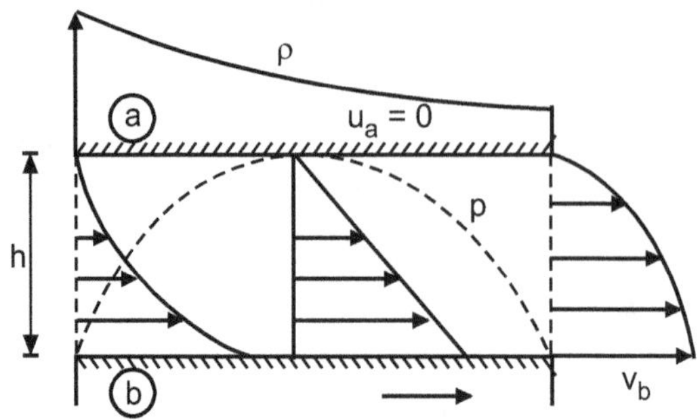

Fig. 3.13

- It is similar to physical wedge showing density gradient in the direction of motion.

- Density wedge = $\dfrac{h(u_a + u_b)}{2} \cdot \dfrac{\partial \rho}{\partial x}$

- It can generate positive pressure if,

$$\frac{\partial \rho}{\partial x} < 0$$

- This term does not contribute to the overall pressure build up and is negligible as compared with physical wedge.

- In this case, mass flow rate = $\rho a v$ = constant as 'a' is constant $\Rightarrow \rho_1 v_1 = \rho_2 v_2$.

(iv) Geometric Squeeze Term (Translational Squeeze Term) :

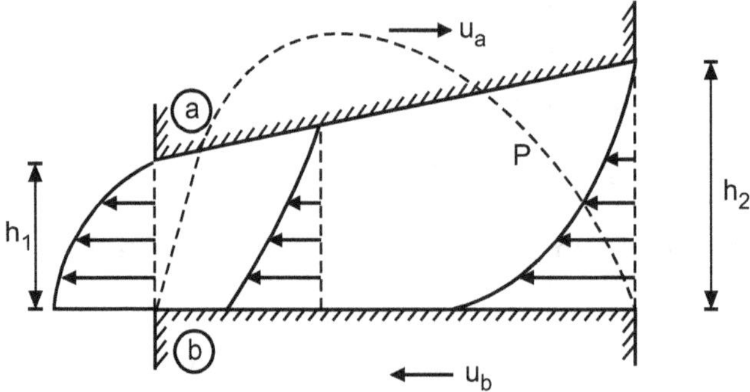

Fig. 3.14

- It accounts for the squeeze like action due to geometrical configuration.

- Even in absence of physical squeeze action, there may be a component of velocity in z-direction.

Translational squeeze term = $- \rho \, u_a \cdot \dfrac{\partial h}{\partial x}$

(v) Normal Squeeze Term :

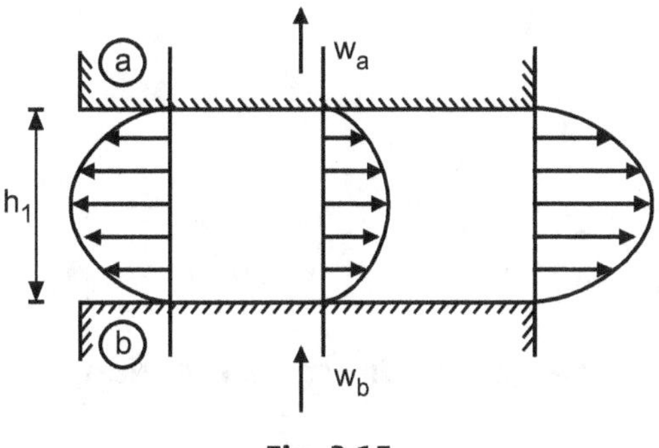

Fig. 3.15

- It occurs due to the relative motion of the surfaces normal to the direction of the motion so that the fluid between two surfaces is physically squeezed.

- Due to the normal squeeze alone, a substantial load-carrying capacity could occur.

- Normal squeeze term = $\rho(w_a - w_b)$

- It provides necessary cushioning effect.

  e.g. Piston pin, journal bearings.

  Here, $w_b > w_a$ to have squeezing action.

(vi) Local Expansion Term :

- It can be expressed as

$$= h\left(\frac{\partial \rho}{\partial t}\right) \rightarrow \text{Rate of change of density w.r.t. time.}$$

- It has negligibly small contribution in generating pressure.

- It is a measure of the change in volume of a given mass of fluid due to expansion as a result of the heat supply to the bearing.

3.4.4 Standard Reduced Forms of Reynold's Equation

(1) For Tangential Motion :

Neglecting normal squeeze term, geometrical squeeze term and local expansion term, Reynold's equation can be given as,

$$\frac{\partial}{\partial x}\left[\frac{\rho h^3}{12\mu}\frac{\partial p}{\partial x}\right] + \frac{\partial}{\partial y}\left[\frac{\rho h^3}{12\mu}\cdot\frac{\partial p}{\partial y}\right] = \frac{\partial}{\partial x}\left[\frac{\rho h(u_a + u_b)}{2}\right] + \frac{\partial}{\partial y}\left[\frac{\rho h(v_a + v_b)}{2}\right]$$

Let
$$\bar{u} = \left(\frac{u_a + u_b}{2}\right)$$

and
$$\bar{v} = \left(\frac{v_a + v_b}{2}\right)$$

$$\frac{\partial}{\partial x}\left[\frac{\rho h^3}{12\mu} \cdot \frac{\partial p}{\partial x}\right] + \frac{\partial}{\partial y}\left[\frac{\rho h^3}{12\mu} \cdot \frac{\partial p}{\partial y}\right] = \bar{u}\,\frac{\partial}{\partial x}(\rho h) + \bar{v}\,\frac{\partial}{\partial y}(\rho h) \qquad \dots (3.24)$$

(2) For Steady-State Conditions (i.e Unidirectional Motion) :

$$v = 0$$

Using this condition in above equation, it becomes

$$\frac{\partial}{\partial x}\left[\frac{\rho h^3}{12\mu} \cdot \frac{\partial p}{\partial x}\right] + \frac{\partial}{\partial y}\left[\frac{\rho h^3}{12\mu}\,\frac{\partial p}{\partial y}\right] = \bar{u}\,\frac{\partial}{\partial x}(\rho h) \qquad \dots (3.25)$$

(3) For Incompressible Fluids e.g. Oils :

$$\rho = \text{Constant}$$

$\therefore$ Above equation becomes,

$$\frac{\partial}{\partial x}\left[h^3\,\frac{\partial p}{\partial x}\right] + \frac{\partial}{\partial y}\left[h^3\,\frac{\partial p}{\partial y}\right] = 12\mu\,\bar{u}\,\frac{\partial h}{\partial x} \qquad \dots (3.26)$$

(4) For Compressible Fluids of Variable Density and Variable Viscosity :

Neglecting the leakages in y-direction and treating pressure constant in y-direction (i.e. along length of bearing),

$$\frac{\partial}{\partial x}\left[\frac{\rho h^3}{\mu}\,\frac{\partial p}{\partial x}\right] = 12\,\bar{u}\,\frac{\partial}{\partial x}(\rho h) \qquad \dots (3.27)$$

(5) Integrated form of Reynold's Equation :

We have an equation for compressible fluid of variable density and variable viscosity.

$$\frac{\partial}{\partial x}\left[\frac{\rho h^3}{\mu} \cdot \frac{\partial p}{\partial x}\right] = 12\,\bar{u}\,\frac{\partial}{\partial x}(\rho h)$$

Integrating above equation w.r.t. x, we get,

$$\frac{\rho h^3}{\mu}\,\frac{\partial p}{\partial x} = 12\,\bar{u}\,(\rho h) + A$$

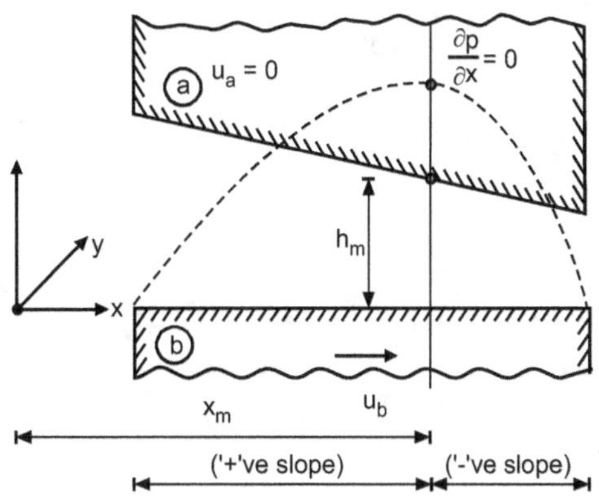

Fig. 3.16

Boundary conditions :

At
$$\frac{\partial p}{\partial x} = 0$$

$$p = p_{max}$$

$$x = x_m$$

$$h = h_m$$

$$\rho = \rho_m$$

$$\mu = \text{constant}$$

Using these values in above equation, we get,

$$0 = 12\,\bar{u}\,\rho_m \cdot h_m + A$$

$\therefore$
$$A = -12\,\bar{u}\,\rho_m \cdot h_m$$

Substituting in above equation, it becomes,

$$\frac{\rho h^3}{\mu} \cdot \frac{\partial p}{\partial x} = 12\,\bar{u}\,(\rho h) - 12\,\bar{u}\,\rho_m \cdot h_m$$

$$\frac{\partial p}{\partial x} = \frac{\mu}{\rho h^3}\left(12\,\bar{u}\,\rho h - 12\,\bar{u}\,\rho_m \cdot h_m\right)$$

$\therefore$
$$\frac{\partial p}{\partial x} = 12\,\bar{u}\cdot\mu\left[\frac{\rho \cdot h - \rho_m \cdot h_m}{\rho h^3}\right] \qquad \dots (3.28)$$

This is called integrated Reynold's equation.

(6) For incompressible fluids e.g. oil,

$$\rho = \text{constant}$$

i.e. $\rho = \rho_m$

∴   Above equation reduces to,

$$\frac{\partial p}{\partial x} = 12\,\bar{u}\,\mu\left[\frac{h - h_m}{h^3}\right]$$

∴ $$\frac{\partial p}{\partial x} = 12\frac{u_b}{2}\cdot\mu\left[\frac{h - h_m}{h^3}\right]$$

∴ $$\frac{\partial p}{\partial x} = 6\cdot u_b\cdot\mu\left[\frac{h - h_m}{h^3}\right] \quad \text{... (3.29)}$$

where, h_m corresponds to p_{max} at which $\dfrac{\partial p}{\partial x} = 0$.

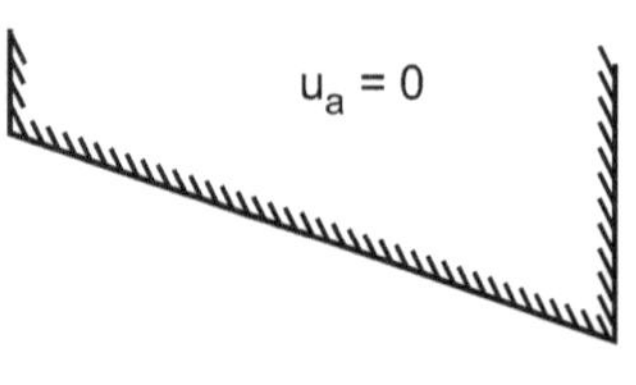

Fig. 3.17

$$\bar{u} = \frac{(u_b - u_a) - 0}{2}$$

$$\bar{u} = \frac{u_b}{2}$$

3.5 HYDRODYNAMIC JOURNAL BEARING

Journal bearings are designed and most widely used to support a radial load which works on the principle of hydrodynamic action.

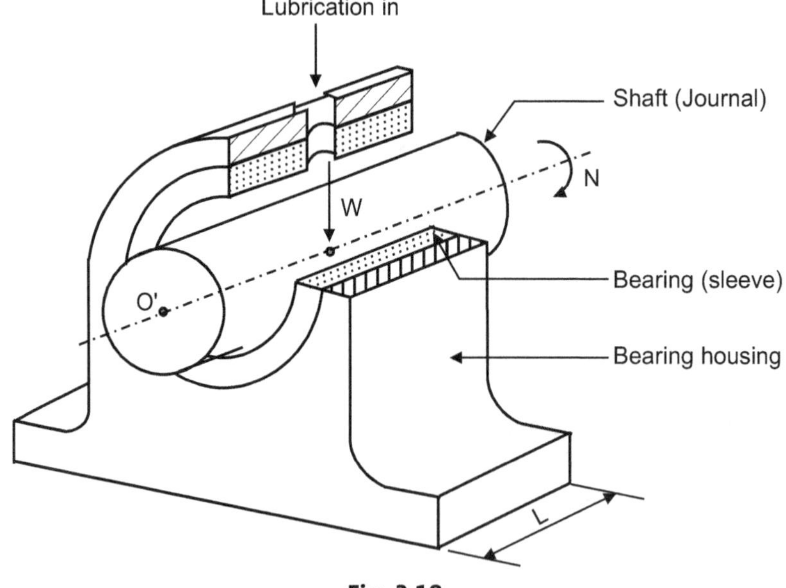

Fig. 3.18

Hydrodynamic Action :

Lubricant is supplied initially in the clearance space between bearing surface and journal, as the journal rotates, the lubricant is pulled into a converging wedge shaped region formed

---

between the moving surfaces. Thus, dynamic pressure built-up, which supports the applied load on journal.

3.5.1 Nomenclature

Fig. 3.19 shows the cross-sectional details of hydrodynamic journal bearing and the terms related with its study. Also the variation of pressure on bearing both circumferentially and along the length of bearing can be illustrated.

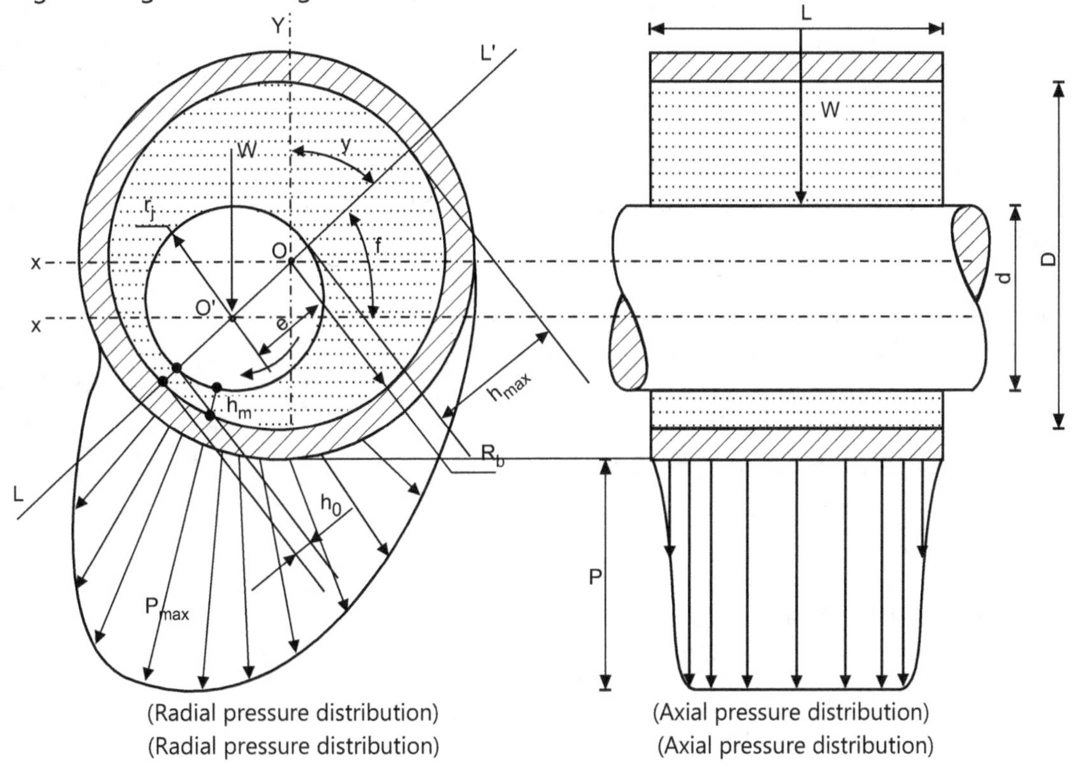

(Radial pressure distribution)   (Axial pressure distribution)

Fig. 3.19

Notations :

O'	–	Centre of journal
O	–	Centre of bearing
W	–	Radial load on journal
R_b	–	Radius of bearing
r_j	–	Radius of journal
h_0	–	Minimum oil-film thickness
h_{max}	–	Maximum oil-film thickness
C	–	Radial clearance

ω_j	–	Angular speed of journal
e	–	Eccentricity
$\in$	–	Eccentricity ratio
ψ	–	Attitude angle
LL'	–	Line of centres
d	–	Diameter of journal
D	–	Diameter of bearing
ϕ	–	Circumferential co-ordinate

Terms Used :

1. Journal :

It is the portion of circular shaft, supported in a circular bush and take radial load called journal.

2. Bearing (Sleeve) :
Journal is made to rotate in a stationary bush or sleeve called bearing, with a complete 360° arc or various arrangements of a partial arc or arcs in a housing structure.

3. Radial Clearance (C) :
The difference between radii of bearing and that of journal is termed as radial clearance. It can be given as below,

$$C = R_b - r_j \qquad \qquad \text{... (3.30)}$$

The bearing and journal operate with a small radial clearance of the order of $\left(\dfrac{1}{1000}\right)$ of the journal radius.

4. Eccentricity (e) :
It is the distance between the centres of bearing and the journal measured along the line of centres.

$$e = O'\,O \text{ from figure}$$

5. Eccentricity Ratio ($\in$) :
It is the ratio of the eccentricity to the radial clearance.

i.e. $$\in = \frac{e}{C} \qquad \qquad \text{... (3.31)}$$

Value of eccentricity ratio varies from 0 to 1.
For concentric bearings,

$$e = 0$$
$$\therefore \qquad \in = 0$$

When journal touches bearing,

$$e = C$$
$$\therefore \qquad \in = 1$$

Eccentricity ratio ($\in$) is a function of,

$$\in = f\,(W_z,\ \omega_j,\ \mu,\ r_j,\ l,\ C)$$

where, r_j – Journal radius
     l – Length of bearing Geometric variables
     C – Radial clearance
     W_z – Radial load
     ω_j – Angular velocity of journal Operating variables
     μ – Dynamic viscosity of lubricant

Also, radial load (W_z) is a function of,

$$W_z = f(e,\ \omega_j,\ \mu,\ r_j,\ l,\ C)$$

6. Minimum Oil-Film Thickness (h_0) :
The oil-film thickness measured along the line joining the centres of journal and bearing. It can be given as,

$$H_0 = R_b - (r_j + e)$$

7. Minimum Oil-Film Thickness Ratio $\left(\dfrac{h_0}{C}\right)$:

It is the ratio of the minimum oil-film thickness to radial clearance.

$\therefore$ Minimum oil-film thickness ratio $= \dfrac{h_0}{C}$

Now,

$$R_b = e + r_j + h_0$$

$$R_b - r_j = e + h_0$$

$$C = e + h_0$$

$$1 = \frac{e}{C} + \frac{h_0}{C}$$

$\therefore$
$$\frac{h_0}{C} = 1 - \frac{e}{C}$$

$\therefore$
$$\frac{h_0}{C} = 1 - \epsilon \qquad\qquad \text{... (3.32)}$$

8. Attitude Angle (ψ) :

It is the angle made by the line of centres with load line (i.e. vertical) such that condition of perfect lubrication occur where film thickness is minimum.

3.5.2 Pressure Distribution

Fig. 3.19 shows the pressure distribution in radial and axial direction.

- **Radial Pressure Distribution :**

    It is maximum at particular angle measured from load line.

    P_{max}–the maximum pressure developed in the fluid film

- **Axial Pressure Distribution :**

    - Pressure distribution along the length of hydrodynamic journal bearing is almost constant.

    - Pressure suddenly falls at ends of bearing due to atmospheric pressure. It is shown in Fig. 3.19.

3.5.3 Principle of Hydrodynamic Lubrication

Principle of hydrodynamic lubrication in journal bearing can be illustrated by using the following three cases :

Case (i) : Journal at rest.

Case (ii) : Journal starts rotating.

Case (iii) : Journal at full speed.

Case (i) Journal at Rest :

- When the journal is at rest, the weight of the journal squeezes out of the oil film so that the journal rests on the bearing surface i.e. in initial stage, under the radial load, the journal touches the inner bearing surface at point P, and metal-to-metal contact is established at P.

- In this case, radial clearance,

$$C = R_b - r_j$$

And at point P, $\quad h_0 = 0$

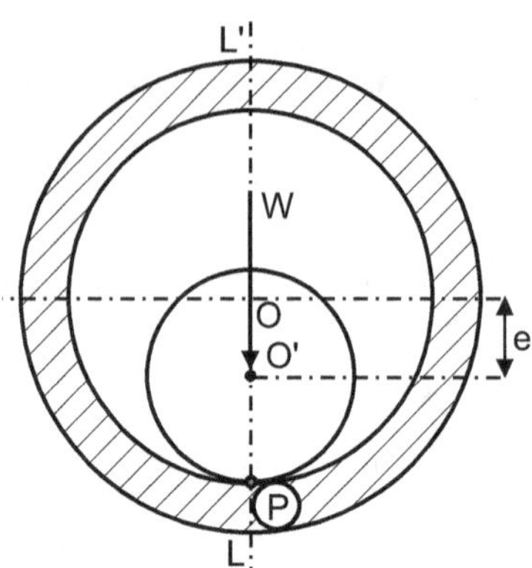

Fig. 3.20

Case (ii) Journal Starts Rotating :

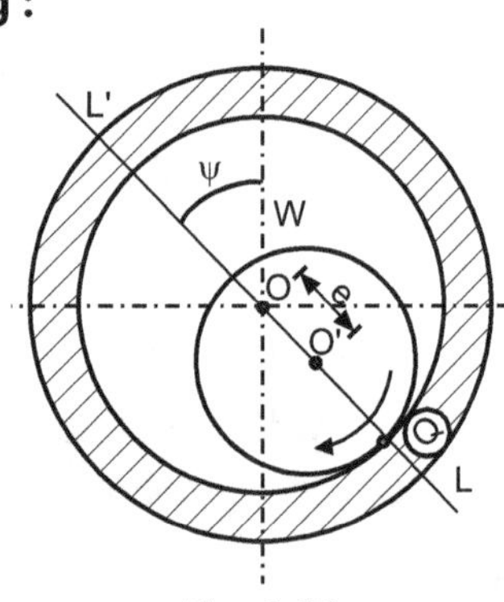

Fig. 3.21

- When journal starts to rotate in clockwise direction inside the bearing, it will climb the bearing wall due to friction up to point Q, such that the line of centres OO' of the bearing and the journal comes to rest at an angle of repose ψ_0.

- At point Q, $\quad h_0 = 0$

Case (iii) Journal at Full Speed :

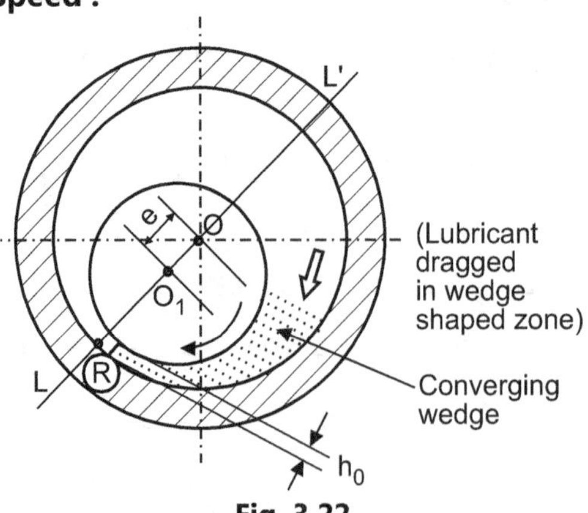

Fig. 3.22

- As the journal speed is further increased, it will drag the fluid into the converging wedge shaped zone; which starts to exert pressure with increasing journal speed.

- At particular journal speed, the pressure becomes sufficient to support the load (W) and the journal is shifted to other side (i.e. to left side) of verticle.

- In this situation, there is minimum clearance and oil-film thickness is minimum (h_{min}) at point R.

- The amount of rotation of the line of centres of journal and bearing from the load line depends on :

  (i) The magnitude of applied radial load

  (ii) The journal speed and

  (iii) The viscosity of lubricant.

- Thus, in hydrodynamic bearings, it is not necessary to supply the lubricant under pressure. The only requirement is to ensure sufficient and continuous supply of the lubricant.

- The minimum thickness of the fluid film increases with an increase in fluid viscosity and surface speed and decreases with an increase in load.

3.6 ANALYSIS OF HYDRODYNAMIC JOURNAL BEARING

More physical insight can be obtained by getting approximate solutions to the hydrodynamic journal bearing. For this purpose, two methods of solution are discussed as follows :

- Infinitely Long-Journal Bearing Solution (ILA) (Sommerfeld Solution).

- Infinitely Short-Journal Bearing Solution (ISA) (Ocvirk-Short Bearing Theory)/Narrow Bearing.

- In above two methods, following parameters are obtained.

- Pressure distribution (i.e. maximum pressure in fluid film) and also dimensionless form of pressure for both infinitely long and short bearings.

- Load-carrying capacity of bearings.

3.6.1 Infinitely Long Journal Bearing

It is also called Infinitely Long Approximation or 'Sommerfeld Solution'.

- **Definition :**

'A journal bearing whose length is greater than or equal to two times the diameter of its journal can be considered to be infinitely long bearing'.

i.e. this approximation provides results with reasonable accuracy when,

$$\frac{l}{d} \geq 2$$

Thus, $\frac{l}{d} \geq 2$ or $l \geq 2d$ ... according to definition.

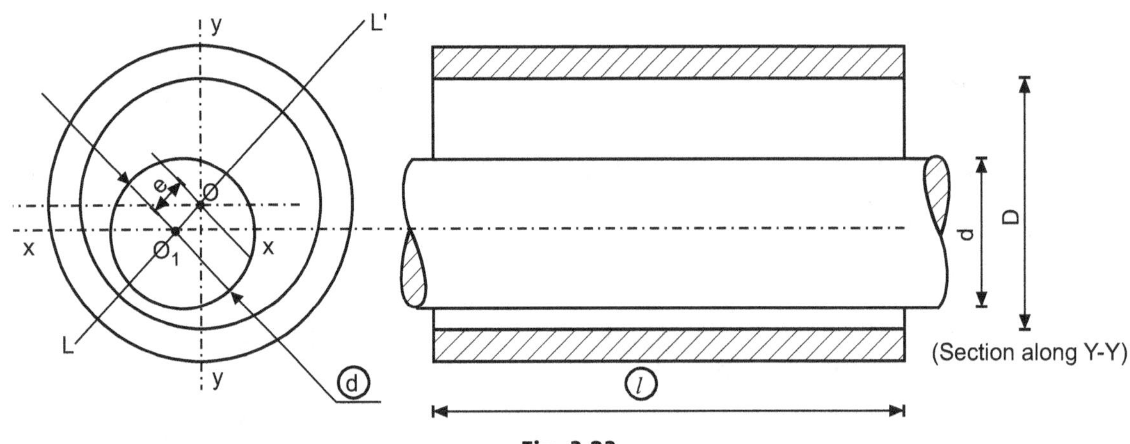

Fig. 3.23

Assumptions :

- As the bearing is much wider in transverse direction than in the direction of motion, therefore it is called infinitely long bearing. For this type of bearing, it is assumed that

$$l \; >> \; d.$$

- There can be little or negligible axial flow of lubricating fluid.

  i.e. $\qquad\qquad Q = 0$

- As the bearing is assumed infinitely long, the pressure variation in axial direction is zero.

  i.e. $\qquad\qquad \frac{\partial p}{\partial y} = 0$

- Density of lubricant remains constant and normal velocity is zero.

  i.e. $\qquad\qquad \rho =$ Constant and normal velocity $= 0$

Above assumptions can be applied to write Reynold's equation for infinitely long bearing analysis in the following manner.

$$\frac{\partial}{\partial x}\left[h^3 \frac{\partial p}{\partial x} \right] = 6\mu \cdot u_b \cdot \frac{\partial h}{\partial x}$$

Integrating this equation w.r.t. dx,

$$h^3 \frac{\partial p}{\partial x} = 6\mu \cdot u_b \cdot h + A$$

where, A is integration constant and can be evaluated using the condition that,

At $\dfrac{\partial p}{\partial x} = 0 \quad \Rightarrow \quad h = h_m$

Using this condition in above equation,

$$0 = 6\mu \cdot u_b \cdot h_m + A$$

$$\therefore \qquad A = -6\mu \cdot u_b \cdot h_m$$

Substituting constant 'A' in above equation, it becomes

$$h^3 \dfrac{\partial p}{\partial x} = 6\mu \cdot u_b \cdot h - 6\mu \cdot u_b \cdot h_m$$

$$\dfrac{\partial p}{\partial x} = 6\mu \cdot u_b \cdot \left[\dfrac{h - h_m}{h^3}\right]$$

We can write above equation as,

$$\dfrac{dp}{dx} = 6\mu \cdot u_b \left[\dfrac{h - h_m}{h^3}\right]$$

where, h_m – Fluid-film thickness at $\dfrac{dp}{dx} = 0$ or $P = p_{max}$

         u_b – Surface velocity or tangential velocity of shaft

         $u_b = r_j \cdot \omega_j$

Now for analysis, we develop the shaft surface and bearing surface along the line joining the centres. Therefore, consider the unwrapped schematic of the fluid-film shape as shown in Fig. 3.24.

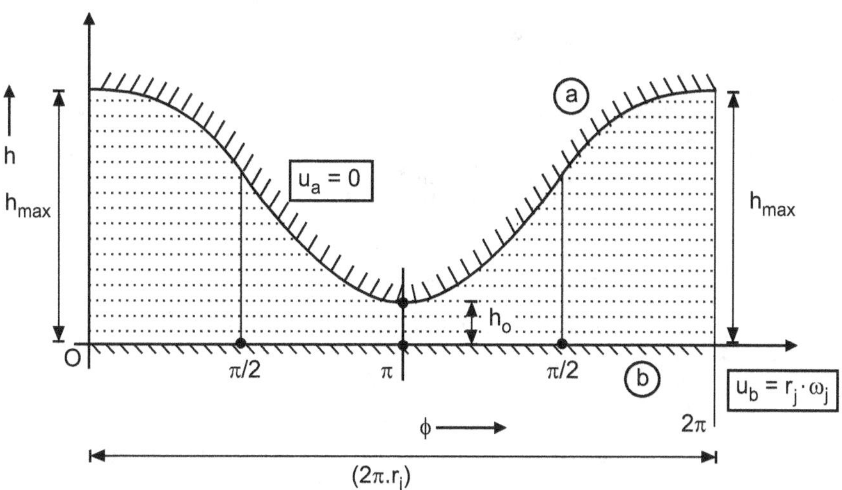

(a) – Development of fixed bearing surface

(b) – Development of rotating (moving) shaft surface

Fig. 3.24 : Film thickness in an unwrapped journal bearing

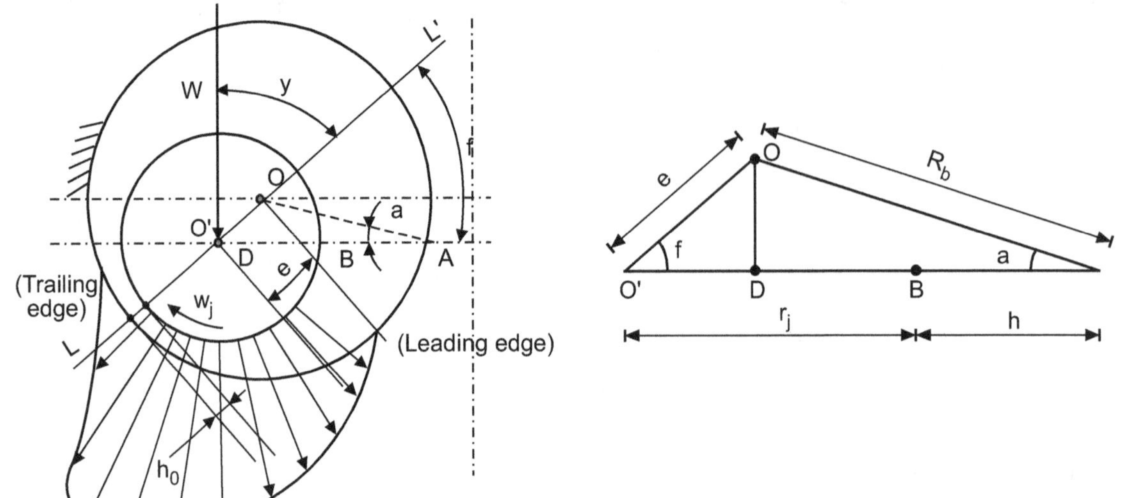

Fig. 3.25

$$OA = \text{Radius of bearing} = R_b$$

$$O'A = r_j + h$$

$$= OO' \cos\phi + OA \cos\alpha$$

$\therefore \qquad O'A = e\cos\phi + R_b \cdot \cos\alpha$

Also, $\qquad O'A = O'D + DA$

But $\qquad OD = e\sin\phi = R_b \sin\alpha$

$\therefore \qquad \sin\alpha = \dfrac{e}{R_b}\cdot\sin\phi$

$\therefore \qquad \cos\alpha = \sqrt{1 - \sin^2\alpha}$

$$= \sqrt{1 - \frac{e^2}{R_b^2}\sin^2\phi}$$

$$= \left[1 - \frac{e^2}{R_b^2}\cdot\sin^2\phi\right]^{1/2}$$

Expanding this form by Taylor's series,

$$\cos\alpha = 1 - \frac{e^2}{R_b^2}\cdot\sin^2\phi + \dots$$

From $\Delta\, O'OA$,

$$h = (O'D + DA) - r_j$$

$$= e\cos\phi + R_b \cdot \cos\alpha - r_j$$

$$= e \cos \phi + R_b \left(1 - \frac{e^2}{2R_b^2} \sin^2 \phi\right) - r_j$$

$$= e \cos \phi + R_b - \frac{e^2}{2R_b} \sin^2 \phi - r_j$$

$$= e \cos \phi + (R_b - r_j) - \frac{e^2}{2R_b} \sin^2 \phi$$

$$= e \cos \phi + C - \frac{e^2}{2R_b} \cdot \sin^2 \phi \qquad \cdots \left(\begin{array}{c}\text{Radial clearance}\\ \because \quad C = R_b - r_j\end{array}\right)$$

$$= C \left[1 + \frac{e}{C} \cos \phi - \frac{e^2}{2R_b \cdot C} \cdot \sin^2 \phi\right]$$

$$= C \left[1 + \frac{e}{C} \cos \phi - \frac{e^2}{C^2} \cdot \frac{C}{2R_b} \cdot \sin^2 \phi\right]$$

$$= C \left[1 + \in \cos \phi - \in^2 \cdot \frac{C}{2R_b} \cdot \sin^2 \phi\right]$$

Neglecting the term $\left(- \in^2 \frac{C}{2R_b} \cdot \sin^2 \phi\right)$, we have,

$$h = C [1 + \in \cos \phi] \qquad \qquad \cdots (3.33)$$

When, $\phi = 0 \Rightarrow h = C(1 + \in)$
$\qquad \phi = \pi \Rightarrow h = C(1 - \in)$
$\qquad \phi = \pi/2 \Rightarrow h = C$

We have,

$$\frac{dp}{dx} = 6u_b \cdot \mu \left[\frac{h - h_m}{h^3}\right]$$

$$\frac{dp}{r_j \cdot d\phi} = 6(r_j \cdot \omega_j) \cdot \mu \left[\frac{h - h_m}{h^3}\right] \qquad \cdots \left(\begin{array}{c}\because \quad dx = r_j \cdot d\phi\\ \text{converting to}\\ \text{polar form}\end{array}\right)$$

$$\frac{dp}{d\phi} = 6 \cdot \omega_j \cdot r_j^2 \cdot \mu \left[\frac{1}{h^2} - \frac{h_m}{h^3}\right]$$

$$\therefore \qquad \frac{dp}{d\phi} = 6 \cdot \omega_j \cdot r_j^2 \cdot \mu \left[\frac{1}{C^2(1 + \in \cos \phi)^2} - \frac{h_m}{C^3(1 + \in \cos \phi)^3}\right]$$

Integrating above equation w.r.t. ϕ,

$$P = 6\omega_j \cdot \left(\frac{r_j}{C}\right)^2 \cdot \mu \left[\int \frac{1}{(1 + \in \cos \phi)^2} \cdot d\phi - \int \frac{h_m}{C(1 + \in \cos \phi)^3} d\phi\right] + A \qquad \cdots (3.34)$$

Let $I_1 = \int \dfrac{1}{(1 + \in \cos \phi)^2} \cdot d\phi$

$$\text{and} \quad I_2 \;=\; \int \frac{h_m}{C(1 + \epsilon \cos \phi)^3} \cdot d\phi$$

(a) Full-Sommerfeld Solution :

The integrals I_1 and I_2 can be conveniently evaluated using standard form of Sommerfeld Substitution (SS).

$$(1 + \epsilon \cos \phi) \;=\; \frac{1 - \epsilon^2}{1 - \epsilon \cos \gamma} \qquad \qquad \text{... (3.35)}$$

where, γ – Sommerfeld variable.

From above substitution, we can easily find $\cos \gamma$.

$$1 - \epsilon \cos \gamma \;=\; \frac{1 - \epsilon^2}{1 + \epsilon \cos \phi}$$

$$1 - \frac{1 - \epsilon^2}{1 + \epsilon \cos \phi} \;=\; \epsilon \cos \gamma$$

$$\frac{1 + \epsilon \cos \phi - 1 + \epsilon^2}{1 + \epsilon \cos \phi} \;=\; \epsilon \cos \gamma$$

$$\frac{\epsilon \, (\epsilon + \cos \phi)}{1 + \epsilon \cos \phi} \;=\; \epsilon \cos \gamma$$

$$\therefore \qquad \cos \gamma \;=\; \frac{\epsilon + \cos \phi}{1 + \epsilon \cos \phi} \qquad \qquad \text{... (3.36)}$$

This is another form of Sommerfeld substitution.

$$\text{Also,} \quad 1 + \epsilon \cos \phi \;=\; \frac{1 - \epsilon^2}{1 - \epsilon \cos \gamma}$$

$$\epsilon \cos \phi \;=\; \frac{1 - \epsilon^2}{1 - \epsilon \cos \gamma} - 1$$

$$\epsilon \cos \phi \;=\; \frac{1 - \epsilon^2 - 1 + \epsilon \cos \gamma}{1 - \epsilon \cos \gamma}$$

$$\epsilon \cos \phi \;=\; \frac{\epsilon \, (\cos \gamma - \epsilon)}{1 - \epsilon \cos \gamma}$$

$$\cos \phi \;=\; \frac{\cos \gamma - \epsilon}{1 - \epsilon \cos \gamma} \qquad \qquad \text{... (3.37)}$$

$$\text{Also,} \qquad \sin \phi \;=\; \sqrt{1 - \cos^2 \phi}$$

$$=\; \sqrt{1 - \frac{(\cos \gamma - \epsilon)^2}{(1 - \epsilon \cos \gamma)^2}}$$

$$=\; \frac{1}{1 - \epsilon \cos \gamma} [(1 - 2\epsilon \cos \gamma + \epsilon^2 \cos^2 \gamma) - (\cos^2 \gamma - 2\epsilon \cos \gamma + \epsilon^2)]^{1/2}$$

$$=\; \frac{1}{1 - \epsilon \cos \gamma} [(1 - \cos^2 \gamma) - \epsilon^2(1 - \cos^2 \gamma)]^{1/2}$$

$$= \frac{1}{1 - \epsilon \cos \gamma} [(1 - \epsilon^2)(1 - \cos^2 \gamma)]^{1/2}$$

$$\therefore \qquad \sin \phi = \frac{\sqrt{1 - \epsilon^2} \cdot \sin \gamma}{1 - \epsilon \cos \gamma} \qquad \qquad \text{... (3.38)}$$

Now substituting $\left(\cos \gamma = \dfrac{e + \cos \phi}{1 + \epsilon \cos \phi} \right)$ in above equation, it becomes,

$$\sin \phi = \frac{\sqrt{1 - \epsilon^2} \cdot \sin \gamma}{1 - \epsilon \left(\dfrac{\epsilon + \cos \phi}{1 + \epsilon \cos \phi} \right)}$$

$$\sin \phi = \frac{\sin \phi}{\sqrt{1 - \epsilon^2}} \left[\frac{1 + \epsilon \cos \phi - \epsilon^2 - \epsilon \cos \phi}{1 + \epsilon \cos \phi} \right]$$

$$= \frac{\sin \phi}{\sqrt{1 - \epsilon^2}} \left[\frac{1 - \epsilon^2}{1 + \epsilon \cos \phi} \right]$$

$$\therefore \qquad \sin \gamma = \frac{\sqrt{1 - \epsilon^2} \, \sin \phi}{1 + \epsilon \cos \phi} \qquad \qquad \text{... (3.39)}$$

Now, differentiating Sommerfeld substitution w.r.t. ϕ,

$$- \epsilon \sin \phi \cdot \frac{d\phi}{d\gamma} = (1 - \epsilon^2) \cdot \frac{d}{d\gamma} (1 - \epsilon \cos \gamma)^{-1}$$

$$= (1 - \epsilon^2)(1 - \epsilon \cos \gamma)^{-2} (-1)(\epsilon \sin \gamma)$$

$$\therefore \qquad \sin \phi \frac{d\phi}{d\gamma} = (1 - \epsilon)(1 - \epsilon \cos \gamma)^{-2} (\sin \gamma)$$

$$\frac{d\phi}{d\gamma} = \frac{1 - \epsilon^2}{(1 - \epsilon \cos \gamma)^2} \cdot \frac{\sin \gamma}{\sin \phi}$$

$$= \frac{1 - \epsilon^2}{(1 - \epsilon \cos \gamma)^2} \cdot \sin \gamma \frac{(1 - \epsilon \cos \gamma)}{\sqrt{1 - \epsilon^2} \cdot \sin \gamma}$$

$$\therefore \qquad d\phi = \frac{\sqrt{1 - \epsilon^2}}{1 - \epsilon \cos \gamma} \cdot d\gamma \qquad \qquad \text{... (3.40)}$$

Applying Boundary Conditions :

When $\phi = 0$ When $\phi = \pi$

Sommerfeld substitution becomes,

$$1 + \epsilon = \frac{1 - \epsilon^2}{1 - \epsilon \cos \gamma} \qquad \qquad 1 + \epsilon \cos \pi = \frac{1 - \epsilon^2}{1 - \epsilon \cos \gamma}$$

$$1 + \epsilon = \frac{(1 - \epsilon)(1 + \epsilon)}{1 - \epsilon \cos \gamma} \qquad \qquad 1 - \epsilon = \frac{(1 - \epsilon)(1 + \epsilon)}{1 - \epsilon \cos \gamma}$$

$$1 - \epsilon \cos \gamma = 1 - \epsilon \qquad \qquad \therefore \; 1 - \epsilon \cos \gamma = 1 + \epsilon$$

$$\cos \gamma = 1 \qquad \qquad \qquad \qquad \cos \gamma = -1$$

$$\gamma = 0 \qquad \qquad \qquad \qquad \qquad \gamma = \pi$$

$$\therefore \; \phi = \gamma = 0 \qquad \qquad \qquad \therefore \; \phi = \gamma = \pi$$

Now, consider integral I_1 for solution.

$$I_1 = \int \frac{d\phi}{(1 + \epsilon \cos \phi)^2}$$

$$= \int \frac{(1 - \epsilon \cos \gamma)^2}{(1 - \epsilon^2)^2} \cdot \frac{\sqrt{1 - \epsilon^2}}{1 - \epsilon \cos \gamma} \cdot d\gamma \qquad \cdots \left(\text{Using } d\phi \text{ and } 1 + \epsilon \cos \phi\right)$$

$$= \frac{1}{(1 - \epsilon^2)^{3/2}} \int (1 - \epsilon \cos \gamma) \, d\gamma$$

$$= \frac{1}{(1 - \epsilon^2)^{3/2}} \cdot [\gamma - \epsilon \sin \gamma] + C_1$$

$$I_2 = \int \frac{h_m}{C(1 + \epsilon \cos \phi)^3} \cdot d\phi$$

$$= \frac{h_m}{C} \int \frac{(1 - \epsilon \cos \gamma)^3}{(1 - \epsilon^2)^3} \cdot \frac{\sqrt{1 - \epsilon^2}}{1 - \epsilon \cos \gamma} \cdot d\gamma$$

$$= \frac{h_m}{C} \cdot \frac{1}{(1 - \epsilon^2)^{5/2}} \int (1 - \epsilon \cos \gamma)^2 \cdot d\gamma$$

$$= \frac{h_m}{C} \cdot \frac{1}{(1 - \epsilon^2)^{5/2}} \left[\int (1 - 2\epsilon \cos \gamma + \epsilon^2 \cdot \cos^2 \gamma) \, d\gamma\right]$$

$$= \frac{h_m}{C} \frac{1}{(1 - \epsilon^2)^{5/2}} \left[\gamma - 2\epsilon \sin \gamma + \frac{\epsilon^2}{2} \gamma + \frac{\epsilon^2}{4} \sin 2\gamma\right] + C_2$$

$$\cdots \left(\because \quad \cos^2 \gamma = \frac{1 + \cos 2\gamma}{2}\right)$$

$$= \frac{C(1 + \epsilon \cos \phi_m)}{C} \cdot \frac{1}{(1 - \epsilon^2)^{5/2}} \left[\gamma - 2\epsilon \sin \gamma + \frac{\epsilon^2}{2} \gamma + \frac{\epsilon^2}{2} \gamma \cdot\right.$$

$$\left. \sin \gamma \cos \gamma\right] + C_2$$

$$\cdots (\because \ h_m = C(1 + \epsilon \cos \phi_m))$$

Substituting I_1 and I_2 in equation for pressure,

$$\therefore \ P = 6\omega_j \cdot \mu \left(\frac{r_j}{C}\right)^2 \left[\frac{\gamma - \epsilon \sin \gamma}{(1 - \epsilon^2)^{3/2}} - \frac{(1 + \epsilon \cos \phi_m)}{(1 - \epsilon^2)^{5/2}} \left(\gamma - 2\epsilon \sin \gamma + \frac{\epsilon^2}{2} \gamma + \frac{\epsilon^2}{4} \sin 2\gamma\right)\right] + A$$

Now, at $\phi = 0$

$$P = 0 \text{ and } A = 0$$

also $\gamma = 0$

$$\therefore \qquad P = 6\omega_j \cdot \mu \left(\frac{r_j}{C}\right)^2 \left[\frac{\gamma - \epsilon \sin \gamma}{(1 - \epsilon^2)^{3/2}} - \frac{(1 - \epsilon^2)}{(1 - \epsilon \cos \gamma)} \cdot \frac{1}{(1 - \epsilon^2)^{5/2}}\right.$$

$$\left.\left(\gamma - 2\epsilon \sin \gamma + \frac{\epsilon^2}{2} \gamma + \frac{\epsilon^2}{2} \sin \gamma \cos \gamma\right)\right]$$

$$\therefore \quad P = \frac{6\omega_j \cdot \mu \left(\dfrac{r_j}{C}\right)^2}{(1 - \epsilon^2)^{3/2}} \left[\gamma - \epsilon \sin \gamma - \frac{1}{1 - \epsilon \cos \gamma} \left(\frac{\gamma(2 + \epsilon^2) - 4\epsilon \sin \gamma + \epsilon^2 \sin \gamma \cos \gamma}{2} \right) \right]$$

Now at $\phi = 2\pi = \gamma$, $\Rightarrow P = 0$

Using this condition in above equation,

$$0 = 2\pi - 0 - \frac{1}{1 - \epsilon \cos \bar{\gamma}} \left[\frac{2\pi(2 + \epsilon^2) - 0 + 0}{2} \right]$$

$$= 2\pi - \frac{2\pi(2 + \epsilon^2)}{2(1 - \epsilon \cos \bar{\gamma})}$$

$$2\pi = \frac{2\pi(2 + \epsilon^2)}{2(1 - \epsilon \cos \bar{\gamma})}$$

$$\therefore \quad 2 - 2\epsilon \cos \bar{\gamma} = 2 + \epsilon^2$$

$$\cos \bar{\gamma} = -\frac{\epsilon}{2} \qquad\qquad \dots (3.41)$$

Equation for pressure,

$$P = \frac{6\omega_j \cdot \mu \left(\dfrac{r_j}{C}\right)^2}{(1 - \epsilon^2)^{3/2}} \left\{ \gamma - \epsilon \sin \gamma - \left[\frac{\gamma(2 + \epsilon^2) - 4\epsilon \sin \gamma + \epsilon^2 \sin \gamma \cos \gamma}{2(1 - \epsilon \cos \gamma)} \right] \right\}$$

$$= \frac{6\omega_j \cdot \mu \left(\dfrac{r_j}{C}\right)^2}{(1 - \epsilon^2)^{3/2}} \left\{ \gamma - \epsilon \sin \gamma - \left[\frac{\gamma(2 + \epsilon^2) - 4\epsilon \sin \gamma + \epsilon^2 \sin \gamma \cos \gamma}{2\left(1 - \epsilon\left(-\dfrac{\epsilon}{2}\right)\right)} \right] \right\}$$

$$\dots \left(\because \ \text{using } \cos \gamma = -\frac{\epsilon}{2} \right)$$

$$= \frac{6\omega_j \cdot \mu \left(\dfrac{r_j}{C}\right)^2}{(1 - \epsilon^2)^{3/2}} \left\{ \gamma - \epsilon \sin \gamma - \left[\frac{r(2 + \epsilon^2) - 4\epsilon \sin \gamma + \epsilon^2 \sin \gamma \cos \gamma}{(2 + \epsilon^2)} \right] \right\}$$

$$= \frac{6\omega_j \cdot \mu \left(\dfrac{r_j}{C}\right)^2}{(1 - \epsilon^2)^{3/2}} \left[\frac{\gamma(2 + \epsilon^2) - \epsilon \sin \gamma(2 + \epsilon^2) - \gamma(2 + \epsilon^2) + 4\epsilon \sin \gamma - \epsilon^2 \sin \gamma \cos \gamma}{(2 + \epsilon^2)} \right]$$

$$= \frac{6\omega_j \cdot \mu \left(\frac{r_j}{C}\right)^2}{(1-\epsilon^2)^{3/2}} \left\{ \frac{-2\epsilon \sin\gamma - \epsilon^3 \sin\gamma + 4\epsilon \sin\gamma - \epsilon^2 \sin\gamma \cos\gamma}{(2+\epsilon^2)} \right\}$$

$$= \frac{6\omega_j \cdot \mu \left(\frac{r_j}{C}\right)^2}{(1-\epsilon^2)^{3/2}} \left\{ \frac{2\epsilon \sin\gamma - \epsilon^2 \sin\gamma (\epsilon + \cos\gamma)}{(2+\epsilon^2)} \right\}$$

$$P = \frac{6\omega_j \cdot \mu \left(\frac{r_j}{C}\right)^2}{(1-\epsilon^2)^{3/2}} \left\{ \frac{2 - \epsilon (\epsilon + \cos\gamma)}{(2+\epsilon^2)} \right\} \epsilon \sin\gamma \qquad \text{... (3.42)}$$

This is an equation for pressure distribution in terms of Sommerfeld variable γ.

Dimensionless form of this equation can be written as,

$$\left(\frac{P}{6\omega_j \cdot \mu \left(\frac{r_j}{C}\right)^2} \right) = \frac{\epsilon \sin\gamma}{(1-\epsilon^2)^{3/2}} \left\{ \frac{2 - \epsilon (\epsilon + \cos\gamma)}{(2+\epsilon^2)} \right\}$$

$$P^* = \frac{\epsilon \sin\gamma}{(1-\epsilon^2)^{3/2}} \left\{ \frac{2 - \epsilon (\epsilon + \cos\gamma)}{(2+\epsilon^2)} \right\} \qquad \text{... (3.43)}$$

Converting above form into 'ϕ' variable,

$$P^* = \frac{\epsilon}{(1-\epsilon^2)^{3/2}} \cdot \frac{\sqrt{1-\epsilon^2} \cdot \sin\phi}{(1+\epsilon \cos\phi)} \left[\frac{2 - \epsilon \left(\epsilon + \dfrac{\epsilon + \cos\phi}{1 + \epsilon \cos\phi} \right)}{(2+\epsilon^2)} \right]$$

$$= \frac{\epsilon \sin\phi}{(1-\epsilon^2)(1+\epsilon \cos\phi)} \left[\frac{2 - \dfrac{\epsilon (\epsilon + \epsilon^2 \cos\phi + \epsilon + \cos\phi)}{(1+\epsilon \cos\phi)}}{(2+\epsilon^2)} \right]$$

$$= \frac{\epsilon \sin\phi}{(1-\epsilon^2)(1+\epsilon \cos\phi)} \left[\frac{2 + 2\epsilon \cos\phi - 2\epsilon^2 - \epsilon^3 \cos\phi - \epsilon \cos\phi}{(1+\epsilon \cos\phi)(2+\epsilon^2)} \right]$$

$$= \frac{\epsilon \sin\phi}{(1-\epsilon^2)(1+\epsilon \cos\phi)^2 (2+\epsilon^2)} [2(1-\epsilon^2) + \epsilon \cos\phi - \epsilon^3 \cos\phi]$$

$$= \frac{\epsilon \sin\phi}{(1-\epsilon^2)(1+\epsilon \cos\phi)^2 (2+\epsilon^2)} [2(1-\epsilon^2) + \epsilon \cos\phi (1-\epsilon^2)]$$

$$= \frac{\epsilon \sin\phi (1-\epsilon^2) [2 + \epsilon \cos\phi]}{(1-\epsilon^2)(1+\epsilon \cos\phi)^2 (2+\epsilon^2)}$$

$$\therefore \quad P^* = \frac{\epsilon \sin\phi (2 + \epsilon \cos\phi)}{(2+\epsilon^2)(1+\epsilon \cos\phi)^2} \qquad \text{... (3.44)}$$

This dimensionless form of pressure in terms of 'ϕ' variable is known as 'Harrison's Equation'.

Pressure in terms of 'ϕ' variable is given by,

$$P = 6\omega_j \cdot \mu \left(\frac{r_j}{C}\right)^2 \cdot \frac{\epsilon \sin \phi \, (2 + \epsilon \cos \phi)}{(2 + \epsilon^2)(1 + \epsilon \cos \phi)^2} \qquad \ldots (3.45)$$

When $\phi = 0$, $\gamma = 0$ $\therefore P^* = 0$

$\phi = \pi$ $P^* = 0$

$\phi = 2\pi$ $P^* = 0$

When $\phi = \phi_m$, $P = P_m$ and $h = h_m$ (i.e. Peak pressure P_m occurs when $\phi = \phi_m$)

We have,

$$h_m = C(1 + \epsilon \cos \phi_m)$$

$$= C\left[\frac{1 - \epsilon^2}{1 - \epsilon \cos \bar{\gamma}}\right]$$

$$= C\left[\frac{1 - \epsilon^2}{1 - \epsilon\left(-\dfrac{\epsilon}{2}\right)}\right] \qquad \ldots \left(\because \text{ Substituting } \cos \bar{\gamma} = -\frac{\epsilon}{2}\right)$$

$$= \frac{C(1 - \epsilon^2)}{1 + \dfrac{\epsilon^2}{2}}$$

$$\therefore \qquad h_m = \frac{2C(1 - \epsilon^2)}{2 + \epsilon^2} \qquad \ldots (3.46)$$

$$\therefore \quad C(1 + \epsilon \cos \phi_m) = \frac{2C(1 - \epsilon^2)}{2 + \epsilon^2}$$

$$\epsilon \cos \phi_m = \frac{2(1 - \epsilon^2)}{2 + \epsilon^2} - 1$$

$$\epsilon \cos \phi_m = \frac{2 - 2\epsilon^2 - 2 - \epsilon^2}{2 + \epsilon^2}$$

$$\epsilon \cos \phi_m = \frac{-3\epsilon^2}{2 + \epsilon^2}$$

$$\therefore \qquad \cos \phi_m = \frac{-3\epsilon}{2 + \epsilon^2} \Rightarrow \phi_m = \cos^{-1}\left(\frac{-3\epsilon}{2 + \epsilon^2}\right)$$

$$\sin \phi_m = \sqrt{1 - \cos^2 \phi_m}$$

$$= \sqrt{1 - \left(\frac{-3\epsilon}{2 + \epsilon^2}\right)^2} = \sqrt{\frac{4 + 4\epsilon^2 + \epsilon^4 - 9\epsilon^2}{(2 + \epsilon^2)^2}}$$

$$\sin \phi_m = \frac{\sqrt{4 - 5\epsilon^2 + \epsilon^4}}{(2 + \epsilon^2)}$$

We have,
$$P^* = \frac{\epsilon \sin \phi}{(2 + \epsilon^2)} \cdot \frac{(2 + \epsilon \cos \phi)}{(1 + \epsilon \cos \phi)^2}$$

$$P_m^* = \frac{\epsilon \sin \phi_m}{2 + \epsilon^2} \cdot \frac{2 + \epsilon \cos \phi_m}{(1 + \epsilon \cos \phi_m)^2}$$

$$= \frac{\epsilon \sqrt{4 - 5\epsilon^2 + \epsilon^4}}{(2 + \epsilon^2)^2} \cdot \frac{2 + \epsilon \left(\dfrac{-3\epsilon}{2 + \epsilon^2}\right)}{\left[1 + \epsilon \left(\dfrac{-3\epsilon}{2 + \epsilon^2}\right)\right]^2}$$

$$= \frac{\epsilon \sqrt{4 - 5\epsilon^2 + \epsilon^4} \,(4 + 2\epsilon^2 - 3\epsilon^2)}{(2 + \epsilon^2)^2 \,(2 + \epsilon^2 - 3\epsilon^2)^2}$$

$$= \frac{\epsilon \sqrt{4 - 5\epsilon^2 + \epsilon^4} \cdot (4 - \epsilon^2)}{(2 + \epsilon^2)^2 \,(2 - 2\epsilon^2)^2}$$

$$\therefore \quad P_m^* = \frac{\epsilon \sqrt{4 - 5\epsilon^2 + \epsilon^4} \,(4 - \epsilon^2)}{4(2 + \epsilon^2)^2 \,(1 - \epsilon^2)^2} \qquad \qquad \text{... (3.47)}$$

Now, when $\epsilon = 0 \Rightarrow \cos \phi_m = \dfrac{-3\epsilon}{2 + \epsilon^2}$

(Concentric bearing condition)

$$\phi_m = \cos^{-1}(0)$$

i.e.
$$\phi_m = \frac{\pi}{2}$$

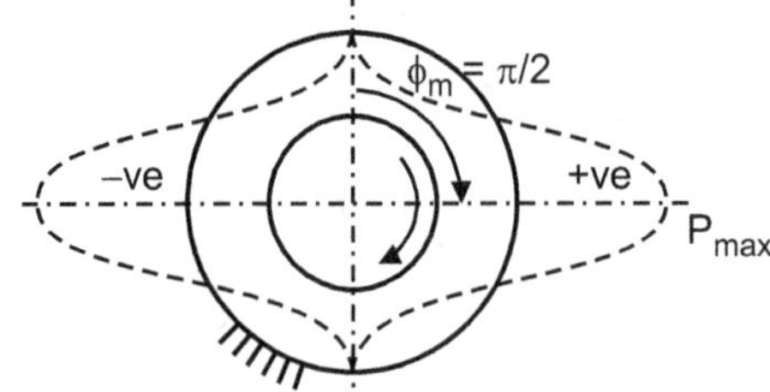

Fig. 3.26

When $\epsilon = 1 \Rightarrow \cos \phi_m = \dfrac{-3}{2 + 1} = -1$

$$\therefore \quad \phi_m = \cos^{-1}(-1)$$

$$m = \pi$$

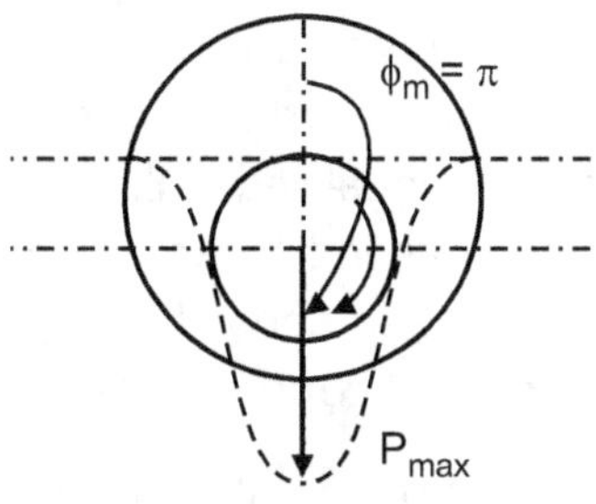

Fig. 3.27

Fig. 3.28 illustrates variation of circumferential pressure distribution (i.e. dimensionless pressure variation) P* versus circumferential co-ordinate ϕ.

- Dimensionless pressure is plotted along y-axis.

- Circumferential co-ordinate ϕ is plotted along x-axis.

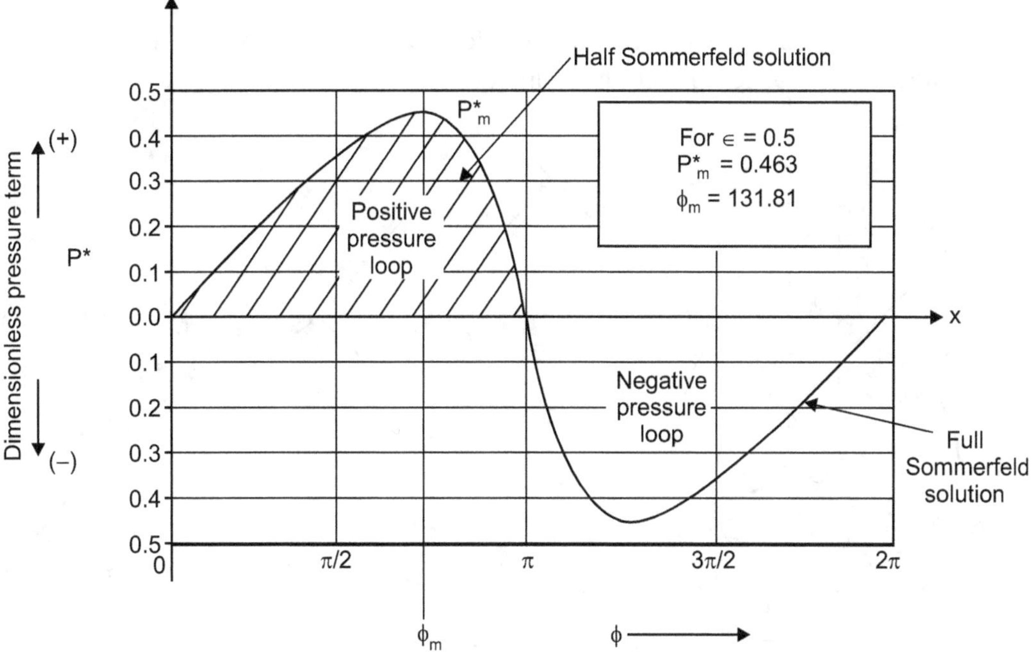

Circumferential dimensionless pressure (P*) variation w.r.t. circumferential co-ordinate (ϕ)

Fig. 3.28

Conclusions :

- The resulting pressure distribution turns out to be antisymmetric about $\theta = \pi$, thus giving negative pressure in one half (i.e. in divergent region from $\phi = \pi$ to $\phi = 2\pi$) of the bearing equal in magnitude to the positive pressure in the other half (i.e. in convergent region from $\phi = 0$ to $\phi = \pi$).

- Large values of negative pressures can be encountered in the presence of high ambient pressures, as in case of a nuclear pressurized water system or a deep submerged submarine. In this situation, conventional lubricants cannot withstand negative pressure, and the liquid fluid in divergent region (from $\phi = \pi$ to $\phi = 2\pi$) will cavitate with gases dissolved in the fluid. Thus, the idealised full journal bearing solution using full Sommerfeld boundary conditions has led to an erroneous result, and it does not take into consideration the cavitation phenomena. This is a major limitation of long journal bearing solution using full Sommerfeld condition (i.e. $\phi = 0$ to $\phi = 2\pi$).

This approach lead to analysis of journal bearing in convergent film region only which is known as half Sommerfeld solution (i.e. from $\phi = 0$ to $\phi = \pi$).

- In dimensionless form, the fluid pressure distribution around the bearing circumference is a function of eccentricity ratio ($\in$). Thus, $\in$ is a parameter which directly affects the load-carrying capacity of bearing.

Load-Carrying Capacity of Infinitely Long Journal Bearing using Full Sommerfeld Condition :

Fig. 3.29 shows the components of load on journal bearing (i.e. radial component in z-direction and tangential component in x-direction).

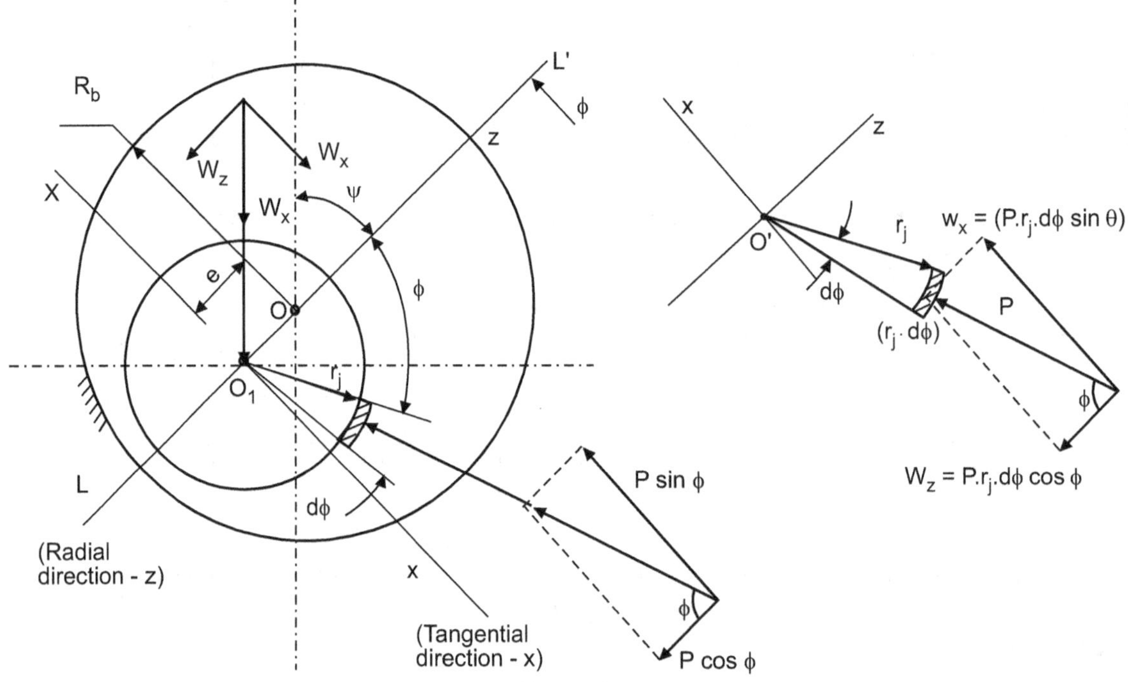

Fig. 3.29

Consider an element $d\phi$ at an angle ϕ from maximum fluid-film thickness (h_{max}), having circumferential length ($r_j \cdot d\phi$).

Let P be the pressure acting on element.

Pressure load acting on element = (Circumferential length of element) $\times$ P

$$= r_j \cdot d\phi \cdot P \times 1$$

Resolving pressure load along x-axis (i.e. perpendicular to the line of centres)

$$= r_j \cdot d\phi \times 1 \times P$$

Total load acting along x-axis,

$$W_x = \int_0^{2\pi} r_j \cdot d\phi \cdot P \cdot \sin \phi$$

$$= r_j \int_0^{2\pi} P \cdot \sin \phi \cdot d\phi$$

Integrating by parts ... $\left[\int AB \, dx = A \int B - \int \int B \cdot \dfrac{dA}{dx} \cdot dx \right]$

$$= r_j \left[P \int_0^{2\pi} \sin \phi - \int \int \sin \phi \frac{dP}{d\phi} \cdot d\phi \right]$$

$$= r_j \left[(- P \cos \phi)_0^{2\pi} - \int_0^{2\pi} - \cos \phi \cdot \frac{dP}{d\phi} \cdot d\phi \right]$$

$$= r_j \left\{ [- P - (-P)] + \int_0^{2\pi} \cos \phi \frac{dP}{d\phi} \cdot d\phi \right\}$$

$$\therefore \qquad W_x = r_j \int_0^{2\pi} \cos \phi \cdot \frac{dP}{d\phi} \cdot d\phi$$

Resolving elemental load along z-direction

$$= - r_j \cdot d\phi \times 1 \times P \cdot \cos \phi$$

Total load along z-axis,

$$W_z = - \int_0^{2\pi} r_j \cdot d\phi \cdot P \cdot \cos \phi$$

$$= - r_j \int_0^{2\pi} P \cdot \cos \phi \cdot d\phi$$

$$= - r_j \left[P \int_0^{2\pi} \cos \phi - \int \int \cos \phi \cdot \frac{dP}{d\phi} \cdot d\phi \right]$$

$$= -r_j \left[P \cdot (\sin \phi)_0^{2\pi} - \int_0^{2\pi} \sin \phi \cdot \frac{dP}{d\phi} \cdot d\phi \right]$$

$$= -r_j \left[0 - \int_0^{2\pi} \sin \phi \cdot \frac{dP}{d\phi} \cdot d\phi \right]$$

$$W_z = r_j \int_0^{2\pi} \sin \phi \cdot \frac{dP}{d\phi} \; d\phi$$

Substituting value of $\left(\dfrac{dP}{d\phi} \right)$ as,

$$\frac{dP}{d\phi} = 6\omega_j \cdot \left(\frac{r_j}{C} \right)^2 \cdot \mu \left[\frac{1}{(1 + \epsilon \cos \phi)^2} - \frac{h_m}{C(1 + \epsilon \cos \phi)^3} \right]$$

$$\therefore \quad W_x = 6\omega_j \cdot r_j \cdot \mu \left(\frac{r_j}{C} \right)^2 \int_0^{2\pi} \left[\underbrace{\frac{\cos \phi}{(1 + \epsilon \cos \phi)^2}}_{I_1} - \underbrace{\frac{h_m \cdot \cos \phi}{C(1 + \epsilon \cos \phi)^3}}_{I_2} \right] d\phi$$

$$\text{and} \quad W_z = 6\omega_j \cdot r_j \cdot \mu \left(\frac{r_j}{C} \right)^2 \int_0^{2\pi} \left[\underbrace{\frac{\sin \phi}{(1 + \epsilon \cos \phi)^2}}_{I_3} - \underbrace{\frac{h_m \cdot \sin \phi}{C(1 + \epsilon \cos \phi)^3}}_{I_4} \right] d\phi$$

Solving integration by parts I_1, I_2, I_3 and I_4,

$$I_1 = \int_0^{2\pi} \frac{\cos \phi}{(1 + \epsilon \cos \phi)^2} \cdot d\phi$$

Substitute,

$$\frac{\cos \phi}{(1 + \epsilon \cos \phi)^2} = \frac{1}{\epsilon (1 + \epsilon \cos \phi)} - \frac{1}{\epsilon (1 + \epsilon \cos \phi)^2}$$

$$\therefore \quad I_1 = \int_0^{2\pi} \left[\frac{1}{\epsilon (1 + \epsilon \cos \phi)} - \frac{1}{\epsilon (1 + \epsilon \cos \phi)^2} \right] d\phi$$

$$= \frac{1}{\epsilon} \int_0^{2\pi} \left[\frac{1 - \epsilon \cos \gamma}{1 - \epsilon^2} - \frac{(1 - \epsilon \cos \gamma)^2}{(1 - \epsilon^2)^2} \right] \frac{(1 - \epsilon^2)^{1/2}}{1 - \epsilon \cos \gamma} \cdot d\gamma$$

$$= \frac{1}{\epsilon} \left[\int_0^{2\pi} \left[\frac{d\gamma}{(1-\epsilon^2)^{1/2}} - \frac{1-\epsilon\cos\gamma}{(1-\epsilon^2)^{3/2}} \, d\gamma \right] \right]$$

$$= \frac{1}{\epsilon} \left[\frac{\gamma}{(1-\epsilon^2)^{1/2}} - \frac{(\gamma-\epsilon\sin\gamma)}{(1-\epsilon^2)^{3/2}} \right]_0^{2\pi} = \frac{1}{\epsilon\,(1-\epsilon^2)^{1/2}} \left[\gamma - \frac{(\gamma-\epsilon\sin\gamma)}{(1-\epsilon^2)} \right]_0^{2\pi}$$

$$= \frac{1}{\epsilon\,(1-\epsilon^2)^{1/2}} \left[2\pi - \frac{(2\pi-0)}{1-\epsilon^2} \right]$$

$$= \frac{1}{\epsilon\,(1-\epsilon^2)^{1/2}} \left[\frac{2\pi - 2\pi\epsilon^2 - 2\epsilon}{1-\epsilon^2} \right] = \frac{1}{\epsilon\,(1-\epsilon^2)^{1/2}} \left[-\frac{2\pi\epsilon^2}{1-\epsilon^2} \right]$$

$$\therefore \quad I_1 = \frac{-2\pi\epsilon}{(1-\epsilon^2)^{3/2}}$$

$$I_2 = \int_0^{2\pi} \frac{\cos\phi}{(1+\epsilon\cos\phi)^3} \cdot d\phi$$

$$= \int_0^{2\pi} \left(\frac{\cos\gamma-\epsilon}{1-\epsilon\cos\gamma} \right) \cdot \left(\frac{1-\epsilon\cos\gamma}{1-\epsilon^2} \right)^3 \cdot \frac{(1-\epsilon^2)^{1/2}}{(1-\epsilon\cos\gamma)} \cdot d\gamma$$

$$= \int_0^{2\pi} \frac{(\cos\gamma-\epsilon)\,(1-\epsilon\cos\gamma)}{(1-\epsilon^2)^{5/2}} \cdot d\gamma$$

$$= \int_0^{2\pi} \frac{\cos\gamma - \epsilon\cos^2\gamma - \epsilon + \epsilon^2\cos\gamma}{(1-\epsilon^2)^{5/2}} \cdot d\gamma$$

$$= \int_0^{2\pi} \frac{\cos\gamma - \epsilon\left(\dfrac{1+\cos 2\gamma}{2}\right) - \epsilon + \epsilon^2\cos\gamma}{(1-\epsilon^2)^{5/2}} \cdot d\gamma$$

$$= \frac{1}{(1-\epsilon^2)^{5/2}} \cdot \int_0^{2\pi} \left[(1+\epsilon^2)\cos\gamma - \epsilon\left(\frac{3+\cos 2\gamma}{2}\right) \right] d\gamma$$

$$= \frac{1}{(1-\epsilon^2)^{5/2}} \left[(1+\epsilon^2)\sin\gamma - \epsilon\left(\frac{3\gamma + \dfrac{\sin 2\gamma}{2}}{2}\right) \right]_0^{2\pi}$$

$$= \frac{1}{(1-\epsilon^2)^{5/2}} \left[(1+\epsilon^2) \sin\gamma - \frac{3\epsilon\gamma}{2} - \frac{\epsilon\sin 2\gamma}{4} \right]_0^{2\pi}$$

$$= \left[0 - \frac{3\epsilon \cdot 2\pi}{2} - 0 \right] \frac{1}{(1-\epsilon^2)^{5/2}}$$

$$\therefore \quad I_2 = \frac{-3\pi\epsilon}{(1-\epsilon^2)^{5/2}}$$

$$I_3 = \int_0^{2\pi} \frac{\sin\phi}{(1+\epsilon\cos\phi)^2} \cdot d\phi$$

Let
$$(1+\epsilon\cos\phi) = z$$
$$-\epsilon\sin\phi \cdot d\phi = dz$$
$$\sin\phi \, d\phi = \frac{dz}{-\epsilon}$$

$$I_3 = \int_0^{2\pi} -\frac{dz}{z^2\epsilon} = -\frac{1}{\epsilon}\left[-\frac{3}{z} \right]_0^{2\pi}$$

$$= \frac{3}{\epsilon}\left[\frac{1}{(1+\epsilon\cos\phi)} \right]_0^{2\pi} = 0 \Rightarrow I_3 = 0$$

$$I_4 = \int_0^{2\pi} \frac{\sin\phi}{(1+\epsilon\cos\phi)^3} \cdot d\phi = \int_0^{2\pi} \left(\frac{dz}{-\epsilon} \right) \frac{1}{z^3}$$

$$= -\frac{1}{\epsilon}\left[\frac{-4}{z^2} \right]_0^{2\pi} = 0 \Rightarrow I_4 = 0$$

Substituting values of integrals I_1 to I_4 in equation for W_x,

$$\therefore \quad W_x = 6\omega_j \cdot r_j \cdot \mu \left(\frac{r_j}{C} \right)^2 \left[\frac{-2\pi\epsilon}{(1-\epsilon^2)^{3/2}} + \frac{h_m}{C} \cdot \frac{3\pi\epsilon}{(1-\epsilon^2)^{5/2}} \right]$$

$$= 6\omega_j \cdot r_j \cdot \mu \left(\frac{r_j}{C} \right)^2 \left[\frac{-2\pi\epsilon}{(1-\epsilon^2)^{3/2}} + \frac{2C(1-\epsilon^2)}{C(2+\epsilon^2)} \cdot \frac{3\pi\epsilon}{(1-\epsilon^2)^{5/2}} \right]$$

$$\dots \left(\because \text{ using value of } h_m = \frac{2C(1-\epsilon^2)}{2+\epsilon^2} \right)$$

$$= 6\omega_j \cdot r_j \cdot \mu \left(\frac{r_j}{C} \right)^2 \left[\frac{-2\pi\epsilon}{(1-\epsilon^2)^{3/2}} + \frac{6\pi\epsilon}{(2+\epsilon^2)(1-\epsilon^2)^{3/2}} \right]$$

$$= 6\omega_j \cdot r_j \cdot \mu \left(\frac{r_j}{C} \right)^2 \left[-2\pi\epsilon + \frac{6\pi\epsilon}{(2+\epsilon^2)} \right] \frac{1}{(1-\epsilon^2)^{3/2}}$$

$$= 6\omega_j \cdot r_j \cdot \mu \left(\frac{r_j}{C}\right)^2 \frac{1}{(1 - \epsilon^2)^{3/2}} \left[\frac{-4\pi\epsilon - 2\pi\epsilon^3 + 6\pi\epsilon}{(2 + \epsilon^2)}\right]$$

$$= 6\omega_j \cdot r_j \cdot \mu \left(\frac{r_j}{C}\right)^2 \frac{1}{(1 - \epsilon^2)^{3/2}} \left[\frac{2\pi\epsilon(1 - \epsilon^2)}{(2 + \epsilon^2)}\right]$$

$$W_x = 12\omega_j \cdot r_j \cdot \mu \left(\frac{r_j}{C}\right)^2 \left[\frac{\pi\epsilon}{(1 - \epsilon^2)^{1/2} \cdot (2 + \epsilon^2)}\right]$$

and
$$W_z = 0$$

$\therefore$ Resultant load-carrying capacity,

$$W_r = \sqrt{W_x^2 + W_z^2}$$

$\therefore$
$$W_r = 12\omega_j \cdot r_j \cdot \mu \left(\frac{r_j}{C}\right)^2 \left[\frac{\pi\epsilon}{(1 - \epsilon^2)^{1/2} (2 + \epsilon^2)}\right] \qquad \text{... (3.48)}$$

Now,
$$\tan \psi = \frac{W_x}{W_z} = \infty$$

$\therefore$
$$\psi = 90°$$

$\therefore$ Locus of centre of shaft is perpendicular to the load vector.

Thus,   as $\epsilon \to 0 \Rightarrow W_r \to 0$

as $\epsilon \to 1 \Rightarrow W_r \to \infty$

From above condition as eccentricity ratio increases, the load-carrying capacity of hydrodynamic bearing increases.

3.6.2 Infinitely Short Journal Bearing

It is also called Infinitely Short Approximation or Ocvirk Short Bearing Theory (1952).

Definition :

A journal bearing whose length to diameter ratio $\left(\text{i.e. } \dfrac{l}{d}\right)$ is less than or equals to $\dfrac{1}{2}$, then it can be considered to be infinitely short bearing or narrow bearing.

i.e. for infinitely short bearing,

$$\frac{l}{d} \le 0.5 \quad \text{or} \quad l \le 0.5\,d$$

where, $\dfrac{l}{d}$ is important geometric parameter in the design of journal bearing.

Ocvirk's Equation :

DuBois and Ocvirk in 1952 derived a solution of Reynold's equation applicable for bearing whose length is much shorter than their diameter.

Considerations or Assumptions :

- As the length to diameter ratio is less than 0.5, the flow in axial direction

  (i.e. y-direction) and end leakage is much larger.

- Michell (1929) and Cardullo (1930) suggested that the flow conditions in the direction of rotation do not affect the pressure.

- According to Ocvirk (1952), the pressure induced circumferential flow is very very small and can be neglected.

  i.e. $\qquad\qquad q_\phi' = 0$

- For pure tangential and unidirectional motion, squeeze term is zero and $\bar{v} = \dfrac{v_a + v_b}{2} = 0$.

  Also tangential velocity of bearing surface $u_a = 0$.

  $$\therefore \qquad \bar{u} = \frac{u_a + u_b}{2} = \left(\frac{u_b}{2}\right)$$

- Fluid is incompressible for which dynamic viscosity is constant (μ = constant) and also density ρ = constant.

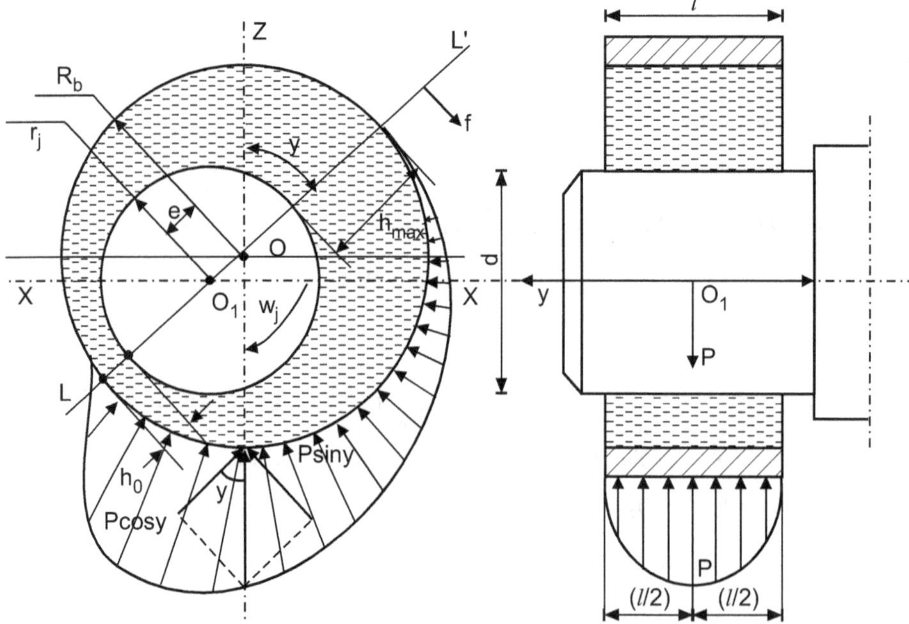

Fig. 3.30 : Infinitely short journal bearing

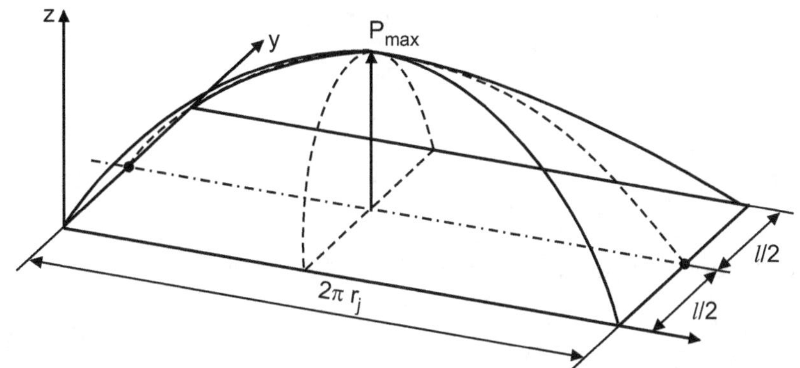

Fig. 3.31 : Development of the shaft surface

Now, fluid flow rate per unit width,

$$q_x = -\frac{h^3}{12\mu} \cdot \frac{\partial P}{\partial x} + \frac{(u_a + u_b)}{2} \cdot h$$

$$= -\frac{h^3}{12\mu} \cdot \frac{\partial P}{\partial x} + \frac{u_b \cdot h}{2} \qquad \text{... (Referring to assumption (iv))}$$

Now, converting translational co-ordinates to rotational co-ordinates,

$$dx = r_j \cdot d\phi$$

$$\therefore \qquad q_\phi = -\frac{h^3}{12\mu} \cdot \frac{\partial P}{r_j \cdot d\phi} + \frac{u_b \cdot h}{2}$$

Neglecting $\qquad q_\phi = -\frac{h^3}{12\mu} \cdot \frac{\partial P}{r_j \cdot d\phi} \qquad \text{... (As per assumption (iii))}$

$$\therefore \qquad q_\phi = \frac{u_b \cdot h}{2}$$

Also, $\qquad q_y = -\frac{h^3}{12\mu} \cdot \frac{\partial P}{\partial y} + \frac{v_a + v_b}{2} \cdot h$

$$q_y = -\frac{h^3}{12\mu} \cdot \frac{\partial P}{\partial y} \qquad \text{... [From assumption (iv)]}$$

Now, $\qquad \dfrac{\partial P_{max}}{\partial y} = \dfrac{P_{max}}{(L/2)} = \dfrac{2P_{max}}{L}$

and $\qquad \dfrac{\partial P_{max}}{\partial x} = \dfrac{P_{max}}{\pi \cdot r_j}$

According to proposition of Michell (1929) and Cardullo (1930) that the term $\left(\dfrac{\partial P}{\partial y}\right)$ be

retained and $\left(\dfrac{\partial P}{\partial x}\right)$ be dropped, i.e. $\begin{bmatrix} \text{Pressure variation along} \\ \text{axial i.e. Y-direction} \end{bmatrix} >> \begin{bmatrix} \text{Pressure variation along} \\ \text{X-direction} \end{bmatrix}$

$$\frac{\partial P}{\partial y} >> \frac{\partial P}{\partial x}$$

We have general equation,

$$\frac{\partial}{\partial x}\left[h^3 \frac{\partial P}{\partial x}\right] + \frac{\partial}{\partial y}\left[h^3 \frac{\partial P}{\partial y}\right] = 12\,\bar{u}\,\mu \cdot \frac{\partial h}{\partial x}$$

Using above conditions in given general equation, it becomes,

$$\frac{\partial}{\partial y}\left[h^3 \cdot \frac{\partial P}{\partial y}\right] = 12\left(\frac{u_b}{2}\right) \cdot \mu \frac{\partial h}{\partial x} \qquad \text{... (Refer assumption (iv))}$$

$$\therefore \qquad \frac{\partial}{\partial y}\left[h^3 \frac{\partial P}{\partial y}\right] = 6u_b \cdot \mu \cdot \frac{\partial h}{\partial x}$$

which is a form of Reynold's equation derived by Ocvirk and is governing equation for ISA.

Ocvirk Solution (Short Bearing Approximation) :

We have, $\qquad \dfrac{\partial}{\partial y}\left[h^3 \cdot \dfrac{\partial P}{\partial y}\right] = 6u_b \cdot \mu \cdot \dfrac{\partial h}{\partial x}$

$$\frac{\partial}{\partial y}\left[h^3 \cdot \frac{\partial P}{\partial y}\right] = 6 \cdot r_j \cdot \omega_j \cdot \mu \cdot \frac{\partial h}{r_j\,\partial\phi}$$

Now film thickness is not a function of 'y'.

$\therefore$ Integrating above equation w.r.t. y,

$$h^3 \frac{\partial P}{\partial y} = 6 \cdot \omega_j \cdot \mu \frac{\partial h}{\partial\phi} \int dy$$

$$\frac{\partial P}{\partial y} = \frac{6 \cdot \omega_j \cdot \mu}{h^3} \cdot \frac{\partial h}{\partial\phi} \cdot y + \frac{A}{h^3}$$

Fig. 3.32 : Variation of pressure over length of bearing

Once again integrating above equation w.r.t. 'y',

$$P = \frac{6\,\omega_j \cdot \mu}{h^3} \cdot \frac{\partial h}{\partial \phi} \cdot \frac{y^2}{2} + \frac{A}{h^3} \cdot y + B$$

Substituting initial conditions P = 0 at $y = \pm \dfrac{l}{2}$

(i) Using $y = +\dfrac{l}{2}$,

$$0 = \frac{6\,\omega_j \cdot \mu}{h^3} \cdot \frac{\partial h}{\partial \phi} \cdot \frac{\left(\frac{l}{2}\right)^2}{2} + \frac{A}{h^3}\left(\frac{l}{2}\right) + B$$

$$= \frac{6\,\omega_j \cdot \mu}{h^3} \cdot \frac{\partial h}{\partial \phi} \cdot \frac{l^2}{8} + \frac{A}{h^3} \cdot \frac{l}{2} + B$$

(ii) Using $y = -\dfrac{l}{2}$,

$$0 = \frac{6\,\omega_j \cdot \mu}{h^3} \cdot \frac{\partial h}{\partial \phi} \cdot \frac{l^2}{8} - \frac{A}{h^3} \cdot \frac{l}{2} + B$$

Adding (i) and (ii), we get,

$$0 = 2\left[\frac{6\,\omega_j \cdot \mu}{h^3} \cdot \frac{\partial h}{\partial \phi} \frac{l^2}{8} + B\right]$$

$$B = -\frac{6\,\omega_j \cdot \mu}{h^3} \cdot \frac{\partial h}{\partial \phi} \frac{l^2}{8}$$

Using value of B in equation (ii), we get,

$$A = 0$$

$$\therefore \qquad P = \frac{6\,\omega_j \cdot \mu}{h^3} \cdot \frac{\partial h}{\partial \phi} \cdot \frac{y^2}{2} - \frac{6\,\omega_j \cdot \mu}{h^3} \cdot \frac{\partial h}{\partial \phi} \cdot \frac{l^2}{8}$$

$$P = \frac{3\,\omega_j \cdot \mu}{h^3} \cdot \frac{\partial h}{\partial \phi}\left[y^2 - \frac{l^2}{4}\right] \qquad \qquad \text{... (3.49)}$$

We know that, $\qquad h = C(1 + \epsilon \cos \phi)$

$$\therefore \qquad \frac{\partial h}{\partial \phi} = -C \epsilon \sin \phi$$

$$\therefore \qquad P = \frac{3\,\omega_j \cdot \mu}{h^3}(-C \epsilon \sin \phi)\left[y^2 - \frac{l^2}{4}\right]$$

$$= \frac{3\,\omega_j \cdot \mu}{C^3(1 + \epsilon \cos \phi)^3}(-C \epsilon \sin \phi)\left[y^2 - \frac{l^2}{4}\right]$$

$$\therefore \qquad P = \frac{3\,\omega_j \cdot \mu \epsilon \sin \phi}{C^2(1 + \epsilon \cos \phi)^3}\left[\frac{l^2}{4} - y^2\right] \qquad \qquad \text{... (3.50)}$$

This is the equation for pressure distribution in infinitely short journal bearing and known as 'Ocvirk equation'.

Conclusions :

- Pressure equation is comprising of two terms one related to axial flow and other to the film thickness.

- As similar to long bearing approximation, the term $\sin \phi$ gives a positive circumferential pressure from 0 to π and a negative circumferential pressure from π to 2π.

- $\left[\dfrac{l^2}{4} - y^2\right]$ term indicates that pressure distribution along length (i.e. axial pressure distribution along Y) is 'parabolic' and the term $\left[\dfrac{\sin \phi}{(1 + \in \cos \phi)^3}\right]$ indicates that pressure distribution along circumference (i.e. circumferential pressure distribution) is of trigonometric form.

Maximum Pressure in Fluid Film for Short Journal Bearing :

$$\frac{\partial P}{\partial \phi} = 0$$

$$P = \frac{3\, \omega_j \cdot \mu}{h^3} \cdot \frac{\partial h}{\partial \phi}\left(y^2 - \frac{l^2}{4}\right)$$

$$\frac{\partial P}{\partial \phi} = \left[3\,\mu\,\omega_j \cdot \left(y^2 - \frac{l^2}{4}\right)\right] \cdot \frac{\partial}{\partial \phi}\left(\frac{1}{h^3} \cdot \frac{\partial h}{\partial \phi}\right) = 0$$

$$\therefore 3\,\mu\,\omega_j \cdot \left(y^2 - \frac{l^2}{4}\right)\frac{\partial}{\partial \phi}\left(\frac{1}{h^3} \cdot \frac{\partial h}{\partial \phi}\right) = 0$$

$$\frac{\partial}{\partial \phi}\left(\frac{1}{h^3} \cdot \frac{\partial h}{\partial \phi}\right) = 0$$

$$-3\,h^{-4}\frac{\partial h}{\partial \phi} + \frac{1}{h^3} \cdot \frac{\partial^2 h}{\partial \phi^2} = 0$$

$$-\frac{3}{h} \cdot \frac{\partial h}{\partial \phi} + \frac{\partial^2 h}{\partial \phi^2} = 0$$

Substituting $h = C(1 + \in \cos \phi)$, we can get quadratic equation,

$$2\in \cos^2 \phi_m - \cos \phi_m - 3\in = 0$$

$$\therefore \qquad \cos \phi_m = \frac{1 \pm \sqrt{1 + 24\in^2}}{4\in}$$

Ignoring positive sign,

$$\cos \phi_m = \frac{1 - \sqrt{1 + 24\in^2}}{4\in} \cdot \frac{1 + \sqrt{1 + 24\in^2}}{1 + \sqrt{1 + 24\in^2}} = \frac{1 - (1 + 24\in^2)}{4\in(1 + \sqrt{1 + 24\in^2})}$$

$$\cos \phi_m = \frac{-24\in^2}{4\in + 4\in(\sqrt{1 + 24\in^2})} \qquad \qquad \text{... (3.51)}$$

when $\in \rightarrow 0$, $\phi_m = \pm\dfrac{\pi}{2}$ and when $\in \rightarrow 1$, $\phi_m = \pm\pi$

Maximum pressure at $\phi = \phi_m$

$$P = \frac{3\mu \cdot \omega_j \cdot \in}{C^2} \left[\frac{l^2}{4} - y^2 \right] \frac{\sin \phi}{(1 + \in \cos \phi)^3} \qquad \text{... (for } 0 \le \phi \le \pi)$$

$P = P_{max}$ at $\phi = \phi_m$ and $y = 0$.

$$P_{max} = \frac{3\mu \cdot \omega_j \cdot \in}{C^2} \left(\frac{l^2}{4} \right) \frac{\sin \phi_m}{(1 + \in \cos \phi_m)^3}$$

Using value of $\cos \phi_m$,

$$\phi_m = \cos^{-1} \left[\frac{-24\in^2}{4\in + 4\in \sqrt{1 + 24\in^2}} \right]$$

$$P_{max} = \frac{3\mu \cdot \omega_j \cdot \in l^4}{4C^2(1 + \in \cos \phi_m)^3} \cdot \sin \left[\cos^{-1} \left(\frac{-24\in^2}{4\in + 4\in \sqrt{1 + 24\in^2}} \right) \right] \qquad \text{... (3.52)}$$

Load-Carrying Capacity of Short Journal Bearing :

Load component of pressure perpendicular to the line of centres i.e. W_x is given by,

$$W_x = 2 \int_0^\pi \int_0^{l/2} P \cdot r_j \cdot d\phi \cdot \sin \phi \cdot dy$$

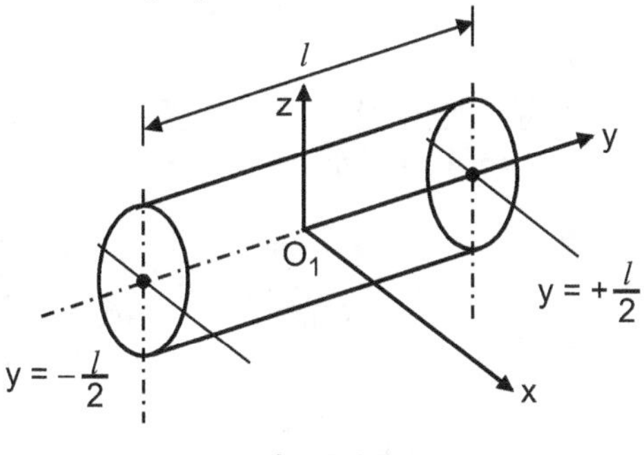

Fig. 3.33

And load component of pressure along the line of centres i.e. W_z,

$$W_z = -2 \int_0^\pi \int_0^{l/2} P \cdot r_j \cdot d\phi \cdot \cos \phi \cdot dy$$

Now,

$$W_x = 2 \int_0^\pi \int_0^{l/2} \frac{3\mu \cdot \omega_j \cdot \in}{C^2} \left(\frac{l^2}{4} - y^2 \right) \cdot \frac{\sin \phi}{(1 + \in \cos \phi)^3} \cdot r_j \cdot \sin \phi \cdot d\phi \cdot dy$$

$$= -6 \int_0^\pi \frac{\mu \cdot \omega_j \cdot \in \cdot r_j}{C^2} \frac{\sin^2 \phi}{(1 + \in \cos \phi)^3} \cdot d\phi \int_0^{l/2} \left(y^2 - \frac{l^2}{4} \right) dy$$

Let,

$$I_1 = \int_0^{l/2} \left(y^2 - \frac{l^2}{4}\right) dy = \left[\frac{y^3}{3} - \frac{l^2}{4} \cdot y\right]_0^{l/2} = \frac{l^3}{24} - \frac{l^3}{8}$$

$\therefore$

$$I_1 = -\frac{13}{12}$$

$$I_2 = \int_0^{\pi} \frac{\mu \cdot \omega_j \cdot r_j \cdot \in}{C^2} \cdot \frac{\sin^2 \phi}{(1 + \in \cos \phi)^3} \cdot d\phi$$

$$W_x = \frac{-6\mu \cdot \omega_j \cdot r_j \cdot \in}{C^2} \left(-\frac{l^3}{12}\right) \int_0^{\pi} \frac{\sin^2 \phi}{(1 + \in \cos \phi)^3} \cdot d\phi$$

$$= \frac{\mu \cdot \omega_j \cdot r_j \cdot \in \cdot l^3}{2C^2} \cdot \int_0^{\pi} \frac{\sin^2 \phi}{(1 + \in \cos \phi)^3} \cdot d\phi$$

Solving the integral,

$$\int_0^{\pi} \frac{\sin^2 \phi}{(1 + \in \cos \phi)^3} \cdot d\phi$$

$$= \int_0^{\pi} \frac{(1 - \in^2) \sin^2 \gamma}{(1 - \in \cos \gamma)^2} \cdot \frac{(1 - \in \cos \gamma)^3}{(1 - \in^2)^3} \cdot \frac{(1 - \in^2)^{1/2}}{(1 - \in \cos \gamma)} \cdot d\gamma$$

$$= \int_0^{\pi} \frac{\sin^2 \gamma}{(1 - \in^2)^{3/2}} \cdot d\gamma = \frac{1}{(1 - \in^2)^{3/2}} \int_0^{\pi} \frac{1 - \cos 2\gamma}{2} \cdot d\gamma$$

$$= \frac{1}{(1 - \in^2)^{3/2}} \left[\frac{\gamma - \frac{\sin 2\gamma}{2}}{2}\right]_0^{\pi} = \frac{1}{(1 - \in^2)^{3/2}} \left[\frac{\pi - 0}{2}\right]$$

$$= \frac{\pi}{2(1 - \in^2)^{3/2}}$$

Substituting in equation for 'W_x',

$$W_x = \frac{\mu \cdot \omega_j \cdot r_j \cdot \in \cdot l^3 \cdot \pi}{4C^2(1 - \in^2)^{3/2}}$$

Now,

$$W_z = -2 \int_0^{\pi} \int_0^{l/2} P \cdot r_j \cdot \cos \phi \cdot d\phi \cdot dy$$

Substituting value of P,

$$W_z = -2 \int_0^\pi \int_0^{l/2} \frac{3\mu \cdot \omega_j \cdot \in}{C^2} \left(\frac{l^2}{4} - y^2\right) \cdot \frac{\sin \phi}{(1 + \in \cos \phi)^3} \cdot r_j \cdot \cos \phi \cdot d\phi \cdot dy$$

$$= -\frac{6\mu \cdot \omega_j \cdot \in \cdot r_j}{C^2} \int_0^\pi \frac{\sin \phi \cdot \cos \phi \cdot d\phi}{(1 + \in \cos \phi)^3} \int_0^{l/2} \left(\frac{l^2}{4} - y^2\right) dy$$

$$= \frac{6\mu \cdot \omega_j \cdot \in \cdot r_j}{C^2} \int_0^{l/2} \left(y^2 - \frac{l^2}{4}\right) \cdot dy \int_0^\pi \frac{\sin \phi \cdot \cos \phi}{(1 + \in \cos \phi)^3} \cdot d\phi$$

We get,

$$\int_0^{l/2} \left(y^2 - \frac{l^2}{4}\right) dy = -\frac{l^3}{12}$$

and $\displaystyle \int_0^\pi \frac{\sin \phi \cdot \cos \phi}{(1 + \in \cos \phi)^3} \cdot d\phi$

$$= \int_0^\pi \frac{(1 - \in^2)^{1/2} \cdot \sin \gamma}{1 - \in \cos \gamma} \cdot \left(\frac{\cos \gamma - \in}{1 - \in \cos \gamma}\right) \cdot \frac{(1 - \in \cos \gamma)^3}{(1 - \in^2)^3} \cdot \left(\frac{(1 - \in^2)^{1/2}}{1 - \in \cos \gamma}\right) \cdot d\gamma$$

$$= \frac{1}{(1 - \in^2)^2} \cdot \int_0^\pi \sin \gamma (\cos \gamma - \in) \cdot d\gamma$$

Let $\qquad \cos \gamma - \in = z$

$\qquad\qquad - \sin \gamma \, d\gamma = dz$

$$= \frac{1}{(1 - \in^2)^2} \cdot \int_0^\pi - z \, dz = -\frac{1}{(1 - \in^2)^2} \int_0^\pi z \, dz$$

$$= -\frac{1}{(1 - \in^2)^2} \left[\frac{z^2}{2}\right]_0^\pi = -\frac{1}{2(1 - \in^2)^2} [(\cos \gamma - \in)^2]_0^\pi$$

$$= -\frac{1}{2(1 - \in^2)^2} [(-1 - \in)^2 - (1 - \in)^2]$$

$$= -\frac{1}{2(1 - \in^2)^2} [1 + 2\in + \in^2 - (1 - 2\in + \in^2)]$$

$$= -\frac{4\in}{2(1 - \in^2)^2}$$

$$= -\frac{2\in}{2(1 - \in^2)^2}$$

Using integrals in equation for W_z, it becomes

$$W_z = \frac{6\mu \cdot \omega_j \cdot \epsilon \cdot r_j}{C^2} \left(-\frac{l^3}{12}\right) \cdot \left(\frac{-2\epsilon}{(1-\epsilon^2)^2}\right)$$

$$\therefore \quad W_z = \frac{\mu \cdot \omega_j \cdot r_j \cdot l^3}{C^3} \cdot \frac{\epsilon^2}{(1-\epsilon^2)^2}$$

$\therefore$ Total load (W_r),

$$\therefore \quad W_r = \sqrt{W_x^2 + W_z^2}$$

$$\therefore \quad = \sqrt{\left[\frac{\mu \cdot \omega_j \cdot r_j \cdot l^3}{4C^2} \cdot \frac{\pi\epsilon}{(1-\epsilon^2)^{3/2}}\right]^2 + \left[\frac{\mu \cdot \omega_j \cdot r_j \cdot l^3}{C^2} \cdot \frac{\epsilon^2}{(1-\epsilon^2)^2}\right]^2}$$

$$\therefore \quad = \frac{\mu \cdot \omega_j \cdot r_j \cdot l^3}{C^2} \sqrt{\frac{\pi^2\epsilon^2}{16(1-\epsilon^2)^3} + \frac{\epsilon^4}{(1-\epsilon^2)^4}}$$

$$\therefore \quad W_r = \frac{\mu \cdot \omega_j \cdot r_j \cdot l^3}{C^2} \sqrt{\frac{\pi^2\epsilon^2(1-\epsilon^2) + 16\epsilon^4}{16(1-\epsilon^2)^4}}$$

$$\therefore \quad = \frac{\mu \cdot \omega_j \cdot r_j \cdot l^3}{C^2} \sqrt{\frac{\epsilon^2}{16(1-\epsilon^2)^4}(\pi^2(1-\epsilon^2) + 16\epsilon^2)}$$

$$\therefore \quad W_r = \frac{\mu \cdot \omega_j \cdot r_j \cdot l^3}{4C^2} \cdot \frac{\epsilon}{(1-\epsilon^2)^2} [\pi^2(1-\epsilon^2) + 16\epsilon^2]^{1/2} \qquad \text{... (3.53)}$$

This is an equation for total load-carrying capacity of infinitely short journal bearing.

Attitude Angle (ψ) :

Taking ratio of W_x to W_z,

$$\tan\psi = \frac{W_x}{W_z} = \frac{\left[\mu \cdot \dfrac{\omega_j \cdot r_j \cdot l^3}{4C^2} \dfrac{\pi\epsilon}{(1-\epsilon^2)^{3/2}}\right]}{\left[\mu \cdot \dfrac{\omega_j \cdot r_j \cdot l^3}{C^2} \cdot \dfrac{\epsilon^2}{(1-\epsilon^2)^2}\right]} = \frac{\dfrac{\pi}{4}}{\dfrac{\epsilon}{(1-\epsilon^2)^{1/2}}}$$

$$\therefore \quad \tan\psi = \frac{\pi(1-\epsilon^2)^{1/2}}{4\epsilon}$$

$$\therefore \quad \psi = \tan^{-1}\left[\frac{\pi(1-\epsilon^2)^{1/2}}{4\epsilon}\right] \qquad \text{... (3.54)}$$

As $\epsilon \to 0$, $\psi \to \dfrac{\pi}{2}$ and as $\epsilon \to 1$, $\psi \to 0$.

We have,

$$W_r = \frac{\mu \cdot \omega_j \cdot r_j \cdot l^3}{4C^2} \frac{\epsilon}{(1-\epsilon^2)^2} [\pi^2(1-\epsilon^2) + 16\epsilon^2]^{1/2}$$

$$\frac{4\,\omega_r \cdot C^2}{\mu \cdot u_b \cdot l^3} = \frac{\epsilon}{(1-\epsilon^2)^2} [\pi^2 - \pi^2\epsilon^2 + 16\epsilon^2]^{1/2}$$

$$= \frac{\pi\in}{(1-\in^2)^2}\left[1-\in^2+\frac{16\in^2}{\pi^2}\right]^{1/2} = \frac{\pi\in}{(1-\in^2)^2}\left[\in^2\left(\frac{16}{\pi^2}-1\right)+1\right]^{1/2}$$

$$\therefore \quad \frac{4\,\omega_r\cdot C^2}{\mu\cdot u_b\cdot l^3} = \frac{\pi\in}{(1-\in^2)^2}[0.62\in^2+1]^{1/2} \qquad \text{... (3.55)}$$

Dimensionless form of Load-Carrying Capacity (W_r^*) for Infinitely Short Journal Bearing :

We have an equation for load-carrying capacity,

$$W_r = \frac{\mu\cdot\omega_j\cdot r_j\cdot l^3}{4C^2}\cdot\frac{\in}{(1-\in^2)^2}[\pi^2(1-\in^2)+16\in^2]^{1/2}$$

$$\therefore \quad \frac{4C^2\cdot W_r}{\mu\cdot\omega_j\cdot r_j\cdot l^3} = \frac{\pi\in}{(1-\in^2)^2}[1+0.62\in^2]^{1/2}$$

$$\therefore \quad \left[\frac{\dfrac{W_r}{l}}{\mu\cdot r_j\cdot\omega_j}\cdot\left(\frac{C}{r_j}\right)^2\right]\left[\frac{4r_j^2}{l^2}\right] = \frac{\pi\in}{(1-\in^2)^2}[1+0.62\in^2]^{1/2}$$

The bracketed quantity $\left[\dfrac{\dfrac{W_r}{l}}{\mu\cdot\omega_j\cdot r_j}\left(\frac{C}{r_j}\right)^2\right] = W_r^*$ is non-dimensional form of load, therefore, above equation becomes

$$W_r^*\cdot\frac{4r_j^2}{l^2} = \frac{\pi\in}{(1-\in^2)^2}[1+0.62\in^2]^{1/2}$$

Introducing $(d^2=4r_j^2)$ in above equation, it becomes

$$W_r^*\times\left(\frac{d}{l}\right)^2 = \frac{\pi\in}{(1-\in^2)^2}[1+0.62\in^2]^{1/2}$$

$$W_r^* = \left(\frac{l}{d}\right)^2\frac{\pi\in}{(1-\in^2)^2}[1+0.62\in^2]^{1/2} \qquad \text{... (3.56)}$$

Relation between Sommerfeld Number (S) and Non-Dimensional Load (W_r^*) :

We have a standard non-dimensional form of Sommerfeld number S as,

$$S = \mu\cdot\omega_j\cdot\frac{l\cdot d}{W_r}\left(\frac{r_j}{C}\right)^2 \qquad \text{... (3.57)}$$

Rearranging the terms, we can write above equation as,

$$S = \frac{\mu\cdot\omega_j\cdot 2r_j}{\dfrac{W_r}{l}}\cdot\left(\frac{r_j}{C}\right)^2 = 2\frac{\mu\cdot r_j\cdot\omega_j}{\dfrac{W_r}{l}}\left(\frac{r_j}{C}\right)^2$$

$$S = 2 \cdot \frac{1}{W_r^*} \qquad\qquad \cdots \left(\because \quad W_r^* = \frac{\frac{W_r}{l}}{\mu \cdot r_j \cdot \omega_j} \left(\frac{C}{r_j}\right)^2 \right)$$

Taking reciprocal on both sides, we can write,

$$\frac{1}{S} = \frac{W_r^*}{2}$$

Substituting W_r^* in above equation, it becomes

$$\frac{1}{S} = \left(\frac{l}{d}\right)^2 \cdot \frac{\pi \in}{2(1 - \in^2)^2} [1 + 0.62 \in^2]^{1/2} \qquad\qquad \cdots (3.58)$$

The above relation between Sommerfeld number and eccentricity ratio $\in$ is plotted below, for short journal bearing.

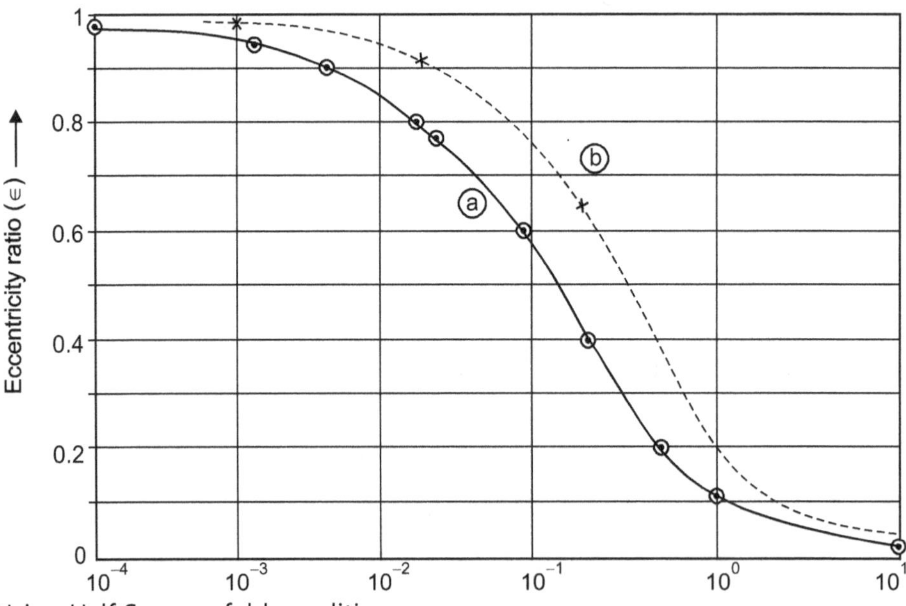

(a) Using Half Sommerfeld conditions
(b) Using Full Sommerfeld conditions

Fig. 3.34

3.7 FRICTION IN HYDRODYNAMIC JOURNAL BEARING

A torque must be continuously supplied through a film of viscous lubricant between the journal and the bearing in order to maintain rotation of the bearing elements. In order to analyse the amount of friction, we will take into account the following two cases.

- Friction in lightly loaded journal bearing (i.e. friction in concentric bearing).
- Friction in hydrodynamic journal bearing for general loadings.

3.7.1 Petroff's Equation (Friction in Concentric Bearing)

Petroff, a Russian Scientist was a first person to explain friction phenomenon in hydrodynamic journal bearing in 1883. It is the analysis carried out for friction in lightly loaded journal bearing.

Assumption :

Petroff made an assumption that for full journal bearing, journal runs almost concentrically with bearing and the eccentricity (e) between the journal and the bearing is zero.

Conditions :

The above assumption is based on the following basic conditions :

- The load is almost equal to zero or light.

- The journal speed of rotation is high or infinite.

- Viscosity of lubricant is high or infinite.

Consider the following figure for calculating friction force and coefficient of friction without considering hydrodynamics of fluid film.

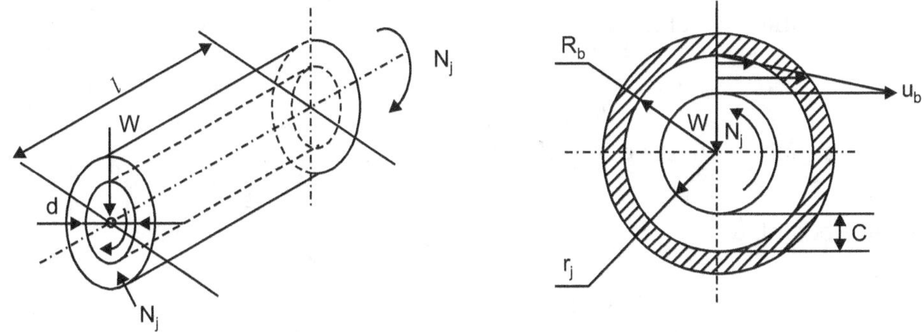

(a) Cross-section of concentric bearing

$A = 2\pi \cdot r_j \cdot l$

$u_b = (2\pi N_j) \cdot r_j$

$F = fW$

$f = \dfrac{F}{W}$

(b)

Fig. 3.35 : Development of journal and bearing surfaces

Consider a full journal bearing and the space between journal and bearing completely filled with the lubricating oil.

Let,

W_r – Radial load on journal (N)

N_j – Journal or shaft speed (rps)

C – Radial clearance (here $h = C$ – for concentric bearing)

$(C = R_b - r_j)$

F – Friction force

r_j – Radius of journal

R_b – Radius of bearing

τ – Shear stress on journal surface

A – Journal surface area (mm^2)

where, $A = (2\pi r_j) \cdot l$

l – Length of bearing (mm)

μ – Absolute viscosity of lubricant (N·s/mm^2)

f – Coefficient of friction

u_b – Journal surface velocity

$u_b = 2\pi r_j \cdot N_j$

P – Bearing pressure

$$P = \frac{W_r}{2l \cdot r_j}$$

Friction force resisting relative motion of the surface is,

$$F = \tau \cdot A$$

From Newton's postulate,

$$\tau = \mu \cdot \frac{u_b}{h}$$

Substituting in above equation, it becomes

$$F = \left(\mu \cdot \frac{u_b}{h}\right) \cdot A$$

$\therefore$ Frictional force (F),

$$F = \mu \frac{(2\pi r_j \cdot N_j)(2\pi r_j \cdot l)}{C} \qquad \dots (\because h = C)$$

$\therefore$

$$F = \frac{4\pi^2 \cdot r_j^2 \cdot N_j \cdot l \cdot \mu}{C}$$

$\therefore$ Frictional torque (T_f),

$$T_f = F \cdot r_j$$

$\therefore$

$$T_f = \frac{4\pi^2 \cdot r_j^3 \cdot N_j \cdot l \cdot \mu}{C}$$

∴ Coefficient of friction (f),

$$f \ = \ \frac{F}{W_r}$$

∴

$$f \ = \ \frac{4\pi^2 \cdot r_j^2 \cdot N_j \cdot l \cdot \mu}{W_r \cdot C}$$

This equation can be rearranged as,

$$f \ = \ \frac{2\pi^2 \cdot \mu \cdot N_j}{\left(\dfrac{W_r}{2 \cdot l \cdot r_j}\right)} \left(\frac{r_j}{C}\right)$$

∴

$$f \ = \ 2\pi^2 \cdot \frac{\mu \cdot N_j}{P} \left(\frac{r_j}{C}\right) \qquad\qquad \text{... (3.59)}$$

where, P – Bearing pressure.

$$P \ = \ \frac{W_r}{2 \cdot l \cdot r_j}$$

This equation is known as 'Petroff's equation'.

- This equation shows that coefficient of friction is directly proportional to the journal speed (N_j) and viscosity of lubricant.

- Coefficient of friction is inversely proportional to the radial load on journal (W_r).

- This equation can be used to provide a quick estimate of the frictional effects in a real design, even when the actual operating value of ∈ is unknown.

3.7.2 Friction in Loaded Bearing

Causes of friction in hydrodynamic journal bearing.

(i) Viscosity of Lubricating Oil :

The resistance to relative motion arises from viscous resistance of the fluid, thus, the performance of the bearing is affected by the viscosity of the lubricant. The oil is assumed to be coherent i.e. cavitation does not diminish the viscosity of the oil.

(ii) Converging (Wedging) Action of Film :

Once the journal starts to rotate the fluid between the clearance space is dragged into a gradually narrowing converging space, building a dynamic pressure self-sufficient to support radial load on journal. Friction is lower for lower journal speed (i.e. for lower bearing modulus). Thus, friction results from wedging action.

(iii) Moderate Load :

The loading conditions affect the amount of friction in journal bearing case.

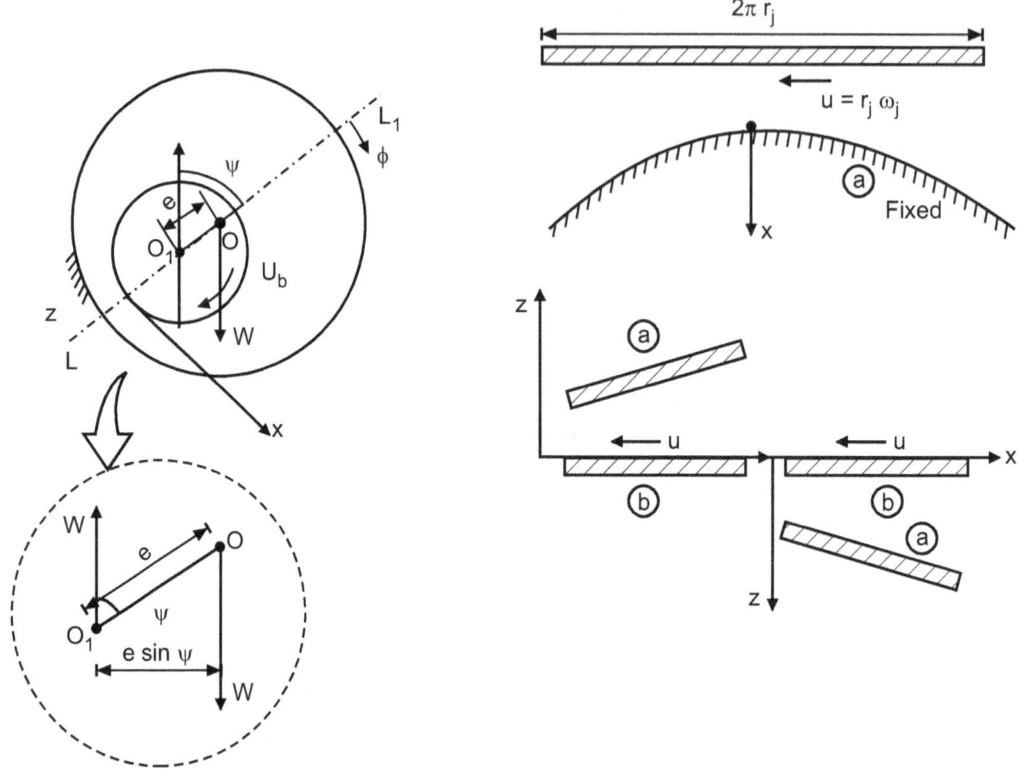

Fig. 3.36 : Developed view of shaft (b) and bearing (a)

(iv) Speed of Rotation :

Friction force (in turn coefficient of friction) is directly proportional to the journal speed (N_j).

Thus, friction depends on speed of rotation also.

Consider journal rotating at moderate speed u_b inside the bearing. Developed view of journal surface and bearing surface is as shown above.

$$\text{Here, } u = r_j \cdot \omega_j$$

Now, we have an equation for u.

$$u = \frac{z^2}{2\mu} \cdot \frac{\partial P}{\partial x} + \left[(u_a - u_b) - \frac{h^2}{2\mu} \cdot \frac{\partial P}{\partial x} \right] \frac{z}{h} + u_a$$

$$\frac{\partial u}{\partial z} = \frac{z}{\mu} \cdot \frac{\partial P}{\partial x} + \left[(u_a - u_b) - \frac{h^2}{2\mu} \cdot \frac{\partial P}{\partial x} \right] \frac{1}{h}$$

$$\mu \cdot \frac{\partial u}{\partial z} = \frac{\partial P}{\partial x} \left(z - \frac{h}{2} \right) + \mu \frac{u_a - u_b}{h}$$

$$\therefore \quad \mu \frac{\partial u}{\partial z} = \frac{\partial P}{\partial x} \left(\frac{2z - h}{2} \right) + \mu \left(\frac{u_a - u_b}{h} \right)$$

$$= \tau_{zx}$$

$$\tau_{zx} \big|_{z=0} \Rightarrow u_b = - u_b = - r_j \cdot \omega_j \} \text{ on journal surface}$$

$$\tau_{zx}\big|_{z=0} \Rightarrow \tau_0 = -\frac{\partial P}{\partial x}\frac{h}{2} + \mu \cdot \frac{u_b}{h} \} \text{ Shear stress on shaft surface} \dots (3.60)$$

$$\tau_{zx}\big|_{z=h} \Rightarrow \tau_h = \frac{\partial P}{\partial x}\frac{h}{2} + \mu \cdot \frac{u_b}{h} \} \text{ Shear stress on bearing surface}$$

Total frictional force on the journal surface or bearing surface,

$$F_{h,\,0} = \int_0^l \int (\tau_{h,\,0}) \cdot dx \cdot dy$$

$$= \int_0^l \int \left(\pm \frac{\partial P}{\partial x} \cdot \frac{h}{2} + \mu \cdot \frac{u}{h} \right) dx\, dy$$

$$= \int_0^l \int \left(\pm \frac{\partial P}{r_j \cdot \partial \phi} \cdot \frac{h}{2} + \mu \cdot \frac{u}{h} \right) r_j \cdot d\phi \cdot dy$$

$$= \int_0^l \left[\int \pm \frac{\partial P}{\partial \phi} \cdot \frac{1}{r_j} \cdot \frac{h}{2} \cdot r_j \cdot d\phi + \mu \frac{u}{h} r_j \cdot d\phi \right] dy$$

$$= \int_0^l \left[\int_0^\pi \pm \frac{\partial P}{\partial \phi} \cdot \frac{h}{2}\, d\phi + \int_0^{2\pi} \frac{\mu \cdot r_j \cdot u}{h} \cdot d\phi \right] dy$$

Let

$$I_1 = \int_0^l \int_0^\pi \left(\pm \frac{\partial P}{\partial \phi} \cdot \frac{h}{2} \cdot d\phi \right) dy = \int_0^\pi \pm \frac{\partial P}{\partial \phi} \cdot \frac{h}{2} \cdot d\phi \int_0^l dy$$

Let

$$h = C(1 + \epsilon \cos \phi) \Rightarrow \frac{\partial h}{\partial \phi} = -C\,\epsilon \sin \phi$$

$\therefore$

$$I_1 = \int_0^\pi \pm \left(\frac{\partial P}{\partial \phi} \right) \left(\frac{h}{2} \right) d\phi \int_0^l dy \qquad \int AB$$

$$= l \left[\left(P \cdot \frac{h}{2} \right)_0^\pi + \int_0^\pi \frac{P}{2} \cdot \frac{\partial h}{\partial \phi} \cdot d\phi \right] = A \int B - \int \int B \cdot \frac{dA}{dx} \cdot dx$$

$$= l \left[\pm \frac{P}{2} \int_0^\pi (-C\,\epsilon \sin \phi) \cdot d\phi \right]$$

Multiplying and dividing by r_j

$$= l\left[\pm\frac{P}{2r_j}\int_0^\pi (-C\in\sin\phi)\, r_j\cdot d\phi\right]$$

$$= \pm\frac{lC\in}{2r_j}\int_0^\pi P(r_j\cdot d\phi)\sin\phi$$

Shows integration of load component per unit width perpendicular to line of centres for half Sommerfeld condition $= W_x$

$$= \pm\frac{C\in}{2r_j}\cdot W_x$$

$$I_1 = \pm\frac{C\in}{2r_j}\cdot W\sin\psi$$

Now, second part of integral,

i.e.

$$I_2 = \int_0^l \int_0^{2\pi} \frac{\mu\cdot r_j\cdot u_b}{h}\cdot d\phi\cdot dy$$

$$= \int_0^{2\pi} \mu\cdot\frac{r_j\cdot u_b}{h}\cdot d\phi \int_0^l dy$$

$$= l\int_0^{2\pi}\left(\frac{\mu\cdot r_j\cdot u_b}{h}\right)d\phi$$

$$= l\cdot\mu\cdot r_j\cdot u_b\int_0^{2\pi}\frac{d\phi}{C(1+\in\cos\phi)}$$

$$= \mu\cdot\frac{r_j\cdot u_b\cdot l}{C}\int_0^{2\pi}\frac{d\phi}{1+\in\cos\phi}$$

$$= \mu\cdot\frac{r_j\cdot u_b\cdot l}{C}\int_0^{2\pi}\frac{1-\in\cos\gamma}{1-\in^2}\cdot\frac{(1-\in^2)^{1/2}}{1-\in\cos\gamma}\cdot d\gamma$$

$$= \frac{\mu\cdot r_j\cdot u_b\cdot l}{C(1-\in^2)^{1/2}}\int_0^{2\pi} d\gamma \qquad\qquad \text{At } \phi = 0 \to \gamma = 0$$

$$= \frac{\mu \cdot r_j \cdot u_b \cdot l}{C(1 - \epsilon^2)^{1/2}} [\gamma]_0^{2\pi} \qquad \text{and } \phi = 2\pi \rightarrow \gamma = 2\pi$$

$$\therefore \qquad I_2 = \frac{2\pi \mu \cdot r_j \cdot u_b \cdot l}{C(1 - \epsilon^2)^{1/2}}$$

Substituting parts I_1 and I_2 in equation for friction force, it becomes

$$F_{h,\,0} = \pm \frac{C\epsilon}{2r_j} \cdot W \sin \psi + \frac{2\pi \mu \cdot r_j \cdot u_b \cdot l}{C(1 - \epsilon^2)^{1/2}} \qquad \text{... (3.61)}$$

This is an equation for friction force in hydrodynamic journal bearing.

Now, torque $\qquad T = W(e \sin \psi)$

Force on journal surface,

$$F = \frac{W e \sin \psi}{r_j}$$

When $\epsilon \rightarrow 0 \in$ shaft is almost concentric.

$$F = \frac{2\pi \mu \cdot u_b \cdot r_j \cdot l}{C}$$

Torque T_f becomes,

$$T_f = F \cdot r_j$$

$$= \frac{2\pi \mu \cdot u_b \cdot r_j^2 \cdot l}{C}$$

Now, $\qquad u_b = r_j \cdot \omega_j = r_j(2\pi N_j)$

Using the previous equation, we get,

$$T_f = \frac{2\pi \mu \cdot r_j \cdot (2\pi) N_j \cdot r_j^2 \cdot l}{C}$$

$$\therefore \qquad T_f = \frac{4\pi^2 \cdot \mu \cdot r_j^3 \cdot N_j \cdot l}{C} \qquad \text{... (3.62)}$$

Power, $\qquad P_f = T_f \cdot \omega_j$

$$= T_f \cdot 2\pi \cdot N_j$$

$\therefore \qquad$ Equivalent coefficient of friction in case of hydrodynamic journal bearing (f'),

$$f' = \frac{F}{W} = \frac{e}{2r_j} \cdot \sin \psi + \frac{2\pi \mu \cdot u_b \cdot r_j \cdot l}{C(1 - \epsilon^2)^{1/2} \cdot W} \qquad \text{... (3.63)}$$

3.8 SOMMERFELD NUMBER (S)

Now, we have Petroff's equation,

$$f = 2\pi^2 \frac{\mu \cdot N_j}{P}\left(\frac{r_j}{C}\right)$$

Multiplying both sides of above equation by $\left(\dfrac{r_j}{C}\right)$,

$$f\left(\frac{r_j}{C}\right) = 2\pi^2 \cdot \frac{\mu \cdot N_j}{P}\left(\frac{r_j}{C}\right)^2$$

$$f\left(\frac{r_j}{C}\right) = 2\pi^2\left[\frac{\mu \cdot N_j}{P}\left(\frac{r_j}{C}\right)^2\right]$$

$$f\left(\frac{r_j}{C}\right) = 2\pi^2 \cdot S$$

where,
$$S = \frac{\mu \cdot N_j}{P}\left(\frac{r_j}{C}\right)^2 \qquad\qquad \dots (3.64)$$

is called Sommerfeld number, it depends on $\in$ and $\left[f\left(\dfrac{r_j}{C}\right)\right]$ is called friction variable

$= \dfrac{1 + 2\in^2}{3\in}$ plotting friction variable against Sommerfeld number (S).

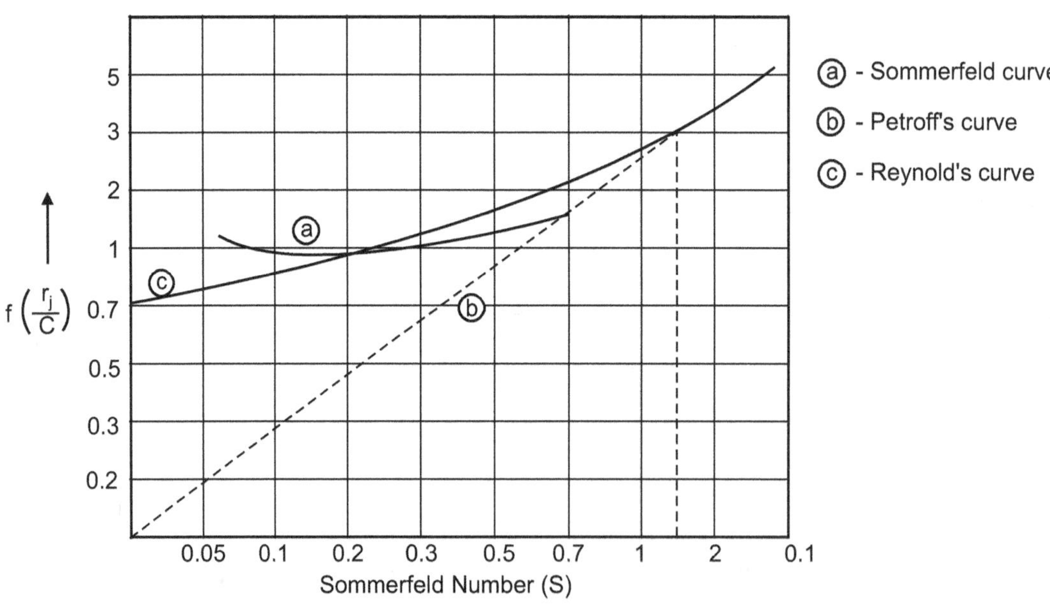

Fig. 3.37 : Bearing friction variable versus Sommerfeld number
for full journal bearings with _l/d_ > 1

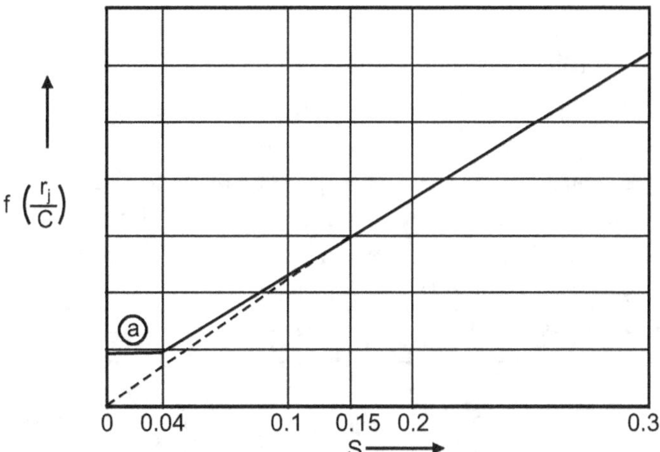

Fig. 3.38 : Friction variable versus Sommerfeld number for concentric journal bearing

- Friction variable is a function of eccentricity ratio $\in$ which is very small in case of lightly loaded bearings.
- Curve (a) (i.e. Sommerfeld curve) and curve (b) (i.e. Petroff's curve) coincide when $S \geq 0.15$.
- Thus, one can define lightly loaded journal bearing as a bearing operating under such conditions that the Sommerfeld number is equal to or greater than 0.15.

3.9 DESIGN CONSIDERATIONS IN HYDRODYNAMIC JOURNAL BEARINGS

The variables used in the design of hydrodynamic journal bearings are categorised into two groups :

1. Design variables.
2. Performance variables.

1. Design Variables :

The **design variables** are those whose values are either given or are under the control of the designer.

Following design variables are used in hydrodynamic journal bearings.

- μ, Viscosity
- p, Unit bearing pressure
- N_j, Journal speed
- r_j, C, l and arc of bearing β, bearing dimensions.

2. Performance Variables :

The **performance variables** are those which tell us how well the bearing is performing.

Following performance variables are used in hydrodynamic journal bearings :

- f, Coefficient of friction
- ΔT, Temperature rise

- Q, Flow rate of lubrication
- h_0, Minimum oil-film thickness

The designer is not having any control over performance variables. For the satisfactory performance of the bearing, certain limits are imposed on the values of performance variables based on the characteristics of bearing materials and the lubricant.

Design of hydrodynamic journal bearing is nothing but defining satisfactory limits for the performance variables and then finding out the values of design variables such that the performance variables do not exceed the defined limits.

3.10 RAIMONDI AND BOYD METHOD

- **Objectives :**

  For a hydrodynamic journal bearing of finite length, there is no exact solution, and there is being need to establish the relationship between different variables (i.e. design variables and performance variables) in the design of hydrodynamic journal bearing).

- A. A. Raimondi and John Boyd of Westinghouse Research Laboratories, solved the Reynolds equation on the digital computer by using iteration technique. While analysing it, they used different dimensionless parameters comprising of different design variables (e.g. Dynamic viscosity (μ), Unit bearing pressure (P), Journal speed (N_j), Bearing dimensions (r_j, C, l, β, etc.)) and performance variables (e.g. Coefficient of friction (f), Temperature rise (ΔT), the lubricant flow rate, (Q), Minimum oil-film thickness (h_0)).

- Refer Fig. 3.39 for various bearing performance parameters.

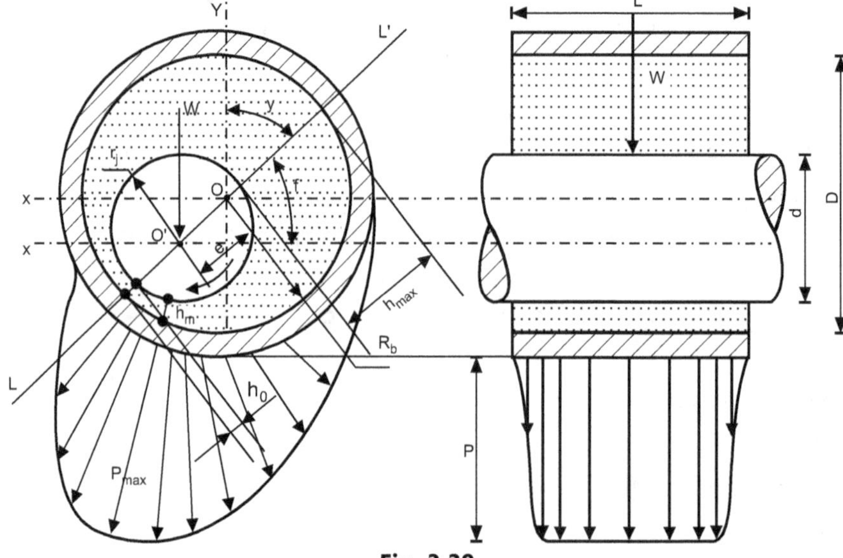

Fig. 3.39

- The dimensionless parameters are given for full journal bearing with side leakage in the form of charts and tables by A. A. Raimondi and John Boyd in 1958.
- Fig. 3.39 shows the numerical solutions for eccentricity ratio ($\in$) versus Sommerfeld number (S) for a wide range of L/D ratios.

- **Dimensionless Parameters :**

  - Length to diameter ratio $\left(\dfrac{l}{d}\right)$

  - Eccentricity ratio $(\in)$

$$\in \; = \; \frac{e}{C} \hspace{4cm} \text{... (By definition)}$$

Referring to Fig. 3.39,

$$R_b \; = \; e + r_j + h_0$$
$$R_b - r_j \; = \; e + h_0$$
$$e + h_0 \; = \; C$$
$$\frac{e}{C} + \frac{h_0}{C} \; = \; 1$$
$$\in + \frac{h_0}{C} \; = \; 1$$
$$\in \; = \; 1 - \frac{h_0}{C}$$

  - Minimum film thickness variable $\left(\dfrac{h_0}{C}\right)$.

  - Sommerfeld number (S).

It is an important non-dimensional parameter more generally used for the description of bearing performance. It bears a relationship to journal bearing theory. The equation for Sommerfeld number contains different variables which can be controlled to give better design.

Sommerfeld number can be given by the relation,

$$S \; = \; \frac{\mu \cdot N_j}{P} \left(\frac{r_j}{C}\right)^2$$

where,   S – Sommerfeld number
     μ – Viscosity of the lubricant (N-s/mm^2)
     N_j – Journal speed (rps)
     P – Unit bearing pressure (N/mm^2)

Designer can control all the variables in Sommerfeld number.

  - Coefficient of friction variable (CFV),

$$CFV \; = \; f\left(\frac{r_j}{C}\right) \hspace{3cm} \text{... (3.65)}$$

  - Flow variable (FV),

$$FV \; = \; \frac{Q}{r_j \cdot C \cdot N_j \cdot l} \hspace{3cm} \text{... (3.66)}$$

where, Q – Total oil flow rate.

- Flow ratio $\left(\dfrac{Q_s}{\overline{Q}}\right)$

- Maximum film pressure ratio $\left(\dfrac{P}{P_{max}}\right)$.

- Maximum film pressure angle $(\phi_{P_{max}})$.

- Zero pressure angle (ϕ_{P_0}).

- Minimum film thickness angle (θ).

- Temperature rise variable.

$$\left[\frac{\rho \cdot C_p \cdot \Delta T}{P}\right]$$

where, ρ – Density (kg/m³)

C_p– Specific heat of lubricant (J/kg °C)

P – Bearing pressure (N/m²)

ΔT – Temperature difference (°C)

Fig. 3.40 shows eccentricity $(\in)$ and $\left(\dfrac{h_0}{C}\right)$ ratio versus (S) for wide range of $\left(\dfrac{l}{d}\right)$ ratios.

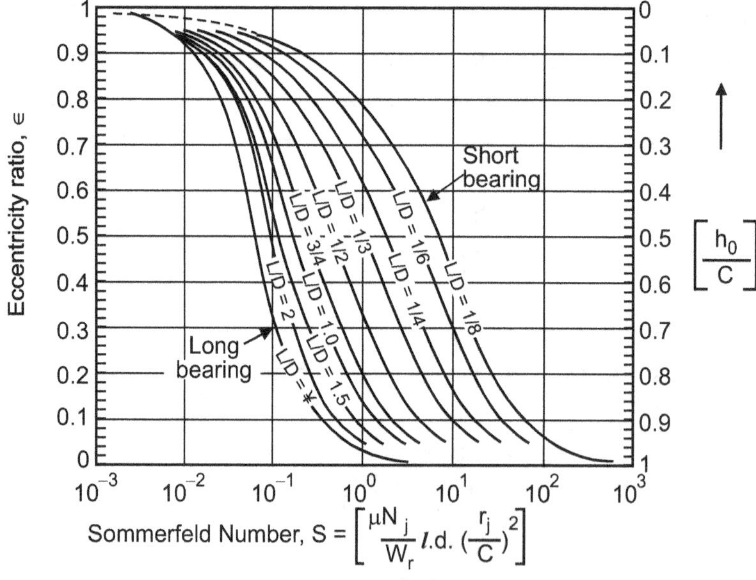

Fig. 3.40 : $\in$ and $\left(\dfrac{h_0}{C}\right)$ versus 'S'

- Table 3.2 shows the values of dimensionless parameters for full journal bearings with side leakage.

Table 3.2

$\left(\dfrac{l}{d}\right)$	ϵ	$\dfrac{h_0}{C}$	S	$CFV = f \cdot \left(\dfrac{r_j}{C}\right)$	$FV = \dfrac{Q}{r_j \cdot C \cdot N_j \cdot l}$	$FR = \left(\dfrac{Q_s}{Q}\right)$	$\dfrac{P}{P_{max}}$	ψ
∞	1.0	0	0	0	0	0	0	0
	0.97	0.03	–	–	–	0	–	–
	0.9	0.1	0.0115	0.756	0.411	0	0.358	31.62
	0.8	0.2	0.021	0.961	0.760	0	0.495	42.22
	0.6	0.4	0.0389	1.20	1.56	0	0.667	54.31
	0.4	0.6	0.0626	1.52	2.26	0	0.764	61.94
	0.2	0.8	0.123	2.57	2.83	0	0.814	67.26
	0.1	0.9	0.240	4.80	3.03	0	0.826	69.10
	0	1.0	∞	∞	3.147	0	–	70.92
∞	1.0	0	0	0	0	1.0	–	0
	0.97	0.03	0.00474	0.514	4.82	0.973	0.152	15.47
	0.9	0.1	0.0188	1.05	4.74	0.913	0.247	26.45
	0.8	0.2	0.0446	1.70	4.62	0.842	0.313	36.24
	0.6	0.4	0.121	3.22	4.33	0.680	0.415	50.58
	0.4	0.6	0.264	5.79	3.99	0.497	0.484	63.10
	0.2	0.8	0.631	12.8	3.59	0.280	0.529	74.02
	0.1	0.9	1.33	26.4	3.37	0.150	0.540	79.5
	0	1.0	∞	∞	3.142	0	–	85
$\left(\dfrac{1}{2}\right)$	1.0	0	0	0	–	1.0	0	0
	0.97	0.03	0.00609	0.610	5.88	0.980	0.126	13.75
	0.9	0.1	0.0313	1.60	5.69	0.939	0.206	23.66
	0.8	0.2	0.0923	3.26	5.41	0.874	0.267	33.31
	0.6	0.4	0.319	8.10	4.85	0.730	0.365	48.14
	0.4	0.6	0.779	17.0	4.29	0.552	0.441	61.45
	0.2	0.8	2.03	40.9	3.72	0.318	0.506	74.94
	0.1	0.9	4.31	85.6	3.43	0.173	0.523	81.62
	0	1.0	∞	∞	3.142	0	–	88.5

Contd...

$\left(\dfrac{1}{4}\right)$	1.0	0	0	0	–	1.0	0	0
	0.97	0.03	0.0101	0.922	6.12	0.984	0.108	12.22
	0.9	0.1	0.0736	3.50	5.91	0.945	0.180	21.85
	0.8	0.2	0.261	8.8	5.60	0.884	0.240	31.04
	0.6	0.4	1.07	26.7	4.99	0.746	0.334	46.72
	0.4	0.6	2.83	61.1	4.37	0.567	0.415	60.86
	0.2	0.8	7.57	153.0	3.76	0.330	0.489	75.18
	0.1	0.9	16.2	322.0	3.45	0.180	0.515	82.31
	0	1.0	∞	∞	3.142		–	89.5

3.11 TEMPERATURE RISE IN HYDRODYNAMIC JOURNAL BEARING

- Generation of heat in hydrodynamic journal bearing is due to the fact that frictional work in bearing is converted to heat which increases the temperature of the lubricating oil. As temperature increases, the viscosity of lubricating oil decreases. The analysis is based on constant viscosity. The viscosity should be determined at average temperature (T_{AV}) of lubricating oil.

- Heat generated in bearing gets dissipated by three basic modes :

   (i) Conduction, (ii) Convection, (iii) Radiation.

   Instead of calculating the heat generated by three basic modes, it is assumed that heat generated is carried away by the flowing lubricating oil in the bearing.

- Temperature rise in the hydrodynamic journal bearings can be calculated as below.

Power Lost in Friction

(a) Friction Power Lost

$$P_F = T_F \cdot \omega_j$$

$$= \frac{\mu\, W_r \cdot r_j}{10^3}\, 2\pi N_j \ (W)$$

$$P_F = \frac{\mu\, W_r \cdot r_j \cdot 2\pi N_j}{10^6} \ (kW) \qquad \ldots (3.67)$$

where, T_F – Frictional torque

        ω_j – Angular velocity

        P_F – Power lost in friction (kW)

        W_r – Radial load on journal (N)

        N_j – Journal speed (rps)

        r_j – Journal radius (mm)

(b) Heat Generation

Rate of Heat Generation

$$H_G = P_F$$

$$= \frac{2\pi N_j \cdot f \cdot W_r}{10^6} \quad (\text{kJ/s})$$

Substituting

$$CFV = f\left(\frac{r_j}{C}\right)$$

where, f – Coefficient of friction

$$\therefore \ f = \left(\frac{C}{r_j}\right) CFV$$

and $P = \dfrac{W_r}{2l \cdot r_j}$

$$\therefore \ W_r = 2l \cdot r_j \cdot P$$

$$\therefore \ H_G = \frac{2\pi N_j \cdot CFV}{10^6}\left(\frac{C}{r_j}\right) 2 \cdot P \cdot l \cdot r_j \qquad \text{... (3.68)}$$

(c) Heat Dissipation

Rate of Heat Dissipation

$$H_D = m \cdot C_p \cdot \Delta T$$

Substituting,

Mass flow rate, $m = \dfrac{\rho Q}{10^9}$

where, ρ – Mass density of lubricating oil (kg/m^3)

Q – Total lubricating oil flow rate ($mm^3/sec.$)

Now, $FV = $ Flow variable $= \dfrac{Q}{r_j \cdot C \cdot N_j \cdot l}$

$$\therefore \ Q = FV(r_j \cdot C \cdot N_j \cdot l)$$

$$\therefore \ m = \frac{\rho\,FV(r_j \cdot C \cdot N_j \cdot l)}{10^9}$$

$$\therefore \ H_D = \frac{\rho \cdot FV(r_j \cdot C \cdot N_j \cdot l)\,\Delta T}{10^9} \qquad \text{... (3.69)}$$

Expressing temperature rise ΔT in dimensionless form,

$\therefore$ Equating (b) part and (c) part,

$$H_G = H_D$$

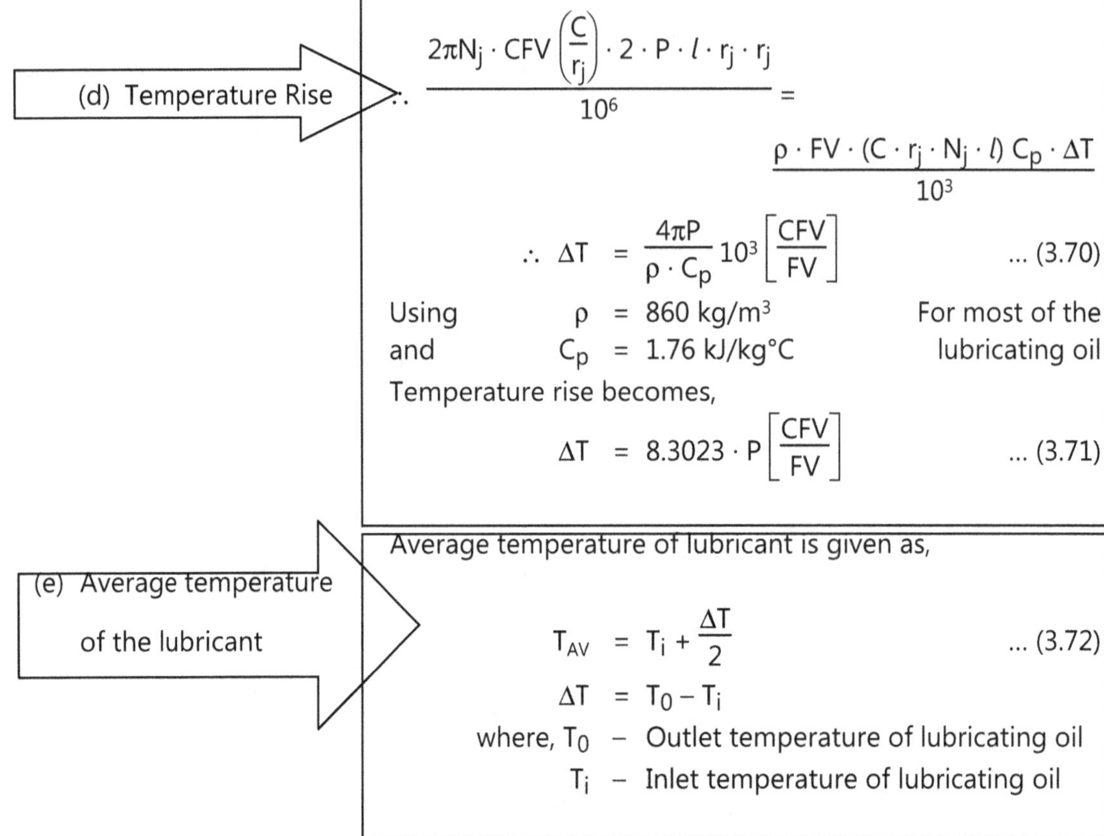

$$\therefore \ \frac{2\pi N_j \cdot CFV \left(\dfrac{C}{r_j}\right) \cdot 2 \cdot P \cdot l \cdot r_j \cdot r_j}{10^6} =$$

$$\frac{\rho \cdot FV \cdot (C \cdot r_j \cdot N_j \cdot l) \, C_p \cdot \Delta T}{10^3}$$

$$\therefore \ \Delta T \ = \ \frac{4\pi P}{\rho \cdot C_p} \, 10^3 \left[\frac{CFV}{FV}\right] \qquad \ldots (3.70)$$

Using ρ = 860 kg/m³   For most of the
and C_p = 1.76 kJ/kg°C   lubricating oil
Temperature rise becomes,

$$\Delta T \ = \ 8.3023 \cdot P \left[\frac{CFV}{FV}\right] \qquad \ldots (3.71)$$

Average temperature of lubricant is given as,

$$T_{AV} \ = \ T_i + \frac{\Delta T}{2} \qquad \ldots (3.72)$$

$$\Delta T \ = \ T_0 - T_i$$

where, T_0 – Outlet temperature of lubricating oil
        T_i – Inlet temperature of lubricating oil

Total Flow of Lubricating Oil (Q) :

While estimating the temperature rise (ΔT), it is assumed that total heat generated is carried away by the total oil flow (Q) in the bearing which is given by,

Total oil flow = (Circumferential flow) + (Axial flow or side leakage)

$$Q \ = \ Q_{CF} + Q_S$$

where, Q_{CF} i.e. circumferential flow is due to the constant circulation of oil round the circumference of journal where, major part of heat is absorbed by lubricating oil and temperature rise takes place.

$$\Delta T \ = \ T_0 - T_i$$

where, T_i – Inlet temperature of lubricating oil (°C)

       T_0 – Outlet temperature of lubricating oil (°C)

Q_S i.e. Axial flow or side leakage. It is through the bearing ends. Assuming that axial flow takes place at average temperature T_{AV}. If we take into account Q_S, the heat dissipation rate can be changed as follows.

$$H_D \ = \ \begin{bmatrix} \text{Heat carried due to} \\ \text{circumferential flow} \end{bmatrix} + \begin{bmatrix} \text{Heat carried due to} \\ \text{side leakage} \end{bmatrix}$$

$$= m_c \cdot C_p \cdot \Delta T + m_s \cdot C_p \frac{\Delta T}{2}$$

$$= \frac{\rho \cdot Q_{CF} \cdot C_p \cdot \Delta T}{10^9} + \frac{\rho \cdot Q_s \cdot C_p \cdot \frac{\Delta T}{2}}{10^9}$$

$$= \frac{\rho \cdot C_p \cdot \Delta T}{10^9}\left[Q_{CF} + \frac{Q_s}{2}\right] = \frac{\rho \cdot C_p \cdot \Delta T}{10^9}\left[(Q - Q_s) + \frac{Q_s}{2}\right]$$

$$= \frac{\rho \cdot C_p \cdot \Delta T}{10^9}\left[Q - \frac{Q_s}{2}\right] = \frac{\rho \cdot C_p \cdot \Delta T \cdot Q}{10^9}\left[1 - \frac{Q_s}{2Q}\right]$$

and $\qquad H_G = \dfrac{2\pi N_j \cdot f \cdot W_r \cdot r_j}{10^6}$

Equating H_D and H_G,

$$\frac{\rho \cdot C_p \cdot \Delta T \cdot Q}{10^9}\left[1 - \frac{Q_s}{2Q}\right] = \frac{2\pi N_j \cdot f \cdot W_r \cdot r_j}{10^6}$$

$$\Delta T = \frac{2\pi \cdot N_j \cdot f \cdot W_r \cdot r_j}{\rho \cdot Q \cdot C_p\left(1 - \frac{1}{2} \cdot \frac{Q_s}{Q}\right)} \cdot 10^3 \qquad\qquad \text{... (3.73)}$$

3.12 PARAMETERS OF BEARING DESIGN

While designing journal bearing, it is required to select the suitable values for the following variables :

- Length to diameter ratio $\left(\dfrac{l}{d}\right)$.

- Radial clearance (C).

- Unit bearing pressure (P).

- Minimum oil-film thickness (h_0).

3.12.1 Length to Diameter Ratio $\left(\dfrac{l}{d}\right)$

- $\left(\dfrac{l}{d}\right)$ ratio plays significant role in designing journal bearing. It influences the performance of the journal bearing.

- In case of long bearings : Because of larger projected area, load-carrying capacity is high and can be increased with an increase in bearing length. As the length of bearing increases, the rate of oil flow decreases. Thus, longer bearing gives high load-carrying capacity and less oil flow rate.

  Rigidity of journal and bearing is also an important part for calculating correct $\left(\dfrac{l}{d}\right)$ ratio.

  There could be damage to journal due to metal to metal contact if the bearing is rigidly supported and cannot deflect with the journal. Thus, this problem is prominent for relatively long bearing possessing poor comformability.

- **In Case of Short Bearings :** Because of smaller projected area, load-carrying capacity is low. Also the oil flow rate is high at the ends and it has improved heat dissipation. The short journal bearing possesses high coefficient of friction (e.g. in aircraft engine).

  It is desirable to use short journal bearing when heat dissipation problem in the bearing becomes critical and also when the shaft deflection is likely to be severe.

- Fig. 3.41 shows pressure distribution along the length of bearing for $\left(\dfrac{l}{d}\right)$ ratio 2 and 1 respectively.

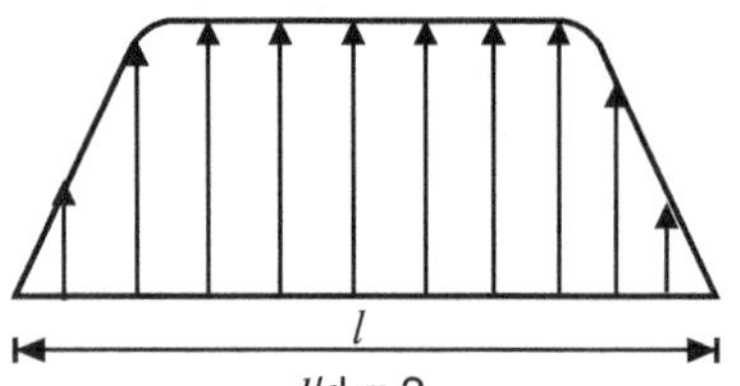

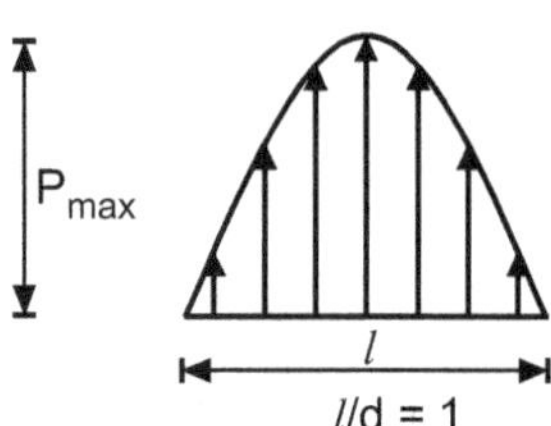

Fig. 3.41

- In practical situation, $\left(\dfrac{l}{d}\right)$ ratio varies from 0.5 to 2. But for most of the applications, it is taken as 1.

3.12.2 Unit Bearing Pressure (p)

- It can be defined as the load per unit projected area of bearing. It is given as,

$$p = \frac{W_r}{2 \cdot l \cdot r_j}$$

where, p – Bearing pressure

   W_r – Radial load on journal

   $(2 \cdot l \cdot r_j)$ – Projected area of journal

- It is a function of Sommerfeld number

$$S = \frac{\mu \cdot N_j}{P}\left(\frac{r_j}{C}\right)^2$$

- where, S is inversely proportional to bearing pressure P. Unit bearing pressure depends on number of factors such as :
  - Material of bearing
  - Temperature during operation
  - Type of loading
  - Frequency of load application (i.e. Fatigue strength of bearing)

- Service conditions :
    - (a) Low and uniform loading
    - (b) Medium shock loading
    - (c) Heavy duty shock loading.
- For some of the applications, values of unit bearing pressure are given in the Table 3.3.

Table 3.3 : Permissible Values of Unit Bearing Pressure for Variety of Applications

Sr. No.	Application Area	Unit Bearing Pressure (N/mm²)
1.	Low and uniform loading	
	(a) Light duty transmission shaft	0.12 – 0.16
	(b) Heavy duty transmission shaft	0.5 – 1
	(c) Main bearings in centrifugal pump	0.5 – 1.2
	(d) Main bearings in electric motors	0.6 – 1.5
2.	Medium shock loading	
	(a) Main bearings in air compressor	1 – 1.8
	(b) Crank-pin in air compressor	1.8 – 3.5
	(c) Main bearing in machine tools	1.5 – 2.5
3.	Heavy duty shock loading	
	(a) Main bearings in diesel engine	5 – 12
	(b) Crank-pin in diesel engine	7 – 15
	(c) Gudgeon pin	13 – 15
	(d) Main bearing in petrol engine	3 – 4
	(e) Crank-pin in petrol engine	10 – 15

3.12.3 Radial Clearance (C)

- For given operating conditions, radial clearance (C) in a journal bearing significantly affects the load-carrying capacity and flow rate.
- For particular operating condition keeping constant, an increase in radial   clearance –
    - (i)   decreases the load-carrying capacity.
    - (ii) increases the oil flow rate.
    - (iii) decreases the extent of the active film around the journal.
- Also, as $Q \propto (C)^3$

    For above relation, a slight increase in clearance will increase the oil flow rate substantially, thus, decreasing the temperature of bearing.

- Radial clearance should be kept small to provide necessary velocity gradient. But this requires costly finishing processes, rigid mountings of the bearing assembly and lubricating oil free from foreign particles. This will increase the initial and maintenance costs.

Practically, $\left(\dfrac{C}{r_j}\right)$ ratio is taken as 0.001.

- Table 3.4 gives values of radial clearance for some of the bearing materials.

Table 3.4 : Radial Clearance for Various Bearing Materials

Bearing Material	Radial Clearance 'C'
Babbits (Tin base)	$0.001\ r_j - 0.0016\ r_j$
Copper-lead and silver lead indium	$0.001\ r_j - 0.009\ r_j$
Aluminium and its alloys	$0.0015\ r_j - 0.0025\ r_j$

3.12.4 Minimum Oil-Film Thickness (h_0)

- The minimum oil-film thickness plays significant role in the design of journal bearing. As h_{min} decreases, the load-carrying capacity increases. However, the value of minimum oil-film thickness is limited from the practical considerations like –

(i)   Surface finish of the bearing.

(ii) Rigidity of journal.

(iii) Geometry of bearing surface.

(iv) Type of loading.

- In practical situations, the lower limit for the minimum oil-film thickness is given by,

$$h_0 \ = \ 0.0002\ r_j - 0.00025\ r_j \qquad \qquad \text{... (3.74)}$$

Below this value of lower limit of (h_0), metal to metal contact occurs.

- Bearing can be designed for the following two conditions :

(i)   Design of bearing for maximum load-carrying capacity.

(ii) Design of bearing for minimum frictional loss.

- Designer can use the following values of the minimum oil-film thickness ratio $\left(\dfrac{h_0}{C}\right)$ under optimum conditions.

$\left[\dfrac{l}{d}\right]$ Ratio	$\left[\dfrac{h_0}{C}\right]$ for Maximum Load	$\left[\dfrac{h_0}{C}\right]$ for Friction Loss
∞	0.65	0.60
1	0.54	0.29
0.5	0.44	0.12
0.25	0.28	0.03

SOLVED EXAMPLES

Example 3.1 : Following data refers to full journal bearing.

(i)   Length of bearing   =   75 mm

(ii) Diameter of bearing   =   75 mm

(iii) Load on bearing   =   12 kN

(iv) Speed of journal   =   1800 rpm

(v) $\dfrac{d}{C}$ ratio   =   2000

(vi) Viscosity of oil   =   10 cP

at operating temperature

Determine the coefficient of friction by using Raimondi and Boyd chart. 'd' is the journal diameter, 'C' is the radial clearance in the bearing.

S	$\left(\dfrac{r_j}{C}\right) f$
0.264	5.79
0.121	3.22
0.0446	1.70

Solution :

Given :

$$l \;=\; 75 \text{ mm}$$
$$d \;=\; 75 \text{ mm}$$
$$W_r \;=\; 12 \text{ kN} = 12 \times 10^3 \text{ N}$$
$$N_j \;=\; 1800 \text{ rpm} = \frac{1800}{60} = 30 \text{ rps}$$
$$\frac{d}{C} \;=\; 2000, \;\; \in \frac{r}{C} = 1000$$
$$\mu \;=\; 10 \text{ cP} = 10 \times 10^{-9} \text{ N-s/mm}^2$$

To find out : f = ? using Raimondi and Boyd chart.

We know the equation for Sommerfeld number as,

$$S \;=\; \frac{\mu \cdot N_j}{P}\left(\frac{r_j}{C}\right)^2$$

$$P = \frac{W}{ld} \;=\; \frac{12 \times 10^3}{75 \times 75} = 2.1333 \text{ N/mm}^2$$

$$\therefore \qquad S \;=\; \frac{\mu \cdot N_j}{P}\left(\frac{r_j}{C}\right)^2$$

$$=\; \frac{10 \times 10^{-9} \times 30}{2.1333}\,(1000)^2$$

$$S \;=\; 0.140625$$

Evaluating value of $\left[\left(\dfrac{r_j}{C}\right)f\right]$ by linear interpolation,

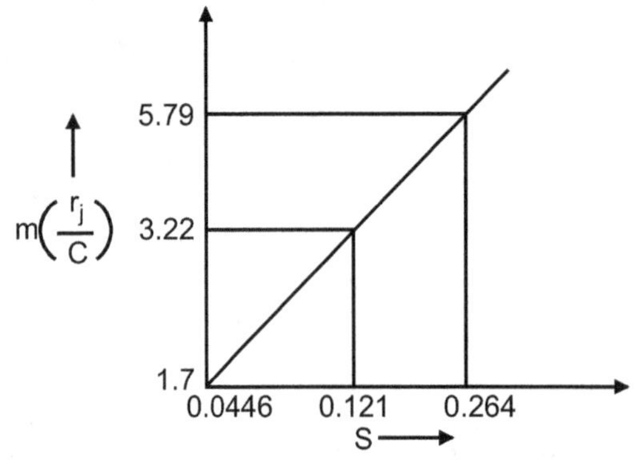

Fig. 3.42

$$S_1 = 0.0446 \quad \Rightarrow \quad \left[\left(\dfrac{r_j}{C}\right)f\right]_1 = 1.70$$

$$S_2 = 0.121 \quad \Rightarrow \quad \left[\left(\dfrac{r_j}{C}\right)f\right]_2 = 3.22$$

$$S_3 = 0.140625 \quad \Rightarrow \quad \left[\left(\dfrac{r_j}{C}\right)f\right]_3 = \ ?$$

$$S_4 = 0.264 \quad \Rightarrow \quad \left[\left(\dfrac{r_j}{C}\right)f\right]_4 = 5.79$$

$$\therefore \quad \frac{S_3 - S_2}{S_4 - S_2} = \frac{\left[\left(\dfrac{r_j}{C}\right)f\right]_3 - \left[\left(\dfrac{r_j}{C}\right)f\right]_2}{\left[\left(\dfrac{r_j}{C}\right)f\right]_4 - \left[\left(\dfrac{r_j}{C}\right)f\right]_2}$$

$$\therefore \quad \frac{0.140625 - 0.121}{0.264 - 0.121} = \frac{\left[\left(\dfrac{r_j}{C}\right)f\right]_3 - 3.22}{5.79 - 3.22}$$

$$f\left(\dfrac{r_j}{C}\right) = 3.57270105$$

$$\therefore \quad f = \frac{3.57270105}{\left(\dfrac{r_j}{C}\right)}$$

$$= \frac{3.57270105}{1000}$$

$\therefore$ Coefficient of friction,

$$f = 3.57270105 \times 10^{-3}$$

Example 3.2 : The following data refers to a 360° hydrodynamic bearing :

(i) Radial load	= 3.5 kN
(ii) Journal diameter	= 70 mm
(iii) Bearing length	= 70 mm
(iv) Journal speed	= 1450 rpm
(v) Radial clearance	= 50 μm
(vi) Viscosity of lubricant	= 25 cP
(vii) Density of lubricant	= 860 kg/m³
(viii) Specific heat of lubricant	= 1.76 kJ/kg·°C

Assuming that the total heat generated in the bearing is carried by the total oil flow in the bearing, calculate :

   (i) The minimum oil-film thickness.

   (ii) The coefficient of friction.

   (iii) Power lost in friction.

   (iv) The total flow rate of the lubricant in l/min.

   (v) The side leakages.

   (vi) The temperature rise neglecting the side leakage.

Solution :

Given :

$$W = 3.5 \text{ kN} = 3.5 \times 10^3 \text{ N};$$

$$d = 70 \text{ mm}; \quad \Rightarrow \quad \therefore \ r_j = \frac{d}{2} = 35 \text{ mm}$$

$$l = 70 \text{ mm};$$

$$N_j = \frac{1450}{60} = 24.1667 \text{ rps};$$

$$C = 50 \ \mu m = 50 \times 10^{-6} \text{ m} = 50 \times 10^{-3} \text{ mm};$$

$$\mu = 25 \text{ cP} = 25 \times 10^{-9} \text{ N-s/mm}^2;$$

$$\rho = 860 \text{ kg/m}^3$$

$$C_p = 1.76 \text{ kJ/kg·°C}$$

To find :

(i) h_0 = ?, (ii) f = ?,

(iii) E_F = ?, (iv) Q = ?,

(v) Q_S = ?, (vi) ΔT = ?

   $\therefore$ Bearing pressure,

$$P = \frac{W_r}{l \cdot d} = \frac{3.5 \times 10^3}{70 \times 70} = 0.714286 \text{ N/mm}^2$$

$$\text{Sommerfeld Number (S)} = \left(\frac{r_j}{C}\right)^2 \frac{\mu \cdot N_j}{P}$$

$$= \left(\frac{35}{0.05}\right)^2 \frac{25 \times 10^{-9} \times 24.1667}{0.714286}$$

$$S = 0.41446$$

From table, we have the following values :

$$\frac{l}{d} = 1$$

(i) Minimum oil-film thickness :

$$\frac{\left(\dfrac{h_0}{C}\right) - 0.6}{0.8 - 0.6} = \frac{0.41446 - 0.264}{0.631 - 0.264}$$

$$\frac{h_0}{C} = 0.08199455$$

$$\therefore \quad h_0 = 0.08199455 \times 0.05$$

$$\therefore \quad h_0 = 4.0997 \times 10^{-3} \text{ mm}$$

$S_1 = 0.264 \quad \Rightarrow \quad \left(\dfrac{h_0}{C}\right)_1 = 0.6$

$S_1 = 0.631 \quad \Rightarrow \quad \left(\dfrac{h_0}{C}\right)_2 = 0.8$

$S = 0.4146 \quad \Rightarrow \quad \dfrac{h_0}{C} = ?$

(ii) Coefficient of friction :

$$\frac{\left(\dfrac{r_j}{C}\right) f - 5.79}{12.8 - 5.79} = \frac{0.41446 - 0.264}{0.631 - 0.264}$$

$$\therefore \quad \left(\frac{r_j}{C}\right) f = 2.87391$$

$$\therefore \quad \frac{35}{0.05} f = 2.87391$$

$$\therefore \quad f = 0.0041056$$

$S_1 = 0.264 \quad \Rightarrow \quad \left[\left(\dfrac{r_j}{C}\right) f\right]_1 = 5.79$

$S_1 = 0.631 \quad \Rightarrow \quad \left[\left(\dfrac{r_j}{C}\right) f\right] = 12.8$

$S = 0.41446 \quad \Rightarrow \quad \left[\left(\dfrac{r_j}{C}\right) f\right] = ?$

(iii) Power lost in friction (E_F) :

$$E_F = \frac{2\pi \, N_j \cdot (f \, W_r \cdot r_j)}{10^6}$$

$$= \frac{2\pi \times 24.1667 \, (0.0041056 \times 3.5 \times 10^3 \times 35)}{10^6}$$

$$\therefore \quad E_F = 0.076368 \text{ kW}$$

(iv) Total flow rate of lubricant (l/min) :

$$\frac{\left(\dfrac{Q}{r_j \cdot C \cdot N_j l}\right) - 3.99}{3.59 - 3.99} = \frac{0.41446 - 0.264}{0.631 - 0.264}$$

$$\frac{Q}{r_j \cdot C \cdot N_j \cdot l} = 3.826011$$

$S_1 = 0.264 \quad \Rightarrow \quad \left(\dfrac{Q}{r_j \cdot C \cdot N_j \cdot l}\right)_1 = 3.99$

$S_1 = 0.631 \quad \Rightarrow \quad \left(\dfrac{Q}{r_j \cdot C \cdot N_j \cdot l}\right)_2 = 3.59$

$S = 0.41446 \quad \Rightarrow \quad \left(\dfrac{Q}{r_j \cdot C \cdot N_j \cdot l}\right) = ?$

$$\therefore \quad Q = 3.826011 \, (r_j \cdot C \cdot N_j \cdot l)$$

$$= 3.826011 \times 35 \times 0.05 \times 24.1667 \times 70$$

$$= 11326.60235 \text{ mm}^3/\text{s} = 11326.60235 \times 10^{-9} \text{ m}^3/\text{s}$$

$$= (11326.60235 \times 10^{-9}) \times 10^3 \times 60 \ l/\text{min}$$

$$Q = 0.679596 \ l/\text{min}$$

(v) Side leakage (Q_S) :

$$\frac{\left(\dfrac{Q_S}{Q}\right) - 0.497}{0.280 - 0.497} = \frac{0.41446 - 0.264}{0.631 - 0.264}$$

$$\frac{Q_S}{Q} = 0.4080359$$

$$Q_S = 0.4080359 \times 0.679596$$

$$S_1 = 0.264 \Rightarrow \left(\frac{Q_S}{Q}\right)_1 = 0.497$$

$$S_2 = 0.631 \Rightarrow \left(\frac{Q_S}{Q}\right)_2 = 0.280$$

$$S = 0.4146 \Rightarrow \frac{Q_S}{Q} = ?$$

$$\therefore \quad Q_S = 0.277299 \ l/\text{min}$$

(vi) Temperature rise (ΔT) neglecting the effect of side leakage :

$$E_F = \frac{\rho \cdot Q \cdot C_p \cdot \Delta T \,(1 - 0)}{10^9}$$

$$\therefore \quad 0.076368 = \frac{860 \times 11326.60235 \times 1.76 \times \Delta T}{10^9}$$

$$\therefore \quad \Delta T = 4.4545°C$$

Example 3.3 : Following data is given for a 360° hydrodynamic bearing :
(i)   Radial load = 3.2 kN
(ii) Journal diameter = 50 mm
(iii) Journal speed = 1490 rpm
(iv) Bearing length = 50 mm
(v)   Radial clearance = 50 μm
(vi) Viscosity of lubricant = 25 cP
(vii) Density of lubricant = 860 kg/m³
(viii) Specific heat of lubricant = 1.76 kJ/kg °C.

Assuming that the total heat generated in the bearing is carried by the total oil flow in the bearing, calculate :

   (i)   Coefficient of friction
   (ii) Minimum oil-film thickness
   (iii) Power lost in friction
   (iv) The total flow of lubricant in l/min
   (v)   The side leakage
   (vi) The temperature rise :
   (a)   Considering effect of side leakage
   (b)   Neglecting effect of side leakage.

Solution :

Given : $W_r = 3.2 \times 10^3$ N; $N_j = \dfrac{1490}{60} = 24.8333$ rps;

$l = 50$ mm; $\mu = 25$ cP $= 25 \times 10^{-9}$ N-s/mm^2;

$d = 50$ mm; $\rho = 860$ kg/m^3

$C = 50$ μm $C_p = 1.76$ kJ/kg °C

$ = 50 \times 10^{-6}$ m

$ = 50 \times 10^{-3}$ mm;

To calculate :

(i) $f = ?$,   (ii) $E_F = ?$,

(iii) $Q_S = ?$, (iv) $h_0 = ?$,

(v) $Q = ?$, (vi) $\Delta T = ?$

$$\text{Bearing pressure,} \quad P = \frac{W_r}{l \cdot d}$$

$$= \frac{3.2 \times 10^3}{50 \times 50}$$

$$P = 1.28 \text{ N/mm}^2$$

$$\text{Sommerfeld Number,} \quad S = \left(\frac{r_j}{C}\right)^2 \cdot \frac{\mu \cdot N_j}{P}$$

$$= \left(\frac{25}{0.05}\right)^2 \cdot \frac{25 \times 10^{-9} \times 24.8333}{1.28}$$

$$S = 0.121256$$

From Raimondi and Boyd chart,

for $\left[\dfrac{l}{d}\right] = 1$ and $S = 0.121$,

we can write,

$$\frac{h_0}{C} = 0.4; \quad \left[\frac{Q}{r_j \cdot C \cdot N_j \cdot l}\right] = 4.33;$$

$$f\left(\frac{r_j}{C}\right) = 3.22; \quad \frac{Q_S}{Q} = 0.68;$$

(i) Coefficient of friction (μ) :

We know,

$$f\left(\frac{r_j}{C}\right) = 3.22$$

$$f = 3.22 \times \left(\frac{C}{r_j}\right)$$

$$= 3.22 \times \frac{0.05}{25}$$

$$f = 0.00644$$

(ii) Minimum oil-film thickness (h_0) :

$$\frac{h_0}{C} = 0.4$$

$$\therefore \quad h_0 = 0.4 \times C$$

$$h_0 = 0.4 \times 0.05$$

$$h_0 = 0.02 \text{ mm}$$

(iii) Power lost in friction (E_F) :

$$E_F = \frac{2\pi \cdot N_j \cdot (f \cdot W_r \cdot r_j)}{10^6}$$

$$= \frac{2\pi \times 24.8333 \times 0.00644 \times 3.2 \times 10^3 \times 25}{10^6}$$

$$\therefore \quad E_F = 0.080388 \text{ kW}$$

(iv) Total flow of lubricant (l/min) :

$$\left(\frac{Q}{r_j \cdot C \cdot N_j \cdot l}\right) = 4.33$$

$$\therefore \quad Q = 4.33 \, (r_j \cdot C \cdot N_j \cdot l)$$

$$= 4.33 \times 25 \times 0.05 \times 24.8333 \times 50$$

$$= 6720.512 \text{ mm}^3/\text{sec}$$

$$= 6720.512 \times 10^{-9} \text{ m}^3/\text{sec}$$

$$= (6720.512 \times 10^{-9}) \times 10^3 \times 60 \text{ } l/\text{min}$$

$$\therefore \quad Q = 0.403231 \text{ } l/\text{min}$$

(v) Side leakage (Q_S) :

$$\frac{Q_S}{Q} = 0.680$$

$$\therefore \quad Q_S = 0.680 \times Q$$

$$\therefore \quad Q_S = 0.680 \times 0.403231$$

$$\therefore \quad Q_S = 0.274197 \text{ } l/\text{min}$$

(vi) Temperature rise (ΔT) :

(a) Considering effect of side leakage,

$$\text{Heat generated} = \text{Heat dissipated}$$

$$\therefore \qquad E_F = \frac{\rho \cdot Q \cdot C_P \cdot \Delta T \left[1 - \dfrac{Q_S}{2Q}\right]}{10^9}$$

$$\therefore \qquad 0.080388 = \frac{860 \times 6720.512 \times 1.76 \left[1 - \dfrac{0.68}{2}\right] \cdot \Delta T}{10^9}$$

$$\therefore \qquad \Delta T = 11.9738°C$$

(b) Neglecting effect of side leakage :

$$E_F = \frac{\rho \cdot Q \cdot C_P \cdot \Delta T \,(1 - 0)}{10^9}$$

$$0.080388 = \frac{860 \times 6720.512 \times 1.76 \times \Delta T}{10^9}$$

$$\Delta T = 7.903°C$$

Example 3.4 : A 360° hydrodynamic bearing has the following data :
(i)   Journal diameter = 50 mm
(ii) Length of journal = 50 mm
(iii) Radial load on journal = 15 kN
(iv) Journal speed = 1450 rpm
(v)   Eccentricity ratio = 0.75
(vi) Radial clearance = 20 μm
(vii) Specific gravity of the oil = 0.86
(viii) Specific heat = 2.09 kJ/kg °C

Evaluate :

   (i)   Probable coefficient of friction;

   (ii) Viscosity of oil;

   (iii) Minimum oil-film thickness;

   (iv) Quantity of oil in circulation;

   (v)   Oil leakage through sides, and

   (vi) The average oil temperature if the oil is supplied at 28°C.

Solution :

Given :

$$W_r = 15 \text{ kN}$$
$$= 15 \times 10^3 \text{ N}$$
$$N_j = \frac{1450}{60} = 24.1667 \text{ rps}$$
$$\epsilon = 0.75 = \frac{e}{C}$$
$$l = 50 \text{ mm}$$

$$d = 50 \text{ m}$$

$$\therefore \frac{l}{d} = 1 \text{ and } r_j = 25 \text{ mm}$$

$$C = 20 \ \mu m$$
$$= 0.02 \text{ mm}$$
$$C_P = 2.09 \text{ kJ/kg } °C$$

To find :

(i) $f = ?$,   (ii) $\mu = ?$,

(iii) $h_0 = ?$, (iv) $Q = ?$,

(v) $Q_S = ?$, (vi) $T_{AV} = ?$

Now,
$$\epsilon = 1 - \frac{h_0}{C}$$

$$0.75 = 1 - \frac{h_0}{C}$$

$$\therefore \qquad \frac{h_0}{C} = 0.25$$

Sommerfeld Number (S) :

From table,

$$\left(\frac{h_0}{C}\right)_1 = 0.2 \Rightarrow S_1 = 0.0446$$

$$\left(\frac{h_0}{C}\right)_2 = 0.4 \Rightarrow S_2 = 0.121$$

$$\left(\frac{h_0}{C}\right) = 0.25 \Rightarrow S = ?$$

$\therefore$ Using linear interpolation to find S at $\left(\dfrac{h_0}{C}\right) = 0.25$

$$\therefore \qquad \frac{S - 0.0446}{0.121 - 0.0446} = \frac{0.25 - 0.2}{0.4 - 0.2}$$

$$\therefore \qquad S = 0.0637$$

(i) Probable coefficient of friction (μ) :

From table,

$$\left(\frac{h_0}{C}\right)_1 = 0.2 \Rightarrow \left[\left(\frac{r_j}{C}\right)f\right]_1 = 1.70$$

$$\left(\frac{h_0}{C}\right)_2 = 0.4 \Rightarrow \left[\left(\frac{r_j}{C}\right)f\right]_2 = 3.22$$

$$\left(\frac{h_0}{C}\right)_3 = 0.25 \Rightarrow \left[\left(\frac{r_j}{C}\right)f\right] = ?$$

$$\therefore \qquad \frac{\left[\left(\dfrac{r_j}{C}\right)f\right] - 1.70}{3.22 - 1.70} = \frac{0.25 - 0.2}{0.4 - 0.2}$$

$$\left(\frac{r_j}{C}\right)f = 2.08$$

$$\therefore \qquad f = 2.08 \times \frac{C}{r_j}$$

$$= 2.08 \times \frac{0.02}{25}$$

$$f = 0.001664$$

(ii) Viscosity of oil (μ) :

$$S = \left(\frac{r_j}{C}\right)^2 \frac{\mu \cdot N_j}{P}$$

$$= \left(\frac{r_j}{C}\right)^2 \frac{\mu \cdot N_j}{\left(\dfrac{W_r}{l \cdot d}\right)}$$

$$\therefore \qquad \mu = \frac{S \cdot \left(\dfrac{W_r}{l \cdot d}\right)}{\left(\dfrac{r_j}{C}\right)^2 \cdot N_j}$$

$$= \frac{0.0637 \cdot \left(\dfrac{15 \times 10^3}{50 \times 50}\right)}{\left(\dfrac{25}{0.02}\right)^2 \cdot 24.1667}$$

$$= 10.1216 \times 10^{-9} \text{ N-s/mm}^2$$

$$\mu = 10.1216 \text{ cP}$$

(iii) Minimum oil-film thickness (h_0) :

$$\frac{h_0}{C} = 0.25$$

$$\therefore \qquad h_0 = 0.02 \times 0.25$$

$$\therefore \qquad h_0 = 0.005 \text{ mm}$$

(iv) Quantity of oil in circulation (Q) :

From table,

$$\left(\frac{h_0}{C}\right)_1 = 0.2 \Rightarrow \left[\frac{Q}{r_j \cdot C \cdot N_j \cdot l}\right]_1 = 4.62$$

$$\left(\frac{h_0}{C}\right)_2 = 0.4 \Rightarrow \left[\frac{Q}{r_j \cdot C \cdot N_j \cdot l}\right]_2 = 4.33$$

$$\left(\frac{h_0}{C}\right) = 0.25 \Rightarrow \left[\frac{Q}{r_j \cdot C \cdot N_j \cdot l}\right] = \ ?$$

$$\frac{\left[\dfrac{Q}{r_j \cdot C \cdot N_j \cdot l}\right] - 4.62}{4.33 - 4.62} = \frac{0.25 - 0.2}{0.4 - 0.2}$$

$$\left[\frac{Q}{r_j \cdot C \cdot N_j \cdot l}\right] = 4.5475$$

$$\therefore \qquad Q = 4.5475 \ (r_j \cdot C \cdot N_j \cdot l)$$

$$= 4.5475 \ (25 \times 0.02 \times 24.1667 \times 50)$$

$$= 2747.45 \ \text{mm}^3/\text{s}$$

$$= 2747.45 \times 10^{-9} \ \text{m}^3/\text{s}$$

$$= (2747.45 \times 10^{-9}) \times 10^3 \times 60 \ l/\text{min}$$

$$Q = 0.164847 \ l/\text{min}$$

(v) Oil leakage through sides (Q_S) :

$$\left(\frac{h_0}{C}\right)_1 = 0.2 \Rightarrow \left(\frac{Q_S}{Q}\right)_1 = 0.842$$

$$\left(\frac{h_0}{C}\right)_2 = 0.4 \Rightarrow \left(\frac{Q_S}{Q}\right)_2 = 0.680$$

$$\left(\frac{h_0}{C}\right) = 0.25 \Rightarrow \left(\frac{Q_S}{Q}\right) = \ ?$$

$$\therefore \qquad \frac{\left(\dfrac{Q_S}{Q}\right) - 0.842}{0.680 - 0.842} = \frac{0.25 - 0.2}{0.4 - 0.2}$$

$$\frac{Q_S}{Q} = 0.8015$$

$$\therefore \qquad Q_S = 0.8015 \times 0.164847$$

$$\therefore \qquad Q_S = 0.132125 \ l/\text{min}$$

(vi) Average oil temperature if the oil is supplied at 28°C :

Considering oil leakage through sides,

$$E_F = \frac{\rho \cdot Q \cdot C_P \cdot \Delta T \left(1 - \dfrac{Q_S}{2Q}\right)}{10^9}$$

Now,

$$E_F = \frac{2\pi \cdot N_j \,(f \cdot W_r \cdot r_j)}{10^6}$$

$$= \frac{2\pi \times 24.1667 \,(0.001664 \times 15 \times 10^3 \times 25)}{10^6}$$

$$E_F = 0.094751 \text{ kW Power lost in friction.}$$

Using in above equation,

$$0.094751 = \frac{860 \times 2747.45 \times 2.09 \times \Delta T \left(1 - \dfrac{1 \times 0.8015}{2}\right)}{10^9}$$

$$\Delta T = 32.0185°C$$

∴ Average temperature of lubricating oil,

$$T_{AV} = T_i + \frac{\Delta T}{2} = 28 + \frac{32.0185}{2}$$

∴ $T_{AV} = 44.00925°C$

Example 3.5 : The following data is given for a 360° hydrodynamic bearing :

(i) Radial load = 10 kN

(ii) Journal speed = 1450 rpm

(iii) $\dfrac{l}{d}$ ratio = 1

(iv) Bearing length = 50 mm

(v) Radial clearance = 20 microns

(vi) Eccentricity = 15 microns

(vii) Specific gravity of lubricant = 0.86

(viii) Specific heat of lubricant = 2.09 kJ/kg°C

Calculate :

 (i) The minimum oil film thickness

 (ii) The coefficient of friction

 (iii) The power lost in friction

 (iv) The viscosity of lubricant in cP

 (v) The total flow rate of lubricant in lit/min

 (vi) Side leakage

(vii) The average temperature, if makeup oil is supplied at 30°C.

Dimensionless parameters are as follows :

$\dfrac{l}{d}$	$\dfrac{h_0}{C}$	$\in$	s	$\left(\dfrac{r}{c}\right)f$	$\dfrac{Q}{r \cdot C \cdot n \cdot l}$	$\dfrac{Q_L}{Q}$	$\dfrac{P_{max}}{p}$
	0.2	0.8	0.0446	1.7	4.62	0.842	3.195
1	0.4	0.6	0.121	3.22	4.33	0.680	2.409
	0.6	0.4	0.264	5.79	3.99	0.497	2.066

(P.U. June 2012, 14 marks)

Note : Assume linear interpolation for intermediate values.   **(P.U. Dec. 2011, 14 marks)**

Solution :

Given : $W = 10 \text{ kN} = 10 \times 10^3 \text{ N}$

$n = \dfrac{1450}{60} = 24.1667 \text{ rps}$

$\in = 0.75 = \dfrac{e}{C}$

$e = 15 \times 10^{-3} \text{ mm} = 0.015 \text{ mm}$

$l = 50 \text{ mm}$

$\dfrac{l}{d} = 1$

$C = 20 \times 10^{-3} = 0.020 \text{ mm}$

$\rho = 860 \text{ kg/m}^3$

$C_p = 2.09 \text{ kJ/kg °C}$

$T_i = 30°C$

1. Minimum oil film thickness (h_0) :

$$1 - \dfrac{h_0}{C} = e$$

$\therefore \qquad \dfrac{h_0}{C} = 1 - \in = 1 - 0.75$

$\therefore \qquad \dfrac{h_0}{C} = 0.25$

$\therefore \qquad h_0 = 0.25 \times 0.020 = 0.005 \text{ mm} = 5 \text{ μm}$

As $\dfrac{h_0}{C} = 0.25$, the dimensionless parameters that correspond to this value can be evaluated based on linear interpolation.

2. Coefficient of friction (f) :

$$\left(\dfrac{h_0}{C}\right)_1 = 0.2 \; ; \left(\dfrac{r}{C}\right)f = 1.7$$

$$\left(\dfrac{h_0}{C}\right)_2 = 0.4 \; ; \left(\dfrac{r}{C}\right)f = 3.22$$

$$\left(\frac{h_0}{C}\right)_3 = 0.25 \; ; \left(\frac{r}{C}\right)f = ?$$

Using linear interpolation,

$$\therefore \quad \frac{\left(\frac{r}{C}\right)f - 1.7}{3.22 - 1.7} = \frac{0.25 - 0.2}{0.4 - 0.2}$$

$$\left(\frac{r}{C}\right)f = 2.08$$

$$\therefore \quad f = 2.08 \times \frac{0.02}{25}$$

$$\mathbf{f = 0.001664}$$

3. Power lost in friction (E_F) :

$$E_F = \frac{2\pi n\,(f \cdot W \cdot r)}{10^6} = \frac{2 \times \pi \times 24.1667 \times 0.001664 \times 10 \times 10^3 \times 25}{10^6}$$

$$\mathbf{E_F = 0.0631 \ kW}$$

4. Viscosity of lubricant (μ) :

$$P = \frac{W}{l \cdot d} = \frac{10 \times 10^3}{50 \times 50} = 4 \ N/mm^2$$

From the given table,

$$\left(\frac{h_0}{C}\right)_1 = 0.2 \; ; s_1 = 0.0466$$

$$\left(\frac{h_0}{C}\right)_2 = 0.4 \; ; s_2 = 0.121$$

$$\left(\frac{h_0}{C}\right)_3 = 0.25 \; ; s_3 = ?$$

Using linear interpolation

$$\frac{s - 0.0446}{0.25 - 0.2} = \frac{0.121 - 0.0446}{0.4 - 0.2}$$

$$s = 0.0637$$

Now, Sommerfeld number

$$s = \left(\frac{r}{C}\right)^2 \frac{\mu \cdot n}{P}$$

$$\therefore \quad 0.0637 = \left(\frac{25}{0.02}\right)^2 \times \frac{\mu \times 24.1667}{4}$$

$$\therefore \quad \mu = 6.7482 \times 10^{-9} \ N\text{-}s/mm^2$$

$$\text{or} \quad \mathbf{\mu = 6.7482 \ cP}$$

5. Total flow rate of lubricant (l/min) Q :

From the given table, $\left(\dfrac{h_0}{C}\right)_1 = 0.2$; $\left(\dfrac{Q}{r \cdot C \cdot n \cdot l}\right)_1 = 4.62$

$\left(\dfrac{h_0}{C}\right)_2 = 0.4$; $\left(\dfrac{Q}{r \cdot C \cdot n \cdot l}\right)_2 = 4.33$

$\left(\dfrac{h_0}{C}\right)_3 = 0.25$; $\left(\dfrac{Q}{r \cdot C \cdot n \cdot l}\right) = ?$

Using linear interpolation,

$$\frac{\left(\dfrac{Q}{r \cdot C \cdot n \cdot l}\right) - 4.33}{0.4 - 0.25} = \frac{4.62 - 4.33}{0.4 - 0.2}$$

$\therefore \qquad \left(\dfrac{Q}{r \cdot C \cdot n \cdot l}\right) = 4.5475$

$\therefore \qquad\qquad Q = 4.5475 \,(25 \times 0.02 \times 24.1667 \times 50)$

$\qquad\qquad\qquad = 2747.45 \text{ mm}^3/\text{sec}$

$\qquad\qquad\qquad = 2747.45 \times 10^{-9} \text{ m}^3/\text{s}$

$\qquad\qquad\qquad = (2747.45 \times 10^{-9}) \times 10^3 \times 60 \; l/\text{min}$

$\therefore \qquad\qquad \mathbf{Q = 0.164847} \; \boldsymbol{l}/\textbf{min}$

6. Side leakage (Q_s) :

From the given table,

$\left(\dfrac{h_0}{C}\right)_1 = 0.2$; $\left(\dfrac{Q_s}{Q}\right)_1 = 0.842$

$\left(\dfrac{h_0}{C}\right)_2 = 0.4$; $\left(\dfrac{Q_s}{Q}\right)_2 = 0.68$

$\left(\dfrac{h_0}{C}\right)_3 = 0.25$; $\left(\dfrac{Q_s}{Q}\right) = ?$

Using linear interpolation,

$$\frac{\left(\dfrac{Q_s}{Q}\right) - 0.68}{0.4 - 0.25} = \frac{0.842 - 0.68}{0.4 - 0.2}$$

$\therefore \qquad\qquad \dfrac{Q_s}{Q} = 0.8015$

$\qquad\qquad\qquad Q_s = 0.8015 \times 0.164847$

$\qquad\qquad\qquad \mathbf{Q_s = 0.132125} \; \boldsymbol{l}/\textbf{min}$

7. Average temperature of make up oil is supplied at 30°C (T_{AV}) :

Power lost in friction

$$E_F = \frac{\rho \cdot Q \cdot C_p \cdot \Delta T \left(1 - \frac{Q_s}{2Q}\right)}{10^9}$$

$$0.0631 = \frac{860 \times 2747.45 \times 2.09 \times \Delta T \left(1 - \frac{1 \times 0.8015}{2}\right)}{10^9}$$

$\therefore \qquad \Delta T = 21.322°C$

$\therefore$ Average temperature of lubricant

$$T_{AV} = T_i + \frac{\Delta T}{2}$$

$$= 30 + \frac{21.322}{2}$$

$$= 30 + 10.661$$

$$\mathbf{T_{AV} = 40.661°C}$$

Example 3.6 : A hydrodynamic journal bearing is subjected to a radial load of 10 kN. The permissible unit bearing pressure is 1000 kPa. The length to diameter ratio is 1. The radius of journal is about 800 times the radial clearance. The viscosity of lubricating oil in working condition is 30 MPa-s. Calculate :

   (i)   The length of bearing.

   (ii) The diameter of journal.

   (iii) Coefficient of friction.

   (iv) Power lost in friction and

   (v) Total flow of the oil.

The journal rotates at 1440 rpm.

Solution :

Given : $W_r = 10$ kN $= 10 \times 10^3$ N

$$P = 1000 \text{ kPa} = 1000 \times 10^3 \text{ N/m}^3$$

$$= 1 \text{ N/mm}^2$$

$$\frac{l}{d} = 1 \Rightarrow \therefore \quad l = d$$

$$r_j = 800 \, (C)$$

$\therefore \qquad \dfrac{r_j}{C} = 800$

$$\mu = 30 \text{ MPa-s}$$

$$= 30 \times 10^6 \text{ Pa-s}$$

$$= 30 \text{ N-s/mm}^2 = 30 \times 10^{-9} \text{ N-s/m}^2 = 30 \text{ cP}$$

$$N_j = \frac{1440}{60} = 24 \text{ rps}$$

To calculate :

(i) l = ?,   (ii)   d = ?,

(iii) f = ?,   (iv) E_F = ?,

(v) Q = ?

(i) The length of bearing :

$$\text{Bearing pressure, P} = \frac{W_r}{l \cdot d}$$

$$\text{As } l = d \Rightarrow P = \frac{W_r}{l^2}$$

$$\therefore \qquad l^2 = \frac{W_r}{P}$$

$$= \frac{10 \times 10^3}{1}$$

$$= 10^4 \text{ mm}^2$$

$$\therefore \qquad l = 100 \text{ mm}$$

(ii) The diameter of journal :

$$d = 100 \text{ mm} \qquad\qquad (\because l = d)$$

Sommerfeld Number (S),

$$S = \left(\frac{r_j}{C}\right)^2 \frac{\mu \cdot N_j}{P}$$

$$= (800)^2 \cdot \frac{30 \times 10^{-9} \times 24}{1}$$

$$S = 0.4608$$

(iii) Coefficient of friction (μ) :

Now, from table,

$$\text{For} \qquad S_1 = 0.264 \Rightarrow \left[\left(\frac{r_j}{C}\right)f\right]_1 = 5.79$$

$$S_2 = 0.631 \Rightarrow \left[\left(\frac{r_j}{C}\right)f\right]_2 = 12.8$$

$$S = 0.4608 \Rightarrow \left[\left(\frac{r_j}{C}\right)f\right] = ?$$

$\therefore$ Using linear interpolation technique,

$$\frac{\left[\left(\frac{r_j}{C}\right)f\right] - 5.79}{12.8 - 5.79} = \frac{0.4608 - 0.264}{0.631 - 0.264}$$

$$\left(\frac{r_j}{C}\right) f = 9.54904$$

$$\therefore \quad f = 9.54904 \times \left(\frac{C}{r_j}\right)$$

$$\therefore \quad f = 0.011936$$

(iv) Power lost in friction (E_F) :

$$E_F = \frac{2\pi \cdot N_j \, (f \, W_r \cdot r_j)}{10^6}$$

$$= \frac{2\pi \times 24 \, (0.011936 \times 10 \times 10^3 \times 50)}{10^6}$$

$$E_F = 0.89995 \text{ kW}$$

(v) Total flow of the oil (Q) :

From table,

For,

$$S_1 = 0.264 \Rightarrow \left[\frac{Q}{r_j \cdot C \cdot N_j \cdot l}\right]_1 = 3.99$$

$$S_2 = 0.631 \Rightarrow \left[\frac{Q}{r_j \cdot C \cdot N_j \cdot l}\right]_2 = 3.59$$

$$S = 0.4608 \Rightarrow \left[\frac{Q}{r_j \cdot C \cdot N_j \cdot l}\right] = ?$$

$$\therefore \quad \frac{\left[\dfrac{Q}{r_j \cdot C \cdot N_j \cdot l}\right] - 3.99}{3.59 - 3.99} = \frac{0.4608 - 0.264}{0.631 - 0.264}$$

$$\left[\frac{Q}{r_j \cdot C \cdot N_j \cdot l}\right] = 3.775504$$

$$\therefore \quad Q_T = 3.775504 \, (r_j \cdot C \cdot N_j \cdot l)$$

$$= 3.775504 \, (50 \times 0.0625 \times 24 \times 100)$$

$$\left(\because \ \frac{r_j}{C} = 800 \quad \therefore \ C = 0.0625\right)$$

$$\therefore \quad Q = 28316.28 \text{ mm}^3/\text{sec}$$

$$= 28316.28 \times 10^{-9} \text{ m}^3/\text{s}$$

$$= (28316.28 \times 10^{-9}) \times 60 \times 10^3 \ l/\text{min}$$

Also, $\quad Q = 1.69898 \ l/\text{min}$

Example 3.7 : Following data is given for a 360° hydrodynamic bearing :
(i)   Length to diameter ratio = 1
(ii) Minimum film-thickness variable = 0.3
(iii) Journal diameter = 100 mm
(iv) Diametral clearance = 100 μm
(v)   External load = 9000 N
(vi) Journal speed = 1350 rpm
Find :
   (i)   The viscosity of oil that need to be used and
   (ii) The coefficient of friction.

Solution :

Given : W_r = 9000 N

$$\frac{l}{d} = 1 \quad \Rightarrow \qquad \therefore \quad l = d$$

$$\frac{h_0}{C} = 0.3$$

$$d = 100 \text{ mm} \quad \therefore \quad l = 100 \text{ mm}$$

$$C = \frac{\text{Diametral clearance}}{2}$$

$$= \frac{100}{2}\ \mu\text{m}$$

$$= 50\ \mu\text{m} = 0.05 \text{ mm}$$

$$N_j = \frac{1350}{60} = 22.5 \text{ rps}$$

To calculate :

(i) μ = ?,   (ii) f = ?

Now, bearing pressure, $P = \dfrac{W_r}{l\,d} = \dfrac{9000}{100 \times 100}$

$\therefore$ P = 0.9 N/mm²

Now, for $\left(\dfrac{l}{d}\right)$ = 1, from table,

and $\left(\dfrac{h_0}{C}\right)$ = 0.3

For $\left(\dfrac{h_0}{C}\right)_1$ = 0.2 $\Rightarrow S_1$ = 0.0446

$$\left(\frac{h_0}{C}\right)_2 = 0.4 \Rightarrow S_2 = 0.121$$

$$\left(\frac{h_0}{C}\right) = 0.3 \Rightarrow S = ?$$

Using linear interpolation,

$$\frac{S - 0.0446}{0.121 - 0.0446} = \frac{0.3 - 0.2}{0.4 - 0.2}$$

$$\therefore \qquad S = 0.0828$$

(i) Viscosity of oil to be used :

Now,
$$S = \left(\frac{r_j}{C}\right)^2 \frac{\mu \cdot N_j}{P}$$

$$\therefore \qquad \mu = \frac{S \cdot P}{\left(\frac{r_j}{C}\right)^2 \cdot N_j}$$

$$= \frac{0.0828 \times 0.9}{\left(\frac{50}{0.05}\right)^2 \times 22.5}$$

$$\therefore \qquad \mu = 3.312 \times 10^{-9} \ \text{N-s/mm}^2$$

$$= 3.312 \ \text{cP}$$

(ii) Coefficient of friction (μ) :

From table,

For
$$\left(\frac{h_0}{C}\right)_1 = 0.2 \Rightarrow \left[\left(\frac{r_j}{C}\right)f\right]_1 = 1.7$$

$$\left(\frac{h_0}{C}\right)_2 = 0.4 \Rightarrow \left[\left(\frac{r_j}{C}\right)f\right]_2 = 3.22$$

$$\left(\frac{h_0}{C}\right) = 0.3 \Rightarrow \left[\left(\frac{r_j}{C}\right)f\right] = ?$$

Using linear interpolation,

$$\frac{\left[\left(\frac{r_j}{C}\right)f\right] - 1.7}{3.22 - 1.7} = \frac{0.3 - 0.2}{0.4 - 0.2}$$

$$\left(\frac{r_j}{C}\right)f = 2.46$$

$$\therefore \qquad f = 2.46 \times \frac{C}{r_j}$$

$$= 2.46 \times \frac{0.05}{50}$$

$$\therefore \qquad f = 0.00246$$

Example 3.8 : The following data refers to a 360° hydrodynamic journal bearing :

(i) Radial load = 30000 N

(ii) Nominal journal diameter = 75 mm

(iii) Bearing width = 75 mm

(iv) Radial clearance = 0.15 mm

(v) Operating speed = 3600 rpm

(vi) Inlet oil temperature = 40°C

The temperature-viscosity relationship is as follows :

t°C	40	41	42	43	44	45	46	47	48	49	50
μ (cP)	52.5	50	47.5	45	43	41	39	37.5	36	34	33

Assume that the total heat produced in the bearing is carried by the total oil flow. The specific gravity and specific heat of the lubricant are 0.86 and 1.76 kJ/kg °C respectively. Calculate :

    (i) Minimum oil-film thickness,

    (ii) Power lost in friction,

    (iii) Requirement of lubricant flow, and

    (iv) Outlet lubricant temperature.

Solution :

Given :

$$W_r = 30000 \text{ N}$$
$$d = 75 \text{ mm}$$
$$l = 75 \text{ mm}$$
$$C = 0.15 \text{ mm}$$
$$N_j = \frac{3600}{60} = 60 \text{ rps}$$
$$T_i = 40°C$$
$$\rho = 860 \text{ kg/m}^3$$
$$C_P = 1.76 \text{ kJ/kg °C}$$

To find :

(i) h_0 = ?, (ii) E_F = ?,

(iii) Q = ?, (iv) T_0 = ?

Here, viscosity of lubricant is to be specified to evaluate the Sommerfeld Number. And viscosity varies with temperature and the average working temperature is not known at initial stage. Therefore, such problems are solved by the trial and error method.

$$\text{Bearing pressure, } P \;=\; \frac{W_r}{l \cdot d} = \frac{30000}{75 \times 75}$$

$$=\; 5.3333 \text{ N/mm}^2$$

$$\text{Sommerfeld Number, } S \;=\; \left(\frac{r_j}{C}\right)^2 \frac{\mu \cdot N_j}{P}$$

$$=\; \left(\frac{37.5}{0.15}\right)^2 \cdot \frac{\mu \times 10^{-9} \times 60}{5.3333}$$

$$S \;=\; 703129.395 \times 10^{-9} \cdot \mu$$

Now, viscosity at inlet temperature of 40°C is 52.5 cP. The average temperature will be more than 40°C.

Trial Case (i) :

$$\text{Assuming viscosity, } \mu \;=\; 45 \text{ cP}$$

$$\therefore \qquad\qquad\qquad\qquad S \;=\; 703129.395 \times 10^{-9} \times 45$$

$$S \;=\; 0.03164$$

From table,

For
$$\left(\frac{l}{d}\right) \;=\; 1$$

For
$$S_1 \;=\; 0.0188 \Rightarrow \left[\left(\frac{r_j}{C}\right)f\right]_1 = 1.05$$

$$S_2 \;=\; 0.0446 \Rightarrow \left[\left(\frac{r_j}{C}\right)f\right]_2 = 1.70$$

$$S \;=\; 0.03164 \Rightarrow \left[\left(\frac{r_j}{C}\right)f\right] = \;?$$

$\therefore$ Using linear interpolation,

$$\frac{\left[\left(\frac{r_j}{C}\right)f\right] - 1.05}{1.7 - 1.05} \;=\; \frac{0.03164 - 0.0188}{0.0446 - 0.0188}$$

$$\therefore \qquad\qquad \left(\frac{r_j}{C}\right)f \;=\; 1.3735 = CFV$$

Also from table,

For
$$\left(\frac{l}{d}\right) \;=\; 1$$

For
$$S_1 \;=\; 0.0188 \Rightarrow \left[\frac{Q}{r_j \cdot C \cdot N_j \cdot l}\right]_1 = 4.74$$

$$S_2 \;=\; 0.0446 \Rightarrow \left[\frac{Q}{r_j \cdot C \cdot N_j \cdot l}\right]_2 = 4.62$$

$$S \;=\; 0.03164 \;\Rightarrow\; \left[\frac{Q}{r_j \cdot C \cdot N_j \cdot l}\right] = \;?$$

$$\therefore \quad \frac{\left[\dfrac{Q}{r_j \cdot C \cdot N_j \cdot l}\right] - 4.74}{4.62 - 4.74} \;=\; \frac{0.03164 - 0.0188}{0.0446 - 0.0188}$$

$$\left[\frac{Q}{r_j \cdot C \cdot N_j \cdot l}\right] \;=\; 4.6803 \;=\; FV$$

Now, temperature rise,

$$\Delta t \;=\; 8.3 \, P \, \frac{(CFV)}{(FV)}$$

$$=\; 8.3 \times 5.3333 \, \frac{(1.3735)}{(4.6803)}$$

$$\Delta t \;=\; 12.9905°C$$

Average temperature,

$$T_{AV} \;=\; T_i + \frac{\Delta t}{2}$$

$$=\; 40 + \frac{12.9905}{2}$$

$$T_{AV} \;=\; 46.4953°C$$

From viscosity-temperature table, it is clear that the viscosity corresponding to 46.5°C is approximately 38 cP, but the assumed value is 45 cP.

Therefore, we assume viscosity as 39 cP as second trial.

Trial Case (ii) :

$$\mu \;=\; 39 \text{ cP}$$

$$\therefore \quad S \;=\; 703129.395 \times 10^{-9} \times 39$$

$$S \;=\; 0.027422$$

From table,

For

$$\left(\frac{l}{d}\right) \;=\; 1$$

For

$$S_1 \;=\; 0.0188 \;\Rightarrow\; \left[\left(\frac{r_j}{C}\right) f\right]_1 = 1.05$$

$$S_2 \;=\; 0.0446 \;\Rightarrow\; \left[\left(\frac{r_j}{C}\right) f\right]_2 = 1.7$$

$$S = 0.027422 \Rightarrow \left[\left(\frac{r_j}{C}\right)f\right] = \,?$$

$\therefore$ Using linear interpolation,

$$\frac{\left[\left(\frac{r_j}{C}\right)f\right] - 1.05}{1.7 - 1.05} = \frac{0.027422 - 0.0188}{0.0446 - 0.0188}$$

$$\left[\left(\frac{r_j}{C}\right)f\right] = 1.2672 = CFV$$

Also,

For

$$S_1 = 0.0188 \Rightarrow \left[\frac{Q}{r_j \cdot C \cdot N_j \cdot l}\right] = 4.74$$

$$S_2 = 0.0446 \Rightarrow \left[\frac{Q}{r_j \cdot C \cdot N_j \cdot l}\right] = 4.62$$

$$S = 0.027422 \Rightarrow \left[\frac{Q}{r_j \cdot C \cdot N_j \cdot l}\right] = \,?$$

$\therefore$

$$\frac{\left[\dfrac{Q}{r_j \cdot C \cdot N_j \cdot l}\right] - 4.74}{4.62 - 4.74} = \frac{0.027422 - 0.0188}{0.0446 - 0.0188}$$

$$\left[\frac{Q}{r_j \cdot C \cdot N_j \cdot l}\right] = 4.6999 = FV$$

And temperature rise,

$$\Delta T = 8.3\, P\, \frac{(CFV)}{FV}$$

$$= 8.3 \times 5.3333 \times \frac{1.2672}{4.6999}$$

$$\Delta T = 11.9352°C$$

Average temperature,

$$T_{AV} = T_i + \frac{\Delta T}{2}$$

$$= 40 + \frac{11.9352}{2}$$

$$T_{AV} = 45.9676°C \approx 46°C$$

It is seen from viscosity-temperature table, that the viscosity at 46°C is 39 cP.

$\therefore$ The assumed value in Trial Case (ii) is correct.

$$\therefore \qquad \left(\frac{r_j}{C}\right) f = 1.2672$$

$$\therefore \qquad f = 1.2672 \times \frac{C}{r_j}$$

$$= 1.2672 \times \frac{0.15}{37.5}$$

$\therefore$ Coefficient of friction,

$$f = 0.0050688$$

(i) Minimum oil-film thickness :

From table,

For
$$\left(\frac{l}{d}\right) = 1$$

$$S_1 = 0.0188 \Rightarrow \left(\frac{h_0}{C}\right)_1 = 0.1$$

$$S_2 = 0.0446 \Rightarrow \left(\frac{h_0}{C}\right)_2 = 0.2$$

$$S = 0.027422 \Rightarrow \left(\frac{h_0}{C}\right) = ?$$

$$\therefore \qquad \frac{\left(\frac{h_0}{C}\right) - 0.1}{0.2 - 0.1} = \frac{0.027422 - 0.0188}{0.0446 - 0.0188}$$

$$\frac{h_0}{C} = 0.13342$$

$$\therefore \qquad h_0 = 0.13342 \times 0.15$$

$$\therefore \qquad h_0 = 0.020013 \text{ mm}$$

(ii) Power lost in friction (E_F) :

$$E_F = \frac{2\pi \cdot N_j \cdot (f\, W_r \cdot r_j)}{10^6}$$

$$= \frac{2\pi \times 60 \times 0.0050688 \times 30000 \times 37.5}{10^6}$$

$$\therefore \qquad E_F = 2.14975 \text{ kW}$$

(iii) Requirement of lubricant flow :

$$\left[\frac{Q}{r_j \cdot C \cdot N_j \cdot l}\right] = 4.6999$$

$$\therefore \qquad Q = 4.6999\,(r_j \cdot C \cdot N_j \cdot l)$$

$$= 4.6999\,(37.5 \times 0.15 \times 60 \times 75)$$

$$\therefore \qquad Q \;=\; 118966.219 \text{ mm}^3/\text{s} = 118966.219 \times 10^{-9} \text{ m}^3/\text{s}$$
$$\qquad\qquad =\; (118966.219 \times 10^{-9}) \times 60 \times 10^3 \; l/\text{min}$$
$$\therefore \qquad Q \;=\; 7.13797 \; l/\text{min}$$

(iv) Outlet lubricant temperature :

$$T_O \;=\; T_i + \Delta t = 40 + 11.9352$$
$$\therefore \qquad T_O \;=\; 51.9352°C$$

Example 3.9 :

The following data is given for 360° hydrodynamic bearing :

(i) $\dfrac{l}{d} = 0.5$

(ii) Journal diameter = 100 mm

(iii) Journal speed = 1500 rpm

(iv) Minimum oil-film thickness = 15 microns

(v) Viscosity of lubricant = 30 cP

(vi) Specific gravity of lubricant = 0.86

(vii) Specific heat of lubricant = 2.09 kJ/kg °C

(viii) Fit between journal and bearing = $H_7 e_7$

Calculate :

    (i)   The load-carrying capacity of bearing

    (ii) The coefficient of friction

    (iii) The power lost in friction

    (iv) The total lubricant flow rate

    (v)   The side leakage and

    (vi) The temperature rise considering effect of side leakage.

Use following data.

Diameter, mm	Tolerances, mm	
	H_7	e_7
100	+ 0.035	− 0.072
	+ 0.000	− 0.107

    (**Note :** Use Raimondi and Boyd chart/table for $\dfrac{l}{d} = 0.5$).

Solution :

Given :

$$\frac{l}{d} = 0.5$$

$$d = 100 \text{ mm} \quad \Rightarrow \quad \therefore \quad l = 50 \text{ mm}$$

$$N_j = \frac{1500}{60} = 25$$

$$h_0 = 15 \text{ μm} = 15 \times 10^{-6} \text{ m} = 0.015 \text{ mm}$$

$$\mu = 30 \text{ cP} = 30 \times 10^{-9} \text{ N-s/mm}^2$$

$$C_P = 2.09 \text{ kJ/kg °C}$$

$$\rho = 860 \text{ kg/m}^3$$

Calculating average diameters of bearing and journal are :

$$D_a = 100 + \left(\frac{0.00 + 0.035}{2}\right) = 100.0175 \text{ mm}$$

$$d_a = 100 - \left(\frac{0.107 + 0.072}{2}\right) = 99.9105 \text{ mm}$$

$$\text{Radial clearance} = \frac{D_a - d_a}{2} = \frac{100.0175 - 99.9105}{2}$$

$$C = 0.0535 \text{ mm}$$

Minimum oil-film thickness variable,

$$\frac{h_0}{C} = \frac{0.015}{0.0535} = 0.28$$

(i) Load-carrying capacity of bearing :

From table,

For

$$\left(\frac{l}{d}\right) = 0.5$$

$$\left(\frac{h_0}{C}\right)_1 = 0.2 \quad \Rightarrow \quad S_1 = 0.0923$$

$$\left(\frac{h_0}{C}\right)_2 = 0.4 \quad \Rightarrow \quad S_2 = 0.319$$

$$\left(\frac{h_0}{C}\right) = 0.28 \quad \Rightarrow \quad S = ?$$

By linear interpolation,

$$\frac{S - 0.0923}{0.319 - 0.0923} = \frac{0.28 - 0.2}{0.4 - 0.2}$$

$$S = 0.18298$$

Now,

$$S = \left(\frac{r_j}{C}\right)^2 \frac{\mu \cdot N_j}{P}$$

$\therefore$

$$P = \left(\frac{r_j}{C}\right)^2 \cdot \frac{\mu \cdot N_j}{S}$$

$$= \left(\frac{50}{0.0535}\right)^2 \cdot \frac{30 \times 10^{-9} \times 25}{0.18298}$$

$$P = 3.58005818 \ \text{N/mm}^2$$

But,

$$P = \frac{W_r}{l \cdot d}$$

$\therefore$

$$W_r = P \cdot l \cdot d$$

$$W_r = 17900.291 \ \text{N}$$

(ii) Coefficient of friction (μ) :

From table,

For

$$\left(\frac{h_0}{C}\right)_1 = 0.2 \ \Rightarrow \ \left[\left(\frac{r_j}{C}\right) f\right]_1 = 3.26$$

$$\left(\frac{h_0}{C}\right)_2 = 0.4 \ \Rightarrow \ \left[\left(\frac{r_j}{C}\right) f\right]_2 = 8.10$$

$$\left(\frac{h_0}{C}\right) = 0.28 \ \Rightarrow \ \left[\left(\frac{r_j}{C}\right) f\right] = ?$$

$\therefore$

$$\frac{\left[\left(\frac{r_j}{C}\right) f\right] - 3.26}{8.10 - 3.26} = \frac{0.28 - 0.2}{0.4 - 0.2}$$

$$\left[\left(\frac{r_j}{C}\right) f\right] = 5.196$$

$\therefore$

$$f = 5.196 \times \frac{C}{r_j}$$

$$= 5.196 \times \frac{0.0535}{50}$$

$$f = 0.00556$$

(iii) Power lost in friction (E_F) :

$$E_F = \frac{2\pi \cdot N_j \ (f \cdot W_r \cdot r_j)}{10^6}$$

$$= \frac{2\pi \times 25 \ (0.00556 \times 17900.291 \times 50)}{10^6}$$

$$E_F = 0.7816724 \ \text{kW}$$

(iv) Total lubricant flow rate :

From table,

For
$$\left(\frac{h_0}{C}\right)_1 = 0.2 \ \Rightarrow \left[\frac{Q}{r_j \cdot C \cdot N_j \cdot l}\right]_1 = 5.41$$

$$\left(\frac{h_0}{C}\right)_2 = 0.4 \ \Rightarrow \left[\frac{Q}{r_j \cdot C \cdot N_j \cdot l}\right]_2 = 4.85$$

$$\left(\frac{h_0}{C}\right) = 0.28 \Rightarrow \left[\frac{Q}{r_j \cdot C \cdot N_j \cdot l}\right] = \ ?$$

$$\therefore \quad \frac{\left[\dfrac{Q}{r_j \cdot C \cdot N_j \cdot l}\right] - 5.41}{4.85 - 5.41} = \frac{0.28 - 0.2}{0.4 - 0.2}$$

$$\left[\frac{Q}{r_j \cdot C \cdot N_j \cdot l}\right] = 5.186$$

$$\therefore \qquad Q = 5.186 \times (r_j \cdot C \cdot N_j \cdot l)$$

$$= 5.186 \times 50 \times 0.0535 \times 25 \times 50$$

$$\therefore \qquad Q = 17340.688 \ \text{mm}^3/\text{s}$$

$$= 17340.688 \times 10^{-9} \ \text{m}^3/\text{s}$$

$$= (17340.688 \times 10^{-9}) \times 60 \times 10^3 \ l/\text{min}$$

$$\therefore \qquad Q = 1.04044 \ l/\text{min}$$

(v) Side leakage (Q_S) :

From table,

For
$$\left(\frac{h_0}{C}\right)_1 = 0.2 \ \Rightarrow \ \left(\frac{Q_s}{Q}\right)_1 = 0.874$$

$$\left(\frac{h_0}{C}\right)_2 = 0.4 \ \Rightarrow \ \left(\frac{Q_s}{Q}\right)_2 = 0.730$$

$$\left(\frac{h_0}{C}\right) = 0.28 \Rightarrow \qquad \left(\frac{Q_S}{Q}\right) = ?$$

$$\therefore \quad \frac{\left(\dfrac{Q_S}{Q}\right) - 0.874}{0.730 - 0.874} = \frac{0.28 - 0.2}{0.4 - 0.2}$$

$$\frac{Q_S}{Q} = 0.8164$$

$$\therefore \quad Q_S = 0.8164 \times Q$$

$$= 0.8164 \times 1.04044$$

$$\therefore \quad Q_S = 0.894942 \; l/min$$

(vi) Temperature rise considering effect of side leakage :

$$\text{Heat generated} = \text{Heat dissipated}$$

$$E_F = \frac{\rho \cdot Q_T \cdot C_P \cdot \Delta T \left(1 - \dfrac{Q_S}{2Q}\right)}{10^9}$$

$$\therefore \quad 0.7816724 = \frac{860 \times 17340.688 \times 2.09 \times \Delta T \left(1 - \dfrac{0.8164}{2}\right)}{10^9}$$

$$\Delta T = 42.378°C$$

Example 3.10 : A 50 mm diameter hardened and ground steel journal rotates at 1440 rpm in a lathe turned bronze bushing which is 50 mm long. For hydrodynamic lubrication, the minimum oil-film thickness should be five times the sum of surface roughness (clearance values) of journal and bearing. The data about machining methods is as follows :

Elements	Machining Methods	Clearance Values
Shaft	Grinding	1.6 micron
Bearing	Turning/Boring	0.8 micron

The class of fit is $H_8 \cdot d_8$ and the viscosity of the lubricant is 18 cP. Determine the maximum radial load that the journal can carry and still operate under hydrodynamic conditions.

$$\text{Journal diameter} = 50^{\,-0.080}_{\,-0.119} \; mm$$

$$\text{Bearing diameter} = 50^{\,+0.039}_{\,+0.000} \; mm$$

Also, determine quantity of lubricating oil required.

Solution :

Given :

$$d = 50 \; mm$$

$$l = 50 \; mm$$

$$N_j = \frac{1440}{60} = 24 \text{ rps}$$

$$r_j = 25 \text{ mm}$$

$$h_0 = 5(1.6 + 0.8)$$

$$= 12 \ \mu m = 0.012 \text{ mm}$$

$$\mu = 18 \text{ cP}$$

To find out :

(i) $W_r = ?$,

(ii) $Q = ?$

For manufacturing process to be centred, the average diameter of the bearing and journal are :

$$D_a = 50 + \left(\frac{0.00 + 0.039}{2}\right) = 50.0195 \text{ mm}$$

$$d_a = 50 - \left(\frac{0.119 + 0.08}{2}\right) = 49.9005 \text{ mm}$$

$$\therefore \ \text{Radial clearance,} \quad C = \frac{\text{Diametral clearance}}{2}$$

$$= \frac{50.0195 - 49.9005}{2}$$

$$C = 0.0595 \text{ mm}$$

$$\therefore \quad \frac{h_0}{C} = \frac{0.012}{0.0595} = 0.2017$$

$$\text{and} \quad \frac{l}{d} = 1$$

$\therefore$ From table,

Corresponding to above values, we get,

$$S = 0.0446 \quad \text{and} \quad \left[\frac{Q}{r_j \cdot C \cdot N_j \cdot l}\right] = 4.62$$

(i) Radial load carried by journal :

$$P = \left(\frac{r_j}{C}\right)^2 \frac{\mu \cdot N_j}{S}$$

$$= \left(\frac{25}{0.0595}\right)^2 \cdot \frac{18 \times 10^{-9} \times 24}{0.0446}$$

$$P = 1.709995 \text{ N/mm}^2$$

$$\therefore \qquad P = \frac{W_r}{l \cdot d}$$

$$\therefore \qquad W_r = P \cdot l \cdot d$$
$$= 1.709995 \times 50 \times 50$$
$$\therefore \qquad W_r = 4274.988 \ N$$

(ii) Quantity of lubricating oil required (Q_T) :

$$\left[\frac{Q}{r_j \cdot C \cdot N_j \cdot l} \right] = 4.62$$

$$Q = 4.26 \ (r_j \cdot C \cdot N_j \cdot l)$$
$$= 4.26 \ (25 \times 0.0595 \times 24 \times 50)$$
$$\therefore \qquad Q = 8246.7 \ mm^3/s$$
$$= 8246.7 \times 10^{-9} \ m^3/s$$
$$= (8246.7 \times 10^{-9}) \times 60 \times 10^3 \ l/min$$
$$\therefore \qquad Q = 0.494802 \ l/min$$

Example 3.11 : A oil-ring type of bearing is as shown in Fig. 3.43. There is no hydrodynamic action over the width of 4 mm of the oil ring. The total radial load acting on the journal is 30 kN and the journal rotates at 1500 rpm. The viscosity of the lubricant is 18 cP. If the radial clearance is 15 microns, calculate :

   (i)   The minimum oil-film thickness.

   (ii) Quantity of lubricating oil that flows in l/min.

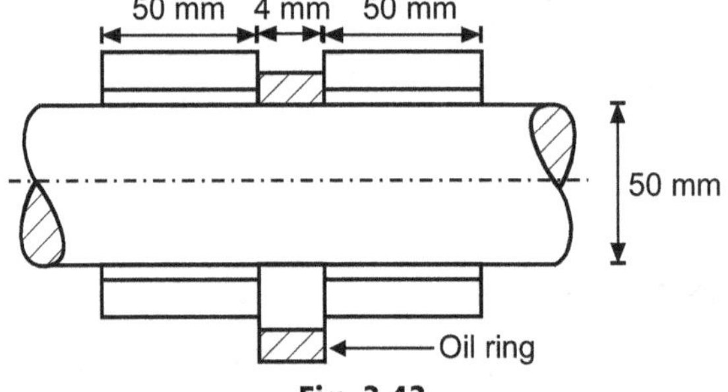

Fig. 3.43

Solution : Given :
$$W_r = 30 \times 10^3 \ N$$
$$\mu = 18 \ cP = 18 \times 10^{-9} \ N\text{-}s/mm^2$$
$$N_j = \frac{1500}{60} = 25 \ rps$$
$$C = 15 \ microns = 0.015 \ mm$$
$$d = 50 \ mm$$

As the oil ring divides the bearing into two parts, each part can be treated as separate hydrodynamic bearing carrying a load of $\left(\dfrac{30}{2} \right)$ or 15 kN.

For each part, $\dfrac{l}{d} = 1$

$$W_r = \dfrac{W}{2} = \dfrac{30 \times 10^3}{2} = 15 \times 10^3 \text{ N}$$

$$P = \dfrac{W_r}{l \cdot d} = \dfrac{15 \times 10^3}{50 \times 50} = 6 \text{ N/mm}^2$$

$$S = \left(\dfrac{r_j}{C}\right)^2 \dfrac{\mu \cdot N_j}{P}$$

$$= \left(\dfrac{25}{0.015}\right)^2 \cdot \dfrac{18 \times 10^{-9} \times 25}{6}$$

$$S = 0.20833$$

(i) Minimum oil-film thickness (h_0) :

From table,

For $\dfrac{l}{d} = 1$

For $S_1 = 0.121 \quad \Rightarrow \quad \left(\dfrac{h_0}{C}\right)_1 = 0.4$

$S_2 = 0.264 \quad \Rightarrow \quad \left(\dfrac{h_0}{C}\right)_2 = 0.6$

$S = 0.20833 \quad \Rightarrow \quad \left(\dfrac{h_0}{C}\right) = \ ?$

$\therefore$ Using linear interpolation,

$$\dfrac{\left(\dfrac{h_0}{C}\right) - 0.4}{0.6 - 0.4} = \dfrac{0.20833 - 0.121}{0.264 - 0.121}$$

$$\dfrac{h_0}{C} = 0.52214$$

$$h_0 = 0.52214 \times C$$

$$= 0.52214 \times 0.015$$

$\therefore \qquad h_0 = 0.007832 \text{ mm}$

(ii) Quantity of lubricating oil flowing :

From table,

For $S_1 = 0.121 \quad \Rightarrow \quad \left[\dfrac{Q}{r_j \cdot C \cdot N_j \cdot l}\right] = 4.33$

$$S_2 = 0.264 \quad \Rightarrow \quad \left[\frac{Q}{r_j \cdot C \cdot N_j \cdot l}\right] = 3.99$$

$$S = 0.20833 \quad \Rightarrow \quad \left[\frac{Q}{r_j \cdot C \cdot N_j \cdot l}\right] = \;?$$

$$\therefore \quad \frac{\left[\dfrac{Q}{r_j \cdot C \cdot N_j \cdot l}\right] - 4.33}{3.99 - 4.33} = \frac{0.20833 - 0.121}{0.264 - 0.121}$$

$$\therefore \quad \left[\frac{Q}{r_j \cdot C \cdot N_j \cdot l}\right] = 4.1224$$

$$\therefore \quad Q = 4.1224\,(r_j \cdot C \cdot N_j \cdot l)$$

$$= 4.1224\,(25 \times 0.015 \times 25 \times 50)$$

$$\therefore \quad Q = 1932.375 \text{ mm}^3/\text{s}$$

$$= 1932.375 \times 10^{-9} \text{ m}^3/\text{s}$$

$$= (1932.375 \times 10^{-9}) \times 60 \times 10^3 \; l/\text{min}$$

$$\therefore \quad Q = 0.115942 \; l/\text{min}$$

$\therefore$ For two part, total oil flow rate gets doubled.

$$\therefore \quad Q = 2 \times 0.115942$$

$$\therefore \quad Q = 0.231885 \; l/\text{min}$$

Example 3.12 : A 360° journal bearing has the following features :

(i)   Ratio of bearing length to journal diameter = 0.5

(ii) Bearing length = 25 mm

(iii) Radial load = 5 kN

(iv) Journal speed = 1000 rpm

(v)   Radial clearance = 0.05 mm

(vi) Oil viscosity = 30 cP

Find :

    (i)   Friction coefficient,   (ii) Oil flow,

    (iii) Eccentricity,   (iv) Power in churning.

Refer : Dimensionless parameters for full journal bearing with side flow $\left(\dfrac{l}{d}\right) = \dfrac{1}{2}$

Solution :

Given :

$$\frac{l}{d} = \frac{1}{2}$$

$$l = 25 \text{ mm} \quad \Rightarrow \quad d = 50 \text{ mm}$$

$$\therefore \quad r_j = 25 \text{ mm}$$

$$W_r = 5 \text{ kN} = 5000 \text{ N}$$

$$N_j = \frac{1000}{60} = 16.667 \text{ r.p.s.}$$

$$C = 0.05 \text{ mm}$$

$$\mu = 30 \text{ cP} = 30 \times 10^{-9} \text{ N-s/mm}^2$$

To find out :

(i)　$f = ?$,　　　　(ii)　$Q = ?$,

(iii)　$e = ?$,　　　　(iv)　$E_F = ?$

$$\text{Bearing pressure, } \quad P = \frac{W_r}{l \cdot d}$$

$$= \frac{5000}{25 \times 50}$$

$$P = 4 \text{ N/mm}^2$$

$$\text{Sommerfeld Number, } \quad S = \left(\frac{r_j}{C}\right)^2 \cdot \frac{\mu \cdot N_j}{P}$$

$$= \left(\frac{25}{0.05}\right)^2 \cdot \frac{30 \times 10^{-9} \times 16.667}{4}$$

$$S = 0.031251$$

(i)　Friction coefficient (f) :

From table,

For
$$\left(\frac{l}{d}\right) = \frac{1}{2}$$

For
$$S_1 = 0.00609 \quad \Rightarrow \quad \left[\left(\frac{r_j}{C}\right)f\right]_1 = 0.610$$

$$S_2 = 0.0313 \quad \Rightarrow \quad \left[\left(\frac{r_j}{C}\right)f\right]_2 = 1.60$$

$$S = 0.031251 \quad \Rightarrow \quad \left[\left(\frac{r_j}{C}\right)f\right] = ?$$

∴　Using linear interpolation,

$$\frac{\left[\left(\frac{r_j}{C}\right)f\right] - 0.610}{1.6 - 0.610} = \frac{0.031251 - 0.00609}{0.0313 - 0.00609}$$

$$\left[\left(\frac{r_j}{C}\right)f\right] = 1.59808$$

$$\therefore \quad f = 1.59808 \times \frac{C}{r_j} = 1.59808 \times \frac{0.05}{25}$$

$$f = 0.0031962$$

(ii) Oil flow (Q) :

From table,

For $\quad \left(\frac{l}{d}\right) = \frac{1}{2}$

For $\quad S_1 = 0.00609 \Rightarrow \left[\frac{Q}{r_j \cdot C \cdot N_j \cdot l}\right]_1 = 5.88$

$\quad S_2 = 0.0313 \Rightarrow \left[\frac{Q}{r_j \cdot C \cdot N_j \cdot l}\right]_2 = 5.69$

$\quad S = 0.031251 \Rightarrow \left[\frac{Q}{r_j \cdot C \cdot N_j \cdot l}\right] = ?$

$$\therefore \quad \frac{\left[\dfrac{Q}{r_j \cdot C \cdot N_j \cdot l}\right] - 5.88}{5.69 - 5.88} = \frac{0.031251 - 0.00609}{0.0313 - 0.00609}$$

$$\frac{Q}{r_j \cdot C \cdot N_j \cdot l} = 5.6903693$$

$$\therefore \quad Q = 5.6903693 \, (r_j \cdot C \cdot N_j \cdot l)$$

$$= 5.6903693 \, (25 \times 0.05 \times 16.667 \times 25)$$

$$Q = 2963.7932 \text{ mm}^3/\text{s} = 2963.7932 \times 10^{-9} \text{ m}^3/\text{s}$$

$$= (2963.7932 \times 10^{-9}) \times 60 \times 10^3 \text{ l/min}$$

$$Q = 0.177828 \text{ l/min}$$

(iii) Eccentricity (e) :

From table, $\quad$ for $\left(\frac{l}{d}\right) = \frac{1}{2}$

For $\quad S_1 = 0.00609 \Rightarrow \left(\frac{h_0}{C}\right)_1 = 0.03$

$$S_2 = 0.0313 \quad \Rightarrow \quad \left(\frac{h_0}{C}\right)_2 = 0.1$$

$$S = 0.031251 \quad \Rightarrow \quad \left(\frac{h_0}{C}\right) = \ ?$$

$$\therefore \quad \frac{\left(\frac{h_0}{C}\right) - 0.03}{0.1 - 0.03} = \frac{0.031251 - 0.00609}{0.0313 - 0.00609}$$

$$\frac{h_0}{C} = 0.099864$$

$$\therefore \quad \frac{h_0}{C} = 1 - \frac{e}{C} = 0.099864$$

$$\therefore \quad \frac{e}{C} = 0.900136$$

$$\therefore \quad e = 0.900136 \times 0.05$$

$$\therefore \quad e = 0.045007 \text{ mm}$$

(iv) Power in churning (E_F) :

$$E_F = \frac{2\pi \cdot N_j \, (f \cdot W_r \cdot r_j)}{10^6}$$

$$E_F = \frac{2\pi \times 16.667 \, (0.0031962 \times 5000 \times 25)}{10^6}$$

$$\therefore \quad E_F = 0.041839 \text{ kW}$$

Example 3.13 : A hydrodynamic journal bearing has following features :
(i)   Length of bearing = 50 mm
(ii) Journal diameter = 50 mm
(iii) $\left(\dfrac{r_j}{C}\right)$ ratio = 1000

(iv) Viscosity of oil = 50 MPa-s
(v)   Journal speed = 950 r.p.m.
(vi) Eccentricity ratio = 0.5

Calculate :
(i)   Load-carrying capacity.
(ii) Coefficient of friction and power lost in friction, considering infinitely long journal bearing.
(iii) Maximum pressure and its location if the inlet oil pressure at $\phi = 185°$ is 200×10^3 Pa.

Solution :

Given :

$$\mu = 50 \text{ MPa-s}$$
$$= 50 \times 10^6 \text{ Pa-s}$$
$$= 50 \text{ N-s/mm}^2 = 50 \times 10^{-9} \text{ N-s/m}^2 = 50 \text{ cP}$$

$$l = 50 \text{ mm}; \qquad N_j = \frac{950}{60} = 15.833 \text{ r.p.s.}$$

$$\in = 0.5$$
$$\omega_j = 2\pi N_j = 2\pi \times 15.833 = 99.483767$$

$$\frac{r_j}{C} = 1000$$

$$r_j = 25 \text{ mm}$$
$$\phi = 185°$$
$$P_i = 200 \times 10^3 \text{ Pa}$$

(i) Load-carrying capacity (W_r) :

For infinitely long journal bearing, load-carrying capacity is given by,

$$W_r = 12 \, \omega_j \cdot r_j \cdot \eta \cdot \left(\frac{r_j}{C}\right)^2 \left[\frac{\pi \in}{(1 - \in^2)^{1/2} \cdot (2 + \in^2)}\right] \cdot l$$

$$= \{12 \times 99.483767 \times 8025 \times 50 \times 10^{-9} \times (1000)^2$$

$$\left[\frac{\pi \times 0.5}{(1 - (0.5)^2)^{1/2} \, (2 + 0.5)^2}\right]\} \times 50$$

$$\therefore \qquad W_r = 60147.8644 \text{ N}$$

(ii) Coefficient of friction (f) :

Coefficient of friction at journal surface can be calculated using following relationship :

$$f = \left(\frac{C}{r_j}\right)\left[\frac{1 + 2\in^2}{3\in}\right]$$

$$= \frac{1}{1000}\left[\frac{1 + 2\,(0.5)^2}{3\,(0.5)}\right]$$

$$f = 10^{-3}$$

$$\therefore \qquad f = 0.001$$

Power lost in friction :

Tangential force acting on journal,

$$F_T = f \cdot W_r = 0.001 \times 60147.8644$$

$$F_T = 60.14786 \text{ N}$$

$\therefore$ Power lost in friction,

$$E_F = 2\pi\, N_j \cdot T$$

$$= 2\pi\, N_j \cdot (F_T \cdot r_j)$$

$$= 2\pi \times 15.833\,(60.14786 \times 25) \times 10^{-3}$$

$$\therefore \quad E_F = 149.590 \text{ W}$$

$$\therefore \quad E_F = 0.14959 \text{ kW}$$

(iii) Maximum pressure and its location (P_{max}) :

Now,

Pressure in bearing, $P = P_i - P_0$

$$= \text{Inlet supply pressure} - \text{Outlet pressure}$$

We know,

$$P = 6\,\omega_j \cdot \mu \left(\frac{r_j}{C}\right)^2 \frac{\in \sin\phi\,(2 + \in \cos\phi)}{(2 + \in^2)(1 + \in \cos\phi)^2}$$

$$= 6 \times 99.483767 \times 50 \times 10^{-9} \times (1000)^2$$

$$\left\{\frac{0.5 \sin(185)\,[2 + 0.5 \times \cos(185)]}{(2 + 0.5^2)(1 + 0.5\cos(185))^2}\right\} \quad \omega_j = 2\pi\, N_j$$

$$= -3.446353133 \text{ MPa}$$

$$\therefore \quad P_0 = P_i - P$$

$$= 200 \times 10^3 + 3.446353133 \times 10^6$$

$$P_0 = 3.646353 \times 10^6 \text{ Pa}$$

Location of maximum pressure,

$$\phi_{max} = \cos^{-1}\left[\frac{-3\in}{2 + \in^2}\right]$$

$$= \cos^{-1}\left[\frac{-3 \times 0.5}{2 + 0.5^2}\right]$$

$$\therefore \quad \phi_{max} = 131.8103°$$

$\therefore$ Maximum pressure occurs at $\phi_{max} = 131.8103°$

$$\therefore \quad P_m = 6 \times 99.483767 \times 50 \times 10^{-9} \times (1000)^2$$

$$\left\{\frac{0.5 \sin(131.8103)\,[2 + 0.5 \cos(131.8103)]}{(2 + 0.5^2)(1 + 0.5\cos(131.8103))}\right\}$$

$$= 12.3585 \text{ MPa}$$

Maximum pressure,

$$P_{max} = P_m + P_0$$

$$= 12.3585 + 3.646353$$

$$P_{max} = 16.0048 \text{ MPa}$$

Example 3.14 : Following data is given for a short-journal bearing :

(i)   Journal speed = 1440 r.p.m.

(ii) Length of bearing = 25 mm

(iii) Journal diameter = 50 mm

(iv) Eccentricity ratio = 0.5

(v)   Viscosity of lubricant = 50 MPa.sec.

(vi) $\left(\dfrac{r_j}{C}\right)$ ratio = 1000

Calculate :

    (i)   Load-carrying capacity

    (ii) Attitude

    (iii) Power lost in friction.

Solution :

Given :

$$N_j = \frac{1440}{60} = 24 \text{ r.p.s.}$$

$$l = 25 \text{ mm}$$

$$d = 50 \text{ mm}$$

$$\epsilon = 0.5$$

$$\mu = 50 \text{ MPa.sec} = 50 \times 10^{-9} \text{ N-s/m}^2$$

$$= 50 \text{ cP}$$

$$\frac{r_j}{C} = 1000$$

To calculate :

(i) $W_r = ?$, (ii) $\psi = ?$,   (iii) $E_F = ?$

(i) Load-carrying capacity (W_r) :

Load-carrying capacity of short-journal bearing is given by,

$$W_r = \frac{\mu \cdot \omega_j \cdot r_j \cdot l^3}{4C^2} \cdot \frac{\epsilon}{(1 - \epsilon^2)^2} [\pi^2 (1 - \epsilon^2) + 1 \, \sigma \, E^2]^{1/2}$$

Here, $\omega_j = 2\pi N_j = 2\pi \times 24 = \quad 150.79645$

Using in above equation, $W_r = \dfrac{50 \times 10^{-9} \times 150.79645 \times 25 \times (25)^3}{4\left(\dfrac{25}{1000}\right)^2} \cdot \dfrac{0.5}{(1 - 0.5^2)^2}$

$$\{\pi^2(1 - 0.5^2) + 16\,(0.5)^2\}^{1/2}$$

$$W_r = 3.5360875 \times 10^3 \text{ N}$$

(ii) Attitude angle (ψ) :

$$\psi = \tan^{-1}\left[\frac{\pi(1 - \in^2)^{1/2}}{4\in}\right]$$

$$= \tan^{-1}\left[\frac{\pi(1 - 0.5)^{1/2}}{4 \times 0.5}\right]$$

$$\therefore \quad \psi = 48.0028°$$

(iii) Power lost in friction (E_F) :

Frictional force on journal is given by,

$$F_T = \frac{4\mu \cdot \pi^2\,(r_j)^2 \cdot N_j \cdot l}{C \cdot (1 - \in^2)^{1/2}}$$

$$= \frac{4 \times 50 \times 10^{-9} \times \pi^2 \times (25)^2 \times 24 \times 25}{\left(\dfrac{25}{1000}\right)(1 - 0.5^2)^{1/2}}$$

$$F_T = 34.1893 \text{ N}$$

$\therefore$ Power lost in friction,

$$E_F = (2\pi r_j \cdot N_j)\,F_T$$

$$= (2 \times \pi \times 25 \times 24 \times 34.1893) \times 10^{-3}$$

$$E_F = 128.8906 \text{ W}$$

Example 3.15 : Following data is given for 360° hydrodynamic bearing :

[P.U. May/June 2006; June 2009, 8 Marks]

Radial load	= 6.5 kN
Journal speed	= 1200 rpm
Journal diameter	= 60 mm
Bearing length	= 60 mm
Minimum oil-film thickness	= 0.009 mm

The class of fit is H_7e_7 (fine) normal running fit. For this fit,

$$\text{Hole limits} = 60 \begin{array}{c} +0.00 \\ +0.03 \end{array} \text{ mm}$$

$$\text{Shaft limits} = 60 \begin{array}{c} -0.06 \\ -0.09 \end{array} \text{ mm}$$

Specify the viscosity of the lubricating oil that you will recommend for this application.

Solution :

Given :
$$\frac{l}{d} = \frac{60}{60} = 1 \qquad\qquad r_j = 30 \text{ mm}$$

$$N_j = 1200 \text{ rpm}$$

$$W_r = 6.5 \text{ kN} = 6.5 \times 10^3 \text{ N}$$

$$h_0 = 0.009 \text{ mm}$$

Class of fit is H_7e_7 :

$\Rightarrow$ $\therefore$ Calculating average diameters of bearing and journal are :

$$D_a = 60 + \left(\frac{0.00 + 0.03}{2}\right) = 60.015 \text{ mm}$$

$$d_a = 60 - \left(\frac{0.09 + 0.06}{2}\right) = 59.925 \text{ mm}$$

$\therefore$ $\qquad$ Radial clearance $= \left(\dfrac{D_a - d_a}{2}\right)$

$$= \frac{60.015 - 59.925}{2}$$

$$C = 0.045 \text{ mm}$$

$\therefore$ Minimum oil-film thickness variable

$$\left(\frac{h_0}{C}\right) = \frac{0.009}{0.045} = 0.2$$

From Table 3.2,

For $\qquad \left(\dfrac{l}{d}\right) = 1$ and $\left(\dfrac{h_0}{C}\right) = 0.2$

We get, $\qquad S = 0.0446$

and $\qquad F_v = \left(\dfrac{Q}{r_j \cdot C \cdot N_j \cdot l}\right) = 4.62$

$\therefore$ **Viscosity of lubricating oil :**

Bearing pressure $\qquad P = \dfrac{W_r}{l \cdot d}$

$$= \frac{6.5 \times 10^3}{60 \times 60}$$

$$P = 1.80555 \ \text{N/mm}^2$$

Sommerfeld Number, $\quad S = \left(\dfrac{r_i}{C}\right)^2 \dfrac{\mu \cdot N_i}{P}$

$$\mu = \frac{S \cdot P}{N_j} \Big/ \left(\frac{r_i}{C}\right)^2$$

$$= \left(\frac{0.0446 \times 1.80555}{1200}\right) \Big/ \left(\frac{30}{0.45}\right)^2$$

$$= 15.0989 \times 10^{-9} \ \text{N-s/mm}^2$$

$\therefore$ Viscosity of lubricating oil $= \mu = 0.150989 \times 10^{-9} \ \text{N-s/mm}^2$

OR

$$\mu = 0.150989 \ \text{cP}$$

Example 3.16 : The following data is given for a 360° hydrodynamic bearing :

[P.U. Dec. 2006]

- Journal diameter $\quad = 50 \begin{smallmatrix} -0.080 \\ -0.119 \end{smallmatrix}$

- Bearing diameter $\quad = 50 \begin{smallmatrix} +0.039 \\ +0.000 \end{smallmatrix}$

- Bearing length $\quad = 50 \ \text{mm}$

- Journal speed $\quad = 1500 \ \text{r.p.m.}$

- Radial load $\quad = 5 \ \text{kN}$

The bearing is machined on a lathe from bronze casting, while the steel journal is hardened and ground. The surface roughness values for turning and grinding are 3.2 and 0.8 microns respectively. For thick-film hydrodynamic lubrication, the minimum film thickness should be six times the sum of surface roughness values for the journal and bearing. Determine the quality and the quantity of the lubrication required.

Solution :

Given : $\qquad d = 50 \ \text{mm}$

$$l = 50 \ \text{mm}$$

$$N_j = 1500 \ \text{r.p.m.} = \frac{1500}{60} = 25 \ \text{r.p.s.}$$

$$W_r = 5 \ \text{kN} = 5000 \ \text{N}$$

$$r = \frac{d}{2} = 25 \text{ mm}$$

$$h_0 = 6 (3.2 + 0.8) = 24 \text{ μm}$$

$$h_0 = 0.024 \text{ mm}$$

For manufacturing process to be centered, the average diameter of the bearing and journal are

$$D_a = 50 + \left[\frac{0.000 + 0.039}{2}\right] = 50.0195 \text{ mm}$$

And

$$d_a = 50 - \left[\frac{0.119 + 0.09}{2}\right] = 49.9005 \text{ mm}$$

Radial clearance (C) :

$$C = \frac{D_a - d_a}{2} = \frac{50.0195 - 49.9005}{2}$$

$$C = 0.0595 \text{ mm}$$

Minimum film thickness variable,

$$\frac{h_0}{C} = \frac{0.024}{0.0595} = 0.4$$

and length to diameter ratio,

$$\frac{l}{d} = \frac{50}{50} = 1$$

From Table 3.2,

$$\text{For} \left(\frac{l}{d}\right) = 1 \text{ and } \left(\frac{h_0}{C}\right) = 0.4$$

we get, $$S = 0.121$$

and   Flow Variable, $$FV = \frac{Q}{r_j \cdot C \cdot N_j \cdot l} = 4.33$$

(i) Quality of Lubrication :

$$\text{Bearing pressure, } P = \frac{\text{Radial load}}{\text{Bearing area}}$$

$$= \frac{W_r}{l \cdot d}$$

$$= \frac{5000}{50 \times 50}$$

$$P = 2 \text{ N/mm}^2$$

Now, Sommerfeld Number,

$$S = \left(\frac{f_i}{C}\right)^2 \frac{\mu \cdot N_i}{P}$$

$$\therefore \quad 0.121 = \left(\frac{25}{0.0595}\right)^2 \cdot \frac{\mu \times 25}{2}$$

$$\therefore \quad \mu = 54.8314 \text{ N-s/mm}^2$$

$$\mu = 54.8314 \text{ cP}$$

(ii) Quantity of Lubrication :

$$FV = \frac{Q}{r_j \cdot C \cdot N_j \cdot l} = 4.33$$

$$\therefore \quad Q = 4.33 \times r_j \cdot C \cdot N_j \cdot l$$

$$= 4.33 \times 25 \times 0.0595 \times 25 \times 50$$

$$= 8051.0938 \text{ mm}^3/\text{s}$$

$$= 8051.0938 \times 10^{-9} \text{ m}^3/\text{s}$$

$$= (8051.0938 \times 10^{-9}) \times 60 \times 10^3 \text{ } l/\text{min}$$

$$Q = 0.483065 \text{ } l/\text{min}$$

Example 3.17 : A Petroff's sleeve bearing consists of a sleeve having a bore diameter of 90 mm and a length of 90 mm. A shaft having 89.9 mm diameter supports a load of 3600 N. A shaft runs at 3000 r.p.m. in the sleeve. If the frictional torque on the shaft is 12 N-m, find

   (i)   The absolute viscosity of lubricant;

   (ii) The bearing pressure;

   (iii) The coefficient of friction; and

   (iv) The power lost in bearing.

Solution :

Given :

$$D = 90 \text{ mm}$$

$$d = 89.9 \text{ mm}$$

$$l = 90 \text{ mm}$$

$$W_r = 3600 \text{ N}$$

$$N_j = \frac{3000}{60} = 50 \text{ r.p.s.}$$

$$T = 12 \text{ N-m} = 12 \times 10^3 \text{ N-mm}$$

Radial clearance, $\quad C = \dfrac{D - d}{2} = \dfrac{90 - 89.9}{2} = 0.05 \text{ mm}$

$$r_j = \frac{d}{2} = \frac{89.9}{2} = 44.95 \text{ mm}$$

(i) The absolute viscosity of lubricant :

$$\text{Frictional torque, } T_f = \frac{4\pi^2 \cdot r_j^3 \cdot N_j \cdot l \cdot \mu}{C}$$

$$12 \times 10^3 = \frac{4 \times \pi^2 \times (44.95)^3 \times 50 \times 90 \times \mu}{0.05}$$

$$\mu = 37.18689 \times 10^{-9} \text{ N-s/mm}^2$$

i.e. $\qquad\qquad \mu = 37.1869 \text{ cP}$

(ii) The bearing pressure :

$$P = \frac{W_r}{2l \cdot r_j}$$

$$= \frac{3600}{2 \times 90 \times 44.95}$$

$$P = 0.445 \text{ N/mm}^2$$

(iii) The coefficient of friction (f) :

$$f = \frac{4\pi^2 \cdot r_j^2 \cdot N_j \cdot l \cdot \mu}{W_r \cdot C}$$

$$= \frac{4\pi^2 \times (44.95)^2 \times 50 \times 90 \times 37.1869 \times 10^{-9}}{3600 \times 0.05}$$

$$f = 0.07416$$

(iv) Power lost in friction (P_F) :

$$P_F = \frac{2\pi \cdot N_j \cdot T}{10^6}$$

$$= \frac{2\pi \times 50 \times 12 \times 10^3}{10^6}$$

$$P_F = 3.7699 \text{ kW}$$

Example 3.18 : In a lightly-loaded journal bearing wherein it is assumed that the journal runs concentric to the bush at 1500 r.p.m. and supports a radial load of 750 N, the viscosity of lubricating oil is 35 cP. The effective coefficient of friction in bearing is 0.025. The $\left(\dfrac{l}{d}\right)$ ratio for the bearing is 1.0, while the radial clearance between the journal and the bush is 100 microns. Evaluate :

    (i)   The diameter of journal and bush,

    (ii) Length of bearing,

    (iii) The power lost in friction.

Solution :

Given :

$$N_j = 1500 \text{ rpm}$$
$$= \frac{1500}{60} = 25 \text{ r.p.s.}$$
$$W_r = 750 \text{ N}$$
$$\mu = 35 \text{ cP} = 35 \times 10^{-9} \text{ N-s/mm}^2$$
$$f = 0.025$$
$$\frac{l}{d} = 1.0$$
$$C = 100 \text{ }\mu m = 100 \times 10^{-3} \text{ mm}$$

For lightly-loaded journal wherein the journal runs concentric to the bush, Petroff's equation can be used.

(i) The diameter of journal :

According to Petroff's equation,

$$T_f = \frac{4\pi^2 \cdot r_j^3 \cdot N_j \cdot l \cdot \mu}{C}$$

Here, $\dfrac{l}{d} = 1 \Rightarrow l = d = 2 \cdot r_j$

∴ Equivalent coefficient of friction,

$$f = \frac{4\pi^2 \cdot r_j^2 \cdot N_j \cdot l \cdot \mu}{W_r \cdot C}$$

$$f \cdot W_r = \frac{4\pi^2 \cdot r^2 \cdot N_j \cdot l \cdot \mu}{C}$$

∴
$$f \cdot W_r = \frac{8\pi^2 \cdot r_j^3 \cdot \mu \cdot N_j}{C} \qquad \dots (\because l = d = 2 \cdot r_j)$$

∴
$$0.025 \times 750 = \frac{8\pi^2 \times r_j^3 \times 35 \times 10^{-9} \times 25}{100 \times 10^{-3}}$$

$$r_j^3 = 27139.6028$$
$$r_j = 30.052 \text{ mm}$$

∴ Diameter of journal,

$$d = 2 \cdot r_j$$
$$= 2 \times 30.052$$
$$d = 60.10 \text{ mm}$$

(ii) Length of bearing :

$$\frac{l}{d} = 1 \Rightarrow l = d$$

$$\therefore \qquad l = 60.10 \text{ mm}$$

Diameter of bearing,

$$D = d + 2C$$

$$= 60.10 + 2 \times (100 \times 10^{-3})$$

$$D = 60.303 \text{ mm}$$

(iii) Power lost in bearing :

Frictional torque,

$$T_f = f \cdot W_r \cdot r_j$$

$$= 0.025 \times 750 \times 30.052$$

$$T_f = 563.475 \text{ N-mm}$$

Power lost in friction,

$$P_F = \frac{2\pi \cdot N_j \cdot T_f}{10^6}$$

$$= \frac{2\pi \times 25 \times 563.475}{10^6}$$

$$P_F = 0.08851 \text{ kW} = 88.51 \text{ W}$$

Example 3.19 : A 360° hydrodynamic bearing has the following features :

[P.U. June 2007]

$$\text{Journal diameter} = 50 \text{ mm}$$

$$\text{Bearing length} = 25 \text{ mm}$$

$$\text{Radial load} = 7.5 \text{ kN}$$

$$\text{Journal speed} = 1400 \text{ rpm}$$

$$\text{Radial clearance} = 0.006 \text{ mm}$$

$$\text{Oil viscosity} = 30 \text{ cP}$$

Find :

(i) The minimum oil-film thickness (h_0).

(ii) Friction coefficient (f).

(iii) Oil flow (Q).

(iv) Side flow (Q_S).

(v) Maximum film pressure.

(vi) Eccentricity and

(vii) Power lost in churning.

Refer : Dimensionless parameters for full journal bearing with side flow $\left(\dfrac{l}{d}\right) = \dfrac{1}{2}$.

Solution :

Given :

$$\frac{l}{d} = \frac{1}{2}$$

$$l = 25 \text{ mm}$$

$$d = 50 \text{ mm} \Rightarrow r_j = 25 \text{ mm}$$

$$W_r = 7.5 \text{ kN}$$

$$N_j = \frac{1400}{60}$$

$$= 23.333 \text{ r.p.s.}$$

$$C = 0.006 \text{ mm}$$

$$\mu = 30 \text{ cP} = 30 \times 10^{-9} \text{ N-s/mm}^2$$

To find out :

(i) $h_0 = ?$ (ii) $f = ?$ (iii) $Q = ?$

(iv) $Q_S = ?$ (v) $P_{max} = ?$ (vi) $e = ?$

(vii) $E_F = ?$

Solution :

(i) Minimum oil-film thickness (h_0) :

From Table 3.2,   For $\dfrac{l}{d} = \dfrac{1}{2}$

Bearing pressure, $P = \dfrac{W_r}{l \cdot d} = \dfrac{7500}{25 \times 50}$

$$P = 6 \text{ N/mm}^2$$

Sommerfeld Number, $S = \left(\dfrac{r_j}{C}\right)^2 \cdot \dfrac{\mu \cdot N_j}{P}$

$$= \left(\frac{25}{0.006}\right)^2 \cdot \frac{30 \times 10^{-9} \times 23.333}{6}$$

$$= 2.025434$$

For $\quad S_1 = 0.779 \Rightarrow \left(\dfrac{h_0}{C}\right)_1 = 0.6$

$\qquad S_2 = 2.03 \Rightarrow \left(\dfrac{h_0}{C}\right)_2 = 0.8$

$\quad S = 2.025434 \Rightarrow \left(\dfrac{h_0}{C}\right) = ?$

Using linear interpolation,

$$\frac{\left(\dfrac{h_0}{C}\right) - 0.6}{0.8 - 0.6} = \frac{2.025434 - 0.779}{2.03 - 0.779}$$

$$\left(\frac{h_0}{C}\right) = \left\{\left[\frac{1.246434}{1.251}\right] \times 0.2\right\} + 0.6$$

$$\left(\frac{h_0}{C}\right) = 0.79927$$

$\therefore \qquad h_0 = 0.79927 \times C$

$\therefore \qquad h_0 = 0.79927 \times 0.006$

$$h_0 = 0.0047956 \text{ mm}$$

(ii) Friction coefficient (f) :

From Table 3.2,

$$\text{For} \left(\frac{l}{d}\right) = \frac{1}{2}$$

$$\text{For} \left(\frac{h_0}{C}\right)_1 = 0.6 \Rightarrow \left[\left(\frac{r_i}{C}\right) \cdot f\right]_1 = 17$$

$$\left(\frac{h_0}{C}\right)_2 = 0.8 \Rightarrow \left[\left(\frac{r_i}{C}\right) \cdot f\right]_2 = 40.9$$

$$\left(\frac{h_0}{C}\right) = 0.79927 \Rightarrow \left[\left(\frac{r_i}{C}\right) \cdot f\right] = ?$$

Using linear interpolation,

$$\therefore \quad \frac{\left[\left(\dfrac{r_i}{C}\right) \cdot f\right] - 17}{40.9 - 17} = \frac{0.79927 - 0.6}{0.8 - 0.6}$$

$$\left[\left(\frac{r_i}{C}\right) \cdot f\right] = 40.812765$$

$$\therefore \quad f = 40.812765 \times \frac{0.006}{25}$$

$$f = 0.0097951$$

(iii) Oil flow (Q) :

From Table 3.2,

For $\quad \dfrac{l}{d} = \dfrac{1}{2}$

For

$$S_1 = 0.779 \qquad \Rightarrow \quad \left[\frac{Q}{r_j \cdot C \cdot N_j \cdot l}\right]_1 = 4.29$$

$$S_2 = 0.03 \qquad \Rightarrow \quad \left[\frac{Q}{r_j \cdot C \cdot N_j \cdot l}\right]_2 = 3.72$$

$$S = 2.025434 \qquad \Rightarrow \quad \left[\frac{Q}{r_j \cdot C \cdot N_j \cdot l}\right] = ?$$

$$\frac{\left[\dfrac{Q}{r_j \cdot C \cdot N \cdot l}\right] - 4.29}{3.72 - 4.29} = \frac{2.025434 - 0.779}{2.03 - 0.779}$$

$$\left[\frac{Q}{r_j \cdot C \cdot N_j \cdot l}\right] = [(0.99635) \times (-0.57)] + 4.29$$

$$= 3.7220804$$

$$\therefore \quad Q = 3.7220804 \times r_j \cdot C \cdot N_j \cdot l$$
$$Q = 3.7220804 \times 25 \times 0.006 \times 23.333 \times 25$$
$$Q = 325.6774 \ mm^3/s$$
$$= 325.6774 \times 10^{-9} \ m^3/s$$
$$= 325.6774 \times 10^{-9} \times 60 \times 10^3 \ l/min$$
$$\therefore \quad Q = 0.01954 \ l/min$$

(iv) Side flow (Q$_S$) :

From Table 3.2,

For $\quad \dfrac{l}{d} = \dfrac{1}{2}$

For

$$\left(\frac{h_0}{C}\right)_1 = 0.6 \qquad \Rightarrow \qquad \left(\frac{Q_s}{Q}\right)_1 = 0.552$$

$$\left(\frac{h_0}{C}\right)_2 = 0.8 \qquad \Rightarrow \qquad \left(\frac{Q_s}{Q}\right)_2 = 0.318$$

$$\left(\frac{h_0}{C}\right) = 0.79927 \qquad \Rightarrow \qquad \left(\frac{Q_s}{Q}\right) = ?$$

$$\frac{\left(\dfrac{Q_S}{Q}\right) - 0.552}{0.318 - 0.552} = \frac{0.79927 - 0.6}{0.8 - 0.6}$$

$$= 0.99635$$

$$\therefore \qquad \frac{Q_S}{Q} = 0.318854$$

$$Q_S = 0.318854 \times 0.01954$$

$$Q_S = 0.00623 \; l/min$$

(v) Maximum film pressure (P_{max}) :

From Table 3.2,

$$\text{For} \qquad \frac{l}{d} = \frac{1}{2}$$

$$\text{For} \qquad \left(\frac{h_0}{C}\right)_1 = 0.6 \qquad \Rightarrow \qquad \left(\frac{P}{P_{max}}\right)_1 = 0.441$$

$$\left(\frac{h_0}{C}\right)_2 = 0.8 \qquad \Rightarrow \qquad \left(\frac{P}{P_{max}}\right)_2 = 0.506$$

$$\left(\frac{h_0}{C}\right) = 0.79927 \qquad \Rightarrow \qquad \left(\frac{P}{P_{max}}\right) = \;?$$

$$\therefore \qquad \frac{\left(\dfrac{P}{P_{max}}\right) - 0.441}{0.506 - 0.441} = \frac{0.79927 - 0.6}{0.8 - 0.6}$$

$$\left(\frac{P}{P_{max}}\right) = (0.99635 \times 0.065) + 0.441$$

$$\frac{P}{P_{max}} = 0.505763$$

$$P_{max} = \frac{P}{0.505763} = \frac{6}{0.505763}$$

$$P_{max} = 11.86327 \; N/mm^2$$

(vi) Eccentricity (e) :

We know,
$$\frac{h_0}{C} = 0.79927$$

Also,
$$\frac{h_0}{C} = 1 - \frac{e}{C}$$

$$\therefore \qquad \frac{e}{C} = 1 - \frac{h_0}{C} = 1 - 0.79927$$

$$\frac{e}{C} = 0.20073$$

$\therefore$

$$e = 0.20073 \times 0.006$$

$$e = 0.0012044 \text{ mm}$$

(vii) Power lost in churning (E_F) :

$$E_F = \frac{2\pi \cdot N_j \, (f \cdot W_r \cdot r_j)}{10^6}$$

$$= \frac{2\pi \times 23.333 \, (0.0097951 \times 7500 \times 25)}{10^6}$$

$$E_F = 0.269256 \text{ kW}$$

OR $E_F = 269.256 \text{ W}$

Example 3.20 : A 360° hydrodynamic bearing has the following features :

[P.U. Nov./Dec. 2007]

$$\text{Journal diameter} = 40 \text{ mm}$$
$$\text{Bearing length} = 20 \text{ mm}$$
$$\text{Radial load} = 6.5 \text{ kN}$$
$$\text{Journal speed} = 1500 \text{ r.p.m.}$$
$$\text{Radial clearance} = 0.007 \text{ mm}$$
$$\text{Oil viscosity} = 25 \text{ cP}$$

Find :

  (i) The minimum oil-film thickness, (h_0)

  (ii) Friction coefficient, (f)

  (iii) Oil flow, (Q)

  (iv) Side flow, (Q_S)

  (v) Maximum film pressure, (P_{max})

  (vi) Eccentricity

  (vii) Power lost in churning

Refer : Dimensionless parameters for full journal bearing with side flow $\left(\frac{l}{d}\right) = \frac{1}{2}$.

Solution :

Given :

$$\frac{l}{d} = \frac{l}{2}$$

$$l = 20 \text{ mm} \quad , \quad d = 40 \text{ mm}$$

$$r_j = 20 \text{ mm}$$

$$W_r = 6.5 \text{ kN}$$

$$N_j = \frac{1500}{60} = 25 \text{ r.p.s.}$$

$$C = 0.007 \text{ mm}$$

$$\mu = 25 \text{ cP} = 25 \times 10^{-9} \text{ N-s/mm}^2$$

To find out :

(a) h_0 = ?, (b) f = ?, (c) Q = ?, (d) Q_S = ?, (e) P_{max} = ?, (f) e = ?, (g) E_F = ?

$$\text{Bearing pressure,} \quad P = \frac{W_r}{l \cdot d} = \frac{6500}{20 \times 40}$$

$$P = 8.125 \text{ N/mm}^2$$

$$\text{Sommerfeld Number,} \quad S = \left(\frac{r_j}{C}\right)^2 \cdot \frac{\mu \cdot N_j}{P}$$

$$= \left(\frac{20}{0.007}\right)^2 \frac{25 \times 10^{-9} \times 25}{8.125}$$

$$S = 0.6279434$$

(a) Minimum oil-film thickness (h_0) :

$$\text{For} \qquad S_1 = 0.319 \qquad \Rightarrow \left(\frac{h_0}{C}\right)_1 = 0.4$$

$$S_2 = 0.779 \qquad \Rightarrow \left(\frac{h_0}{C}\right)_2 = 0.6$$

$$S = 0.6279434 \Rightarrow \left(\frac{h_0}{C}\right) = ?$$

Using linear interpolation,

$$\frac{\left(\frac{h_0}{C}\right) - 0.4}{0.6 - 0.4} = \frac{0.6279434 - 0.319}{0.779 - 0.319}$$

$$\left(\frac{h_0}{C}\right) = (0.671616 \times 0.2) + 0.4$$

$$\frac{h_0}{C} = 0.534323$$

$$h_0 = 0.534323 \times 0.007$$

$$h_0 = 0.0037403 \text{ mm}$$

(b) Friction coefficient (f) :

From Table 3.2,

For $\left(\dfrac{l}{d}\right) = \dfrac{1}{2}$

For $\left(\dfrac{h_0}{C}\right)_1 = 0.4 \quad \Rightarrow \quad \left[\left(\dfrac{r_i}{C}\right)\cdot f\right] = 8.1$

$\left(\dfrac{h_0}{C}\right)_2 = 0.6 \quad \Rightarrow \quad \left[\left(\dfrac{r_i}{C}\right)\cdot f\right] = 17.0$

$\left(\dfrac{h_0}{C}\right) = 0.534323 \quad \Rightarrow \quad \left[\left(\dfrac{r_i}{C}\right)\cdot f\right] = ?$

Using linear interpolation,

$$\dfrac{\left[\left(\dfrac{r_i}{C}\right)\cdot f\right] - 8.1}{17 - 8.1} = \dfrac{0.534323 - 0.4}{0.6 - 0.4}$$

$$\left[\left(\dfrac{r_i}{C}\right)\cdot f\right] = (0.671615 \times 8.9) + 9.1$$

$$\dfrac{r_i}{C}\cdot f = 14.07737$$

$$f = 14.07737 \times \dfrac{0.007}{20}$$

$$f = 0.0049271$$

(c) Oil-flow (Q) :

From Table 3.2,

For $\dfrac{l}{d} = \dfrac{1}{2}$

For $S_1 = 0.319 \quad \Rightarrow \quad \left(\dfrac{Q}{r_j \cdot C \cdot N_j \cdot l}\right)_1 = 4.85$

$S_2 = 0.779 \quad \Rightarrow \quad \left(\dfrac{Q}{r_j \cdot C \cdot N_j \cdot l}\right)_2 = 4.29$

$S = 0.6279434 \quad \Rightarrow \quad \left(\dfrac{Q}{r_j \cdot C \cdot N_j \cdot l}\right) = ?$

$$\dfrac{\left(\dfrac{Q}{r_j \cdot C \cdot N_j \cdot l}\right) - 4.85}{4.29 - 4.85} = \dfrac{0.6279434 - 0.319}{0.779 - 0.319}$$

$$\dfrac{Q}{r_j \cdot C \cdot N_j \cdot l} = (0.6716161 \times -0.56) + 4.85$$

$$\frac{Q}{r_j \cdot C \cdot N_j \cdot l} = 4.473895$$

$$Q = 4.473895 \times r_j \cdot C \cdot N_j \cdot l$$
$$= 4.473895 \times 20 \times 0.007 \times 25 \times 20$$
$$= 313.17265 \text{ mm}^3/\text{s}$$
$$= 313.17265 \times 10^{-9} \text{ m}^3/\text{s}$$
$$= 313.17265 \times 10^{-9} \times 60 \times 10^3 \text{ l/min}$$
$$Q = 0.01879 \text{ l/min}$$

(d) Side flow (Q_s) :

From Table 3.2,

For $\qquad \dfrac{l}{d} = \dfrac{1}{2}$

For $\qquad \left(\dfrac{h_0}{C}\right)_1 = 0.4 \qquad \Rightarrow \qquad \left(\dfrac{Q_s}{Q}\right)_1 = 0.73$

$\qquad\qquad \left(\dfrac{h_0}{C}\right)_2 = 0.6 \qquad \Rightarrow \qquad \left(\dfrac{Q_s}{Q}\right)_2 = 0.552$

$\qquad\qquad \left(\dfrac{h_0}{C}\right) = 0.534323 \qquad \Rightarrow \qquad \left(\dfrac{Q_s}{Q}\right) = \;?$

Using linear interpolation,

$$\frac{\left(\dfrac{Q_s}{Q}\right) - 0.73}{0.73 - 0.552} = \frac{0.534323 - 0.4}{0.6 - 0.4}$$

$$\frac{Q_s}{Q} = (0.671615 \times 0.178) + 0.73$$

$$\frac{Q_s}{Q} = 0.849547$$

$$Q_s = 0.849547 \times 0.01879$$
$$Q_s = 0.015963 \text{ l/min}$$

(e) Maximum film pressure (P_{max}) :

From Table 3.2,

For $\qquad \dfrac{l}{2} = \dfrac{1}{2}$

For $\qquad \left(\dfrac{h_0}{C}\right)_1 = 0.4 \qquad \Rightarrow \qquad \left(\dfrac{P}{P_{max}}\right)_1 = 0.365$

$$\left(\frac{h_0}{C}\right)_2 = 0.6 \quad \Rightarrow \quad \left(\frac{P}{P_{max}}\right)_2 = 0.441$$

$$\left(\frac{h_0}{C}\right) = 0.534323 \quad \Rightarrow \quad \left(\frac{P}{P_{max}}\right) = ?$$

Using linear interpolation,

$$\frac{\left(\dfrac{P}{P_{max}}\right) - 0.365}{0.441 - 0.365} = \frac{0.534323 - 0.4}{0.6 - 0.4}$$

$$\frac{P}{P_{max}} = (0.671615 \times 0.076) + 0.365$$

$$P_{max} = \frac{P}{(0.41604274)}$$

$$\therefore \quad P_{max} = \frac{8.125}{0.41604274}$$

$$P_{max} = 19.52924 \ \text{N/mm}^2$$

(f) Eccentricity (e) :

We know,

$$\frac{h_0}{C} = 1 - \frac{e}{C}$$

$$\therefore \quad \frac{e}{C} = 1 - \frac{h_0}{C}$$

$$e = \left(1 - \frac{h_0}{C}\right) \cdot C$$

$$e = (1 - 0.534323) \times 0.007$$

$$e = 0.00325974 \ \text{mm}$$

(g) Power lost in churning (E_F) :

$$E_F = \frac{2\pi \cdot N_i \cdot (f \cdot W_r \cdot r_j)}{10^6}$$

$$= \frac{2\pi \times 25 \, (0.0049271 \times 6500 \times 20)}{10^6}$$

$$E_F = 0.100613 \ \text{kW}$$

$$\text{or} \quad 100.613$$

EXERCISE

1. Explain the mechanism of pressure development in oil film of hydrodynamic journal bearing.

2. Discuss different regimes of lubrication with the help of Stribeck curve.

[P.U. Dec. 2010, 6 Marks]

3. State assumptions made while deriving Reynold's equation.

4. Derive from basic principles two-dimensional Reynold's equation taking usual notations.   **[P.U. Dec. 2008, 12 Marks; Dec. 2010, 8 Marks; June 2011, 12 Marks]**

5. Starting with Navier-Stroke's equation, derive two dimensional Reynold's equation for unidirectional motion.

6. Derive from basic principles,

$$q_x = -\frac{h^3}{12\mu} \cdot \frac{\partial P}{\partial x} + \left[\frac{u_a + u_b}{2}\right] \cdot h$$

where, $\left\{\left[\dfrac{u_a + u_b}{2}\right] h\right\}$ Couette velocity induced flow term

and $\left\{\left[-\dfrac{h^3}{12\mu} \cdot \dfrac{\partial P}{\partial x}\right]\right\}$ Poiseuille pressure induced flow term

7. Explain :

   (i) Couette velocity induced flow

   (ii) Poiseuille pressure induced flow

8. State meaning of each term involved in Reynold's equation.

9. Explain physical interpretation of each term involved in Reynold's equation.

10. Derive

$$E_F = 0.100613 \text{ kW}$$

$$\frac{\partial P}{\partial x} = 6 \cdot u_b \cdot \mu \left[\frac{h - h_m}{h^3}\right]$$

where, μ – Viscosity of oil h_0 – Minimum oil-film thickness

             h – Oil-film thickness u_b – Journal velocity

11. Derive integrated form of Reynold's equation.

12. Draw radial pressure distribution and axial pressure distribution for hydrodynamic journal bearing.

13. Define :

   (i) Journal   (v) Eccentricity ratio
   (ii) Sleeve   (vi) Minimum oil-film thickness
   (iii) Radial clearance   (vii) Minimum oil-film thickness ratio
   (iv) Eccentricity   (viii) Attitude angle

14. Derive the relation $\dfrac{h_0}{C} = 1 - \epsilon$ for hydrodynamic journal bearing.

[P.U. Dec. 2008, 6 Marks; June 2010 2 Marks]

15. Explain principle of hydrodynamic lubrication in journal bearing.

16. Define :   **[P.U. Dec. 2010, 2 Marks]**

    (i)   Infinitely long journal bearing

    (ii) Infinitely short journal bearing

17. Compare long and short journal bearing with the help of following points :

    (i) Fluid film pressure, (ii) Pressure gradient, (iii) Fluid flow, (iv) Load carrying capacity.

                                                      [P.U. June 2010, 6 Marks]

18. State assumptions made for analysis of :

    (i)   Infinitely long journal bearing

    (ii) Infinitely short journal bearing

19. Derive :   **[P.U. June 2009, 5 Marks; June 2011, 6 Marks]**

$$h = C (1 + \epsilon \cos \phi)$$

where, h = Oil-film thickness

                    C = Radial clearance

                    ϵ = Eccentricity ratio

                    ϕ = Angle measured from maximum oil-film thickness

20. Derive an equation for pressure distribution in case of infinitely long journal bearing.

$$P = 6\, \omega_j \cdot \mu \cdot \left(\frac{r_j}{C}\right)^2 \frac{\epsilon \sin \phi\, (2 + \epsilon \cos \phi)}{(2 + \epsilon^2)\, (1 + \epsilon \cos \phi)^2}$$

                                                 [P.U. June 2009, 10 Marks]

21. Derive dimensionless form of pressure distribution in case of infinitely long journal bearing (or Derive Harrison's equation).

$$P^* = \frac{\epsilon \sin \phi\, (2 + \epsilon \cos \phi)}{(2 + \epsilon^2)\, (1 + \epsilon \cos \phi)^2}$$

22. Derive :

$$h_m = \frac{2C(1 - \epsilon^2)}{2 + \epsilon^2} \qquad \text{In case of infinitely long journal bearing}$$

$$\phi_m = \cos^{-1}\left(\frac{-3\epsilon}{2 + \epsilon^2}\right)$$

where,

                    h_m = Maximum oil-film thickness

                    ϵ = Eccentricity ratio

                    C = Radial clearance

23. Discuss variation of dimensionless pressure term with respect to circumferential co-ordinate using half Sommerfeld solution for infinitely long journal bearing.

24. Derive :

$$W_r = 12 \cdot \omega_j \cdot r_j \cdot \mu \left(\frac{r_j}{C}\right)^2 \left[\frac{\pi \epsilon}{(1 - \epsilon^2)^{1/2} (2 + \epsilon^2)}\right]$$

for infinitely long journal bearing,

where, W_r – Resultant load-carrying capacity

25. Derive :   **[P.U. Dec. 2009, 12 Marks; June 2010, 12 Marks; June 2011, 10 Marks]**

$$P = 3 \, \omega_j \cdot \mu \cdot \frac{\epsilon \sin \phi}{C^2(1 + \epsilon \cos \phi)^3} \left[\frac{l^2}{4} - y^2\right]$$

for infinitely short journal bearing

where, P is pressure distribution

and show variation of pressure graphically.

26. Derive an equation for load-carrying capacity of infinitely short journal bearing using half Sommerfeld condition.

$$W_r = \frac{\mu \cdot \omega_j \cdot r_j \cdot l^3}{4C^2} \cdot \frac{\epsilon}{(1 - \epsilon^2)^2} [\pi^2 (1 - \epsilon^2) + 16 \, \epsilon^2]^{1/2}$$

27. Derive the following expressions for infinitely short journal bearing usual using notation :

    (i) Pressure distribution, (ii) Load-carrying capacity.   **[P.U. Dec. 2008, 18 Marks]**

28. Derive for short journal bearing,

$$W_r = \frac{1}{4C^2} \mu \cdot u_b \cdot l^3 \frac{\pi \, \epsilon}{(1 - \epsilon^2)^2} [0.62 \, \epsilon^2 + 1]^{1/2}$$

29. Derive an equation for coefficient of friction in concentric bearing using with usual notations.   **[P.U. June 2009, 5 Marks]**

30. State assumptions made while deriving Petroff's equation and derive Petroff's equation.

31. Write Petroff equation. State its usefulness.   **[P.U. Dec. 2010, 4 Marks]**

32. Derive an equation for frictional force in a journal of radius R and length L as,

$$F = \frac{C \epsilon}{2R} \cdot W \sin \psi + \frac{2\pi \, \mu \cdot u \, R \cdot L}{C \sqrt{1 - \epsilon^2}}$$

    where,   W = Radial load   ;   C = Radial clearance

$$\psi \;\; = \;\; \text{Attitude angle} \quad ; \quad \mu \;\; = \;\; \text{Dynamic viscosity of oil}$$
$$\in \;\; = \;\; \text{Eccentricity ratio} \quad ; \quad u \;\; = \;\; \text{Shaft surface speed}$$

33. Write short notes on :   **[P.U. June 2009, 8 Marks]**

    (i)   Sommerfeld Number

    (ii) Design considerations in hydrodynamic journal bearing

    (iii) Temperature rise in hydrodynamic journal bearing

    (iv) Ocvirk short bearing theory

    (v)   Finite length bearing theory

34. Explain Raimondi and Boyd method with reference to each variable involved in it.

35. State the parameters of bearing design. Explain any two in detail.

                                                                         [P.U. June 2011, 8 Marks]

36. Explain how selection of following parameters affect performance of hydrodynamic journal bearing :

    (i)   Length to diameter ratio

    (ii) Unit bearing pressure

    (iii) Radial clearance

    (iv) Minimum oil-film thickness

37. Explain the following terms with reference to hydrodynamic journal bearings :

    (i) Design variables, (ii) Performance variables, (iii) Sommerfeld number.

                                                                         [P.U. June 2009, 6 Marks]

38. Explain energy losses in case of hydrodynamic journal bearing.

39. Explain the heat balance for hydrodynamic journal bearings with feed lubrication.

                                                                         [P.U. June 2009, 6 Marks]

EXAMPLES FOR PRACTICE

1. The following data refers to a 360° hydrodynamic bearing :

    (i)   Radial load = 5 kN

    (ii) Journal speed = 1500 r.p.m.

    (iii) Journal diameter = 50 mm

    (iv) Bearing diameter = 50 mm

    (v)   Bearing length = 50 mm

    (vi) Tolerance values on journal diameter and bearing diameter are
    $50\,^{-0.080}_{-0.119}$ mm and $50\,^{+0.039}_{+0.000}$ mm.

The hardened and ground steel journal rotates in a lathe turned bronze bushing, for hydrodynamic lubrication, the minimum oil-film thickness should be six times the sum of surface roughness values (c.*l*.a) for the journal and bearing. The data about machining methods is as follows :

Elements	Machining Methods	Clearance Values
Bearing	Turning / Boring	0.8 μm
Shaft	Grinding	3.2 μm

Determine :

(i) Minimum oil-film thickness variable.

(ii) Viscosity of the lubricating oil, and

(iii) Lubricant oil flow required in *l*/min.

(**Ans. :** (i) $\left(\dfrac{h_0}{C}\right) = 0.4,$ (ii) $\mu = 54.833 \times 10^{-9}$ N-s/mm²

(iii) Q = 0.48308 *l*/min)

2. An oil-ring type of hydrodynamic bearing is as shown in Fig. 3.44. The total radial load acting on the journal is 20 kN and the journal rotates at 1450 r.p.m. The radial clearance and viscosity of lubricant are 20 μm and 6.75×10^{-9} N-s/mm² respectively. There is no hydrodynamic action over the width of 4 mm of the oil ring.

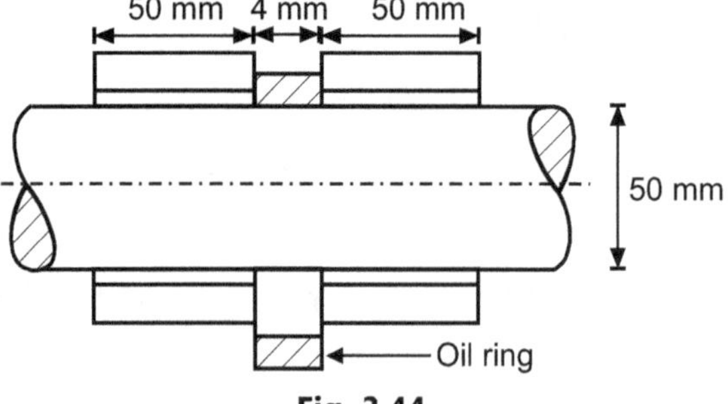

Fig. 3.44

Determine :

(i) Minimum oil-film thickness

(ii) Flow variable (FV)

(iii) Overall lubricant flow rate in *l*/m

(**Ans. :** (i) $h_0 = 5$ μm, (ii) FV = 4.5475

(iii) Q = 0.329640 *l*/min)

3. A 360° hydrodynamic bearing has following data : **[P.U. June 2010, 12 Marks]**

(i) Journal diameter = 50 mm

(ii) Radial load = 10 kN

(iii)   Journal speed = 1450 r.p.m.

(iv)   Bearing length = 50 mm

(v)   Radial clearance = 20 μm

(vi)   Eccentricity ratio = 15 μm

(vii)   Specific gravity of lubricating oil = 0.86

(viii) Specific heat of lubricant = 2.09 kJ/kg °C

Evaluate :

(i)   Coefficient of friction

(ii) Viscosity of oil

(iii) Minimum oil-film thickness

(iv) Quantity of oil in circulation

(v) Oil leakage through sides

(vi) Power lost in friction

(vii) The average oil temperature if the oil is supplied at 27°C

(**Ans. :**   (i)   f = 0.001664,   (ii)   μ = 6.7482 × 10⁻⁹ N-s/mm²

(iii) h_0 = 0.005 mm,   (iv)   Q = 2747.485 mm³/s

(v) Q_S = 2202.109 mm³/sec   (vi) E_F = 0.0631 kW

(vii)   37.66°C)

4. For a 360° hydrodynamic bearing,

(i) $\left(\dfrac{l}{d}\right) = 1$

(ii) Bearing length = 100 mm

(iii) Radial load = 50 kN

(iv) Journal speed = 24 r.p.s.

(v) Radial clearance = 120.0 microns

(vi) Viscosity of lubricating oil = 16 × 10⁻⁹ N-s/mm²

Evaluate :

(i)   Minimum oil-film thickness

(ii) Coefficient of friction

(iii) Power lost in friction

(**Ans. :**   (i) h_0 = 0.00871 mm,   (ii) μ = 0.0020213,

(iii) E_F = 0.7609 kW)

5. Following data refers to a 360° hydrodynamic bearing :

(i) $\left(\dfrac{l}{d}\right)$ ratio = 1

(ii) Radial load = 25000 N

(iii) Journal speed = 15 r.p.s.

(iv) Unit bearing pressure = 2.5 N/mm²

(v) Viscosity of lubricant = 20×10^{-9} N-s/mm²

(vi) Tolerance values on bearing diameter and journal diameter are as follows,

$$D^{\,+\,0.00}_{\,+\,0.03} \text{ mm and } d^{\,-\,0.06}_{\,-\,0.09} \text{ mm respectively.}$$

Calculate :

(i) Bearing specifications

(ii) Minimum oil-film thickness

(iii) Lubricant flow rate in l/min

(**Ans. :**   (i) D × d = (100 × 100) mm,   (ii) h_0 = 0.019107 mm,

(iii) 1.056813 l/min)

6. Following specifications are given for a full-journal bearing.

(i) $\left(\dfrac{l}{d}\right)$ ratio = 1

(ii) Journal diameter = 100 mm

(iii) Journal speed = 3000 r.p.m.

(iv) Radial clearance = 0.025 mm

(v) Eccentricity ratio = 0.6

(vi) Average viscosity of lubricating oil = 0.02 Pa-s

Calculate :

(a) Assuming infinitely long bearing.

   (i)   Load-carrying capacity using full Sommerfeld condition

   (ii)   Coefficient of friction

   (iii) Attitude angle

(b) Assuming infinitely short bearing,

   (i)   Load-carrying capacity

   (ii)   Coefficient of friction

(iii)   Attitude angle

(iv)   Oil flow rate

(Ans. :   (a)   (i) W_r = 1505.31 kN,   (ii) f = 0.47813 × 10⁻³,

(iii) ψ = 64.483°

(b)   (i) W_r = 639.7 kN,   (ii) f = 0.6172 × 10⁻³,

(iii) ψ = 46.317°,   (iv) Q = 0.02421 m³/s)

7. The specifications are given for short-journal bearing.

(i)   Length of bearing = 20 mm

(ii) Diameter of journal = 30 mm

(iii) Journal speed = 1460 r.p.m.

(iv) Eccentricity ratio = 0.6

(v) $\left(\dfrac{r_j}{C}\right)$ ratio = 1000

(vi) Viscosity of the lubricant = 55 MPa.sec

Calculate :

(i)   Load-carrying capacity

(ii) Attitude angle

(iii) Power lost in friction

(Ans. :   (i) W_r = 3.6532 × 10³ N,   (ii) ψ = 51.4881°,

(iii) E_F = 45.4219 W)

NUMERICALS ASKED IN VARIOUS UNIVERSITY EXAMINATIONS

1. Following data is given for a 360° hydrodynamic bearing :

(i)   Radial load = 3.2 kN

(ii)   Journal diameter = 50 mm

(iii)   Journal speed = 1490 rpm

(iv)   Bearing length = 50 mm

(v)   Radial clearance = 50 µm

(vi)   Viscosity of lubricant = 25 cP

(vii)   Density of lubricant = 860 kg/m³

(viii) Specific heat of lubricant = 1.76 kJ/kg °C.

Assuming that the total heat generated in the bearing is carried by the total oil flow in the bearing, calculate :

(i)   Coefficient of friction

(ii) Minimum oil-film thickness

(iii) Power lost in friction

(iv) The total flow of lubricant in l/min

(v) The side leakages

(vi) The temperature rise :

      (a) Considering effect of side leakage

      (b) Neglecting effect of side leakage.   **(P. U. Dec. 2004/May 2004)**

Solution :

Refer Example 3.3 on page 3.83.

2.   The following data is given for 360° hydrodynamic bearing :

(i) $\dfrac{l}{d} = 0.5$

(ii)   Journal diameter = 100 mm

(iii)   Journal speed = 1500 rpm

(iv)   Minimum oil-film thickness = 15 microns

(v)   Viscosity of lubricant = 30 cP

(vi)   Specific gravity of lubricant = 0.86

(vii)   Specific heat of lubricant = 2.09 kJ/kg °C

(viii) Fit between journal and bearing = $H_7 e_7$

Calculate :

(i)   The load-carrying capacity of bearing

(ii) The coefficient of friction

(iii) The power lost in friction

(iv) The total lubricant flow rate

(v) The side leakage and

(vi) The temperature rise considering effect of side leakage.

Use following data.

Diameter, mm	Tolerances, mm	
	H_7	e_7
100	+ 0.035	− 0.072
	+ 0.000	− 0.107

(**Note :** Use Raimondi and Boyd chart/table for $\dfrac{l}{d} = 0.5$).   **(May 2003)**

Solution :

Refer Example 3.9 on page 3.104.

3. Following data refers to full journal bearing.

 (i) Length of bearing   = 75 mm

 (ii) Diameter of bearing   = 75 mm

 (iii) Load on bearing   = 12 kN

 (iv) Speed of journal   = 1800 rpm

 (v) $\dfrac{d}{C}$ ratio   = 2000

 (vi) Viscosity of oil   = 10 cP

at operating temperature

Determine the coefficient of friction by using Raimondi and Boyd chart. 'd' is the journal diameter, 'C' is the radial clearance in the bearing.

S	$\left(\dfrac{r_j}{C}\right) f$
0.264	5.79
0.121	3.22
0.0446	1.70

                     (Dec. 2002)

Solution :

Refer Example 3.1 on page 3.79.

4. The following data refers to a 360° hydrodynamic journal bearing :

 (i) Radial load = 30000 N

 (ii) Nominal journal diameter = 75 mm

 (iii) Bearing width = 75 mm

 (iv) Radial clearance = 0.15 mm

 (v) Operating speed = 3600 rpm

 (vi) Inlet oil temperature = 40°C

The temperature-viscosity relationship is as follows :

t°C	40	41	42	43	44	45	46	47	48	49	50
μ (cP)	52.5	50	47.5	45	43	41	39	37.5	36	34	33

Assume that the total heat produced in the bearing is carried by the total oil flow. The specific gravity and specific heat of the lubricant are 0.86 and 1.76 kJ/kg °C respectively. Calculate :

    (i)   Minimum oil-film thickness

    (ii) Power lost in friction

    (iii) Requirement of lubricant flow and

    (iv) Outlet lubricant temperature.   **(June 2002)**

Solution :

Refer Example 3.8 on page 3.99.

5. A hydrodynamic journal bearing is subjected to a radial load of 10 kN. The permissible unit bearing pressure is 1000 kPa. The length to diameter ratio is 1. The radius of journal is about 800 times the radial clearance. The viscosity of lubricating oil in working condition is 30 MPa-s. Calculate :

    (i)   The length of bearing.

    (ii) The diameter of journal.

    (iii) Coefficient of friction.

    (iv) Power lost in friction and

    (v) Total flow of the oil.

The journal rotates at 1440 rpm.   **(Dec. 2000 and 2003)**

Solution :

Refer Example 3.6 on page 3.94.

6. A 360° hydrodynamic journal bearing has the following data :

    (i)   Journal diameter = 50 mm

    (ii)   Length of journal = 50 mm

    (iii)   Radial load on journal = 15 kN

    (iv)   Journal speed = 1450 rpm

    (v)   Eccentricity ratio = 0.75

    (vi)   Radial clearance = 20 μm

    (vii) Specific gravity of the oil = 0.86

    (viii) Specific heat = 2.09 kJ/kg °C

Evaluate :

    (i)   Probable coefficient of friction;

    (ii)   Viscosity of oil;

    (iii)   Minimum oil-film thickness;

    (iv)   Quantity of oil in circulation;

    (v)   Oil leakage through sides, and

    (vi)   The average oil temperature if the oil is supplied at 28°C.   **(June 2000)**

Solution :

Refer Example 3.4 on page 3.86.

7. Following data is given for 360° hydrodynamic bearing :   **(P.U. May/June 2006)**

                       Radial load   =   6.5 kN

                   Journal speed   =   1200 rpm

                  Journal diameter   =   60 mm

$$\text{Bearing length} \quad = \quad 60 \text{ mm}$$
$$\text{Minimum oil-film thickness} \quad = \quad 0.009 \text{ mm}$$

The class of fit is $H_7 e_7$ (fine) normal running fit. For this fit,

$$\text{Hole limits} \quad = \quad 60 \,^{+0.00}_{+0.03} \text{ mm}$$

$$\text{Shaft limits} \quad = \quad 60 \,^{-0.06}_{-0.09} \text{ mm}$$

Specify the viscosity of the lubricating oil that you will recommend for this application.

Solution :

Refer Example 3.15 on page 3.119.

8.　The following data is given for a 360° hydrodynamic bearing :　　　**(P.U. Dec. 2006)**

- Journal diameter　　　　　　　$= \quad 50 \,^{-0.080}_{-0.119}$

- Bearing diameter　　　　　　　$= \quad 50 \,^{+0.039}_{+0.000}$
- Bearing length　　　　　　　　$= \quad 50 \text{ mm}$
- Journal speed　　　　　　　　$= \quad 1500 \text{ r.p.m.}$
- Radial load　　　　　　　　　$= \quad 5 \text{ kN}$

The bearing is machined on a lathe from bronze casting, while the steel journal is hardened and ground. The surface roughness values for turning and grinding are 3.2 and 0.8 microns respectively. For thick-film hydrodynamic lubrication, the minimum film thickness should be six times the sum of surface roughness values for the journal and bearing. Determine the quality and the quantity of the lubrication required.

Solution :

Refer Example 3.16 on page 3.121.

9.　A 360° hydrodynamic bearing has the following features :　　　**(P.U. June 2007)**

$$\text{Journal diameter} \quad = \quad 50 \text{ mm}$$
$$\text{Bearing length} \quad = \quad 25 \text{ mm}$$
$$\text{Radial load} \quad = \quad 7.5 \text{ kN}$$
$$\text{Journal speed} \quad = \quad 1400 \text{ rpm}$$
$$\text{Radial clearance} \quad = \quad 0.006 \text{ mm}$$
$$\text{Oil viscosity} \quad = \quad 30 \text{ cP}$$

Find :

(i)　The minimum oil-film thickness (h_0).

(ii)　Friction coefficient (f).

(iii)　Oil flow (Q).

(iv)　Side flow (Q_s).

(v)　Maximum film pressure.

(vi) Eccentricity and

(vii) Power lost in churning.

Refer : Dimensionless parameters for full journal bearing with side flow $\left(\dfrac{l}{d}\right) = \dfrac{1}{2}$.

Solution :

Refer Example 3.19 on page 3.126.

10. A 360° hydrodynamic bearing has the following features :   **(P.U. Nov./Dec. 2007)**

Journal diameter = 40 mm

Bearing length = 20 mm

Radial load = 6.5 kN

Journal speed = 1500 r.p.m.

Radial clearance = 0.007 mm

Oil viscosity = 25 cP

Find :

(a) The minimum oil-film thickness, (h_0)

(b) Friction coefficient, (f)

(c) Oil flow, (Q)

(d) Side flow, (Q_S)

(e) Maximum film pressure, (P_{max})

(f) Eccentricity

(g) Power lost in churning

Refer : Dimensionless parameters for full journal bearing with side flow $\left(\dfrac{l}{d}\right) = \dfrac{1}{2}$.

Solution :

Refer Example 3.20 on page 3.131.

✠ ✠ ✠

Chapter 4

HYDRODYNAMIC THRUST BEARING

4.1 INTRODUCTION

Hydrodynamic thrust bearing comprises of two planes and non-parallel surfaces separated by a lubricant film, one of the surfaces is held stationary while other moves with a constant speed. Thus, this type of bearing can support, a thrust load i.e. the load perpendicular to the direction of relative sliding motion.

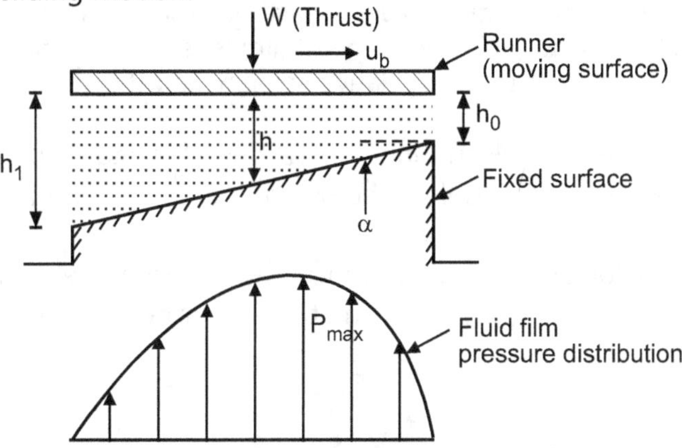

Fig. 4.1 : Hydrodynamic thrust bearing

- The direction of motion and the inclination (α) are chosen in such a way that convergent film is formed. The stationary plane can either be fixed or pivoted so that it can assume any inclination relative to the moving plane.
- Thus, a sufficient fluid-film pressure is generated to balance an applied thrust-load with suitable separation of the stationary and rotating surfaces to avoid wear. Thus, it gives low friction and avoids excessive temperature rise.
- Hydrodynamic thrust bearing is also called 'fixed-pad slider bearing' or 'hydrodynamic plane slider bearing'.

4.2 MECHANISM OF PRESSURE DEVELOPMENT IN HYDRODYNAMIC THRUST BEARING

One plate is kept inclined with respect to other plate.

In this case, the top plate is kept inclined with respect to the lower plate. Due to this inclination, the converging oil film separates two plates which will cause different types of velocity distribution at different sections. The velocity variation at sections PP' and QQ' be assumed to vary linearly from the velocity u_a of moving plate to zero of the stationary plate. Considering this variation, the flow continuity is not satisfied.

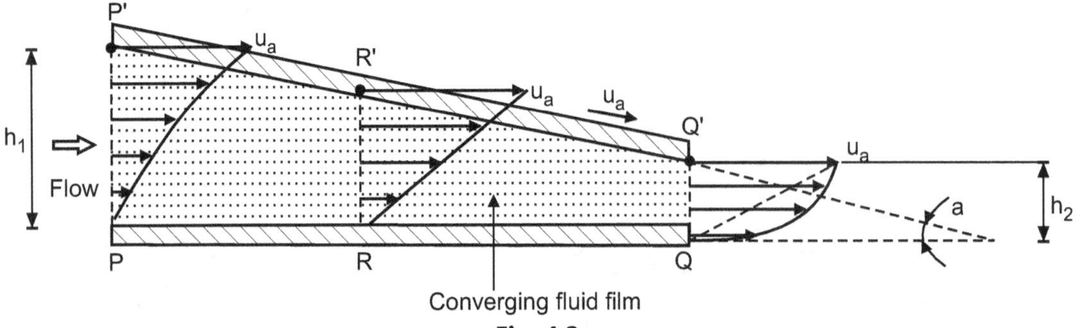

Converging fluid film

Fig. 4.2

Assuming that at particular section RR', the velocity be linear, and in order to satisfy the flow continuity, the velocity variation at sections PP' and QQ' are to be given by the solid lines. Pressure build up automatically as the flow will have both pressure induced term (Poiseuille) and velocity induced term (Couette). Such type of film is termed as convergent film. This film can produce positive pressure if there is relative velocity and the surfaces are separated by a viscous fluid film.

Poiseuille Flow : The velocity distribution for a fluid flowing under laminar conditions through a small clearance 'h' as a result of the pressure gradient, $\partial p/\partial z$ is termed as pressure induced flow or Poiseuille flow.

Couette Flow : The velocity distribution which results from the motion of the bearing surfaces alone, under constant pressure condition, is termed as velocity induced flow or couette flow.

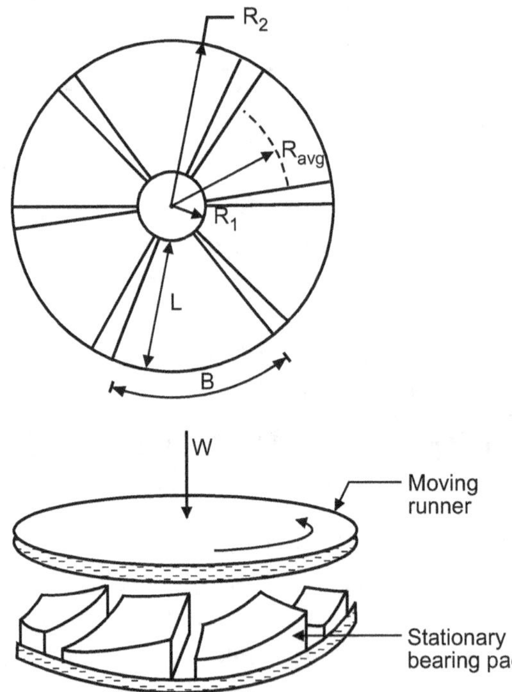

Fig. 4.3 : Configuration of a fixed-pad thrust bearing

Thus, the operating principle involved can be explained by considering a flat surface sliding over a tapered land. Motion of the flat surface or thrust runner draws fluid into a wedge-shaped zone over the tapered land. Pumping of fluid into the zone of reducing downstream clearance by shearing action of the runner, pressurizes the oil. The change in film thickness 'h' adjusts the inflow and outflow to provide a balance of the integrated pressure over the bearing area with the applied load. A group of these tapered land thrust pads are arranged with oil distribution grooves in an annular configuration to form a complete thrust bearing as shown in Fig. 4.3.

4.3 TYPES OF HYDRODYNAMIC THRUST BEARING

Following are common types of hydrodynamic thrust bearing.

- Flat plate thrust bearing (Tapered-pad thrust bearing).

- Tilting pad thrust bearing (Kingsburry thrust bearing).

- Tapered land fixed-pad bearings.

- Rayleigh step bearings (Stepped film bearing).

- Spring support thrust bearings.

- Convergent thrust bearings.

- Convergent-divergent thrust bearing.

4.3.1 Flat-Plate Thrust Bearing (Tapered-Pad Thrust Bearing)

Hydrodynamic thrust bearing comprises of two planes and non-parallel surfaces separated by a lubricant film, one of the surfaces is held stationary while other moves with a constant speed. Thus, this type of bearing can support a thrust load i.e. the load perpendicular to the direction of relative sliding motion.

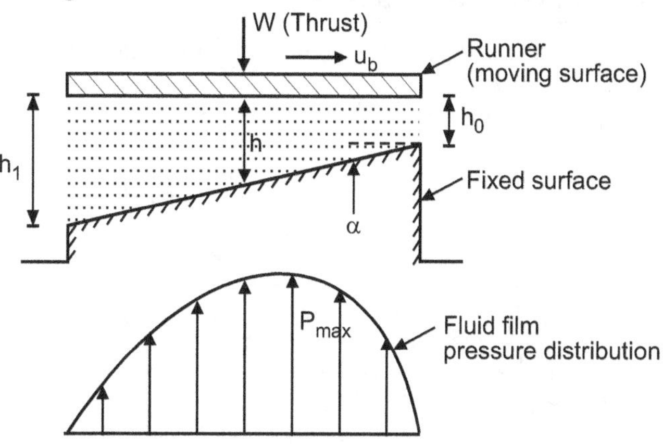

Fig. 4.4 : Hydrodynamic thrust bearing

- The direction of motion and the inclination (α) are chosen in such a way that convergent film is formed. The stationary plane can either be fixed or pivoted so that it can assume any inclination relative to the moving plane.

- Thus, a sufficient fluid-film pressure is generated to balance an applied thrust-load with suitable separation of the stationary and rotating surfaces to avoid wear. Thus, it gives low friction and avoid excessive temperature rise.

- Hydrodynamic thrust bearing is also called 'fixed-pad slider bearing' or 'hydrodynamic plane slider bearing'.

4.3.2 Tilting-Pad Thrust Bearing (Kingsburry Thrust Bearing)

It is a type of tapered-pad bearings consisting of a moving runner plate and self-adjusting pad called tilting pad, therefore called tilting-pad thrust bearing. Tilting pads are pivoted at a point, sometimes called pivoted-pad thrust bearings. Pads can be adjusted to form a nearly optimum oil wedge for supporting high loads.

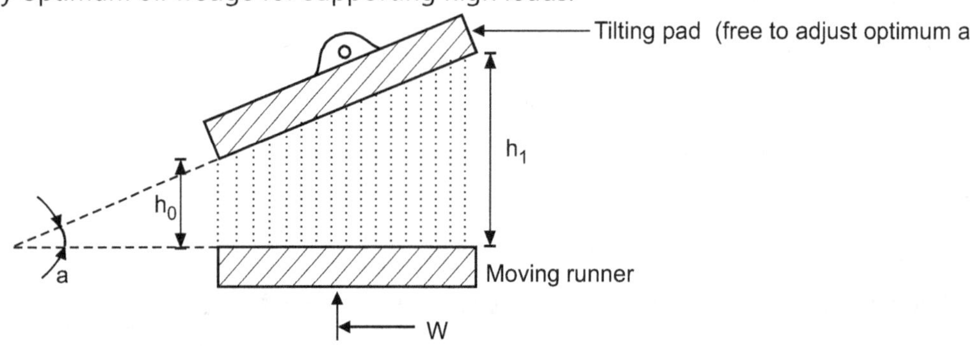

Fig. 4.5 : Tilting-pad thrust bearing

These type of bearings are being used more frequently in turbines, compressors, pumps and marine drives.

4.3.3 Tapered-Land Fixed Pad Bearing

It consists of moving runner and a tapered-land fixed pad, which gives load-carrying capacity better than fixed-pad bearings.

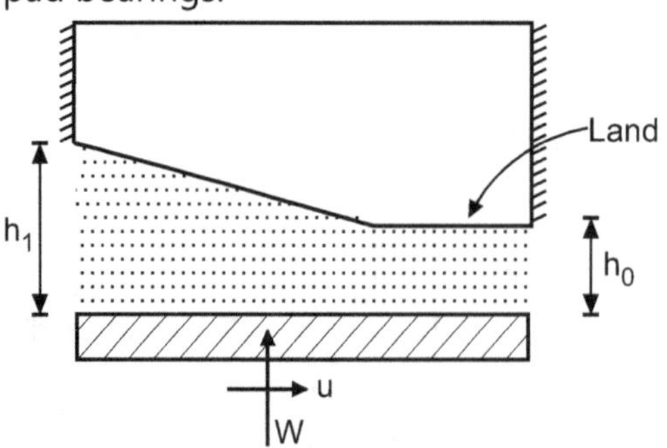

Fig. 4.6 : Tapered-land fixed pad bearing

It provides reliable, compact designs for a large variety of midsize to large, high speed machines such as turbines, compressors, and pumps. The flat land provides higher load-carrying capacity and minimize wear during starting, stopping and at low speeds. Operation of this bearing is sensitive to load, speed and lubricant viscosity.

4.3.4 Rayleigh Step Bearing (Stepped Film Bearing)

It is also called stepped film bearing. It provides simple design for smaller bearings.

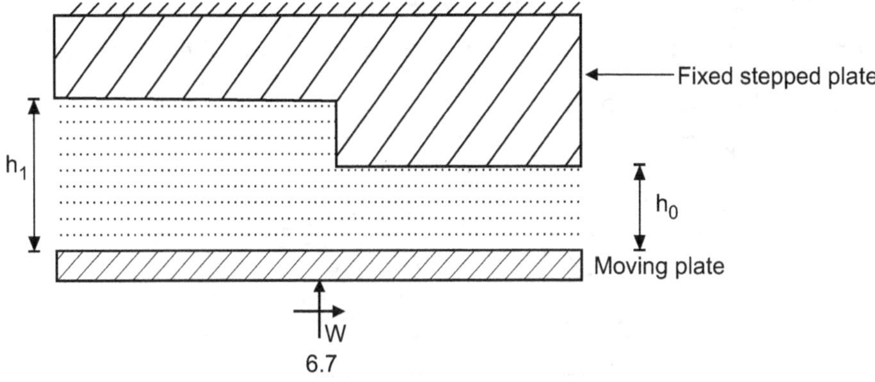

Fig. 4.7 : Rayleigh step bearing

It consists of a stepped plate which is held fixed and a flat runner plate. Step height must be small with the same order of thickness as the minimum film thickness for optimum load capacity. These bearings are well suited for use with low-viscosity fluids such as water, gasoline, and solvents. Two parallel sections forming step give maximum load-carrying capacity.

4.3.5 Spring Support Thrust Bearing

In some of the largest thrust bearings carrying millions of pounds of thrust, springs or other flexible supports are used for the thrust segments. It is shown in Fig. 4.8.

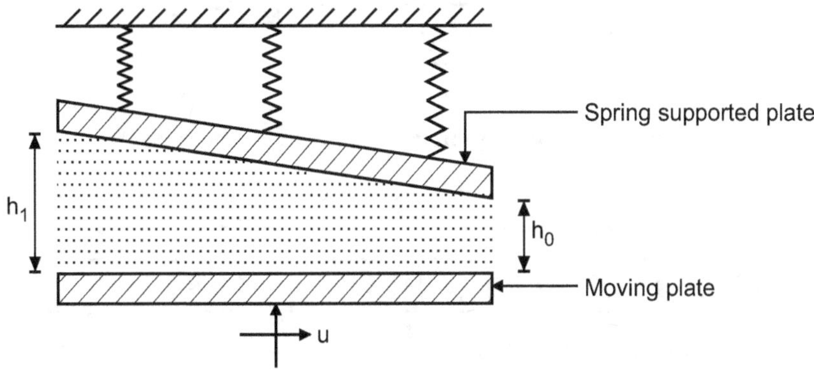

Fig. 4.8 : Spring support thrust bearing

In these type of bearings, the flexible mounting avoids the high contact stresses imposed by loading individual pivots.

Rubber backing for each thrust pad can be used to provide this flexible support in smaller bearings and where axial space is at a premium.

4.3.6 Convergent Thrust Bearing

In this type of bearing, the film shape is non-linear.

e.g. Exponential converging shape provides the pumping action of fluid with less shock.

It gives better load-carrying capacity.

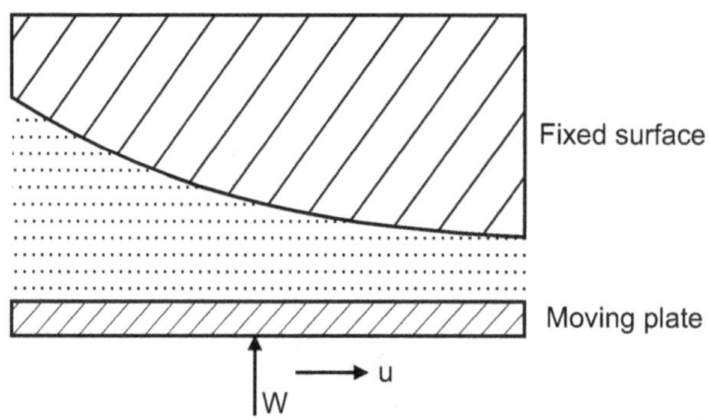

Fig. 4.9

4.3.7 Convergent-Divergent Thrust Bearing

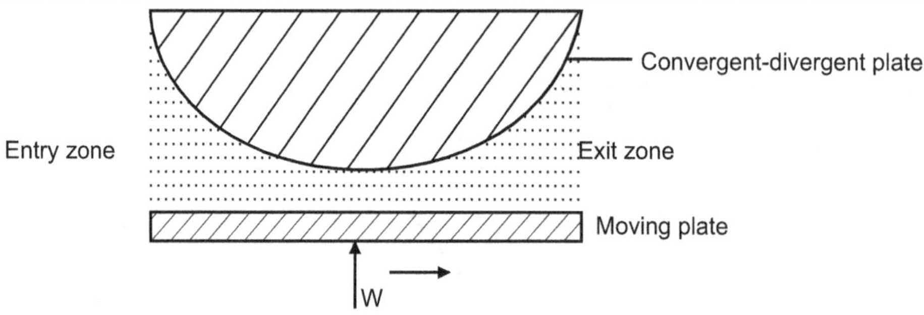

Fig. 4.10 : Convergent-divergent thrust bearing

In this type, both convergent and divergent zones are combined which give smooth pumping action of fluid from entry zone to exit zone without any shocks.

4.4 ANALYSIS OF FLAT-PLATE THRUST BEARING

Fig. 4.11 shows the flat-plate thrust bearing with moving runner plate and fixed pad. Bearing is assumed as infinite length tapered-pad bearing (i.e. Length 'L' along 'y'-direction).

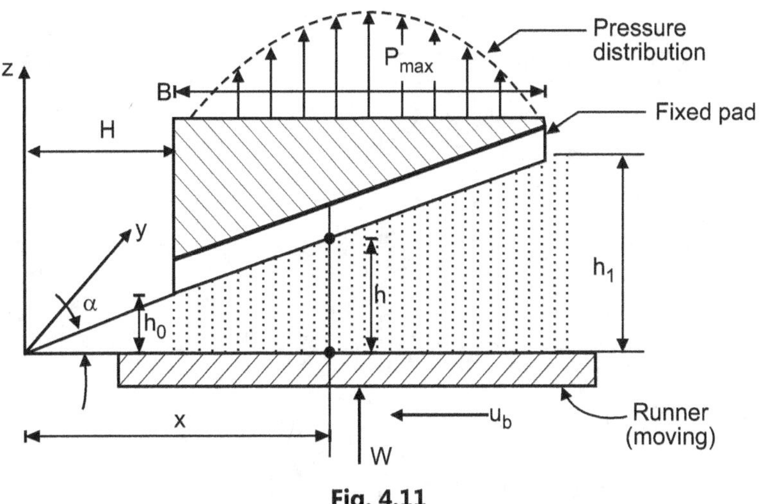

Fig. 4.11

4.4.1 Pressure Distribution

Let,

h_0– Minimum oil thickness

h_1– Maximum oil film thickness

B– Width of bearing (along 'x'-direction)

L – Length of bearing along 'y'-direction (infinite)

K– Bearing parameter where, $K = \dfrac{h_1 - h_0}{h_0}$

α– Film thickness at a distance x

H– Distance of minimum film thickness from co-ordinate axis.

$$\therefore \quad \tan \alpha = \frac{h_0}{H} = \frac{h_1}{H + B} = \frac{h}{x} = \frac{h_1 - h_0}{B}$$

$$\therefore \quad \frac{h_0}{H} = \frac{h}{x} \Rightarrow x = \frac{h}{h_0} \cdot H$$

$$\text{and} \quad \frac{h_0}{H} = \frac{h_1 - h_0}{B} \Rightarrow \frac{B}{H} = \frac{h_1 - h_0}{h_0}$$

$$= K$$

$$\therefore H = \frac{B}{K} \Rightarrow \therefore x = \frac{h}{h_0} \cdot \frac{B}{K} \text{ i.e. } K = \frac{h_1 - h_0}{h_0} \quad \dots (4.1)$$

Fig. 4.12

Now, we have reduced form of Reynold's equation for incompressibe fluids (oil bearings).

$$\frac{dP}{dx} = -6 \cdot u_b \cdot \mu \left[\frac{h - h_m}{h^3}\right] \qquad \dots \ (\because \ u_b \text{ in opposite direction to } x)$$

$$= -6u_b \cdot \mu \left[\frac{1}{h^3} - \frac{h_m}{h^3}\right]$$

$$dP = -6u_b \cdot \mu \left[\frac{1}{h^2} - \frac{h_m}{h^3}\right] \cdot dx \qquad\qquad x = \frac{h}{h_0} \cdot \frac{B}{K}$$

$$\therefore \qquad dP = -6u_b \cdot \mu \left[\frac{1}{h^2} - \frac{h_m}{h^3}\right]\left(\frac{B}{h_0 \cdot K}\right) \cdot dh \qquad dx = \left(\frac{B}{h_0 \cdot K}\right) \cdot dh$$

Integrating above equation,

$$\int dP = -6u_b \cdot \mu \frac{B}{h_0 \cdot K} \int \left(\frac{1}{h^2} - \frac{h_m}{h^3}\right) dh$$

$$P = -6u_b \cdot \mu \frac{B}{h_0 \cdot K}\left[-\frac{1}{h} + \frac{h_m}{2h^2} + C\right]$$

Applying boundary conditions,

Pressure at $h = h_1 = h_0$, $\qquad P = 0$ $\qquad\qquad\qquad\qquad\qquad$ ... (Ambient condition)

$$\therefore \qquad\qquad 0 = -6u_b \cdot \mu \frac{B}{K \cdot h_0}\left[-\frac{1}{h_0} + \frac{h_m}{2h_0^2} + C\right]$$

$$\therefore \qquad -\frac{1}{h_0} + \frac{h_m}{2h_0^2} + C = 0 \qquad\qquad\qquad\qquad\qquad\qquad\qquad \dots (1)$$

At $h = h_0 = h_1$, pressure is atmospheric i.e. 0

$$0 = -6u_b \cdot \mu \frac{B}{K \cdot h_0}\left[-\frac{1}{h_1} + \frac{h_m}{2h_1^2} + C\right]$$

$$\therefore \qquad -\frac{1}{h_1} + \frac{h_m}{2h_1^2} + C = 0 \qquad\qquad\qquad\qquad\qquad\qquad\qquad \dots (2)$$

Solving equations (1) and (2) $\Rightarrow$ (1) $-$ (2), we get,

$$-\frac{1}{h_0} + \frac{1}{h_1} + \frac{h_m}{2}\left(\frac{1}{h_0^2} - \frac{1}{h_1^2}\right) = 0$$

$$\frac{h_0 - h_1}{h_1 h_0} + \frac{h_m}{2}\left(\frac{h_1^2 - h_0^2}{h_0^2 - h_1^2}\right) = 0$$

$$\frac{h_0 - h_1}{h_1 h_0} = \frac{h_m}{2} \left(\frac{h_0^2 - h_1^2}{h_1^2 h_0^2} \right)$$

$$1 = \frac{h_m}{2} \frac{(h_0 + h_1)}{h_1 h_0}$$

$$h_m = \frac{2h_1 h_0}{h_1 + h_0} \qquad \qquad \dots (4.2)$$

$$\therefore \qquad -\frac{1}{h_1} + \frac{2h_1 h_0}{2h_1^2 (h_1 + h_0)} + C_1 = 0$$

$$C = \frac{1}{h_1} - \frac{h_0}{h_1(h_1 + h_0)}$$

$$= \frac{h_1^2 + h_1 h_0 - h_1 h_0}{h_1^2(h_1 + h_0)} \Rightarrow C = \frac{1}{h_1 + h_0}$$

$$\therefore \qquad P = \frac{-6u_b \cdot \mu\, B}{K \cdot h_0} \left[-\frac{1}{h} + \frac{h_m}{2h^2} + \frac{1}{h_1 + h_0} \right]$$

$$= \frac{6u_b \cdot \mu \cdot B}{K\, h_0} \left[\frac{1}{h} - \frac{2h_1 h_0}{2h^2(h_1 + h_0)} - \frac{1}{h_1 + h_0} \right]$$

$$P = \frac{6u_b \cdot \mu \cdot B}{K\, h_0} \left[\frac{1}{h} - \frac{h_1 h_0}{h^2(h_1 + h_0)} - \frac{1}{h_1 + h_0} \right] \qquad \dots (4.3)$$

This is an equation for the pressure distribution in flat-plate thrust bearing (tapered pad bearing) of infinite length L (along 'y'-direction).

Dimensionless Form of Pressure :

$$h^* = \frac{h}{h_0} \quad \text{and} \quad P^* = \frac{h_0^2 P}{6u_b \cdot \mu \cdot B}$$

$$\uparrow$$

Dimensionless form

Multiply and divide by 'h_0' on both sides,

$$P = \frac{6u_b \cdot \mu \cdot B}{K\, h_0^2} \cdot h_0 \left[\frac{1}{h} - \frac{h_0 h_1}{h^2(h_1 + h_0)} - \frac{1}{h_1 + h_0} \right]$$

$$P^* = \frac{P \cdot h_0^2}{6u_b \cdot \mu \cdot \beta} = \frac{1}{K} \left[\frac{h_0}{h_1} - \frac{h_0^2 \cdot h_1}{h^2(h_1 + h_0)} - \frac{h_0}{h_1 + h_0} \right]$$

Bearing parameter, $\quad K = \dfrac{h_1 - h_0}{h_0} = \dfrac{h_0}{h_0} - 1 \;\Rightarrow\; \dfrac{h_1}{h_0} = K + 1 \quad \dfrac{h_1}{h_0} + 1 = K + 2$

$$= \frac{1}{K}\left[\frac{1}{h^*} - \left(\frac{h_0}{h}\right)^2 \frac{h_1}{h_1 + h_0} - \frac{h_0}{h_1 + h_0}\right]$$

$$= \frac{1}{K}\left[\frac{1}{h^*} - \frac{h_1/h_0}{h^{*2}\,\dfrac{(h_1 + h_0)}{h_0}} - \frac{h_0/h_0}{(h_1 + h_0/h_0)}\right]$$

$$= \frac{1}{K}\left[\frac{1}{h^*} - \frac{K + 1}{h^{*2}\,(K + 2)} - \frac{1}{K + 2}\right]$$

$$P^* = \frac{P \cdot h_0^2}{6u_b \cdot \mu \cdot \beta} = \frac{1}{K}\left[\frac{1}{h^*} - \frac{K + 1}{h^{*2}\,(K + 2)} - \frac{1}{K + 2}\right] \qquad \dots (4.4)$$

which is an equation for dimensionless form of pressure in terms of K.

Dimensionless Peak Pressure P_m^* :

$$P_m = \frac{6u_b \cdot \mu \cdot \beta}{K \cdot h_0}\left[\frac{1}{h_m} - \frac{h_0 h_1}{h_m^2\,(h_1 + h_0)} - \frac{1}{h_1 + h_0}\right]$$

$$= \frac{6u_b \cdot \mu \cdot \beta}{K \cdot h_0}\left[\frac{h_1 + h_0}{2h_0 \cdot h_1} - \frac{h_1 h_0}{\dfrac{4h_1^2 h_0^2}{(h_1 + h_0)^2}} - \frac{1}{h_1 + h_0}\right]$$

$$= \frac{6u_b \cdot \mu \cdot \beta}{K \cdot h_0}\left[\frac{h_1 + h_0}{2h_0 h_1} - \frac{h_1 + h_0}{4h_1 h_0} - \frac{1}{h_1 + h_0}\right]$$

$$= \frac{6u_b \cdot \mu \cdot \beta}{K \cdot h_0}\left[\frac{2(h_1 + h_0)^2 - (h_1 + h_0)^2 - 4h_1 h_0}{4h_1 h_0(h_1 + h_0)}\right]$$

$$= \frac{6u_b \cdot \mu \cdot \beta}{K \cdot h_0}\left[\frac{h_1^2 + 2h_1 h_0 + h_0^2 - 4h_1 h_0}{4h_1 h_0(h_1 + h_0)}\right]$$

$$P_m = \frac{6u_b \cdot \mu \cdot \beta}{K \cdot h_0}\left[\frac{(h_1 - h_0)^2}{4h_1 h_0(h_1 + h_0)}\right]$$

$$\therefore \quad P_m^* = \frac{P_m \cdot h_0^2}{6u_b \cdot \mu \cdot \beta} = \frac{1}{K}\left[\frac{(h_1 - h_0)^2}{4h_1(h_1 + h_0)}\right] \qquad \dots (4.5)$$

Divide the numerator and denominator by h_0^2.

$$P^*_m = \frac{1}{K}\left[\frac{(h_1 - h_0)^2/h_0^2}{4h_1(h_1 + h_0)/h_0^2}\right]$$

$$P^*_m = \frac{1}{K}\left[\frac{K^2}{4(K + 1)(K + 2)}\right] \qquad \ldots (4.6)$$

This is equation for dimensionless form of peak pressure in terms of Bearing parameter 'K'.

where, $\quad K = \dfrac{h_1 - h_0}{h_0}$

$$K + 1 = \frac{h_1}{h_0}$$

$$K + 2 = \frac{h_1 + h_0}{h_0}$$

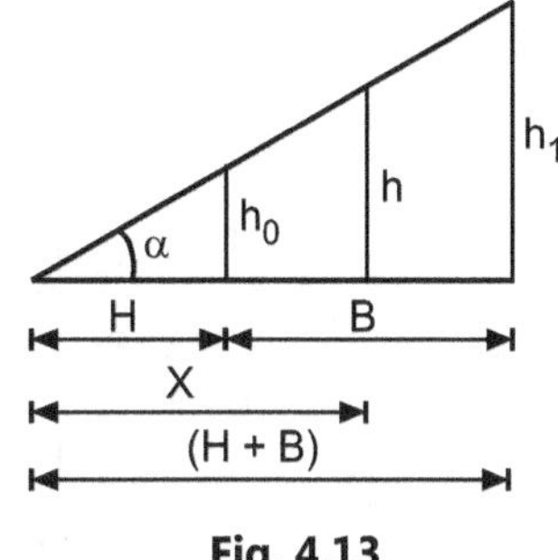

Fig. 4.13

4.4.2 Load-Carrying Capacity

Load-carrying capacity per unit length 'L'

$$W_{z'} = \frac{W}{L}$$

$$= \int_{H}^{(H+B)} P \cdot dx \cdot 1 = \int_{H}^{(H+B)} P \cdot dx$$

$$= \int_{h_0}^{h_1} \left(\frac{B}{h_0 \cdot K}\right) \cdot P \cdot dh \qquad\qquad \left(\because x = \frac{h}{h_0} \cdot \frac{B}{K}\right)$$

$$= \frac{B}{h_0 \cdot K} \int_{h_0}^{h_1} P \cdot dh \qquad\qquad \text{At} \quad x = H, h = h_0$$

and $\quad x = (H + B), h = h_1$

$$= \frac{B}{h_0 \cdot K} \int_{h_0}^{h_1} \left[\frac{6u_b \cdot \mu \cdot B}{K \cdot h_0}\left(\frac{1}{h} - \frac{h_0 \cdot h_1}{h^2(h_1 + h_0)} - \frac{1}{h_1 + h_0}\right)\right] dh$$

$$= \frac{6u_b \cdot \mu \cdot B^2}{K^2 \cdot h_0^2}\left[\log_e \cdot h\,\frac{h_0 \cdot h_1}{h(h_1 + h_0)} - \frac{h}{h_1 + h_0}\right]_{h_0}^{h_1}$$

$$= \frac{6u_b \cdot \mu \cdot B^2}{K^2 \cdot h_0^2}\left[\log_e \frac{h_1}{h_0} + \frac{h_0 h_1}{h_1 + h_0}\left(\frac{1}{h_1} + \frac{1}{h_0}\right) - \frac{h_1 - h_0}{h_1 + h_0}\right]$$

$$= \frac{6u_b \cdot \mu \cdot B^2}{K^2 \cdot h_0^2}\left[\log_e \frac{h_1}{h_0} + \frac{h_0 \cdot h_1}{h_1 + h_0}\left(\frac{h_0 - h_1}{h_0 \cdot h_1}\right) - \frac{h_1 - h_0}{h_1 + h_0}\right]$$

$$= \frac{6u_b \cdot \mu \cdot B^2}{K^2 \cdot h_0^2}\left[\log_e \frac{h_1}{h_0} + \frac{h_0 - h_1 - h_1 + h_0}{h_1 + h_0}\right]$$

$$= \frac{6u_b \cdot \mu \cdot B^2}{K^2 \cdot h_0^2}\left[\log_e \frac{h_1}{h_0} + \frac{2h_0 - 2h_1}{h_1 + h_0}\right]$$

$$W_{z'} = \frac{6u_b \cdot \mu \cdot B^2}{K^2 \cdot h_0^2}\left[\log_e \frac{h_1}{h_0} - \frac{2(h_1 - h_0)}{h_1 + h_0}\right] \qquad \ldots (4.7)$$

This is an equation for load-carrying capacity of flat-plate thrust bearing (Tapered pad bearing) of infinite length 'L' (along 'y'-direction).

$$\therefore \qquad W_{z'} = \frac{W}{L} = \frac{6u_b \cdot \mu\, B^2}{K^2 \cdot h_0^2} \cdot C_1$$

$$W = 6C_1 \frac{u_b \cdot \mu \cdot B^2 \cdot L}{K^2 \cdot h_0^2} \qquad \cdot_\cdot\, h_1, h_0 \text{ are parameters and}$$
$$\text{constant for various loads}$$

$$W = C_0 \cdot \frac{u_b \cdot \mu \cdot B^2 \cdot L}{K^2 \cdot h_0^2}$$

where, $C_0 = 6C_1$

Maximum Load-Carrying Capacity :

It has been found that, for an attitude, bearing will provide maximum load-carrying capacity.

i.e. $\dfrac{h_1}{h_0} = 2,$ $C_0 = 0.1589 \approx 0.159$

and $K = 1$

$$K = \frac{h_1 - h_0}{h_0}$$

$$= \frac{h_1}{h_0} - 1 = 2 - 1 \qquad K = 1$$

For $\dfrac{h_1}{h_0} = 2$, C_1 becomes

$$C_1 \;=\; \log_e(2) - \frac{2\left(\dfrac{h_1}{h_0} - 1\right)}{\left(\dfrac{h_1}{h_0} + 1\right)} \;=\; 0.0264805$$

$$C_0 \;=\; 6C_1$$

$$= 6 \times 0.0264805$$

$$\therefore \qquad W_{max} \;=\; 0.159 \cdot \frac{u_b \cdot \mu \cdot B^2 \cdot L}{h_0^2} \qquad\qquad \ldots (4.8)$$

which is an equation for maximum load carried by tapered-pad thrust bearing.

Now dimensionless form of load can be written as,

$$W^* \;=\; \frac{W_{z'}\, h_0^2}{6 u_b \cdot \mu \cdot B^2} \;=\; \frac{1}{K^2}\left[\log_e \frac{h_1}{h_0} - \frac{2(h_1 - h_0)}{(h_1 + h_0)/h_0}\right]$$

$$=\; \frac{W \cdot h_0^2}{6 u_b \cdot \mu \cdot B^2 \cdot L} \;=\; \frac{1}{K^2}\left[\log_e \frac{h_1}{h_0} - \frac{2(h_1 - h_0)/h_0}{(h_1 + h_0)/h_0}\right]$$

$$W^* \;=\; \frac{1}{K^2}\left[\log_e(K + 1) - \frac{2K}{K + 2}\right] \qquad\qquad \ldots (4.9)$$

This is a dimensionless form of load carried by tapered-pad thrust bearing in terms of 'K'.

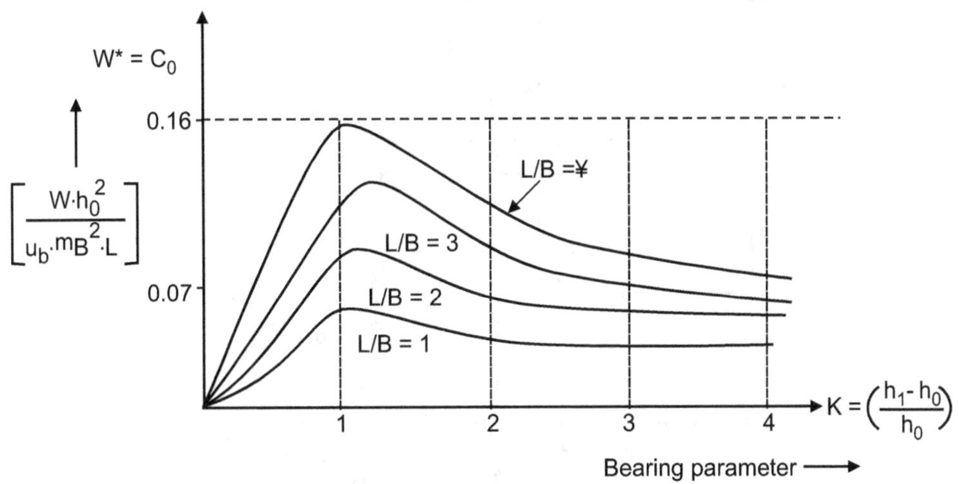

Fig. 4.14

- It is found that maximum load can be obtained for definite $\left(\dfrac{h_1}{h_0}\right)$ when dimensions of bearing, viscosity of lubricant, sliding velocity and minimum film thickness are held constant.
- For given u_b, μ and h_0, there is a definite value of 'α' which gives minimum friction.
- Thus, a bearing with fixed shoe will give satisfactory performance in a narrow range of operating conditions.
- It is found that, W is maximum at attitude $= \dfrac{h_1}{h_0} = 2$.
- For this bearing, for efficient operation of bearing, manufacturing taper inclination is difficult and slider should be moved in one direction only.

4.5 ANALYSIS OF TILTING-PAD THRUST BEARING/ KINGSBURRY THRUST BEARING

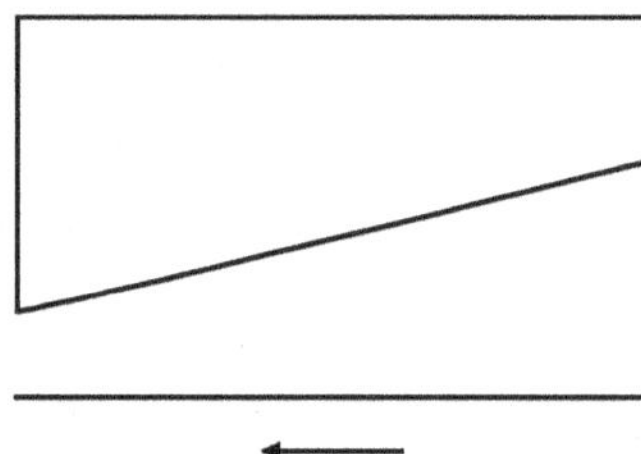

Fig. 4.15

4.5.1 Load-Carrying Capacity

The analysis of tilting-pad thrust bearings is similar to that of tapered-pad bearings. Thus, the expressions for pressure distribution, 'p' load-carrying capacity W, are same for tapered-pad as well as tilting-pad bearings.

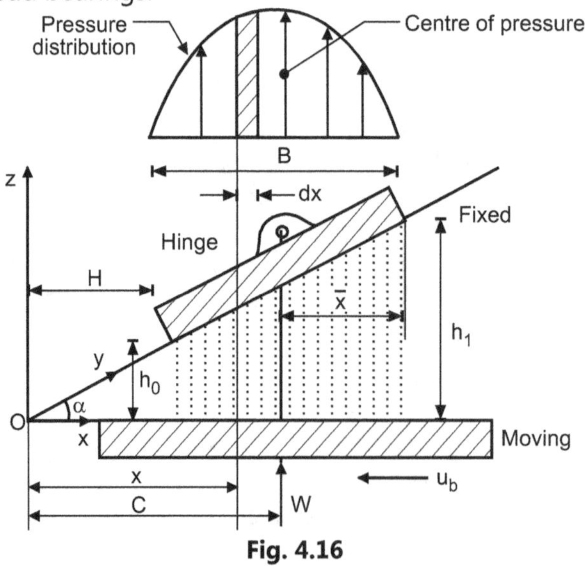

Fig. 4.16

Convention :

This type of geometry is used for the **"flying heads"** of **magnetic disc** memory systems in computer applications. The discs spin and the "heads" or tilting pads are supported by a hydrodynamic air film. For maximum packing density on the discs, the air-film thickness under the shoes is designed to be about 20 millionth of an inch or even less.

4.5.2 Centre of Pressure

It is the resultant of all hydrodynamic pressures and must be at the pivot position. This is

located at a distance of $\bar{x}$ from right corner of pad C from left margin.

- The pressure variation within the bearing is not symmetrical about the mid-point. Thus, peak in pressure curve always occurs towards the exit or trailing edge of the bearing.

- The position of centre of pressure, that is, the location of the line of action of normal force W, can be found by taking moments about the leading edge of the bearing.

- Load per unit length of bearing

$$W_{z'} = \frac{W}{L}$$

- Taking moment about point 0,

$$\frac{W}{L} \times C = \int_{H}^{(H+B)} (P \times 1 \times dx) \times x$$

$$= \int_{H}^{(H+B)} Px \, dx$$

Substituting

$$x = \frac{h}{h_0} \cdot \frac{B}{K}$$

Differentiating,

$$dx = \frac{B}{h_0 \cdot K} \cdot dh$$

Now, at $x = H$, $h = h_0$

and at $x = H + B$, $h = h_1$

$$= \int_{h_0}^{h_1} P \cdot \left(\frac{h}{h_0} \cdot \frac{B}{K}\right) \cdot \frac{B}{h_0 \cdot K}\, dh$$

$$= \frac{B^2}{h_0^2 \cdot K^2} \int_{h_0}^{h_1} \frac{6u_b \cdot \mu \cdot B}{K \cdot h_0} \left[\frac{1}{h} - \frac{h_0 h_1}{h^2(h_1 + h_0)} - \frac{1}{h_1 + h_0}\right]$$

$$\frac{W}{L} \times C = \frac{6u_b \cdot \mu \cdot B^3}{h_0^3 \cdot K^3} \left[\int_{h_0}^{h_1} \left(1 - \frac{h_0 h_1}{h(h_1 + h_0)} - \frac{h}{h_1 + h_0}\right) dh\right]$$

$$\frac{W}{L} \times C = \frac{6u_b \cdot \mu \cdot B^3}{K^3 \cdot h_0^3} \left[h - \frac{h_0 \cdot h_1}{h_1 + h_0} \cdot \log_e \cdot h - \frac{h^2}{2(h_1 + h_0)}\right]_{h_0}^{h_1}$$

$$\frac{W}{L} \times C = \frac{6u_b \cdot \mu \cdot B^3}{K^3 \cdot h_0^3} \left[(h_1 - h_0) - \frac{h_0 \cdot h_1}{h_1 + h_0} \log_e \left(\frac{h_1}{h_0}\right) - \frac{(h_1^2 - h_0^2)}{2(h_1 + h_0)}\right]$$

$$\frac{W}{L} \times C = \frac{6u_b \cdot \mu \cdot B^3}{K^3 \cdot h_0^3} \left[\frac{2(h_1^2 - h_0^2) - (h_1^2 - h_0^2)}{2(h_1 + h_0)} - \frac{h_0 \cdot h_1}{h_1 + h_0} \log_e \left(\frac{h_1}{h_0}\right)\right]$$

$$\frac{W}{L} \times C = \frac{6 \cdot u_b \cdot \mu \cdot B^3}{K^3 \cdot h_0^3} \left[\frac{h_1^2 - h_0^2}{2(h_1 + h_0)} - \frac{h_0 \cdot h_1}{h_1 + h_0} \cdot \log_e \left(\frac{h}{h_0}\right)\right]$$

$$\frac{W}{L} \times C = \frac{6u_b \cdot \mu \cdot B^3}{K^3 \cdot h_0^3} \left[\frac{(h_1 - h_0)(h_1 + h_0)}{2(h_1 + h_0)} - \frac{h_0 \cdot h_1}{h_1 + h_0} \cdot \log_e \left(\frac{h_1}{h_0}\right)\right]$$

$$\frac{W}{L} \times C = \frac{6u_b \cdot \mu \cdot B^3}{K^3 \cdot h_0^3} \left[\frac{h_1 - h_0}{2} - \frac{h_0 \cdot h_1}{h_1 + h_0} \log_e \left(\frac{h_1}{h_0}\right)\right] \qquad \ldots (4.10)$$

$$\left[\frac{\left(\frac{W}{L}\right) C \cdot h_0^3}{6u_b \cdot \mu \cdot B^3}\right] = \frac{1}{K^3} \left[\frac{h_1 - h_0}{2} - \frac{h_0 \cdot h_1}{h_1 + h_0} \cdot \log_e \left(\frac{h_1}{h_0}\right)\right]$$

$$\left[\frac{\left(\frac{W}{L}\right) \cdot h_0^2}{6u_b \cdot \mu \cdot B^2}\right] \cdot \frac{C \cdot h_0}{B} = \frac{1}{K^3} \left[\frac{h_1 - h_0}{2} - \frac{h_0 \cdot h_1}{h_1 + h_0} \cdot \log_e \left(\frac{h_1}{h_0}\right)\right]$$

$$\therefore \quad W^* \cdot \frac{C}{B} \cdot h_0 = \frac{1}{K^3}\left[\frac{h_1 - h_0}{2} - \frac{h_0 \cdot h_1}{h_1 + h_0}\log_e\left(\frac{h_1}{h_0}\right)\right]$$

$$\therefore \quad \frac{C}{B} = \frac{1}{W^* \cdot h_0 \cdot K^3}\left[\frac{h_1 - h_0}{2} - \frac{h_0 \cdot h_1}{h_1 + h_0}\log_e\frac{h_1}{h_0}\right]$$

$$\frac{C}{B} = \frac{1}{W^* \cdot K^3}\left[\frac{h_1 - h_0}{2h_0} - \frac{h_1}{h_1 + h_0}\log_e\left(\frac{h_1}{h_0}\right)\right]$$

$$\frac{C}{B} = \frac{1}{W^* \cdot K^3}\left[\frac{h_1 - h_0}{2h_0} - \frac{h_1/h_0}{(h_1 + h_0)/h_0}\log_e\left(\frac{h_1}{h_0}\right)\right]$$

$$\frac{C}{B} = \frac{1}{W^* \cdot K^3}\left[\frac{K}{2} - \left(\frac{K + 1}{K + 2}\right)\log_e (K + 1)\right]$$

Substituting, $\quad W^* = \dfrac{1}{K^2}\left[\log_e (K + 1) - \dfrac{2K}{K + 2}\right]$

in above equation, we get,

$$\frac{C}{B} = \frac{1}{\left\{\dfrac{1}{K^2}\left[\log_e (K + 1) - \dfrac{2K}{K + 2}\right]\right\} K^3}\left[\frac{K}{2} - \left(\frac{K + 1}{K + 2}\right)\log_e (K + 1)\right]$$

$$\frac{C}{B} = \frac{\left[\dfrac{1}{2} - \dfrac{(K + 1)\log_e (K + 1)}{K(K + 2)}\right]}{\left[\log_e (K + 1) - \dfrac{2K}{K + 2}\right]} \qquad \ldots (4.11)$$

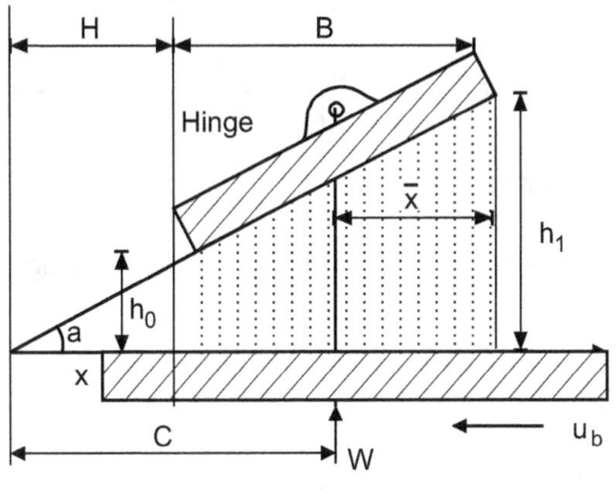

Fig. 4.17

Now, $\quad C + \bar{X} = H + B$

$$\overline{X} = H + B - C$$

$$= \frac{B}{K} + B - C$$

$$\overline{X} = B\left[\frac{1}{K} + 1 - \frac{C}{B}\right]$$

Now

$$\overline{X}^* = \frac{\overline{X}}{B} = \frac{1}{K} + 1 - \frac{C}{B}$$

$$\overline{X}^* = \frac{\overline{X}}{B} = \frac{1}{K} + 1 - \frac{\left[\dfrac{1}{2} - \dfrac{(K+1)\log_e(K+1)}{K(K+2)}\right]}{\left[\log_e(K+1) - \dfrac{2K}{K+2}\right]}$$

$$= \frac{1+K}{K} - \frac{\left[\dfrac{K(K+2) - 2(K+1)\log_e(K+1)}{2K(K+2)}\right]}{\left[\dfrac{(K+2)\log_e(K+1) - 2K}{(K+2)}\right]}$$

$$= \frac{1+K}{K} - \frac{\left[K(K+2) - 2(K+1)\log_e(K+1)\right]}{2K\left[(K+2)\log_e(K+1) - 2K\right]}$$

$$= \frac{(1+K)\left[K(K+2)\log_e(K+1) - 2K^2\right] - K(K+2) + (K+1)\log_e(K+1)}{K^2}$$

$$\therefore \quad \overline{X}^* = \frac{\overline{X}}{B} = \frac{2(3+K)(1+K)\log_e(1+K) - K(6+5K)}{2K\{(2+K)\log_e(1+K) - 2K\}}$$

$$\Rightarrow \overline{X} = \left\{\frac{2(3+K)(1+K)\log_e(1+K) - K(6+5K)}{2K(2+K)\log_e(1+K)}\right\} B \qquad \ldots (4.12)$$

$$- 2K$$

where, $\overline{X}$ – Distance of centre of pressure from leading edge (maximum oil-film thickness side)

Jakobson and Floberg :

K	0	$\frac{1}{2}$	1	$1\frac{1}{2}$	2	3	4
$\overline{X}^*$	$\frac{1}{2}$	0.5404	0.5687	0.5982	0.6074	0.6338	0.6536

$\dfrac{L}{B}$	∞	2	1.5	1.0	0.75	0.5
$\bar{X}^* = \dfrac{\bar{X}}{B}$	0.5687	0.5730	0.3756	0.5818	0.5838	0.6005
$6W^* = C_o$	0.1589	0.1096	0.09457	0.06894	0.05037	0.02892

Conclusions :

- As pad is pivoted, it is free to take up its own optimum angle to the slider depending upon load and speed and viscosity of oil film.

- The correct position for the pivot will be at (or atleast very close to) the centre of pressure or somewhat nearer the trailing edge of the bearing than its geometric centre.

- A pad centrally pivoted has the advantage that it allows motion of the slider in either direction.

and $\dfrac{X_1}{B}$ ratio is usually **0.556** in practice.

4.5.3 Friction in Tilting-Pad Thrust Bearing

$$\tau \propto S$$

$$= \mu S$$

where, S – Shear strain rate - velocity gradient

τ – Shear stress

μ – Dynamic viscosity

Shear stress,

$$\tau_{ij} = \mu \left[\frac{\partial u_i}{\partial x_j} + \frac{\partial u_j}{\partial x_i} \right] \text{Measure of shear strain rate in 3-dimensional flow}$$

μ – Dynamic viscosity (Mg/m^2)

u – Component of velocity vector (m/s)

$(u_x = u, u_y \ v, u_z = w)$

x – Component of co-ordinate vector

$(x_x = x, x_y = y, x_z = z)$

τ_{zx} = Shear stress perpendicular to z and along x-co-ordinates.

$$= \mu \left(\frac{\partial u_x}{\partial x_z} + \frac{\partial u_z}{\partial x_x} \right)$$

$$= \mu \left(\frac{\partial u}{\partial z} + \frac{\partial w}{\partial x} \right)$$

$$\tau_{zx} = \mu \frac{\partial u}{\partial z} \qquad \dots \left(\because \frac{\partial w}{\partial x} = 0 \right) \qquad \dots (4.13)$$

$$\tau_{zx} = \mu \left[\frac{\partial u_z}{\partial x_y} + \frac{\partial u_y}{\partial x_z} \right] = \mu \left[\frac{\partial w}{\partial y} + \frac{\partial v}{\partial z} \right]$$

$$\tau_{zy} = \mu \frac{\partial v}{\partial z} \quad \dots \left(\because \frac{\partial w}{\partial y} = 0 \right) \qquad \dots (4.14)$$

Considering unidirectional tangential motion,

$$\tau_{zx} = \mu \cdot \frac{\partial u}{\partial z} \qquad\qquad \because \frac{\partial v}{\partial z} = 0; \quad \tau_{zy} = \mu \frac{\partial v}{\partial z} = 0$$

Shear forces acting on the solid bearing surfaces a and b.

Shear stress on body b,

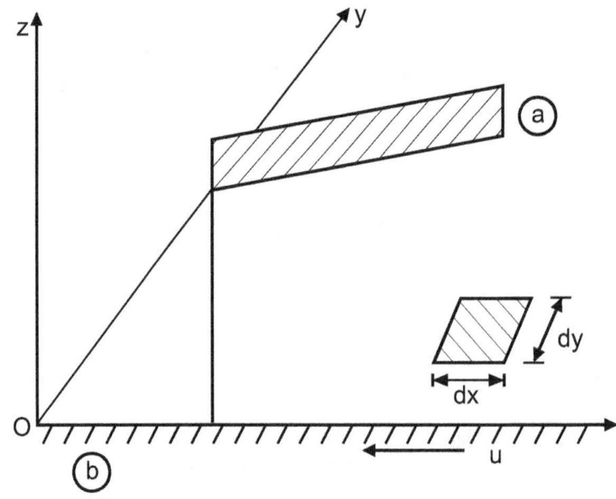

Fig. 4.18

$$\tau_{zx}\Big|_{z=0} = \mu \left. \frac{\partial u}{\partial z} \right|_{z=0} = \tau_0$$

Shear stress on body a,

$$\tau_{zx}\Big|_{z=h} = \mu \left. \frac{\partial u}{\partial z} \right|_{z=h} = \tau_h$$

$$u = \frac{z^2}{2\mu} \cdot \frac{\partial p}{\partial x} + \left[(u_a - u_b) - \frac{h^2}{2\mu} \cdot \frac{\partial p}{\partial x}\right]\frac{z}{h} + u_b$$

$$\frac{\partial u}{\partial z} = \frac{z}{\mu} \cdot \frac{\partial p}{\partial x} + \left[(u_a - u_b) - \frac{h^2}{2\mu}\frac{\partial p}{\partial x}\right] \cdot \frac{1}{h} + 0$$

For $u_a = 0$, $u_b = -u$

$$\frac{\partial u}{\partial z} = \frac{z}{\mu} \cdot \frac{\partial p}{\partial x} + \left[0 - (-u) - \frac{h^2}{2\mu} \cdot \frac{\partial p}{\partial x}\right]\frac{1}{h}$$

$$\mu \cdot \frac{\partial u}{\partial z} = z\frac{\partial p}{\partial x} + \left[u \cdot \mu - \frac{h^2}{2} \cdot \frac{\partial p}{\partial x}\right]\frac{1}{h}$$

$$= z \cdot \frac{\partial p}{\partial x} + \left[\frac{u \cdot \mu}{h} - \frac{h}{2} \cdot \frac{\partial p}{\partial x}\right]$$

$$= \left(\frac{2z - h}{2}\right)\frac{\partial p}{\partial x} + \frac{u \cdot \mu}{h}$$

$$\tau_0 = \tau_{z=0}\bigg| = \mu\left.\frac{\partial u}{\partial z}\right|_{z=0} = -\frac{h}{2}\frac{\partial p}{\partial x} + \frac{u\mu}{h} = -\frac{\partial p}{\partial x} \cdot \frac{h}{2} + \mu\frac{u}{h}$$

$$\tau_h = \tau_{zx}\big|_h = \mu\left.\frac{\partial u}{\partial z}\right|_{z=h} = \frac{h}{2} \cdot \frac{\partial p}{\partial x} + \mu\frac{u}{h} = \frac{\partial p}{\partial x} \cdot \frac{h}{2} + \mu \cdot \frac{u}{h}$$

$$\tau_{h,0} = \pm\frac{\partial p}{\partial x} \cdot \frac{h}{2} + \mu \cdot \frac{u}{h} \qquad \ldots (4.15)$$

Frictional force,

$$F_{h,0} = \int_0^L \int_0^{H+B} (\tau_{h,0}) \cdot \partial x \cdot \partial y$$

$$F_{h,0} = \int_0^L \int_H^{H+B} \left(\pm\frac{\partial p}{\partial x} \cdot \frac{h}{2} + \mu \cdot \frac{u}{h}\right) \partial x \cdot \partial y$$

$$= \underbrace{\int_0^L \int_H^{H+B} \left(\pm\frac{\partial p}{\partial x} \cdot \frac{h}{2}\right) \partial x\, \partial y}_{\text{I}} + \underbrace{\int_0^L \int_H^{H+B} \mu \cdot \frac{u}{h} \cdot dx\, dy}_{\text{II}}$$

$$I = \int_0^L \left[\int_H^{H+B} \pm\frac{\partial p}{\partial x} \cdot \frac{h}{2}\, dx\right] dy = \int_0^L \left[\left\{\frac{h}{2} \cdot P\right\}_H^{H+B} \mp \int_H^{H+B} \frac{P}{2} \cdot \frac{\partial h}{\partial x} \cdot dx\right] dy$$

When $\quad \begin{aligned} h &= H, \, P = 0 \\ h &= H + B, \, P = 0 \end{aligned}$

and $\qquad \dfrac{dh}{dx} = \tan \alpha$

$$= \mp \int\limits_{H}^{H+B} \dfrac{P}{2} \cdot \tan \alpha \cdot dx \int\limits_{0}^{L} dy$$

$$= \mp \dfrac{\tan \alpha}{2} \int\limits_{H}^{H+B} P \, dx \cdot L$$

Now, $\displaystyle\int\limits_{H}^{H+B} P \, dx =$ Load-carrying capacity per unit width

$$= \mp \dfrac{\tan \alpha}{2} \cdot \dfrac{W}{L} \cdot L$$

$$I \;=\; \mp \dfrac{\tan \alpha}{2} \cdot W \qquad\qquad\qquad \dots (4.16)$$

$$II \;=\; \int\limits_{0}^{L} \int\limits_{H}^{H+B} \left(\mu \, \dfrac{u}{h} \right) dx \, dy$$

$$= \int\limits_{H}^{H+B} \left(\mu \, \dfrac{u}{h} \right) dx \int\limits_{0}^{L} dy$$

Here, $\qquad x \;=\; \dfrac{h \cdot B}{h_0 \cdot K} = \dfrac{1}{h} = \dfrac{B}{h_0 \cdot K} \cdot \dfrac{1}{x}$

$$II \;=\; \int\limits_{H}^{H+B} \dfrac{\mu \cdot u \, B}{h_0 \cdot K} \cdot \dfrac{1}{x} \cdot dx \int\limits_{0}^{L} dy$$

$$= \mu \, \dfrac{u \, B}{h_0 \cdot K} \cdot \left[\log_e (x) \right]_{H}^{H+B} \cdot L$$

$$= \mu \, \dfrac{u \, B \, L}{h_0 \cdot K} \cdot \log_e \left[1 + \dfrac{B}{H} \right]$$

Substituting $\left(\dfrac{B}{H} \right) = K$

$$II = \mu \frac{u\,B\,L}{h_0 \cdot K} \cdot \log_e (1 + K) \qquad \dots (4.17)$$

$$F_{h,\,0} = \mp \frac{W}{2} \tan \alpha + \mu \frac{u\,B\,L}{h_0} \cdot \frac{\log_e (1 + K)}{K} \qquad \dots (4.18)$$

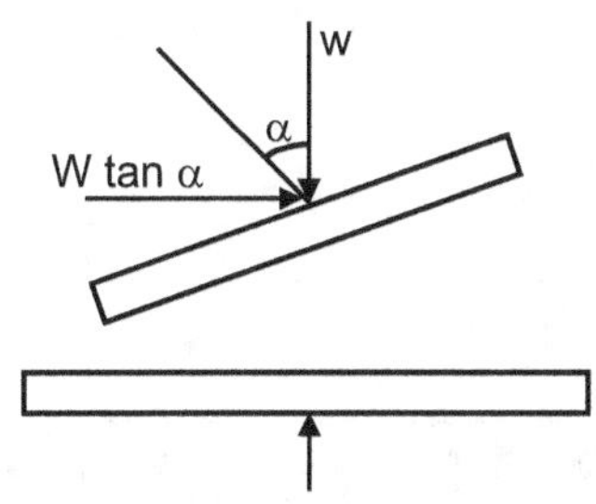

Fig. 4.19

Horizontal component of integrated pressure

$$= W \cdot \tan \alpha$$

When added to the force on the fixed pad.

Equivalent Coefficient of Friction :

$$\mu = \frac{F}{W} = \frac{\tan \alpha}{2} + \frac{\mu\,u\,B\,L}{h_0} \log_e (1 + K) \qquad \dots (4.19)$$

Oil Flow Rate :

Volume flow rate per unit width,

$$\dot{q}_x = -\frac{h^3}{12\mu} \cdot \frac{\partial p}{\partial x} + \frac{h}{2} (u_a + u_b)$$

Flow rate at $P = P_m$ or $h = h_m$ or $x = x_m$ and $\dfrac{dp}{dx} = 0$

$$\dot{q}_x = 0 + \frac{h_m (0 - u)}{2}$$

$$= -\frac{h_m \cdot u}{2}$$

$$\dot{q}_x = \frac{h_m \cdot u}{2}$$

$$= u \left(\frac{h_0 - h_1}{h_0 + h_1} \right) = \frac{u h_1}{\left(\dfrac{h_0 + h_1}{h_0} \right)} = \frac{u \cdot h_1}{K + 2}$$

Dimensionless flow rate,

$$Q = \frac{q_x'}{u(h_1 - h_0)} = \frac{h_1/h_0}{(K + 2)(h_1 - h_0)/h_0}$$

Let us divide numerator and denominator by h_0, then above equation becomes

$$Q = \frac{K + 1}{(K + 2) \cdot K}$$

$$Q = \frac{K + 1}{K(K + 2)} \qquad \qquad \text{... (4.20)}$$

4.6 ANALYSIS OF TAPERED LAND FIXED-PAD BEARING

- As the relative sliding motion of the two elements of the bearing ceases, then all the hydrodynamic load-carrying capacity falls to zero and the bearing collapses.

- To avoid this effect an obvious practical solution is to provide a parallel 'land' at the end of the taper, which can carry any residual static load safely. The configuration is then known as a "Tapered-land bearing".

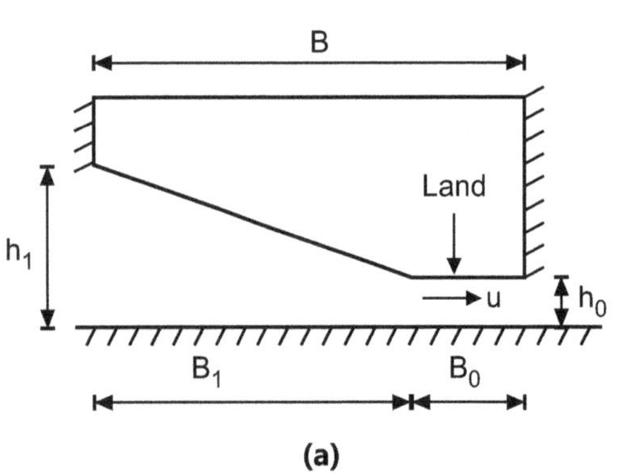

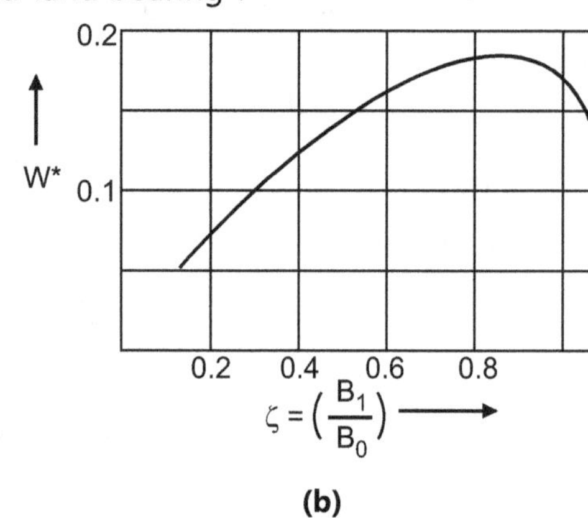

Fig. 4.20

- For the infinitely wide bearing, optimum configuration occurs at, Refer Fig. 4.20 (a).

$$\xi = \frac{B_1}{B} = 0.8$$

$$\frac{h_1}{h_0} = 2.25 \Rightarrow \text{Then, } 6W^* = C_0$$

For optimum value of $K \approx 1 = 0.192$ Refer Fig. 4.20 (b).

$$K = \frac{h_1 - h_0}{h_0} = 1$$

$$\frac{h_1}{h_0} = 2$$

$$C_0 = 0.159$$

- Tapered-land fixed-pad bearing has more load-carrying capacity than fixed pad.

4.7 ANALYSIS OF RAYLEIGH STEP BEARING (STEPPED FILM BEARING)

- Lord Rayleigh, in 1918, analysed various possible profiles a bearing might have in order to optimize load-carrying capacity.

- He used the calculus of variations to find best possible film shape to give maximum load-carrying capacity and found two parallel sections/zones, known as 'Rayleigh-step bearing'.

- This is true with no side leakage (side flow) for an infinitely wide bearing.

4.7.1 Pressure Distribution

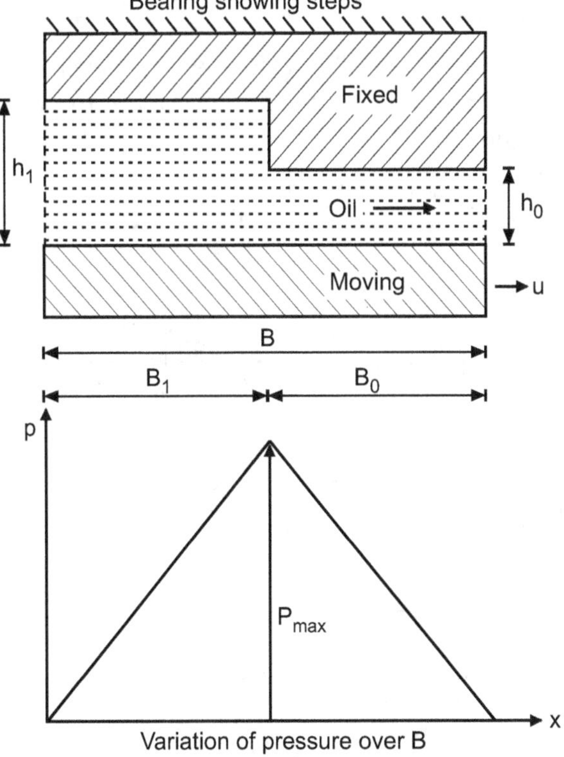

Fig. 4.21

Reynold's Equation :

- For unidirectional tangential motion of incompressible fluid with constant viscosity,

$$\frac{\partial}{\partial x}\left(h^3\frac{\partial p}{\partial x}\right) + \frac{\partial}{\partial y}\left(h^3\frac{\partial p}{\partial y}\right) = 12\mu\,\bar{u}\,\frac{\partial p}{\partial x}$$

Neglecting side leakages and for uniform film thickness,

$$\frac{\partial}{\partial x}\left(h^3\cdot\frac{\partial p}{\partial x}\right) = 0$$

$$\frac{\partial^2 p}{\partial x^2} = 0$$

$$\frac{\partial p}{\partial x} = 0$$

$\therefore$ Rate of change of pressure along x-direction is constant i.e. slope is constant.

$$\left[\frac{\partial p}{\partial x}\right]_1 = \frac{P_{max}}{B_1} \text{ and } \left[\frac{\partial p}{\partial x}\right]_0 = \frac{-P_{max}}{B_0}$$

- where, P_{max} is the peak pressure at the step and B_1, B_0 are lengths of the input and exit regions respectively.

- Since the fluid is incompressible and we are idealising the bearing as being infinitely long, it follows that q, the volume flow rate per unit width, must be the same at every section.

$$\therefore \qquad q'_x = -\frac{h^3}{12\mu}\left(\frac{\partial p}{\partial x}\right)_1 + \left(\frac{u_a + u_b}{2}\right)h$$

Here, using for first step $h = h_1$, $u_a = 0$, $u_b = u$.

$$\therefore \qquad q'_x = -\frac{h_1^3}{12\mu}\left[\frac{\partial p}{\partial x}\right]_1 + \frac{uh_1}{2} = -\frac{h_0^3}{12\mu}\left[\frac{\partial p}{\partial x}\right]_0 + \frac{uh_0}{2}$$

$\therefore$ Equating volume flow rates,

$$-\frac{h_1^3}{12\mu}\left[\frac{P_{max}}{B_1}\right] + \frac{uh_1}{2} = -\frac{h_0^3}{12\mu}\left[-\frac{P_{max}}{B_0}\right] + \frac{uh_0}{2}$$

$$\frac{u(h_1 - h_0)}{2} = \frac{P_{max}}{12\mu}\left[\frac{h_0^3}{B_0} + \frac{h_1^3}{B_1}\right]$$

$$P_{max} = \frac{12\mu\,u(h_1 - h_0)}{2\left[\dfrac{h_0^3}{B_0} + \dfrac{h_1^3}{B_1}\right]}$$

$$P_{max} \;=\; \frac{6\mu\, u(h_1 - h_0)}{\left(\dfrac{h_0^3}{B_0} + \dfrac{h_1^3}{B_1}\right)} \qquad \text{... (4.21)}$$

Divide numerator and denominator by h_0^3,

$$\therefore \qquad P_{max} \;=\; \frac{6\mu \cdot u(h_1 - h_0)/h_0^3}{\left(\dfrac{h_1^3}{B_1} + \dfrac{h_0^3}{B_0}\right)/h_0^3}$$

$$P_{max} \;=\; \frac{6\mu\, u\left(\dfrac{h_1}{h_0} - 1\right)/h_0^2}{\left[\dfrac{\left(\dfrac{h_0}{h_0}\right)^3}{B_1} + \dfrac{1}{B_0}\right]}$$

$$P_{max} \;=\; \frac{6\mu\, u(h^* - 1)/h_0^2}{\left[\dfrac{h^*}{B_1} + \dfrac{1}{B_0}\right]} \qquad\qquad h^* \;=\; \frac{h_1}{h_0} \qquad \text{... (4.22)}$$

Average pressure, $\quad P_{avg} \;=\; \dfrac{W}{L \cdot B}$

4.7.2 Load-Carrying Capacity

Load-carrying capacity per unit width of bearing,

$$\frac{W}{L} \;=\; \int_0^B P \times 1 \times dx$$

$$=\; \frac{1}{2} \cdot P_{max} \times B$$

$$=\; \frac{B}{2}\, \frac{6\mu\, u(h^* - 1)\,(B_1 - B_0)}{h_0^2\,(h^{*3} \cdot B_0 + B_1)} \qquad W \;=\; \text{Area of } \Delta$$

$$=\; 3B\, \frac{\mu\, u\left(\dfrac{h_1}{h_0} - 1\right)(B_1)}{h_0^2\left[\left(\dfrac{h_1}{h_0}\right)^3 + \dfrac{B_1}{B_0}\right]} \frac{W}{L} \;=\; \frac{1}{2} P_{max} \cdot B$$

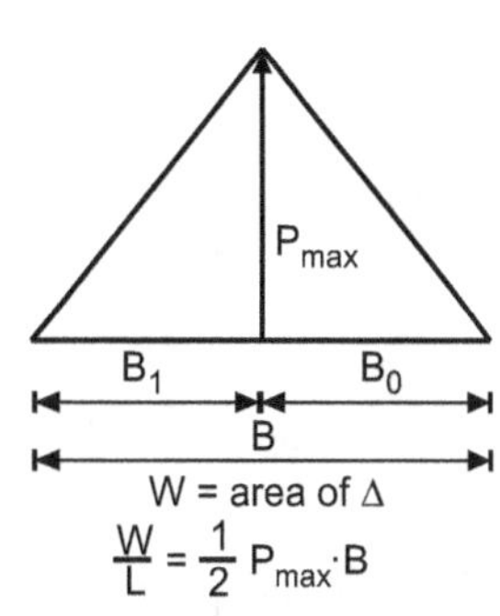

Fig. 4.22

$$W = \frac{3B\,\mu\,u\left(\dfrac{h_1}{h_0} - 1\right)B_1 \cdot L}{h_0^2\left[\left(\dfrac{h_1}{h_0}\right)^3 + \dfrac{B_1}{B_0}\right]} \qquad \ldots (4.23)$$

This is an equation for load-carrying capacity of Rayleigh step bearing.

For optimization,

$$\frac{B_1}{B_0} = 2.588 \text{ and}$$

$$\frac{h_1}{h_0} = 1.87$$

$$\therefore \qquad W = \frac{0.206\,\mu\,u\,B^2 \cdot L}{h_0^2} > \text{ for flat tilting-pad bearing} \qquad \ldots (4.24)$$

i.e. for tilting pad bearings,

$$W = \frac{0.160\,\mu\,u\,B^2\,L}{h_0^2} \qquad \ldots (4.25)$$

4.7.3 Archibald Approximation

(a)   Load-carrying capacity for square step bearing including slide flow,

$$W = \frac{0.0275\,\mu\,u\,B^2\,L}{h_0^2} \qquad \ldots (4.26)$$

With $\qquad \dfrac{h_1}{h_0} = 1.7$ and $C_0 = 0.103 \qquad \ldots (4.27)$

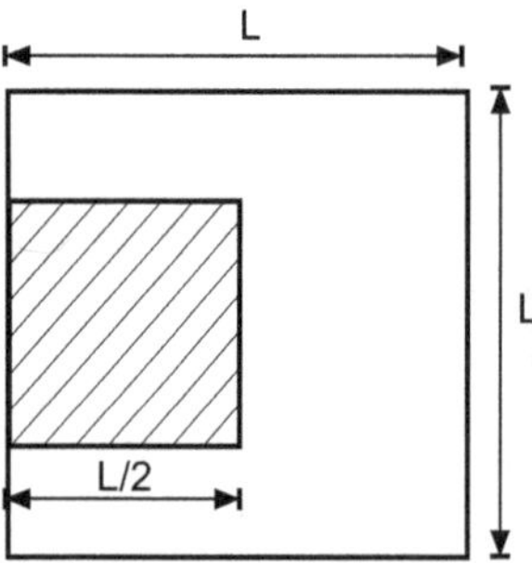

Fig. 4.23

(b)   For square tilting pad bearing with side flow factor of 0.44,

$$W = \frac{0.0704\,\mu\,u\,B^2\,L}{h_0^2} \qquad \ldots (4.28)$$

4.7.4 Cameron Approximation

(a)   For semicircular step of radius u_2 and $\dfrac{h_1}{h_0} = 1.7$ ... (4.29)

$$C_0 = 0.105$$

$$W = \frac{0.105\,\mu\,u\,B^2\,L}{h_0^{\,2}}$$ ... (4.30)

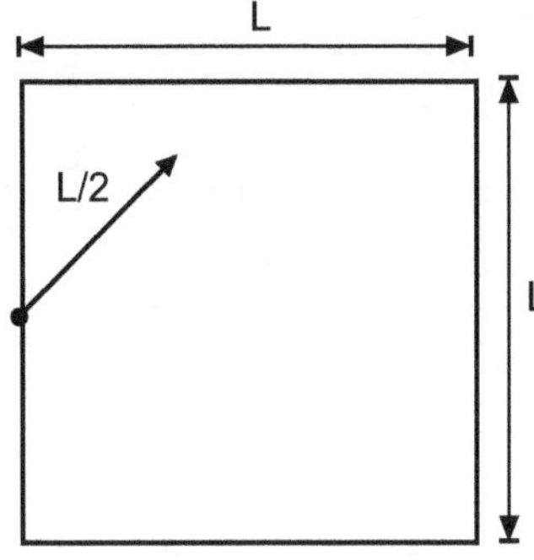

Fig. 4.24

(b)   For triangular step with $\dfrac{h_1}{h_0} = 2.12$

$$W = \frac{0.121\,\mu\,u\,B^2 L}{h_0^{\,2}}$$ ... (4.31)

4.7.5 Akers Approximation

$$\frac{h_1}{h_0} = 2.05$$

$$C_0 = 0.124$$

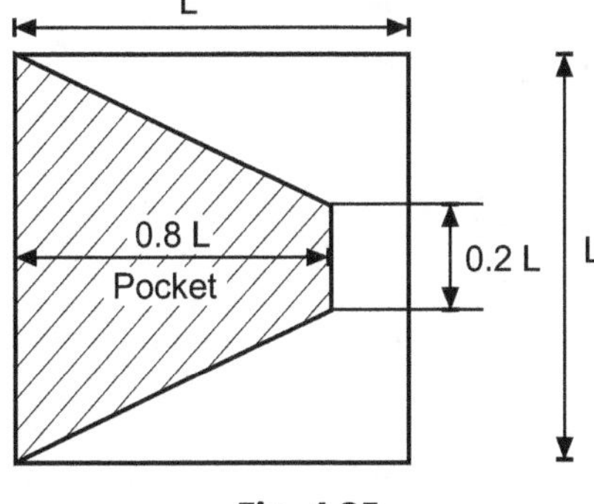

Fig. 4.25

SOLVED EXAMPLES

Example 4.1 : Following data is given for the hydrodynamic tapered-pad bearing.

- Length of pad = 900 mm
- Width of pad = 150 mm
- Maximum oil-film thickness = 120×10^{-3} mm
- Minimum oil-film thickness = 60×10^{-3} mm
- Viscosity of lubricant = 0.06 Pa·s
- Sliding velocity = 4 m/s

Evaluate :

(i)   The load-carrying capacity.

(ii) The pressure at a distance of 130 mm from the leading edge.

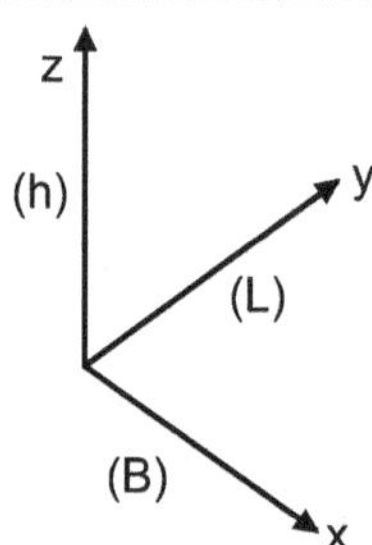

Fig. 4.26

Given :

$$L = 900 \text{ mm}$$
$$B = 150 \text{ mm}$$
$$h_1 = 120 \times 10^{-3} \text{ mm}$$
$$h_0 = 60 \times 10^{-3} \text{ mm}$$
$$\mu = 0.06 \text{ Pa·s}$$
$$= 0.06 \times 10^{-6} \text{ MPa·s} = 0.06 \times 10^{-6} \text{ N-s/mm}^2$$

Solution :

As

$$\frac{L}{B} = \frac{900}{150} = 6 > 5$$

Bearing is assumed to be infinitely long.   ... ($\because$ for infinitely long bearing L > 5 B)

(i)   Load-carrying capacity :

Bearing parameter, $K = \dfrac{h_1 - h_0}{h_0}$

$$= \frac{120 \times 10^{-3} - 60 \times 10^{-3}}{60 \times 10^{-3}}$$

Load-carrying capacity is given by,

$$W = \frac{6\, u_b \cdot \mu\, B^2 \cdot L}{K^2 - h_0^2} \left[\log_e \frac{h_1}{h_0} - \frac{2(h_1 - h_0)}{h_1 + h_0} \right]$$

$$W = \frac{6 \times 4 \times 10^3 \times 0.06 \times 10^{-6} \times (150)^2}{1 \times (60 \times 10^{-3})^2}$$

$$\left[\log_e \frac{120 \times 10^{-3}}{60 \times 10^{-3}} - \frac{2(120 \times 10^{-3} - 60 \times 10^{-3})}{(120 \times 10^{-3} + 60 \times 10^{-3})} \right]$$

$$W = 214.492 \times 10^3 \text{ N}$$

$$W = 214.492 \text{ kN}$$

(ii) Pressure at a distance of 130 mm from the leading edge :

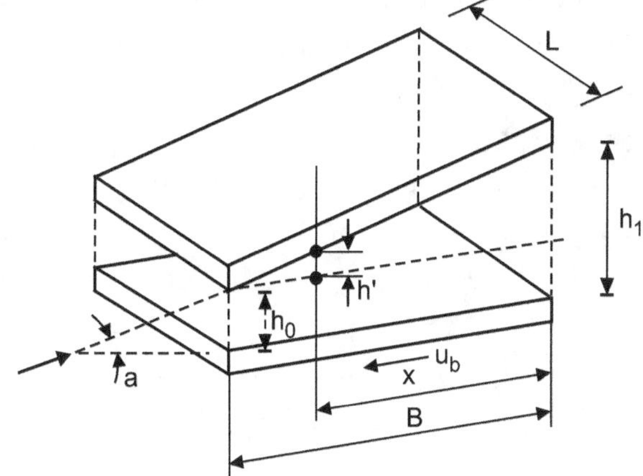

Fig. 4.27

We have, $x = 130$ mm.

$$\alpha = \frac{h_1 - h_0}{B} = \frac{120 \times 10^{-3} - 60 \times 10^{-3}}{150} = 4 \times 10^{-4} \text{ rad}$$

Now, $h = h_1 - \alpha \cdot x = 120 \times 10^{-3} - 4 \times 10^{-4} \times 130$

$$= 0.068 \text{ mm}$$

Now, $P = \dfrac{6\, u_b \cdot \mu \cdot B}{K \cdot h_0} \left[\dfrac{1}{h} - \dfrac{h_0 \cdot h_1}{h^2\,(h_1 + h_0)} - \dfrac{1}{h_1 + h_0} \right]$

$$= \frac{6 \times 4 \times 10^3 \times 0.06 \times 10^{-6} \times 150}{1 \times 60 \times 10^{-3}}$$

$$\left[\frac{1}{0.068} - \frac{120 \times 10^{-3} \times 60 \times 10^{-3}}{(0.068)^2 \, (120 \times 10^{-3} + 60 \times 10^{-3})}\right.$$

$$\left. - \frac{1}{120 \times 10^{-3} + 60 \times 10^{-3}}\right]$$

$$= \frac{194400}{60} \, [14.70588 - 8.650519031 - 5.55555]$$

$$P = 1.7993 \text{ N/mm}^2$$

Example 4.2 : A rectangular plane slider bearing is operating under the following conditions :

$$\text{Bearing width} = 80 \text{ mm (in the direction of motion)}$$
$$\text{Bearing length} = 150 \text{ mm (across the direction of motion)}$$
$$\text{Sliding speed} = 2 \text{ m/s}$$
$$\text{Oil viscosity} = 0.02 \text{ Pa·s}$$
$$\text{Maximum oil-film thickness} = 0.04 \text{ mm}$$
$$\text{Minimum oil-film thickness} = 0.02 \text{ mm}$$

Find :

(i) Load-carrying capacity.

(ii) Pressure at a distance of 50 mm from the leading end of the pad. Disregard slide leakage.

Given : $B = 80 \text{ mm}$ $h_1 = 0.04 \text{ mm}$

$\qquad\qquad\qquad L = 150 \text{ mm}$ $h_0 = 0.02 \text{ mm}$

$\qquad\qquad u_b = 2 \text{ m/s} = 2 \times 10^3 \text{ mm/s}$ $\mu = 0.02 \text{ Pa·s}$

$\qquad\qquad\qquad = 0.02 \times 10^{-6} \text{ N-s/mm}^2$

Solution :

(i)   Load-carrying capacity :

Bearing parameter, $K = \dfrac{h_1 - h_0}{h_0} = \dfrac{0.04 - 0.02}{0.02} = 1$

As $\dfrac{L}{B} = \dfrac{150}{80} = 1.875$

As the side leakage is neglected, the bearing can be considered as infinitely long bearing.

$\therefore \qquad W = \dfrac{6 \cdot u_b \cdot \mu \cdot B^2 \cdot L}{K^2 \cdot h_0^2} \left[\log_e \dfrac{h_1}{h_0} - \dfrac{2(h_1 - h_0)}{h_1 + h_0}\right]$

$$= \frac{6 \times 2 \times 10^{+3} \times 0.02 \times 10^{-6} \times (80)^2 \cdot (150)}{1^2 \cdot (0.02)^2}$$

$$\left[\log_e \frac{0.04}{0.02} - \frac{2(0.04 - 0.02)}{0.04 + 0.02}\right]$$

$$W = 207.253 \text{ kN}$$

(ii) Pressure at a distance of 50 mm from the leading end of the shaft,

Here, $x = 50$ mm

Inclination of the pad,

$$\alpha = \frac{h_1 - h_0}{B} = \frac{0.04 - 0.02}{80} \Rightarrow \alpha = 2.5 \times 10^{-4} \text{ rad.}$$

$\therefore$ Oil-film thickness at $x = 50$ mm from the leading end

$$h = h_1 - \alpha \cdot x$$

$$= 0.04 - 2.5 \times 10^{-4} (50)$$

$$h = 0.0275 \text{ mm}$$

Now,

$$P = \frac{6 \cdot u_b \cdot \mu \cdot B}{K \cdot h_0}\left[\frac{1}{h} - \frac{h_0 \cdot h_1}{h^2 (h_1 + h_0)} - \frac{1}{(h_1 + h_0)}\right]$$

$$= \frac{6 \times 2 \times 10^3 \times 0.02 \times 10^{-6} \times 80}{1 \times 0.02}$$

$$\left(\frac{1}{0.0275}\right) - \left(\frac{0.04 \times 0.02}{(0.0275)^2 (0.04 + 0.02)}\right) - \left(\frac{1}{0.04 + 0.02}\right)$$

$$= 0.96 \, [36.363636 - 17.63085 - 16.66668]$$

$$= 0.96 \, [2.066115699]$$

$$P = 1.98347 \text{ N/mm}^2$$

Example 4.3 : A plane slider with fixed shoe operates under hydrodynamic conditions and has the following details.

Width B = 50 mm

Length to width ratio = 1

Slider velocity = 2.5 m/s

Minimum oil-film thickness = 15 micron

Absolute viscosity of oil = 0.025 Pa·s

Assuming ratio of oil-film thickness as 2, find maximum load-carrying capacity of bearing.

Given : $B = 50$ mm

$$\frac{L}{B} = 1 \qquad\qquad\qquad u_b = 2.5 \times 10^3 \text{ mm/s}$$

$$\therefore \qquad L = B \qquad\qquad h_0 = 15 \text{ micron}$$

$$\mu = 0.025 \text{ Pa·s} \qquad\qquad = 15 \times 10^{-3} \text{mm}$$

$$= 0.025 \times 10^{-6} \text{ N-s/mm}^2$$

Solution : $\qquad h = \dfrac{h_1}{h_0} = 2$

Assuming bearing as infinitely long,

Bearing parameter, $\quad K = \dfrac{h_1 - h_0}{h_0}$

$$= \dfrac{h_1}{h_0} = 1 = 2 - 1$$

$$K = 1$$

Load-carrying capacity

$$W = \dfrac{6 \cdot u_b \cdot \mu \cdot B^2\, L}{K^2 \cdot h_0^{\,2}} \left[\log_e \dfrac{h_1}{h_0} - \dfrac{2(h_1 - h_0)}{h_1 + h_0} \right]$$

For $\dfrac{h_1}{h_0} = 2$, above equation becomes,

$$W = \dfrac{6\, u_b \cdot \mu \cdot B^2\, L}{K^2 - h_0^{\,2}} \left[\log_e (2) - \dfrac{2(2 - 1)}{2 + 1} \right]$$

$$= \dfrac{6\, u_b \cdot \mu \cdot B^2 \cdot L}{K^2 \cdot h_0^{\,2}} [0.0264805]$$

$$= 0.1589\, \dfrac{u_b \cdot \mu \cdot B^2 \cdot L}{h_0^{\,2}}$$

$$= 0.1589 \times \dfrac{2.5 \times 10^3 \times 0.025 \times 10^{-6} \times (50)^2 \times 50}{(15 \times 10^{-3})^2}$$

$$= 5517.36 \text{ N}$$

$$W = 5.51736 \text{ kN}$$

Maximum load-carrying capacity.

Example 4.4 : A hydrodynamic plane slider bearing with fixed shoe is operating under following conditions. **(P.U. Dec. 2006)**

- Length of bearing = 300 mm

- Length to width ratio = 2
- Sum of surface roughness for fixed shoe and moving plate $= 6 \times 10^{-3}$ mm
- Minimum oil-film thickness = 5 × (Sum of surface roughness)
- Viscosity of oil = 30 MPa·s
- Sliding velocity = 150 m/min

Neglect side leakage.

Evaluate :

(i)   Maximum load carrying capacity

(ii)   Maximum pressure

(iii) Optimum oil-film thickness

(iv)   Position of point of application of load

(v)   Power lost in friction.

Solution :

Given :

$$L = 300 \text{ mm}$$

$$\frac{L}{B} = 2$$

$$\therefore \quad B = \frac{L}{2} = 150 \text{ mm}$$

$$\Sigma R_a = 6 \times 10^{-3} \text{ mm}$$

$$h_0 = 5\,(\Sigma R_a)$$

$$= 5\,(6 \times 10^{-3}) \qquad = 30 \times 10^{-3} \text{ mm}$$

$$\mu = 30 \text{ m Pa·s} \qquad = 30 \times 10^{-9} \text{ m Pa·s}$$

$$= 30 \times 10^{-9} \text{ N-s/mm}^2$$

$$u_b = 150 \text{ m/min} \qquad = \frac{150 \times 10^3}{60} = 2.5 \times 10^3 \text{ mm/s}$$

As side leakage is neglected, bearing is considered as infinitely long.

(i)   Load-carrying capacity :

Bearing parameter, $K = \dfrac{h_1 - h_0}{h_0}$

Optimum value of maximum oil-film thickness

$$\frac{h_1}{h_0} = 2.18 \Rightarrow \therefore h_1 = 2.18 \times h_0$$

$$= 2.18 \times 30 \times 10^{-3}$$

$$h_1 = 65.4 \times 10^{-3} \text{ mm}$$

$$\therefore \quad K = \frac{65.4 \times 10^{-3} - 30 \times 10^{-3}}{30 \times 10^{-3}} = 1.18$$

$$W = \frac{6\, u_b \cdot \mu\, B^2 \cdot L}{K^2\, h_0^2} \left[\log_e \frac{h_1}{h_0} - \frac{2(h_1 - h_0)}{h_1 + h_0} \right]$$

$$= \frac{6\, u_b \cdot \mu\, B^2 \cdot L}{K^2 - h_0^2} \left[\log_e (2.18) - \frac{2(2.18 - 1)}{(2.18 + 1)} \right] \cdots \left(\because \frac{h_1}{h_0} = 2.18 \right)$$

$$W = \frac{6 \times 2.5 \times 10^3 \times 30 \times 10^{-9} \times (150)^2 \times 300}{(1.18)^2 \cdot (30 \times 10^{-3})^2} [0.0371865]$$

$$W = 90135.3329 \text{ N}$$

(ii) Maximum pressure :

$$P_m = \frac{6\, u_b \cdot \mu \cdot B}{K \cdot h_0} \left[\frac{(h_1 - h_0)^2}{4\, h_1\, h_0\, (h_1 + h_0)} \right]$$

$$= \frac{6 \times 2.5 \times 10^3 \times 30 \times 10^{-9} \times 150}{1.18 \times 30 \times 10^{-3}}$$

$$\left[\frac{(65.4 \times 10^{-3} - 30 \times 10^{-3})^2}{4 \times 65.4 \times 10^{-3} \times 30 \times 10^{-3} \times (65.4 \times 10^{-3} + 30 \times 10^{-3})} \right]$$

$$P_m = 3.19154 \text{ N/mm}^2$$

(iii) Position of point of application of load :

The distance of centre of pressure from leading edge under optimum condition is approximately given by,

$$\overline{X} = 0.576\, B$$

$$= 0.576 \times 150$$

$$\overline{X} = 86.4 \text{ mm}$$

(iv) Power lost in friction :

We know the equation for frictional force,

$$F = \frac{W}{2} \tan \alpha + \frac{\mu\, u \cdot B \cdot L}{h_0} \cdot \frac{\log_e (k + 1)}{k}$$

$$\text{where,} \qquad \tan \alpha = \frac{h_1 - h_0}{B}$$

$$= \frac{65.4 \times 10^{-3} - 30 \times 10^{-3}}{150}$$

$$= 2.36 \times 10^{-4} \text{ rad.}$$

$$\mathbf{h_0} = \mathbf{30 \times 10^{-3} \ mm}$$

$$k = \frac{h_1 - h_0}{h_0}$$

$$= \frac{65.4 \times 10^{-3} - 30 \times 10^{-3}}{30 \times 10^{-3}}$$

$$\mathbf{k} = \mathbf{1.18}$$

Using these values in above equation, we get,

$$F = \left[\frac{90135.3329}{2} \times 2.36 \times 10^{-4} \right] \times$$

$$\left[\frac{30 \times 10^{-9} \times 2.5 \times 10^3 \times 300 \times 150}{30 \times 10^{-3}} \cdot \frac{\log_e (1.18 + 1)}{1.18} \right]$$

$$= [10.63596928] \times [74.48567]$$

$$F = 85.1216 \text{ N}$$

$\therefore$ Power lost in friction

$$P_F = F \cdot u$$

$$= 85.1216 \times 2.5 \times 10^3$$

$$P_F = 212.804 \text{ W}$$

Example 4.5 : For a taper land bearing operating under hydrodynamic condition, width and length of shoe is 75 mm. Velocity of slide is 6 m/s. Viscosity is 25 MPa. Film thickness at entry is 0.3 mm and that at exit is 0.15 mm. Effect of leakage is to lower the load-carrying capacity by 30% of the ideal value. Estimate the load on the shoe.

Given :

$$B = 75 \text{ mm}, L = 75 \text{ mm}$$

$$u_b = 6 \times 10^3 \text{ mm/s}$$

$$\mu = 25 \text{ MPa·s} = 25 \times 10^{-9} \text{ N-s/mm}^2$$

$$h_0 = 0.03 \text{ mm}$$

$$h_1 = 0.15 \text{ mm}$$

Solution :

(i)   Load-carrying capacity :

$$\text{Bearing parameter,} \quad K = \frac{h_1 - h_0}{h_0} = \frac{0.15 - 0.03}{0.03}$$

$$K = 4$$

As side leakage is neglected, bearing is considered as infinitely long bearing.

$$\therefore \quad W = \frac{6\, u_b \cdot \mu\, B^2\, L}{K^2 - h_0^2} \left[\log_e \frac{h_1}{h_0} - \frac{2(h_1 - h_0)}{h_1 + h_0} \right]$$

$$= \frac{6 \times 6 \times 10^3 \times 25 \times 10^{-9} \times 75^2 \times 75}{(4)^2 \times (0.03)^2}$$

$$\left[\log_e \left(\frac{0.15}{0.03}\right) - \frac{2(0.15 - 0.03)}{0.15 + 0.03} \right]$$

$$W = 7280.10 \text{ N}$$

But actual load-carrying capacity

$$W_a = 70\% \text{ of } (W)$$

$$W_a = 0.7\, W$$

$$= 0.7 \times 7280.10$$

$$W_a = 5097.071 \text{ N}$$

Example 4.6 : The Rayleigh step bearing is having following details.

- Length of bearing = 850 mm
- Width of bearing = 250 mm
- Load on bearing = 200 kN
- Sum of surface roughness on contacting surfaces = 5 μ
- Minimum oil-film thickness = 18 (Sum of surfaces roughness value)
- Sliding velocity = 7.5 m/s

Calculate :

(i)   Step dimensions B_1 and B_0

(ii)   Maximum oil-film thickness

(iii) Viscosity of lubricant

(iv)   Maximum pressure at step.

Given :

$$B = 250 \text{ mm}$$

$$L = 850 \text{ mm}$$

$$W = 200 \text{ kN} = 200 \times 10^3 \text{ N}$$

$$u = 7.5 \times 10^3 \text{ mm/s}$$

$$\frac{L}{B} = \frac{850}{250} = 3.4$$

$$h_0 = 18\,(5 \times 10^{-3}) = 90 \times 10^{-3} \text{ mm}$$

Bearing is considered as infinitely long.

(i) Step bearing (B_1 and B_0) :

For optimum condition,

$$\frac{B_1}{B_0} = 2.588$$

$$\therefore \quad B_1 = 2.588\, B_0$$

$$\text{and} \quad B_1 + B_0 = B = 250 \text{ mm}$$

$$\therefore \quad 2.588\, B_0 + B_0 = 250$$

$$3.588\, B_0 = 250$$

$$\therefore \quad B_0 = 69.677 \text{ mm}$$

$$\therefore \quad B_1 = 2.588\, B_0 = 2.588 \times 69.677$$

$$\therefore \quad B_1 = 180.32 \text{ mm}$$

(ii) Maximum oil-film thickness (h_1) :

Under optimum condition,

$$\frac{h_1}{h_0} = 1.87$$

$$\therefore \quad h_1 = 1.87\, h_0$$

$$= 1.87 \times 90 \times 10^{-3}$$

$$h_1 = 0.1683 \text{ mm}$$

(iii) Viscosity of Lubricant (μ) :

$$W = \frac{3\,B\,\mu \cdot \left(\dfrac{h_1}{h_0} - 1\right) B_1 \cdot L \cdot u}{h_0^2 \left[\left(\dfrac{h_1}{h_0}\right)^3 + \dfrac{B_1}{B_0}\right]}$$

$$\mu = \frac{W \cdot h_0^2 \left[\left(\dfrac{h_1}{h_0}\right)^3 + \dfrac{B_1}{B_0}\right]}{3\,B \cdot B_1 \cdot L \cdot u \left(\dfrac{h_1}{h_0} - 1\right)}$$

$$= \frac{200 \times 10^3 \,(90 \times 10^{-3})^2 \left[\left(\dfrac{0.1683}{0.09}\right)^3 + \dfrac{180.32}{69.677}\right]}{3 \times 250 \times 180.32 \times 850 \times 7.5 \times 10^3 \left(\dfrac{0.1683}{0.09} - 1\right)}$$

$$\mu \;=\; \frac{14785.97409}{7.5007485 \times 10^{11}}$$

$$\therefore \qquad \mu \;=\; 19.712665 \times 10^{-9} \text{ N-s/mm}^2$$

$$\mu \;=\; 19.713 \text{ cP}$$

(iv) Maximum pressure (P_{max}) :

$$P_{max} \;=\; \frac{6\,\mu \cdot u\,(h_1 - h_0)}{\left(\dfrac{h_0^{\,3}}{B_0} + \dfrac{h_1^{\,3}}{B_1}\right)}$$

Also,

$$W \;=\; \frac{1}{2}\,P_{max} \cdot L \cdot B$$

$$P_{max} \;=\; \frac{2W}{L \cdot B}$$

$$\;=\; \frac{2 \times 200 \times 10^3}{850 \times 250}$$

$$P_{max} \;=\; 1.88235 \text{ N/mm}^2$$

Example 4.7 : The following data is given for a hydrostatic thrust bearing : **(P.U. June 2006)**

$$\begin{aligned}
\text{Thrust load} &\;=\; 500 \text{ kN}\\
\text{Shaft speed} &\;=\; 720 \text{ rpm}\\
\text{Shaft diameter} &\;=\; 500 \text{ mm}\\
\text{Recess diameter} &\;=\; 300 \text{ mm}\\
\text{Film thickness} &\;=\; 0.15 \text{ mm}\\
\text{Viscosity of lubricant} &\;=\; 29.3 \text{ cP}
\end{aligned}$$

Calculate :

  (i)   Supply pressure.

  (ii) Flow requirement in l/min.

  (iii) Power loss in pumping.

  (iv) Power loss in friction.

Given :

$$\begin{aligned}
R_0 &\;=\; 250 \text{ mm}\\
R_i &\;=\; 150 \text{ mm}\\
h_0 &\;=\; 0.15 \text{ mm}
\end{aligned}$$

$$W = 500 \text{ kN} = 500 \times 10^3 \text{ N}$$

$$N = 720 \text{ rpm}$$

$$\mu = 29.3 \text{ cP} = 29.3 \times 10^{-9} \text{ N·s/mm}^2$$

Calculate :

(i) $P_i = ?$, (ii) $Q = ?$, (iii) $E_P = ?$, (iv) $E_F = ?$

Solution :

(i) Supply pressure :

$$W = \frac{\pi \cdot P_i \, (R_0^2 - R_i^2)}{2 \cdot \log_e \left(\dfrac{R_0}{R_i}\right)}$$

$$P_i = \frac{2 \cdot W \cdot \log_e \left(\dfrac{R_0}{R_i}\right)}{\pi \, (R_0^2 - R_i^2)}$$

$$= \frac{2 \times 500 \times 10^3 \times \log_e \left(\dfrac{250}{150}\right)}{\pi \, (250^2 - 150^2)}$$

$$P_i = 4.065 \text{ N/mm}^2$$

(ii) Flow requirement in *l*/min :

$$Q = \frac{\pi \cdot P_i \cdot h_0^3}{6 \cdot \mu \cdot \log_e \left(\dfrac{R_0}{R_i}\right)}$$

$$= \frac{\pi \times 4.065 \times (0.15)^3}{6 \times 29.3 \times 10^{-9} \times \log_e \left(\dfrac{250}{150}\right)}$$

$$Q = 479946.31 \text{ mm}^3\text{/s}$$

$$= 479946.31 \times 10^{-9} \text{ m}^3\text{/s}$$

$$= (479946.31 \times 10^{-9}) \times 60 \times 10^3 \; l\text{/min}$$

$$Q = 28.7968 \; l\text{/min}$$

(iii) Power loss in pumping :

$$E_P = \frac{P_i \cdot Q}{10^6} = \frac{4.065 \times 479946.31}{10^6}$$

$$E_P = 1.95098 \text{ kW}$$

(iv) Power loss in friction :

$$E_P = \frac{\mu \cdot N^2 \cdot (R_0^4 - R_i^4)}{(58.053 \times 10^6) \cdot h_0} = \frac{29.3 \times 10^{-9} \times (720)^2 \times (250^4 - 150^4)}{(58.053 \times 10^6) \times 0.15}$$

$$E_F = 5.93056 \text{ kW}$$

Example 4.8 : The Rayleigh step bearing of length 213 mm and width 860 mm is required to support 150 kN load. The sum of surface roughness on contacting surfaces of bearing is 5 microns. The minimum oil-film thickness required is 20 times the sum of surface roughness on contacting surfaces. The sliding velocity is 8 m/s. Using optimum conditions.

Calculate :   **(P.U. Dec. 2006)**

   (i)   The location of step.

   (ii)   The maximum oil-film thickness.

   (iii)   The viscosity of lubricating oil.

   (iv)   The maximum pressure and

   (v)   The ratio of maximum pressure to average pressure.

Solution :

Given : Length of bearing along 'y' direction, B = 213 mm

Width of bearing along 'x' direction, L = 860 mm.

$$W = 150 \text{ kN} = 150 \times 10^3 \text{ N}$$

$$u = 8 \text{ m/s} = 8000 \text{ mm/s}$$

$$\frac{B}{L} = \frac{860}{213} = 4.038 \Rightarrow \left\{ \text{Hence, bearing is considered as infinitely long.} \right.$$

$$h_0 = 20 \,(5 \times 10^{-3})$$

$$= 100 \times 10^{-3}$$

$$h_0 = 0.1 \text{ mm}$$

(i) Location of step :

Using optimum conditions,

$$\frac{B_1}{B_0} = 2.588$$

$$B_1 = 2.588 \cdot B_0$$

and $B_1 + B_0 = B = 213$

$\therefore$ $2.588\, B_0 + B_0 = 213$

            $3.588\, B_0 = 213$

$$B_0 = 59.365 \text{ mm}$$

$$\therefore \quad B_1 = 2.588\, B_0 = 2.588 \times 59.365$$

$$B_1 = 153.635 \text{ mm}$$

(ii) Maximum oil-film thickness :

For optimum conditions,

$$\frac{h_1}{h_0} = 1.87$$

$$h_1 = 1.87\, h_0$$

$$= 1.87 \times 0.1$$

$$h_1 = 0.187 \text{ mm}$$

(iii) The viscosity of lubricating oil :

$$W = \frac{3\, B \cdot \mu \left[\dfrac{h_1}{h_0} - 1 \right] B_1 \cdot L \cdot u}{h_0^2 \left[\left(\dfrac{h_1}{h_0} \right)^3 + \dfrac{B_1}{B_0} \right]}$$

$$\mu = \frac{W \cdot h_0^2 \left[\left(\dfrac{h_1}{h_0} \right)^3 + \dfrac{B_1}{B_0} \right]}{3B \left[\dfrac{h_1}{h_0} - 1 \right] B_1 \cdot L \cdot u}$$

$$= \frac{150 \times 10^3 \times (0.1)^2 \left[\left(\dfrac{0.187}{0.1} \right)^3 + \dfrac{153.635}{59.365} \right]}{3 \times 213 \left[\dfrac{0.187}{0.1} - 1 \right] \times 153.635 \times 860 \times 8000}$$

$$= \frac{13690.7636}{5.87623 \times 10^{11}}$$

$$= 23.29855 \times 10^{-9} \text{ N-s/mm}^2$$

$$\mu = 23.29855 \text{ cP}$$

(iv) The maximum pressure :

$$P_{max} = \frac{6\, \mu \cdot u\, (h_1 - h_0)}{\left(\dfrac{h_0^3}{B_0} + \dfrac{h_1^3}{B_1} \right)} = \frac{6 \times 23.29855 \times 10^{-9} \times 8000\, (0.187 - 0.1)}{\left[\dfrac{(0.1)^3}{59.365} + \dfrac{(0.187)^3}{153.635} \right]}$$

$$= \frac{9.72947448 \times 10^{-5}}{5.940817985 \times 10^{-5}}$$

$$\therefore \quad P_{max} = 1.637733 \text{ N/mm}^2$$

Alternatively,

We can also find 'P_{max}' using

$$W = \frac{1}{2} P_{max} \cdot L \cdot B$$

$$\therefore \qquad P_{max} = \frac{2W}{L \cdot B} = \frac{2 \times 150 \times 10^3}{213 \times 860}$$

$$P_{max} = 1.637733 \text{ N/mm}^2$$

(v) The ratio of maximum pressure to average pressure :

Average pressure,

$$P_{av} = \frac{\text{Load}}{\text{Surface area}} = \frac{W}{B \cdot L}$$

$$P_{av} = \frac{150 \times 10^3}{860 \times 213}$$

$$P_{av} = 0.8188666 \text{ N/mm}^2$$

$$\therefore \qquad \frac{P_{max}}{P_{av}} = \frac{1.637733}{0.8188666}$$

$$\frac{P_{max}}{P_{av}} = 1.999 \approx 2$$

Example 4.9 : A fixed-inclined self-acting thrust pad of slider bearing has pad width five times the length. The viscosity of lubricant is 0.06 N-s/mm^2, the sliding velocity is 8 m/s, the pad length is 0.25 m, the minimum film thickness is 25 μm and the film thickness ratio is adjusted to have maximum load-carrying capacity. Calculate the maximum load-carrying capacity, the shear force experienced by the sliding and the coefficient of friction.

(P.U. May 2007)

Solution :

Given :   Width of bearing (L)

(along y direction)

Length of pad (B) = 0.25 m = 0.25×10^{-3} mm

$$\frac{L}{B} = 5 \quad \text{... (Given)}$$

$$\therefore \qquad L = 5\,B = 5 \times 0.25 \text{ m} = 1.25 \text{ m} = 1.25 \times 10^3 \text{ mm}$$

$$\mu = 0.06 \text{ N-s/m}^2$$

$$\mu = 0.06 \times 10^{-6} \text{ N-s/mm}^2$$

$$u_b = 8 \text{ m/s} = 8 \times 10^3 \text{ mm/s}$$

$$h_0 = 25\ \mu m = 25 \times 10^{-3}\ mm$$

$$\frac{h_1}{h_0} = 2.18 \quad \dots (\because \text{ For maximum load-carrying}$$

$$\text{capacity}, \frac{h_1}{h_0} = 2.18)$$

$$\therefore \quad h_1 = 2.18 \cdot h_0 = 2.18 \times 25 \times 10^{-3}$$

$$h_1 = 0.0545\ mm$$

As

$$\frac{L}{B} = 5 \qquad \text{(Bearing is considered to be infinitely wide)}$$

Bearing parameter (k) :

$$k = \frac{h_1 - h_0}{h_0} = \frac{h_1}{h_0} - 1 = 2.18 - 1 = 1.18$$

Maximum load-carrying capacity :

$$W_{max} = \frac{6\ u_b \cdot \mu \cdot B^2 \cdot L}{k^2 \cdot h_0^2}\left[\log_e \frac{h_1}{h_0} - \frac{2\,(h_1 - h_0)}{h_1 + h_0}\right]$$

$$= \frac{1.25 \times 10^3 \times 6 \times 8 \times 10^3 \times 0.06 \times 10^{-6} \times (0.25 \times 10^3)^2}{(1.18)^2 \times (25 \times 10^{-3})^2}$$

$$\left[\log_e (2.18) - \frac{2\,(0.0545 - 25 \times 10^{-3})}{0.0545 + 25 \times 10^{-3}}\right]$$

$$= \frac{180 \times 1.25 \times 10^3}{8.7025 \times 10^{-4}}\,[0.0371865]$$

$$W_{max} = 9614438.616\ N$$

Shear force experienced by the sliding pad :

$$F = \frac{W}{2}\tan\alpha + \frac{\mu\ u_b \cdot B \cdot L}{h_0} \cdot \frac{\log_e (1 + k)}{k}$$

$$= \frac{W}{2}\left(\frac{h_1 - h_0}{B}\right) + \frac{\mu\ u\ B \cdot L}{h_0}\frac{\log_e (1 + k)}{k} \qquad (\because \ \tan\alpha = \frac{h_1 - h_0}{B})$$

$$= \frac{9614438.616}{2}\left(\frac{0.0545 - 25 \times 10^{-3}}{0.25 \times 10^3}\right)$$

$$+ \frac{0.06 \times 10^{-6} \times 8 \times 10^3 \times 0.25 \times 10^3 \times 1.25 \times 10^3}{25 \times 10^{-3}} \cdot \frac{\log_e (1 + 1.18)}{1.18}$$

$$= 567.2519 + 3962.6689$$

$$= 4529.9207\ N$$

Coefficient of friction :

$$f = \frac{F_S}{W_{max}} = \frac{4529.9207}{9614438.616} \Rightarrow f = 4.7116 \times 10^{-4}$$

Example 4.10 : A fixed-inclined self-acting thrust pad of slider bearing has pad width five times the length. The viscosity of the lubricant is 0.05 N-s/m^2, the sliding velocity is 10 m/s, the pad length is 0.3 m, the minimum film thickness is 15 μm and the film thickness ratio is adjusted to have maximum load carrying capacity. Calculate the maximum load-carrying capacity, the shear force experienced by the sliding pad and the coefficient of friction.

(P.U. Dec. 2007)

Solution :

Given :

$$\text{Pad width (L)} \ =$$

$$\text{Pad length (B)} \ = \ 0.3 \text{ m} = 0.3 \times 10^{+3} \text{ mm}$$

$$\frac{L}{B} = 5 \Rightarrow L = 5\,B = 5 \times 0.3 = 1.5 \text{ m} = 1.5 \times 10^3 \text{ mm}$$

$$\mu \ = \ 0.05 \text{ N-s/m}^2 = 0.05 \times 10^{-6} \text{ N-s/mm}^2$$

$$u_b \ = \ 10 \text{ m/s} = 10 \times 10^3 \text{ mm/s}$$

$$h_0 \ = \ 15 \text{ μm} = 15 \times 10^{-3} \text{ mm}$$

$$\frac{h_1}{h_0} \ = \ 2.18 \ \ ... \ (\text{For maximum load-carrying capacity } h_1/h_0 = 2.18)$$

$$\therefore \quad h_1 \ = \ 2.18\, h_0 = 2.18 \times 15 \times 10^{-3}$$

$$h_1 \ = \ 0.0327 \text{ mm}$$

$$\text{As} \quad \frac{L}{B} = 5 \Rightarrow \text{Bearing is considered to be infinitely wide}$$

Bearing parameter (k) :

$$k \ = \ \frac{h_1 - h_0}{h_0} \ = \ \frac{h_1}{h_0} - 1 = 2.18 - 1 = 1.18$$

Maximum load-carrying capacity :

$$W_{max} \ = \ \frac{6\,u_b \cdot \mu \cdot B^2 \cdot L}{k^2 \cdot h_0^2}\left[\log_e \frac{h_1}{h_0} - \frac{2\,(h_1 - h_0)}{h_1 + h_0}\right]$$

$$= \ \frac{6 \times 10 \times 10^3 \times 0.05 \times 10^{-6} \times (0.3 \times 10^3)^2 \times 1.5 \times 10^3}{(1.18)^2 \times (15 \times 10^{-3})^2}$$

$$\times \left[\log_e (2.18) - \frac{2\,(0.0327 - 15 \times 10^{-3})}{0.0327 + 15 \times 10^{-3}} \right]$$

$$= \ \frac{405000}{3.1329 \times 10^{-4}} \, [0.0371865] = 1292731974 \, [0.0371865]$$

$$W_{max} \ = \ 48072193.09 \text{ N}$$

Shear force experienced by the sliding pad :

$$F_s \ = \ \frac{W}{2} \tan \alpha + \frac{\mu \cdot u_b \cdot B \cdot L}{h_0} \cdot \frac{\log_e (1 + k)}{k}$$

$$= \frac{W}{2}\left(\frac{h_1 - h_0}{B}\right) + \frac{\mu\, u_b \cdot B \cdot L}{h_0} \frac{\log_e (1 + k)}{k} \quad \ldots \left(\because \tan\alpha = \frac{h_1 - h_0}{B}\right)$$

$$= \frac{48072193.09}{2}\left(\frac{0.0327 - 15 \times 10^{-3}}{0.3 \times 10^3}\right)$$

$$+ \frac{0.05 \times 10^{-6} \times 10 \times 10^3 \times 0.3 \times 10^3 \times 1.5 \times 10^3}{15 \times 10^{-3}} \frac{\log_e (2.18)}{1.18}$$

$$= 1418.1297 + 9906.6721$$

$$F_s = 11324.802 \text{ N}$$

Coefficient of friction (f) :

$$f = \frac{F_s}{W_{max}} = \frac{11324.802}{48072193.09}$$

$$f = 2.3558 \times 10^{-4}$$

EXERCISE

1. Enumerate types of hydrodynamic thrust bearing.

2. Explain working principle of hydrodynamic thrust bearing.

3. Explain the mechanism of pressure development in hydrodynamic thrust bearing.
   [P.U. Dec. 2008, 8 Marks]

4. Derive equation for pressure and load-carrying capacity for flat plate thrust bearing. **[P.U. Dec. 2010, 12 Marks]**

5. For fixed inclined slider bearing with usual notations derive an expression for –
   (i) Pressure distribution, (ii) Dimensionless Pressure (P^*), (iii) Dimensionless peak pressure (P^*_m), (iv) Maximum load carrying capacity (W_{max}).
   [P.U. June 2011, 16 Marks]

6. For optimum conditions, derive an equation for load-carrying capacity of tapered-pad thrust bearing.

7. Derive for inclined slider bearing

$$W_{max} = 0.1589 \cdot \frac{u_b \cdot \mu \cdot B^2 \cdot L}{h_0^2}$$

where, u_b – Slider velocity

   μ – Dynamic viscosity

   B – Width of slider

   L – Length of slider

   h_0 – Minimum oil-film thickness

8. Explain tilting-pad thrust bearing with one application. Define centre of pressure and derive an equation for centre of pressure from the leading edge of bearing.

9. Write short notes on :
   (i)   Tapered pad thrust bearing
   (ii) Tapered-land fixed pad bearing
   (iii) Rayleigh step bearing
   (iv) Friction in tilting pad thrust bearing

10. Derive an equation for maximum pressure and load-carrying capacity for Rayleigh step bearing.

11. What is Rayleigh step bearing ? State advantages, limitations and applications of it.   **[P.U. Dec. 2008, 8 Marks]**

12. Derive for Rayleigh step bearing

$$W = \frac{0.206\, \mu \cdot u \cdot B^2 \cdot L}{h_0^2}$$

   where, μ – Dynamic viscosity of lubricant
                 u – Sliding velocity
                 B – Width of bearing
                 L – Length of bearing

13. Derive an expression for load-carrying capacity of Rayleigh step bearing which has entry zone gap of h_1 over a length of B_1 and exit zone gap of h_0 over a length of B_0 and sliding with a velocity of U.

$$\left[\frac{h_1}{h_0} = 1.87 \text{ and } \frac{B_1}{B_2} = 2.588\right]$$ **[P.U. June 2010, 9 Marks]**

14. Derive an equation for friction force in tilting pad thrust bearing.

15. Write short notes on :
    (i)   Stepped film bearing
    (ii) Michell pad thrust bearing
    (iii) Centre of pressure of tilting pad thrust bearing

16. State assumptions made while deriving an equation for pressure in infinitely wide tapered-pad bearing.

NUMERICALS ASKED IN VARIOUS UNIVERSITY EXAMINATIONS

1. Following data is given for a hydrostatic thrust bearing :
   (i)   Thrust load = 850 kN
   (ii) Shaft speed = 900 r.p.m.
   (iii) Shaft diameter = 450 mm
   (iv) Recess diameter = 250 mm
   (v)   Viscosity of lubricant = 30 cP

Calculate optimum film thickness for minimum power loss. Show the variation of energy losses against film thickness graphically. Also calculate total power loss.

(May 2004)

Solution :

Refer Example 4.7 on page 41.

2. The following data is given for a hydrostatic step bearing of a vertical turbogenerator : **(Dec. 2003)**
   (i)   Thrust load = 500 kN
   (ii)   Shaft speed = 1000 r.p.m.
   (iii) Supply pressure = 6 N/mm^2
   (iv)   Ratio of recess diameter to shaft diameter = 0.6
   (v)   Oil-film thickness = 0.15 mm
   (vi)   Viscosity of lubricant = 170 SUS
   (vii) Specific heat of lubricant = 2.09 kJ/kg °C
   (viii) Density of lubricant = 860 kg/m^3
   Calculate :
   (i)   Shaft and recess diameters
   (ii)   Flow rate of lubricant in l/min
   (iii) Frictional power loss
   (iv)   Pumping power loss
   (v)   Temperature rise
   (vi)   Optimum oil-film thickness so that total power loss is minimum and
   (vii) The performance parameters corresponding to optimum oil-film thickness.
   Assume that the total power loss in the bearing is converted into frictional heat.

Solution :

Refer Example 4.7 on page 41.

3. A step bearing supports the vertical shaft of a turbo-generator. The recess diameter to shaft diameter ratio is 0.6 and supply pressure is 5 MPa. The thrust load is 400 kN. The shaft rotates at 800 r.p.m. If the viscosity of oil is 30 cP, calculate optimum oil-film thickness to be maintained so that the total power loss in the bearing is minimum. **(Dec. 2002)**

Solution :

Refer Example 4.6 on page 39.

4. The hydrostatic thrust bearing of a generator consists of six pads as shown in Fig. 4.28. The total thrust load is 900 kN and the film thickness is 0.05 mm. Viscosity of the lubricant is 60 cP. Neglecting the flow over the corners, each pad can be approximated as a circular area of 500 mm and 100 mm as outer and inner diameters respectively, as shown in Fig. 4.28. The density of the lubricant oil is 0.9 gm/cc.

Calculate :

(i) Supply pressure   (ii) Flow requirement   **(May 2005 and Dec. 2001)**

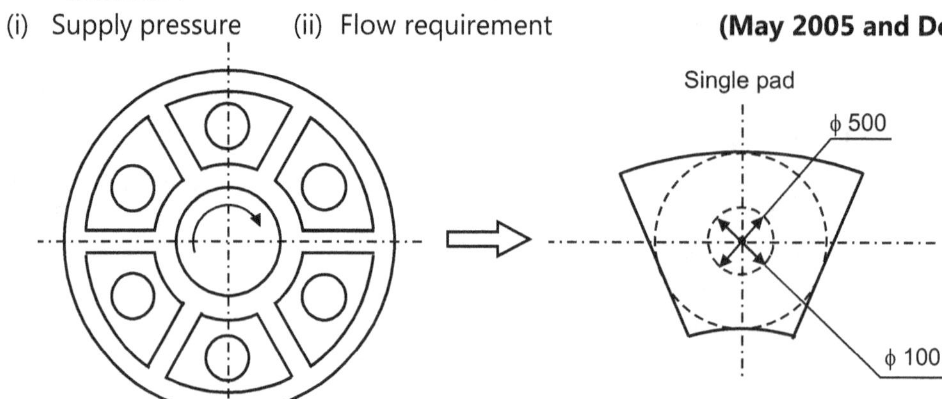

Fig. 4.28

5. A hydrostatic step bearing has 115 mm diameter recess concentric with 200 mm diameter of the shaft. The step is to carry a load of 15 kN, while maintaining lubricant film of 0.10 mm. If lubricant viscosity is 105 cP and shaft speed is 720 r.p.m., Estimate :

   (i)   Recess pressure
   (ii)   Lubricant flow required
   (iii) Power lost in pumping and
   (iv)   Power lost in friction.   **(P.U. Dec. 2006, 8 Marks)**

6. The following data is given for hydrostatic step bearing :   **(P.U. Nov./Dec. 2007)**

Thrust load	=	600 kN
Supply pressure	=	8 MPa
Shaft speed	=	1200 r.p.m.
Oil-film thickness	=	0.2 mm
Viscosity of lubricant	=	170 SUS
Specific gravity of lubricant	=	0.84
Ratio of recess diameter to shaft diameter	=	0.7

   Suggest the optimum oil-film thickness, so that the total power loss is minimum.

7. Determine the mass flow rate of fluid through the slot where two reservoirs are connected by a slot having size 300 mm × 200 mm × 0.3 mm. The reservoirs are filled with an oil of viscosity 105 cP and the pressures in the two reservoirs are 10 bar and 3 bar respectively and the relative density of oil is 0.8.

                    (P.U. Nov./Dec. 2008)

✠ ✠ ✠

Chapter 5

HYDROSTATIC LUBRICATION

5.1 PRINCIPLE OF HYDROSTATIC LUBRICATION

The term 'Hydrostatic Lubrication' was coined and introduced by D. D. Fuller in 1947. The load supporting fluid films are not the result of sliding surfaces in case of hydrostatic bearings. In case of hydrodynamic bearings, the pressure is developed by relative motion of the mating surfaces.

So, unlike the hydrodynamic bearings, hydrostatic bearings do not require motion of one surface relative to another.

Thus, hydrostatic bearing can be defined as one in which the loaded surfaces are separated by a fluid film which is forced between them by an externally generated pressure, thus formation of fluid film and the successful operation of the bearing requires a supply pump which can operate continuously.

In hydrostatic bearings, high pressure lubricating fluid film is created by external source, as the lubricating fluid is supplied between two surfaces under pressure, these bearings are often called externally pressurised bearings.

In operation the loaded member as shown in Fig. 5.1 is raised by the pressure in the recess acting on the bearing surface until flow through the restriction is equal to flow from the recess. The integrated product of pressure and bearing area is then equal to the applied load.

Thus, the bearing clearance changes will accommodate load changes. As the fluid is supplied to the recess at certain high pressure, a particular pressure profile exists over the area of bearing.

This pressure distribution can be maintained only if fluid is supplied to the recess at a rate equal to the rate at which it escapes over the lands of bearings. The film thickness and lubricating fluid pressure profile are fairly uniform across the interface.

Usually, more than one bearing is supplied with fluid by the same pump. These bearings are designed for use with both incompressible and compressible fluids.

Hydrostatic bearing can fulfil some of the extreme requirements :

- Extreme low frictional resistance.

- Heavy loadings at low speeds.

- High positional accuracy e.g. in machine tool spindles.

Constructional Features of Hydrostatic Bearing System :

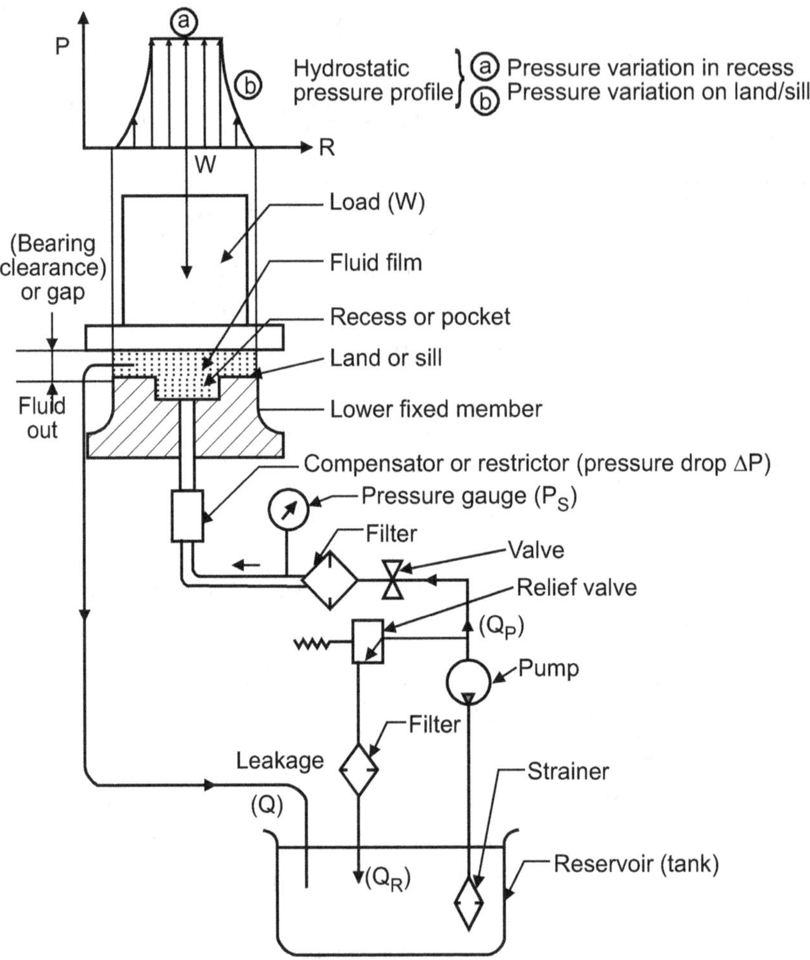

Fig. 5.1 : Hydrostatic lubrication system

The general arrangement of the lubricating fluid supply system of a typical installation is as shown in Fig. 5.1. The pump draws fluid from reservoir through a coarse filter or strainer. Further the pumped fluid under pressure is supplied to the bearing compensator or restrictor (which merely provides resistance to flow). Compensator fixes some of the variables as viscosity of oil, oil flow, film gap and radii. The oil is supplied to the compensator through a line filter at a pressure of P_S, whose value is determined by setting the pressure relief valve, which ensures that the fluid is delivered to compensator at a constant pressure regardless of the rate at which fluid flows. A second filter in the return line from this valve allows debris to be flushed from the system by operating the pump with on-off valve in the line to the bearing closed.

5.2 ARRANGEMENT OF HYDROSTATIC LUBRICATION SYSTEM

There are two basic arrangements of hydrostatic lubrication :

(i)   Lubrication at constant pressure.   (ii)   Lubrication at constant flow.

5.2.1 Lubrication at Constant Pressure

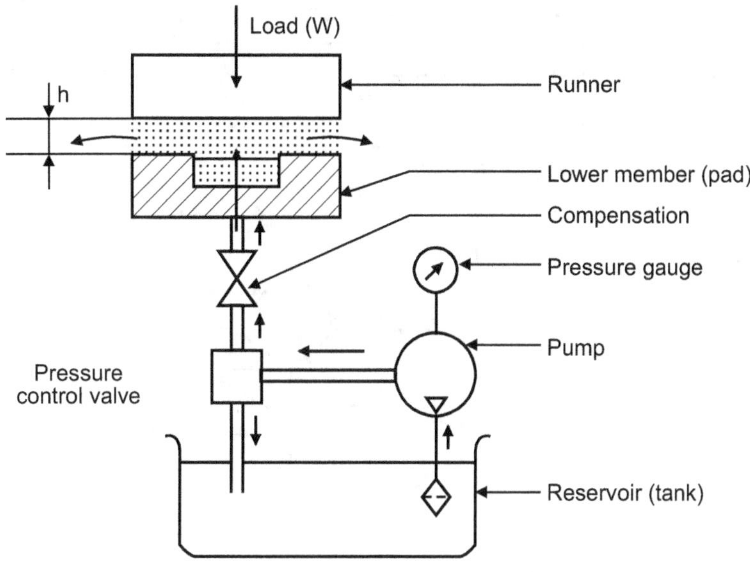

Fig. 5.2

Fig. 5.2 shows the arrangement of simple hydrostatic thrust bearing with constant pressure lubrication system. It consists of –

- Lower fixed member called pad. The pad has a central recess also called pocket. Land or sills surrounds the recess.

- The upper moving member is called as runner. The load is usually applied to the runner. The lubricant is supplied at constant pressure (P_s) through a compensator (or restrictor). When the system is to be started up, the pressure builds up in the recess. In the recess, the supply pressure P_s drops to recess pressure P_r. The pressure drop from (P_s) to (P_r) can be controlled by –

   (a)   The fixed compensator placed between the supply manifold and the bearing.

   (b)   Gap between the land and the runner (i.e. bearing clearance or the outflow passage).

Thus, the flow of lubricant (Q), recess pressure (P_r) and the land clearance or gap are interdependent. The equilibrium position will be reached when the flow is such as to build the pressure necessary to balance the load. Equilibrium is restored in a way that as load increases, it reduces the flow by decreasing the bearing clearance (h), also the recess pressure (P_r) increases. And as the load decreases, it reduces the pressure (P_r) by increasing bearing clearance (h). Thus, bearing stiffness term can be defined as the rate at which the load changes with respect to the bearing clearance or land clearance valve.

5.2.2 Lubrication at Constant Flow

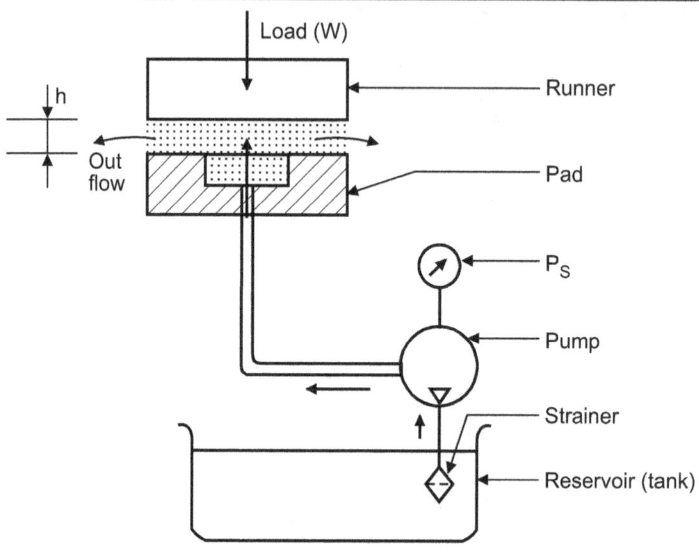

Fig. 5.3

Fig. 5.3 shows the simplest arrangement of hydrostatic thrust bearing with constant flow lubrication system. This system is free from restrictor, which means that –

Supply pressure (P_S) = Recess pressure

In this arrangement, a high pressure pump is assumed to deliver fluid from a reservoir at a constant rate of flow regardless of the pressure which exists in the recess.

For an increase in load causes land clearance (h) to decrease and the recess pressure (P_r) must increase provided the flow is kept at a constant value to balance the load. The flow is kept constant by pressure compensated flow-regenerating valves, one at each pocket, fed at a constant supply pressure from a common system.

5.3 ADVANTAGES OF HYDROSTATIC BEARINGS

Hydrostatic bearings have following advantages :

- **It Can Take High Loads at Extremely Low Speeds :**

The loaded surfaces are separated by a full fluid film even at zero speed.

$$\therefore \quad \text{Friction force (F)} = \left(\mu \frac{u_b}{h} \right) \cdot A$$

$$\therefore \quad F \propto u_b$$

During starting, when $u_b = 0 \Rightarrow F = 0$.

The resulted lubrication with full fluid film at all times is with virtually zero wear. This feature of zero static friction was used first time in the Mount Palomar Telescope and in large radar installations. As the hydrostatic bearings can take up very heavy loads at low speed, they are used in large telescopes.

- **Low Frictional Characteristics :**

Due to low frictional characteristics, these bearings are used in gyroscopes where extreme low friction is the necessary requirement.

- **High Stiffness and Good Damping Characteristics :**

Hydrostatic bearings possess high stiffness and good damping ability. Thus, by appropriate design, the stiffness in turns the vibration characteristics of the bearing can be controlled and significant amount of mechanical damping introduced.

- **High Positional Accuracy :**

Hydrostatic bearings have high positional accuracy. e.g. In case of machine tool spindle, high stiffness and good damping coupled with extremely good rotational accuracy, results in very accurate use.

5.4 LIMITATIONS OF HYDROSTATIC BEARINGS

- For operation of hydrostatic bearings, number of auxiliary equipments are required e.g. high-pressure pumps, filter and strainer unit, relief valve, oil supply line, etc. which make the overall system more complicated.

- Hydrostatic lubrication requires space for fluid cleaning requirement.

- They are expensive and have high maintenance cost.

- Overall power loss comprising of pumping power loss and frictional power loss is not necessarily low.

5.5 APPLICATIONS OF HYDROSTATIC BEARINGS

- In vertical turbo generator.

- Ball mills.

- Telescope machine – where a hydrostatic bearing can take up very high loads at low speeds.

- In precision machine tools – as a hydrostatic bearing provide high positional (i.e. high rotational accuracy) in case of machine tools) accuracy.

- In force measuring equipments.

- In laboratory equipments.

- In gyroscopes – As hydrostatic bearing pressures low friction characteristics.

- In ultra centrifuges (running as high as 90000 rpm) and have been supported by means of step bearings using air as lubricant.

- In high speed dental drills (operating at 500,000 rpm).

5.6 VISCOUS FLOW THROUGH RECTANGULAR SLOT

The basic theory of viscous flow through rectangular slot has been utilized for design of the load-carrying system of the Hale's Telescope.

Flow of lubricating fluid through rectangular slot will give a fundamental equation in lubrication. The viscous fluid flow through rectangular slot is as shown in Fig. 5.4.

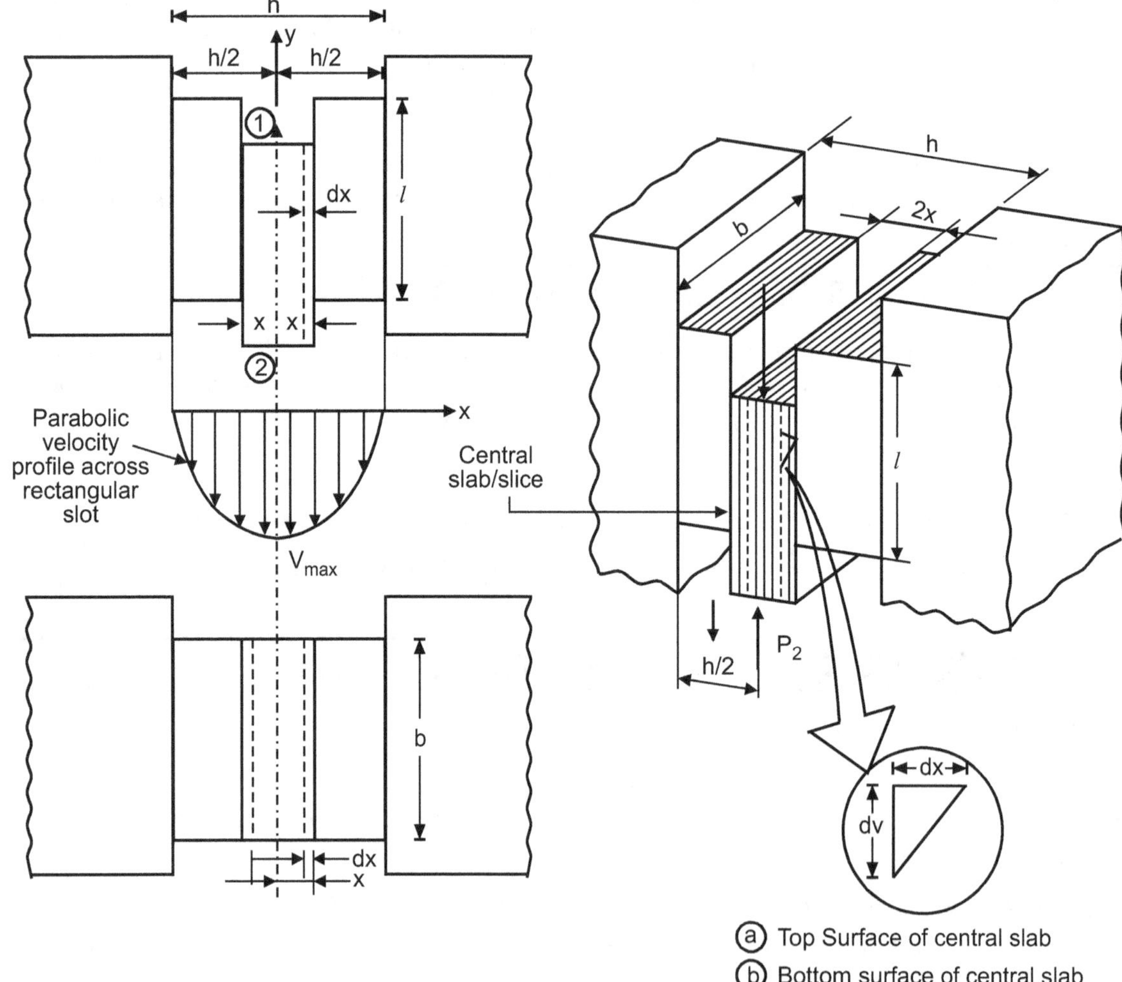

Fig. 5.4 : Viscous flow through rectangular slot

Let, l = Slot length in the direction of fluid flow (mm)

b = Width of slot perpendicular to the direction of flow (mm)

h = Slot thickness or thickness of fluid flow (mm)

ΔP = $(P_1 - P_2)$ – Pressure difference between the two sides of the middle slice (N/mm^2).

μ = Absolute viscosity of the fluid ($N\text{-}s/mm^2$)

5.6.1 Assumptions

- The width of slot (b) is assumed to be very large as compared to the film thickness h, therefore, the losses at the ends of the slot can be neglected.

- The length of the slot (l) is assumed to be large, therefore the losses at entrance and exit can be neglected.

- It is assumed that pressure at end (1) is larger than at end (2), therefore a pressure difference between the two points (1) and (2) causes flow of fluid.

- It is assumed that middle rectangular slab of fluid is being extruded down through the slot due to the downward force created by pressure difference $(P_1 - P_2)$. The thickness of middle fluid slab is '2x', width is 'b' and length is 'l' as shown.

5.6.2 Analysis

The downward force on the middle slab of fluid due to pressure difference, $\Delta P = P_1 - P_2$ is given by,

$$F_y\ (\downarrow) = (2x) \cdot b \cdot \Delta P$$

Now, due to viscosity of fluid flowing in downward direction, the shear resistance will act on both surfaces of the slab in upward direction.

$\therefore$ The upward resisting force acting on the slab,

$$F_y\ (\uparrow) = -\mu \cdot A \cdot \frac{dv}{dx}$$

$$F_y\ (\uparrow) = -\mu\ (2\,b \cdot l)\ \frac{dv}{dx}$$

The negative sign shows that the velocity v decreases as x increases i.e. velocity gradient $\frac{dv}{dx}$ is negative.

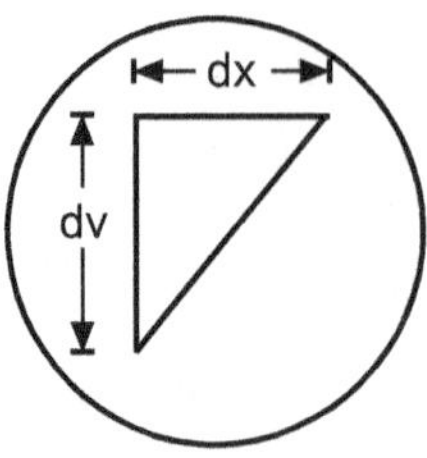

Fig. 5.5

Equating forces in vertical direction for static equilibrium,

$$F_y (\downarrow) \;=\; F_y (\uparrow)$$

$$\therefore \qquad (2x) \cdot b \cdot \Delta P \;=\; -\mu \cdot (2 \cdot b \cdot l) \cdot \frac{dv}{dx}$$

$$dv \;=\; -\frac{\Delta P}{\mu l} \cdot x \cdot dx$$

Integrating above equation to get velocity,

$$\therefore \qquad \int dv \;=\; \int -\frac{\Delta P}{\mu l} \cdot x \cdot dx$$

$$v \;=\; -\frac{\Delta P \cdot x^2}{2\mu \cdot l} + C \qquad \qquad \dots (5.1)$$

where, C is constant of integration and evaluated for the boundary condition.

$$\left(\text{At } x = \pm \frac{h}{2} \;\Rightarrow\; v = 0 \right)$$

Substituting boundary condition in equation (5.1)

$$0 \;=\; -\frac{\Delta P}{2\mu \cdot l} \left(\pm \frac{h}{2} \right)^2 + C$$

$$\therefore \qquad C \;=\; \frac{\Delta P\, h^2}{8\mu l}$$

Using value of C in equation (5.1) for v, it becomes,

$$v \;=\; -\frac{\Delta P\, x^2}{2\,\mu \cdot l} + \frac{\Delta P\, h^2}{8\,\mu \cdot l}$$

$$v \;=\; \frac{\Delta P}{2\mu \cdot l} \left[\frac{h^2}{4} - x^2 \right] \qquad \qquad \dots (5.2)$$

This equation shows that the velocity distribution across the rectangular slot is parabolic in nature.

The maximum velocity when x = 0, will be at the centre (shown in Fig. 5.5), and is given by,

$$v_{max} = \frac{\Delta P}{2\mu \cdot l}\left[\frac{h^2}{4} - 0\right]$$

$$v_{max} = \frac{\Delta P \cdot h^2}{8\mu \cdot l} \qquad \text{... (5.3)}$$

Average Velocity of the Lubricating Fluid :

It is equal to two third of the maximum velocity.

i.e. $\qquad v_{av} = \frac{2}{3} v_{max}$

$$v_{av} = \frac{2}{3}\left[\frac{\Delta P\, h^2}{8\mu \cdot l}\right]$$

$$v_{av} = \frac{\Delta P \cdot h^2}{12\mu \cdot l} \qquad \text{... (5.4)}$$

Volume Flow Rate of Fluid through Rectangular Slot (Q) :

It is the average velocity multiplied by area of cross-section.

i.e. $\qquad$ Q = Average velocity × Area of cross-section of the slot

$\qquad$ Q = $v_{av} \times (b \cdot h)$

$$Q = \frac{\Delta P\, h^2}{12\,\mu \cdot l}\,(b \cdot h)$$

$\therefore \qquad Q = \dfrac{\Delta P \cdot h^3 \cdot b}{12 \cdot \mu \cdot l} \qquad \text{... (5.5)}$

5.6.3 Application

It is used for design or evaluation of the load-carrying system of the Hale's telescope.

5.7 HYDROSTATIC STEP BEARING ANALYSIS

It is also called circular step bearing.

Fig. 5.6 illustrates the principle of a hydrostatic step bearing action.

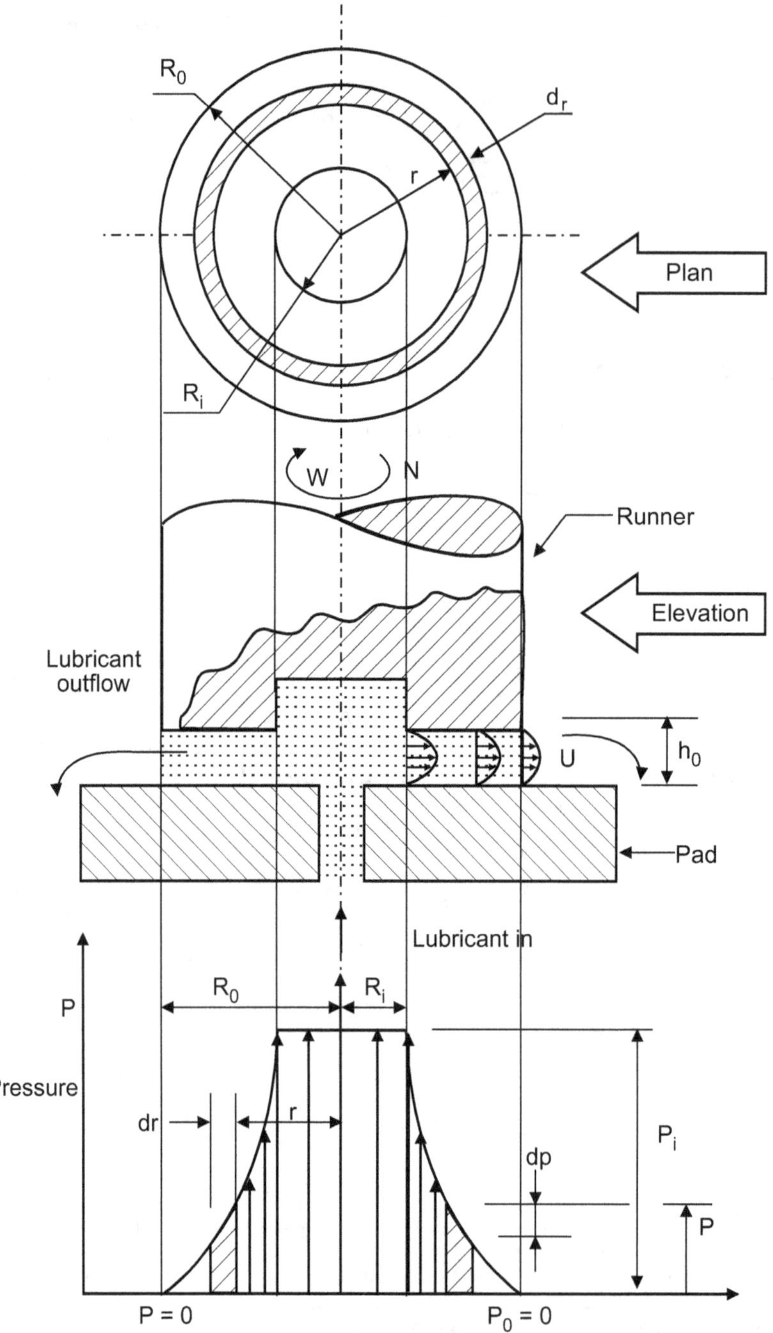

Fig. 5.6 : Pressure distribution in hydrostatic step bearing

Let, W = Vertical thrust load on runner, (N)

R_0 = Outer radius of shaft, (mm)

R_i = Radius of recess or pocket, (mm)

P_0 = Outlet lubricant pressure, (N/mm²)

P_i = Inlet lubricant pressure, (N/mm²) or supply pressure

h_0 = Fluid-film thickness (annulus depth), (mm)

μ = Absolute viscosity of lubricant, (N-s/mm²)

Q = Flow rate of lubricant, (mm³/sec.)

N = Shaft speed, (rpm)

5.7.1 Principle of Working

Lubricant from a reservoir is pumped by a constant displacement pump and is forced into a central circular recess and then flows outwards between the bearing surfaces, developing pressure and separation and returning to a reservoir for recirculation. The thrust load is supported by the fluid within the pocket and land. The outside pressure is usually equal to zero or ambient.

5.7.2 Assumptions

Following assumptions are made in order to derive the load-carrying capacity, flow requirement and frictional power lost.

- The recess depth is quite enough for the pressure in it to be fairly uniform or almost constant.

- For pressure development, the bearing is assumed to have low rotational velocity and its effect is neglected for pressure development.

- The flow can be considered as laminar across the land of the pad.

5.7.3 Analysis

5.7.3.1 Pressure Distribution

For deriving an equation for the total load-carrying capacity of hydrostatic step bearing, it is first necessary to find the pressure distribution on an annular area between the radii R_i and R_0.

We know equation (5.5) for flow rate of lubricant through a slot and is given by,

$$Q = \frac{\Delta P \cdot h^3 \cdot b}{12 \cdot \mu \cdot l}$$

where, ΔP = Pressure difference causing fluid flow, (N/mm²)

b = Width of the slot across the fluid flow, (mm)

l = Length of the slot in the direction of fluid flow, (mm)

h = Thickness of the slot or fluid film, (mm)

μ = Absolute viscosity of the lubricant, (N-s/mm^2)

Consider an annular ring at radius r, where ($R_i < r < R_0$) and of width 'dr', along the flow of lubricant. Apply above equation for the flow rate of lubricant across the annular ring.

$$\Delta P = dp; \quad b = 2\pi r; \quad l = dr; \quad h = h_0.$$

Using these quantities in above equation,

$$Q = -\frac{dp \cdot (2\pi r) \cdot h_0^3}{12 \cdot \mu \cdot dr}$$

The negative sign is due to the fact that as radius increases, pressure decreases or $\left(\dfrac{dp}{dr}\right)$ is negative.

$$dp = -\frac{6\mu \cdot Q}{\pi \cdot h_0^3} \cdot \frac{dr}{r}$$

Integrating above equation, we get,

$$\int dp = \int -\frac{6\mu \cdot Q}{\pi \cdot h_0^3} \cdot \frac{dr}{r}$$

$$P = -\frac{6\mu \cdot Q}{\pi \cdot h_0^3} \cdot \log_e r + C \qquad \qquad \dots (5.6)$$

where, C is constant of integration and can be calculated from,

First Boundary Condition :

At $r = R_0$, $P = 0$.

Using this condition in equation (5.6), for P,

$$0 = -\frac{6\mu Q}{\pi h_0^3} \log_e R_0 + C$$

$$\therefore \qquad C = \frac{6\mu Q}{\pi h_0^3} \cdot \log_e R_0$$

Substituting value of C in equation (5.6), for pressure,

$$\therefore \qquad P = \frac{6\mu Q}{\pi h_0^3} \log_e r + \frac{6\mu Q}{\pi h_0^3} \cdot \log_e R_0$$

$$\therefore \qquad P = \frac{6\mu Q}{\pi h_0^3} \log_e \frac{R_0}{r} \qquad\qquad \text{... (5.7)}$$

5.7.3.2 Flow Rate of Lubricant

Using second boundary condition,

At $r = R_i$, $P = P_i$

Using this condition in above equation,

$$\therefore \qquad P_i = \frac{6\mu \cdot Q}{\pi h_0^3} \log_e \frac{R_0}{R_i}$$

$$\therefore \qquad Q = \frac{\pi \cdot P_i \cdot h_0^3}{6\mu \cdot \log_e\left(\dfrac{R_0}{R_i}\right)} \qquad\qquad \text{... (5.8)}$$

This is an equation for flow rate of lubricant.

Pressure Distribution in Bearing Clearance of Hydrostatic Step Bearing :

Dividing equation for P by equation for P_i,

$$\frac{P}{P_i} = \frac{\log_e\left(\dfrac{R_0}{r}\right)}{\log_e\left(\dfrac{R_0}{R_i}\right)}$$

$$\therefore \qquad P = \left[\frac{\log_e\left(\dfrac{R_0}{r}\right)}{\log_e\left(\dfrac{R_0}{R_i}\right)}\right] P_i \qquad\qquad \text{... (5.9)}$$

which gives the pressure distribution on an annular ring from radius R_i to R_0.

5.7.3.3 Load-Carrying Capacity

The total load-carrying capacity of hydrostatic step bearing is equal to summation of two components i.e.

- Load supported by the central recess area (where pressure P_i is constant).

- Load supported by the annular area from R_i to R_0 (where pressure P_i varies).

$$\therefore \qquad \text{Total load, } W = W_R + W_A$$

$$\text{i.e.} \quad W = \begin{bmatrix} \text{Load supported by} \\ \text{central recess} \end{bmatrix} + \begin{bmatrix} \text{Load supported by} \\ \text{annular area} \end{bmatrix}$$

$$= (P_i \cdot \pi \cdot R_i^2) + \left(\int_{R_i}^{R_0} P \cdot 2\pi \, r \cdot dr \right)$$

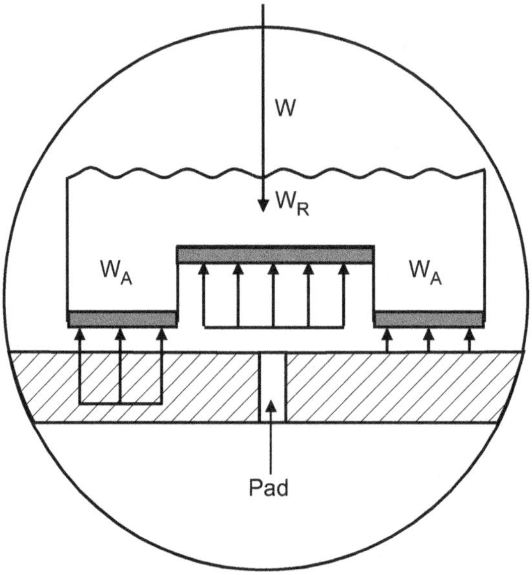

Fig. 5.7

Using equation for pressure distribution in an annular area from radius R_i to R_0,

$$W = P_i \cdot \pi \cdot R_i^2 + \int_{R_i}^{R_0} \frac{P_i \cdot \log_e\left(\dfrac{R_0}{r}\right)}{\log_e\left(\dfrac{R_0}{R_i}\right)} \cdot 2\pi \, r \cdot dr$$

$$W = \pi \cdot P_i \cdot R_i^2 + \frac{2\pi \cdot P_i}{\log_e\left(\dfrac{R_0}{R_i}\right)} \int_{R_i}^{R_0} \log_e\left(\dfrac{R_0}{r}\right) \cdot r \cdot dr$$

$$W = \pi \cdot P_i \left[R_i^2 + \frac{2}{\log_e\left(\dfrac{R_0}{R_i}\right)} \int_{R_i}^{R_0} \log_e\left(\dfrac{R_0}{r}\right) \cdot r \cdot dr \right]$$

Now, integrating by parts,

$$\left[\because \ \int AB \cdot dx = A \int B \, dx + \int \int B \cdot \frac{dA}{dx} \cdot dx \right]$$

Let,

$$I = \int_{R_i}^{R_0} \log_e \left(\frac{R_0}{R_i} \right) \cdot r \cdot dr$$

$$= \left\{ \log_e \left(\frac{R_0}{r} \right) \int r \, dr - \int \left[\left(\int r \, dr \right) \cdot \frac{d}{dr} \log_e \left(\frac{R_0}{r} \right) \right] \cdot dr \right\}_{R_i}^{R_0}$$

$$= \left\{ \log_e \left(\frac{R_0}{r} \right) \cdot \frac{r^2}{2} - \int \frac{r^2}{2} \cdot \frac{r}{R_0} \cdot \left(-\frac{R_0}{r^2} \right) \cdot dr \right\}_{R_i}^{R_0}$$

$$= \left\{ \log_e \left(\frac{R_0}{r} \right) \cdot \frac{r^2}{2} + \frac{r^2}{4} \right\}_{R_i}^{R_0}$$

$$= \left\{ \left[\log_e \left(\frac{R_0}{R_0} \right) \cdot \frac{R_0^2}{2} + \frac{R_0^2}{4} \right] - \left[\log_e \left(\frac{R_0}{R_i} \right) \cdot \frac{R_i^2}{2} + \frac{R_i^2}{4} \right] \right\}$$

$$\therefore \qquad I = \frac{R_0^2 - R_i^2}{4} - \frac{R_i^2}{2} \cdot \log_e \left(\frac{R_0}{R_i} \right) \qquad \ldots \left(\because \ \log_e (1) = 0 \right)$$

Using I in above integral,

$$W = \pi \cdot P_i \left\{ R_i^2 + \frac{2}{\log_e \left(\frac{R_0}{R_i} \right)} \left[\frac{R_0^2 - R_i^2}{4} - \frac{R_i^2}{2} \log_e \left(\frac{R_0}{R_i} \right) \right] \right\}$$

$$= \pi \cdot P_i \left\{ R_i^2 + \frac{R_0^2 - R_i^2}{2 \cdot \log_e \left(\frac{R_0}{R_i} \right)} - R_i^2 \right\}$$

$$W = \frac{\pi \cdot P_i \, (R_0^2 - R_i^2)}{2 \log_e \left(\frac{R_0}{R_i} \right)} \qquad \ldots (5.10)$$

This equation is used to evaluate load-carrying capacity of hydrostatic step bearing and it is used even if there is no recess, in which case R_i will be the radius of the oil supply-pipe.

Also, we can write equation for P_i in terms of W as below.

$$P_i = \frac{2W \log_e\left(\dfrac{R_0}{R_i}\right)}{\pi\left(R_0^2 - R_i^2\right)} \qquad \ldots (5.11)$$

5.7.3.4 Dimensionless Form of Flow Rate and Load-carrying Capacity

The flow rate and load-carrying capacity for a hydrostatic step bearing can often be conveniently expressed in non-dimensional terms as discussed in the following.

(i)   Dimensionless form of Flow Rate (Q*) :

We have an equation (5.8), for flow rate of lubricant for circular hydrostatic step bearing.

$$Q = \frac{\pi \cdot P_i \cdot h_0^3}{6\mu \cdot \log_e\left(\dfrac{R_0}{R_i}\right)}$$

$$\therefore \qquad \frac{Q}{\pi \cdot P_i \cdot h_0^3} = \frac{1}{6\mu \cdot \log_e\left(\dfrac{R_0}{R_i}\right)}$$

$$\therefore \qquad Q^* = \frac{1}{6\mu \cdot \log_e\left(\dfrac{R_0}{R_i}\right)} \qquad \ldots (5.12)$$

where, $Q^* = \dfrac{Q}{\pi \cdot P_i \cdot h_0^3}$ is called normalized or non-dimensional flow rate for circular pad bearing.

Dimensionless form of Load-Carrying Capacity (W*) :

We know the equation for load-carrying capacity of circular pad hydrostatic step bearing,

$$W = \frac{P_i \cdot \pi \cdot (R_0^2 - R_i^2)}{2 \cdot \log_e\left(\dfrac{R_0}{R_i}\right)}$$

$$\therefore \qquad W = \frac{P_i \cdot \pi \cdot R_0^2\left[1 - \left(\dfrac{R_i}{R_0}\right)^2\right]}{2 \cdot \log_e\left(\dfrac{R_0}{R_i}\right)}$$

$$\therefore \quad \frac{W}{P_i \cdot \pi \cdot R_0^{\,2}} = \frac{1 - \left(\dfrac{R_i}{R_0}\right)^2}{2 \cdot \log_e\left(\dfrac{R_0}{R_i}\right)}$$

$$\therefore \quad W^* = \frac{1 - \left(\dfrac{R_i}{R_0}\right)^2}{2 \cdot \log_e\left(\dfrac{R_0}{R_i}\right)} \qquad \text{... (5.13)}$$

where, $W^* = \dfrac{W}{P_i \cdot \pi \cdot R_0^{\,2}}$ is called normalized or non-dimensional load for circular-pad bearing.

W^* and Q^* both depend on shape of the bearing. The variation in these quantities with the ratio of the outer land to inner land radii i.e. $\left(\dfrac{R_0}{R_i}\right)$ are plotted in Fig. 5.8.

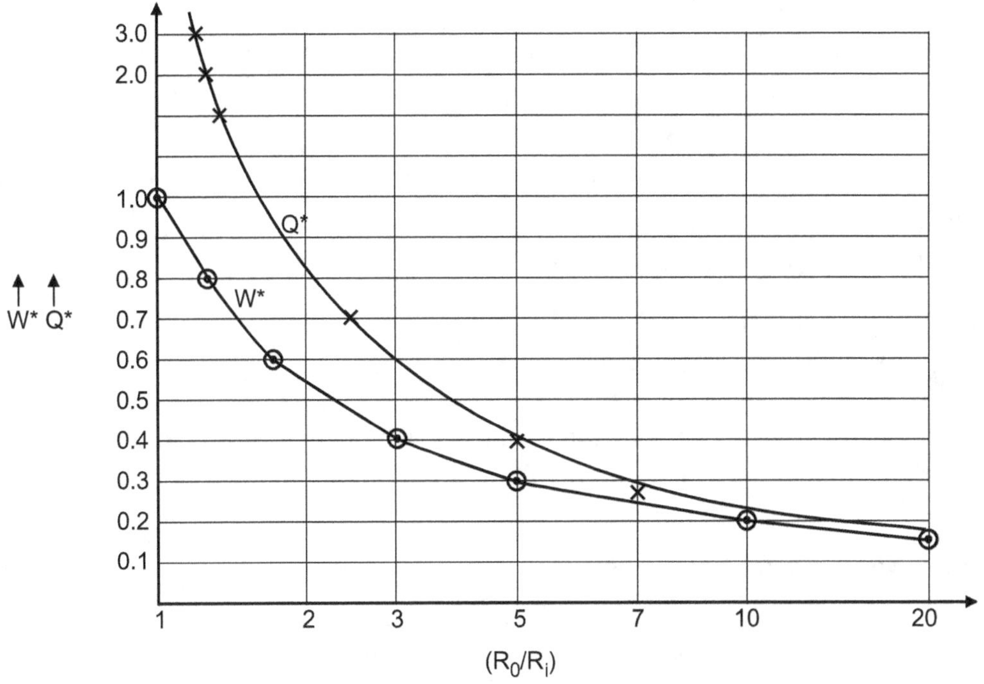

Fig. 5.8 : Variation of non-dimensional load and non-dimensional flow rate with $\left(\dfrac{R_0}{R_i}\right)$ ratio

5.8 ENERGY LOSSES IN HYDROSTATIC STEP BEARING

During the operation of hydrostatic bearing, the lubricant is continuously pumped from reservoir and supplied in the recess. Thus, there is loss of energy associated with pumping of the lubricant, called pumping power loss and also the energy loss due to viscous friction, called viscous power loss.

Therefore, total power loss is given by,

$$\text{Total power loss} = \begin{bmatrix} \text{Energy loss due} \\ \text{to viscous friction} \end{bmatrix} + \begin{bmatrix} \text{Pumping power} \\ \text{loss} \end{bmatrix}$$

$$\therefore \qquad E_T = E_F + E_P$$

Let E_F be Part–I and E_P be Part–II.

5.8.1 Viscous Power Loss (Frictional Power Loss (E_F))

Energy loss is associated in order to overcome the viscous frictional resistance on the step bearing during rotation of shaft. The frictional or viscous power loss can be evaluated as below.

Applying Newton's law of viscosity,

Shear force on area is given by,

$$F = \mu \cdot A \cdot \frac{U}{h}$$

Here, we consider elemental area as annular ring of radius r (where, $R_i < r < R_0$) and width dr across which lubricant is flowing.

The area of elemental ring, $A = 2\pi r \cdot dr$

Velocity at annular ring, $U = v = \dfrac{2\pi r \cdot N}{60}$

and Fluid-film thickness, $h = h_0$.

Using these quantities in above equation for shear force on annular ring (dF), it becomes,

$$dF = \mu \cdot (2\pi r \cdot dr)\frac{v}{h_0}$$

Substituting velocity v in above equation,

$$F = \mu \cdot (2\pi r \cdot dr)\frac{2\pi N \cdot r}{60} \cdot \frac{1}{h_0}$$

$$= \frac{4\pi^2 \cdot \mu \cdot N}{60 \cdot h_0} \cdot r^2 \cdot dr$$

$$\therefore \quad \text{Frictional torque on annular ring is given by,}$$

$$dT = r \cdot dF$$

$$= \frac{4\pi^2 \cdot \mu \cdot N}{60 \cdot h_0} \cdot r^3 \cdot dr$$

$\therefore$ Total frictional torque on the step is given by,

$$T = \int_{R_i}^{R_0} dT = \int_{R_i}^{R_0} \frac{4\pi^2 \cdot \mu \cdot N}{60 \cdot h_0} \cdot r^3 \cdot dr$$

$$= \frac{4\pi^2 \cdot \mu \cdot N}{60 \cdot h_0} \left[\frac{1}{4} \cdot r^4 \right]_{R_i}^{R_0}$$

$$T = \frac{\pi^2 \cdot \mu \cdot N}{60\, h_0} [R_0^4 - R_i^4] \qquad \qquad \qquad \dots (5.14)$$

$\therefore$ Frictional or viscous power loss is given by,

$$E_F = \frac{2\pi\, N \cdot T}{60 \times 10^6}\ (kW)$$

Substituting value of frictional torque in above equation, it becomes

$$= \frac{2\pi \cdot N}{60 \times 10^6} \left[\frac{\pi^2 \cdot \mu \cdot N}{60\, h_0} (R_0^4 - R_i^4) \right] = \frac{2\pi^3 \cdot \mu \cdot N^2\, (R_0^4 - R_i^4)}{3600 \times 10^6\, h_0}$$

$\therefore$
$$E_F = \frac{\mu \cdot N^2\, (R_0^4 - R_i^4)}{(58.053 \times 10^6)\, h_0}\ (kW) \qquad \qquad \dots (5.15)$$

This is an equation for viscous or frictional power loss and it shows that frictional power loss is inversely proportional to the film thickness (h_0), i.e.

$$E_F \propto \frac{1}{h_0} \qquad \qquad \qquad \dots (5.16)$$

where, E_F = Friction or viscous power loss, (kW)

  μ = Absolute viscosity of lubricant, (N-s/mm^2)

  R_0 = Outer radius of the shaft, (mm)

  R_i = Radius of recess or pocket in shaft, (mm)

  N = Speed of shaft (rpm)

5.8.2 Pumping Power Loss (E_P)

Power is consumed by the external pump therefore, the energy loss associated with pumping of lubricant is called pumping power loss and is given by,

$$E_P = Q \cdot \Delta P \qquad \qquad \qquad \dots (5.17)$$

where, $\Delta P = (P_i - P_0)$

$$= \frac{(Q \times 10^{-9}) \cdot (\Delta P \times 10^6)}{\mu_p \cdot 10^3}, \text{ (kW)}$$

$$E_P = \frac{Q(P_i - P_0)}{\mu_p \cdot 10^6}, \text{ (kW)} \qquad \qquad ...(5.18)$$

where, $\quad E_P$ = Pumping power loss, (kW)

$\qquad \qquad P_i$ = Inlet lubricant pressure, (N/mm^2)

$\qquad \qquad P_0$ = Outlet lubricant pressure, (N/mm^2)

$\qquad \qquad \mu_p$ = Pump efficiency

$\qquad \qquad Q$ = Lubricant flow rate, (mm^3/sec.)

Now, for $P_0 = 0$, $\mu_p = 1$, above equation becomes,

$$E_P = \frac{P_i \cdot Q}{10^6} \qquad \qquad ...(5.19)$$

Using value of Q in above equation, it becomes,

$$E_P = \frac{\pi \cdot P_i^2 \cdot h_0^3}{6\mu \cdot \log_e\left(\dfrac{R_0}{R_i}\right)} \cdot \frac{1}{10^6}, \text{ (kW)}$$

$$\therefore \quad E_P = \frac{1}{1.91 \times 10^6}\left[\frac{P_i^2 \cdot h_0^3}{\mu \cdot \log_e\left(\dfrac{R_0}{R_i}\right)}\right], \text{ (kW)} \qquad \qquad ...(5.20)$$

$\therefore$ This equation shows that pumping power loss is directly proportional to the cube of film thickness.

i.e. $\qquad \qquad E_P \propto h_0^3 \qquad \qquad ...(5.21)$

Adding Part-I and Part-II for total power loss,

$\therefore$ Total power loss in hydrostatic step bearing,

$$E_T = \left\{\frac{1}{58.053 \times 10^6}\left[\frac{\mu \cdot N^2(R_0^4 - R_i^4)}{h_0}\right]\right\} + \left\{\frac{1}{1.91 \times 10^6}\left[\frac{P_i^2 \cdot h_0^3}{\mu \cdot \log_e\left(\dfrac{R_0}{R_i}\right)}\right]\right\} \qquad ...(5.22)$$

$\therefore$ For most of the bearings, pumping losses are predominent compared to viscous or frictional losses.

$\therefore$ Neglecting viscous losses,

Total power loss,

$$E_T = \frac{1}{1.91 \times 10^6} \frac{(P_i^2 \cdot h_0^3)}{\mu \cdot \log_e\left(\dfrac{R_0}{R_i}\right)} \qquad \text{... Neglecting effect of viscous power} \quad \text{... (5.23)}$$

5.9 OPTIMUM DESIGN OF HYDROSTATIC STEP BEARING

Optimization is an act of obtaining better results with an aim of minimizing or maximizing the objective function subjected to constraints.

Now, optimum design of step bearing includes optimization of following design parameters.

(a) Optimum Recess Size :

Where recess size can be influenced by three parameters :

* Minimizing inlet pressure, (P_i)

* Minimizing flow rate of lubricant, (Q)

* Minimizing pumping power, (E_P)

(b) Oil-Film Thickness :

Optimum oil-film thickness can be evaluated for total power loss in step bearing.

(c) Stiffness of Hydrostatic Step Bearing.

5.9.1 Optimum Recess Size

5.9.1.1 Minimizing Inlet Pressure

We can find optimum recess size for non-dimensional recess pressure, non-dimensional flow rate (Q) and non-dimensional pumping power (E_P).

(i) Recess Pressure (P_i) : We have an equation for load-carrying capacity for hydrostatic step bearing.

$$W = \frac{P_i \cdot \pi \cdot (R_0^2 - R_i^2)}{2 \cdot \log_e\left(\dfrac{R_0}{R_i}\right)} = \frac{P_i \cdot \pi}{2} \cdot \frac{R_0^2\left[1 - \left(\dfrac{R_i}{R_0}\right)^2\right]}{\log_e\left(\dfrac{R_0}{R_i}\right)}$$

$$\therefore \qquad P_i = \frac{W}{\pi \cdot R_0^2} \cdot \frac{2 \log_e\left(\dfrac{R_0}{R_i}\right)}{1 - \left(\dfrac{R_i}{R_0}\right)^2}$$

$$\therefore \qquad P_i = \frac{W}{A} \cdot k_p \qquad \qquad \dots (5.24)$$

$$\text{where,} \qquad A = \pi \cdot R_0^2$$

$$\text{and} \qquad k_p = P_i \cdot \frac{A}{W}$$

$$= \frac{2 \cdot \log_e \left(\dfrac{R_0}{R_i}\right)}{1 - \left(\dfrac{R_i}{R_0}\right)^2}$$

$$\therefore \qquad k_p = \frac{2 \cdot \log_e \left(\dfrac{R_0}{R_i}\right)}{1 - \left(\dfrac{R_i}{R_0}\right)^2} \qquad \qquad \dots (5.25)$$

where, k_p is dimensionless number in terms of recess pressure for various $\left(\dfrac{R_0}{R_i}\right)$ ratio.

5.9.1.2 Minimizing Flow Rate of Lubricant (Q)

We have an equation (5.8), for flow rate of lubricant through hydrostatic step bearing and is given as,

$$Q = \frac{\pi \cdot P_i \cdot h_0^3}{6\mu \cdot \log_e \left(\dfrac{R_0}{R_i}\right)}$$

Using $\left(P_i = \dfrac{W}{A} \cdot k_p\right)$ in above equation,

$$Q = \frac{\pi \cdot \left(\dfrac{W}{A} \cdot k_p\right) \cdot h_0^3}{6\mu \cdot \log_e \left(\dfrac{R_0}{R_i}\right)}$$

$$= \frac{W \, k_p \cdot \pi \cdot h_0^3}{A \cdot 6\mu \cdot \log_e \left(\dfrac{R_0}{R_i}\right)}$$

Rearranging the terms, we get,

$$= \left(\frac{2 \cdot k_p \cdot \pi}{\log_e\left(\frac{R_0}{R_i}\right)}\right) \frac{W}{A} \cdot \frac{h_0^3}{12\mu}$$

$$\therefore \qquad Q = k_q \cdot \frac{W}{A} \cdot \frac{h_0^3}{12\mu} \qquad \qquad \dots (5.26)$$

where, $A = \pi R_0^2$

$$k_q = \frac{2 \cdot k_p \cdot \pi}{\log_e\left(\frac{R_0}{R_i}\right)} \qquad \qquad \dots (5.27)$$

where, k_q is dimensionless number in terms of flow rate for $\left(\frac{R_0}{R_i}\right)$ ratio.

5.9.1.3 Minimizing Pumping Power Loss

We know the equation for pumping power loss.

$$E_P = P_i \cdot Q$$

Using equation (5.26) for 'Q' in above equation, it becomes,

$$E_P = P_i \cdot k_q \cdot \frac{W}{A} \cdot \frac{h_0^3}{12\mu}$$

Substituting equation (5.26) $\left(\text{i.e. } P_i = \frac{W}{A} \cdot k_p\right)$ in above equation, it becomes,

$$E_P = \left(\frac{W}{A} \cdot k_p\right) \cdot k_q \cdot \frac{W}{A} \cdot \frac{h_0^3}{12\mu}$$

$$\therefore \qquad E_P = k_p \cdot k_q \cdot \frac{W^2}{A^2} \cdot \frac{h_0^3}{12\mu}$$

$$E_P = k_r \left(\frac{W}{A}\right)^2 \cdot \frac{h_0^3}{12\mu} \qquad \qquad \dots (5.28)$$

where, $A = \pi \cdot R_0^2$

$k_r = k_p \cdot k_q$

$$= \left[\frac{2 \cdot \log_e\left(\frac{R_0}{R_i}\right)}{1 - \left(\frac{R_i}{R_0}\right)^2} \right] \cdot \frac{2k_p \cdot \pi}{\log_e\left(\frac{R_0}{R_i}\right)} = \left[\frac{2 \cdot \log_e\left(\frac{R_0}{R_i}\right)}{1 - \left(\frac{R_i}{R_0}\right)^2} \right] \frac{2 \cdot \pi}{\log_e\left(\frac{R_0}{R_i}\right)} \left[\frac{2 \cdot \log_e\left(\frac{R_0}{R_i}\right)}{1 - \left(\frac{R_i}{R_0}\right)^2} \right]$$

$$= \left[\frac{2 \cdot \log_e\left(\frac{R_0}{R_i}\right)}{1 - \left(\frac{R_i}{R_0}\right)^2} \right]^2 \cdot \frac{2\pi}{\log_e\left(\frac{R_0}{R_i}\right)}$$

$$k_r = \frac{8\pi \log_e\left(\frac{R_0}{R_i}\right)}{1 - \left(\frac{R_i}{R_0}\right)^2} \qquad \qquad \dots (5.29)$$

where, k_r = dimensionless number for pumping power.

Thus, we have three equations for k_p, k_q and k_r expressed in terms of $\left(\frac{R_i}{R_0}\right)$ ratio.

Values of k_p, k_q and k_r are tabulated for various values of $\left(\frac{R_i}{R_0}\right)$.

Table 5.1 : Optimum Values of Design Parameters for a
Circular Bearing with a Single Circular Recess

Sr. No.	$\left(\frac{R_i}{R_0}\right)$ Ratio	Dimensionless Numbers			Optimum Value
		k_p (Recess Pressure)	k_q (Flow Rate)	k_r (Pumping Power)	
1.	0.1	4.6517	12.6933	59.0454	
2.	0.2	3.3530	13.0899	43.8904	
3.	0.3	2.6461	13.8092	36.5405	
4.	0.4	2.1816	14.9597	32.6361	
5.	0.5	1.8484	16.7552	30.9703 ←	Optimum
6.	0.6	1.5963	19.6346	31.3427	Value
7.	0.7	1.3987	24.6395	34.4633	
8.	0.8	1.2397	34.9070	43.2742	
9.	0.9	1.1091	66.1413	73.3573	

Thus, from above values, it is seen that the optimum $\left(\dfrac{R_i}{R_0}\right)$ ratio for minimum pumping power losses is 0.5.

    i.e.   For minimum pumping losses,

$$\frac{R_i}{R_0} = 0.5$$

$\therefore$ $R_i = 0.5\,R_0$ ... (5.30)

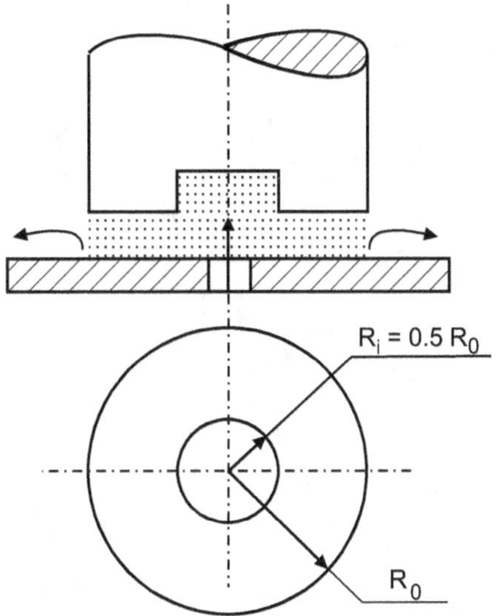

Fig. 5.9 : Optimised $\left(\dfrac{R_i}{R_0}\right)$ **ratio i.e. recess size for minimum pumping losses**

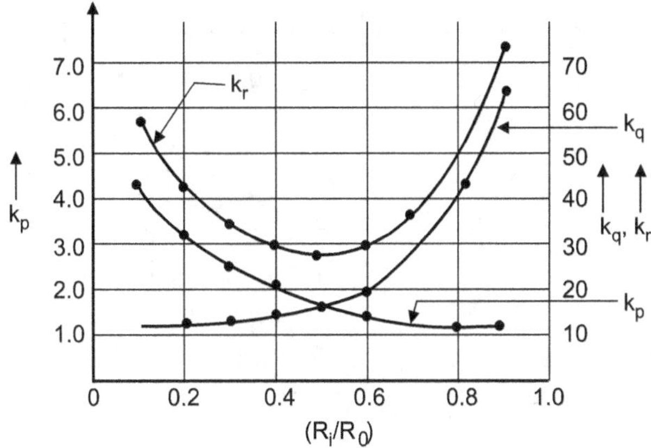

Fig. 5.10

Alternative Approach to Find $\left(\dfrac{R_i}{R_0}\right)$ Ratio for Minimum Pumping Losses :

We can find the optimum value of design parameter $\left(\dfrac{R_0}{R_i}\right)$ for minimum pumping losses.

For most of bearings, speeds are low.

$\therefore$ Pumping losses are predominant as compared to viscous power losses.

$\therefore$ Viscous losses are neglected.

$\therefore$ Total power losses, from equation (5.23),

$$E_T = E_P = \frac{1}{1.91 \times 10^6} \cdot \frac{P_i^2 \cdot h_0^3}{\mu \cdot \log_e \left(\dfrac{R_0}{R_i}\right)}$$

We have,

$$W = \frac{P_i \cdot \pi \cdot (R_0^2 - R_i^2)}{2 \cdot \log_e \left(\dfrac{R_0}{R_i}\right)}$$

$\therefore$

$$P_i = \frac{2 W \log_e \left(\dfrac{R_0}{R_i}\right)}{\pi (R_0^2 - R_i^2)}$$

Using in above equation for E_T,

$$E_T = \frac{1}{1.91 \times 10^6} \left[\frac{2 W \cdot \log_e \left(\dfrac{R_0}{R_i}\right)}{\pi (R_0^2 - R_i^2)}\right]^2 \cdot h_0^3 \; \frac{1}{\mu \cdot \log_e \left(\dfrac{R_0}{R_i}\right)}$$

$$= \frac{1}{1.91 \times 10^6} \cdot \frac{4 W^2 \log_e \left(\dfrac{R_0}{R_i}\right) \cdot h_0^3}{\mu \cdot \pi (R_0^2 - R_i^2)}$$

$$= \frac{4 W^2 \cdot h_0^3}{\mu \cdot \pi} \left[\frac{\log_e \left(\dfrac{R_0}{R_i}\right)}{(R_0^2 - R_i^2)}\right]$$

$$= C \cdot \frac{\log_e\left(\dfrac{R_0}{R_i}\right)}{(R_0^2 - R_i^2)}$$

where, C is constant.

Optimum recess size for minimum pumping loss occurs when,

$$\frac{d(E_T)}{dr_i} = 0 \qquad \qquad \text{... (5.31)}$$

$$\therefore \quad C\left[\frac{(R_0^2 - R_i^2) \cdot \dfrac{1}{\left(\dfrac{R_0}{R_i}\right)} \cdot \left(-\dfrac{R_0}{R_i^2}\right) - \log_e\left(\dfrac{R_0}{R_i}\right) \cdot 2\,(R_0^2 - R_i^2)\,(0 - 2R_i)}{(R_0^2 - R_i^2)^4}\right] = 0$$

Dividing both sides by $(R_0^2 - R_i^2)$,

$$-\frac{(R_0^2 - R_i^2)}{R_i} + \log_e\left(\frac{R_0}{R_i}\right) \cdot 4\,R_i = 0$$

$$4\,R_i^2 \cdot \log_e\left(\frac{R_0}{R_i}\right) - (R_0^2 - R_i^2) = 0$$

$$4\,R_i^2 \cdot \log_e\left(\frac{R_0}{R_i}\right) = R_0^2 - R_i^2$$

$$\log_e\left(\frac{R_0}{R_i}\right) = \frac{1}{4}\left[\left(\frac{R_0}{R_i}\right)^2 - 1\right]$$

Substituting $x = \dfrac{R_0}{R_i}$, above equation becomes,

$$\log_e x = \frac{1}{4}\,[x^2 - 1]$$

$$\therefore \quad x^2 - 4 \cdot \log_e x - 1 = 0$$

Solving above equation, we get,

$$x = \frac{R_0}{R_i} = 1.861$$

$$\therefore \quad \frac{R_i}{R_0} = 0.535 \quad \Rightarrow \quad R_i = 0.535\,R_0 \qquad \text{... (5.32)}$$

5.9.2 Optimum Oil-film Thickness

The oil-film thickness for which the total power loss is minimum is known as optimum oil-film thickness.

We have an equation (5.15), for viscous power loss or friction power loss.

$$E_F = \frac{1}{58.053 \times 10^6}\left[\frac{\mu \cdot N^2 (R_0^4 - R_i^4)}{h_0}\right]$$

$$\therefore \qquad E_F \propto \frac{1}{h_0}$$

and equation (5.23), for pumping power loss,

$$E_P = \frac{1}{1.91 \times 10^6}\left[\frac{P_i^2 \cdot h_0^3}{\mu \cdot \log_e\left(\dfrac{R_0}{R_i}\right)}\right]$$

$$\therefore \qquad E_P \propto h_0^3$$

$\therefore$ The oil-film thickness h_0 should be selected such that total power loss is minimum.

$\therefore$ Total power loss,

$$E_T = \frac{1}{58.053 \times 10^6}\left[\frac{\mu\, N^2 (R_0^4 - R_i^4)}{h_0}\right] + \frac{1}{1.91 \times 10^6}\left[\frac{P_i^2 \cdot h_0^3}{\mu \cdot \log_e\left(\dfrac{R_0}{R_i}\right)}\right]$$

$$\text{Let,} \qquad x_1 = \frac{\mu\, N^2 (R_0^4 - R_i^4)}{58.053 \times 10^6}$$

$$\text{and} \qquad x_2 = \frac{P_i^2}{1.91 \times 10^6 \times \mu \cdot \log_e\left(\dfrac{R_0}{R_i}\right)}$$

Substituting these values in above equation for E_T, it becomes,

$$E_T = \frac{x_1}{h_0} + x_2 \cdot h_0^3$$

For optimum oil-film thickness, the derivative of total power loss with respect to oil-film thickness is equal to zero.

$$\frac{dE_T}{dh_0} = 0 \qquad \text{... (5.33)}$$

$$\therefore \quad \frac{d}{dh_0}\left[\frac{x_1}{h_0} + x_2 \cdot h_0^3\right] = 0$$

$$\therefore \quad -\frac{x_1}{h_0^2} + 3x_2 \cdot h_0^2 = 0$$

$$\therefore \quad 3x_2 \cdot h_0^2 = \frac{x_1}{h_0^2}$$

$$h_0^4 = \frac{1}{3} \cdot \frac{x_1}{x_2}$$

$$\therefore \quad h_0 = \left[\frac{x_1}{3x_2}\right]^{1/4} \qquad \text{... (5.34)}$$

which is an equation for optimum oil-film thickness for minimum total power loss.

where, $\quad x_1 = \dfrac{\mu \cdot N^2 (R_0^4 - R_i^4)}{58.053 \times 10^6}$ and $\quad x_2 = \dfrac{P_i^2}{1.91 \times 10^6 \, \mu \cdot \log_e\left(\dfrac{R_0}{R_i}\right)}$

Total power loss is plotted against oil-film thickness.

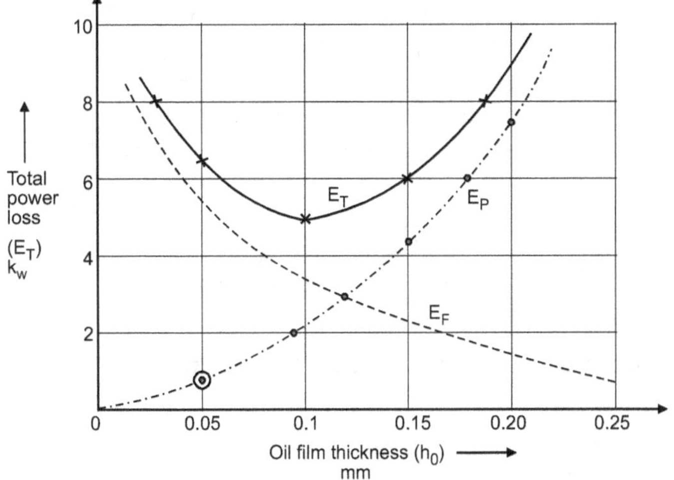

E_T = Total power loss

E_P = Pumping power loss

E_F = Viscous or frictional power loss

Fig. 5.11 : Total power loss (E_T) versus oil-film thickness (h_0)

5.9.3 Optimum Stiffness of Bearing

It can be defined as the rate of change of load capacity with film thickness. It is an important design parameter which can be evaluated by differentiating load with respect to oil-film thickness.

Now, the load-carrying capacity of hydrostatic step bearing is given by equation (5.10).

$$W = \frac{P_i \cdot \pi \cdot (R_0^2 - R_i^2)}{2 \cdot \log_e\left(\dfrac{R_0}{R_i}\right)}$$

For constant flow rate Q,

$$Q = \frac{\pi \cdot P_i \cdot h_0^3}{6\mu \cdot \log_e\left(\dfrac{R_0}{R_i}\right)}$$

$$\therefore \qquad P_i = \frac{6\mu \cdot Q \cdot \log_e\left(\dfrac{R_0}{R_i}\right)}{\pi \cdot h_0^3}$$

Using above equation in equation for load,

$$W = \frac{6\mu \cdot Q \cdot \log_e\left(\dfrac{R_0}{R_i}\right)}{\pi\, h_0^3} \cdot \frac{\pi\, (R_0^2 - R_i^2)}{2 \cdot \log_e\left(\dfrac{R_0}{R_i}\right)}$$

$$W = \frac{3\mu \cdot Q\, (R_0^2 - R_i^2)}{h_0^3} \qquad\qquad \text{... (5.35)}$$

Differentiating equation (5.35) with respect to oil-film thickness,

$$\frac{dW}{dh_0} = \frac{3\mu \cdot Q \cdot (R_0^2 - R_i^2)}{h_0^4}\, (-3)$$

$$= \frac{-9\mu \cdot Q(R_0^2 - R_i^2)}{h_0^4}$$

$$= \frac{-9\mu \cdot (R_0^2 - R_i^2)}{h_0^4} \cdot \frac{\pi \, h_0^3 \cdot P_i}{6\mu \cdot \log_e\left(\dfrac{R_0}{R_i}\right)} \qquad \left[\because Q = \frac{\pi \, h_0^3 \cdot P_i}{6\mu \cdot \log_e\left(\dfrac{R_0}{R_i}\right)} \right]$$

$$= -\frac{3}{2h_0} \cdot \mu \cdot \frac{\pi \, P_i (R_0^2 - R_i^2)}{\log_e\left(\dfrac{R_0}{R_i}\right)}$$

$$= -\frac{3}{h_0} \left[\frac{\pi \cdot P_i \cdot (R_0^2 - R_i^2)}{\log_e\left(\dfrac{R_0}{R_i}\right)} \right]$$

$$= -\frac{3}{h_0} \cdot W$$

$$\therefore \qquad \text{Stiffness, } S = \frac{dW}{dh_0} = -\frac{3W}{h_0} \qquad\qquad \text{... (5.36)}$$

The negative sign indicates that the stiffness (S) decreases as oil-film thickness increases. It has no physical significance.

Also the load-carrying capacity W increases as the film thickness decreases.

This can be shown graphically as below.

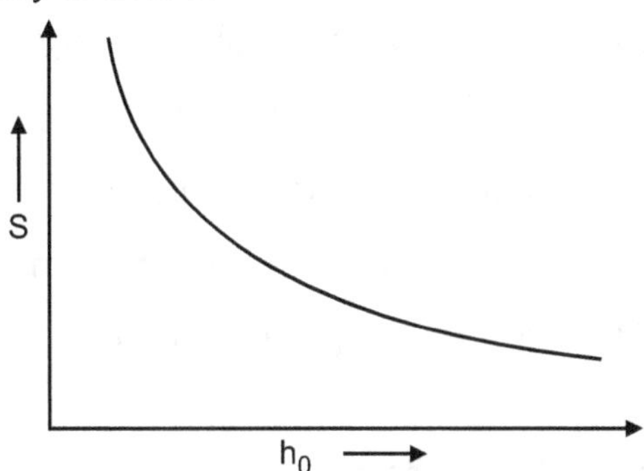

Fig. 5.12 : Stiffness (S) versus oil-film thickness (h₀)

5.10 TEMPERATURE RISE IN HYDROSTATIC STEP BEARING

It is assumed that the total power loss in hydrostatic step bearing is converted into heat. This leads to increase in the temperature of lubricant. The heat generated in the bearing is carried away by the lubricant. The temperature rise in hydrostatic step bearing is obtained as follows.

The total power loss in hydrostatic step bearing is given by,

$$E_T = E_F + E_P \qquad \text{... (5.37)}$$

where,

E_T – Total power loss in kW

E_F – Frictional (viscous) power loss in kW

E_P – Pumping power loss in kW

1.   Rate of Heat Generation (H_G) :

The rate of heat generation is given by,

$$H_G = E_T = E_F + E_P \qquad \text{... (5.38)}$$

2.   Rate of Heat Dissipation (H_D) :

The rate of heat dissipation is given by,

$$H_D = m\, C_p\, \Delta T \qquad \text{... (5.39)}$$

or

$$H_D = \frac{\rho\, Q\, C_p\, \Delta T}{10^9} \qquad \text{... (5.40)}$$

where,

m – Mass flow rate of lubricant, kg/s

C_p – Specific heat of lubricant, kJ/kg °C

ΔT – Temperature rise in lubricant, °C

ρ – Mass density of lubricant, kg/m^3

Q – Flow rate of lubricant, mm^3/s

3.   Heat Balance :

Rate of heat generation = Rate of heat dissipation

$$H_G = H_D$$

$$\therefore \qquad E_F + E_P = m\, C_p\, \Delta T$$

$$\therefore \qquad \Delta T = \frac{E_F + E_P}{m\, C_p} \qquad \text{... (5.41)}$$

or

$$\Delta T = \frac{E_F + E_P}{\rho\, Q\, C_p} \times 10^9 \qquad \text{... (5.42)}$$

5.11 HYDROSTATIC CONICAL THRUST BEARING

Fig. 5.13 illustrates the principle of a hydrostatic conical thrust bearing.

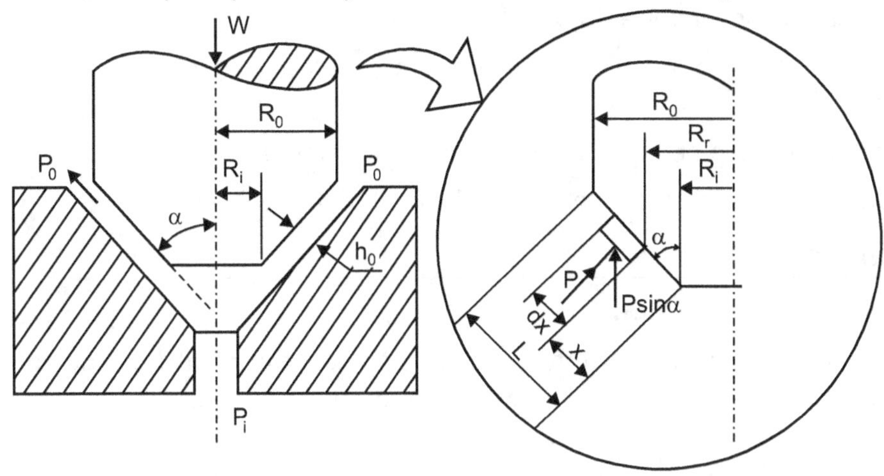

Fig. 5.13 : Hydrostatic conical thrust bearing

Let,

W = Vertical thrust load on runner, (N)

R_0 = Outer radius of conical shaft, (mm)

R_i = Inner radius of conical shaft, (mm)

L = Length of pad, (mm)

α = Semi-cone angle

P_0 = Outlet lubricant pressure, (N/mm^2)

P_i = Inlet lubricant pressure, (N/mm^2)

h_0 = Distance between conical shaft surface and conical pad, or fluid film thickness, (mm)

μ = Absolute viscosity of lubricant, (N-s/mm^2)

Q = Flow rate of lubricant, (mm^3/sec)

N = Shaft speed, (r.p.m.)

5.11.1 Principle of Working

Lubricant from reservoir is pumped by a constant displacement pump and is forced into a central circular recess and then flows outwards between the conical bearing surface and developing pressure and separation and returning to a reservoir for recirculation. The thrust load is supported by the fluid film within the conical pocket and conical land. The outside pressure is usually equal to zero or ambient.

5.11.2 Assumptions

Following assumptions are made in order to derive the load-carrying capacity, flow requirement and frictional power loss.

- The recess depth is quite enough for the pressure in it to be fairly uniform or almost constant.
- For pressure development, the effect of rotational velocity is neglected.
- The flow is considered as laminar across the land of the pad.

5.11.3 Analysis

5.11.3.1 Pressure Distribution

For deriving an equation for the total load-carrying capacity of hydrostatic conical thrust bearing, it is first necessary to find the pressure distribution on an annular area between the radii 'R_i' and 'R_0'.

We know equation (5.5) for the flow rate of lubricant through a slot and is given by,

$$Q = \frac{\Delta P \cdot h^3 \cdot b}{12 \cdot \mu \cdot l} \qquad \ldots (5.43)$$

where,

ΔP = Pressure difference causing fluid flow, (N/mm^2)

b = Width of the slot across the fluid flow, (mm)

l = Length of the slot in the direction of fluid flow

h = Thickness of the slot or fluid film, (mm)

μ = Absolute viscosity of the lubricant, (N-s/mm^2)

Consider an elemental ring of thickness 'dx' at a distance of 'x' from the inner radius.

$$\therefore \qquad \sin \alpha = \frac{R_0 - R_i}{L} \qquad \ldots (5.44)$$

$$r = R_i + x \sin \alpha \qquad \ldots (5.45)$$

$$\text{and} \qquad R_0 = R_i + L \cdot \sin \alpha \qquad \ldots \text{(From equation 5.44)}$$

From equation (5.43),

$$\Delta P = dP$$

$$b = 2\pi r$$

$$\therefore \qquad b = 2\pi (R_i + x \sin \alpha) \qquad \ldots \text{(From equation 5.45)}$$

$$l = dx$$

$$h = h_0$$

Substituting these values in equation (5.43),

$$Q = -\frac{dP \cdot h_0^3 \cdot [2\pi (R_i + x \sin \alpha)]}{12 \cdot \mu \cdot dx} \qquad \ldots (5.46)$$

The negative sign is due to the fact that as radius increases, pressure decreases or $\left[\dfrac{dP}{dx}\right]$ is negative.

$$\therefore \qquad dP = -\left[\frac{6\mu \cdot Q}{\pi \cdot h_0^3}\right]\frac{dx}{(R_i + x \sin \alpha)}$$

Integrating above equation, we get,

$$\int dP = \int -\left[\frac{6 \cdot \mu \cdot Q}{\pi \cdot h_0^3}\right]\frac{dx}{(R_i + x \sin \alpha)}$$

$$\therefore \qquad P = -\frac{6 \cdot \mu \cdot Q}{\pi\, h_0^3} \cdot \log_e (R_i + x \sin \alpha) \cdot \frac{1}{\sin \alpha} + C \qquad \ldots (5.47)$$

where, 'C' is constant of integration and can be evaluated.

At $x = L$; $P = P_0 = 0$.

Using this condition in equation (5.47),

$$0 = -\left[\frac{6 \cdot \mu \cdot Q}{\pi \cdot h_0^3}\right]\frac{\log_e (R_i + L \cdot \sin \alpha)}{\sin \alpha} + C$$

$$\therefore \qquad C = \left[\frac{6\,\mu \cdot Q}{\pi \cdot h_0^3}\right]\frac{\log_e R_0}{\sin \alpha} \qquad \ldots (5.48)$$

Substituting value of 'C' from equation (5.48) in equation (5.47), we get,

$$P = \left\{-\left[\frac{6 \cdot \mu \cdot Q}{\pi\, h_0^3}\right]\frac{\log_e (R_i + x \cdot \sin \alpha)}{\sin \alpha}\right\} + \left\{\left[\frac{6 \cdot \mu \cdot Q}{\pi\, h_0^3}\right]\frac{\log_e R_0}{\sin \alpha}\right\}$$

$$\therefore \qquad P = \left[\frac{6 \cdot \mu \cdot Q}{\pi \cdot h_0^3 \cdot \sin \alpha}\right]\left[\log_e \left(\frac{R_0}{R_i + x \sin \alpha}\right)\right] \qquad \ldots (5.49)$$

- Using second boundary condition :

At $x = 0$, $P = P_i$

Equation (5.49) becomes,

$$P_i = \left(\frac{6 \cdot \mu \cdot Q}{\pi \cdot h_0^3 \cdot \sin \alpha}\right)\left(\log_e \left(\frac{R_0}{R_i}\right)\right) \qquad \ldots (5.50)$$

Dividing equation (5.49) by equation (5.50), we get,

$$\frac{P}{P_i} = \frac{\log_e\left(\dfrac{R_0}{R_i + x \cdot \sin \alpha}\right)}{\log_e\left(\dfrac{R_0}{R_i}\right)}$$

$$\therefore \quad P = \frac{P_i \log_e\left(\dfrac{R_0}{R_i + x \cdot \sin \alpha}\right)}{\log_e\left(\dfrac{R_0}{R_i}\right)} \qquad \qquad \ldots (5.51)$$

This equation gives the pressure distribution on annular area from radius 'R_i' to 'R_0'. This pressure is perpendicular to the cone surface.

5.11.3.2 Flow Rate of Lubricant

From equation (5.50),

$$P_i = \left[\frac{6 \cdot \mu \cdot Q}{\pi \cdot h_0^3 \cdot \sin \alpha}\right]\left[\log_e\left(\frac{R_0}{R_i}\right)\right]$$

$$Q = \frac{\pi \cdot P_i \cdot h_0^3 \cdot \sin \alpha}{6 \cdot \mu \cdot \log_e\left(\dfrac{R_0}{R_i}\right)} \qquad \qquad \ldots (5.52)$$

which is an equation for flow rate of lubricant.

5.11.3.3 Load Carrying Capacity

The total load-carrying capacity of hydrostatic conical thrust bearing is equal to the summation of two components i.e.

- Load supported by the central recess area (where P_i is constant), and
- Load supported by the annular area from R_i to R_0 (where pressure P_i varies).

$$\therefore \quad \text{Total load} = \begin{bmatrix}\text{Load supported} \\ \text{by central recess}\end{bmatrix} + \begin{bmatrix}\text{Load supported by} \\ \text{annular area}\end{bmatrix}$$

$$W = [P_i \cdot \pi \cdot R_i^2] + \left[\int_0^L (P \cdot \sin \alpha)(2\pi r \cdot dx)\right]$$

Using equation (5.51) above,

$$W = (P_i \cdot \pi \cdot R_i^2) + \int_0^L \frac{P_i \cdot \log_e\left(\dfrac{R_0}{R_i + x \cdot \sin \alpha}\right)}{\log_e(R_0/R_i)} \times \sin \alpha \times (2\pi r \cdot dx)$$

$$= P_i \cdot \pi \cdot R_i^2 + \int_0^L 2\pi \cdot \frac{P_i \cdot \log_e\left(\dfrac{R_0}{R_i + x \cdot \sin \alpha}\right)}{\log_e (R_0/R_i)} \cdot \sin \alpha \cdot (R_i + x \sin \alpha)\, dx$$

$$= P_i \cdot \pi \cdot R_i^2 + \frac{2\pi \cdot P_i \cdot \sin \alpha}{\log_e (R_0/R_i)} \int_0^L \log_e\left(\frac{R_0}{R_i + x \cdot \sin \alpha}\right)(R_i + x \cdot \sin \alpha)\, dx$$

$$= \pi \cdot P_i \left[R_i^2 + \frac{2 \cdot \sin \alpha}{\log_e (R_0/R_i)} \int_0^L \log_e\left(\frac{R_0}{R_i + x \cdot \sin \alpha}\right)(R_i + x \cdot \sin \alpha) \cdot dx\right] \qquad \ldots (5.53)$$

$$\text{Let } I = \int_0^L \log_e\left(\frac{R_0}{R_i + x \sin \alpha}\right)(R_i + x \cdot \sin \alpha)\, dx$$

Substituting
$$y = R_i + x \cdot \sin \alpha$$
$$dy = \sin \alpha \cdot dx$$
$$dx = \frac{dy}{\sin \alpha}$$

Conditions :

When $x = 0$; $y = R_i$

When $x = L$; $y = R_i + L \cdot \sin \alpha = R_0$

$\therefore$ 'I' becomes,

$$I = \int_{R_i}^{R_0} \log_e\left(\frac{R_0}{y}\right) \cdot y \cdot \frac{dy}{\sin \alpha}$$

$$= \frac{1}{\sin \alpha} \int_{R_i}^{R_0} \log_e\left(\frac{R_0}{y}\right) \cdot y \cdot dy$$

$$= \frac{1}{\sin \alpha} \left\{ \log_e\left(\frac{R_0}{y}\right) \int y\, dy - \int \left[\left(\int y\, dy \cdot \frac{d}{dy} \log_e\left(\frac{R_0}{y}\right)\right) dy\right] \right\}_{R_i}^{R_0}$$

$$= \frac{1}{\sin \alpha} \left\{ \log_e\left(\frac{R_0}{y}\right) \cdot \frac{y^2}{2} - \int \frac{y^2}{2} \cdot \frac{y}{R_0} \cdot - \frac{R_0}{y^2} \cdot dy \right\}_{R_i}^{R_0}$$

$$= \frac{1}{\sin \alpha} \left\{ \log_e\left(\frac{R_0}{y}\right) \cdot \frac{y^2}{2} + \int \frac{y}{2} \cdot dy \right\}_{R_i}^{R_0} = \frac{1}{\sin \alpha} \left\{ \log_e\left(\frac{R_0}{y}\right) \cdot \frac{y^2}{2} + \frac{y^2}{4} \right\}_{R_i}^{R_0}$$

$$= \frac{1}{\sin \alpha} \left\{ \left[\log_e\left(\frac{R_0}{R_0}\right) \cdot \frac{R_0^2}{2} + \frac{R_0^2}{4} \right] - \left[\log_e\left(\frac{R_0}{R_i}\right) \cdot \frac{R_i^2}{2} + \frac{R_i^2}{4} \right] \right\}$$

$$I = \frac{1}{\sin \alpha} \left[\left(\frac{R_0^2 - R_i^2}{4}\right) - \frac{R_i^2}{2} \log_e\left(\frac{R_0}{R_i}\right) \right] \dots \left(\text{since } \log_e\left(\frac{R_0}{R_0}\right) = 0 \right) \qquad \dots (5.54)$$

Substituting equation (5.54) in equation (5.53), we get,

$$W = \pi \cdot P_i \left\{ R_i^2 + \frac{2 \cdot \sin \alpha}{\log_e\left(\frac{R_0}{R_i}\right)} \cdot \left[\frac{1}{\sin \alpha} \left[\left(\frac{R_0^2 - R_i^2}{4}\right) - \frac{R_i^2}{2} \log_e\left(\frac{R_0}{R_i}\right) \right] \right] \right\}$$

$$= \pi \cdot P_i \left\{ R_i^2 + \frac{2}{\log_e\left(\frac{R_0}{R_i}\right)} \cdot \frac{\log_e\left(\frac{R_0}{R_i}\right)}{2} \left[\frac{R_0^2 - R_i^2}{2 \cdot \log_e\left(\frac{R_0}{R_i}\right)} - R_i^2 \right] \right\}$$

$$= \pi \cdot P_i \left\{ R_i^2 + \left[\frac{R_0^2 - R_i^2}{2 \cdot \log_e\left(\frac{R_0}{R_i}\right)} \right] - R_i^2 \right\}$$

$$W = \frac{\pi \cdot P_i \, (R_0^2 - R_i^2)}{2 \cdot \log_e \, (R_0/R_i)} \qquad \dots (5.55)$$

which is an equation for load-carrying capacity of hydrostatic conical thrust bearing.

5.12 FLOW OF FLUID THROUGH ANNULAR AREA BETWEEN METAL PIN AND CYLINDER (BETWEEN PISTON AND CYLINDER)

The lubricant flow rate through a slot is given by an equation

$$Q = \frac{\Delta P \cdot h^3 \cdot b}{12 \cdot \mu \cdot l}$$

where,

ΔP = Pressure difference causing fluid flow, (N/mm^2)

b = Width of the slot across the fluid flow, (mm)

l = Length of the slot in the direction of fluid flow, (mm)

h = Thickness of the slot or fluid film, (mm)

$$\mu \;=\; \text{Absolute viscosity of the lubricant, (N-s/mm}^2)$$

Consider an arrangement of piston and cylinder with fluid film as shown in Fig. 5.14.

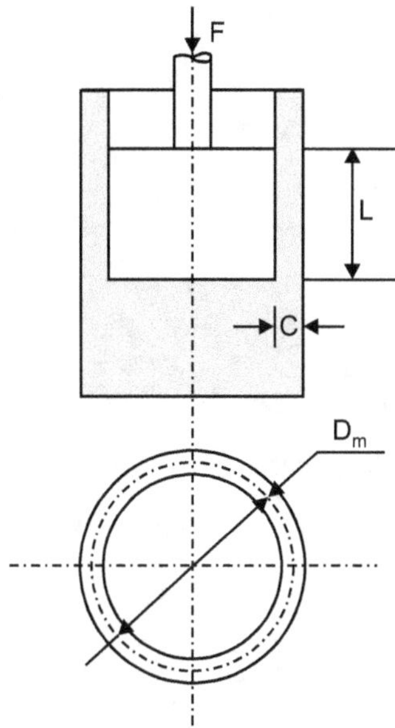

Fig. 5.14 : Arrangement of piston and cylinder

Let

A = Area of cross-section of the piston, (mm)

L = Length of piston, (mm)

l = Length of piston in fluid, (mm)

C = Radial clearance between piston and cylinder, (mm)

D_m = Mean diameter of an annular area between piston and cylinder, (mm)

μ = Absolute viscosity of the fluid (N-s/mm^2)

ΔP = Pressure difference across the two ends of the piston, (N/mm^2)

F_P = Force acting on the piston, (N)

Q = Fluid flow rate through an annular area between piston and cylinder, (mm^3/s)

V_P = Piston velocity, (mm/s)

Here,

$b = \pi \cdot D_m$

$l = 1$

and

$h = c$

Using above equations in the equation for 'Q', it becomes

$$Q = \frac{\Delta P \cdot h^3 \cdot b}{12 \cdot \mu \cdot l}$$

$$\therefore \qquad Q = \frac{\Delta P \cdot (\pi \cdot D_m) \cdot c^3}{12 \cdot \mu \cdot l}$$

Force acting on the piston $F_P = \Delta P \cdot A$

$$\therefore \qquad \Delta P = \frac{F_P}{A}$$

$\therefore$ Q becomes
$$Q = \frac{\pi \cdot F_P \cdot D_m \cdot c^3}{12 \cdot \mu \cdot l \cdot A} \qquad \qquad \dots (5.56)$$

This equation gives flow rate of lubricant through the annular area between piston and cylinder.

Also, $\qquad \qquad Q = V_P \cdot A$

$$\therefore \qquad V_P \cdot A = \frac{\pi \cdot F_P \cdot D_m \cdot c^3}{12 \cdot \mu \cdot l \cdot A}$$

$$\therefore \qquad V_P = \frac{\pi \cdot F_P \cdot D_m \cdot c^3}{12 \cdot \mu \cdot l \cdot A^2} \qquad \qquad \dots (5.57)$$

which is an equation for the piston velocity.

SOLVED EXAMPLES

Example 5.1 : Following data is given for a hydrostatic, flat, foot-step bearing :

    (i)   Shaft diameter = 60 mm

    (ii)   Step diameter = 40 mm

    (iii) Thrust load = 5000 N

    (iv) Minimum oil-film thickness = 150 μm

    (v)   Viscosity of oil = 20 MPa

    (vi) Shaft speed = 1500 r.p.m.

Calculate :

    (i)   Quantity of oil supplied to the bearing.

    (ii)   Total power lost in the bearing.

Solution :

Given : $\qquad \qquad R_0 = \frac{60}{2} = 30$ mm $\qquad ; \qquad \mu = 20$ MPa

$$R_i = \frac{40}{2} = 20 \text{ mm} \quad ; \quad = 20 \times 10^{-9} \text{ N-s/mm}^2$$

$$h_0 = 150 \ \mu m = 0.15 \text{ mm};$$

$$W = 5000 \text{ N}$$

To calculate :

(i) $Q = ?$

(ii) $E_T = ?$

We know,

Load-carrying capacity of hydrostatic bearing is given by,

$$W = \frac{\pi \cdot P_i \ (R_0^2 - R_i^2)}{2 \log_e \left(\dfrac{R_0}{R_i} \right)}$$

$\therefore \qquad$
$$P_i = \frac{2 \ W \log_e \left(\dfrac{R_0}{R_i} \right)}{\pi \cdot \left(R_0^2 - R_i^2 \right)} = \frac{2 \times 5000 \times \log_e \left(\dfrac{30}{20} \right)}{\pi \ (30^2 - 20^2)}$$

$$P_i = 2.5813 \text{ N/mm}^2$$

(i)   Quantity of oil supplied to the bearing :

We know, $\qquad$
$$Q = \frac{\pi \cdot P_i \cdot h_0^3}{6\mu \cdot \log_e \left(\dfrac{R_0}{R_i} \right)}$$

$$= \frac{\pi \times 2.5813 \times (0.15)^3}{6 \times 20 \times 10^{-9} \cdot \log_e \left(\dfrac{30}{20} \right)}$$

$\therefore \qquad Q = 562506.31 \text{ mm}^3/\text{s}$

$\qquad\qquad = 562506.31 \times 10^{-9} \text{ m}^3/\text{s}$

$\qquad\qquad = (562506.31 \times 10^{-9}) \times 10^{-3} \times 60 \ l/\text{min}$

$\therefore \qquad Q = 33.7504 \ l/\text{min}$

(ii) Total power lost in bearing (E_T) :

$\qquad$ Total power lost = (Power lost due to viscous friction) + (Pumping power loss)

$$E_T = E_F + E_P$$

$\therefore$ Power lost due to viscous friction (E_F) is given by,

$$E_F = \frac{\mu \cdot N^2 (R_0^4 - R_i^4)}{(58.053 \times 10^6)\, h_0}$$

$$= \frac{20 \times 10^{-9} \times (1500)^2 (30^4 - 20^4)}{(58.053 \times 10^6) \times 0.15}$$

$$E_F = 3.358999 \times 10^{-3} \text{ kW}$$

Pumping power loss is given by,

$$E_P = \frac{Q(P_i - P_0)}{\mu_p \cdot 10^6}$$

$$= \frac{562506.31\,(2.5813)}{1 \times 10^6}$$

$\therefore$ $E_P = 1.451998 \text{ kW}$

$\therefore$ Total power lost in bearing

$$= E_F + E_P$$

$$= 3.358999 \times 10^{-3} + 1.451998$$

$\therefore$ $E_T = 1.455357 \text{ kW}$

Example 5.2 : The following data refers to a hydrostatic thrust bearing :

(i)   Shaft diameter = 500 mm

(ii)   Recess diameter = 300 mm

(iii)   Shaft speed = 750 r.p.m.

(iv)   Supply pressure = 6 N/mm^2

(v)   Film thickness = 0.18 mm

(vi)   Viscosity of lubricant = 28 cP

(vii)   Specific gravity of lubricant = 0.86

(viii) Specific heat of lubricant = 1.76 kJ/kg °C

Calculate :

(i)   Load-carrying capacity of the bearing

(ii)   Flow requirement in l/min

(iii)   Viscous power loss

(iv)   Pumping power loss

(v)   Temperature rise

Assume that the total power loss in the bearing is converted into frictional heat.

Solution :

Given :

R_0 = 250 mm	;	h_0 = 0.18 mm
R_i = 150 mm	;	μ = 28 cP = 28×10^{-9}
N = 750 r.p.m.	;	ρ = 860 kg/m³
P_i = 6 N/mm²	;	C_p = 1.76 kJ/kg °C

To calculate :

(i)　W = ?,　　　　(ii)　Q = ?,

(iii)　E_F = ?,　　　　(iv)　E_p = ?,

(v)　ΔT = ?

(i) Load-carrying capacity of the bearing (W) :

We know,

$$W = \frac{\pi \cdot P_i \, (R_0^2 - R_i^2)}{2 \cdot \log_e\left(\dfrac{R_0}{R_i}\right)} = \frac{\pi \times 6 \, (250^2 - 150^2)}{2 \cdot \log_e\left(\dfrac{250}{150}\right)}$$

$$W = 738003.5396 \text{ N}$$

(ii) Flow requirement in l/min (Q) :

We know,

$$Q = \frac{\pi \cdot P_i \cdot h_0^3}{6 \cdot \mu \cdot \log_e\left(\dfrac{R_0}{R_i}\right)}$$

$$= \frac{\pi \times 6 \times (0.18)^3}{6 \times 28 \times 10^{-9} \cdot \log_e\left(\dfrac{250}{150}\right)}$$

$$Q = 1280963.287 \text{ mm}^3/\text{s}$$

$$= 1280963.287 \times 10^{-9} \text{ m}^3/\text{s}$$

$$= (1280963.287 \times 10^{-9}) \times 10^3 \times 60 \text{ l/min}$$

$$Q = 76.8578 \text{ l/min}$$

(iii) Viscous power loss (E_F) :

$$E_F = \frac{\mu \cdot N^2 \, (R_0^4 - R_i^4)}{(58.053 \times 10^6) \cdot h_0}$$

$$= \frac{28 \times 10^{-9} \times (750)^2 \, (250^4 - 150^4)}{(58.053 \times 10^6) \times 0.18}$$

$$E_F = 5.12463 \text{ kW}$$

(iv) Pumping power loss (E_P) :

$$E_P = \frac{Q \cdot P_i}{10^6}$$

$$= \frac{1280963.287 \times 6}{10^6}$$

$$E_P = 7.6857797 \text{ kW}$$

(v) Temperature rise (ΔT) :

Total power lost in bearing,

$$E_T = E_F + E_P$$

$$= 5.12463 + 7.6857797$$

$$= 12.81041 \text{ kW}$$

Given assumption :

Total power loss in the bearing is converted into frictional heat.

$$\therefore \quad \text{Heat generated} = \text{Total power loss}$$

$$= 12.81041 \text{ kW}$$

and   Heat dissipated $= \rho \cdot Q \cdot C_P \cdot \Delta T$

$$= 860 \times 1280963.287 \times 10^{-9} \times 1.76 \times \Delta T$$

Equating heat generated to heat dissipated as per assumption,

$$\therefore \quad 12.81041 = 860 \times 1280963.287 \times 10^{-9} \times 1.76 \times \Delta T$$

$$\therefore \quad \Delta T = 6.6072 °C$$

Example 5.3 : The following data refers to a hydrostatic step bearing :

  (i)   Shaft diameter = 500 mm

  (ii) Recess diameter = 250 mm

  (iii) Thrust load = 450 kN

  (iv) Shaft speed = 720 r.p.m.

  (v) Oil-film thickness = 0.16 mm

  (vi) Viscosity of lubricant = 170 SUS

  (vii) Specific heat of lubricant = 1.76 kJ/kg °C

(viii) Specific gravity of lubricant = 0.86

Calculate :

(i)   Supply pressure

(ii)   Oil flow rate in l/min

(iii) Frictional power loss

(iv)   Pumping power loss and

(v)   Temperature rise in the bearing.

Assume that the total power loss is converted into frictional heat.

Solution :

Given :

$$R_0 = 250 \text{ mm} \quad ; \quad h_0 = 0.16 \text{ mm}$$
$$R_i = 125 \text{ mm} \quad ; \quad \mu = 170 \text{ SUS}$$
$$W = 450 \times 10^3 \text{ N} \quad ; \quad \rho = 860 \text{ kg/m}^3$$
$$N = 720 \text{ r.p.m.} \quad ; \quad C_P = 1.76 \text{ kJ/kg °C}$$

To calculate :

(i) $P_i = ?$,   (ii) $Q = ?$,

(iii) $E_F = ?$,   (iv) $E_P = ?$,

(v) $\Delta T = ?$

(i)   Supply pressure (P_i) :

$$W = \frac{\pi \cdot P_i \cdot (R_0^2 - R_i^2)}{2 \cdot \log_e\left(\dfrac{R_0}{R_i}\right)}$$

$$\therefore \quad P_i = \frac{2W \cdot \log_e\left(\dfrac{R_0}{R_i}\right)}{\pi \cdot (R_0^2 - R_i^2)} = \frac{2 \times 450 \times 10^3 \cdot \log_e\left(\dfrac{250}{125}\right)}{\pi \,(250^2 - 125^2)}$$

$$\therefore \quad P_i = 4.2362 \text{ N/mm}^2$$

(ii)   Oil-flow rate in l/min :

$$Q = \frac{\pi \cdot P_i \cdot h_0^3}{6 \cdot \mu \cdot \log_e\left(\dfrac{R_0}{R_i}\right)}$$

$$= \frac{\pi \times 4.2362 \times (0.16)^3}{6 \times 31.2534 \times 10^{-9} \times \log_e\left(\frac{250}{125}\right)}$$

$$Q = 419384.42 \text{ mm}^3/\text{s}$$

$$= 419384.42 \times 10^{-9} \text{ m}^3/\text{s}$$

$$= (419384.42 \times 10^{-9}) \times 60 \times 10^3 \text{ } l/\text{min}$$

$$Q = 25.1631 \text{ } l/\text{min}$$

Absolute viscosity,

$$\mu = \rho\left(0.22 \text{ SUS} - \frac{180}{\text{SUS}}\right) \times 10^{-6} \text{ N-s/m}^2$$

$\therefore$
$$\mu = 860\left(0.22 \times 170 - \frac{180}{170}\right) \times 10^{-6}$$

$$= 31.2534 \times 10^{-3} \text{ N-s/m}^2$$

(iii) Frictional power loss (E_F) :

$$E_F = \frac{\mu \cdot N^2 (R_0^4 - R_i^4)}{(58.053 \times 10^6) \cdot h_0}$$

$$= \frac{31.2534 \times 10^{-9} \times (720)^2 \times (250^4 - 125^4)}{(58.053 \times 10^6) \times 0.16}$$

$$E_F = 6.387765 \text{ kW}$$

(iv) Pumping power loss (E_P) :

$$E_P = \frac{P_i \cdot Q}{10^6}$$

$$= \frac{4.2362 \times 419384.42}{10^6}$$

$$E_P = 1.776596 \text{ kW}$$

(v) Temperature rise in the bearing (ΔT) :

As total power loss is converted into frictional heat,

Total power loss,

$$E_T = E_F + E_P$$

$$= 6.387765 + 1.776596$$

$$E_T = 8.164361 \text{ kW}$$

$\therefore$ Heat generated = Total power loss

$$= 8.164361$$

$$\text{Heat dissipated} = \rho \cdot Q \cdot C_P \cdot \Delta T, \text{ kW}$$

$$= 860 \times 419384.42 \times 10^{-9} \times 1.76 \times \Delta T$$

$\therefore \qquad$ Heat generated $=$ Heat dissipated $\qquad \ldots \ (\because \text{ as per assumption})$

$\therefore \qquad 8.164361 = 860 \times 419384.42 \times 10^{-9} \times 1.76 \times \Delta T$

$$\Delta T = 12.862°C$$

Example 5.4 : Following data is given for a hydrostatic thrust bearing :

(i)   Shaft diameter = 450 mm

(ii)   Recess diameter = 250 mm

(iii) Shaft speed = 750 r.p.m.

(iv) Thrust load = 900 kN

(v)   Viscosity of lubricant = 30 cP

Calculate :

(i)   The optimum film thickness for minimum energy losses.

(ii)   The total power loss

(iii) Temperature rise

Assume that total power loss is converted into frictional heat. Indicate the energy losses as a function of film thickness graphically.

Solution :

Given : $\qquad W = 900 \times 10^3$ N $\qquad ; \qquad R_i = 125$ mm

$\qquad\qquad\qquad N = 750$ r.p.m. $\qquad ; \qquad \mu = 30$ cP $= 30 \times 10^{-9}$ N-s/mm^2

$\qquad\qquad\qquad R_0 = 225$ mm

To find out :

(i) $h_{opt} = ?,$ (ii)$E_T = ?,$ (iii)$\Delta T = ?$

Supply pressure (P_i) :

$$W = \frac{\pi \cdot P_i \cdot (R_0^2 - R_i^2)}{2 \cdot \log_e \left(\dfrac{R_0}{R_i} \right)}$$

$$\therefore \qquad P_i = \frac{2W \cdot \log_e \left(\dfrac{R_0}{R_i} \right)}{\pi \cdot (R_0^2 - R_i^2)}$$

$$= \frac{2 \times 900 \times 10^3 \times \log_e \left(\frac{225}{125}\right)}{\pi \left(225^2 - 125^2\right)}$$

$$P_i = 9.6222 \ \text{N/mm}^2$$

Frictional power loss (E_F) :

$$E_F = \frac{\mu \cdot N^2 \left(R_0^4 - R_i^4\right)}{(58.053 \times 10^6) \cdot h_0}$$

$$= \frac{30 \times 10^{-9} \times (750)^2 \left(225^4 - 125^4\right)}{(58.053 \times 10^6) \times h_0}$$

$$E_F = \frac{0.67402}{h_0}, \ \text{kW}$$

Pumping power loss (E_P) : Oil flow rate :

$$E_P = \frac{P_i \cdot Q}{10^6} \qquad\qquad Q = \frac{\pi \cdot P_i \cdot h_0^3}{6 \cdot \mu \cdot \log_e \left(\frac{R_0}{R_i}\right)}$$

$$= \frac{9.6222 \times 2857 \times 14326.8 \ h_0^3}{10^6} \qquad = \frac{\pi \times 9.6222 \times h_0^3}{6 \times 30 \times 10^{-9} \cdot \log_e \left(\frac{225}{125}\right)}$$

$$E_P = 2749.2 \ h_0^3 \qquad\qquad\qquad = 285714326.8 \cdot h_0^3 \ \text{mm}^3/\text{s}$$

(ii)   Total power loss :

$$E_T = E_F + E_P$$

$$E_T = \frac{0.67402}{h_0} + 2749.2 \ h_0^3$$

(i)   Optimum film thickness for minimum energy losses :

In order to find optimum film thickness, differentiate total power loss with respect to oil-film thickness and equate it to zero.

$$\therefore \qquad \frac{dE_T}{dh_0} = 0$$

$$\therefore \qquad \frac{d}{dh_0}\left[\frac{0.67402}{h_0}\right] + 2749.2 \ h_0^3 = 0$$

$$\therefore \quad -\frac{0.67402}{h_0^2} + 3 \times 2749.2 \cdot h_0^2 = 0$$

$$\therefore \quad 8247.6\, h_0^2 = \frac{0.67402}{h_0^2}$$

$$\therefore \quad h_0^4 = 8.172317 \times 10^{-5}$$

$$\therefore \quad h_0 = 0.09508 \text{ mm}$$

optimum oil-film thickness for minimum power loss.

$\therefore$ Frictional power loss (E_F),

$$E_F = \frac{0.67402}{h_0} = \frac{0.67402}{0.09508}$$

$$E_F = 7.08898 \text{ kW}$$

Pumping power loss (E_P),

$$E_P = 2749.2\, h_0^3 = 2749.2 \times (0.09508)^3$$

$$E_P = 2.363055 \text{ kW}$$

$\therefore$ Total power loss,

$$E_T = E_F + E_P = 7.08898 + 2.363055$$

$$\therefore \quad E_T = 9.452033 \text{ kW}$$

Values of power losses for few values of h_0 are tabulated as under :

Table 5.2

h_0	E_P	E_F	E_T
0.025	0.043	26.960	27.003
0.050	0.344	13.480	13.824
0.075	1.160	8.987	10.146
0.100	2.749	6.740	9.489
0.125	5.369	5.392	10.761
0.150	9.278	4.493	13.771
0.175	14.733	3.851	18.585
0.200	21.993	3.370	25.363

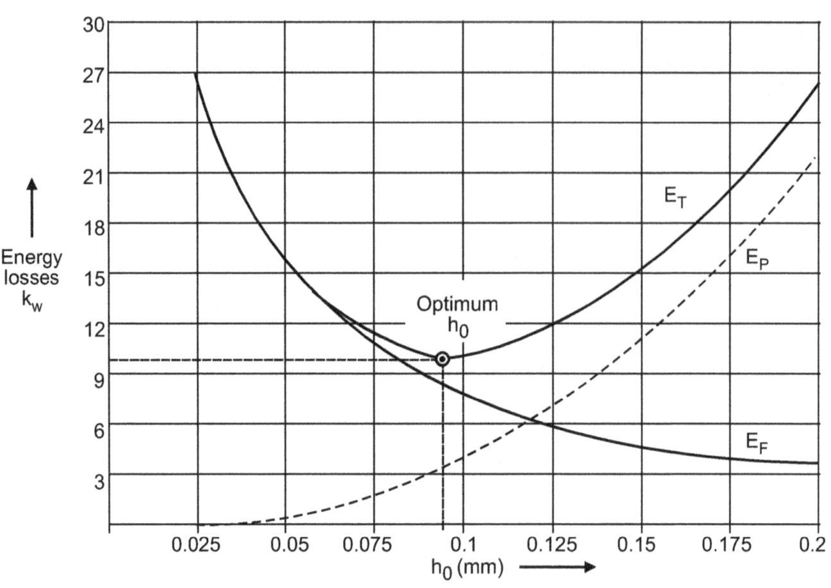

Fig. 5.15 : Plot of energy losses against oil-film thickness

(iii) Temperature rise (ΔT) in the bearing :

As,

$$Q = 285714326.8 \; h_0^3$$

$$= 285714326.8 \times (0.09508)^3$$

$$Q = 245583.699 \text{ mm}^3/s \Rightarrow \text{ oil flow rate}$$

$$= 245583.699 \times 10^{-9} \text{ m}^3/s$$

$$= (245583.699 \times 10^{-9}) \times 60 \times 10^3 \text{ l/sec}$$

$$Q = 14.735 \text{ l/min}$$

Heat generated = Heat dissipated $\quad ... (\because \text{ as per assumption})$

$\therefore \qquad 9.452033 = \rho \cdot Q \cdot C_P \cdot \Delta T$

$$= 860 \times 0.2455837 \times 10^{-3} \times 2 \times \Delta T \quad ... (\because C_P = 2 \text{ kJ/kg °C})$$

$\therefore \qquad \Delta T = 22.3768°C$

Example 5.5 : The following data refers to a hydrostatic thrust bearing.

(i)   Shaft diameter = 400 mm

(ii) Recess diameter = 250 mm

(iii) Shaft speed = 720 rpm

(iv) Supply pressure = 5 N/mm^2

(v)   Film thickness = 0.15 mm

(vi)　Viscosity of lubricant = 30 cP

(vii)　Specific heat of lubricant = 1.76 kJ/kg °C

(viii)　Specific gravity of lubricant = 0.86

Calculate :

(i)　Load-carrying capacity of the bearing

(ii)　Oil flow rate

(iii)　Total power loss

(iv)　Temperature rise

Assume that the total power loss in the bearing is converted into frictional heat.

Solution :

Given :　　　　　　　R_0 = 200 mm　　　　;　　　P_i = 5 N/mm^2

R_i = 125 mm　　　　;　　　h_0 = 0.15 mm

μ = 30 cP　　　　;　　　ρ = 860 kg/m^3

= 30×10^{-9} N-s/mm^2　　　C_p = 1.76 kJ/kg °C

N = 720 rpm

To calculate :

(i) W = ?, (ii) Q = ?, (iii) E_T = ?, (iv) ΔT = ?

(i)　Load-carrying capacity (W) of the bearing :

$$W = \frac{\pi \cdot P_i \left(R_0^2 - R_i^2\right)}{2 \cdot \log_e \left(\dfrac{R_0}{R_i}\right)}$$

$$= \frac{\pi \times 9 \times (200^2 - 125^2)}{2 \cdot \log_e \left(\dfrac{200}{125}\right)}$$

$$= 407317.721 \text{ N}$$

or　　　　　　　**W = 407.31772 kN**

(ii)　Oil flow rate (Q) :

$$Q = \frac{\pi \cdot P_i \cdot h_0^3}{6 \cdot \mu \cdot \log_e \left(\dfrac{R_0}{R_i}\right)}$$

$$= \frac{\pi \times 5 \times (0.15)^3}{6 \times 30 \times 10^{-9} \times \log_e \left(\frac{200}{125}\right)}$$

$$= 626641.09 \text{ mm}^3/\text{s}$$

$$= 626641.09 \times 10^{-9} \text{ m}^3/\text{s}$$

$$= (626641.09 \times 10^{-9}) \times 10^3 \times 60 \text{ } l/\text{min}$$

$$Q = 37.59832 \text{ } l/\text{min}$$

(iii) Total power loss :

$$E_T = \quad E_F \quad + \quad E_P$$

$$\text{(Frictional power loss)} + \text{(Pumping power loss)}$$

$$= \frac{\mu \cdot N^2 (R_0^4 - R_i^4)}{(58.053 \times 10^6) \cdot h_0} + \frac{P_i \cdot Q}{10^6}$$

$$= \left\{ \frac{30 \times 10^{-9} \times (720)^2 [200^4 - 125^4]}{58.053 \times 10^6 \times 0.15} \right\} + \left\{ \frac{5 \times 626641.09}{10^6} \right\}$$

$$= (2.4231) + (3.1333)$$

$$\therefore \quad E_T = 5.55646 \text{ kW}$$

(iv) Temperature rise (ΔT) :

$$\text{Heat generated} = \text{Total power loss}$$

$$= 5.55646 \text{ kJ/s}$$

Heat dissipated

$$= \rho \cdot Q \cdot C_P \cdot \Delta T \text{ kW}$$

$$= 860 \times 626641.09 \times 10^{-9} \times 1.76 \times \Delta T$$

$$\text{Heat generated} = \text{Heat dissipated}$$

$$\therefore \quad \Delta T = 5.85642 °C$$

Example 5.6 : A step bearing supports the vertical shaft of a turbo-generator. The recess diameter to shaft diameter ratio is 0.6 and supply pressure is 5 MPa. The thrust load is 400 kN. The shaft rotates at 800 r.p.m. If the viscosity of oil is 30 cP, calculate optimum oil-film thickness to be maintained so that the total power loss in the bearing is minimum.

Solution :

Given : $\dfrac{R_i}{R_0} = 0.6$; $W = 400 \text{ kN} = 400 \times 10^3 \text{ N}$

$P_i = 5 \text{ MPa}$; $N = 800 \text{ r.p.m.}$

$$= 5 \text{ N/mm}^2$$

$$\mu = 30 \text{ cP}$$

$$= 30 \times 10^{-9} \text{ N-s/mm}^2$$

To calculate, $h_0 = ?$

Lubricant flow rate :

$$Q = \frac{\pi \cdot P_i \cdot h_0^3}{6 \cdot \mu \cdot \log_e\left(\dfrac{R_0}{R_i}\right)}$$

$$= \frac{\pi \times 5 \times h_0^3}{6 \times 30 \times 10^{-9} \cdot \log_e\left(\dfrac{1}{0.6}\right)}$$

$$Q = 1.70834153 \times 10^8 \cdot h_0^3, \text{ mm}^3/\text{s}$$

Frictional power loss (E_F) :

$$E_F = \frac{\mu \cdot N^2 (R_0^4 - R_i^4)}{(58.053 \times 10^6) \times h_0}$$

$$= \frac{30 \times 10^{-9} \times (800)^2 \, [R_0^4 - (0.6 \, R_0)^4]}{(58.053 \times 10^6) \cdot h_0}$$

Now, as we know,

$$W = \frac{\pi \cdot P_i (R_0^2 - R_i^2)}{2 \log_e\left(\dfrac{R_0}{R_i}\right)}$$

$$400 \times 10^3 = \frac{\pi \times 5 \, [R_0^2 - (0.6 \, R_0)^2]}{2 \cdot \log_e\left(\dfrac{1}{0.6}\right)}$$

$$= \frac{\pi \times 5 \, R_0^2 \, [1 - 0.36]}{2 \cdot \log_e\left(\dfrac{1}{0.6}\right)}$$

$$\therefore \quad R_0 = 201.62 \text{ mm}$$

$$\therefore \quad R_i = 0.6 \, (201.62) = 120.971 \text{ mm}$$

Using these values in above equation for E_F,

$$\therefore \qquad E_F = \frac{30 \times 10^{-9}\,(800)^2\,[(201.62)^4 - (120.971)^4]}{58.053 \times 10^6 \times h_0}$$

$$E_F = \frac{0.475699}{h_0}, \text{ kW}$$

Pumping power loss (E_P) :

$$E_P = \frac{P_i \cdot Q}{10^6} = \frac{5 \times 1.70834153 \times 10^8 \cdot h_0^3}{10^6}$$

$$E_P = 854.171 \cdot h_0^3, \text{ kW}$$

$\therefore$ **Total power loss (E_T)**

$$E_T = E_F + E_P$$

$$E_T = \frac{0.475699}{h_0} + 854.171 \cdot h_0^3$$

Optimum oil-film thickness (h_0) :

Optimum oil-film thickness can be obtained by differentiating total power loss with respect to h_0 and equating it to zero.

$$\therefore \qquad \frac{dE_T}{dh_0} = 0$$

$$\therefore \quad \frac{d}{dh_0}\left[\frac{0.475699}{h_0} + 854.171 \cdot h_0^3\right] = 0$$

$$\therefore \quad 2562.513\,h_0^2 - \frac{0.475699}{h_0^2} = 0$$

$$\therefore \qquad 2562.513\,h_0^2 = \frac{0.475699}{h_0^2}$$

$$\therefore \qquad h_0 = 0.1167257 \text{ mm}$$

Example 5.7 : The following data is given for a hydrostatic step bearing of a vertical turbo generator :

   (i)   Thrust load = 500 kN

   (ii) Shaft speed = 1000 r.p.m.

   (iii) Supply pressure = 6 N/mm²

(iv) Ratio of recess diameter to shaft diameter = 0.6

(v) Oil-film thickness = 0.15 mm

(vi) Viscosity of lubricant = 170 SUS

(vii) Specific heat of lubricant = 2.09 kJ/kg °C

(viii) Density of lubricant = 860 kg/m³

Calculate :

(i) Shaft and recess diameters

(ii) Flow rate of lubricant in l/min

(iii) Frictional power loss

(iv) Pumping power loss

(v) Temperature rise

(vi) Optimum oil-film thickness so that total power loss is minimum and

(vii) The performance parameters corresponding to optimum oil-film thickness.

Assume that the total power loss in the bearing is converted into frictional heat.

Solution :

Given : $W = 500 \times 10^3$ N   ; $P_i = 6$ N/mm²

$N = 1000$ r.p.m.   ; $h_0 = 0.15$ mm

$\dfrac{R_i}{R_0} = 0.6$; $\rho = 860$ kg/m³

$\mu = 170$ SUS   ; $C_P = 2.09$ kJ/kg °C

To calculate :

(i) $D_0 = ?,\ D_i = ?,$ (ii) $Q = ?,$

(iii) $E_F = ?,$ (iv) $E_P = ?,$

(v) $\Delta T = ?$ (vi) $h_0 = ?$ for minimum E_T

(i) Shaft and recess diameters :

$$W = \frac{\pi \cdot P_i \cdot (R_0^2 - R_i^2)}{2 \cdot \log_e\left(\dfrac{R_0}{R_i}\right)}$$

$$W = \frac{\pi \cdot P_i \cdot R_0^2\,(1 - 0.6^2)}{2 \cdot \log_e\left(\dfrac{1}{0.6}\right)}$$

$$\therefore \quad R_0^2 = \frac{500 \times 10^3 \times 2 \times \log_e\left(\frac{1}{0.6}\right)}{\pi \times 6 \times (0.64)}$$

$$\therefore \quad R_0 = 205.777 \text{ mm}$$

$$\therefore \quad R_i = 123.466 \text{ mm}$$

$$\therefore \quad D_0 = 411.554 \text{ mm}$$

$$\text{and} \quad D_i = 246.932 \text{ mm}$$

(ii) Lubricant flow rate (Q) :

Absolute viscosity,

$$\mu = \rho\left(0.22 \text{ SUS} - \frac{180}{\text{SUS}}\right) \times 10^{-6} \text{ N-s/m}^2$$

$$= 860\left(0.22 \times 170 - \frac{180}{170}\right) \times 10^{-6}$$

$$= 31.2534 \times 10^{-3} \text{ N-s/m}^2$$

$$= (31.2534 \times 10^{-3}) \times 10^{-6} \text{ N-s/mm}^2$$

$$\mu = 31.2534 \times 10^{-9} \text{ N-s/mm}^2$$

We know,

$$Q = \frac{\pi \cdot P_i \cdot h_0^3}{6 \cdot \mu \cdot \log_e\left(\frac{R_0}{R_i}\right)}$$

$$= \frac{\pi \times 6 \times (0.15)^3}{6 \times 31.2534 \times 10^{-9} \times \log_e\left(\frac{205.777}{123.466}\right)}$$

$$Q = 0.6641288 \times 10^6 \text{ mm}^3/\text{s}$$

$$\therefore \quad Q = (0.6641288 \times 10^6) \times 10^{-9} \text{ m}^3/\text{s}$$

$$= [(0.6641288 \times 10^6) \times 10^{-9}] \times 60 \times 10^3 \text{ l/min}$$

$$Q = 39.84773 \text{ l/min}$$

(iii) Frictional power loss (E_F) :

$$E_F = \frac{\mu \cdot N^2 (R_0^4 - R_i^4)}{(58.053 \times 10^6) \times h_0}$$

$$= \frac{31.2534 \times 10^{-9} \times (1000)^2 (205.777^4 - 123.466^4)}{(58.053 \times 10^6) \times 0.15}$$

$$E_F = 5.6013 \text{ kW}$$

(iv) Pumping power loss (E_P) :

$$E_P = \frac{P_i \cdot Q}{10^6}$$

$$= 6 \times \frac{\pi \cdot P_i \cdot h_0^3}{6\mu \cdot \log_e\left(\dfrac{R_0}{R_i}\right)} = \frac{6 \times \pi \times 6 \times (0.15)^3}{6 \times 31.2534 \times 10^{-9} \times \log_e\left(\dfrac{205.777}{123.466}\right)}$$

$$E_P = 3.9848 \text{ kW}$$

$\therefore$ **Total power loss (E_T),**

$$E_T = E_F + E_P$$

$$E_T = \frac{0.840193}{h_0} + 1180.673\, h_0^3$$

$$E_T = 9.5861 \text{ kW}$$

(v) Temperature rise in bearing (ΔT) :

Heat generated = Heat dissipated $\qquad \dots (\because$ as per assumption)

$$E_T = \rho \cdot Q \cdot C_P \cdot \Delta T$$

$\therefore$

$$\Delta T = \frac{E_T}{\rho \cdot Q \cdot C_P}$$

$$= \frac{9.5861}{860 \times 0.6641288 \times 10^{-3} \times 2.09}$$

$$\Delta T = 8.03054°C$$

(vi) Optimum oil-film thickness for minimum total power loss (h_0) :

To obtain optimum oil-film thickness, differentiate total power loss (in terms of h_0) with respect to h_0 and equate it to zero.

$\therefore$

$$\frac{dE_T}{dh_0} = 0$$

$\therefore$

$$\frac{d}{dh_0}\left[\frac{0.840193}{h_0} + 1180.673\, h_0^3\right] = 0$$

$\therefore$

$$3542.019\, h_0^2 - \frac{0.840193}{h_0^2} = 0$$

$\therefore$

$$3542.019\, h_0^2 = \frac{0.840193}{h_0^2}$$

$\therefore$

$$h_0 = 0.1241 \text{ mm}$$

$\therefore$ Optimum oil-film thickness = 0.1241 mm

(vii) Performance parameters corresponding to optimum oil-film thickness :

(a)   Frictional power loss :

$$E_F = \frac{0.840193}{h_0} = \frac{0.840193}{0.1241}$$

$$E_F = 6.7703 \text{ kW}$$

(b)   Pumping power loss :

$$E_P = 1180.673 \, h_0^3$$

$$= 1180.673 \, (0.1241)^3$$

$$E_P = 2.2566 \text{ kW}$$

(c)   Total power loss :

$$E_T = E_F + E_P$$

$$= 6.7703 + 2.2566$$

$$\therefore \qquad E_T = 9.0269 \text{ kW}$$

(d)   Lubricant flow rate (Q) :

$$Q = \frac{\pi \cdot P_i \cdot h_0^3}{6 \cdot \mu \cdot \log_e \left(\dfrac{R_0}{R_i}\right)}$$

$$= \frac{\pi \times 6 \times (0.1241)^3}{6 \times 31.2534 \times 10^{-9} \times \log_e \left(\dfrac{205.777}{123.466}\right)}$$

$$Q = 0.376092 \times 10^6 \text{ mm}^3/s$$

$$= (0.376092 \times 10^6) \times 10^{-9} \text{ m}^3/s$$

$$= [(0.376092 \times 10^6) \times 10^{-9}] \times 60 \times 10^3 \text{ } l/min$$

$$Q = 22.5655 \text{ } l/min$$

(e)   Temperature rise (ΔT) :

$$\text{Heat generated} = \text{Heat dissipated} \qquad\qquad ... (\because \text{ as per assumption})$$

$$\therefore \qquad 9.0269 = \rho \cdot Q \cdot C_P \cdot \Delta T$$

$$\therefore \qquad \Delta T = \frac{9.0269}{860 \times 0.376092 \times 10^3 \times 2.09}$$

$$\therefore \qquad \Delta T = 13.354 °C$$

where, ρ is in kg/m^3, Q is in m^3/s, C_P is in kJ/kg °C, ΔT is in °C.

Example 5.8 : Following data is given for a hydrostatic thrust bearing :

   (i)   Thrust load = 850 kN

   (ii)   Shaft speed = 900 r.p.m.

   (iii) Shaft diameter = 450 mm

   (iv) Recess diameter = 250 mm

   (v)   Viscosity of lubricant = 30 cP

Calculate optimum film thickness for minimum power loss. Show the variation of energy losses against film thickness graphically. Also calculate total power loss.

Solution :

    Given :

$$W = 850 \times 10^3 \text{ N} \quad ; \quad R_0 = 225 \text{ mm}$$

$$N = 900 \text{ r.p.m.} \quad ; \quad R_i = 125 \text{ mm}$$

$$\mu = 30 \text{ cP}$$

$$= 30 \times 10^{-9} \text{ N-s/mm}^2$$

To find out :

$$h_0 = ?$$

Supply pressure (P_i) :

$$W = \frac{\pi \cdot P_i \, (R_0^2 - R_i^2)}{2 \cdot \log_e\left(\dfrac{R_0}{R_i}\right)}$$

$$P_i = \frac{2\,W \cdot \log_e\left(\dfrac{R_0}{R_i}\right)}{\pi \, (R_0^2 - R_i^2)}$$

$$= \frac{2 \times 850 \times 10^3 \times \log_e\left(\dfrac{225}{125}\right)}{\pi \, (225^2 - 125^2)}$$

$$P_i = 9.08763 \text{ N/mm}^2$$

Frictional power loss (E_F) :

$$E_F = \frac{\mu \cdot N^2 \cdot (R_0^4 - R_i^4)}{(58.053 \times 10^6) \cdot h_0}$$

$$= \frac{30 \times 10^{-9} \times (900)^2 \, (225^4 - 125^4)}{(58.053 \times 10^6) \times h_0}$$

$$\therefore \qquad E_F = \frac{0.970589}{h_0}, \text{ kW}$$

Pumping power loss (E_P) : Oil flow rate (Q)

$$E_P = \frac{P_i \cdot Q}{10^6}$$

$$= \frac{9.08763 \times 269841209.7 \cdot h_0^3}{10^6} \qquad Q = \frac{\pi \cdot P_i \cdot h_0^3}{6 \cdot \mu \cdot \log_e\left(\dfrac{R_0}{R_i}\right)}$$

$$E_P = 2452.217 \, h_0^3, \text{ kW} \qquad\qquad = \frac{\pi \times 9.08763 \times h_0^3}{6 \times 30 \times 10^{-9} \times \log_e\left(\dfrac{225}{125}\right)}$$

$$= 269841209.7 \, h_0^3, \text{ mm}^3/s$$

$\therefore$ **Total power loss (E_T),**

$$E_T = E_F + E_P = \frac{0.970589}{h_0} + 2452.217 \, h_0^3$$

Optimum oil-film thickness for minimum energy losses :

Differentiate total energy loss with respect to h_0 and equate it to zero.

$$\therefore \qquad \frac{dE_T}{dh_0} = 0$$

$$\therefore \qquad \frac{d}{dh_0}\left[\frac{0.970589}{h_0} + 2452.217 \, h_0^3\right] = 0$$

$$\therefore \qquad 7356.651 \, h_0^2 - \frac{0.970589}{h_0^2} = 0$$

$$\therefore \qquad 7356.651 \, h_0^2 = \frac{0.970589}{h_0^2}$$

$$\therefore \qquad h_0 = 0.10717 \text{ mm}$$

$\therefore$ Frictional power loss (E_F),

$$E_F = \frac{0.970589}{h_0} = \frac{0.970589}{0.10717}$$

$$\therefore \qquad E_F = 9.05654 \text{ kW}$$

Pumping power loss (E_P),

$$E_P = 2452.217 \, h_0^3 = 2452.217 \, (0.10717)^3$$

$$E_P = 3.0184 \text{ kW}$$

$\therefore$ Total power loss (E_T),

$$E_T = E_F + E_P$$

$$= 9.05654 + 3.0184$$

$$E_T = 12.0749 \text{ kW}$$

Table 5.3 shows values of power losses for few values of h_0.

Table 5.3

h_0	E_P	E_F	E_T
0	0	∞	∞
0.025	0.038	38.82	38.83
0.050	0.030	19.4	19.7
0.075	1.032	12.93	13.96
0.100	2.4481	9.7	12.14
0.125	4.781	7.76	12.54
0.150	8.262	6.46	14.72
0.175	13.120	5.54	18.66
0.200	19.58	4.85	24.43

Fig. 5.16 shows variation of energy losses against oil-film thickness and total power loss corresponding to the optimum oil-film thickness.

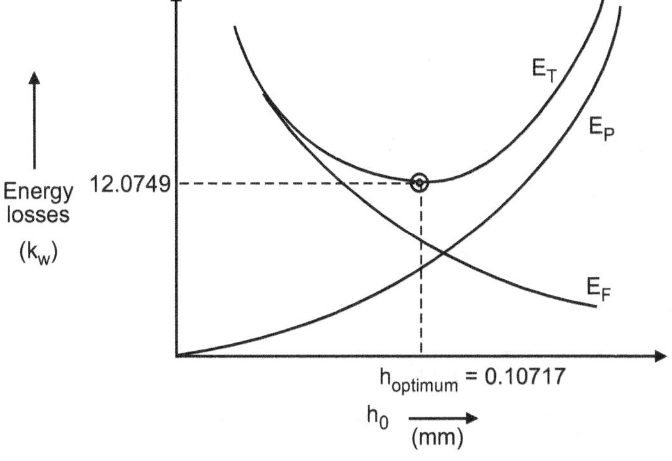

Fig. 5.16 : Plot of energy losses against oil-film thickness

Example 5.9 : A hydrostatic step bearing has following details :

Shaft diameter = 10 cm

Recess diameter = 6 cm

Film thickness = 0.05 mm

Supply pressure = 5.5 bar

Viscosity of oil = 30 cP

Recess depth = 0.5 mm

Find the load-carrying capacity and oil flow rate required.

Solution :

Given :

$$R_0 = 5\text{ cm} = 50\text{ mm} \quad ; \quad \mu = 30\text{ cP}$$

$$R_i = 3\text{ cm} = 30\text{ mm} \quad ; \quad = 30 \times 10^{-9}\text{ N-s/mm}^2$$

$$h_0 = 0.05\text{ mm}$$

$$P_i = 5.5\text{ bar}$$

$$= 5.5 \times 10^5\text{ N/m}^2$$

$$= 5.5 \times 10^5 \times 10^{-6}\text{ N/mm}^2$$

$$= 0.55\text{ N/mm}^2$$

To find out :

(i) W = ? (ii) Q = ?

(i) Load-carrying capacity (W) :

$$W = \frac{\pi \cdot P_i \cdot (R_0^2 - R_i^2)}{2 \cdot \log_e\left(\dfrac{R_0}{R_i}\right)}$$

$$= \frac{\pi \times 0.55 \times (50^2 - 30^2)}{2 \cdot \log_e\left(\dfrac{50}{30}\right)}$$

$$W = 2706.013\text{ N}$$

(ii) Oil flow rate (Q) :

$$Q = \frac{\pi \cdot P_i \cdot h_0^3}{6 \cdot \mu \cdot \log_e\left(\dfrac{R_0}{R_i}\right)}$$

$$= \frac{\pi \times 0.55 \times (0.05)^3}{6 \times 30 \times 10^{-9} \times \log_e\left(\frac{50}{30}\right)}$$

$$Q = 2348.9696 \ mm^3/s$$

$$= 2348.9696 \times 10^{-9} \ m^3/s$$

$$= (2348.9696 \times 10^{-9}) \times 60 \times 10^3 \ l/min$$

$$Q = 0.14094 \ l/min$$

Example 5.10 : Following data is given for a hydrostatic thrust bearing :

Supply pressure = 5 MPa

Shaft speed = 1000 r.p.m.

Shaft diameter = 500 mm

Recess diameter = 300 mm

Viscosity of lubricant = 35 cP

Specific gravity of lubricant = 0.86

Specific heat of lubricant = 2 kJ/kg °C

Calculate :

(i)   Load-carrying capacity

(ii)   Optimum oil-film thickness

(iii) Flow rate of lubricant

(iv)   Total power loss and

(v)   Temperature rise

Solution :

Given :

P_i = 5 MPa   ; μ = 35 cP = 35×10^{-9} N-s/mm²

$\quad$ = 5 N/mm²   ; ρ = 860 kg/m³

N = 1000 r.p.m.   ; C_P = 2 kJ/kg °C

R_0 = 250 mm   ;

R_i = 150 mm   ;

To find out :

(i) W = ?,   (ii) Q = ?,

(iii) E_T = ?,   (iv) h_0 = ?,

(v) ΔT = ?

(i)　Load-carrying capacity (W) :

$$W = \frac{\pi \cdot P_i \cdot (R_0^2 - R_i^2)}{2 \cdot \log_e\left(\dfrac{R_0}{R_i}\right)} = \frac{\pi \times 5 \times (250^2 - 150^2)}{2 \cdot \log_e\left(\dfrac{250}{150}\right)}$$

$$W = 615002.95 \text{ N}$$

(ii)　Flow rate of lubricant (Q) :

$$Q = \frac{\pi \cdot P_i \cdot h_0^3}{6 \cdot \mu \cdot \log_e\left(\dfrac{R_0}{R_i}\right)}$$

$$= \frac{\pi \times 5 \times h_0^3}{6 \times 35 \times 10^{-9} \times \log_e\left(\dfrac{250}{150}\right)}$$

$$= 146429273.7 \, h_0^3, \text{ mm}^3/\text{s}$$

(iii)　Total power loss :

Total power loss = (Frictional power loss) + (Pumping power loss)

$$E_T = E_F + E_P$$

$\therefore$　**Frictional power loss (E_F),**

$$E_F = \frac{\mu \cdot N^2 \cdot (R_0^4 - R_i^4)}{(58.053 \times 10^6) \cdot h_0}$$

$$= \frac{35 \times 10^{-9} \times (1000)^2 \, (250^4 - 150^4)}{(58.053 \times 10^6) \, h_0}$$

$$E_F = \frac{2.049851}{h_0}, \text{ kW}$$

Pumping power loss (E_P),

$$E_P = \frac{P_i \cdot Q}{10^6}$$

$$= \frac{5 \times 146429273.7 \, h_0^3}{10^6}$$

$$E_P = 732.1464 \, h_0^3, \text{ kW}$$

∴　Total power loss,

$$E_T = \frac{2.049851}{h_0} + 732.1464\, h_0^3$$

(iv)　Optimum oil-film thickness :

It is obtained by differentiating total power loss with respect to oil-film thickness and equating it to zero.

$$\therefore \quad \frac{dE_T}{dh_0} = 0$$

$$\therefore \frac{d}{dh_0}\left[\frac{2.049851}{h_0} + 732.1464\, h_0^3\right] = 0$$

$$\therefore 2196.439\, h_0^2 - \frac{2.049851}{h_0^2} = 0$$

$$\therefore \quad 2196.439\, h_0^2 = \frac{2.049851}{h_0^2}$$

$$\therefore \Rightarrow \quad h_0 = 0.17478 \text{ mm} \rightarrow \text{Optimum oil-film thickness}$$

Performance parameters corresponding to optimum oil-film thickness.

Flow rate of lubricant (Q) :

$$Q = 146429273.7\, h_0^3$$

$$= 146429273.7 \times (0.17478)^3$$

$$Q = 781813.406 \text{ mm}^3/\text{s}$$

$$= (781813.406) \times 10^{-9} \text{ m}^3/\text{s}$$

$$= (781813.406 \times 10^{-9}) \times 60 \times 10^3 \text{ l/min}$$

$$Q = 46.9088 \text{ l/min}$$

Frictional power loss (E_F) :

$$E_F = \frac{2.049851}{h_0} = \frac{2.049851}{0.17478}$$

$$E_F = 11.7282 \text{ kW}$$

Pumping power loss (E_P) :

$$E_P = 732.1464\, h_0^3 = 732.1464\,(0.17478)^3$$

$$E_P = 3.9091 \text{ kW}$$

$\therefore$ Total power loss,

$$E_T = E_F + E_P$$

$\therefore$ $\qquad$ $E_T = 11.7282 + 3.9091$

$\qquad\qquad$ $E_T = 15.6373$ kW

(v)   Temperature rise :

$$\text{Heat generated} = \text{Heat dissipated}$$

$$H_g = H_d$$

$\therefore$ $\qquad$ $15.6373 = \rho \cdot Q \cdot C_P \cdot \Delta T$

$\therefore$ $\qquad$ $\Delta T = \dfrac{15.6373}{860 \times 781813.406 \times 10^{-9} \times 2}$

$\qquad$ $\Delta T = 11.6287°C$

Example 5.11 : A hydrostatic step bearing has 114 mm diameter recess concentric with 200 mm diameter of the shaft. The step is to carry load of 15 kN, while maintaining lubricant film of 0.13 mm. If the lubricant viscosity is 105 cP and shaft speed is 720 r.p.m, estimate recess pressure and lubricant flow required. Also estimate power lost in pumping and in churning.

Solution :

$\quad$ **Given data :** $\qquad$ $R_0 = 100$ mm $\qquad$; $\qquad$ $h_0 = 0.13$ mm

$\qquad\qquad\qquad\qquad\qquad$ $R_i = 57$ mm $\qquad$; $\qquad$ $\mu = 105$ cP

$\qquad\qquad\qquad\qquad\qquad$ $W = 15 \times 10^3$ N $\qquad$; $\qquad\qquad$ $= 105 \times 10^{-9}$ N-s/mm^2

$\qquad\qquad\qquad\qquad\qquad$ $N = 720$ r.p.m.

To calculate :

$\quad$ (i) $\quad$ $P_i = ?,$ $\qquad\qquad$ (ii) $\quad$ $Q = ?,$

$\quad$ (iii) $\quad$ $E_P = ?,$ $\qquad\quad$ (iv) $\quad$ $E_F = ?$

(i)   Recess pressure (P_i) :

$\quad$ We know,

$$W = \frac{\pi \cdot P_i \cdot (R_0^2 - R_i^2)}{2 \cdot \log_e\left(\dfrac{R_0}{R_i}\right)}$$

$\therefore$ $\qquad$ $P_i = \dfrac{2 \cdot W \cdot \log_e\left(\dfrac{R_0}{R_i}\right)}{\pi \cdot (R_0^2 - R_i^2)} = \dfrac{2 \times 15 \times 10^3 \times \log_e\left(\dfrac{100}{57}\right)}{\pi (100^2 - 57^2)}$

$\qquad$ $P_i = 0.79512$ N/mm^2

(ii) Oil flow rate (Q) :

$$Q = \frac{\pi \cdot P_i \cdot h_0^3}{6 \cdot \mu \cdot \log_e\left(\dfrac{R_0}{R_i}\right)} = \frac{\pi \times 0.79512 \times (0.13)^3}{6 \times 105 \times 10^{-9} \times \log_e\left(\dfrac{100}{57}\right)}$$

$\therefore \qquad Q = 15496.87 \text{ mm}^3/\text{s} = 15496.87 \times 10^{-9} \text{ m}^3/\text{s}$

$\qquad\qquad = (15496.87 \times 10^{-9}) \times 60 \times 10^3 \text{ } l/\text{min}$

$\qquad Q = 0.929812 \text{ } l/\text{min}$

(iii) Pumping power loss (E_P) :

$\therefore \qquad E_P = \dfrac{P_i \cdot Q}{10^6} = \dfrac{0.79512 \times 15496.87}{10^6}$

$\qquad E_P = 0.012322 \text{ kW}$

(iv) Churning power loss (E_F) :

$$E_F = \frac{\mu \cdot N^2 (R_0^4 - R_i^4)}{(58.053 \times 10^6) \, h_0} = \frac{105 \times 10^{-9} \times (720)^2 \, (100^4 - 57^4)}{(58.053 \times 10^6) \times 0.13}$$

$\qquad E_F = 0.6451155 \text{ kW}$

$\therefore \quad$ Total power loss,

$\qquad E_T = E_P + E_F = 0.012322 + 0.6451155$

$\therefore \qquad E_T = 0.657438 \text{ kW}$

Example 5.12 : In hydrostatic step bearing the shaft end has diameter of 400 mm and a concentric recess 200 mm in diameter. If the bearing is energized with pressurised oil of 100 cP viscosity to create and retain film of 0.2 mm thickness, calculate the pressure required at starting, pressure required to maintain film, and oil flow rate.

Solution :

Given data : $\qquad R_0 = 200 \text{ mm} \qquad ; \qquad h_0 = 0.2 \text{ mm}$

$\qquad\qquad\qquad R_i = 100 \text{ mm}$

$\qquad\qquad\qquad \mu = 100 \text{ cP} = 100 \times 10^{-9} \text{ N-s/mm}^2$

To find :

(i) $P_i = ?$, $\qquad\qquad$ (ii) $Q = ?$

We know that,

$$W = \frac{\pi \cdot P_i \cdot (R_0^2 - R_i^2)}{2 \cdot \log_e\left(\frac{R_0}{R_i}\right)}$$

$\therefore$

$$P_i = \frac{2\,W \log_e\left(\frac{R_0}{R_i}\right)}{\pi\,(R_0^2 - R_i^2)} = \frac{2\,W \log_e\left(\frac{200}{100}\right)}{\pi\,(200^2 - 100^2)}$$

$$P_i = 1.471 \times 10^{-5}\,W,\ \text{N/mm}^2$$

Oil flow rate (Q),

$$Q = \frac{\pi \cdot P_i \cdot h_0^3}{6 \cdot \mu \cdot \log_e\left(\frac{R_0}{R_i}\right)} = \frac{\pi \times (1.471 \times 10^{-5}\,W) \times (0.2)^3}{6 \times 100 \times 10^{-9} \times \log_e\left(\frac{200}{100}\right)}$$

$$Q = 0.888947\,W\ \text{mm}^3/\text{s}$$

Example 5.13 : A hydrostatic thrust bearing consists of four pads as shown in Fig. 5.17. Each pad can be approximated as a circular area of outer and inner diameters of 200 mm and 50 mm respectively as shown in Fig. 5.17. The total thrust load on bearing is 300 kN, and the film thickness is 0.1 mm. The viscosity and specific gravity of the lubricating oil are 250 SUS and 0.88 respectively. Calculate the supply pressure and flow requirement.

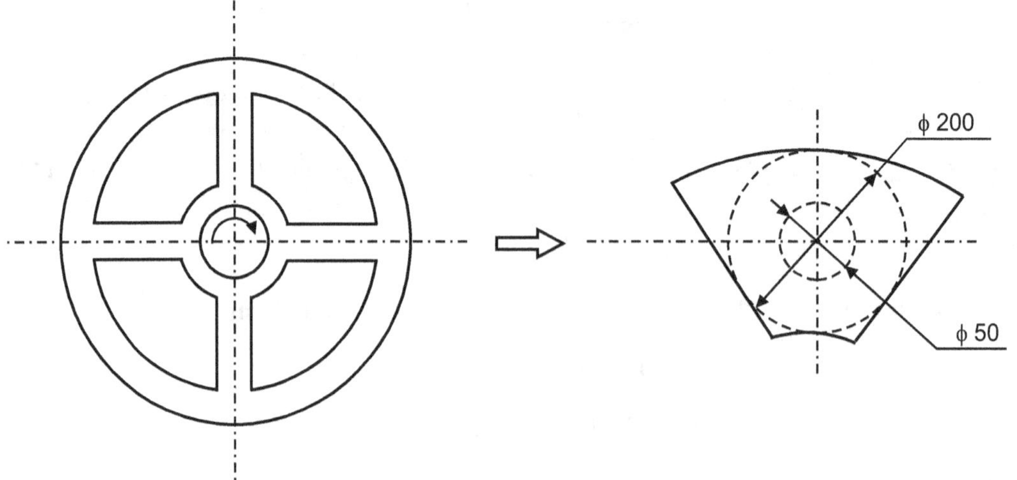

Fig. 5.17

Solution :

Given data :

$$W_T = 300 \times 10^3 \text{ N} \quad ; \quad \mu = 250 \text{ SUS}$$
$$h_0 = 0.1 \text{ mm} \quad ; \quad \rho = 880 \text{ kg/m}^3$$
$$R_0 = 100 \text{ mm} \quad ; \quad n = 4 \text{ (Number of pads)}$$
$$R_i = 25 \text{ mm}$$

To find :

(i) $P_i = ?,$ (ii) $Q = ?$

(i)   Supply pressure (P_i) :

Load on each pad, $(W) = \dfrac{W_T}{n}$

$$= \dfrac{300 \times 10^3}{4}$$

$$W = 75000 \text{ N}$$

$$\therefore \qquad W = \dfrac{\pi \cdot P_i \cdot (R_0^2 - R_i^2)}{2 \cdot \log_e \left(\dfrac{R_0}{R_i} \right)}$$

$$\therefore \qquad P_i = \dfrac{2 W \log_e \left(\dfrac{R_0}{R_i} \right)}{\pi (R_0^2 - R_i^2)}$$

$$= \dfrac{2 \times 75000 \times \log_e \left(\dfrac{100}{25} \right)}{\pi (100^2 - 25^2)}$$

$$P_i = 7.06034 \text{ N/mm}^2$$

(ii)   Oil flow rate (Q) : Absolute viscosity

$$Q = \dfrac{\pi \cdot P_i \cdot h_0^3}{6 \cdot \mu \cdot \log_e \left(\dfrac{R_0}{R_i} \right)} \qquad\qquad \mu = \rho \left(0.22 \text{ SUS} - \dfrac{180}{\text{SUS}} \right) \times 10^{-6} \text{ N-s/m}^2$$

$$= \dfrac{\pi \times 7.06034 \times (0.1)^3}{6 \times 47.7664 \times 10^{-9} \times \log_e \left(\dfrac{100}{25} \right)} \qquad = 880 \left(0.22 \times 250 - \dfrac{180}{250} \right) \times 10^{-6}$$

$Q = 55827.254 \text{ mm}^3/\text{s}$ $= 47.7664 \times 10^{-3} \text{ N-s/m}^2$

This is the oil flow rate through a single pad. $= (47.7664 \times 10^{-3}) \times 10^{-6} \text{ N-s/mm}^2$

$$\mu = 47.7664 \times 10^{-9} \text{ N-s/mm}^2$$

Total oil flow rate,

$$Q_T = n \cdot Q$$
$$= 4 \times 55827.254$$
$$= 223309.018 \text{ mm}^3/\text{s}$$
$$= 223309.018 \times 10^{-9} \text{ m}^3/\text{s}$$
$$= (223309.018 \times 10^{-9}) \times 60 \times 10^3 \text{ } l/\text{min}$$
$$Q_T = 13.3985 \text{ } l/\text{min}$$

Example 5.14 : The hydrostatic thrust bearing of a generator consists of six pads as shown in Fig. 5.18. The total thrust load is 900 kN and the film thickness is 0.05 mm. Viscosity of the lubricant is 60 cP. Neglecting the flow over the corners, each pad can be approximated as a circular area of 500 mm and 100 mm as outer and inner diameters respectively, as shown in Fig. 5.18. The density of the lubricant oil is 0.9 gm/cc.

Calculate :

(i)   Supply pressure

(ii)   Flow requirement

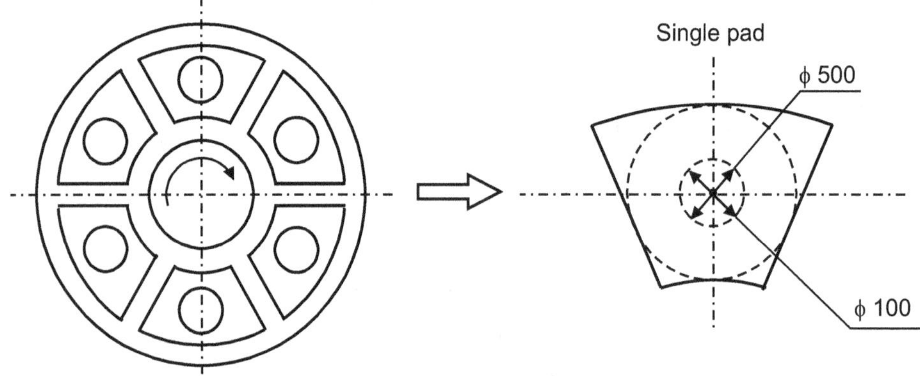

Fig. 5.18

Solution :

Given data :

$W_T = 900$ kN   ; $R_0 = 250$ mm

$= 900 \times 10^3$ N   ; $R_i = 50$ mm

$h_0 = 0.05$ mm   ; $\rho = 0.9$ gm/cc

$\mu = 60$ cP ; $= 0.9 \times 10^{-3} \times 10^6$ kg/m^3

$= 60 \times 10^{-9}$ N-s/mm^2 ; $= 900$ kg/m^3

$n = 6$

To find :

    (i) P_i = ?,   (ii) Q_T = ?

(i)   Supply pressure (P_i) :

$$\text{Load on each pad (W)} = \frac{W_T}{n}$$

$$= \frac{900 \times 10^3}{6}$$

$$W = 150000 \text{ N}$$

Now,

$$W = \frac{\pi \cdot P_i \, (R_0^2 - R_i^2)}{2 \cdot \log_e \left(\dfrac{R_0}{R_i}\right)}$$

$$\therefore \quad P_i = \frac{2\,W \cdot \log_e \left(\dfrac{R_0}{R_i}\right)}{\pi \,(R_0^2 - R_i^2)} = \frac{2 \times 150000 \times \log_e \left(\dfrac{250}{50}\right)}{\pi \,(250^2 - 50^2)}$$

$$P_i = 2.5615 \text{ N/mm}^2$$

(ii)   Flow requirement (Q) :

$$Q = \frac{\pi \cdot P_i \cdot h_0^3}{6 \cdot \mu \cdot \log_e \left(\dfrac{R_0}{R_i}\right)} = \frac{\pi \times 2.5615 \times (0.05)^3}{6 \times 60 \times 10^{-9} \times \log_e \left(\dfrac{250}{50}\right)}$$

$$Q = 1736.111 \text{ mm}^3/\text{s}$$

$$= 1736.111 \times 10^{-9} \text{ m}^3/\text{s} = (1736.111 \times 10^{-9}) \times 60 \times 10^3 \text{ l/min}$$

$$Q = 0.104167 \text{ l/min}$$

This is the oil flow rate through a single pad.

$\therefore$ Total oil flow rate,

$$Q_T = n \cdot Q = 6 \times 0.104167$$

$$\therefore \qquad Q_T = 0.625 \text{ l/min}$$

Example 5.15 : The hydrostatic step bearing consists of six pads as shown in Fig. 5.19. Neglecting the flow over corners each pad can be approximated as a circular area of outer and inner diameters of 500 mm and 200 mm respectively, as shown in Fig. 5.19. The thrust load is 900 kN, and the film thickness is 0.15 mm. The viscosity and density of lubricating oil are 30 cP and 0.9 gm/cc respectively. The specific heat of the lubricant is 2.09 kJ/kg °C.

[P.U. June 2010, 10 Marks]

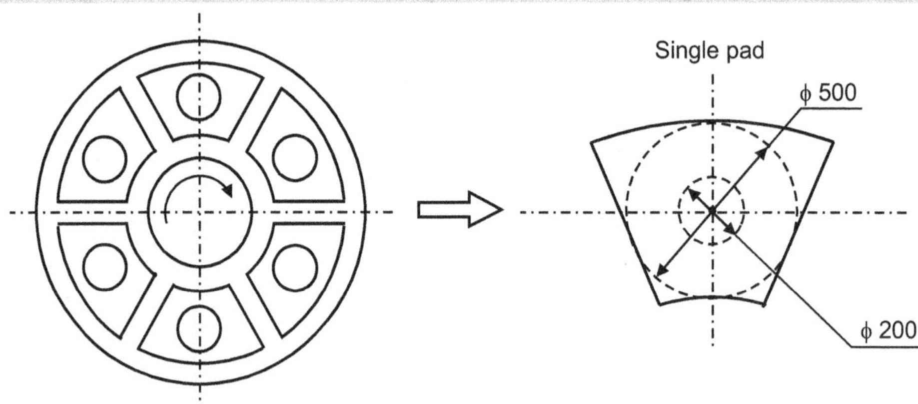

Fig. 5.19

If the shaft is rotating at 720 r.p.m.

Calculate :

(i)   Supply pressure

(ii)   The lubricant flow rate

(iii)   Frictional power loss

(iv)   Pumping power loss and

(v)   Temperature rise

Assume that the total power loss is converted into frictional heat.

Solution :

Given data :

$$W_T = 900 \times 10^3 \text{ N} \quad ; \quad C_P = 2.09 \text{ kJ/kg °C}$$

$$R_0 = 250 \text{ mm} \quad ; \quad N = 720 \text{ r.p.m.}$$

$$R_i = 100 \text{ mm} \quad ; \quad n = 6$$

$$\mu = 30 \text{ cP}$$

$$= 30 \times 10^{-9} \text{ N-s/mm}^2$$

$$h_0 = 0.15 \text{ mm} \quad ; \quad \rho = 0.9 \text{ gm/c.c}$$

$$= 0.9 \times 10^{-3} \times 10^6 \text{ kg/m}^3$$

$$= 900 \text{ kg/m}^3$$

To calculate :

    (i) P_i = ?,   (ii)   Q = ?,

    (iii) E_F = ?,   (iv) E_P = ?,

    (v) ΔT = ?

(i)   Supply pressure (P_i) :

$$\text{Load on each pad, } W = \frac{W_T}{n} = \frac{900 \times 10^3}{6}$$

$$W = 150 \times 10^3 \text{ N}$$

$$W = \frac{\pi \cdot P_i \cdot (R_0^2 - R_i^2)}{2 \cdot \log_e \left(\dfrac{R_0}{R_i} \right)}$$

$$150 \times 10^3 = \frac{\pi \cdot P_i \, (250^2 - 100^2)}{2 \cdot \log_e \left(\dfrac{250}{100} \right)}$$

$$\therefore \qquad P_i = 1.6667 \text{ N/mm}^2$$

(ii)   Lubricant flow rate (Q) :

Oil flow rate for each pad is,

$$Q = \frac{\pi \cdot P_i \cdot h_0^3}{6 \cdot \mu \cdot \log_e \left(\dfrac{R_0}{R_i} \right)}$$

$$= \frac{\pi \times 1.6667 \times (0.15)^3}{6 \times 30 \times 10^{-9} \times \log_e \left(\dfrac{250}{100} \right)}$$

$$= 107145.83 \text{ mm}^3/\text{s}$$

Total oil flow rate is,

$$
\begin{aligned}
Q_T &= n \cdot Q \\
&= 6 \times 107145.83 \\
&= 642874.999 \text{ mm}^3/\text{s} \\
&= 642874.999 \times 10^{-9} \text{ m}^3/\text{s} \\
&= (642874.999 \times 10^{-9}) \times 60 \times 10^3 \text{ } l/\text{min} \\
Q_T &= 38.5725 \text{ } l/\text{min}
\end{aligned}
$$

(iii) Frictional power loss (E_F) :

$$E_F' = \frac{\mu \cdot N^2 \cdot (R_0^4 - R_i^4)}{(58.053 \times 10^6) \times h_0}$$

$$E_F' = \frac{30 \times 10^{-9} \times (720)^2 \, (250^4 - 100^4)}{(58.053 \times 10^6) \times 0.15}$$

$$E_F' = 6.7978 \text{ kW} \qquad \text{... (for single pad)}$$

$\therefore$ Frictional power loss for bearing

$$E_F = n \cdot E_F'$$

$$= 6 \times 6.7978$$

$$E_F = 40.79 \text{ kW}$$

(iv) Pumping power loss (E_P) :

$$E_P' = \frac{P_i \cdot Q}{10^6}$$

$$= \frac{1.6667 \times 107145.83}{10^6}$$

$$= 0.17858 \text{ kW} \qquad \text{... (for single pad)}$$

$\therefore$ Pumping power loss for bearing,

$$E_P = n \cdot E_P'$$

$$= 6 \times 0.17858$$

$$E_P = 1.07148 \text{ kW}$$

(v)   Total power loss (E_T) :

$\therefore$

$$E_T = E_F + E_P = 40.79 + 1.07148$$

$$E_T = 41.8615 \text{ kW}$$

(vi) Temperature rise (ΔT) :

Heat generated = Heat dissipated $\text{... (} \because \text{ as per assumption)}$

$$E_T = \rho \cdot Q_T \cdot C_P \cdot \Delta T$$

$$\Delta T = \frac{E_T}{\rho \cdot Q_T \cdot C_P} = \frac{41.8615}{900 \times 642874.999 \times 10^{-9} \times 2.09}$$

$\therefore$

$$\Delta T = 34.6178°C$$

Example 5.16 : A hydrostatic thrust bearing consists of four pads with four oil pockets of size 180 mm × 180 mm as shown in Fig. 5.20. The thrust load is 650 kN and the oil-film thickness is 0.18 mm. The viscosity of the lubricant is 105 cP. The pressure in area 'X' (i.e. 480 mm × 480 mm), boardering the pockets can be assumed to be uniform and is equal to the supply pressure. The pressure distribution in the area 'Y' (i.e. shaded area) is assumed to be linear, varying from supply pressure at the inner edge to atmospheric pressure at the outer edge. It can be assumed that area 'Y' is straightened out and has length equal to the mean length shown by dotted line.

Calculate :

(i)　Supply pressure and

(ii)　Oil flow rate in *l*/min.

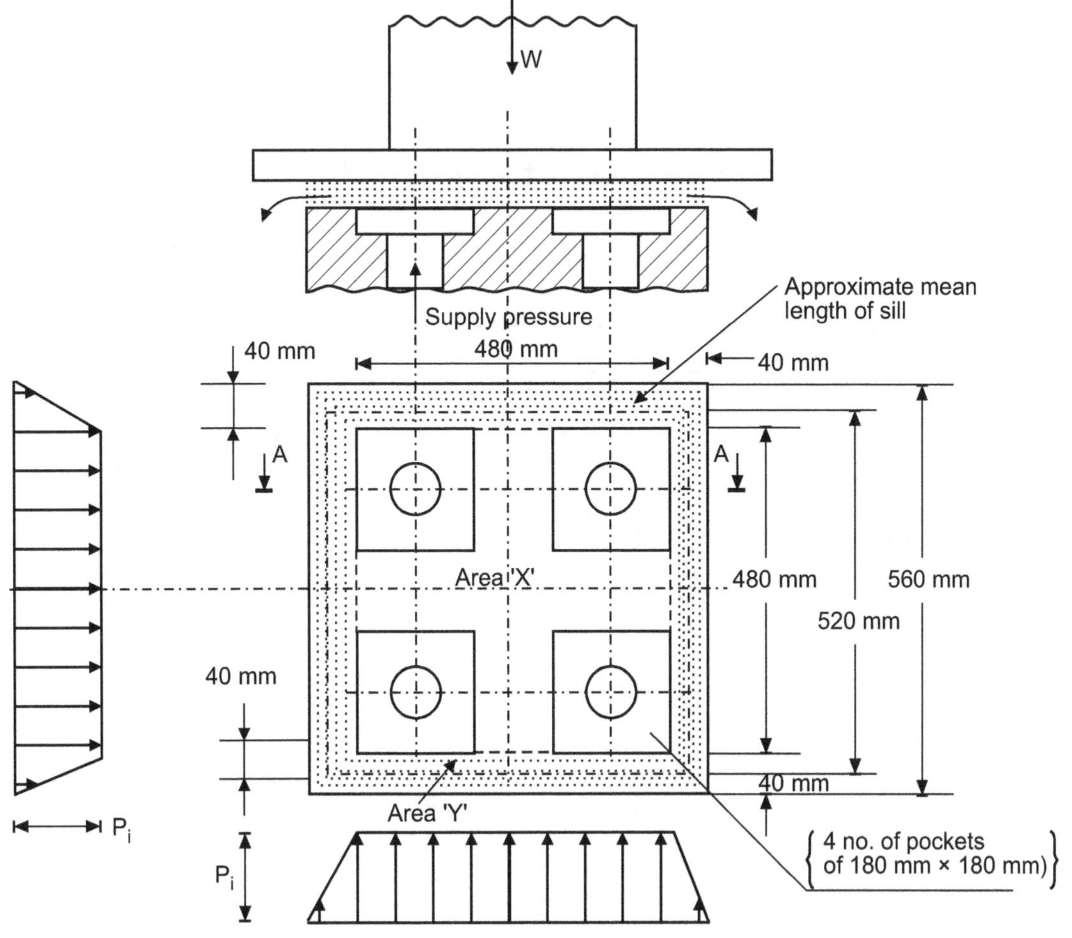

Fig. 5.20

Solution :

Given data :

$$n = 4$$
$$W_T = 650 \times 10^3 \text{ N}$$
$$h_0 = 0.18 \text{ mm}$$
$$\mu = 105 \text{ cP} = 105 \times 10^{-9} \text{ N-s/mm}^2$$

To calculate :

(i) $P_i = ?$,   (ii) $Q_T = ?$

Pressure in area 'X' = Supply pressure = P_i

Pressure in area 'Y' = $\dfrac{P_i}{2}$

(i) Supply pressure (P_i) :

Load on bearing,

$$W = (\text{Area 'X'}) (P_i) + (\text{Area 'Y'}) \left(\dfrac{P_i}{2}\right)$$

$$\therefore \quad 650 \times 10^3 = [480 \times 480]\, P_i + [560 \times 560 - 480 \times 460] \times \dfrac{P_i}{2}$$

$$= 230400\, P_i + 41600\, P_i$$

$$650 \times 10^3 = 272000\, P_i$$

$$\therefore \quad P_i = 2.38971 \text{ N/mm}^2$$

(ii) Oil flow rate (Q) :

When area 'Y' is straightened out, its length,

$$b = 520 \times 4$$
$$b = 2080 \text{ mm}$$

and
$$l = 40 \text{ mm}$$

Oil flow rate is given by,

$$Q = \dfrac{\Delta P \cdot h^3 \cdot b}{12 \cdot \mu \cdot l} = \dfrac{2.38971 \times (0.18)^3 \times 2080}{12 \times 105 \times 10^{-9} \times 40}$$

$$\therefore \quad Q = 575169.06 \text{ mm}^3/\text{s}$$

$$= 575169.06 \times 10^{-9} \text{ m}^3/\text{s}$$

$$= (575169.06 \times 10^{-9}) \times 60 \times 10^3 \text{ l/min}$$

$$Q_T = 34.5101 \text{ l/min}$$

Example 5.17 : The hydrostatic thrust bearing with a rectangular oil groove L (size 150×75) are given in Fig. 5.21. The pressure distribution can be assumed to be linear, varying from supply pressure at the inner edge to atmospheric pressure at the outer edge. Neglect flow over the corners. The thrust load is 200 kN and the oil-film thickness is 0.05 mm. The viscosity of the lubricant is 125 cP.

Calculate :

(i)   Supply pressure and

(ii) Oil flow rate.

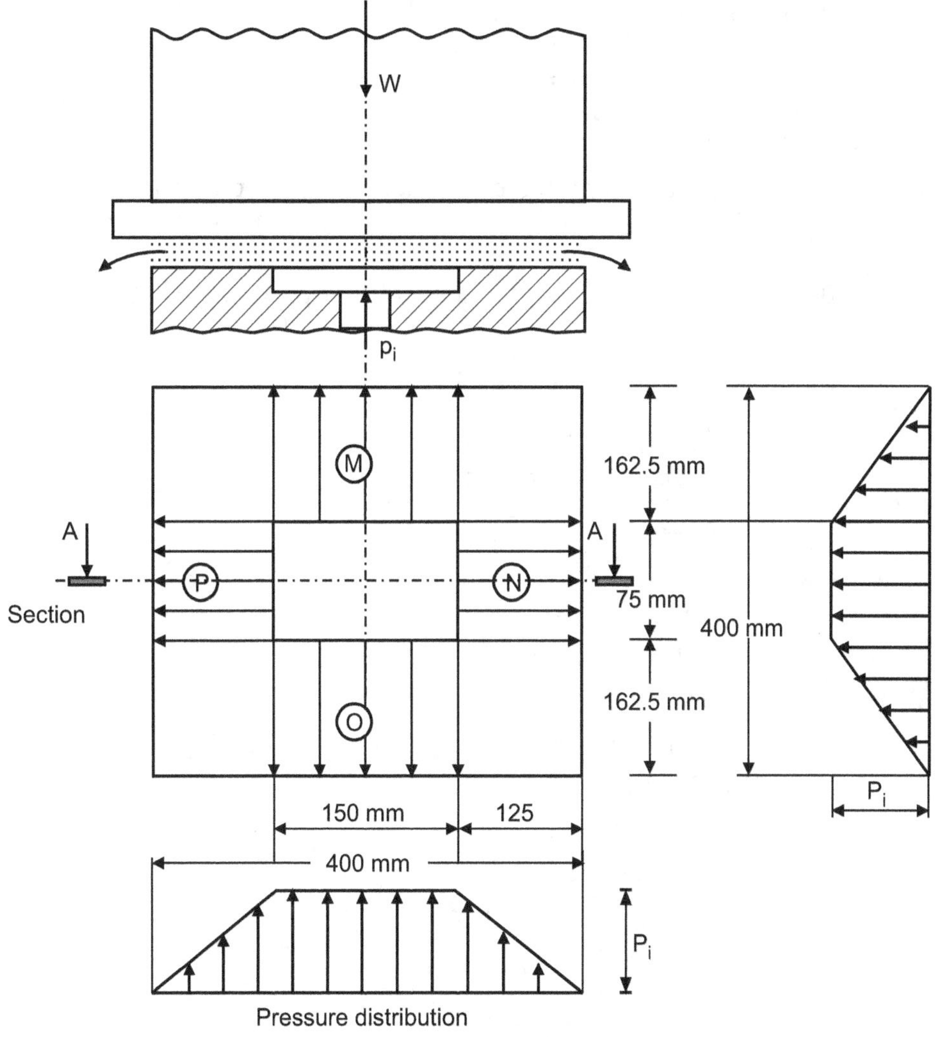

Fig. 5.21

Solution :

$$W_T = 200 \times 10^3 \text{ N}$$

Given data :

$$\text{Groove size} = (150 \text{ mm} \times 75 \text{ mm})$$
$$h_0 = 0.05 \text{ mm}$$
$$\mu = 125 \text{ cP} = 125 \times 10^{-9} \text{ N-s/mm}^2$$

Assumption :

Pressure in area 'L' = Supply pressure P_i

and pressure in areas 'M', 'N', 'O', 'P'

$$= \text{Average pressure} = \frac{P_i}{2}$$

(i) Supply pressure (P_i) :

$$W = \left(\begin{array}{c}\text{Load supported by} \\ \text{area 'L'}\end{array}\right) + \left(\begin{array}{c}\text{Load supported by areas} \\ \text{'M', 'N', 'O' and 'P'}\end{array}\right)$$

$$200 \times 10^3 = (P_i)(\text{Area 'L'}) + \left(\frac{P_i}{2}\right)(\text{Area 'M' + Area 'N' + Area 'O' + Area 'P'})$$

$$200 \times 10^3 = P_i (150 \times 75) + \left(\frac{P_i}{2}\right)[(150 \times 162.5)_M + (75 \times 125)_N$$
$$+ (150 \times 162.5)_O + (75 \times 125)_P]$$

$$200 \times 10^3 = 11250 (P_i) + 33750 (P_i)$$

$$\therefore \qquad P_i = 4.4444 \text{ N/mm}^2$$

(ii) Oil flow rate (Q) :

$$Q = \frac{\Delta P \cdot h^3 \cdot b}{12 \cdot \mu \cdot l}$$

Lubricant flow over area 'M' :

$$\Delta P = 4.4444 \text{ N/mm}^2 \qquad ; \qquad b = 162.5 \text{ mm}$$
$$l = 150 \text{ mm}$$
$$\mu = 125 \times 10^{-9} \text{ N-s/mm}^2$$
$$h = 0.05 \text{ mm}$$

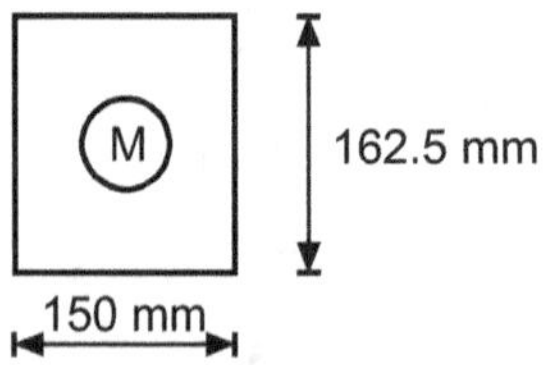

Fig. 5.22

$$\therefore \qquad Q_M = \frac{4.4444 \times (0.05)^3 \times 162.5}{12 \times 125 \times 10^{-9} \times 150}$$

$$= 401.231 \ mm^3/s$$

Lubricant flow over area 'P' :

$$\Delta P = 4.4444 \ N/mm^2 \qquad ; \qquad b = 75 \ mm$$

$$l = 125 \ mm \qquad ; \qquad \mu = 125 \times 10^{-9} \ N\text{-}s/mm^2$$

$$h = 0.05 \ mm$$

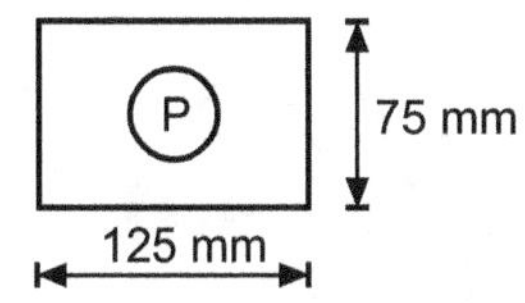

Fig. 5.23

$$\therefore \qquad Q_P = \frac{4.4444 \times (0.05)^3 \times 75}{12 \times 125 \times 10^{-9} \times 125}$$

$$= 222.22 \ mm^3/s$$

$\therefore$ Total lubricant flow rate (Q),

$$Q = 2Q_M + 2Q_P$$

$$= 2 \times 401.231 + 2 \times 222.22$$

$$Q = 1246.902 \ mm^3/s$$

$$= 1246.902 \times 10^{-9} \ m^3/s$$

$$= (1246.902 \times 10^{-9}) \times 60 \times 10^3 \ l/min$$

$$Q = 0.074814 \ l/min$$

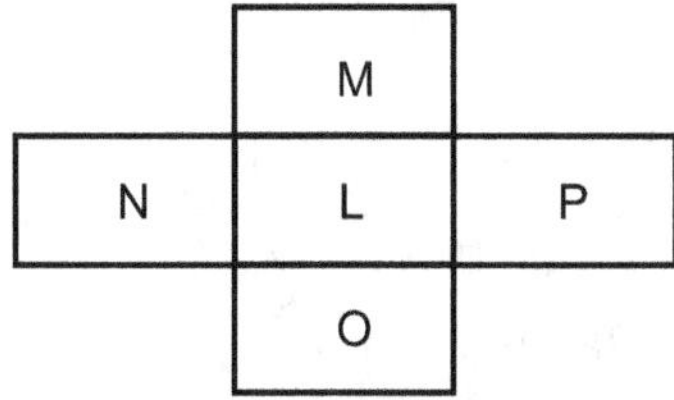

Fig. 5.24

Example 5.18 : A hydrostatic step bearing has 115 mm diameter recess concentric with 200 mm diameter of the shaft. The step is to carry a load of 15 kN, while maintaining lubricant film of 0.10 mm. If lubricant viscosity is 105 cP and shaft speed is 720 r.p.m., estimate :

(P.U. Dec. 2006, 8 Marks)

   (i)   Recess pressure

   (ii)   Lubricant flow required

   (iii) Power lost in pumping and

   (iv) Power lost in friction.

Given :

$$R_0 = \frac{200}{2} = 100 \text{ mm}$$

$$R_i = \frac{115}{2} = 57.5 \text{ mm}$$

$$W = 15 \text{ kN} = 15 \times 10^3 \text{ N}$$

$$h_0 = 0.1 \text{ mm}$$

$$\mu = 105 \text{ cP}$$

$$= 105 \times 10^{-9} \text{ N-s/mm}^2$$

$$N = 720 \text{ r.p.m.}$$

To calculate :

(i) $P_i = ?$, (ii) $Q = ?$, (iii) $E_p = ?$ and (iv) $E_F = ?$

Solution :

(i)   Recess pressure :

We know

$$W = \frac{\pi \cdot P_i \cdot (R_0^2 - R_i^2)}{2 \cdot \log_e \left[\dfrac{R_0}{R_i} \right]}$$

$$P_i = \frac{2W \cdot \log_e \left[\dfrac{R_0}{R_i} \right]}{\pi (R_0^2 - R_i^2)}$$

$$= \frac{2 \times 15 \times 10^3 \times \log_e \left[\dfrac{100}{57.5} \right]}{\pi (100^2 - 57.5^2)}$$

$$P_i = 0.78946 \text{ N/mm}^2$$

(ii) Oil flow rate :

$$Q = \frac{\pi \cdot P_i \cdot h_0^3}{6 \cdot \mu \cdot \log_e \left(\dfrac{R_0}{R_i} \right)}$$

$$= \frac{\pi \times 0.78946 \times (0.1)^3}{6 \times 105 \times 10^{-9} \times \log_e \left(\dfrac{100}{57.5} \right)}$$

$$= 7113.9676 \text{ mm}^3/s = 7113.9676 \times 10^{-9} \text{ m}^3/s$$

$$= (7113.9676 \times 10^{-9}) \times 60 \times 10^3 \text{ } l/min$$

$$Q = 0.42684 \text{ } l/min$$

(iii)　Power lost in pumping :

$$E_P = \frac{P_i \cdot Q}{10^6} = \frac{0.78946 \times 7113.9676}{10^6}$$

$$E_P = 0.0056162 \text{ kW}$$

(iv)　Power lost in friction :

$$E_F = \frac{\mu \cdot N^2 (R_0^4 - R_i^4)}{(58.053 \times 10^6) h_0} = \frac{105 \times 10^{-9} \times (720)^2 (100^4 - 57.5^4)}{(58.053 \times 10^6) \times 0.10}$$

$$E_F = 0.83513 \text{ kW}$$

Example 5.19 : Two reservoirs are connected by a slit 150 mm wide, 250 mm long and 0.25 mm thick. The reservoirs are filled with a lubricating oil of viscosity 90 cP. The pressures in the two reservoirs are 8.5 bar and 2.5 bar respectively. If the relative density of the oil is 0.9, evaluate :

(i)　　The average velocity of an oil flow through the slit; and

(ii)　　The flow rate of fluid through the slit.

Solution :

Given : b = 150 mm

　　　　l = 250 mm

　　　　h = 0.25 mm

　　　　μ = 90 cP = 90×10^{-9} N-s/mm^2

　　　　P_1 = 8.5 bar = 8.5×10^5 N/m^2

　　　　P_2 = 2.5 bar = 2.5×10^5 N/m^2

　　　　ρ = 0.9×1000 kg/m^3

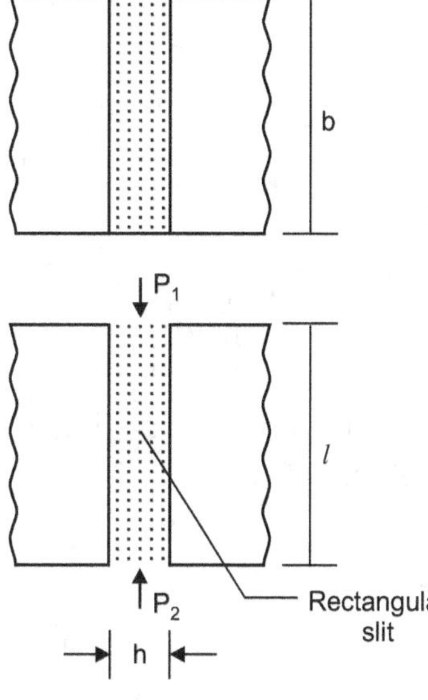

Fig. 5.25

Pressure difference, $\Delta P = P_1 - P_2$

$$= 8.5 \times 10^5 - 2.5 \times 10^5$$

$$= 6 \times 10^5 \text{ N/m}^2 = 6 \times 10^5 \times 10^{-6} \text{ N/mm}^2$$

$$\Delta P = 0.6 \text{ N/mm}^2$$

(i)   The average velocity of an oil through the slit :

$$V_{avg} = \frac{\Delta P \cdot h^2}{12 \cdot \mu \cdot l}$$

$$= \frac{0.6 \times (0.25)^2}{12 \times 90 \times 10^{-9} \times 250}$$

$$V_{avg} = 138.889 \text{ mm/sec.}$$

(ii)   The flow rate of fluid through the slit :

- Volume flow rate of the fluid :

$$Q = \frac{\Delta P \cdot h^3 \cdot b}{12 \cdot \mu \cdot l}$$

$$= \frac{0.6 \times (0.25)^3 \times 150}{12 \times 90 \times 10^{-9} \times 250}$$

$$Q = 5208.33 \text{ mm}^3/\text{s}$$

$$= 5208.33 \times 10^{-9} \text{ m}^3/\text{s}$$

$$= (5208.33 \times 10^{-9}) \times 60 \times 10^3 \text{ } l/\text{min}$$

$$Q = 0.3125 \text{ } l/\text{min}$$

- Mass flow rate of the fluid :

$$m = \rho \cdot Q$$

$$= 800 \times 5208 \times 10^{-9}$$

$$m = 4.1664 \times 10^{-3} \text{ kg/s}$$

Example 5.20 : A low pressure vessel wall is made of two steel plates rolled over each other. A vessel contains a fluid of viscosity 15 cP at 2.2 MPa pressure. A crack of 18 μm is developed between the rolled steel plates. The width of crack is 80 mm. If the length of crack in the direction of possible leakage is 1.5 m, evaluate the leakage of fluid from the pressure vessel in a day.

Solution :

Given : $b = 80$ mm

$$l = 1.5 \text{ m} = 1500 \text{ mm}$$

$$h = 18 \text{ μm} = 0.018 \text{ mm}$$

$$\mu = 15 \text{ cP} = 15 \times 10^{-9} \text{ N-s/mm}^2$$

$$\Delta P = 2 \text{ N/mm}^2$$

The crack acts as a slot of small width.

The leakage rate of fluid :

$$Q = \frac{\Delta P \cdot h^3 \cdot b}{12 \cdot \mu \cdot l}$$

$$= \frac{2 \times (0.018)^3 \times 80}{12 \times 15 \times 10^{-9} \times 1500}$$

$$Q = 3.456 \text{ mm}^3/\text{s}$$

$$= 3.456 \times 10^{-9} \text{ m}^3/\text{s}$$

$$= (3.456 \times 10^{-9}) \times 60 \times 10^3 \text{ }l/\text{min}$$

$$Q = 2.0736 \times 10^{-4} \text{ }l/\text{min}$$

$$\therefore \quad Q = (2.0736 \times 10^{-4}) \times 60 \times 24 \text{ }l/\text{day}$$

$$Q = 0.298598 \text{ }l/\text{day}$$

Example 5.21 : Water leaks through the shaft entry sleeve of the water pump, if the shaft of 30 mm diameter is running concentric in a sleeve having 30.04 bore diameter and 30 mm length. The viscosity of water is 1.2 cP and the pressure inside the casing is 6 bar. Determine the quantity of water leakage in l/min.

Solution :

Given :

$$D_b = 30.04 \text{ mm}$$

$$D = 30 \text{ mm}$$

$$l = 30 \text{ mm}$$

$$\mu = 1.2 \text{ cP} = 1.2 \times 10^{-9} \text{ N-s/mm}^2$$

$$P_i = 6 \text{ bar} = 6 \times 10^5 \text{ N/m}^2 \quad = 6 \times 10^5 \times 10^{-6} \text{ N/mm}^2$$

$$= 0.6 \text{ N/mm}^2$$

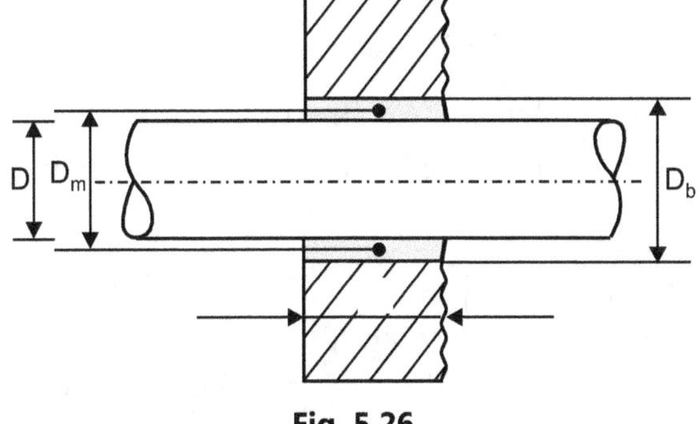

Fig. 5.26

$$\therefore \qquad \Delta P = P_i - P_0$$

$$= 0.6 - 0$$

$$= 0.6 \text{ N/mm}^2$$

Radial clearance from Fig. 5.26,

$$C = \frac{D_b - D}{2}$$

$$\therefore \qquad C = \frac{30.04 - 30}{2}$$

$$= 0.02 \text{ mm}$$

$$\text{Mean diameter, } D_m = \frac{D_b + D}{2}$$

$$= \frac{30.04 + 30}{2}$$

$$= 30.02 \text{ mm}$$

The rate of fluid flow through the slot is given by the following equation,

$$Q = \frac{\Delta P \cdot h^3 \cdot b}{12 \cdot \mu \cdot l}$$

Now, for the annular space between the shaft and sleeve,

$$b = \pi \cdot D_m$$

and $\qquad h = C$

Hence, the above equation for 'Q' becomes,

$$Q = \frac{\Delta P \, (\pi \cdot D_m) \cdot C^3}{12 \cdot \mu \cdot l}$$

$$= \frac{0.6 \times \pi \times 30.02 \times (0.02)^3}{12 \times 1.2 \times 10^{-9} \times 30}$$

$$Q = 1047.8957 \text{ mm}^3/\text{s}$$

$$= 1047.8957 \times 10^{-9} \text{ m}^3/\text{s}$$

$$= (1047.8957 \times 10^{-9}) \times 60 \times 10^3 \text{ } l/\text{min}$$

$$Q = 0.062874 \text{ } l/\text{min}$$

Example 5.22 : A heat exchanger has 500 number of tubes inside it. The outer diameter of single tube is 18 mm, and placed in a 120 mm thick tube plate. After the expansion of tubes in a tube plate, a radial clearance of 0.0015 is left between the tubes and the tube plate. The process fluid which stands on one side of the tube plate has a viscosity of 0.75 cP and a pressure of 1.5 MPa. On the other side of the tube plate, there is a steam at a pressure of 220 kPa. Estimate the loss of process fluid per hour across the tube plate.

Solution :

$$n = 500$$
$$D_o = 18 \text{ mm}$$
$$l = 80 \text{ mm}$$
$$C = 0.0015 \text{ mm}$$
$$\mu = 0.75 \text{ cP} = 0.75 \times 10^{-9} \text{ N-s/mm}^2$$
$$P_1 = 1.5 \text{ MPa} = 1.5 \text{ N/mm}^2$$
$$P_2 = 200 \text{ kPa} = 200 \times 10^{-3} \text{ MPa}$$
$$= 200 \times 10^{-3} \text{ N/mm}^2$$
$$= 0.2$$

Pressure difference on two sides :

$$\Delta P = P_1 - P_2$$
$$= 1.5 - 0.2$$
$$\Delta P = 1.3 \text{ N/mm}^2$$

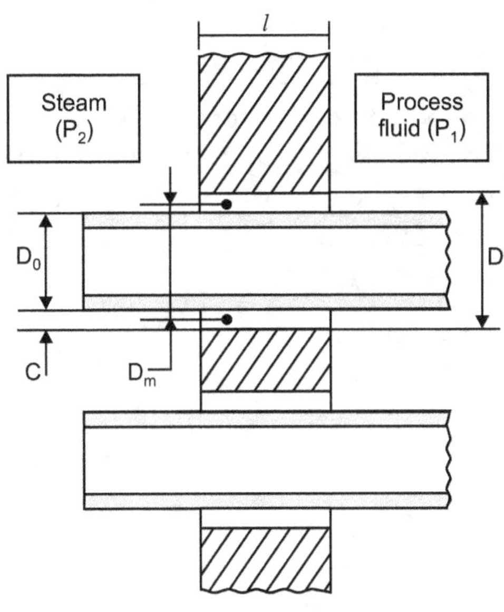

Fig. 5.27

$$D = D_o + 2C$$
$$= 18 + 2 \times 0.0015$$
$$D = 18.003 \text{ mm}$$

$$\text{Mean diameter, } D_m = \frac{D + D_o}{2} = \frac{18.003 + 18}{2} = 18.0015 \text{ mm}$$

The flow rate of fluid through a slot is,

$$Q = \frac{\Delta P \cdot h^3 \cdot b}{12 \cdot \mu \cdot l}$$

For annular space between the tube and plate,

$$b = \pi D_m$$

and

$$h = C$$

Substituting in above equation for 'Q',

$$Q = \frac{\Delta P \cdot C^3 \cdot (\pi \cdot D_m)}{12 \cdot \mu \cdot l}$$

$$= \frac{1.3 \times (0.0015)^3 \times (\pi \times 18.0015)}{12 \times 0.75 \times 10^{-9} \times 80}$$

$$Q = 0.34462 \text{ mm}^3/\text{s}$$

$\therefore$ Total flow rate,

$$Q = n \cdot Q$$

$$= 500 \times 0.34462$$

$$Q = 172.311 \text{ mm}^3/\text{s}$$

Example 5.23 : A cylinder with flat bottom is completely filled with an oil of viscosity 35 cP. Cylinder bore diameter is 90.5 mm and length is 100 mm. A piston of 90 mm diameter and 70 mm length move down concentrically in a cylinder under the load of 220 N. Evaluate the velocity of piston when the flat bottom end of the piston is at a distance of :

(i)   70 mm from the bottom of cylinder.

(ii)   35 mm from the bottom of cylinder.

(iii)   4 mm from the bottom of cylinder.

Solution :

Given :

$$D = 90.5 \text{ mm}$$

$$D_C = 90 \text{ mm}$$

$$l = 100 \text{ mm}$$

$$L = 70 \text{ mm}$$

$$F_P = 220 \text{ N}$$

$$\mu = 35 \text{ cP}$$

$$= 35 \times 10^{-9} \text{ N-s/mm}^2$$

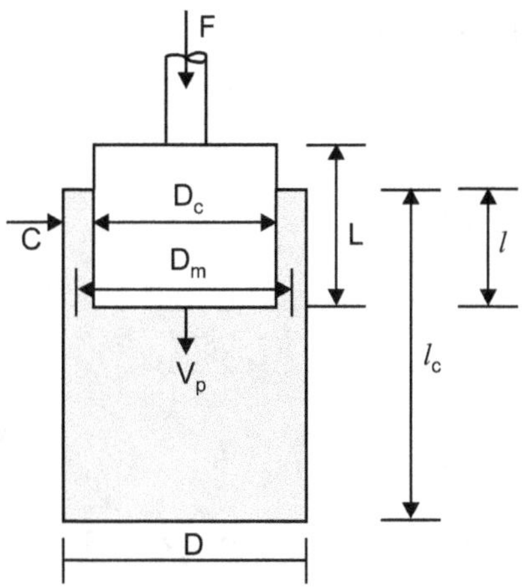

Fig. 5.28

$$\text{Radial clearance, } C = \frac{D - D_C}{2}$$

$$= \frac{90.5 - 90}{2}$$

$$C = 0.25 \text{ mm}$$

Mean diameter :

$$D_m = \frac{D_C + D}{2} = \frac{90.5 + 90}{2}$$

$$= 90.25 \text{ mm}$$

Cross-sectional area of piston :

$$A = \frac{\pi}{4} \cdot D_C^2$$

$$= \frac{\pi}{4} \times (90)^2$$

$$= 6361.725 \text{ mm}^2$$

Velocity of piston :

From equation (5.57),

$$v_p = \frac{\pi \cdot F_P \, D_m \cdot c^3}{12 \cdot \mu \cdot l \cdot A^2} = \frac{\pi \times 220 \times 90.25 \times (0.25)^3}{12 \times 35 \times 10^{-9} \times (l) \times (6361.725)^2}$$

$$v_p = \frac{57.3377}{l} \text{ , mm/s}$$

(i)   When bottom end of piston is at a distance of 70 mm from cylinder bottom :

For this case, length of piston in the fluid is,

$$l_1 = l_c - 70 = 100 - 70$$
$$= 30 \text{ mm}$$

From equation for 'v_p',

$$v_{p_1} = \frac{57.3377}{l_1} = \frac{57.3377}{30}$$

$$v_{p_1} = 1.9113 \text{ mm/s}$$

(ii)   When bottom end of piston is at a distance of 35 mm from cylinder bottom :

For this case, length of piston in the fluid is,

$$l_2 = l_c - 35 = 100 - 35$$
$$l_2 = 65 \text{ mm}$$

For this length, velocity of piston

$$v_{p_2} = \frac{57.3377}{l_2} = \frac{57.3377}{65}$$

$$v_{p_2} = 0.88212 \text{ mm/s}$$

(iii)   When bottom end of piston is at a distance of 4 mm from cylinder bottom :

The length of piston in the fluid is,

$$l_3 = L = 70$$

For this length, velocity of piston

$$v_{p_3} = \frac{57.3377}{70}$$

$$v_{p_3} = 0.81911 \text{ mm/s}$$

Example 5.24 : The following data is given for hydrostatic step bearing :

(P.U. May/June 2007)

Thrust load = 700 kN

Supply pressure = 10 MPa

Shaft speed = 1500 r.p.m.

Oil-film thickness = 0.3 mm

Viscosity of lubricant = 170 SUS

Specific gravity of lubricant = 0.75

Ratio of recess diameter to shaft diameter = 0.8.

Suggest the optimum oil-film thickness, so that the total power loss will be minimum.

Solution :

Given :

$$W = 700 \text{ kN} = 700 \times 10^3 \text{ N}$$

$$P_i = 10 \text{ MPa} = 10 \text{ N/mm}^2$$

$$N = 1500 \text{ r.p.m.}$$

$$h_0 = 0.3 \text{ mm}$$

$$\mu = 170 \text{ SUS}$$

Specific gravity of lubricant $= 0.75$

$\therefore$ Density $(\rho) = 0.75 \times 1000 = 750 \text{ kg/mm}^3$

$$\frac{R_i}{R_0} = 0.8$$

To calculate :

$$h_0 = ? \text{ for minimum total power loss } (E_T)$$

$$W = \frac{\pi \cdot P_i \cdot (R_0^2 - R_i^2)}{2 \cdot \log_e (R_0/R_i)}$$

$$700 \times 10^3 = \frac{\pi \times 10 \times [1 - (0.8)^2] \, R_0^2}{2 \cdot \log_e \left(\dfrac{1}{0.8}\right)}$$

$$\therefore \quad R_0^2 = \frac{700 \times 10^3 \times 2 \cdot \log_e \left(\dfrac{1}{0.8}\right)}{\pi \times 10 \times [1 - (0.8)^2]}$$

$$R_0 = 166.1996 \text{ mm}$$

$$\therefore \quad R_i = 166.1996 \times 0.8$$

$$R_i = 132.9597 \text{ mm}$$

$$\therefore \quad D_o = 332.399 \text{ mm}$$

and $\quad D_1 = 265.92 \text{ mm}$

Absolute viscosity :

$$\mu = \rho \left(0.22 \text{ SUS} - \frac{180}{\text{SUS}}\right) 10^{-6} \text{ N-s/m}^2$$

$$= 750 \left(0.22 \times 170 - \frac{180}{170}\right) 10^{-6}$$

$$= 0.027256 \text{ N-s/m}^2$$

$$= 0.027256 \times 10^{-6} \text{ N-s/mm}^2$$

$$\mu = 27.256 \times 10^{-9} \text{ N-s/mm}^2$$

∴   **Frictional Power Loss (E_F) :**

$$E_F = \frac{\mu \cdot N^2 \, (R_0^4 - R_i^4)}{(58.053 \times 10^6) \, h_0}$$

$$= \frac{27.256 \times 10^{-9} \times (1500)^2 \, (166.1996^4 - 132.9597^4)}{(58.053 \times 10^6) \, h_0}$$

$$E_F = \frac{0.475867}{h_0} \text{ kW}$$

Pumping Power Loss (E_P) :

$$E_P = \frac{P_i \cdot Q}{10^6}$$

$$= \frac{P_i}{10^6} \left[\frac{\pi \cdot P_i \cdot h_0^3}{6 \cdot \mu \cdot \log_e \left(\dfrac{R_0}{R_i} \right)} \right]$$

$$= \frac{10}{10^6} \left[\frac{\pi \times 10 \times h_0^3}{6 \times 27.256 \times 10^{-9} \times \log_e \left(\dfrac{1}{0.8} \right)} \right]$$

$$E_P = 8608.989 \, h_0^3 \text{ kW}$$

Total Power Loss (E_T) :

∴

$$E_T = E_F + E_P$$

$$E_T = \frac{0.475867}{h_0} + 8608.989 \, h_0^3$$

Optimum oil-film thickness for minimum total power loss (h_0) :

To obtain optimum oil-film thickness, differentiate total power loss (in terms of h_0) with respect to h_0 and equate it to zero.

∴

$$\frac{d(E_T)}{d(h_0)} = 0$$

∴

$$\frac{d}{dh_0} \left[\frac{0.475867}{h_0} + 8608.989 \, h_0^3 \right] = 0$$

∴

$$25826.967 \, h_0^2 - \frac{0.475867}{h_0^2} = 0$$

$$\therefore \qquad 25826.967\, h_0^2 = \frac{0.475867}{h_0^2}$$

$$\therefore \qquad h_0^4 = \frac{0.475867}{25826.967}$$

$$h_0 = 0.065517 \text{ mm}$$

Example 5.25 : The following data is given for hydrostatic step bearing :

(P.U. Nov./Dec. 2007)

$$\text{Thrust load} = 600 \text{ kN}$$
$$\text{Supply pressure} = 8 \text{ MPa}$$
$$\text{Shaft speed} = 1200 \text{ r.p.m.}$$
$$\text{Oil-film thickness} = 0.2 \text{ mm}$$
$$\text{Viscosity of lubricant} = 170 \text{ SUS}$$
$$\text{Specific gravity of lubricant} = 0.84$$

Ratio of recess diameter to shaft diameter = 0.7

Suggest the optimum oil-film thickness, so that the total power loss is minimum.

Solution :

  Given :

$$W = 600 \text{ kN} = 600 \times 10^3 \text{ N}$$
$$P_i = 8 \text{ MPa} = 8 \text{ N/mm}^2$$
$$N = 1200 \text{ rpm}$$
$$h_0 = 0.2 \text{ mm}$$
$$\mu = 170 \text{ SUS}$$
$$\text{Specific gravity} = 0.84$$

$$\therefore \qquad \rho = 0.84 \times 1000 = 840 \text{ kg/mm}^3$$

$$\frac{R_i}{R_0} = 0.7$$

To calculate :

$$h_0 = ? \text{ for minimum total power loss } (E_T)$$

$$W = \frac{\pi \cdot P_i \,(R_0^2 - R_i^2)}{2 \cdot \log_e (R_0/R_i)}$$

$$600 \times 10^3 = \frac{\pi \times 8 \times [1 - (0.7)^2]\, R_0^2}{2 \cdot \log_e \left(\dfrac{1}{0.7}\right)}$$

$$R_0^2 = \frac{600 \times 10^3 \times 2 \times \log_e (1/0.7)}{\pi \times 8 \times (1 - (0.7)^2)}$$

$$R_0 = 182.735 \text{ mm} \Rightarrow D_0 = 365.47 \text{ mm}$$

$$\therefore \qquad R_i = 182.735 \times 0.7$$

$$R_i = 127.9145 \text{ mm} \Rightarrow D_i = 255.829 \text{ mm}$$

Absolute Viscosity :

$$\mu = \rho \left(0.22 \, SUS - \frac{180}{SUS} \right) 10^{-6} \ \text{N-s/m}^2$$

$$= 840 \left(0.22 \times 170 - \frac{180}{170} \right) 10^{-6}$$

$$= 0.030527 \ \text{N-s/m}^2 = 0.030527 \times 10^{-6} \ \text{N-s/mm}^2$$

$$= 30.527 \times 10^{-9} \ \text{N-s/mm}^2$$

Frictional Power Loss (E_F) :

$$E_F = \frac{\mu \cdot N^2 \, (R_0^4 - R_i^4)}{(58.053 \times 10^6) \, h_0}$$

$$= \frac{30.527 \times 10^{-9} \times (1200)^2 \, (182.735^4 - 127.9145^4)}{58.053 \times 10^6 \cdot h_0}$$

$$E_F = \frac{0.6416}{h_0} \ \text{kW}$$

Pumping Power Loss (E_P) :

$$E_P = \frac{P_i \cdot Q}{10^6} = \frac{P_i}{10^6} \left[\frac{\pi \cdot P_i \cdot h_0^3}{6 \cdot \mu \cdot \log_e \left(\frac{R_0}{R_i} \right)} \right]$$

$$= \frac{8}{10^6} \left[\frac{\pi \times 8 \times h_0^3}{6 \times 30.527 \times 10^{-9} \times \log_e (1/0.7)} \right]$$

$$E_P = 3077.669 \cdot h_0^3 \ \text{kW}$$

Total Power Loss (E_T) :

$$E_T = E_F + E_P \qquad E_T = \frac{0.6416}{h_0} + 3077.669 \, h_0^3$$

Optimum oil-film thickness for minimum total power loss (h_0) :

To obtain optimum oil-film thickness, differentiate total power loss (in terms of h_0) with respect to h_0 and equate it to zero.

$$\therefore \qquad \frac{d \, (E_T)}{d \, (h_0)} = 0$$

$$\frac{d}{d \, h_0} \left[\frac{0.6416}{h_0} + 3077.669 \, h_0^3 \right] = 0$$

$$9233.01 \, h_0^2 - \frac{0.6416}{h_0^2} = 0$$

$$\therefore \qquad 9233.01 \, h_0^2 = \frac{0.6416}{h_0^2}$$

$$\therefore \qquad h_0^4 = 6.948983 \times 10^{-5}$$

$$\therefore \qquad h_0 = 0.0913 \ \text{mm}$$

Example 5.26 : Determine the mass flow rate of fluid through the slot where two reservoirs are connected by a slot having size 300 mm × 200 mm × 0.3 mm. The reservoirs are filled with an oil of viscosity 105 cP and the pressures in the two reservoirs are 10 bar and 3 bar respectively and the relative density of oil is 0.8.   **(P.U. Nov./Dec. 2008)**

Given :

$$b = 200 \text{ mm}$$
$$l = 300 \text{ mm}$$
$$h = 0.3 \text{ mm}$$
$$\mu = 105 \text{ cP} = 105 \times 10^{-9} \text{ N-s/mm}^2$$
$$P_1 = 10 \text{ bar} = 10 \times 10^5 \text{ N/m}^2$$
$$P_2 = 3 \text{ bar} = 3 \times 10^5 \text{ N/m}^2$$
$$\rho = 0.8 \times 1000 \text{ kg/m}^3$$

Solution :

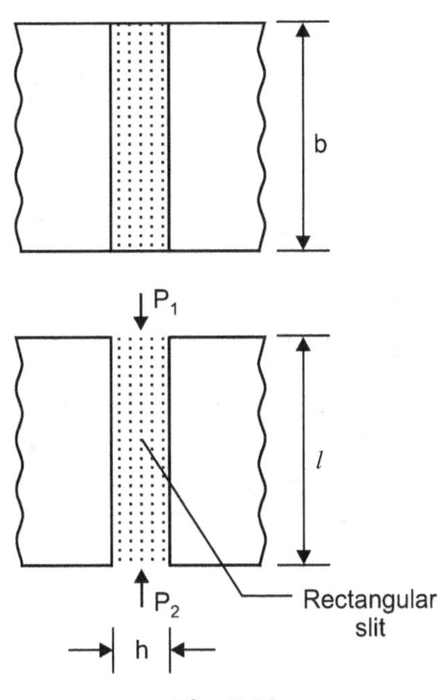

Fig. 5.29

Pressure difference,

$$\Delta P = P_1 - P_2$$
$$= 10 \times 10^5 - 3 \times 10^5$$
$$= 7 \times 10^5 \text{ N/m}^2$$
$$= 7 \times 10^5 \times 10^{-6} \text{ N/mm}^2$$
$$\Delta P = 0.7 \text{ N/mm}^2$$

- The volume flow rate of fluid through slit,

$$Q = \frac{\Delta P \cdot h^3 \cdot b}{12 \cdot \mu \cdot l}$$

$$= \frac{0.7 \times (0.3)^3 \times 200}{12 \times 105 \times 10^{-9} \times 300} = \frac{3.78}{3.78 \times 10^{-4}}$$

$$Q = 10000 \ mm^3/s$$

$\therefore$ The mass flow rate of fluid through slit

$$m = \rho \cdot Q$$

$$= (0.8 \times 1000) \times \text{Volume flow rate in } m^3/s$$

$\therefore$ **Q in l/min :**

$$Q = 10000 \ mm^3/s$$

$$= 10000 \times 10^{-9} \ m^3/s$$

$$= (10000 \times 10^{-9}) \times 60 \times 10^3 \ l/min$$

$$Q = 0.6 \ l/min$$

Substituting in equation for 'm',

$$m = \rho \cdot Q$$

$$= 800 \times 10000 \times 10^{-9}$$

$$m = 8 \times 10^{-3} \ kg/s$$

Example 5.27 : Determine the mass flow rate of fluid through the slot where two reservoirs are connected by a slot having size 290 mm × 190 mm × 0.29 mm. The reservoirs are filled with an oil of viscosity 100 cP and the pressures in the two reservoirs are 10 bar and 3 bar respectively and the relative density of the oil is 0.8. **[P.U. June 2009, 6 Marks]**

Solution :

Given ;

$$b = 190 \ mm$$

$$l = 290 \ mm$$

$$h = 0.29 \ mm$$

$$\mu = 100 \ cP = 100 \times 10^{-9} \ N\text{-}s/mm^2$$

$$P_1 = 10 \ bar; \quad P_2 = 3 \ bar$$

$$\rho = 0.8 \times 1000 \ kg/m^3$$

Pressure difference

$$\Delta P = P_1 - P_2$$

$$= 10 \times 10^5 - 3 \times 10^5$$

$$= 7 \times 10^5 \text{ N/m}^2$$
$$= 7 \times 10^5 \times 10^{-6} \text{ N/mm}^2$$
$$\Delta P = 0.7 \text{ N/mm}^2$$

The volume flow rate of fluid through slit,

$$Q = \frac{\Delta P \, h^3 \cdot b}{12 \, \mu \cdot l}$$

$$= \frac{0.7 \times (0.29)^3 \times 190}{12 \times 100 \times 10^{-9} \times 290}$$

$$Q = 9300 \text{ mm}^3/s$$

The mass flow rate of fluid through slit,

$$m = \rho \cdot Q$$
$$= (0.8 \times 1000) \times \text{Volume flow rate in m}^3/s$$

$\therefore$ Q in l/min

$$Q = 9300 \text{ mm}^3/s$$
$$= 9300 \times 10^{-9} \text{ m}^3/s$$
$$= (9300 \times 10^{-9}) \times 60 \times 10^3 \, l/\text{min}$$

$\therefore$ $$Q = 0.558 \, l/\text{min}$$

Using in equation for 'm',

$$m = \rho \cdot Q$$
$$= (0.8 \times 1000) \times 9300 \times 10^{-9}$$

$\therefore$ $$m = 7.44 \times 10^{-3} \text{ kg/s}.$$

EXERCISE

1. Explain principle of operation of hydrostatic bearing.   **[P.U. June 2009, 4 Marks]**
2. Draw a neat sketch of hydrostatic thrust bearing showing all the accessories required. What is restrictor or compensator ?   **[P.U. June 2011, 5 Marks]**
3. Discuss constructional features of hydrostatic bearing system.
4. Explain in brief the various arrangements of hydrostatic lubrication systems.
   [P.U. Dec. 2009, 6 Marks]
5. State applications of hydrostatic bearings.
   [P.U. May 2010, 2 Marks; Dec. 2010, 2 Marks]
6. State advantages and limitations of hydrostatic bearings.
   [P.U. Dec. 2010, 6 Marks]
7. Derive expression for flow rate through rectangular slot. What are assumptions made while deriving the equation ?
   [P.U. Dec. 2010, 8 Marks; May 2010, 8 Marks]
8. Derive an equation for volume flow rate of fluid through rectangular slot for Hale's Telescope.
9. Explain principle of working of hydrostatic step bearing and state assumptions made for the analysis of the hydrostatic step bearing.

10. Derive an expression for oil flow rate and pressure distribution over an annular ring of hydrostatic step bearing.

11. Derive an expression for load-carrying capacity and oil flow rate for hydrostatic step bearing. State the assumptions made. **[P.U. Dec. 2009, 8 Marks]**

12. Derive an expression for load-carrying capacity for circular step bearing in terms of supply pressure from fundamental equation of viscous flow and hence determine   load-carrying capacity for following data :
    (i)   Shaft diameter = 500 mm
    (ii)   Recess diameter = 300 mm
    (iii) Supply pressure = 6 MPa **[P.U. June 2009, 16 Marks; June 2011, 18 Marks]**

13. State dimensionless form of oil flow rate and load-carrying capacity for hydrostatic step bearing. And plot the variation of these dimensionless parameters with the ratio of the outer land (R_0) to inner land (R_i) i.e. $\left(\dfrac{R_0}{R_i}\right)$.

14. Discuss different types of energy losses in hydrostatic bearings.
    [P.U. June 2009, 6 Marks]

15. Derive an equation for viscous power loss and pumping power loss in case of hydrostatic step bearing.

16. Show that in case of energy losses for hydrostatic thrust bearings,
    (i)   Frictional power loss is inversely proportional to the oil-film thickness.
    (ii)   Pumping power loss is directly proportional to the cube of the oil-film thickness.

17. State different parameters to be optimized in case of hydrostatic thrust bearing.

18. Show that ratio of inner land to outer land of circular hydrostatic thrust bearing i.e. $\dfrac{R_i}{R_0}$ is equal to 0.5; for minimum pumping losses.

19. Show that in case of hydrostatic step bearing with shaft rotating at exceptionally low speed, for a given load carrying capacity and a shaft diameter the power loss is minimum when; Recess diameter = 0.53 × Shaft diameter.
    [P.U. Dec. 2010, 8 Marks]

20. Derive an equation for –

    (i)   Dimensionless number (k_p) for recess pressure for various $\left(\dfrac{R_0}{R_i}\right)$ ratio.

    (ii)   Dimensionless number (k_q) for flow rate for various $\left(\dfrac{R_0}{R_i}\right)$ ratio.

    (iii) Dimensionless number (k_r) for pumping power.

21. What do you mean by 'optimum design of hydrostatic step bearing' ? For given fixed outside diameter of the shaft and neglecting frictional power loss, show that the condition for minimum power loss is,

$$ln\left(\frac{R_0}{R_i}\right) = \frac{1}{4}\left[\frac{R_0^2}{R_i^2} - 1\right]$$

[P.U. June 2011, 6 Marks]

22. Define optimum oil-film thickness and derive an equation for the same.

23. Derive $$h_0 = \left[\frac{x_1}{3x_2}\right]^{1/4}$$

[P.U. Dec. 2008, 6 Marks; Dec. 2009, 8 Marks]

where, h_0 = Optimum oil-film thickness for minimum total power loss. Plot the variation of power loss against oil-film thickness.

24. Derive an equation for stiffness of hydrostatic thrust bearing

i.e. $$S = -\frac{3W}{h_0}$$

where, S = Stiffness

      W = Load on bearing

      h_0 = Oil-film thickness

25. Derive an expression for flow of fluid through annular area between piston and cylinder and velocity of piston. **[P.U. May 2010, 6 Marks]**

26. Show that for circular step bearing the load-carrying capacity is,

$$W = \frac{\pi P_i}{2}\left[\frac{R_0^2 - R_i^2}{\log_e\left(\frac{R_0}{R_i}\right)}\right]$$

Notations have usual meanings. **[P.U. Dec. 2008, 12 Marks]**

EXAMPLES FOR PRACTICE

1. The following data refers to a hydrostatic thrust bearing :
   (i)   Shaft diameter = 400 mm,   (ii)   Recess diameter = 250 mm
   (iii) Shaft speed = 720 r.p.m.,   (iv) Supply pressure = 5 N/mm²
   (v)   Film thickness = 0.15 mm,   (vi) Viscosity of lubricant = 30 cP
   (vii) Specific heat of lubricant = 1.76 kJ/kg °C
   (viii) Specific gravity of lubricant = 0.86
   Calculate :
   (i)   Load-carrying capacity of the bearing   (ii)   Oil flow rate
   (iii) Total power loss   (iv) Temperature rise
   Assume that total power loss in the bearing is converted into frictional heat.
   [Ans. : (i)   W = 407.3181 kN,   (ii)   Q = 37.598419 *l*/min

  (iii) E_T = 5.5552073 kW,   (iv) ΔT = 5.85707°C]

2. The following data is given for hydrostatic step bearing :
 (i) Shaft diameter = 400 mm (ii) Recess diameter = 250 mm
 (iii) Supply pressure = 6 MPa (iv) Shaft speed = 750 r.p.m.
 (v) Oil-film thickness = 0.1 mm (vi) Viscosity of the oil = 30 cP
 Determine :
 (i) Load-carrying capacity (ii) Power lost in friction
 (iii) Heat generated at the bearing
 [**Ans. :** (i) W = 488781.251 N, (ii) E_F = 3.94107 kW
   (iii) H_g = 3.94107 kW]

3. The following data is given for a hydrostatic step bearing :
 (i) Shaft diameter = 480 mm (ii) Recess diameter = 240 mm
 (iii) Shaft speed = 700 r.p.m. (iv) Thrust load = 400 kN
 (v) Oil-film thickness = 0.15 mm (vi) Viscosity of the oil = 160 SUS
 (vii) Specific heat of lubricant = 1.76 kJ/kg °C
 (viii) Specific gravity of lubricant = 0.86
 Calculate :
 (i) Supply pressure (ii) Oil flow requirement in l/min
 (iii) Frictional power loss (iv) Pumping power loss, and
 (v) Temperature rise.
 Assume that the total power loss is converted into frictional heat.
 [**Ans. :** (i) P_i = 4.08581 N/mm^2, (ii) Q = 21.3272 l/min,
   (iii) E_F = 5.12906 kW, (iv) E_P = 1.452527 kW
   (v) ΔT = 12.2287°C]

4. Following data refers to a hydrostatic step bearing : **[P.U. Dec. 2009, 10 Marks]**
 (i) Shaft diameter = 400 mm (ii) Recess diameter = 250 mm
 (iii) Shaft speed = 750 r.p.m. (iv) Thrust load = 450 kN
 (v) Viscosity of the oil = 30 cP (vi) Specific gravity of oil = 0.86
 (vii) Specific heat of the oil = 2 kJ/kg °C
 Calculate :
 (i) Supply pressure
 (ii) Frictional power loss
 (iii) Pumping power loss
 (iv) Optimum oil-film thickness for minimum total power loss.
 (v) Oil flow rate in l/min
 (vi) Temperature rise.

 [**Ans. :** (i) P_i = 5.52421 N/mm^2, (ii) $E_F = \dfrac{0.394106}{h_0}$ kW

   (iii) E_P = 1133.143 h_0^3 kW, (iv) h_0 = 0.103761 mm

(v)   Q = 13.7462 l/min,   (vi) ΔT = 12.8532°C]

5.   Following data is given for hydrostatic thrust bearing :

(i)   Thrust load = 850 kN,   (ii)   Shaft speed = 900 r.p.m.

(iii) Shaft diameter = 450 mm,   (iv)   Recess diameter = 250 mm

(v)   Viscosity of lubricant = 30 cP

Calculate optimum film thickness for minimum power loss. Show the variation of energy losses against film thickness graphically. Also calculate total power loss.

[**Ans. :** h_0 = 0.10717 mm, E_T = 12.0749 kW]

6.   A hydrostatic thrust bearing consists of four pads with four oil pockets of size (150 × 150) as shown in Fig. 5.30. The thrust load is 500 kN and the oil-film thickness is 0.15 mm. The viscosity of lubricant is 250 cP. The pressure in area 'X' (i.e. 400 mm × 400 mm), boardering the pockets can be assumed to be uniform and is equal to the supply pressure. The pressure distribution in the area 'Y' (i.e. shaded area) is assumed to be linear, varying from supply pressure at the inner edge to the atmospheric pressure at the outer edge. It can be assumed that area 'Y' is straightened out and has length equal to the mean length shown by dotted line.

Calculate :

(i)   Supply pressure and   (ii)   Oil flow rate in l/min.

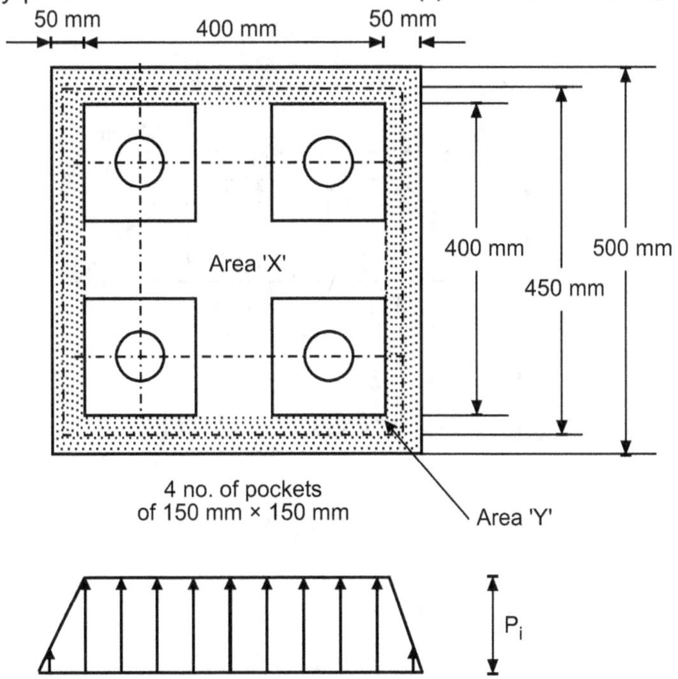

Fig. 5.30

[**Ans. :** (i) P_i = 2.44103 N/mm^2,

    (ii)   Q = 5.93214 l/min]

7.   The hydrostatic thrust bearing with a rectangular oil groove 'P' of size (100 mm × 50 mm) is shown in Fig. 5.31. The thrust load on the bearing is 100 kN and the oil-film thickness is 0.02 mm. The viscosity of the lubricant is 300 cP. The pressure distribution can be assumed to be linear, varying from supply pressure at the inner edge to atmospheric pressure at the outer edge. Neglecting the flow over the corners, calculate

(i)   Supply pressure and

(ii)   Oil flow rate in l/min.

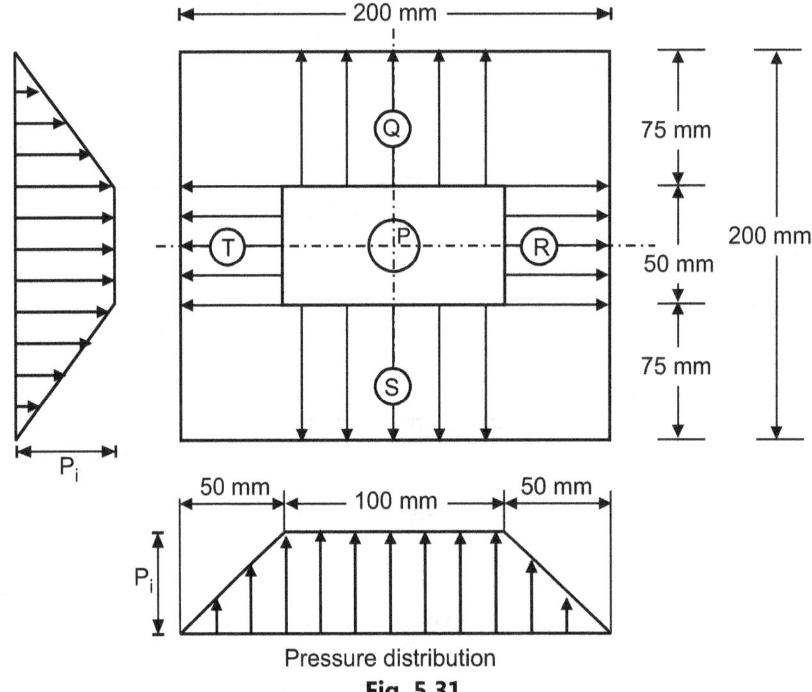

Fig. 5.31

[**Ans. :**   (i) P_i = 6.66713 N/mm^2

    (ii)   Q = 4.14853 × 10^{-3} l/min]

✠ ✠ ✠

Chapter 6

HYDROSTATIC SQUEEZE FILM LUBRICATION

6.1 INTRODUCTION TO HYDROSTATIC SQUEEZE-FILM BEARINGS

Hydrostatic bearings are used where there is very small or no relative tangential velocity, but due to external loading which may be transient or periodic, the relative normal or squeeze velocity may be prominent. And an oil film is maintained between the contacting surfaces even though the relative motion of these bearing surfaces becomes momentarily zero.

The viscous lubricant cannot be instantaneously squeezed out from between two surfaces that are approaching each other. It takes time for these surfaces to meet and during that interval, due to the resistance of lubricant to extrusion, a pressure is built up and the load is supported actually by the oil film. This phenomenon is called squeeze-film lubrication. It can be observed in many practical situations, some of which are discussed in next section.

6.2 PRACTICAL SITUATIONS OF HYDROSTATIC SQUEEZE-FILM LUBRICATION

Squeeze-film action plays an important role in large number of applications such as,

1.   Clutch in Automotive Transmission :

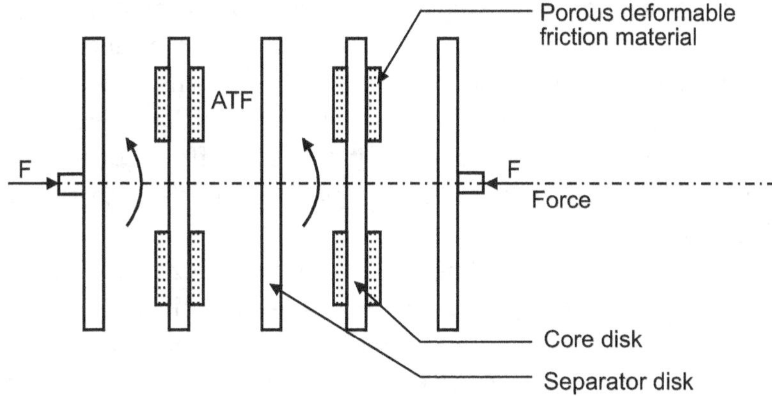

Fig. 6.1 : Clutch in automotive transmission

Main function of clutch pak in automotive transmission is the smooth engagement and disengagement of shafts transmitting motion. There are set of separator discs and friction discs. Automotive Transmission Fluid (ATF) serves as the squeeze-film fluid. During engagement of a set of separator discs and friction discs, ATF is squeezed between the clearance space as the discs approach each other and then lock for full speed operation.

Thus, squeeze-film lubrication takes place due to presence of lubricant on the faces, thereby delaying the physical contact between the active surfaces.

2.   Engine Piston-Pin Bearing :

In engine piston-pin bearing, squeeze-film action of oil can be observed. The squeeze film effect in this case is also called 'cushioning effect'. Thus, cushioning by squeeze film action of the engine oil occurs during power stroke, which provides an oil film despite lack of significant relative velocity usually needed to avoid metal to metal contact.

3.   Piston Rings :

During operation of an I.C. engine, both sliding and squeeze-film components exist. At the top and bottom of the stroke in an engine, ring sliding velocity drops to zero and squeeze film action provides the needed cushioning.

4.   Damper Film for Jet Engine Ball Bearing :

It is also called the squeeze-film vibration absorber. In this case, the bearing supports are completely isolated from the engine support structure by squeeze-film annulus, which absorbs the vibrations to some extent.

Since ball bearings have almost no damping capacity, an annular lubricant film enveloping the fixed outer bearing ring provides damping by squeeze-film action to minimize rotor vibration. The design criteria of this squeeze-film damper is the transmissibility ratio.

5.   Peeling of a Flexible Tape :

The hydrodynamics of peeling a flexible strip from a surface attached by a layer of viscous fluids e.g. adhesives involve negative squeeze analysis in the presence of surface tension.

6.   Mechanism of Walking on Wet or Icy Pavement :

Squeeze film effect is seen in the mechanism of walking on wet or icy pavements with rubber soles e.g. Hydroplaning : i.e. Rolling mechanism of an automobile tyre on a wet road, it is associated with no relative sliding motion of tyre, water film and road surface in the contact area, due to squeeze-film behaviour. Due to this, traction is lost and steering and braking are no longer possible. This phenomenon is called hydroplaning. In landing of airplane during rainstorm, due to hydroplaning, it may skid off the runaway. Also, in case of automobiles, on wet road, it skids out on curves, driver can neither accelerates nor brake.

7.   Human Knee Joint :

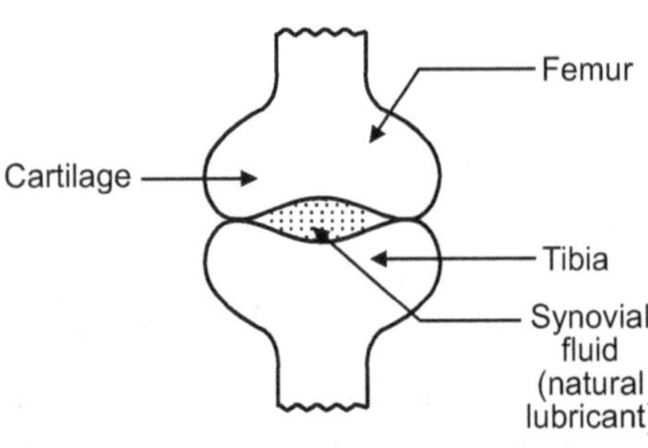

Fig. 6.2 : Human knee joint

Phenomenon of squeeze-film lubrication can be obtained in skeletal joints of man and animals, where relative sliding motion is limited but under dynamic walking or running conditions squeeze-film behaviour contributes to the low friction of the bearing joint. Impact between the femur and tibia in the configuration of Fig. 6.2 is cushioned by the body's natural lubricant called 'synovial fluid' during aerobic exercises.

6.3 ANALYSIS OF HYDROSTATIC SQUEEZE-FILM BEARING

Analysis of hydrostatic squeeze-film bearing can be explained by considering the following two cases :

- Circular plate approaching a plane and
- Rectangular plate approaching a plane.

6.3.1 Circular Plate Approaching a Plane

Squeeze-film effect can be analysed for the two circular flat plates approaching each other or a single circular flat plate approaching a plane. The basic theory of hydrostatic lubrication allows for predicting the action of bearings when there is no relative sliding motion.

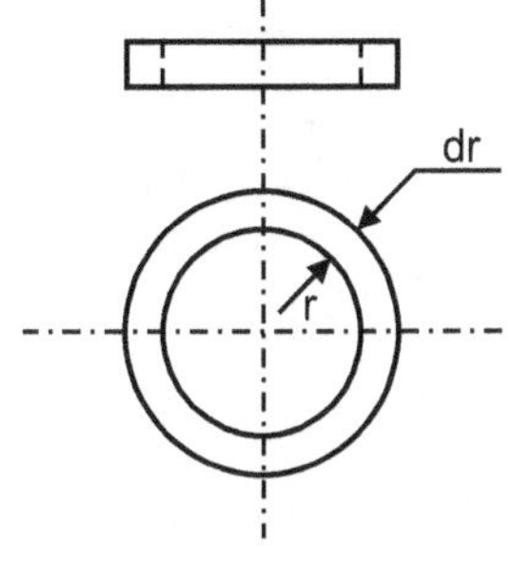

Let, R – The radius of circular plate

r – The radius of elementary circular slot

dr – The depth of slot in the direction of flow

h – The thickness of slot

$\therefore$ Width of slot is given by,

$$b = 2\pi r$$

Fig. 6.3

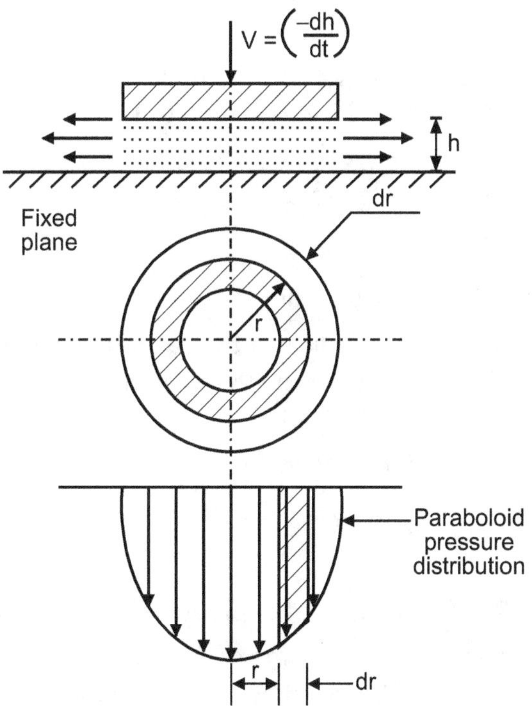

Fig. 6.4 : Circular plate approaching a plane

Consider a circular plate approaching a large plane surface as shown in Fig. 6.3. The clearance space between the plate and the surface is filled with a viscous liquid. Due to squeezing action caused by the relative motion between the plate and the surface, the liquid is displaced radially outward causing an outward flow. Imagine an elementary circular slot through which the liquid is being forced out radially.

For hydrostatic lubrication, we know the equation for the flow of an incompressible viscous fluid through a finite slot.

$$q \;=\; \frac{\Delta P \cdot h^3 \cdot b}{12\,\mu \cdot l} \qquad\qquad \text{... (6.1)}$$

where,

$$\Delta P \;=\; \text{The pressure difference (N/mm}^2\text{)}$$
$$h^3 \;=\; \text{The thickness of finite slot (mm)}$$
$$b \;=\; \text{Width of slot (mm)}$$
$$\mu \;=\; \text{Viscosity of lubricant (N-s/mm}^2\text{)}$$
$$l \;=\; \text{Length of slot (mm)}$$

Now, for differential slot,

$$\frac{\Delta P}{l} \;=\; -\frac{dP}{dr} \quad \text{... (for circular slot)}$$

and

$$b \;=\; 2\pi r$$

Substituting values for width 'b' and $\left(\dfrac{\Delta P}{l}\right)$ in equation (6.1),

$$\therefore \qquad q \;=\; \left(-\frac{dP}{dr}\right) \cdot \frac{h^3 \cdot 2\pi r}{12 \cdot \mu}$$

$$q \;=\; -\frac{\pi r \cdot h^3}{6\mu} \cdot \frac{dP}{dr}$$

Negative sign of the above equation indicates that as radius increases, pressure decreases and the volume of fluid has been displaced by the imaginary plate of radius r, as it moves to the lower plane.

$$q_r \;=\; \text{Area} \times \text{Velocity}$$

$$\;=\; (\pi r^2) \cdot v$$

where,

$$v \;-\; \text{Relative velocity of approach of plane in m/s}$$

$$\begin{bmatrix} \text{The volume of fluid being} \\ \text{forced out through the} \\ \text{differential slot} \end{bmatrix} = \begin{bmatrix} \text{The volume of fluid being} \\ \text{displaced by the imaginary} \\ \text{plate of radius r} \end{bmatrix}$$

$$q = q_r$$

$$\therefore \quad -\frac{\pi r \cdot h^3}{6\,\mu} \cdot \frac{dP}{dr} = (\pi r^2)\, v$$

$$\therefore \quad dP = -\frac{6\,\mu \cdot r \cdot v}{h^3} \cdot dr$$

where, v — the relative velocity of approach of plate in m/s

Integrating above equation to get pressure,

$$\therefore \quad \int dP = -\frac{6\,\mu \cdot v}{h^3} \int r \cdot dr$$

$$P = -\frac{6 \cdot \mu \cdot v}{h^3}\, \frac{r^2}{2} + A$$

$$P = -\frac{3\,\mu \cdot v \cdot r^2}{h^3} + A \qquad \ldots (6.2)$$

where, A is constant of integration and can be evaluated by using boundary conditions.

At $r = R$, $P = 0$

$$\therefore \quad P \text{ becomes,}$$

$$0 = -\frac{3\,\mu \cdot v \cdot R^2}{h^3} + A$$

$$\therefore \quad A = \frac{3\,\mu \cdot v\, R^2}{h^3} \qquad \ldots (6.3)$$

Substituting value of constant A in equation (6.2),

$$\therefore \quad P = -\frac{3\,\mu \cdot v\, R^2}{h^3} + \frac{3\,\mu \cdot v \cdot R^2}{h^3}$$

$$P = \frac{3\,\mu \cdot v}{h^3}\,[R^2 - r^2] \qquad \ldots (6.4)$$

Above equation shows that the pressure distribution is parabolic and an entire surface it is of paraboloid nature.

Condition of Maximum Pressure :

Maximum pressure occurs at $r = 0$, i.e. at centre.

$$\therefore \quad \text{Using this condition,}$$

$P = P_{max}$ at $r = 0$.

$$\therefore \quad P_{max} = \frac{3\,\mu \cdot v}{h^3}\,[R^2 - 0]$$

$$\therefore \qquad P_{max} = \frac{3\,\mu \cdot v \cdot R^2}{h^3} \qquad \qquad \ldots (6.5)$$

Average Pressure over the Entire Circular Plate :

It is equal to one half of the maximum pressure, for a paraboloid, the average pressure,

$$P_{avg} = \frac{1}{2}\,P_{max}$$

$$P_{avg} = \frac{1}{2}\left(\frac{3\,\mu \cdot v \cdot R^2}{h^3}\right) \qquad \qquad \ldots (6.6)$$

Load-Carrying Capacity :

It is the product of the area and the average pressure,

i.e.
$$W = (A)\,(P_{avg})$$

$$W = (\pi R^2)\,(P_{avg})$$

$$W = \pi R^2 \cdot \left(\frac{3\,\mu \cdot v \cdot R^2}{2h^3}\right)$$

$$W = \frac{3\,\pi \cdot \mu \cdot v \cdot R^4}{h^3} \qquad \qquad \ldots (6.7)$$

where,

W –   Load carrying capacity (N)

μ –   Viscosity of lubricant (N-s/mm^2)

v –   Relative velocity of approach of plate (m/s)

h –   Film thickness (mm)

R –   Outer radius of circular plate (mm)

This equation can be used to find load-carrying capacity for given instantaneous velocity of approach and film thickness. Also, the opposite condition can be analyzed where the load is constant.

Conclusions :

- The resisting force increases rapidly as film thickness decreases, it would be almost impossible to maintain a constant approach velocity.

- The fluid becomes more viscous at higher pressures which can prevent a uniform approach velocity.

- Also, an increase in viscosity of lubricant would result in corresponding increase in resisting force between the approaching plate and the surface.

Time Required to Squeeze the Film :

The time that will be elapsed for an oil film to be reduced to some minimum value. The time required to reduce the film thickness can be found out by using the equation given below.

$$W = \frac{3\pi\mu \cdot v R^4}{2h^3}$$

Velocity of Approach :

It can be defined as the rate of change of film thickness with respect to time.

Substituting value for relative velocity of approach of a plate in above equation as,

$$v = -\frac{dh}{dt} \quad \cdots \left(\begin{array}{l} \text{Negative sign indicates} \\ \text{that 'h' decreases with 't'} \end{array} \right)$$

Equation for load becomes,

$$W = -\frac{3}{2} \cdot \frac{\pi\mu \cdot R^4}{h^3} \cdot \frac{dh}{dt}$$

$$dt = -\frac{3}{2} \cdot \frac{\pi\mu \cdot R^4}{W h^3} \cdot dh$$

Now, total time required in seconds for the film thickness to be reduced from an initial value h_1 to some final value h_2 can be calculated by integrating above equation,

$$\int dt = \int -\frac{3}{2} \cdot \frac{\pi\mu \cdot R^4}{W h^3} \cdot dh$$

$$\therefore \quad t = -\frac{3}{2} \frac{\pi\mu \cdot R^4}{W} \int_{h_1}^{h_2} \frac{dh}{h^3}$$

$$t = -\frac{3}{2} \frac{\pi\mu \cdot R^4}{W} \left[-\frac{1}{2h^2} \right]_{h_1}^{h_2}$$

$$t = \frac{3\pi\mu R^4}{4W} \left[\frac{1}{h_2^2} - \frac{1}{h_1^2} \right] \qquad \qquad \text{... (6.8)}$$

where, t = time in seconds for the film thickness to be reduced from h_1 to h_2.

This value will be on safer side because the actual time for approach of the plate towards the surface will be somewhat greater than the theoretical.

6.3.2 Rectangular Plate Approaching a Plane

Consider a rectangular plate approaching a plane as shown in Fig. 6.5, the maximum pressure variation, load-carrying capacity and time of approach can be determined. For analysis, consider an elementary slot through which fluid is being forced by the approach of the plate towards a plane.

Assumptions :

- For the analysis, it is assumed that the ratio of the dimensions of the plate i.e. breadth and length $\left(\dfrac{b}{l}\right)$ is large so that flow will take place only in one direction (i.e. x-direction). In other words, the slide leakage along the y-direction is neglected.

- Flow is assumed to be laminar therefore, the inertia forces are negligible.

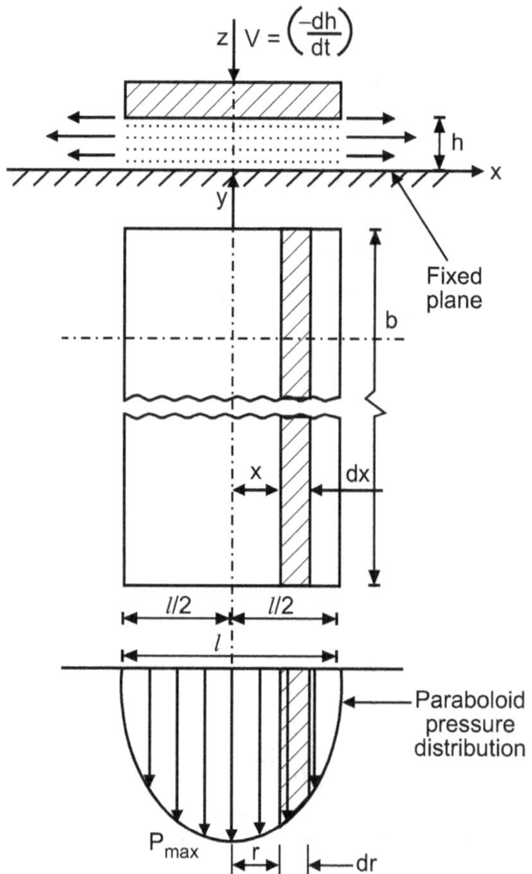

Fig. 6.5 : Rectangular plate approaching a plane

Let,

b = Width of slot along y-direction

l = Length of plate along x-direction

v = Relative velocity of approach = $-\dfrac{dh}{dt}$

x = Distance of an elementary slot from plate centre

dx = Depth of slot in the direction of flow

h = Thickness of slot

We know the equation for the flow of an incompressible viscous fluid through a finite slot.

$$q = \frac{\Delta P \cdot h^3 \cdot b}{12 \cdot \mu \cdot l}$$

where, ΔP = The pressure difference (N/mm²)

h = The thickness of finite slot (mm)

b = Width of the slot (mm)

μ = Viscosity of lubricant (N-s/mm²)

l = Length of slot (mm)

The above equation is modified for the flow through the differential slot where,

$$\frac{\Delta P}{l} = \left(-\frac{dP}{dx}\right)$$

Substituting above relation in the equation for flow, it becomes,

$$q = -\frac{h^3 \cdot b}{12 \cdot \mu} \cdot \frac{dP}{dx}$$

Negative sign shows that as the pressure decreases along the length of plate.

The volume of the fluid being displaced by the rectangular plate of width b and length x is given by,

$$q_x = \text{Area} \times \text{Velocity}$$

$$q_x = (b \cdot x) \cdot v$$

$$q_x = b \cdot x \cdot v$$

Now equating,

$$\begin{bmatrix} \text{Flow through the} \\ \text{differential slot} \end{bmatrix} = \begin{bmatrix} \text{The volume of fluid being displaced by} \\ \text{the plate of width b and length x} \end{bmatrix}$$

$\therefore$ $q = q_x$

$\therefore$ $-\dfrac{h^3 b}{12\mu} \cdot \dfrac{dP}{dx} = b \cdot x \cdot v$

$$dP = \frac{12\mu \cdot x \cdot v}{-h^3} \cdot dx$$

Integrating above equation,

$$\int dP = \int \frac{12\mu \cdot x \cdot v}{-h^3} \cdot dx$$

$$P = -\frac{12\mu \cdot v}{h^3}\left[\int x\, dx\right]$$

$$P = -\frac{12\mu \cdot v}{h^3}\left[\frac{x^2}{2}\right] + C$$

$$P = -\frac{6\mu \cdot v \cdot x^2}{h^3} + C \qquad \ldots (6.9)$$

where, C is constant of integration and can be evaluated using boundary conditions.

$$P = 0 \text{ at } x = \frac{l}{2}$$

Substituting the condition in equation (6.9), we get,

$$0 = -\frac{6\mu\, v\, l^2}{4h^3} + C$$

$$\therefore \qquad C = \frac{6\mu\, v\, l^2}{4h^3}$$

Using the value of constant C in equation for P,

$$P = -\frac{6\mu \cdot v \cdot x^2}{h^3} + \frac{6\mu \cdot v \cdot l^2}{4h^3}$$

$$P = \frac{6\mu \cdot v}{h^3}\left[\frac{l^2}{4} - x^2\right] \qquad \ldots (6.10)$$

This equation is used to calculate pressure at any point along the length of plate, and it shows that pressure distribution is parabolic.

Maximum Pressure :

Maximum pressure occurs at $x = 0$, i.e. at the plate centre line.

Thus, $P = P_{max}$ at $x = 0$.

Using this condition in equation (6.10), it becomes,

$$P_{max} = \frac{6\mu \cdot v}{h^3}\left[\frac{l^2}{4} - 0\right]$$

$$\therefore \qquad P_{max} = \frac{6\mu \cdot v \cdot l^2}{4h^3}$$

$$P_{max} = \frac{3\mu \cdot v \cdot l^2}{2h^3} \qquad \qquad \text{... (6.11)}$$

which is an equation for maximum pressure.

Average Pressure over the Entire Plate :

It can be found by neglecting side leakage. It is equal to two-third of the maximum pressure.

$$\therefore \qquad P_{avg} = \frac{2}{3} \, [\text{Average height of a parabola}]$$

$$= \frac{2}{3} \, [P_{max}]$$

$$= \frac{2}{3} \left[\frac{3\mu \cdot v \cdot l^2}{2h^3} \right]$$

$$\therefore \qquad P_{avg} = \frac{\mu \cdot v \cdot l^2}{h^3} \qquad \qquad \text{... (6.12)}$$

Load-Carrying Capacity :

The instantaneous load-carrying capacity can be determined as the product of the area and the average pressure on plate, and it is given below.

$$W = (\text{Area}) \cdot (\text{Average pressure})$$

$$= (b \cdot l) \cdot \left(\frac{\mu \, v \cdot l^2}{h^3} \right)$$

$$W = \frac{\mu \cdot v \cdot b \cdot l^3}{h^3} \qquad \qquad \text{... (6.13)}$$

where,

$$W = \text{Load-carrying capacity (N)}$$

$$\mu = \text{Velocity of lubricant (N-s/mm}^2)$$

$$v = \text{Relative velocity of approach of plate (m/s)}$$

$$h = \text{Film thickness (mm)}$$

$$b = \text{Width of plate (mm)}$$

$$l = \text{Length of plate (mm)}$$

This equation can be used to find load-carrying capacity for given instantaneous velocity of approach and film thickness.

Hay's and Archibald developed an exact solution for rectangular plates approaching a plane.

$$W = K_s \frac{\mu \cdot v \cdot b \cdot l^3}{h^3} \qquad \qquad ...(6.14)$$

where, K_s – side flow coefficient.

The equation reflects the actual two-dimensional flow under the flat plate in both b and l directions. Following Table 6.1 gives values of K_s for different $\left(\dfrac{b}{l}\right)$ ratios.

Table 6.1 : Side Flow Coefficients for Squeeze Film under Rectangular Plates

$\dfrac{b}{l}$	K_s	$\dfrac{b}{l}$	K_s
∞	1.00	0.9	0.380
10	0.937	0.8	0.330
8	0.922	0.7	0.275
6	0.895	0.6	0.225
4	0.843	0.5	0.175
3	0.790	0.4	0.12
2	0.686	0.3	0.075
1	0.425	0.1	0.01

Time of Approach :

Time required in seconds for the film thickness to reduce from an initial value of h_1 to a final value with a constant force W acting on the rectangular plate can be estimated using the equation as given below.

$$W = \frac{\mu \cdot v \cdot b \, l^3}{h^3}$$

Velocity of approach is given by,

$$v = -\frac{dh}{dt}$$

$\therefore$ Equation for load becomes,

$$W = -\frac{\mu \cdot d l^3}{h^3} \cdot \frac{dh}{dt}$$

$\therefore \qquad dt = -\frac{\mu \cdot b l^3}{W h^3} \cdot dh$

Total time required can be evaluated by integrating above equation,

$$\int dt = \int -\frac{\mu \cdot b l^3}{W h^3} \cdot dh$$

$$t = -\frac{\mu \cdot b \cdot l^3}{W} \left[\int_{h_1}^{h_2} \frac{dh}{h^3} \right]$$

$$t = -\frac{\mu \cdot b\, l^3}{W} \left[-\frac{1}{2h^2} \right]_{h_1}^{h_2}$$

$$t = \frac{\mu \cdot b\, l^3}{2W} \left[\frac{1}{h_2^2} - \frac{1}{h_1^2} \right] \qquad \ldots (6.15)$$

where, t is the time in seconds for the film thickness to reduce from an initial value of h_1 to final value h_2 with a constant force W acting on the plate. According to Hays and Archibald, for an exact analysis,

$$t = K_s \cdot \frac{\mu \cdot b l^3}{2W} \left[\frac{1}{h_2^2} - \frac{1}{h_1^2} \right] \qquad \ldots (6.16)$$

6.4 APPROXIMATION OF A SQUARE PLATE USING A CIRCULAR PLATE

Square plate of dimension (D × D), approaching a plane can be approximated using circular plate of diameter D. Equation for an average pressure for a circular plate is given by,

$$P_{avg} = \frac{3\mu\, v\, R^3}{2h^3}$$

$$P_{avg} = \frac{3}{2} \frac{\mu v}{h^3} \left[\frac{D^2}{4} \right]$$

$$P_{avg} = \frac{3}{8} \cdot \frac{\mu v D^2}{h^3}$$

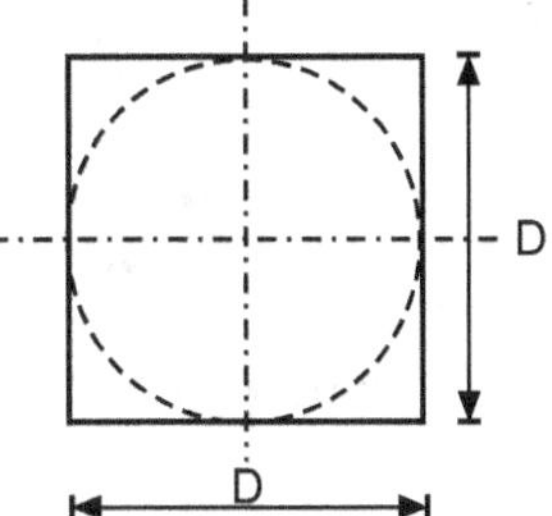

Fig. 6.6 : Square plate approximation using a circular plate

It can be seen that,

- A square plate of dimension (D × D) as shown in Fig. 6.6 will impose a greater restriction on the escape of an oil than a circular plate because of its extra corner area, which will raise the average pressure exerted by the oil film.

- Using a factor $\left(\frac{1}{2} \right)$ to compensate for this effect instead of taking $\left(\frac{3}{8} \right)$.

Average Pressure :

$$\therefore \qquad P_{avg} = \frac{1}{2}\left[\frac{\mu \cdot v \cdot D^2}{h^3}\right] \qquad \qquad \text{... (6.17)}$$

- **The Instantaneous Load-Carrying Capacity :** It can be given by,

$$W = \text{Area} \times P_{avg}$$

$$W = D^2\left[\frac{1}{2}\mu \cdot v \cdot \frac{D^2}{h^3}\right]$$

$$W = \frac{\mu \cdot v\, D^4}{2h^3} \qquad \qquad \text{... (6.18)}$$

- **The Time of Approach :** The time of approach for a square plate will be approximately,

$$t = \frac{\mu\, b\, l^3}{4W}\left[\frac{1}{h_2^2} - \frac{1}{h_1^2}\right] \qquad \qquad \text{... (6.19)}$$

For a square plate,

$$b = l = D$$

$\therefore$ Above equation for t becomes,

$$t = \frac{\mu \cdot D^4}{4W}\left[\frac{1}{h_2^2} - \frac{1}{h_1^2}\right] \qquad \qquad \text{... (6.19 a)}$$

Hay's and Archibald developed an exact solution for rectangular plates approaching a plane.

$$W = K_s \frac{\mu \cdot v \cdot b \cdot l^3}{h^3}$$

$$W = K_s \frac{\mu \cdot v \cdot D^4}{h^3} \qquad \qquad \text{where, } K_s - \text{side flow coefficient}$$

where, for square plate $l = b = 1$ and $K_s = 0.425$

$$\therefore \qquad W = 0.425\,\frac{\mu \cdot v \cdot D^4}{h^3} \qquad \qquad \text{... (6.19 b)}$$

For square plate of dimension D × D

According to Hay's and Archibald, for an exact analysis,

$$t = K_s \cdot \frac{\mu \cdot bl^3}{2W}\left[\frac{1}{h_2^2} - \frac{1}{h_1^2}\right]$$

$$t = 0.2125\,\frac{\mu D^4}{W}\left[\frac{1}{h_2^2} - \frac{1}{h_1^2}\right] \text{ (for } l = b = D\text{)} \qquad \qquad \text{... (6.19 c)}$$

SOLVED EXAMPLES

Example 6.1 : A circular plate of 250 mm diameter is approaching towards a fixed plane surface. Plate and fixed surfaces are separated by an oil-film thickness with the viscosity of oil as 150 cP. A load of 15 kN is supported by the film. Calculate the time required for reducing the film thickness from 0.25 mm to 0.0125 mm.

Solution :

Approximate square plate of dimension (D × D) based on the parameters in above problem, where D is side of square plate and is equal to diameter of circular plate.

Given :

$$D = 250 \text{ mm}$$

$$W = 150 \times 10^3$$

$$\mu = 15 \text{ cP} = 150 \times 10^{-9} \text{ N-s/mm}^2$$

$$h_1 = 0.25 \text{ mm}, \ h_2 = 0.0125 \text{ mm}$$

(i)   For circular plate approaching a plane :

$$R = \frac{D}{2} = \frac{250}{2} = 125 \text{ mm}$$

Time of approach is given by,

$$t = \frac{3}{4} \frac{\pi \mu R^4}{W} \left[\frac{1}{h_2^2} - \frac{1}{h_1^2} \right]$$

$$= \frac{3}{4} \frac{\pi \times 150 \times 10^{-9} \times (125)^4}{15 \times 10^3} \left[\frac{1}{(0.0125)^2} - \frac{1}{(0.25)^2} \right]$$

$$t = 36.724 \text{ s}$$

(ii)   Approximation of square plate :

Time of approach based on Hays equation,

$$t = 0.2125 \frac{\mu D^4}{W} \left[\frac{1}{h_2^2} - \frac{1}{h_1^2} \right]$$

$$= \frac{0.2125 \times 150 \times 10^{-9} \times (250)^4}{15 \times 10^3} \left[\frac{1}{(0.0125)^2} - \frac{1}{(0.25)^2} \right]$$

$$t = 52.992 \text{ s}$$

Time of approach can also be given by an equation

$$t = \frac{\mu D^4}{4W} \left[\frac{1}{h_2^2} - \frac{1}{h_1^2} \right]$$

$$= \frac{150 \times 10^{-9} \times (250)^4}{4 \times 15 \times 10^3} \left[\frac{1}{(0.0125)^2} - \frac{1}{(0.25)^2} \right]$$

$$t = 62.344 \text{ s}$$

Thus, $\left\{ \begin{array}{c} \text{Time of approach for} \\ \text{square plate} \end{array} \right\} > \left\{ \begin{array}{c} \text{Time of approach} \\ \text{for circular plate} \end{array} \right\} \quad \cdots \left(\begin{array}{c} \text{Due to extra corner} \\ \text{area of square plate} \end{array} \right)$

Example 6.2 : A circular plate is approaching a plane surface. Initially, the oil-film thickness was 0.080 mm. A load of 50 kN acts on a plate for a period of 18 seconds. Oil viscosity is 45 cP. After application of load, the oil-film thickness finally reduces to 0.02 mm. Estimate diameter of plate. **[P.U. June 2009, 6 Marks]**

Solution :

Given :

$h_2 = 0.08$ mm ; $W = 50$ kN $= 50 \times 10^3$ N

$h_1 = 0.02$ mm ; $t = 18$ s

$\mu = 45$ cP $= 45 \times 10^{-9}$ N-s/mm^2

Time of approach for circular plate is,

$$t = \frac{3}{4} \frac{\pi \mu R^4}{W} \left[\frac{1}{h_2^2} - \frac{1}{h_1^2} \right]$$

$$18 = \frac{3}{4} \frac{\pi \times 45 \times 10^{-9} R^4}{50 \times 10^3} \left[\frac{1}{(0.02)^2} - \frac{1}{(0.08)^2} \right]$$

$$R^4 = 3621659149$$

$$R = 245.32 \text{ mm}$$

Diameter of plate required $= \textbf{490.63 mm}$

Example 6.3 : A circular plate of diameter 150 mm is approaching a plane at a velocity of 12.5 cm/s at the instant, oil-film thickness is 0.25 mm. The viscosity of the oil is 0.035 Pa·s. Evaluate for squeeze film action **[P.U. Dec. 2008, 8 Marks]**

(i) The maximum pressure

(ii) Average pressure

(iii) Load-carrying capacity

(iv) Time required to squeeze the oil film from 0.25 mm to 0.005 mm.

Solution :

Given :

$D = 150$ mm $\Rightarrow$ $R = 75$ mm

$v = 12.5$ cm/s $\Rightarrow$ 125 mm/s

$h = 0.25$ mm

$$\mu \ = \ 0.035 \ \text{Pa·s}$$
$$= \ 0.035 \ \text{N-s/m}^2$$
$$= \ 0.035 \times 10^{-6} \ \text{N-s/mm}^2$$

(i) Maximum pressure (P_{max}) :

$$P_{max} \ = \ \frac{3 \, \mu \, v \, R^2}{h^3}$$

$$\therefore \qquad P_{max} \ = \ \frac{3 \times 0.035 \times 10^{-6} \times 125 \times (75)^2}{(0.25)^3}$$

$$P_{max} \ = \ 4.725 \ \text{N/mm}^2$$

(ii) Average Pressure (P_{avg}) :

$$P_{avg} \ = \ \frac{1}{2} P_{max} = \frac{1}{2} \times 4.725$$

$$P_{avg} \ = \ 2.3625 \ \text{N/mm}^2$$

(iii) Load-carrying capacity (W) :

$$W \ = \ \frac{3\pi \times \mu \, v \, R^4}{2h^3} = \frac{3\pi \times 0.035 \times 10^{-6} \times 125 \times (75)^4}{2 \times (0.25)^3}$$

$$= \ 41748.82 \ \text{N}$$

$$W \ = \ 41.7488 \ \text{kN}$$

(iv) Time required to squeeze the oil film :

Here, $h_1 = 0.25$ mm and $h_2 \ = \ 0.005$ mm

$$t \ = \ \frac{3}{4} \frac{\pi \, \mu \, R^4}{W} \left[\frac{1}{h_2^2} - \frac{1}{h_1^2} \right]$$

$$= \ \frac{3}{4} \frac{\pi \times 0.035 \times 10^{-6} \times (75)^4}{41748.82} \left[\frac{1}{(0.08)^2} - \frac{1}{(0.25)^2} \right]$$

$$t \ = \ 2.499 \ \text{s}$$

Example 6.4 : A rectangular plate 75 mm long and 225 mm wide is approaching towards a fixed plane surface. At an instant, an oil-film thickness is 0.075 mm, viscosity of oil is 90 cP, load supported by moving plate is 1.5 kN. Calculate the time required to squeeze the film to 0.025 mm.   **[P. U. June 2006; June 2009, 8 Marks]**

Given :

$$b \ = \ 225 \ \text{mm}$$
$$l \ = \ 75 \ \text{mm}$$
$$h_1 \ = \ 0.075 \ \text{m,} \qquad h_2 \ = \ 0.025 \ \text{mm}$$

$$\mu = 90 \text{ cP} = 90 \times 10^{-9} \text{ N-s/mm}^2$$

$$W = 1.5 \text{ kN} = 1500 \text{ N}$$

Solution :

Time required to squeeze the film is given by,

$$t = \frac{\mu \, b \, l^3}{2W}\left[\frac{1}{h_2^2} - \frac{1}{h_1^2}\right]$$

$$= \frac{90 \times 10^{-9} \times 225 \times (75)^3}{2 \times 1500}\left[\frac{1}{(0.025)^2} - \frac{1}{(0.075)^2}\right]$$

$$t = 4.05 \text{ s}$$

Example 6.5 : A rectangular plate having 50 mm length and an infinite width is approaching a fixed plane surface. Initially oil-film thickness is 0.035 mm, and viscosity of oil is 75 cP. Load supported per unit width of plate is 30 kN/m.

Calculate :

(i)   The time required to squeeze the film to 0.008 mm.

(ii)   The maximum pressure.

(iii)   Average pressure,

Solution :

Given : l = 50 mm

$$\frac{W}{b} = 30 \text{ kN/m}$$

$$= 30 \times 10^3 \times 10^{-3} \text{ N/mm}$$

$$= 30 \text{ N/mm}$$

$$h_1 = 0.035 \text{ mm} \quad ; \quad h_2 = 0.008 \text{ mm}$$

$$\mu = 75 \text{ cP} = 75 \times 10^{-9} \text{ N-s/mm}^2$$

(i)   Time required to squeeze the film (t) :

$$t = \frac{\mu \, b \, l^3}{2W}\left[\frac{1}{h_2^2} - \frac{1}{h_1^2}\right]$$

$$= \frac{\mu \, l^3}{2\left(\dfrac{W}{b}\right)}\left[\frac{1}{h_2^2} - \frac{1}{h_1^2}\right]$$

$$= \frac{75 \times 10^{-9} \times (50)^3}{2 \times 30}\left[\frac{1}{(0.008)^2} - \frac{1}{(0.035)^2}\right]$$

$$t = 2.3139 \text{ s}$$

(ii) Maximum pressure (P_{max}) :

$$P_{max} = \frac{3}{2} \cdot \frac{\mu\, v\, l^2}{h^3}$$

Here, velocity of approach,

$$v = \frac{\text{Change in film thickness}}{\text{Time required}}$$

$$= \frac{h_1 - h_2}{t}$$

$$= \frac{0.035 - 0.008}{2.3139}$$

$$v = 0.0116686 \text{ mm/s}$$

$$\therefore \quad P_{max} = \frac{3}{2} \times \frac{75 \times 10^{-9} \times 0.0116686 \times (50)^2}{(0.008)^3}$$

$$\cdots \left(\begin{array}{c} \because \quad \text{Pressure will be maximum at} \\ h = h_2 = 0.008 \text{ mm} \end{array} \right)$$

$$\therefore \quad P_{max} = 6.4098 \text{ N/mm}^2$$

(iii) Average pressure (P_{avg}) :

$$P_{avg} = \frac{2}{3}\,(P_{max})$$

$$= \frac{2}{3} \times 6.4098$$

$$P_{avg} = 4.2732 \text{ N/mm}^2$$

Example 6.6 : A rectangular plate having length to width ratio of 0.25 is approaching towards a fixed plane with an initial oil-film thickness between the plate and plane as 0.05 mm. Load supported by plate is 12 kN for 4 seconds. The viscosity of oil is 35 cP. Calculate bearing length and width for final oil-film thickness as 0.01 mm. Also find maximum pressure value.

Given :

$$\frac{l}{b} = 0.25 \implies l = 0.25\,b$$

$$W = 12 \text{ kN} = 12000 \text{ N}$$

$$h_1 = 0.05 \text{ mm} \; ; \; h_2 = 0.01 \text{ mm}$$

$$t = 4 \text{ seconds}$$

$$\mu = 35 \text{ cP} = 35 \times 10^{-9} \text{ N-s/mm}^2$$

Solution :

(i) Time of approach for rectangular plate is given by,

$$t = \frac{\mu\,b\,l^3}{2W}\left[\frac{1}{h_2^2} - \frac{1}{h_1^2}\right]$$

$$4 = \frac{35 \times 10^{-9} \times b \times (0.25\,b)^3}{2 \times 12000}\left[\frac{1}{(0.01)^2} - \frac{1}{(0.05)^2}\right]$$

$\therefore \qquad b = 367.73$ mm

$\therefore \qquad l = 0.25\,b$

$$= 0.25 \times 367.73$$

$$l = 91.93 \text{ mm}$$

Bearing dimensions ($l = 91.93$ mm,

$b = 367.73$ mm)

(ii) Maximum pressure (P_{max}) :

$$P_{max} = \frac{3}{2}\,\frac{\mu\,v\,l^2}{h^3}$$

Here velocity of approach,

$$v = \frac{h_1 - h_2}{t}$$

$$= \frac{0.05 - 0.01}{4}$$

$$v = 0.01 \text{ mm/s}$$

$$\therefore \qquad P_{max} = \frac{3}{2} \times \frac{35 \times 10^{-9} \times 0.01 \times (91.93)^2}{(0.01)^3}$$

$$\ldots \;(\because\; P_{max} \text{ at } h = h_2 = 0.01 \text{ mm})$$

$$P_{max} = 4.4368 \text{ N/mm}^2$$

Example 6.7 : Two parallel rectangular plates with width to length ratio of 4 are separated by an oil film of thickness 0.1 mm at the beginning of load cycle. The load of 12 kN is applied on the upper plate for 5 seconds, the lower plate being stationary. If the viscosity of oil and the permissible minimum oil film thickness are 30 cP and 0.02 mm respectively, calculate the length and width of plates. **[P.U. Dec. 2010, 4 Marks]**

Given :

$$\frac{b}{l} = 4 \;\Rightarrow b = 4l$$

$$W = 12 \text{ kN} = 12000 \text{ N}$$

$$h_1 = 0.1 \text{ mm}$$

$$h_2 = 0.02 \text{ mm}$$

$$t = 5 \text{ seconds}$$

$$\mu = 30 \text{ cP} = 30 \times 10^{-9} \text{ N-s/mm}^2$$

Solution :

(i)   Time of approach for rectangular plate is given by,

$$t = \frac{\mu \cdot b \cdot l^3}{2W}\left[\frac{1}{h_2^2} - \frac{1}{h_1^2}\right]$$

$$\therefore \qquad 5 = \frac{30 \times 10^{-9} \times 4l \times l^3}{2 \times 12000}\left[\frac{1}{(0.02)^2} - \frac{1}{(0.1)^2}\right]$$

$$\therefore \qquad \frac{50}{30 \times 10^{-9} \times 4} = l^4$$

$$\therefore \qquad l = 142.87 \text{ mm}$$

$$\therefore \qquad b = 571.48 \text{ mm} \left.\right\} \text{ Bearing dimensions}$$

Example 6.8 : A rectangular plate having length to width ratio of 0.25 is approaching towards a fixed plane with an initial oil-film thickness between the plate and plane as 0.05 mm. Load supported by the plate is 12 kN for 4 seconds. The viscosity of oil is 35 cP. Calculate bearing length and width for final oil-film thickness as 0.01 mm. Also find maximum pressure value.   **[P.U. Dec. 2009, 8 Marks]**

Solution :

Given : $\dfrac{l}{b} = 0.25 \Rightarrow l = 0.25\,b \Rightarrow b = 4l$

$$W = 12 \text{ kN} = 12000 \text{ N}$$

$$h_1 = 0.05 \text{ mm}$$

$$h_2 = 0.01 \text{ mm}$$

$$t = 4 \text{ sec.}$$

$$\mu = 35 \text{ cP} = 35 \times 10^{-9} \text{ N-s/mm}^2$$

Time of approach for rectangular plate is given by,

$$t = \frac{\mu \cdot b \cdot l^3}{2W}\left[\frac{1}{h_2^2} - \frac{1}{h_1^2}\right]$$

$$4 = \frac{35 \times 10^{-9} \times 4l \times l^3}{2 \times 12000}\left[\frac{1}{(0.01)^2} - \frac{1}{(0.05)^2}\right]$$

$$l = 91.932 \text{ mm}$$

$$b = 4 \times 91.932 = 367.72 \text{ mm} \left.\right\} \text{ Bearing dimensions}$$

Maximum pressure :

$$P_{max} = \frac{3}{2} \frac{\mu \cdot v \cdot l^2}{h^3}$$

Now, $v = \dfrac{h_1 - h_2}{t}$

$$= \frac{0.05 - 0.01}{4} = 0.01 \text{ mm/sec.}$$

and $h = h_2$ $= 0.01$ ... [Pressure maximum at h_2]

$$\therefore \quad P_{max} = \frac{3}{2} \times \frac{35 \times 10^{-9} \times 0.01 \times (91.932)^2}{(0.01)^3}$$

$$P_{max} = 4.437014 \text{ N/mm}^2$$

Example 6.9 : A circular plate of 60 mm radius is approaching the base plane at a velocity of 150 mm/s at the instant when the oil-film thickness is 0.2 mm. If the absolute viscosity of the oil is 0.025 Pa-s, calculate :

(i)   the load-carrying capacity of the oil-film at the given instant;

(ii) the maximum pressure; and

(iii) the average pressure.

Solution :

Given : $R = 60$ mm

$v = 150$ mm/s

$h = 0.2$ mm

$\mu = 0.025$ Pa-s

$= 0.025$ N-s/m^2

$= 0.025 \times 10^{-6}$ N-s/mm^2

(i) Load-carrying capacity (W) :

$$W = \frac{3\pi \, m \, v \, R^4}{2h^3} = \frac{3\pi \times 0.025 \times 10^{-6} \times 150 \times (60)^4}{2 \times (0.2)^3} = 28627.763 \text{ N}$$

$$W = 28.6277 \text{ kN}$$

(ii) The maximum pressure (P_{max}) :

$$P_{max} = \frac{3\mu \, v \, R^2}{h^3} = \frac{3 \times 150 \times 10^{-6} \times 0.025 \times 10^{-6} (60)^2}{(0.2)^3}$$

$$P_{max} = 6.0625 \text{ N/mm}^2$$

(iii) The average pressure (P_{avg}) :

$$P_{avg} = \frac{1}{2} P_{max} = \frac{5.0625}{2}$$

$$P_{avg} = 2.53125 \text{ N/mm}^2$$

Example 6.10 : Two parallel plates 40 mm long and infinitely wide are separated by an oil film of 30 μm thick having viscosity of 0.75 N-s/mm². If load per unit width of 18000 N/m is applied to the plates, find the time required to reduce the film thickness to 3 μm and the maximum pressure. **(P.U. May/June 2007)**

Solution :

Given : l = 40 mm

$$h_1 = 30 \text{ μm} = 0.030 \text{ mm}$$

$$h_2 = 3 \text{ μm} = 0.003 \text{ mm}$$

$$\mu = 0.75 \text{ N-s/mm}^2$$

$$= 0.75 \times 10^{-6} \text{ N-s/mm}^2$$

$$\frac{w}{b} = 18000 \text{ N/m} = 18000 \times 10^{-3} \text{ N/mm}$$

(i) Time required to reduce the film thickness to 3 μm (t) :

$$t = \frac{\mu \, b \cdot l^3}{2w} \left[\frac{1}{h_2^2} - \frac{1}{h_1^2} \right]$$

$$= \frac{\mu \cdot l^3}{2 \left(\dfrac{w}{b} \right)} \left[\frac{1}{h_2^2} - \frac{1}{h_1^2} \right]$$

$$= \frac{0.75 \times 10^{-6} \times (40)^3}{2 \times 18000 \times 10^{-3}} \left[\frac{1}{(0.003)^2} - \frac{1}{(0.03)^2} \right]$$

$$t = 146.6667 \text{ s}$$

(ii) Maximum pressure (P_{max}) :

$$P_{max} = \frac{3}{2} \cdot \frac{\mu \, v \, l^2}{h^3}$$

$$\text{Velocity of approach, } v = \frac{\text{Change in film thickness}}{\text{Time required}}$$

$$= \frac{h_1 - h_2}{t}$$

$$= \frac{0.03 - 0.003}{146.6667}$$

$$v = 1.84091 \times 10^{-4} \text{ mm/s}$$

$$\therefore \quad P_{max} = \frac{3}{2} \cdot \frac{\mu v l^2}{h^3}$$

$$= \frac{3}{2} \times \frac{0.75 \times 10^{-6} \times 1.84091 \times 10^{-4} \times (40)^2}{(0.003)^2}$$

... ($\because$ Pressure will be maximum at $h = h_2 = 0.003$ mm)

$$P_{max} = 12.27273 \text{ N/mm}^2$$

Example 6.11 : Two parallel plates 30 mm long and infinitely wide are separated by an oil film 25 μm thick having viscosity of 0.65 Ns/m². If load per unit width of 15000 N/m is applied to the plates, find the time required to reduce the film thickness to 2.5 μm and the maximum pressure. **(P.U. Nov./Dec. 2007)**

Solution :

    Given : l = 30 mm

$$h_1 = 25 \text{ μm} = 25 \times 10^{-3} \text{ mm}$$

$$\mu = 0.65 \text{ N-s/m}^2$$

$$= 0.65 \times 10^{-6} \text{ N-s/mm}^2$$

$$\frac{w}{b} = 15000 \text{ N/m} = 15000 \times 10^{-3} \text{ N/mm}$$

$$h_2 = 2.5 \times 10^{-3} \text{ mm}$$

To calculate :

(i)   t = ?

(ii) P_{max} = ?

(i)   Time required to reduce the film thickness to 2.5 μm (t) :

$$t = \frac{\mu \cdot b \cdot l^3}{2w} \left[\frac{1}{h_2^2} - \frac{1}{h_1^2} \right]$$

$$= \frac{\mu \cdot l^3}{2 \left(\dfrac{w}{b} \right)} \left[\frac{1}{h_2^2} - \frac{1}{h_1^2} \right]$$

$$= \frac{0.65 \times 10^{-6} \times (30)^3}{2 \times 15000 \times 10^{-3}} \left[\frac{1}{(0.0025)^2} - \frac{1}{(0.025)^2} \right]$$

$$t = 92.664 \text{ sec}$$

(ii) Maximum pressure (P_{max}) :

$$P_{max} = \frac{3}{2} \cdot \frac{\mu v l^2}{h^3}$$

Velocity of approach,

$$v = \frac{\text{Change in film thickness}}{\text{Time required}}$$

$$= \frac{h_1 - h_2}{t}$$

$$= \frac{0.025 - 0.0025}{92.664}$$

$$v = 2.42813 \times 10^{-4} \text{ mm/s}$$

$$\therefore \quad P_{max} = \frac{3}{2} \times \frac{0.65 \times 10^{-6} \times 2.42813 \times 10^{-4} \times (30)^2}{(0.0025)^3}$$

$$\ldots (\because \text{ Pressure will be maximum at } h = h_2 = 0.0025 \text{ mm})$$

$$P_{max} = 13.63636 \text{ N/mm}^2$$

Example 6.12 : Two parallel plates 3 cm long and infinitely wide are separated by oil of viscosity 0.6 N-s/m^2 and are approaching each other. If a load of 30 kN per meter width is applied, what will be the film thickness after one second ? Initial film thickness is 25 μm.

[P.U. May 2010, 6 Marks]

Solution : Given : $l = 3 \text{ cm} = 30 \text{ mm}$

$$h_1 = 25 \text{ μm} = 25 \times 10^{-3} \text{ mm}$$

$$\mu = 0.6 \text{ N-s/mm}^2$$

$$= 0.6 \times 10^{-6} \text{ N-s/mm}^2$$

$$\frac{w}{b} = 30 \text{ kN} = 30000 \times 10^{-3} \text{ N/mm}$$

$$t = 1 \text{ sec.}$$

$$h_2 = ?$$

To calculate : $h_2 = ?$

Time required to reduce the film thickness to h_2 is 1 sec.

$$t = \frac{\mu \cdot b \cdot l^3}{2w} \left[\frac{1}{h_2^2} - \frac{1}{h_1^2} \right]$$

$$1 = \frac{0.6 \times 10^{-6} \times (30)^3}{2 \times 30000 \times 10^{-3}} \left[\frac{1}{h_2^2} - \frac{1}{(0.025)^2} \right]$$

$$3703.7037 = \frac{1}{h_2^2} - 1600$$

$$\therefore \quad \frac{1}{h_2^2} = 5303.7037$$

$$\therefore \quad h_2^2 = 0.0001885$$

$$\therefore \quad h_2 = 0.0137295 \text{ mm}$$

$$\text{OR } 13.7295 \ \mu m \hspace{3cm} \textbf{... Ans.}$$

Example 6.13 : Derive an expression to evaluate time required to squeeze the oil film from 0.25 mm to 0.005 mm, when a circular plate of diameter 150 mm is approaching a plane at a velocity of 12.5 cm/s at the instant, oil-film thickness is 0.25 mm. The viscosity of the oil is 0.035 Pa-s. **(P. U. Nov./Dec. 2008)**

Solution : Refer Example 6.1, on page 6.15.

Example 6.14 : The two rectangular parallel plates of size 300 mm × 75 mm are separated by an oil-film of 0.1 mm thickness. The thickness of oil is 80 cP. The lower plate is stationary. If the normal load acting on the upper plate is 5000 N, calculate the time required to reduce the film thickness to 0.01 mm. **(P. U. Nov./Dec. 2008)**

Solution :

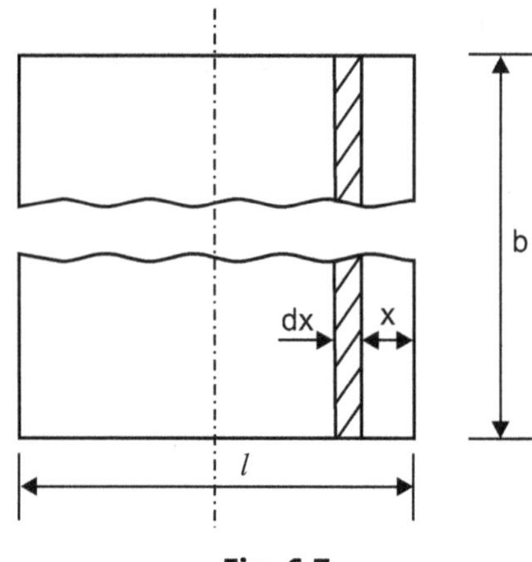

Fig. 6.7

Given : $b = 300$ mm

$l = 75$ mm

$h_1 = 0.1$ mm

$\mu = 80$ cP

$= 80 \times 10^{-9}$ N-s/mm^2

h_2 = 0.01 mm

W = 5000 N

Time required to reduce the film thickness to 0.01 mm

$$t = \frac{\mu \cdot b \cdot l^3}{2W}\left[\frac{1}{h_2^2} - \frac{1}{h_1^2}\right]$$

$$= \frac{80 \times 10^{-9} \times 300 \times (75)^3}{2 \times 5000}\left[\frac{1}{(0.01)^2} - \frac{1}{(0.1)^2}\right]$$

$$= 1.0125 \times 10^{-3}\,[10000 - 100]$$

$$t = 10.02375 \text{ sec.}$$

EXERCISE

1. Give practical situations where hydrostatic squeeze-film lubrication can be observed. **[P.U. May 2010, 6 Marks]**

2. Explain the phenomenon of squeeze-film lubrication ? State two examples where this type of lubrication is observed. **[P.U. Dec. 2010, 4 Marks]**

3. Explain squeeze-film effect in case of circular plate approaching a plane.

4. Derive an equation for load-carrying capacity for given instantaneous velocity of approach and film thickness in case of circular plate approaching a plane.

5. Derive an equation for time required to squeeze the film from h_1 to h_2 for the circular plate approaching the plane.

6. Explain squeeze-film effect in case of rectangular plate approaching a plane.

7. Derive an equation for load-carrying capacity for given instantaneous velocity of approach and film thickness in case of rectangular plate approaching a plane.

[P.U. Dec. 2010, 6 Marks]

8. Derive an equation for time required to squeeze the film from h_1 to h_2 for the rectangular plate approaching the plane.

[P.U. June 2009, 8 Marks; Dec. 2010, 6 Marks; June 2011, 12 Marks]

9. Approximate square plate of dimension (D × D) approaching a plane using circular plate of diameter D.

10. Derive an equation for load carrying capacity and time required to squeeze the film from h_1 to h_2 for square plate approaching a plane.

[P.U. Dec. 2009, 12 Marks]

EXAMPLES FOR PRACTICE

1. A circular plate of 200 mm radius is approaching towards a fixed plane surface. Initially, the oil-film thickness between the plate and plane is 0.2 mm. The viscosity of oil being 105×10^{-9} N-s/mm². A load of 20 kN is supported by the moving circular plate. Calculate time required to squeeze the oil film to a thickness of 0.01 mm.

   Approximate square plate of dimension (D × D), where D is diameter of circular plate and find time of approach for this case.

   (**Ans. :** For circular plate, t = 197.426 s

   For square plate, t = 284.857 s)

2. A circular plate having diameter 120 mm is approaching towards a fixed plane surface with a velocity of 150 mm/s. At this instant, oil-film thickness is 0.2 mm. Viscosity of oil is 25 cP.

   Evaluate :

   (i)   Maximum pressure

   (ii) Average pressure

   (iii) Load-carrying capacity

   (**Ans. :**   (i) P_{max} = 5.06251 N/mm²

   (ii) P_{avg} = 2.5313 N/mm²

   (iii)   W = 28.631)

3. A rectangular plate of length 25 mm and infinite width is approaching towards a plane surface with an initial oil-film thickness of 0.025 mm between the plate and fixed plane. Viscosity of oil is 50 cP. Load supported per unit width, by the plate is 20 kN/m.

   Calculate :

   (i)   Time required to squeeze the film thickness to 0.0025 mm

   (ii) The velocity of approach and

   (iii) The maximum pressure

   (**Ans. :**   (i)   t = 3.093748 s

   (ii)   v = 0.0072731 mm/s

   (iii) P_{max} = 21.8171 N/mm²)

4. A rectangular plate 1.1 m wide and 0.15 m long is approaching towards a fixed plane surface. Initially, the oil-film thickness between plate and surface is 0.08 m.

Plate supports a load of 10000 N for 5.7 seconds. Minimum oil-film thickness is limited to the value equals to 8 times the R_a value on two surfaces (where, R_a is surface roughness value = 5 µm).

Calculate :

(i) Viscosity of oil and

(ii) Initial oil-film thickness, if viscosity reduces by 15%.

(Ans. :   (i) $\mu = 65.6012$ cP

(ii) $h_i = 116.6752 \times 10^{-3}$ mm)

5. A rectangular plate is approaching a fixed plane surface. Specifications of squeeze-film bearings are given below.

- Length of plate = 50 mm
- Width of plate = 200 mm
- Initial oil-film thickness = 0.050 mm
- Final oil-film thickness = 0.01 mm
- Normal load on plate = 1 kN
- Viscosity of oil = 40 cP

Calculate time required to squeeze the oil film from initial value to final limit.

(Ans. : t = 4.801 s).

6. Derive an expression to evaluate time required to squeeze the oil film from 0.075 mm to 0.025 mm. When a rectangular plate of 75 mm long and 225 mm wide is approaching towards a fixed plane surface, supporting a load of 1.5 kN. The viscosity of the oil is 90 cP.   **[P.U. June 2009, 16 Marks]**

(Ans. : t = 4.05 sec.) (Refer Example 6.4 on page 6.17).

NUMERICAL EXAMPLES ASKED IN VARIOUS UNIVERSITY EXAMINATIONS

1. A rectangular plate 75 mm long and 225 mm wide is approaching towards a fixed plane surface. At an instant, an oil-film thickness is 0.075 mm, viscosity of oil is 90 cP, load supported by moving plate is 1.5 kN. Calculate the time required to squeeze the film to 0.025 mm.   **(P. U. June 2006)**

Given :

$$b = 225 \text{ mm}$$
$$l = 75 \text{ mm}$$
$$h_1 = 0.075 \text{ m}, h_2 = 0.025 \text{ mm}$$
$$\mu = 90 \text{ cP} = 90 \times 10^{-9} \text{ N-s/mm}^2$$
$$W = 1.5 \text{ kN} = 1500 \text{ N}$$

Solution :

Refer Example 6.4 on page 6.17.

2. Two parallel plates 40 mm long and infinitely wide are separated by an oil film of 30 μm thick having viscosity of 0.75 N-s/mm^2. If load per unit width of 18000 N/m is applied to the plates, find the time required to reduce the film thickness to 3 μm and the maximum pressure. **(P.U. May/June 2007)**

Solution :

Refer Example 6.10 on page 6.23.

3. Two parallel plates 30 mm long and infinitely wide are separated by an oil film 25 μm thick having viscosity of 0.65 Ns/m^2. If load per unit width of 15000 N/m is applied to the plates, find the time required to reduce the film thickness to 2.5 μm and the maximum pressure.

Solution :

Refer Example 6.10 on page 6.23.

Example 5.10 :

4. Derive an expression to evaluate time required to squeeze the oil film from 0.25 mm to 0.005 mm, when a circular plate of diameter 150 mm is approaching a plane at a velocity of 12.5 cm/s at the instant, oil-film thickness is 0.25 mm. The viscosity of the oil is 0.035 Pa-s.

5. The two rectangular parallel plates of size 300 mm × 75 mm are separated by an oil-film of 0.1 mm thickness. The thickness of oil is 80 cP. The lower plate is stationary. If the normal load acting on the upper plate is 5000 N, calculate the time required to reduce the film thickness to 0.01 mm. **(P. U. Nov./Dec. 2008)**

Solution :

Refer Example 6.14, on page 6.26.

✠ ✠ ✠

Chapter 7

ELASTOHYDRODYNAMIC LUBRICATION AND GAS LUBRICATED BEARINGS

7.1 BASIC CONCEPTS IN ELASTOHYDRODYNAMIC LUBRICATION PRINCIPLE AND APPLICATIONS

The lubrication principles applied to rolling bodies, such as ball or roller bearings, gears, cams, etc. is known as Elastohydrodynamic Lubrication (EHL).

Although lubrication of rolling objects operates on a considerably different principle than sliding objects, the principles of hydrodynamic lubrication can be applied, within limits, to explain lubrication of rolling elements. An oil wedge, similar to that which occurs in hydrodynamic lubrication, exists at the leading edge of the bearing. Adhesion of oil to the sliding element and the supporting surface increases pressure and creates a film between two bodies. **Because the area of contact is extremely small in a roller and ball bearing, the force per unit area or load pressure is extremely high.** Under these pressures, it would appear that the oil would be entirely squeezed from between the bearing surfaces. However, **viscosity increase that occurs under extremely high pressure** prevents the oil from being entirely squeezed out. Consequently, a thin film of oil is maintained. **The surfaces which carry this load are likely to deform.** A very thin lubricating film actually supports the load. **Thus, elastohydrodynamic lubrication deals with the lubrication of elastic contacts.**

All the assumptions used in the classical theory of hydrodynamic lubrication cannot be used especially because the variation of viscosity with pressure must be considered here. In addition to this, a heavy load which causes elastic deformation of solids changes the geometry of the lubricating film. Thus, in the problems of elastohydrodynamic lubrication, it is necessary to solve simultaneously the hydrodynamic as well as the elasticity equations concerned with the contact, since the shape of oil film largely controls pressure distribution.

In elastohydrodynamic lubrication, we are thus, faced with the simultaneous solution of the Reynolds equation, the elastic deformation equations and the equation relating to viscosity of the lubricant and pressure. Thermal effects and shear rate also play an important role and should be taken into account.

Analytical work on elastohydrodynamic lubrication was started with the pioneering work by **Grubin** (1949). He developed an analytical approach to incorporate both the elastic deformation and viscosity pressure properties of the lubricant and obtained the film shape and pressure distribution in line contact.

In rolling element bearings, two common forms of contact are encountered; point contact and line contact. If a sphere comes into contact with a flat surface, point contact is initially formed and the circular size grows with load. For a cylinder coming into contact with a flat surface, a line contact is formed and it grows into a rectangular patch with an increase in load. For the contact between a sphere and a curved surface, the point contact grows into an elliptical footprint. The rolling element bearings, gears and cams and followers are examples of non-conforming contacts.

7.2 ELASTOHYDRODYNAMIC LUBRICATION BETWEEN TWO CONTACTING BODIES

In elastohydrodynamic lubrication, simultaneous solution of the Reynolds equation, the elastic deformation equations and equations relating to the viscosity of lubricant and pressure is considered.

7.2.1 Hydrodynamic Equation (Pressure Viscosity term in Reynold's Equation)

If the two contacting bodies (two rollers in contact) are rotating as shown in Fig. 7.1, then the average velocity can be written as,

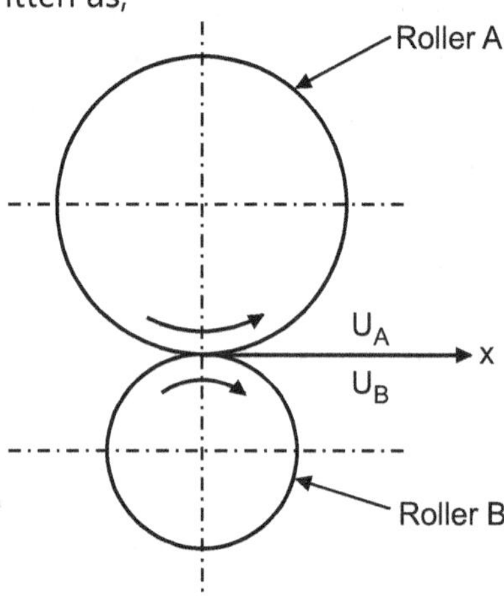

Fig. 7.1 : Two contacting bodies

$$U = U_A + U_B$$

where, U_A – Linear velocity of roller A

U_B – Linear velocity of roller B

U – Average velocity of roller A and roller B

The governing equation for hydrodynamic pressure (i.e. Reynolds equation) for two contacting bodies as shown in Fig. 7.1 is given by,

$$\frac{\partial}{\partial x}\left(\frac{h^3}{12\mu}\frac{\partial P}{\partial x}\right) + \frac{\partial}{\partial z}\left(\frac{h^3}{12\mu}\frac{\partial P}{\partial z}\right) = \frac{U_A + U_B}{2}\frac{\partial h}{\partial x}$$

i.e.
$$\frac{\partial}{\partial x}\left(\frac{h^3}{\mu}\frac{\partial P}{\partial x}\right) + \frac{\partial}{\partial z}\left(\frac{h^3}{\mu}\frac{\partial P}{\partial z}\right) = 6U\frac{\partial h}{\partial x} \qquad \text{... (7.1)}$$

The pressure inside the contact zone is likely to be of considerable magnitude. Thus, the viscosity in this cannot be treated as constant. The variation of viscosity with pressure for different kinds of oils cannot be expressed in a single equation. The two common relationships, based on the kinds of oil are as follows :

(i) **For Napthenic Oils (or Gulf Oils Having Low V.I.)**, viscosity varies as the pressure rises and is given by the following relation –

$$\mu = \mu_0\, e^{\alpha p} \qquad \text{... (7.2)}$$

where,

μ – Viscosity of oil at pressure p

μ_0 – Initial viscosity corresponding to atmospheric pressure

α – Piezo-viscosity coefficient

p – Pressure

(ii) **For Paraffinic Oils (or Pennsylvania Oils Having High V.I.)**, viscosity varies as the pressure rises and is given by the relation –

$$\mu = \mu_0\, (1 + cp)^n \qquad \text{... (7.3)}$$

where, c and n are constant

Substituting either equation (7.2) or equation (7.3) in equation (7.1), we get,

$$\frac{\partial}{\partial x}\left(\frac{h^3}{\mu_0}\frac{\partial q}{\partial x}\right) + \frac{\partial}{\partial z}\left(\frac{h^3}{\mu_0}\frac{\partial q}{\partial z}\right) = 6U\frac{\partial h}{\partial x} \qquad \text{... (7.4)}$$

where, q is regarded as the **modified pressure** and U is the average velocity.

Also, for **Napthenic oils, the modified pressure is,**

$$q = \frac{1 - e^{-\alpha p}}{\alpha} \qquad \text{... (7.5)}$$

q has the property that, as $p \to \infty$, $e^{-\alpha p} \to 0$ and therefore, $q \to \dfrac{1}{\alpha}$, which is a constant.

i.e. as $p \to \infty, q = \dfrac{1}{\alpha} \qquad \text{... (7.6)}$

Next, for **paraffinic oils, the modified pressure is,**

$$q = \frac{1 - (1 + cp)^{1-n}}{(n - 1)\, c} \qquad \text{... (7.7)}$$

Here also, the q has the property that as $p \to \infty$, $(1 + cp)^{1-n} \to 0$ and therefore, $q \to \dfrac{1}{(n-1)\,c}$ which is a constant.

$$\text{i.e. as} \quad p \to \infty, q \;=\; \frac{1}{(n-1)\,c} \qquad \qquad \text{... (7.8)}$$

Equation (7.4) can be used as the governing equation, in which μ_0 is constant and q can be called as modified pressure.

In the case of **line contacts**, the equation (7.4) reduces to,

$$\frac{\partial}{\partial x}\left(h^3 \frac{\partial q}{\partial x}\right) \;=\; 6\,\mu_0\,U\,\frac{\partial h}{\partial x} \qquad \qquad \text{... (7.9)}$$

Equation (7.9) gives the **standard integrated modified form of Reynolds equation** as mentioned below.

$$\frac{\partial q}{\partial x} \;=\; 6\,\mu_0\,U\left(\frac{h - h_m}{h^3}\right) \qquad \qquad \text{... (7.10)}$$

where,

$\qquad\qquad h_m \quad$ – Oil film thickness where the pressure is maximum

and $\qquad h \quad$ – Oil film thickness at the cross-section

7.2.2 Hertz Equations for Deformation and Pressure (Hertz Theory)

The film shape in elastohydrodynamic lubrication is given by elastic deformation of the two contacting surfaces as determined by the classical theory of Hertz.

7.2.2.1 Elastic Deformation

The deformation of a cylindrical disc loaded against a plane or a ball against a plane are similar. They both stem from the same simple relation.

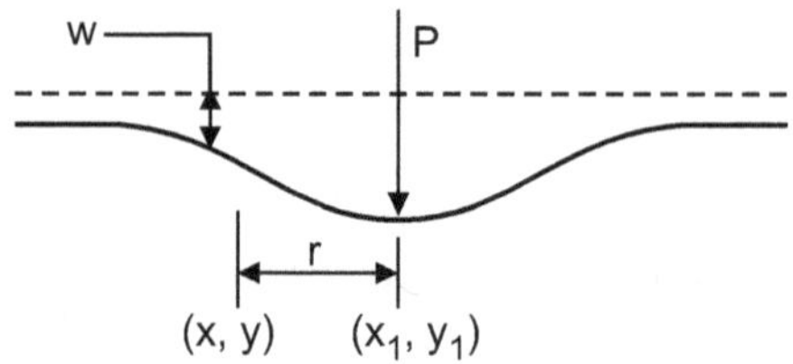

Fig. 7.2 : Deformation due to a point load

A deflection w at a point (x, y) consequent to a point load P at (x_1, y_1) where the distance between (x, y) and (x_1, y_1) is r, is given by,

$$w \;=\; \frac{1 - v^2}{\pi E}\,\frac{P}{r} \qquad \qquad \text{... (7.11)}$$

where,　　　　　　v –　Poisson's ratio

　　　　　　　　　E –　Young's modulus

The term $\dfrac{1 - v^2}{\pi E}$ is known as Lame's Constant.

If there is a distributed pressure p over the area, instead of point load P, then $P = p\,dx_1\,dy_1$, and the **deflection** is given by,

$$w \;=\; \frac{1 - v^2}{\pi E} \int \int \frac{p\,dx_1\,dy_1}{r} \qquad \text{... (7.12)}$$

7.2.2.2 Elastic Pressures

If two dry surfaces are loaded together (without lubricant), there is an **elastic flattening.** The pressures so generated are semi-elliptical as shown in Fig. 7.3.

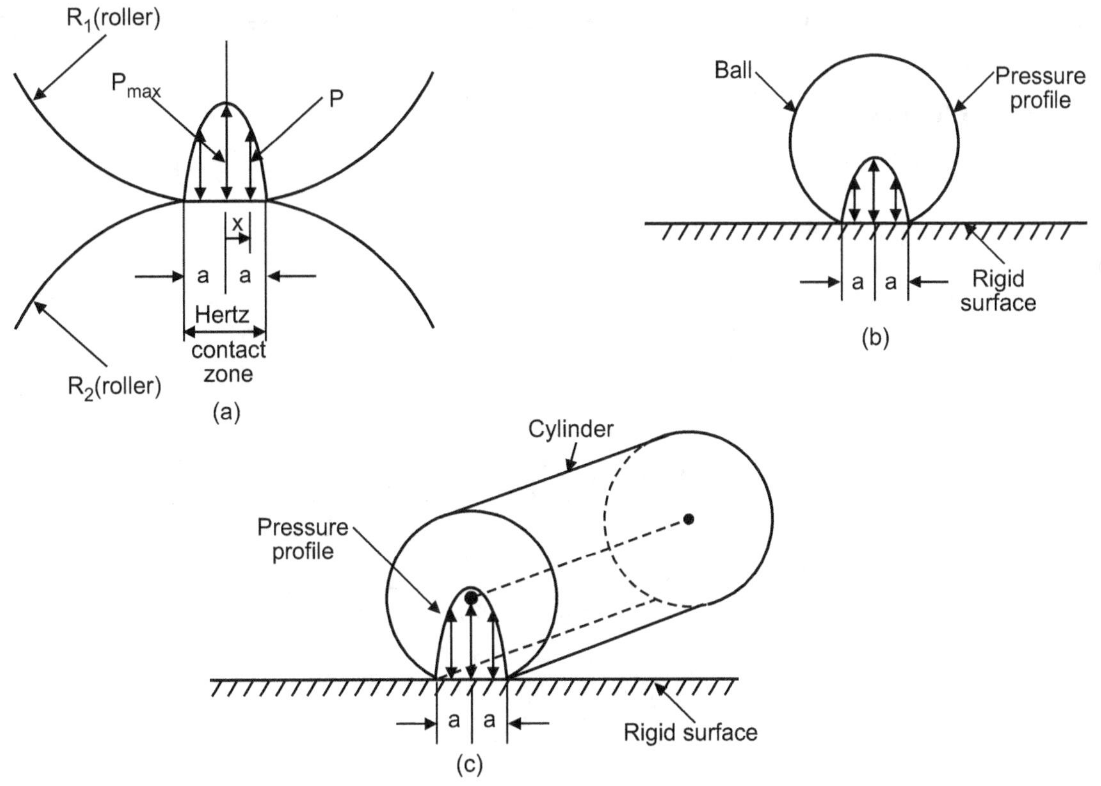

Fig. 7.3 : Semi-elliptical pressure distribution

Because of the generation of pressures of semi-elliptical nature, it means that if the half width of line contact with the cylindrical disc or the radius of point contact with the balls is 'a' and 'x' is the distance from the centre line, the pressure 'p' at any point 'x' is given by,

$$p = p_{max} \left(1 - \frac{x^2}{a^2}\right)^{1/2} \qquad \qquad \text{... (7.13)}$$

It is of course usual to reduce two surfaces of radii R_1 and R_2 to a reduced radius R acting on a plane according to the relation –

$$\frac{1}{R} = \frac{1}{R_1} \pm \frac{1}{R_2} \qquad \qquad \text{... (7.14)}$$

where, '+' (positive sign) for external and '–' (negative sign) for internal contact.

The pressure equation (7.13) also holds good for an elastic cylinder and a ball on a rigid body surface or vice-versa.

7.2.2.3 Relation between Applied Load, Contact Width, Peak Pressures and Deflections

Pressure distribution at contact zone is semi-elliptical with width '2a' and peak pressure 'p_{max}'.

(a)   Ball of Radius 'a' :

$$W = \int_0^a 2\pi x \, p \, dx$$

$$= 2\pi \int_0^a p_{max} \left(1 - \frac{x^2}{a^2}\right)^{1/2} x \, dx$$

$$= \frac{2\pi \, p_{max}}{a} \int_0^a x \sqrt{a^2 - x^2} \, dx$$

$$= \frac{2\pi \, p_{max}}{a} \left[-\frac{1}{3} (a^2 - x^2) \sqrt{a^2 - x^2} \right]_0^a$$

$$= \frac{2\pi \, p_{max}}{a} \cdot \frac{a^3}{3}$$

$$= \frac{2\pi}{3} p_{max} \, a^2$$

$$\therefore \qquad W = \frac{2\pi}{3} p_{max} \, a^2 \qquad \qquad \text{... (7.15)}$$

(b)　Cylinder of Radius 'a' and Length 'L' :

Load per unit length, $W' = \dfrac{W}{L}$

$$\therefore \quad W' = \frac{W}{L} = \int_{-a}^{a} p \, dx$$

$$= \int_{-a}^{a} p_{max}\left(1 - \frac{x^2}{a^2}\right)^{1/2} dx = \frac{p_{max}}{a} \int_{-a}^{a} \sqrt{a^2 - x^2} \, dx$$

$$= \frac{p_{max}}{a}\left[\frac{a^2}{2}\sin^{-1}\frac{x}{a} + \frac{x}{2}\sqrt{a^2 - x^2}\right]_{-a}^{a}$$

$$= \frac{p_{max}}{a}\left[\frac{a^2}{2}\times\frac{\pi}{2} - \frac{a^2}{2}\left(-\frac{\pi}{2}\right) + 0\right]$$

$$= \frac{p_{max}}{a}\left[2\times\frac{a^2\pi}{4}\right] = \frac{p_{max}}{a}\left[\frac{a^2\pi}{2}\right]$$

$$= \frac{p_{max}\times a\pi}{2} = \frac{\pi}{2}p_{max}\,a$$

$$\therefore \quad W' = \frac{W}{L} = \frac{\pi}{2}p_{max}\,a \qquad\qquad \text{... (7.16)}$$

(c)　Elastohydrodynamic Lubrication of Cylinders or Rollers :

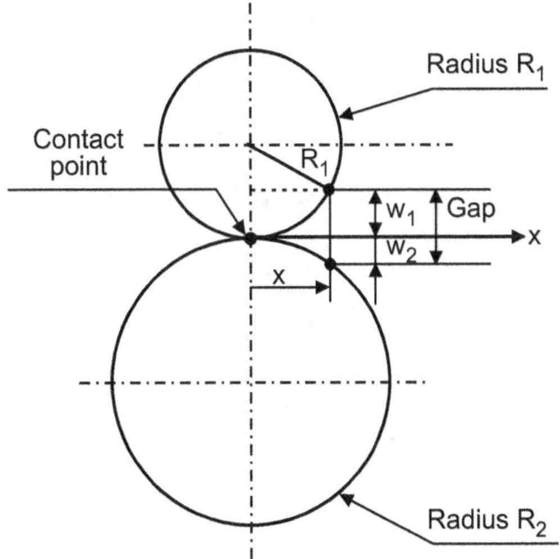

Fig. 7.4 : Cylinders in contact

Fig. 7.4 shows two cylinders or two rollers in contact, the gap between the two cylinders at a distance x from the contact point is given by,

$$\text{Gap} = w_1 + w_2 = \left(R_1 - \sqrt{R_1^2 - x^2}\right) + \left(R_2 - \sqrt{R_2^2 - x^2}\right)$$

$$\therefore \quad w_1 + w_2 = R_1 - R_1\left[1 - \left(\frac{x}{R_1}\right)^2\right]^{1/2} + R_2 - R_2\left[1 - \left(\frac{x}{R_2}\right)^2\right]^{1/2}$$

Further, using Taylor's series,

$$w_1 + w_2 = R_1 - R_1\left[1 - \frac{1}{2}\frac{x^2}{R_1^2} + \ldots\ldots\right] + R_2 - R_2\left[1 - \frac{1}{2}\frac{x^2}{R_2^2} + \ldots\ldots\right]$$

$$= R_1 - R_1 + \frac{x^2}{2R_1} + R_2 - R_2 + \frac{x^2}{2R_2}$$

$$= \frac{x^2}{2}\left(\frac{1}{R_1} + \frac{1}{R_2}\right)$$

$$= \frac{x^2}{2}\left(\frac{1}{R}\right) \quad \ldots \text{ by equation (7.14)}$$

$$\therefore \text{ Gap} = w_1 + w_2 = \frac{x^2}{2R} \qquad \qquad \ldots (7.17)$$

where, R is the reduced radius of a single cylinder on the plane.

Next, if external loads are applied, due to elastic deformation the gap will become zero and 'x' becomes the half contact width 'a', as shown in Fig. 7.5.

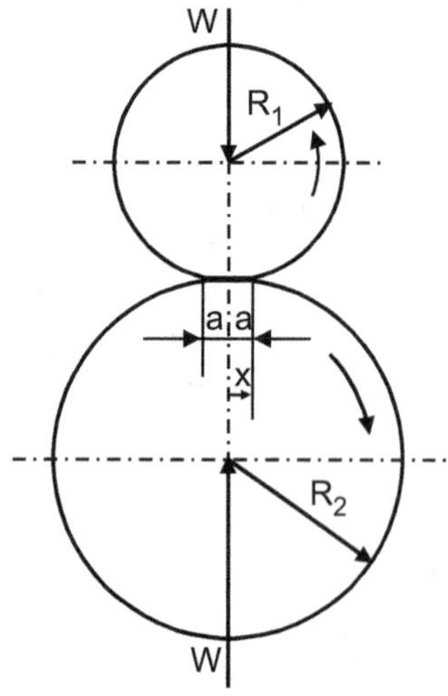

Fig. 7.5 : Cylinders in contact under external load W

Substituting $x = a$ in equation (7.17), we get,

$$w_1 + w_2 = \frac{a^2}{2R} \qquad \qquad ... (7.18)$$

Here, w_1 and w_2 are given by,

$$w_1 = \frac{1 - v_1^2}{E_1} p_{max} \, a \text{ and } w_2 = \frac{1 - v_2^2}{E_2} p_{max} \, a \qquad \qquad ... (7.19)$$

Substituting from equation (7.19) in equation (7.18), we get,

$$w_1 + w_2 = \frac{a^2}{2R} = \frac{1 - v_1^2}{E_1} p_{max} \, a + \frac{1 - v_2^2}{E_2} p_{max} \, a$$

$$\therefore \quad w_1 + w_2 = \frac{a^2}{2R} = \left(\frac{1 - v_1^2}{E_1} + \frac{1 - v_2^2}{E_2} \right) p_{max} \, a \qquad \qquad ... (7.20)$$

Also from equation (7.16), we have,

$$w' = \frac{W}{L} = \frac{\pi}{2} p_{max} \, a$$

$$\therefore \quad p_{max} \, a = \frac{2W}{\pi L} \qquad \qquad ... (7.21)$$

Substituting from equation (7.21) in equation (7.20), we get,

$$\frac{a^2}{2R} = \left(\frac{1 - v_1^2}{E_1} + \frac{1 - v_2^2}{E_2} \right) \times \frac{2W}{\pi L}$$

$$\therefore \quad a^2 = \left(\frac{1 - v_1^2}{E_1} + \frac{1 - v_2^2}{E_2} \right) \times \frac{4WR}{\pi L}$$

$$\therefore \quad a = \sqrt{ \left(\frac{1 - v_1^2}{E_1} + \frac{1 - v_2^2}{E_2} \right) \frac{4WR}{\pi L} } \qquad \qquad ... (7.22)$$

Next, for rollers having similar materials, the half contact width is given by,

$$v = v_1 = v_2 \text{ and } E = E_1 = E_2$$

$$\therefore \quad a = \sqrt{ \left(\frac{1 - v^2}{E} \right) \frac{8WR}{\pi L} } \qquad \qquad ... (7.23)$$

7.2.3 Ertel-Grubin Equation

The study of elastohydrodynamic lubrication of two rollers, deformed by the pressure generated within entrapped fluid whose viscosity is itself altered by the pressure, was firstly carried out by Ertel and which was further completed by Grubin, and therefore, the equation is known as **Ertel-Grubin Equation.**

They made two simplifying assumptions :

- The deformed shape within the contact zone is parallel and constant; and

- The shape outside the Hertzian zone is the same whether there is a lubricant or not.

They argued that, if the two non-conforming surfaces are in contact under normal load, the contact area and the pressure are almost Hertzian. The surfaces undergo elastic deformation and the area of contact can be found by using the Hertzian equation for dry contact conditions. The area of contact is almost a flat surface. The entrapped oil film in the contact zone is parallel and equal to h_0. As the oil is entrapped and subjected to pressure, the pressure remains constant as q (modified pressure) and also the viscosity as μ (viscosity of oil at pressure p).

The above statement is proved as follows :

As soon as the oil enters the Hertzian zone, the pressures get so high that $p \to \infty$, and $e^{-\alpha p} \to 0$. Therefore q is given by equation (7.5) in which $q \to \dfrac{1}{\alpha}$, and is a constant. Thus, if q is constant then $\dfrac{dq}{dx} = 0$. If it is zero, then $h - h_m = 0$ [Refer equation (7.10)] or $h = h_m = h_0$, i.e. constant film thickness. The film thickness, therefore, must be parallel and there is no hydrodynamic pressure variation through the thickness of the film. If the film is parallel (and there is no hydrodynamic pressure variation through the thickness of film), **the pressure in the Hertzian zone is the same whether there is a film or not** and is not affected by the existence of the oil film.

The pressures **outside** the zone are much smaller than the pressures **inside.** Therefore, the shape of the surface outside the contact is determined **solely** by the Hertz pressure inside and the hydrodynamic pressure is considered to have no influence on it. The film shape is therefore known from the Hertz equations already derived for **dry** contact conditions. The oil film in the contact is parallel and equal to h_0. Outside the contact zone, the film shape or thickness h is ($h_0 + h_s$), where h_s is the gap between the distorted bodies found by purely Hertzian contact stress. The shape is not altered by the pressure there, as the pressure is very small. Therefore, **the film thickness outside the contact zone is given by,**

$$h \;=\; h_0 + h_s$$

$$\therefore \quad h \;=\; h_0 + \left(\frac{1 - v_1^2}{E_1} + \frac{1 - v_2^2}{E_2}\right) p_{max}\, a \left[\frac{x}{a}\sqrt{\frac{x^2}{a^2} - 1} - \log_e\left(\frac{x}{a} + \sqrt{\frac{x^2}{a^2} - 1}\right)\right] \quad \text{... (7.24)}$$

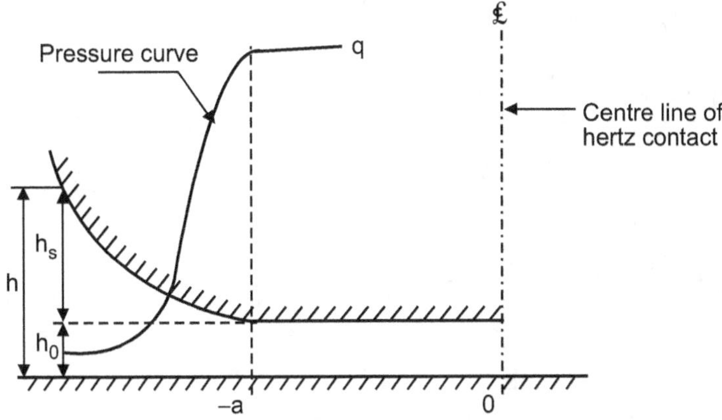

Fig. 7.6 : Reduced pressure curve and oil film thickness for Grubin's theory

The standard integrated form of modified Reynold's equation will be,

$$\frac{dq}{dx} = 6\,\mu_o\,U\left(\frac{h - h_m}{h^3}\right) \qquad \text{... Refer equation (7.10)}$$

where,

$$q = \frac{1 - e^{-\alpha p}}{\alpha} \qquad \text{or} \qquad q = \frac{1 - (1 + cp)^{1-n}}{(n - 1)\,c}$$

As αp or cp and n are very large, q is constant and respectively equal to $\frac{1}{\alpha}$ or $\frac{1}{(n - 1)\,c}$.

As the pressure is constant inside the contact zone, $\frac{dq}{dx}$ must be zero and hence $h_0 = h_m = $ constant, but the equation for q just outside the contact zone is,

$$\frac{dq}{dx} = 6\,\mu_o\,U\left(\frac{h - h_m}{h^3}\right)$$

$$\therefore \quad \frac{dq}{dx} = 6\,\mu_o\,U\left[\frac{(h_0 + h_s) - h_0}{(h_0 + h_s)^3}\right]$$

$$\therefore \quad \frac{dq}{dx} = 6\,\mu_o\,U\,\frac{h_s}{(h_0 + h_s)^3} \qquad \text{... (7.25)}$$

But the equation for gap h at any point outside the contact zone is given by,

$$h = h_0 + h_s$$

where,

$$h_s = \left(\frac{1 - v_1^2}{E_1} + \frac{1 - v_2^2}{E_2}\right) p_{max}\, a\left[\frac{x}{a}\sqrt{\frac{x^2}{a^2} - 1} - \log_e\left(\frac{x}{a} + \sqrt{\frac{x^2}{a^2} - 1}\right)\right] \qquad \text{... (7.26)}$$

Now, from equation (7.16), we have,

Load per unit length $= W' = \dfrac{W}{L} = \dfrac{\pi}{2} p_{max} \, a$

$$\therefore \qquad p_{max} \, a = \frac{2W}{\pi L} \qquad \qquad \text{... (7.27)}$$

$$\text{Let} \qquad \left(\frac{1 - v_1^2}{\pi E_1} + \frac{1 - v_2^2}{\pi E_2} \right) = \frac{1}{E'} \qquad \qquad \text{... (7.28)}$$

$$\text{i.e.} \qquad \left(\frac{1 - v_1^2}{E_1} + \frac{1 - v_2^2}{E_2} \right) = \frac{\pi}{E'} \qquad \qquad \text{... (7.29)}$$

Substituting from equations (7.27) and (7.29) in equation (7.26), we get,

$$h_s = \frac{\pi}{E'} \times \frac{2W}{\pi L} \left[\frac{x}{a} \sqrt{\frac{x^2}{a^2} - 1} - \log_e \left(\frac{x}{a} + \sqrt{\frac{x^2}{a^2} - 1} \right) \right]$$

$$\text{i.e.} \qquad h_s = \frac{2W}{E'L} \left[\frac{x}{a} \sqrt{\frac{x^2}{a^2} - 1} - \log_e \left(\frac{x}{a} + \sqrt{\frac{x^2}{a^2} - 1} \right) \right]$$

$$\text{i.e.} \qquad \frac{h_s E'}{W/L} = 2 \left[\frac{x}{a} \sqrt{\frac{x^2}{a^2} - 1} - \log_e \left(\frac{x}{a} + \sqrt{\frac{x^2}{a^2} - 1} \right) \right] \qquad \text{... (7.30)}$$

If we define,

$$\bar{h} = \frac{hE'}{W/L}, \quad \bar{h}_0 = \frac{h_0 E'}{W/L} \text{ and } \bar{h}_s = \frac{h_s E'}{W/L} \qquad \text{... (7.31)}$$

then,

$$\bar{h} = \bar{h}_0 + \bar{h}_s = \frac{E'}{W/L} (h_0 + h_s) \qquad \qquad \text{... (7.32)}$$

Substituting from equations (7.31) and (7.32) in equation (7.25), we get,

$$\frac{dq}{dx} = 6 \, \mu_0 \, U \, \frac{\bar{h}_s \left(\dfrac{W/L}{E'} \right)}{\left[\bar{h} \left(\dfrac{W/L}{E'} \right) \right]^3}$$

$$\therefore \qquad \frac{dq}{dx} = \frac{6 \, \mu_0 \, U \, \bar{h}_s}{\left(\dfrac{W}{E'L} \right)^2 \, \bar{h}^3} \qquad \qquad \text{... (7.33)}$$

Now, let us define,

$$\bar{q} = \frac{\left(\dfrac{W}{E'L}\right)^2}{6\,\mu_o\,Ua}\,q \qquad \text{... (7.34)}$$

Then, substituting equation (7.34) in equation (7.33), we get,

$$\frac{d\bar{q}}{d\bar{x}} = \frac{\bar{h}_s}{\bar{h}^3} \qquad \text{... (7.35)}$$

Now, to find $\bar{q}$, integrate equation (7.35) numerically between limits $x = -\infty$ and $= -a$ (or $\bar{x} = -\infty$ and $\bar{x} = -1$), where $\bar{x} = \dfrac{x}{a}$.

$$\therefore \qquad \bar{q} = \int_{-\infty}^{-1} \bar{h}_s\,\frac{d\bar{x}}{\bar{h}^3} \qquad \text{... (7.36)}$$

When $\bar{q}$ is solved numerically, it can be transformed to p by using the equation,

$$q = \frac{1 - e^{-\alpha p}}{\alpha}$$

From the solution of the above equation, it will be shown that, at $x = -a$, the pressure, $\bar{q}$ can be approximated by the empirical relation,

$$\bar{q} = 0.0986\,\bar{h}_o^{(-11/8)} \qquad \text{... (7.37)}$$

Further, $q = \dfrac{1}{\alpha}$ at $\bar{x} = \dfrac{x}{a} = -1$ i.e. at $x = -a$ and

$$a^2 = \left(\frac{1-v^2}{\pi E}\right)\frac{8WR}{\pi L} \qquad \text{(for similar materials)}$$

$$\text{or} \qquad a^2 = \left(\frac{1-v_1^2}{E_1} + \frac{1-v_2^2}{E_2}\right)\frac{4WR}{\pi L} \qquad \text{(for dissimilar materials)}$$

$$\text{i.e.} \qquad a^2 = \left(\frac{1-v_1^2}{\pi E_1} + \frac{1-v_2^2}{\pi E_2}\right)\frac{4WR}{L}$$

$$a^2 = \left(\frac{1}{E'}\right)\frac{4WR}{L}$$

$$\text{i.e.} \qquad a = \left(\frac{4}{E'}\,\frac{WR}{L}\right)^{1/2} \qquad \text{... (7.38)}$$

Since $q = \dfrac{1}{\alpha}$ at $x = -a$, therefore, from equation (7.34), q can be written as,

$$q = \frac{6\,\mu_o\,U\,a}{(W/E'L)^2}\quad \bar{q} = \frac{1}{\alpha}$$

$\therefore$
$$\frac{1}{\alpha} = \frac{6\,\mu_o\,U\,a}{(W/E'L)^2} \times 0.0986 \;\bar{h}_o^{\,(-11/8)}$$

i.e.
$$\frac{1}{\alpha} = \frac{6\,\mu_o\,U}{(W/E'L)^2}\left(\frac{4WR}{E'L}\right)^{1/2} \times 0.0986\;\bar{h}_o^{\,(-11/8)}$$

$$\frac{1}{\alpha} = \frac{6\,\mu_o\,U}{(W/E'L)^2}\left(\frac{4WR}{E'L}\right)^{1/2} \times 0.0986\left(\frac{h_0 E'}{W/L}\right)^{-11/8}$$

$\therefore$
$$h_0^{\,11/8} = \frac{6 \times 2 \times 0.0986}{(W/E'L)^2}\left(\frac{WR}{E'L}\right)^{1/2}\left(\frac{W}{LE'}\right)^{11/8}\mu_o\,U\,\alpha$$

$\therefore$
$$h_0^{\,11/8} = \frac{1.1832\,\mu_o\,U\,\alpha\,R^{1/2}}{(W/E'L)^{1/8}}$$

$\therefore$
$$h_0 = \left[\frac{1.1832\;\mu_o\,U\,\alpha\,R^{1/2}}{\left(\dfrac{W}{E'L}\right)^{1/8}}\right]^{8/11}$$

$\therefore$
$$h_0 = \frac{1.130\,(\mu_o\,U\,\alpha)^{8/11}\,R^{4/11}}{\left(\dfrac{W}{E'L}\right)^{1/11}} \qquad\qquad \text{... (7.39)}$$

Now,

$$\frac{1}{E'} = \left(\frac{1-v_1^2}{\pi E_1} + \frac{1-v_2^2}{\pi E_2}\right) \qquad\qquad \text{... from equation (7.28)}$$

For both surfaces of similar materials,

$$\frac{1}{E'} = \frac{2}{\pi}\left(\frac{1-v^2}{E}\right)$$

$\therefore$
$$\left(\frac{1}{E'}\right)^{1/11} = \left(\frac{2}{\pi}\right)^{1/11}\left(\frac{1-v^2}{E}\right)^{1/11} = 0.96\left(\frac{1-v^2}{E}\right)^{1/11}$$

Substituting this in equation (7.39), we get,

$$h_0 = \frac{1.130\,(\mu_o\,U\,\alpha)^{8/11}\,R^{4/11}}{\left(\dfrac{W}{L}\right)^{1/11}\left[0.96\left(\dfrac{1-v^2}{E}\right)^{1/11}\right]}$$

$$\therefore \quad h_0 = \frac{1.18 \, (\mu_O \, U \, \alpha)^{8/11} \, R^{4/11}}{\left[(1 - \nu^2) \dfrac{W}{LE}\right]^{1/11}}$$

$$\therefore \quad \frac{h_0}{R} = \frac{1.18 \, (\mu_O \, U \, \alpha)^{8/11} \, R^{4/11}}{\left[(1 - \nu^2) \dfrac{W}{LE}\right]^{1/11}} \times \frac{1}{R}$$

$$\therefore \quad \frac{h_0}{R} = \frac{1.18 \, (\mu_O \, U \, \alpha)^{8/11}}{\left[(1 - \nu^2) \dfrac{W}{LE}\right]^{1/11}} \times \frac{1}{R^{7/11}}$$

$$\therefore \quad \frac{h_0}{R} = \frac{1.18 \, (\mu_O \, U \, \alpha/R)^{8/11}}{\left[(1 - \nu^2) \dfrac{W}{ELR}\right]^{1/11}}$$

Now, $\nu = 0.3$, giving $\dfrac{1}{(1 - \nu^2)^{1/11}} = \dfrac{1}{[1 - (0.3)^2]^{1/11}} = 1.009$

$$\therefore \quad \frac{h_0}{R} = 1.19 \left(\frac{\mu_O \, U \, \alpha}{R}\right)^{8/11} \left(\frac{ELR}{W}\right)^{1/11} \qquad \text{... (7.40)}$$

which is a Ertel-Grubin equation.

The equation (7.40) gives a very accurate representation of the mean oil film thickness upto the midpoint. **The Ertel-Grubin theory takes only the entry region into account when finding the film thickness and it does it remarkably well.**

7.3 APPLICATIONS

Many machine components carry heavy loads with low-geometrical conformity such as gears, cams, rolling-element bearings, etc. In these non-conformity heavily loaded contacts, the elastic deformation of the bounding solids is large and affects the hydrodynamic lubrication process. The elastohydrodynamic lubrication deals with the lubrication of these elastic solids.

The elastohydrodynamic phenomena can also occur in some low-elastic modulus contacts of high geometrical conformity such as lip seals, thrust and journal bearings with soft liners and tape head interfaces of magnetic recording of tape drives.

7.4 INTRODUCTION TO GAS LUBRICATED BEARINGS

For many years, air-lubricated bearings have been a source of interest as air is available in abundant quantity. The basic principle of operation of hydrodynamic bearing or a hydrostatic bearing with gas as a lubricant is same as that of an oil-lubricated bearing. An early research on gas-lubricated bearings revealed that air might be a very desirable lubricant in bearings. Therefore, for many applications, air bearings are employed. There are some marked differences in behaviour of gas-lubricated bearings compared with liquid-lubricated bearings.

7.5 REQUIREMENTS OF GAS LUBRICATION

Following points are taken into account for the successful operation of an aerodynamic bearing.

- **Finished Surfaces of Bearings with High Accuracy :** As film thickness in gas-lubricated bearings is much thinner than oil-lubricated bearings, if the bearing surfaces are not finished with close tolerances, the minimum film thickness may be of the same order as the surface roughness of the journal and bearing.

- **Accurate Alignment between the Journal and Bearing :** The alignment between the journal and bearing must be very good as a slight misalignment of the surfaces will cause the fluid to alternatively expand and compress which distorts the pressure profile and the flow pattern.

- **Accurate Dimensions and Clearances :** In order to get smooth and correct operation of bearings, it must have accurate dimensions. Also the clearances provided must be accurate.

- **Speed must be High :** The basic requirement for every gas-lubricated bearing is that the speed of operation must be high as compared to the oil-lubricated bearings.

- **Load must be Low :** Another important aspect associated with gas-lubricated bearing is the load, which is required to be supported. It should be relatively low as compared to the load supported by an oil-lubricated bearing.

- **Variation of Density with Pressure :** At low speeds, the density may be treated as constant but at high speed operation the density variation with pressure must be taken into account. As a result of which the basic differential equation is of non-linear form.

- **Expansion of Gas is Considered to be Isothermal :** For analysis of gas bearings, the expansion of gas is considered to be isothermal. At moderate speeds the frictional losses are small and there is only a slight rise in temperature. The viscosity of a gas increases with increase in the temperature.

7.6 MERITS OF GAS BEARINGS

Gas bearings have numerous advantages over other bearings, some of which are discussed below.

- **Low Frictional Characteristics :** Gases have extremely low coefficient of absolute viscosity as compared to oils. Therefore, the viscous resistance is very less. In other words, the gas bearing has low frictional characteristics because of which these can be employed in various applications.

- **Operate over Extremely Wide Ranges of Temperature :** As there is no chemical degradation of the lubricant, these bearings can be operated over extremely wide ranges of temperature i.e. cryogenic temperature range of (–450°F) to very high temperature upto (3000°F).

- **Elimination of Losses in Bearing :** Negligible losses are associated with gas- lubricated bearings as compared to the oil bearings. Therefore, there is a reduction in frequent elimination of bearing seals.

- **Cleanliness in Bearing :** Due to elimination of losses and absence of oil, more cleanliness is associated with gas bearings than liquid bearings.

- **Elimination of Contamination :** Contamination is caused by most of the liquid lubricants. Gas bearings can be employed where it is needed to keep environment free from contamination.

- **Stability of Lubricant :** Gas bearings found to be more stable than oil bearings.

- **No Need of Cooling :** Due to its low frictional characteristics, there will be low heating of bearing, and therefore, cooling is not required. Thus, these bearings are also called as constant temperature bearings.

- **Permits High Speeds :** Low frictional and heating characteristics permit practical attainment of high speeds (e.g. 700,000 rpm).

- **No Vaporization, Cavitation, Solidification and Decomposition of Lubricant :** There is no vaporization, cavitation, solidification and decomposition of the gases over extreme high ranges of temperature (e.g. from very low temperature of – 450°F to high temperature of approximately 3000°F).

- **Lower Cost and Easily Available Lubricant :** Air as lubricant is available in abundant quantity and the only cost involved is that for filtering the lubricant.

7.7 DEMERITS OF GAS BEARINGS

Gas bearings possess the following disadvantages.

- **Reduced Unit-Load Carrying Capacity :** Gas bearings have a reduced unit-load carrying capacity, generally with self-acting bearings.

- **Bearings are Larger :** For some of the applications, the bearings are necessarily larger and operate with thinner films than their liquid bearing counterparts.

- **Need Closer Control over Manufacturing Aspects :** Thinner films in gas bearings demand closer control over manufacturing tolerances, surface finishes, thermal and elastic distortions and also the alignment between the journal and bearing.

- **Low Damping Characteristics :** Gas bearings are associated with low damping characteristics, which make it necessary to analyze the dynamic characteristics of the mechanical system using the gas bearing as there may not be enough damping to suppress the instability encountered or to control the instability encountered.

- **Gas Bearings are Less Forgiving than Oil-Lubricated Bearings :** Gas-lubricated bearings are less forgiving of errors in evaluating loads or of deviations from specifications during manufacture and installation and also of distortions associated with rotor bearing components or the housing.

7.8 APPLICATIONS OF GAS BEARINGS

Gas bearings are useful for wide varieties of applications which are listed below.

- Due to its low frictional characteristics, these bearings can be employed in near-static apparatus, such as dynamometers, wind tunnel balances and some other sophisticated mechanical instruments.

- Gas bearings are found in machine tool slideways in order to avoid the stick-slip vibration phenomenon, in high speed grinding spindles and in precision linear and rotational indexing metrology devices, due to their low frictional characteristics.

- Gas bearings can be employed over extremely wide ranges of temperatures e.g. in gas cooled reactors, for various types of expansion gas liquefiers, for cryogenic and pyrogenic turbomachinery where extremes of temperatures are no liability.

- These bearings can be used effectively where it is necessary to keep the environment free from contamination by liquid lubricant e.g. in high purity gas handling plants.

- Gas bearings are found in most of the high speed applications as in truly hermetically sealed high speed blowers and compressors where process gas is used as lubricant, and also in high speed dental and orthopedic drills and cutters operating upto 500,000 rpm.

- These bearings are used in high precision inertial guidance instruments such as gyroscopes and accelerometers.

- These bearings are used in foil type bearings for air cycle turbomachines on air-craft and space borne power generation components.

- Gas bearings are employed in computer peripheral devices including magnetic memory devices, tapes, discs and drums, read-write heads 'flying' with an air gap measured in micro-inches.

7.9 REYNOLDS EQUATION FOR GAS LUBRICATION

We know the Generalized Reynolds equation which can be given as,

$$\frac{\partial}{\partial x}\left[\frac{\rho h^3}{12\mu}\cdot\frac{\partial P}{\partial x}\right] + \frac{\partial}{\partial y}\left[\frac{\rho h^3}{12\mu}\cdot\frac{\partial P}{\partial y}\right] = \frac{\partial}{\partial x}\left[\frac{\rho h(u_a + u_b)}{2}\right] + \frac{\partial}{\partial y}\left[\frac{\rho h(v_a + v_b)}{2}\right]$$

$$+ \rho(\omega_a - \omega_b) - \rho u_a \cdot \frac{\partial h}{\partial x} - \rho v_a \cdot \frac{\partial h}{\partial y} + h \cdot \frac{\partial \rho}{\partial t}$$

This form can be applicable to two-dimensional motion. Now, film thickness is a function of x, y and time t.

∴   Total differential of film thickness will take the following form.

$$Dh \; = \; \frac{\partial h}{\partial t} \cdot dt + \frac{\partial h}{\partial x} \cdot dx + \frac{\partial h}{\partial y} \cdot dy$$

∴
$$\frac{Dh}{dt} \; = \; \frac{\partial h}{\partial t} + \frac{\partial h}{\partial x} \cdot \frac{dx}{dt} + \frac{\partial h}{\partial y} \cdot \frac{dy}{\partial t}$$

$$\frac{Dh}{Dt} \; = \; \frac{\partial h}{\partial t} + u_a \frac{\partial h}{\partial x} + v_a \cdot \frac{\partial h}{\partial y} \qquad \ldots (7.41)$$

Here,

$$\frac{Dh}{dt} \quad - \quad \text{Rate of change of total-film thickness with respect to time}$$

$$\text{t along z-direction}$$

$$\frac{Dh}{Dt} \quad - \quad \text{Approach velocity of two surfaces}$$

$$= \; (\omega_a - \omega_b)$$

Substituting in equation (7.41), it becomes,

$$(\omega_a - \omega_b) \; = \; \frac{\partial h}{\partial t} + u_a \cdot \frac{\partial h}{\partial x} + v_a \cdot \frac{\partial h}{\partial y}$$

$$\frac{\partial h}{\partial t} \; = \; (\omega_a - \omega_b) - u_a \frac{\partial h}{\partial x} - v_a \frac{\partial h}{\partial y}$$

Multiplying both sides by 'ρ' and adding the term $\left(h \frac{\partial \rho}{\partial t} \right)$ on both sides,

$$h \frac{\partial \rho}{\partial t} + \rho \frac{\partial h}{\partial t} \; = \; h \frac{\partial \rho}{\partial t} + \rho \, (\omega_a - \omega_b) - \rho \, u_a \cdot \frac{\partial h}{\partial x} - \rho \, v_a \cdot \frac{\partial h}{\partial y}$$

$$\partial \frac{(h\rho)}{\partial t} \; = \; \rho(\omega_a - \omega_b) - \rho \, u_a \cdot \frac{\partial h}{\partial x} - \rho \, v_a \cdot \frac{\partial h}{\partial y} + h \frac{\partial \rho}{\partial t}$$

Substituting above results in Generalized Reynolds equation, it becomes,

$$\frac{\partial}{\partial x}\left[\frac{\rho h^3}{12\mu}\frac{\partial P}{\partial x}\right] + \frac{\partial}{\partial y}\left[\frac{\rho h^3}{12\mu}\frac{\partial P}{\partial y}\right] = \frac{\partial}{\partial x}\left[\frac{\rho h(u_a + u_b)}{2}\right] + \frac{\partial}{\partial y}\left[\frac{\rho h(v_a + v_b)}{2}\right] + \frac{\partial}{\partial t}(\rho h) \;\ldots (7.42)$$

For unidirectional motion in x-direction and treating bushing fixed,

i.e. $\quad v_a = v_b = 0$

and $\quad u_a = 0$

Equation (7.42) becomes,

$$\frac{\partial}{\partial x}\left[\frac{\rho h^3}{12\mu} \cdot \frac{\partial P}{\partial x}\right] + \frac{\partial}{\partial y}\left[\frac{\rho h^3}{12\mu} \cdot \frac{\partial P}{\partial y}\right] = \frac{u_b}{2}\frac{\partial}{\partial x}(\rho h) + \frac{\partial}{\partial t}(\rho h) \qquad \text{... (7.43)}$$

Assumptions :

- Viscosity is a function of pressure and temperature.
- As pressure is low, the temperature variation is negligible (i.e. the film is isothermal).
- Assume viscosity constant.

i.e. $\quad \mu = $ Constant

Now equation (7.43) becomes,

$$\frac{\partial}{\partial x}\left[\rho h^3 \cdot \frac{\partial P}{\partial x}\right] + \frac{\partial}{\partial y}\left[\rho h^3 \cdot \frac{\partial P}{\partial y}\right] = 6u_b \cdot \mu \cdot \frac{\partial}{\partial x}(\rho h) + 12\mu \frac{\partial}{\partial t}(\rho h) \qquad \text{... (7.44)}$$

This is the governing differential equation of gas-lubricated bearings.

Now, we have two cases of pressure and density relationships.

(i) For Isothermal Condition :

We have $\qquad PV = mRT$

$$P\left(\frac{V}{m}\right) = RT = \text{Constant}$$

$$\frac{P}{\left(\dfrac{m}{V}\right)} = RT = C$$

$$\frac{P}{\rho} = RT = C$$

$\therefore \qquad P = \rho RT = \rho \cdot C \qquad \text{... (7.45)}$

where, R is the gas constant

T is the absolute temperature

ρ is the density of air

P is the pressure of gas.

(ii) For Polytropic Condition :

If it is assumed that a gas obeys a polytropic relationship, then

$$\frac{P}{\rho^n} = C_1 = \text{Constant}$$

$$P = \rho^n \cdot C_1$$

$$\rho = P^{1/n} \cdot C_2 \qquad \text{... (7.46)}$$

where,

$$n \text{ is polytropic index} = \frac{C_p}{C_v}$$

$$= 1 \quad \dots \text{ (for isothermal flow)}$$

Now, substituting equation (7.46) in equation (7.44), it becomes,

$$\frac{\partial}{\partial x}\left[P^{1/n} \cdot h^3 \cdot C_2 \cdot \frac{\partial P}{\partial x}\right] + \frac{\partial}{\partial y}\left[P^{1/n} \cdot h^3 \cdot C_2 \cdot \frac{\partial P}{\partial y}\right] = 6u_b \cdot \mu \cdot \frac{\partial}{\partial x}(P^{1/n} \cdot C_2 \cdot h)$$

$$+ 12\,\mu\,\frac{\partial}{\partial t} \cdot (P^{1/n} \cdot C_2 \cdot h)$$

Cancelling out constant C_2 from both sides, we get,

$$\frac{\partial}{\partial x}\left[P^{1/n} \cdot h^3 \cdot \frac{\partial P}{\partial x}\right] + \frac{\partial}{\partial y}\left[P^{1/n} \cdot h^3 \cdot \frac{\partial P}{\partial y}\right] = 6u_b \cdot \mu \frac{\partial}{\partial x}\left[P^{1/n} \cdot h\right] + 12\,\mu \cdot \frac{\partial}{\partial t}\left[P^{1/n} \cdot h\right] \quad \dots (7.47)$$

This is an equation for gas-lubricated bearings obeying adiabatic process where, $n = \dfrac{C_p}{C_v}$.

For $n = 1$, equation (7.47) takes the form as,

$$\frac{\partial}{\partial x}\left[P \cdot h^3 \cdot \frac{\partial P}{\partial x}\right] + \frac{\partial}{\partial y}\left[P \cdot h^3 \cdot \frac{\partial P}{\partial y}\right] = 6u_b \cdot \mu \frac{\partial}{\partial x}[P \cdot h] + 12\,\mu \frac{\partial}{\partial t}[P \cdot h] \quad \dots (7.48)$$

This is an equation for gas-lubricated bearings following isothermal process where, **n = 1.**

Dimensionless Form :

For analysis of gas bearing, the equation derived for hydrodynamic bearing and hydrostatic bearing can be applied to gas bearings depending upon the degree of compressibility that exists. The extent of compressibility is determined by a dimensionless group of parameters that evolve from mathematical analysis, which is called as compressibility number.

Now, in case of liquid bearings, pressures are considered as gauge pressures while in case of air bearings, pressures are considered as absolute pressures.

Let $\qquad p_a$ = atmospheric pressure

Now, $\qquad P = \dfrac{p}{p_a}$

$\therefore \qquad p = P \cdot p_a$

Also, $\qquad \dfrac{h}{h_m} = H$

Absolute film thickness,

$$h = h_m \cdot H$$

Let,

l – Dimension of bearing in Y-direction

B – Dimension of bearing in X-direction

t – Time variable

T – Any particular time value

Now,

$$\frac{x}{B} = X \;\Rightarrow\; x = X \cdot B = X \cdot \pi D \qquad\qquad \dots (\because B = \pi D)$$

$$\therefore \qquad \partial x = B \cdot \partial X$$

$$\frac{y}{l} = Y \Rightarrow y = Y \cdot l$$

$$\therefore \qquad \partial y = l \cdot dY$$

$$\frac{t}{T} = \frac{1}{\omega} \;\Rightarrow\; t = \frac{T}{\omega}$$

$$\partial t = \frac{1}{\omega} \cdot \partial T$$

Now substituting the above values in equation (7.41), it becomes,

$$\frac{\partial}{\partial x}\left[p_a^{1/n}\, P^{1/n} \cdot h^3 \cdot \frac{\partial P}{\partial x} \right] + \frac{\partial}{\partial y}\left[p_a^{1/n}\, P^{1/n} \cdot h^3 \cdot \frac{\partial P}{\partial y} \right] = 6u_b \cdot \mu \frac{\partial}{\partial x}\left[p_a^{1/n}\, P^{1/n} \cdot h \right] + 12\,\mu \cdot \frac{\partial}{\partial t}\left[P^{1/n} \cdot h \right]$$

$$\therefore \quad \frac{\partial}{B\,\partial X}\left[p_a^{1/n} \cdot P^{1/n} \cdot h_m^3 \cdot H^3 \cdot p_a \cdot \frac{\partial P}{B\,\partial X} \right] + \frac{\partial}{l\,\partial Y}\left[p_a^{1/n} \cdot P^{1/n} \cdot h_m^3 \cdot H^3 \cdot p_a \cdot \frac{\partial P}{l\,\partial Y} \right]$$

$$+ 6u_b \cdot \mu \frac{\partial}{B\,\partial X}\left[p_a^{1/n} \cdot P^{1/n} \cdot h_m \cdot H \right] + 12\,\mu \cdot \omega \cdot \frac{\partial}{\partial T}\left[p_a^{1/n} \cdot P^{1/n} \cdot h_m \cdot H \right] \qquad \dots (7.49)$$

Multiplying both sides by $\left[\dfrac{B^2}{h_m^3 \cdot p_a} \right]$,

$$\frac{\partial}{\partial X}\left[p_a^{1/n} \cdot H^3 \cdot \frac{\partial P}{\partial X} \right] + \left(\frac{B}{l}\right)^2 \frac{\partial}{\partial Y}\left[P^{1/n} \cdot H^3 \cdot \frac{\partial P}{\partial Y} \right] =$$

$$\frac{B^2}{h_m^3 \cdot p_a}\left[\frac{6u_b \cdot \mu}{B} \cdot h_m \frac{\partial}{\partial X}(P^{1/n} \cdot H) + 12\,\mu \cdot \omega \cdot h_m \cdot \frac{\partial}{\partial T}(P^{1/n} \cdot H) \right]$$

$$\frac{\partial}{\partial X}\left[P^{1/n} \cdot H^3 \cdot \frac{\partial P}{\partial X}\right] + \left(\frac{B}{l}\right)^2 \frac{\partial}{\partial Y}\left[P^{1/n} \cdot H \cdot \frac{\partial P}{\partial Y}\right] = \frac{6u_b \cdot \mu \cdot B}{h_m^2 \cdot p_a} \frac{\partial}{\partial X}[P^{1/n} \cdot H] + \frac{12\,\mu \cdot \omega \cdot B^2}{h_m^2 \cdot p_a}$$

$$\frac{\partial}{\partial T}[P^{1/n} \cdot H] \quad \dots (7.50)$$

Let,
$$\lambda = \left(\frac{B}{l}\right) \Rightarrow \text{width to length ratio}$$

and
$$\wedge_g = \frac{6u_b \cdot \mu \cdot B}{p_a \cdot h_m^2} \quad - \quad \text{Dimensionless bearing number suggested by Cap. Sawyer}$$

$$\sigma_g = \frac{12\,\mu \cdot \omega \cdot B^2}{p_a \cdot h_m^2} \quad - \quad \text{Dimensionless squeeze number}$$

Using these notations, equation (7.50) becomes,

$$\frac{\partial}{\partial X}\left[P^{1/n} \cdot H^3 \cdot \frac{\partial P}{\partial X}\right] + \lambda^2 \frac{\partial}{\partial Y}\left[P^{1/n} \cdot H \cdot \frac{\partial P}{\partial Y}\right] + \wedge_g \cdot \frac{\partial}{\partial X}[P^{1/n} \cdot H] + \rho_g \frac{\partial}{\partial T}[P^{1/n} \cdot H] \quad \dots (7.51)$$

This is a generalized equation for gas bearings in terms of dimensionless numbers $\wedge_g$ and σ_g.

For Isothermal Condition, n = 1

$$\frac{\partial}{\partial X}\left[PH^3 \frac{\partial P}{\partial X}\right] + \lambda^2 \frac{\partial}{\partial Y}\left[PH^3 \cdot \frac{\partial P}{\partial Y}\right] = \wedge_g \frac{\partial}{\partial X}[P \cdot H] + \sigma_g \cdot \frac{\partial}{\partial T}[PH] \quad \dots (7.52)$$

Under Steady-State Conditions :

$$\frac{\partial}{\partial X}\left[PH^3 \cdot \frac{\partial P}{\partial X}\right] + \lambda^2 \frac{\partial}{\partial Y}\left[PH^3 \cdot \frac{\partial P}{\partial Y}\right] = \wedge_g \cdot \frac{\partial}{\partial X}[PH] \quad \dots (7.53)$$

Two cases are discussed below.

(i)   Infinitely Long Bearing :

For which it is assumed that side leakage is negligible.

$$\therefore \qquad \lambda^2 = \left(\frac{B}{l}\right)^2$$

$$\frac{\partial}{\partial X}\left[PH^3 \cdot \frac{\partial P}{\partial X}\right] = \wedge_g \cdot \frac{\partial(PH)}{\partial X}$$

(ii)   Infinitely Short Bearing :

$$\lambda^2 \frac{\partial}{\partial Y}\left[PH^3 \cdot \frac{\partial P}{\partial Y}\right] = \wedge_g \cdot \frac{\partial(PH)}{\partial X}$$

There are two limiting cases.

(i) Extremely Low Speed :

The operation of the bearing approaches that of the incompressible case, thus, resulting in very small bearing number $\wedge_g$.

For small bearing numbers as u_b approaches to zero,

Bearing number $\wedge_g \Rightarrow 0$.

And $P \Rightarrow 1$.

$$\left(\text{i.e. } P = \frac{p}{p_a} = 1 \right)$$

$$\text{i.e.} \qquad p = p_a$$

$$\therefore \qquad \Delta P \Rightarrow 0$$

On differentiating equation (7.53),

$$P \frac{\partial}{\partial X}\left[H^3 \frac{\partial P}{\partial X} \right] + H^3 \frac{\partial P}{\partial X}\frac{\partial P}{\partial X} + \lambda^2 P \cdot \frac{\partial}{\partial Y}\left[H^3 \cdot \frac{\partial P}{\partial Y} \right] + H^3 \frac{\partial P}{\partial Y} \cdot \frac{\partial P}{\partial Y} = \wedge_g \left[P \cdot \frac{\partial H}{\partial X} + H \cdot \frac{\partial P}{\partial X} \right]$$

Dividing both sides by P,

$$\frac{\partial}{\partial X}\left[H^3 \cdot \frac{\partial P}{\partial X} \right] + \frac{H^3}{P}\left[\frac{\partial P}{\partial X} \right]^2 + \lambda^2 \frac{\partial}{\partial Y}\left[H^3 \frac{\partial P}{\partial Y} \right] + \frac{X^2}{P} H^3 \left[\frac{\partial P}{\partial Y} \right]^2 = \wedge_g \left[\frac{\partial H}{\partial X} + \frac{H}{P}\frac{\partial P}{\partial X} \right]$$

$$\frac{\partial}{\partial X}\left[H^3 \frac{\partial P}{\partial X} \right] + \frac{H^3}{P}\left[\left(\frac{\partial P}{\partial X}\right)^2 + \lambda^2 \left(\frac{\partial P}{\partial Y}\right)^2 \right] + \lambda^2 \frac{\partial}{\partial Y}\left(H^3 \cdot \frac{\partial P}{\partial Y} \right)$$

$$= \wedge_g \left[\frac{\partial H}{\partial X} + \frac{H}{P} \cdot \frac{\partial P}{\partial X} \right]$$

Here, $\qquad u_b \to 0$

$$\wedge_g \to 0$$

$$\Delta \to 0 \qquad \text{and} \qquad P \to 1$$

As $\qquad \left(\frac{\partial P}{\partial X}\right)^2 << \left(\frac{\partial P}{\partial X}\right) \qquad\qquad \left(\because \frac{\partial P}{\partial X} << \frac{\partial H}{\partial X} \right)$

and $\qquad \left(\frac{\partial P}{\partial X}\right)^2 << \left(\frac{\partial P}{\partial Y}\right)$

$\therefore$ Neglecting small terms,

$$\frac{\partial}{\partial X}\left(H^3 \cdot \frac{\partial P}{\partial X} \right) + \lambda^2 \frac{\partial}{\partial Y}\left(H^3 \cdot \frac{\partial P}{\partial Y} \right) = \wedge_g \left[\frac{\partial H}{\partial X} \right] \qquad\qquad \text{... (7.54)}$$

This is the equation for gas-lubricated bearings supplied for extremely low speed applications.

(ii)   Extremely High Speed :

When $\wedge_g$ approaches one, operation of the bearing approaches that of the compressible case. As $\wedge_g$ gets larger with lower ambient pressure or high speed, the compressibility effects become very significant. Thus, for large bearing number,

If u_b approaches ∞

$\therefore$ $\wedge_g$ approaches ∞

and for pressure to be finite,

$$\frac{\partial}{\partial X}(PH) \Rightarrow 0 = 0$$

$\therefore$ $P \cdot H$ must be constant.

$$\therefore \qquad P = \frac{p}{p_a}$$

$$H = \frac{h}{h_m}$$

Substituting in above equation,

$$\therefore \qquad \frac{p}{p_a} \times \frac{h}{h_m} = \text{Constant}$$

$$\therefore \qquad p \cdot h = p_a \cdot h_m = \text{Constant} \qquad \qquad \text{... (7.55)}$$

Conclusion :

In oil-lubricated bearings, the pressure is proportional to the speed and viscosity of lubricant and is independent of the ambient pressure, whereas in gas-lubricated bearings at high speeds, the pressure is independent of speed and viscosity and is dependent on ambient pressure.

7.10 SLIP AT THE FLUID SOLID INTERFACE

When gas films become very thin, while operating in a partial vacuum, the gas may no longer be considered as a continuous fluid, with the bulk viscosity of that fluid.

While deriving Reynolds equation it was assumed that the distributed film velocity is replaced by the film surface velocities. When the bearing film thickness is comparable to the mean free molecular path of the gas, continum flow theory is not valid and the slip flow occurs at the boundary between the bearing surface and the gas.

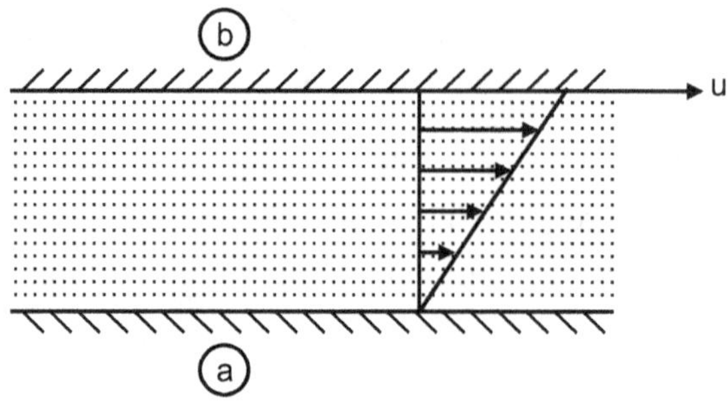

Fig. 7.7 : Slip at the fluid solid interface

Knudsen Number (K_n) :

It is defined as the ratio of the mean free molecular path and the film thickness. It is a measure of the average number of molecular collisions in a given length i.e. Knudsen number is a measure of slip flow.

i.e. $\qquad K_n = \dfrac{\lambda_m}{h}$ $\qquad\qquad\qquad$ ... (7.56)

where, $\qquad K_n$ – Knudsen number

$\qquad\qquad \lambda_m$ – Mean free path of molecules (MFMP)

$\qquad\qquad h$ – Film thickness

Following Table 7.1 shows values of λ_m for different gases.

Table 7.1 : Values of λ_m for Different Gases

Gases	λ_m (µm)
Air	0.064
Hydrogen	0.1125
Neon	0.132
Helium	0.186

Knudsen Number	Type of Flow
(i)　　$K_n < 0.01$	The flow is treated as continuum or laminar flow.
(ii)　　$0.01 < K_n < 1.5$	The flow is treated as slip flow.
(iii)　　$K_n > 1.5$	Fully developed molecular flow.

e.g. At atmospheric pressure and temperature,

$\qquad\qquad \lambda_m = 0.064$ µm

Let $\qquad\qquad h = 2.54$ µm

$\therefore \qquad K_n = \dfrac{\lambda_m}{h} = \dfrac{0.064}{2.54} = 0.025$

$$\therefore \qquad 0.01 \ \leq \ K_n \ \leq \ 1.5$$

Thus, flow is slip flow.

Now for laminar flow, $K_n < 0.01$

$$\therefore \qquad \frac{\lambda_m}{h} \ < \ 0.01$$

At atmospheric pressure and temperature,

$$\lambda_m \ = \ 0.064 \ \mu m$$

$$\therefore \qquad \frac{0.064}{h} \ < \ 0.01 \ \Rightarrow \ h \ > \ \frac{0.064}{0.01}$$

$$\therefore \qquad h \ > \ 6.4 \ \mu m$$

7.11 PRINCIPLES OF AIR BEARINGS

- For low speed operation of bearings, the behaviour of aerodynamic bearing is similar to that of hydrodynamic bearing.

- For extremely low speeds, load-carrying capacity is not a function of velocity and viscosity but is a function of ambient pressure.

- For extremely high speeds, side leakage is not important. Results of infinitely long bearing are the same as that for infinitely short bearing.

Following Fig. 7.8 shows discrepancy in load-carrying capacity between results based on incompressible and compressible lubricants.

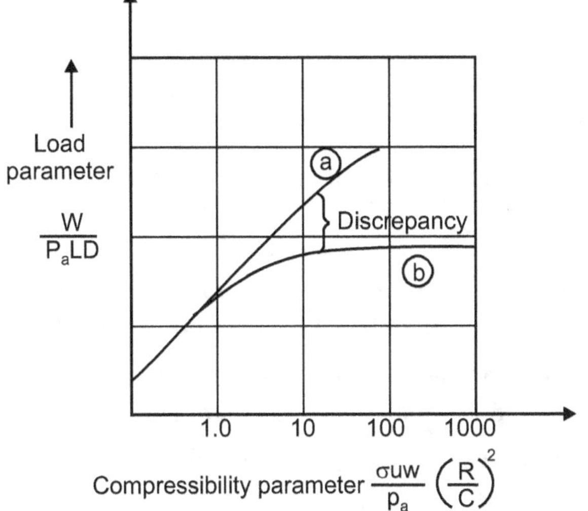

Fig. 7.8 : Discrepancy in load-carrying capacity between results based on incompressible and compressible lubricants

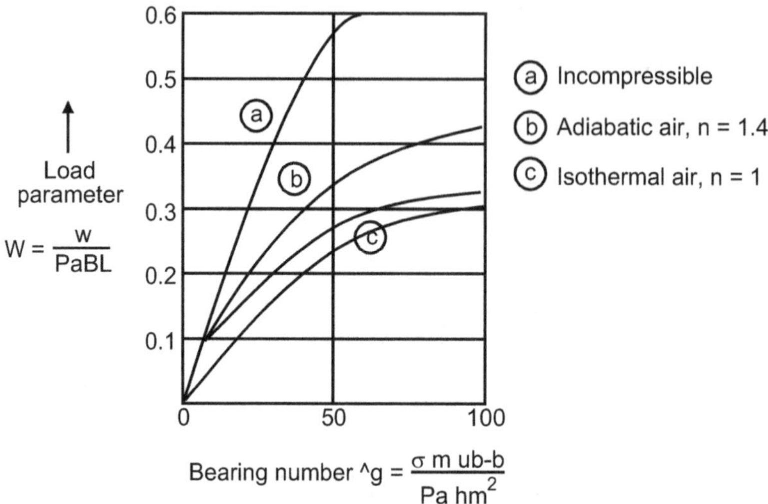

Bearing number $\wedge g = \dfrac{\sigma\, m\, ub\text{-}b}{Pa\, hm^2}$

Fig. 7.9 : Effect of bearing number on isothermal and adiabatic load for plane slider bearing operating in air with film thickness ratio $\dfrac{h_1}{h_2} = 2$ and $\dfrac{L}{B} = 1$

7.12 ACTIVE AND PASSIVE MAGNETIC BEARINGS

7.12.1 Qualities of Magnetic Bearings

- They do not require any maintenance.

- They have a long operating life.

- There are no losses through mechanic friction, a non-contact system avoids fatigue and wear, which occur with ball bearings.

- They do not heat.

- They are noiseless.

- There is no danger of contamination with lubricating oil near the bearing.

7.12.2 Applications

- **Use in Extreme Conditions :** Magnetic bearings can be used in extreme conditions, especially at high rotation speeds with a wide range of operating temperature.

- **Use in Chemically Aggressive Environment :** It can be used in chemically aggressive environment, e.g. liquefied oxygen and methane, etc., sea water and vacuum.

- **Require No Cooling and Lubrication :** Magnetic suspension system of the rotor eliminates a need for cooling and lubrication. Therefore oil emissions are reduced, which provides direct environmental benefits. The removal of oil in the system makes it more fire safe as well.

- **Use in Special Purpose Machineries :** Magnetic bearings are used for special purposes, such as turbo-compressors, vacuum pumps, gyroscopes, rotating accumulators of mechanical energy. It ensures increased reliability and efficiency of turbomachines.

- **Maglev Train :** The Maglev trains essentially use a linear version of the active magnetic bearing, a very high-speed trains that are safe, reliable, and emit less noise compared to regular trains.

- **In Space Applications :** It can be also found in space engineering.

7.12.3 Active Magnetic Bearings (AMB)

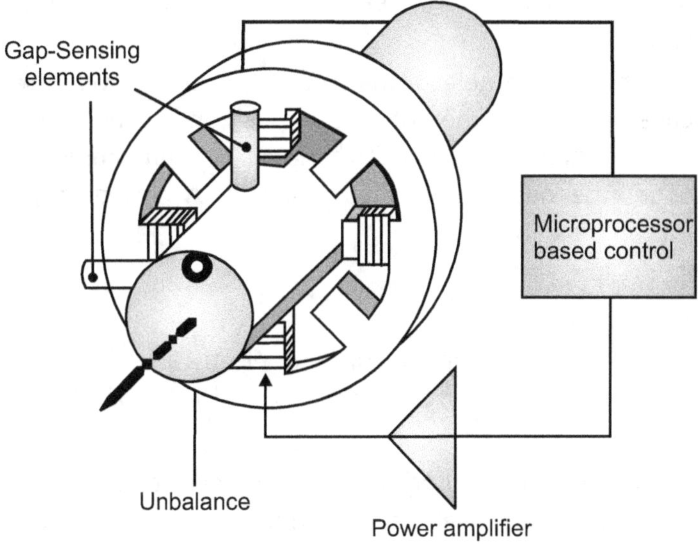

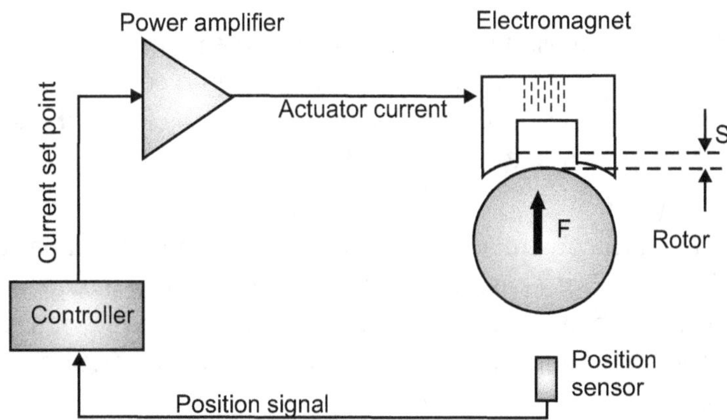

Fig. 7.10 : Principle of Active magnetic bearing carrying a rotor load

The magnetic force used in magnetic bearings can be divided into two categories of how the force is created :

- Reluctance force and
- Lorentz force.

The Reluctance Force : It results from a difference of permiabilities between two materials.

The Lorentz Force : It results from the movement of charges in a magnetic field.

The force of a magnet is inversely proportional to the square of an increase in distance. As the distance between the magnet and the object subjected to its force decreases, the force levels off at a point when the material becomes saturated with the magnetic flux. For a mechatronic system, higher order relationships complicate matters and make it more difficult to implement a controller. For this reason the magnetic force must be linearized around the operating point.

A magnetic rotor is suspended by an electromagnet. Its position is measured by a position sensor, to get an active control of the rotor. The position signal is then treated by a controller, which gives a current set point. This signal is then amplified by the power amplifier, in order to get the necessary actuator current. A closed loop control is thus realized and the system can be stabilized.

Components of AMB :

- **Electromagnets**

  They are composed of a soft magnetic core and electrical coils. They look somewhat like the stator of an electrical motor.

- **Iron Core**

  The iron core is a material conducting the magnetic field to the air gap. Its magnetic permeability has to be high, as well as its magnetic saturation. In order to minimize eddy current losses, the core usually consists of insulated lamination sheets.

- **Windings**

  The current through the winding is the source of magnetic field. The winding is made of an insulated conductor wound on the soft magnetic core. In order to improve the efficiency of the AMB, the conductor has to have a low electrical resistance and must be wound with a high fill-factor.

- **Rotor**

  The rotor, in standard constructions, is realized with a lamination packet shrinked on a non magnetic shaft. Tight manufacturing tolerances are needed in order to avoid unbalances. The mechanical properties of the rotor lamination have to be good, in order to overcome the centrifugal stress due to high speed rotation.

- **Position Sensors**

  In most applications, there are position sensors in AMBs. Since AMBs are actively controlled regarding to the sensor signal, the control performance strongly depends on the sensor performance. Several sensor types are used in AMBs : inductive, eddy current, capacity and optical displacement sensors.

- **Controller**

  Today controllers are mainly based on digital technology. They provide a great flexibility and high computation speed. Digital controllers enable principally an adaptative control, unbalance compensation and provide a great tool for system diagnosis. For real time processing, Digital Signal Processors (DSPs) are used.

  AMBs are controlled in closed-loop. Different methods such as PD, PID, optimal output feedback or observer based state feedback are in use.

- **Power Amplifiers**

  The power amplifiers convert the control signals into control currents. Switching amplifiers are usually used because of their low losses. The amplifier is often the limiting component in an AMB system. This single actuator enables the levitation along only one axis and only in one direction. In AMB systems, several actuators are used in order to control the rotor levitation along several degrees-of-freedom (DOF). Actuators are typically arranged as pairs facing each-other.

This enables to attract the rotor in two opposite directions along one axis.

Active magnetic bearings require complicated control hardware, such as digital signal processor ampliers, digital-to-analog converters, analog-to-digital converters, and software. The active magnetic bearings (AMB) use the feedback loop between position of rotor in the air gap and the magnetic force. These consist of rotor position sensor, a system for automatic rotor position control, a power amplifier and electromagnetic actuators. The active magnetic system ensures high precision of rotor location, but this system is the most expensive solution. Thus System monitoring is then possible by using the AMB as a sensor, which provides indications about the changes in shaft dynamics

The load carrying capacity of AMB depends on the arrangement and geometry of the electromagnets, the magnetic properties of the material, of the power electronics, and of the control laws - a set-up with main elements is as shown in Fig. 7.11

Static and Dynamic Stiffness : It the ratio of the supported load with respect to the resulting displacement of that load. In classical bearings the stiffness stems for example from the elasticity of the oil film or the deformation of balls and inner ring of a ball bearing.

In an AMB the force is generated by a control current, which can be adjusted to the needs and opens a novel way of shaping the stiffness and even the overall dynamic behavior, and thus the term "stiffness" may not be the best way to describe the performance of an AMB, but is still used for comparison reasons with classical bearings.

One way of obtaining a high *static stiffness* is by applying PID-control. In that way, the current i, and implicitly the force as well, is shaped depending on the displacement x of the rotor within the air gap as

$$i \;=\; P_x + I \int x \cdot dt + D\left(\frac{d_x}{d_t}\right)$$

The integral part of the PID control brings the position x to the same value before and after the load step, and thus the rotor shows a behavior that cannot be obtained with classical bearings

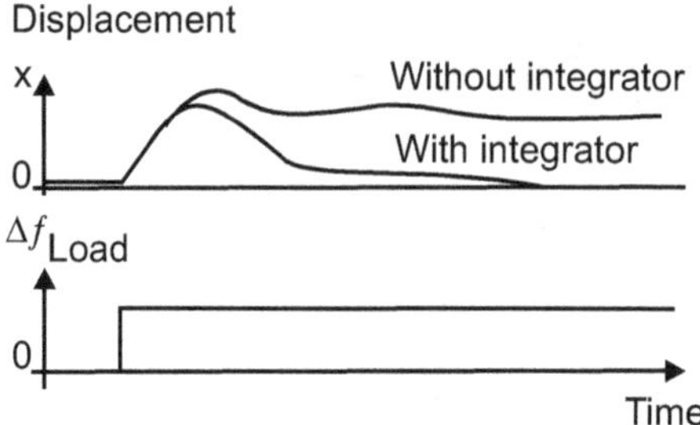

Fig. 7.11 : Step response of rotor position to a change in load force with PD and PID control

Types of AMB :

- **Radial AMB**

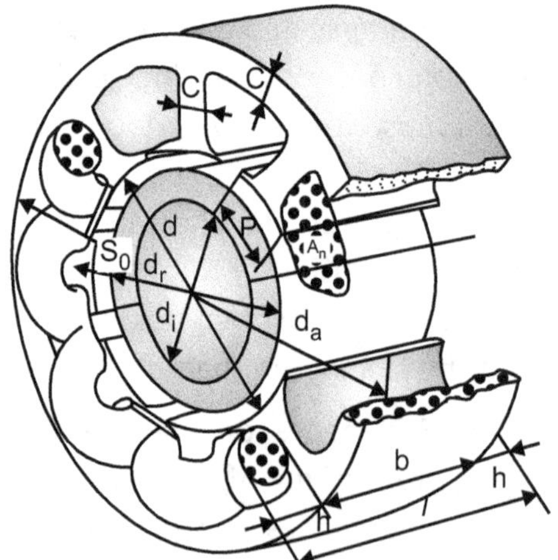

d	Inner diameter (bearing diameter)	d_a	Outer diameter
c	Leg width	d_i	Shaft diamter
h	Winding head height	b	Bearing width (magnetically active part)
A_n	Slot cross section (winding space)	p	Pole shoe width
D_r	Rotor diameter	I	Bearing length
S_0	Nominal air gap		

Fig. 7.12 : Radial ABM (Schweitzer 1994)

- **Axial AMB Bearing**

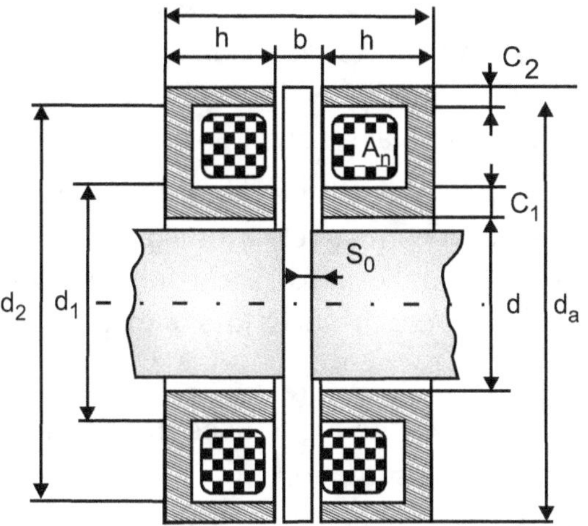

d	Inner diameter (or bearing diameter)	d_a	Outer diameter
c_1	Inner leg width	d_1	Inner winding space diameter
d_2	Outer winding space diamter	A_n	Slot cross section (winding space)
h	pot magnet height	c_2	Outer leg width
S_0	Nominal air gap	l	Bearing length

Fig. 7.13 : Axial AMB bearing

7.12.4 Passive Magnetic Bearing (PMB)

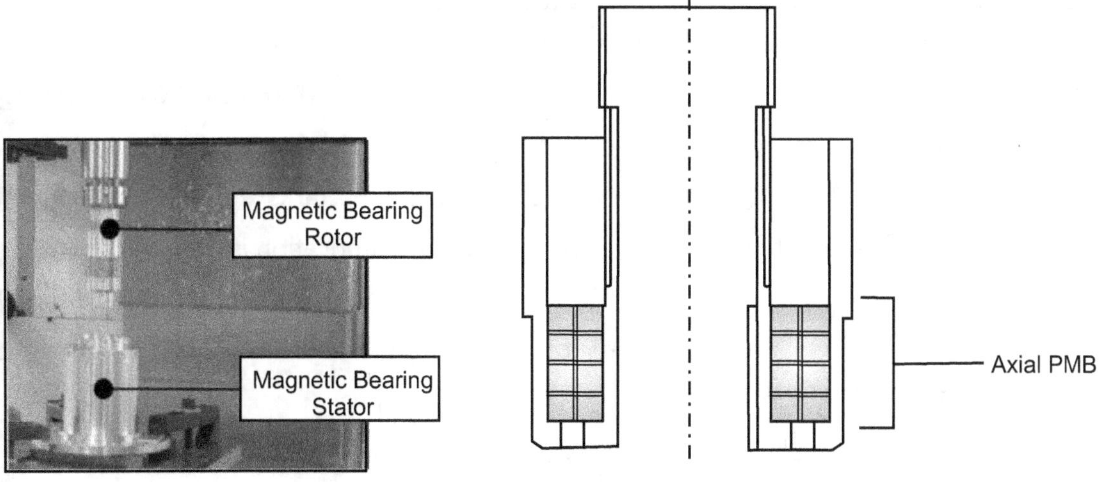

Fig. 7.14 : PMB configuration

This arrangement is achieved by placing two concentric magnets so that the repulsive reaction forces will center the magnets relative to each other. Figure shows the positioning of a rotor magnet (inside) and a stator magnet (outside). Moreover, it has been demonstrated that it is possible to modify global magnetic field and increase the generated forces by stacking many magnets with alternating poles.

The passive magnetic bearings are built of the permanent magnets. They use the repelling or attractive magnetic forces between magnets for magnetic levitation. The repelling forces are used in a large majority of applications. The configuration of the passive magnetic bearing with attractive magnetic forces menaces loss of magnetic levitation.

Advantages of PMB :

- Passive magnetic bearings, unlike the active ones, are simple (and thus actually trouble-free), they do not have power consumption,

- They take up only little space and their price is low.

- The passive magnetic bearing (PMB) has no feedback loop.

- PMBs have a significant advantage - it is a cheaper solution in comparison to active magnetic bearing.

Disadvantage

- It has a lower loading capacity and dynamic stiffness.
- The position of rotor is superposition of the magnetic repelling forces and external forces. It does not ensure precise location of the rotor.
- There is a steady state error, which is proportional to external forces.

EXERCISE

1. Explain the phenomenon of elastohydrodynamic lubrication.

[P.U. Dec. 2010, 6 Marks]

2. How elastohydrodynamic lubrication differs from hydrodynamic lubrication ?

[P.U. Dec. 2008, 6 Marks; Dec. 2010, 6 Marks; June 2011, 7 Marks]

3. State the applications where elastohydrodynamic lubrication is observed.

[P.U. June 2010, 2 Marks]

4. Using modified Reynold's equation for elastohydrodynamic lubrication, derive Ertel-Grubin equation as,

$$\frac{h_0}{R} = 1.19 \left(\frac{\mu_0 \, U \, \alpha}{R}\right)^{8/11} \left(\frac{ELR}{W}\right)^{1/11}$$

Explain the various terms involved.

5.　Write short notes on the following :

   (i)　Width of contact of two cylinders under radial load

   (ii)　Standard modified forms of Reynold's equation

6.　Explain the phenomenon of elastohydrodynamic lubrication. State the applications where EHD lubrication is observed.　**[P.U. Dec. 2009, 8 Marks]**

7.　State basic requirements of gas lubrication.

8.　Explain requirements of gas lubrication.

9.　Write short notes on :

   (i)　Gas lubricated bearing　　　　　　**[P.U. Dec. 2010, 6 Marks]**

   (ii)　Features of gas lubricated bearing

10.　Explain merits and demerits of gas bearings.

[P.U. Dec. 2010, 8 Marks; Dec. 2009, 4 Marks]

11.　State the advantages and limitations of gas lubricated bearing.

[P.U. May 2010, 4 Marks]

12.　Explain merits, demerits and applications of gas bearings.

[P.U. June 2009, 6 Marks; June 2011, 6 Marks]

13.　Give applications of gas bearings.　　　　**[P.U. June 2009, 2 Marks]**

14.　Derive governing differential equation for gas-lubricated bearings.

15.　Derive Reynolds equation for gas-lubricated bearings obeying –

   (i)　Isothermal process　　　　　　　(ii)　Adiabatic process

16.　Explain dimensionless bearing number $\wedge_g$ and dimensionless squeeze number σ_g.

17.　Derive an equation for gas-lubricated bearings in terms of bearing number $\wedge_g$ and squeeze number σ_g.

18.　Derive an equation for gas-lubricated bearings applied for extremely low speed applications.

19.　Explain the phenomenon of slip at the fluid solid interface.

20.　Discuss Knudsen number and give its significance.

21. Explain principles of air bearings.

22. Discuss in brief

    (i)   Active magnetic bearing

    (ii) Passive magnetic bearing

23. Explain the working of active magnetic bearing with it's advantages and applications.

24. Explain the need of passive magnetic bearing stating it's advantages and disadvantages.

✠ ✠ ✠

Chapter 8

TRIBOLOGICAL ASPECTS

8.1 LUBRICATION IN METAL WORKING

8.1.1 Introduction

In manufacturing, the required shape of parts is obtained by plastic deformation. Most of the metals are subjected to bulk or primary deformation processes which include :

- Rolling

- Forging

- Drawing and

- Extrusion

An important consideration in metal deformation process is the friction developed between the workpiece and the forming tool or tools. Metal-forming operations involve a hard, non-deforming tool interacting with a soft workpiece at pressures sufficient to cause plastic flow in the weaker material. Wear behaviour is also a significant concern. Lubrication is of immense importance during metal forming. The workpiece surface frequently undergoes a very substantial extension, which leads to exposure of fresh metal surface. Therefore, lubricant is required to protect the old surface as well as the new formed surface.

Lubricants are selected to reduce friction and suppress tool wear.

8.1.2 Considerations in Selecting a Lubricant for Metal Working

- Its ability to act as a thermal barrier, keeping heat in the workpiece away from the tooling.

- Its ability to act as a coolant and remove heat from the tools.

- Its ability to retard corrosion if left on the formed product.

- Ease of application and removal.

- Lack of toxicity, odour and flammability.

- Reactivity or lack of reactivity with material surfaces.

- Adaptability over a useful range of pressure, temperature and velocity.

- Surface wetting characteristics.

- Cost, availability and its ability to flow or thin and still function.

- Behaviour of a given lubricant will change with variation in the interface conditions e.g. the surface finish of both surfaces, area of contact, load, speed, temperature, and amount of lubricant.

8.1.3 Rolling

It is the process of reducing the thickness or changing the cross-section of a long workpiece by compressive forces applied through a set of rolls. The basic operation is flat rolling or simply rolling where the rolled products are flat plate and sheet.

In rolling the thickness of a strip of metal is reduced by passing it through a sets of rolls where some minimum friction is required to pull the metal into the roll gap. The slab moves at the same speed as the surface of the rolls at the neutral point, but moves slower towards the entry (called as backward slip) and faster towards the exit (called as forward slip). Interface pressure reaches maximum at the neutral point. Since the position of the neutral point is governed by friction in the roll gap, forward slip is a very sensitive measure of the efficiency of lubricants. With decreasing friction, forward slip diminishes.

Rolling may be hot rolling or cold rolling as discussed below.

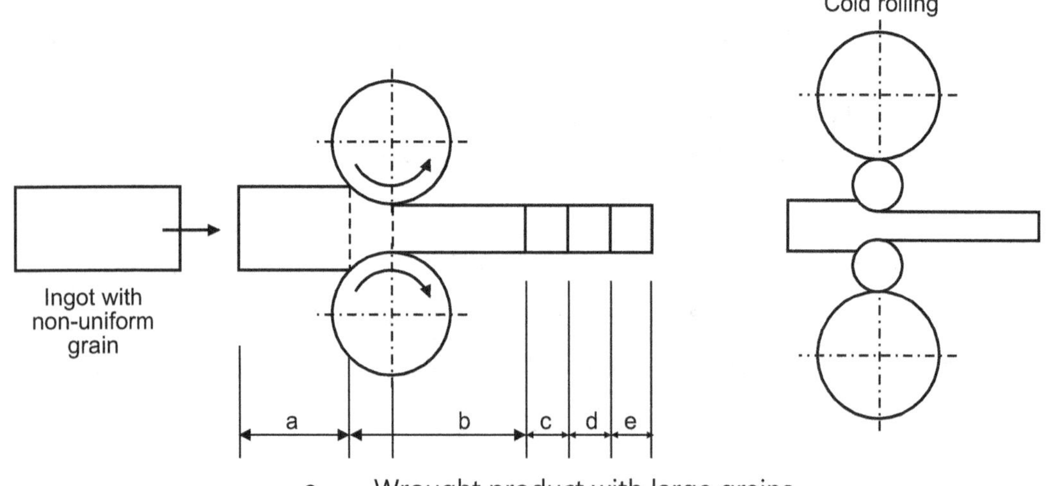

a　–　Wrought product with large grains

b　–　Deformed elongated grains

c　–　New grains forming

d　–　New grains growing

e　–　Wrought product with small uniform grains

Fig. 8.1

- In rolling, although the rolls cannot pull the strip into the roll gap without some friction, force and power requirement rise with increasing friction.

- In cold rolling, the coefficient of friction 'f' usually ranges between 0.02 to 0.3, depending on the materials and lubricants used. The low ranges of the coefficient of friction are obtained with effective lubricants and regimes approaching hydrodynamic lubrication such as in cold rolling of aluminium at high speeds.

- In hot rolling, 'f' may range from about 0.2, with effective lubrication to as high as 0.7, indicating sticking which usually occurs with steels, stainless steels and high temperature alloys.

- Camber can be controlled by varying the location of coolant (lubricant) on the rolls in hot rolling.

- Lubrication is also important for good surface finish and to minimize defects.

Lubricants for Rolling :

- Ferrous alloys are usually hot rolled without a lubricant, although graphite may be used.

- Aqueous solutions are used to cool the rolls and breakup the scale on the workpiece.

- Non-ferrous alloys are hot rolled with a variety of compounded oils, emulsions and fatty acids.

- Cold rolling is done with low viscosity lubricants, including mineral oils, emulsions, paraffin and fatty oils.

8.1.4 Forging

It is the plastic working of a metal by means of localized compressive forces exerted by manual or power hammers, presses or special forging machines. It may be done either hot or cold. The material flow in forging takes place in the direction of least resistance.

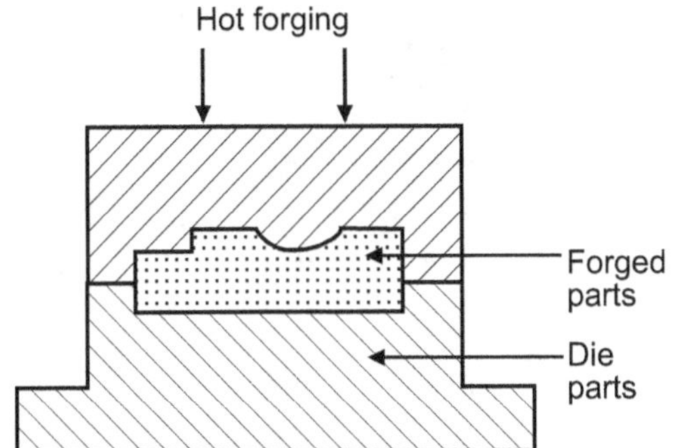

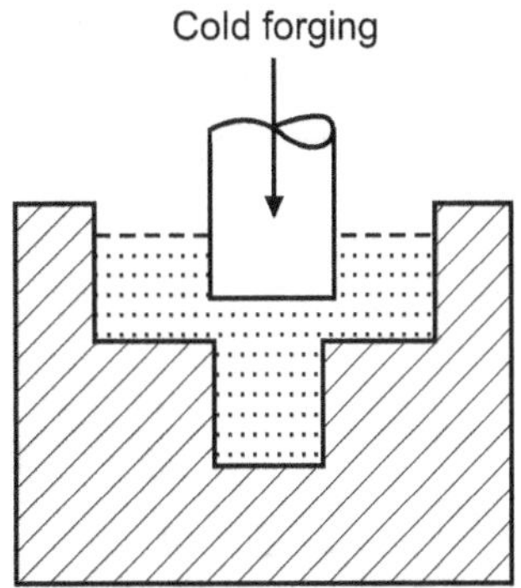

Fig. 8.2 : Triaxial compression

Lubrication in forging plays an important role and it serves the following purposes :

- It affects friction and wear and consequently the flow of metal into the die cavities, thus facilitating easy and smooth flow of metal in the die cavity with reduced sliding friction between workpiece and die.

- It controls metal flow and reduces pressure requirements.

- Lubricants can also serve as thermal barrier between the hot forging and the relatively cool dies, thus, slowing the rate of cooling of the workpiece.

- Lubricant serves as a parting agent, thus preventing the forging from sticking to dies.

- It coats die surfaces uniformly thus preventing uneven metal flow.

- It can significantly affect the wear pattern in forging dies and does not attack or abrase die surfaces.

- It assists in forging ejection.

A wide variety of metal working fluids can be used in forging.

  For **hot forging :** Graphite, molybdenum disulphide and sometimes glass.

  For **cold forging :** Mineral oils and soaps are common lubricants.

8.1.5 Drawing

It is an operation in which the cross-sectional area of a bar or tube is reduced by pulling it through a converging die. The die opening may be of any shape.

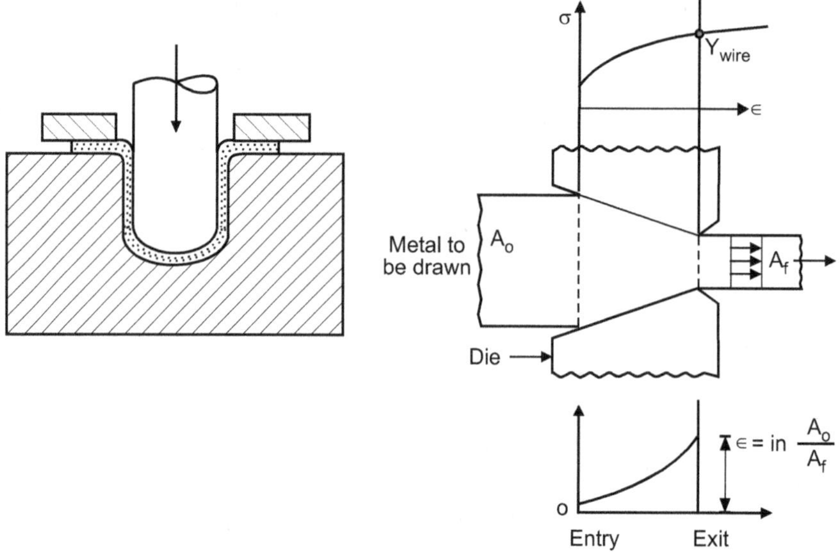

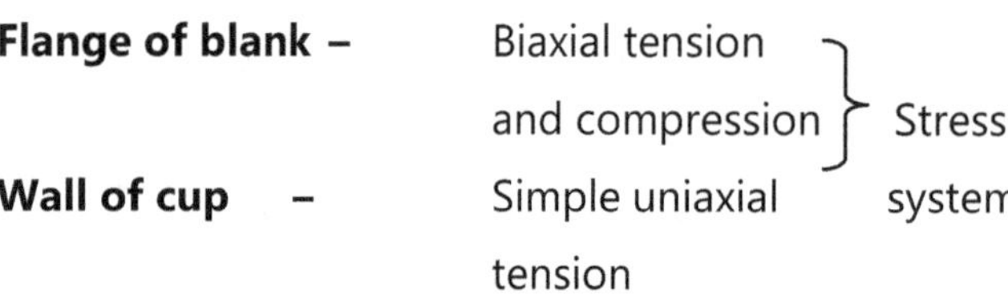

Fig. 8.3

- All sliding is unidirectional and the draw force is opposed by frictional stresses at the interface. If the strength of the drawn product is insufficient to carry the draw force, the product will tear off.

- Interface pressures are always below the compressive flow strength of the material.

- In tube drawing, without an internal die, frictional conditions are the same as in wire drawing, but mandrel controls the internal diameter.

- Wire drawing involves smaller diameter materials than rod drawing with sizes as small as 0.025 mm. Rod and wire drawing are usually finishing processes with good lubrication. The value of 'f' ranges from 0.03 to 0.1.

Lubrication Requirements in Drawing :

- Proper lubrication is essential in rod, tube and wire drawing regardless of whether the process is dry or wet drawing.

- In dry drawing, the surface of the wire is coated with various lubricants, depending on its strength and frictional characteristics. The most common lubricant used is soap. The rod to be drawn is first surface treated by pickling. This treatment removes the surface scale that could lead to surface defects and being quite abrasive, would considerably reduce the die life. The soap is picked up by the wire as it goes through a box filled with soap powder.

- With high strength material such as steels, stainless steels and high temperature alloy, the surface of the rod or wire may be coated either with a softer metal or with a conversion coating. Copper or tin can be chemically deposited on the surface of the metal. This thin layer of softer metal acts as a solid lubricant during drawing. Conversion coating may consist of sulphate or oxalate coating on the rod, which are then typically coated with soap, as a lubricant. Polymers are also used as solid lubricants, such as in drawing of titanium.

- In wet drawing, the dies and rod are completely immersed in a lubricant. Typical lubricants are oils and emulsions containing fatty or chlorinated additives and various chemical compounds.

8.1.6 Extrusion

It is the process in which a round billet placed in a chamber is forced through a die opening by a ram. Thus, the metal is compressed and forced to flow through a suitably shaped die to form a product with reduced cross-section. The die may be round or of various other shapes. Extrusion may be either hot or cold. Following are the types of extrusion processes :

- Direct extrusion

- Indirect extrusion

- Hydrostatic extrusion

- Impact extrusion

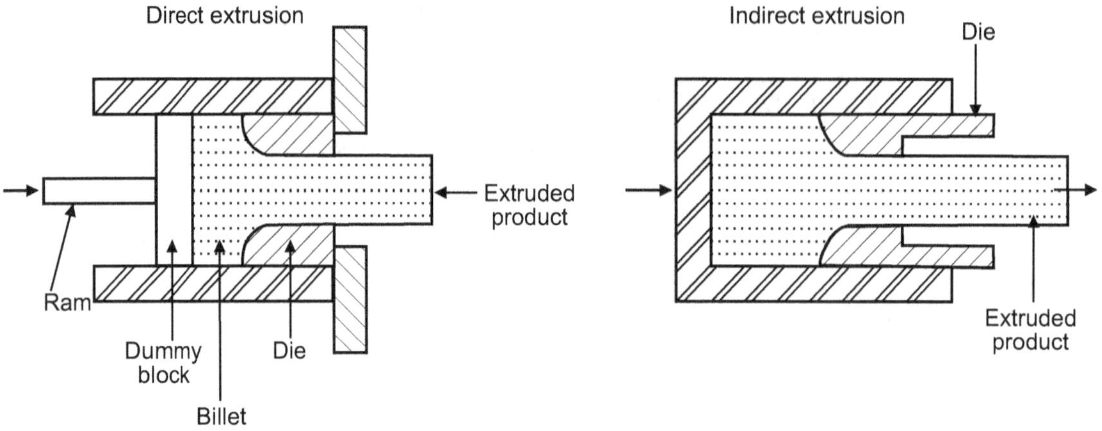

Fig. 8.4

In forward extrusion the stresses necessary to overcome friction add to the die pressure, often limiting the length of billet that can be extruded. When a lubricant is used, the die entry must be tapered to facilitate material flow along the die face. To minimize friction in reverse extrusion of tubes, the container is kept as short as possible and a short land is formed on the punch. Lubricant between the workpiece and punch and end face must be gradually metered out to protect the freshly formed, highly extended surfaces. Lubrication is desirable to prevent metal pick-up and punch wear.

The most homogeneous flow pattern is obtained when there is no friction at the billet container-die-interfaces. This type of flow occurs when the lubricant is very effective or with direct extrusion. The two factors that greatly influence the metal flow in extrusion are :

- Frictional conditions at billet-container-die interfaces which can be imposed by effective lubrication.

- Thermal gradients in the billet.

Lubrication in Extrusion

Cold Extrusion :

Lubrication is crucial, especially with steels, because of the generation of new surfaces and the possibility of seizure between the metal and the tooling caused by the breakdown of lubrication. The most effective lubrication is phosphate conversion coating on the workpiece and soap (or wax in some cases) as the lubricant. Temperature rise in cold extrusion is an important factor especially at high extrusion ratios. The temperature may be sufficiently high to initiate and complete the recrystallization process of cold worked metal, thus reducing the advantages of cold working.

Hot Extrusion :

For steels, stainless steels and high temperature materials, glass is an excellent lubricant. It maintains its viscosity at elevated temperatures, it has good wetting characteristics and acts as a thermal barrier between the billet and the container and the die, thus, minimizing cooling. A circular glass pad is usually placed at the die entrance. This pad softens and melts away slowly as extrusion progresses and forms an optimal die geometry. The viscosity-temperature index of glass is an important factor in this application. Solid lubricants such as graphite and molybdenum disulphide are also used in hot extrusion. Non-ferrous metals are usually extruded without a lubricant although graphite may be used.

Lubricants Commonly Used for Metal Working Operations:

Table 8.1 shows lubricants commonly used in metal working operations.

Table 8.1

CC – Conversion coating		J – Canned or jacketed	
CL – Chlorinated paraffin		L – Lanolin	
CD – Compound oil		MO – Mineral oil	
CP – Copper plate		MS – Molybdenum disulphide	
CSN – Chemicals and synthetics		PI – Polymer	
D – Dry		S – Soap	
E – Emulsion		Sa – Salt	
Ep – Extreme pressure		T – Tallow	
FA – Fatty acid		W – Water	
FO – Fatty oil		Wa – Wax	
G – Graphite			
GI – Glass			

Table 8.2

Materials and Alloy	Temperature	Forging	Rolling	Extrusion	Rod and Wire Drawing
Aluminium	Cold	FA + MO, S	FA + MO, MO	D, G, MS, L, S	MO, E, Wa, FA + MO
	Hot	MO + G, MS	FA + CO, FA + E	D, G, PI	–
Beryllium	Hot	MO + G, J	G	MS, G, J	G
Copper	Cold	S, E, T	E, MO	S, T, L, Wa, G, MS	FO + E + S, MO, Wa
	Hot	G	D, E	D, MO + G	–
Lead	Cold	FO + MO	FA + MO, EM	D, S, T, E, FO, D	FO
	Hot	–	–		–

Contd...

Magnesium	Cold	FA + MO, CC + S	D, FA + MO	D, T	–
	Hot	W + G, MO + G	MO + FA + EM, D, G	D, PI	–
Nickel	Cold	–	MO + CL	CC + S	CC + S, MO + CL
	Hot	MO + G, W + G, GI	W, E	GI, J	–
Refractory	Hot	GI, G, MS	G + MS	J + GI	G + MS, PI
Steel (Carbon	Cold	EP + MO, CC + S	E, CO, MO	CC + S, T, W + MS	S, CC + S
and low alloy)	Hot	MO + G, Sa, GI	W, MO, CO, G + E	GI, G	–
Stainless Steel	Cold	CL + MO, CC + S	CL + EM, CL + MO	CC + S, CP, MO	CC + S, CL + MO
	Hot	MO + G, GI	D, W, E	GI	–
Titanium	Cold	S, MO	MO, CC + FO, G	CC + G, CC + S	CC + PI
	Hot	W + G, GI, MI	PI, CC, G, MS	J + GI, GI	–

8.2 MECHANICS OF TYRE ROAD INTERACTION

8.2.1 Tyre Road Interaction

A tyre fitted on the wheel can be modelled as an elastic body in rolling contact with the ground. As such, it is subjected to creep and microslip. Tangential force and twisting arising from the lateral creep and usually referred to as the cornering force and the self-aligning torque, play a significant role in the steering process of a vehicle. Therefore, the analysis which is possible for solid isotropic bodies cannot be done in the case of a tyre. One-dimensional models have been proposed to describe the experimentally observed behaviour. An approximately elliptically shaped contact area is created when a toroidal membrane with internal pressure is pressed against a rigid plane surface. The size of the contact area can be compared with that created by the intersection of the plane with the undeformed surface of the toroid, at such a location as to give an area which is sufficient to support the applied load by the pressure inside the toroid. The apparent dimensions of the contact ellipse x and y (as shown in Fig. 8.5 below) are a function of the vertical deflection of the tyre.

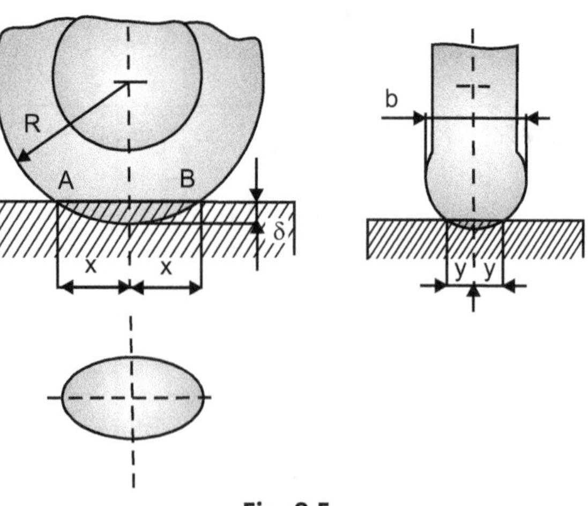

Fig. 8.5

Where,

$$x = [(2R - \delta)\delta]^{\frac{1}{2}}$$

$$y = [(b - \delta)\delta]^{\frac{1}{2}}$$

The apparent contact area is

$$xy = \pi\delta[(b - \delta)(2R - \delta)]^{\frac{1}{2}} \, 2\pi bR\delta$$

- It is known that the tyre is tangential to the flat surface at the edge of the contact area and therefore the true area is only about 80 % of the apparent area.
- It has been found that approximately 80 to 90 % of the external load is supported by the inflation pressure.
- On the other hand, an automobile tyre having a stiff tread on its surface forms an almost rectangular contact zone when forced into contact with the road.

The external load is transmitted through the walls to the rim. Fig. 8.6below shows, both unloaded and loaded automobile tyres in contact with the road. As a result of action of the external load, W, the tension in the walls decreases and as a consequence of that the curvature of the walls increases. An effective up-thrust on the hub is created in this way. In the ideal case of a membrane model the contact pressure is uniformly distributed within the contact zone and is equal to the pressure inside the membrane. The real tyre case is different because the contact pressure tends to be concentrated in the centre of the contact zone.

This is mainly due to the tread.

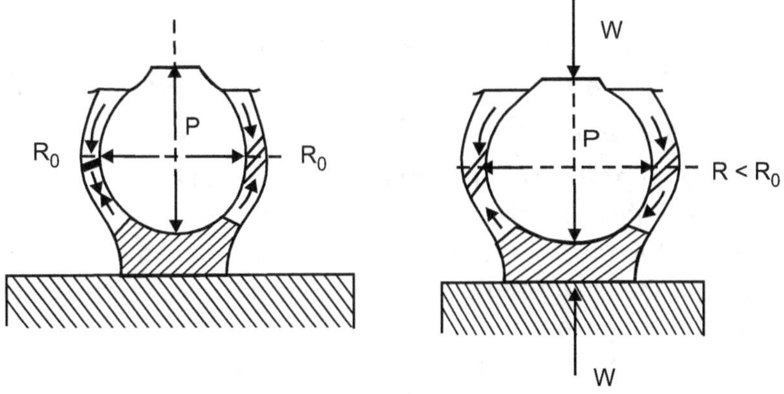

Fig. 8.6

8.2.2 Rolling Friction and Road Grip

Rolling friction Fr can be seen as

$$M/R,$$

Where, M is a torque and R the radius of the rolling body.

For an elastic wheel the reaction force acts through the wheel center and therefore the moment

$$M = 0.$$

For a visco-elastic wheel the reaction force moves towards the loading side, because stresses are lower in unloading,

$$M = Wz$$

where W is the normal load and z the distance from the wheel center, as seen in Fig. 8.6. Displacement of the center of pressure, and hence the coefficient of friction μ_r, depends on speed and temperature in the same way as the loss factor $\tan \delta$,

$$\mu_r = 0.33$$

$$\mu_r = 0.33 \left(\frac{W}{G * R^2} \right)^{\frac{1}{3}} \tan\delta$$

... [A formulation for μ_r as proposed by Greenwood et al. (1961)] where $G\_$ is the complex shear modulus. Rolling friction is mainly due to energy dissipated as rubber is compressed and released in the contact patch.

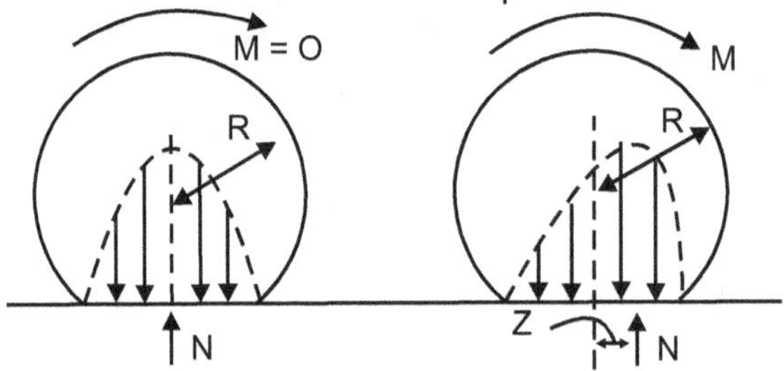

Fig. 8.7 (Source: Gent 2007)

8.2.3 Two Stress Mechanisms are Involved in the Relative Slippage between the Elastomer and the Road Surface

1. Frequency Excitation of the Material by the Road Texture

The rubber is distorted when it slips over the rough spots on the road, the size of which varies from 1 centimetre (macrotexture range) to 1 micron (microtexture range). This mechanism is known as the **road roughness effect**. The flexibility of the rubber enables it to adapt to the shape of rough points on the road surface. Because rubber is viscous, the deformation of a tread block, as it moves over the road surface, can be compared to flow. The block strikes the rough spot and distorts, but, because of hysteresis, does not immediately return to its initial height on the other side of the rough spot. It is also described using the word **indentation**, which emphasizes the penetration of road roughness into the rubber of the tyre tread.

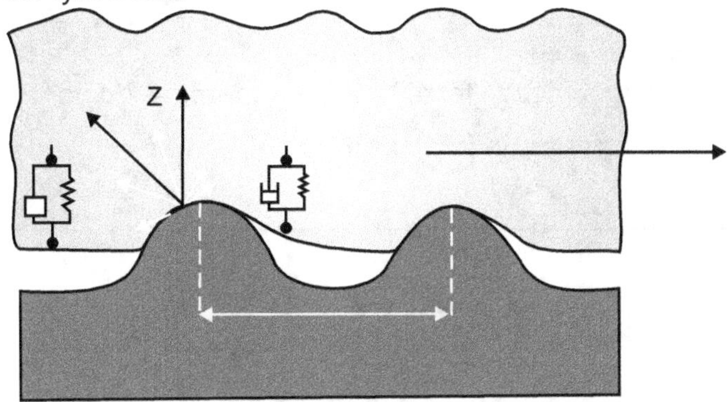

Fig. 8.8

We can model the indentation by using a spring-damper assembly which undergoes a compression-relaxation cycle for a given deformation value. This generates hysteresis (and therefore an energy loss) in the damper at each cycle. The asymmetrical deformation of the rubber block around the rough spot generates a force field, in which the tangential force X opposes slippage.

2. Molecular Adhesion

It comes into play at a scale of one hundredth of micron, and is amplified by slippage.

In both cases, the visco-elastic properties of the rubber, and particularly its hysteresis, play animportant role. Adhesion results from molecular interactions occurring at the rubber/ground interface (Van der Waals* bonding). Bonds form, stretch and then break, to form again farther on. The rubber's molecular chains therefore follow a cycle of stretching and breaking which generates visco-elastic work (friction between molecular chains in a certain volume of material). This work multiplies the bonding energy by a factor which can vary from 100 to 1000 depending on the temperature and the speed of slippage of the rubber over the road surface.

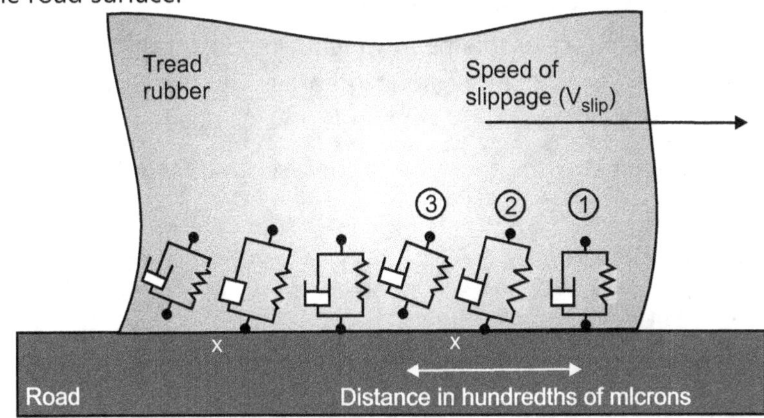

Fig. 8.9

Stress Cycle :

- The bond is created.

- The molecular chain is stretched: its viscous properties, represented by the piston, resist deformation, generating a friction force X which opposes skidding.

- The bond breaks and forms again farther on.

8.2.4 Wheel on Rail Road

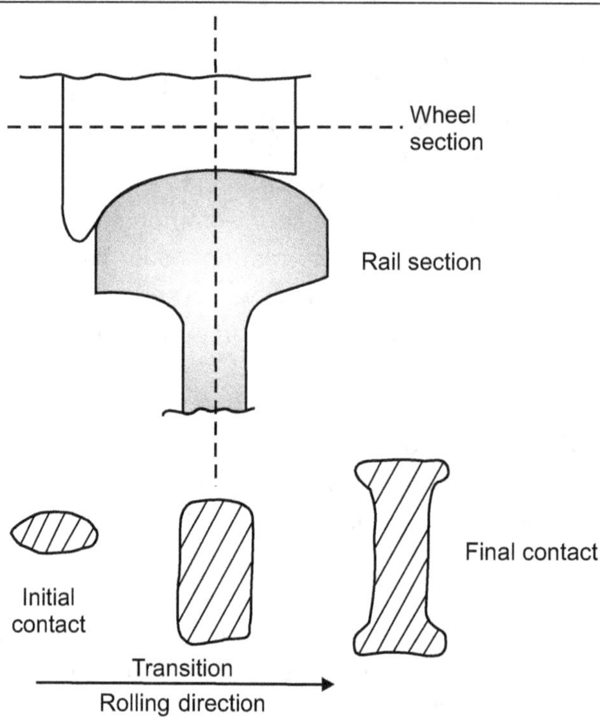

Fig. 8.10

The Solution of Hertzian contact problems in which the contact area is semi-ellipsoidal are given in closed from involving complete elliptic integrals. This classic theory can not be used for non-conformal contacts where area of contact is non-elliptical.

The actual nature of contact stresses and area of contact are affected by,

- Normal load, F

- Tangential traction

- Breaking condition and

- Dynamic behavior of locomotive during negotiating curve

- For new rails and wheels stresses induced frequently exceed the elastic limit loading to plastic flow and residual stresses. During repeated rolling contact the material is subjected to combination of contact stresses due to contact load together with residual stresses introduced during previous passes of the load. After some cycles of loading the steady state is reached in which material is no longer stresses beyond its elastic limit. The process in rail-road is the 'Shakedown Limit'. of the track.

- During combined rolling and sliding the critical shear stress approaches the surface with increasing tangential traction. It lies on the surface when the ratio of tangential traction and normal load reaches a value of about 0.25, which is usually experienced in high speed trains in curved tracks.

- When rolling stock experiences a load in excess of the shakedown limit, it experiences continuous plastic deformation with repeated rolling and there is forward shearing of the surface.

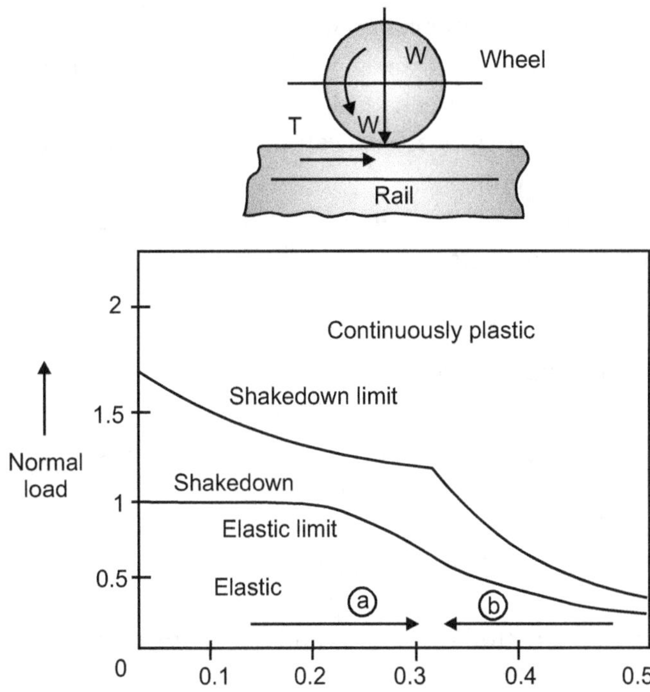

Fig. 8.11 : Ratio of traction force to normal load T/W)

(a)   Critical stress beneath surface.

(b)   Critical stress at surface.

8.3 INTRODUCTION TO SURFACE ENGINEERING

The term *surface engineering* was coined for the first time in England in 1970s. *Surface engineering is a multidisciplinary activity intended to advocate the properties of the surfaces of engineering components so that their function and serviceability can be improved.*

The *ASM Handbook* defines surface engineering as *"treatment of the surface and near-surface regions of a material to allow the surface to perform functions that are distinct from those functions demanded from the bulk of the material"*.

Surface engineering encompasses the modification of a surface by application of a thin film, plasma enhancement, ion bombardment, self-assembly, nanomachining, chemical treatment, or other processes. Surface engineering techniques are now being used in virtually every area of technology, including automotive, aerospace, missile, power, electronic, biomedical, textile, petroleum, petrochemical, chemical, steel, power, cement, machine tools, and construction industries. They are being used to develop a wide range of advanced functional properties, including physical, chemical, electrical, electronic, magnetic, mechanical, wear-resistant, and corrosion-resistant properties at the required substrate surfaces. Almost all types of materials, including metals, ceramics, polymers, and composites, can be deposited onto similar or dissimilar materials.

The properties such as corrosion resistance, oxidation and/or sulfidation resistance, wear resistance, frictional energy losses, mechanical properties, electronic or electrical properties, thermal insulation and aesthetic appearance can be enhanced metallurgically, mechanically, chemically, or by adding a coating.

Surface engineering will remain a growth industry well into the next decade because

- Surface engineered products increase and improve performance,
- Add functionality,
- Reduce costs,
- Improve materials usage efficiency, and
- Provide performance not possible with bulk materials.

Thus Surface Engineered component results in

- Creation of entirely new and revolutionary products.
- Solution of previously unsolved engineering problems.
- Improved functionality of existing products; engineering, medical, and decorative functionalities.
- Production of nanostructured coatings and nanocomposites.
- Conservation of scarce materials.
- Ecological considerations – reduction of effluent output and power consumption.

8.3.1 Surface Engineering for Wear and Corrosion Resistance

8.3.1.1 Diffusion

The diffusion coatings described in this section involve heat treating processes that cause carbon, nitrogen, or a combination of the two to diffuse into the surface of a ferrous part to alter the surface chemistry/properties. These processes include carburizing, nitriding, and carbonitriding. Each of these depends on the concentration gradient of the diffusing species, the diffusivity of the atomic species in the host material, and the time and temperature at which the process takes place.

Table 8.3

Process	Name of Case	Process temperature °C (°F)	Case hardness, typical case depth	Hardness HRC	Typical base metals	Process characteristics
Carburizing						
Pack	Diffused carbon	815-1090 (1500-2000)	125 μm-1.5 mm (5-60 mils)	50-63(a)	Low-carbon steels, low-carbon alloy steels	Low equipment costs, difficult to control case depth accurately.
Gas	Diffused carbon	815-980 (1500-1800)	75 μm-1.5 mm (3-60 mils)	50-63 (a)	Low-carbon steels, low-carbon alloy steels	Good control of case depth, suitable for continuous operation, good gas controls required, can be dangerous.
Liquid	Diffused carbon and possibly nitrogen	815-980 (1500-1800)	50 μm-1.5 mm (2-60 mils)	50-65 (a)	Low-carbon steels, low-carbon alloy steels	Faster than pack and gas processes, can pose salt disposal problem, salt baths require frequent maintenance
Vacuum	Diffused carbon	815-1090 (1500-2000)	75 μm-1.5 mm (3-60 mils)	50-63 (a)	Low-carbon steels, low-carbon alloy steels	Excellent process control, bright parts, faster than gas carburizing high equipment costs.
Nitriding						
Gas	Diffused nitrogen, nitrogen compounds	480-590 (900-1000)	125 μm-0.75 mm (5-30 mils)	50-70	Alloy steels, nitriding steels, stainless steels	Hardest cases from nitriding steels, quenching not required, low distortion, process is low, is usually a batch process.
Salt	Diffused nitrogen, nitrogen compounds	510-565 (950-1050)	2.5 μm-0.75 mm (0.1-30 mils)	50-70	Most ferrous metals including cast iron	Usually used for thin hard cases < 25 μm (< 1 mil), no white layer, most are proprietary processes.
Ion	Diffused nitrogen, nitrogen compounds	340-565 (650-1050)	75 μm-0.75 mm (3-30 mils)	50-70	Alloy steels, nitriding steels, stainless steels	Faster than gas nitriding, no white layer, high equipment costs, close case control.
Carbonitriding						
Gas	Diffused carbon and nitrogen	760-870 (1400-1600)	75 μm-0.75 mm (3-30 mils)	50-65(a)	Low-carbon steels, low-carbon alloy steels, stainless steels	Lower temperature than carburizing (less distortion), slightly harder case than carburizing, gas control critical.
Liquid (cyaniding)	Diffused carbon and nitrogen	760-870 (1400-1600)	2.5-125 μm (0.1-5 mils)	50-65(a)	Low-carbon steels	Good for thin cases on non-critical parts, batch process, salt disposal problems.
Ferritic nitrocarburizing	Diffused carbon and nitrogen	480-590 (900-1090)	2.5-25 μm (0.1-1 mil)	40-60(a)	Low-carbon steels	Low-distortion process for thin case on low-carbon steel, most processes are proprietary.

(a) Carburizing :

Carburizing is the addition of carbon to the surface of low-carbon steels at temperatures (generally between 850 and 950°C, at which austenite, with its high solubility for carbon, is the stable crystal structure. Hardening of the component is accomplished by removing the part and quenching or allowing the part to slowly cool and then reheating to the austenitizing temperature to maintain the very hard surface property.

On quenching, a good wear- and fatigue-resistant high-carbon martensitic case is superimposed on a tough, low-carbon steel core. Carburized steels used in case hardening usually have base carbon contents of about 0.2 wt %, with the carbon content of the carburized layer being fixed between 0.8 and 1.0 wt %. Carburizing methods include gas carburizing, vacuum carburizing, plasma (ion) carburizing, salt-bath carburizing, and pack carburizing.

(b) Nitriding :

Nitriding is a process similar to carburizing, in which nitrogen is diffused into the surface of a ferrous product to produce a hard case. Unlike carburizing, nitrogen is introduced between 500 and 550°C, which is below the austenite formation temperature (A_{c1}) for ferritic steels, and quenching is not required. As a result of not austenitizing and quenching to form martensite, nitriding results in minimum distortion and excellent control. The various nitriding processes include gas nitriding, liquid nitriding, and plasma (ion) nitriding.

All hardenable steels must be quenched and tempered prior to nitriding. The nitriding process is used to obtain a high surface hardness, improve wear resistance, increase fatigue resistance and improve corrosion resistance (except Stainles steel). The diffusion zone is the original core microstructure with the addition of nitride precipitates and nitrogen solid solution.

The following steels can be nitrided for specific applications :

* Aluminium-containing low-alloy steels : Nitralloys.
* Medium-carbon, chromium-containing low-alloy steels : 4100, 4300, 5100, 6100, 8600, 8700, and 9800 series.
* Low-carbon, chromium-containing low-alloy steels : 3300, 8600, and 9300 series.
* Hot-working die steels containing 5% Cr : H_{11}, H_{12}, and H_{13}.
* Air-hardenable tool steels : A_2, A_6, D_2, D_3, and S_7.
* High-speed tool steels : M_2 and M_4.
* Nitronic stainless steels : 30, 40, 50, and 60.
* Ferritic and martensitic stainless steels : 400 series
* Austenitic stainless steels : 200 and 300 series
* Precipitation-hardened stainless steels : 13-8 PH, 15-5 PH, 17-4 PH, 17-7 PH, A-286, AM 350, and AM 355

(c) Carbonitriding :

It introduces both carbon and nitrogen into the austenite of the steel. The process is similar to carburizing in that the austenite composition is enhanced and the high surface hardness is produced by quenching to form martensite. This process is a modified form of gas carburizing in which ammonia is introduced into the gas-carburizing atmosphere. As in gas nitriding, elemental nitrogen forms at the workpiece surface and diffuses along with carbon into the steel. Typically, carbonitriding takes place at a lower temperature and a shorter time than gas carburizing, producing a shallower case.

Steels with carbon contents upto 0.2% are commonly carbonitrided; these include 1000, 1100, 1200, 1300, 1500, 4000, 4100, 4600, 5100, 6100, 8600, and 8700 series.

8.3.1.2 Plating and Coating Methods

It is a layer of material, formed naturally or synthetically or deposited artificially on the surface of an object made of another material, with the aim of obtaining required technical or decorative properties.

The substrate, in other words, the coated object, or, its superficial layer, constitutes one phase of the system. The coating constitutes the second phase. Between the coating and the substrate there exists an interface in the form of a layer of certain volume, with intermediate properties, usually facilitating adherence of the coating to the substrate.

In the case of some coatings this layer bears the name of **intermediate**. In some cases it is difficult to distinguish between the coating and the superficial layer, particularly in incremental diffusion layers.

It involves an intentional buildup or addition of a new layer on a metal substrate, that is, the application of a coating or lining. A wide range of processes are used to deposit metal, ceramic, and organic (paints or plastic and rubber linings) coatings or combinations of these materials (composite coatings).

(a) Electro and Electroless Plating :

Electroplating :

Electroplating (i.e. Electrodeposition) is defined as the deposition of a coating by electrolysis, that is, depositing a substance on an electrode immersed in an electrolyte by passing electric current through the electrolyte.

Aqueous Solution Electroplating

The process can take place in an aqueous electrolyte near ambient temperatures (called aqueous solution electroplating) or in a fused metal salt at high temperatures (called metalliding or fused-salt electroplating).

Aqueous solution electroplating provides decorative and protective finishes for use at ambient temperatures and in a variety of environments.

Drawbacks :

- A main drawback in electroplating is the inability of achieving uniform deposition, which is related to the throwing power of the electrolyte. Throwing power is substrate-shape dependent and also depends on the anode/cathode configuration and the current density, as well as on the composition and conductivity of the electrolyte.

- A second difficulty is that not all metallic elements can be deposited.

- Another problem with electroplating is evolution of hydrogen at the electrodes when the cathode efficiency is less than 100%. If a ferrous substrate is to be plated, absorbed atomic hydrogen can cause embrittlement of the part. Unless the parts are heat treated to remove the absorbed hydrogen, they will be brittle and unusable for any application involving elastic strain.

Substrate Preparation for Plating

Substrate preparation for plating is critical to ensure good adhesion and surface quality. Maximum adhesion depends on both the elimination of surface contaminants in order to induce a metallurgical bond and the generation of a completely active surface to initiate plating on all areas. The cleaning steps for steel substrates usually involve precleaning, intermediate alkaline cleaning, electrocleaning, acid treatments, and anodic desmutting. Electrodeposited metals can have a very good bond to the substrate, but that bond will never be the same as a fusion bond, and poor bonds can go undetected unless techniques are used to test the actual bond strength. The electrodeposited coating usually ends up with a surface texture that is the same as the starting substrate surface texture, unless an intermediate leveling coating (such as copper) is used.

Advantages :

The electroplating process produces a coating with distinct advantages :

- The workpiece will not undergo distortion or metallurgical changes because the operating temperature of the bath does not exceed 100°C.

- It is possible to adjust the plating conditions in order to modify hardness, internal stress, and metallurgical characteristics of the coating.

- These coatings are dense and adherent to the substrate.

- The coating thickness is proportional to the current density and length of time of the deposition.

- Deposition rate can be accelerated by forced circulation of the electrolyte for some metals in high-speed plating.

- There is no technical limit to the thickness of electrodeposits.

- Application of coatings is not confined to the line of sight. Although throwing power may be limited, the freedom of anode design and location is helpful.

- Those areas not requiring deposition can be masked.
- Only the tank size of the bath limits the dimensions of the part, although large parts such as gun barrels can be the tank itself; or brush plating can also be used.
- This process is suitable for automation and has economic advantages over other coating processes.

Nickel Plating :

- It is widely used for a corrosion-and wear-resistant finish.
- Typical applications, with a thin top coat of electrodeposited chromium, are decorative trim for automotive and consumer products and office furniture.
- Nickel deposits are also used for nondecorative purposes for improved wear resistance, for example, on pistons, cylinder walls, ball studs, etc.

Chromium Electroplating :

- It is also used as decorative and hard coating.
- Colored and tarnish-resistant chromium decorative coatings are produced over a base deposit of copper and/or nickel for applications such as those noted above for nickel.
- Hard chromium coatings are used for hydraulic pistons and cylinders, piston rings, aircraft engine parts, and plastic molds, where resistance to wear, heat abrasion, and/or corrosion are required.

Cadmium and Zinc Electroplating :

- It provides galvanic corrosion protection when coated on steel.
- Cadmium is preferred for the protection of steel in marine environments, whereas zinc is preferred in industrial environments.
- Cadmium is also preferred for fastening hardware and connectors because its coefficient of friction is less than zinc.
- Cadmium is toxic and should not be used in parts that will have contact with food.
- Precautions for minimizing hydrogen embrittlement should be taken because cadmium plating is more susceptible to such embrittlement than any other plated metal.

Electroless Plating :

Electroless plating baths have been developed for copper, nickel, silver, gold, and a number of other metals, but the systems for corrosion and wear applications are the nickel-phosphorus and nickel-boron systems.

Process :

Electroless Nickel Plating is used to deposit nickel without the use of an electric current; thus it is sometimes called autocatalytic plating. In this process, the part is immersed in an aqueous solution containing metal salts, a reducing agent, and other chemicals that control the pH and reaction rates. The part acts as a catalyst for the reduction of the nickel ions by the reducing agent. The reducing agent causes the metal ion reduction and the nickel coating on the part continues to act as a catalyst as the plating process continues, unlike in electroplating where the ions pick up electrons from the cathode. When the process takes place using a hypophosphite-reducing agent, the finished nickel coating is not pure nickel, but contains phosphorus inclusions. Phosphorus content can be as high as 13%. When the process takes place using a borohydride compound reducing agent, the finished product is a nickel-boron alloy. The boron content can be as high as 5%.

Characteristics :

- Nickel-phosphorus coatings are uniform, hard, relatively brittle, lubricious, easily solderable, and highly corrosion resistant. Wear resistance equivalent to hard chromium coatings can be obtained when the coating is heat treated at low temperatures to produce a very hard precipitation-hardened structure.

- Most of these coatings are amorphous metal glasses that when heated first form nickel phosphate (Ni3P) particles; at temperatures above 320°C, the deposit crystallizes.

- Internal stresses are primarily a function of coating composition, and coating thickness uniformity can be easily controlled.

- Adhesion to most metals is excellent, and frictional properties are also excellent and similar to chromium.

- Nickel-boron coatings have excellent resistance to wear and abrasion, but because they are not completely amorphous they have reduced resistance to corrosive environments. Also, they are much more costly than nickel-phosphorus coatings.

- The microhardness of electroless nickel-phosphorus coating is about 48-50 HRC, equivalent to many hardened steels.

- After precipitation hardening, hardness values as high as 1100 HVN are reported, which is equivalent to commercial hard-chromium coatings. Because of their high hardness, electroless nickel coatings have excellent wear and abrasion resistance in both the deposited and hardened condition.

- Electroless nickel coatings can be easily soldered and are used in electronic applications to facilitate soldering of light metals such as aluminium.

- Electroless nickel is often used as a barrier coating; to be effective, the deposit must be free of pores and defects.

8.3.1.2.1 Hot Dip Coatings

Hot dip coatings are predominantly used to improve the aqueous corrosion of steel.

Hot Dip Coatings

In hot dip process, coating materials in the form of solids are melted in a tank furnace, using the energy of gas burned in burners, or by electric resistance heating. Since coating materials are predominantly metals and the melting point of used coating materials is usually several hundred degrees Celsius i.e. not exceeding 1000°C, coatings made from them are traditionally called **hot dip**.

Properties of hot dip coatings are decided by,

- Surface preparation,

- Chemical composition of the metallic material (purity and composition of alloy) and its temperature,

- Time of soaking of the objects in the bath and

- The substrate material.

Before dipping into the bath, the object is degreased, sand blasted and covered with fluxes by immersion or spraying. The fluxes (most often mixtures of zinc chloride and ammonium chloride with foaming agents as carbohydrates, glycerine, tallow may also be added to the bath. Metallic materials are hot dip coated by tin, zinc, aluminium, lead and their alloys.

Batch and Continuous Processing

Processing of hot dip coatings involves either batch or continuous processing.

The continuous process is more advantageous for sheet steels, whereas the batch process is normally used for individual parts. In the batch galvanizing process, the two types of conventional practices are the wet process and the dry process.

- The wet process involves a flux blanket on the top of the molten zinc bath to remove impurities from the surface of the steel and also to keep that portion of the surface of the zinc bath, through which the steel is immersed, free from oxides.

- In the dry process the steel is usually cleaned, treated with an aqueous solution, dried, and then dipped in the molten zinc bath. The molten zinc bath is maintained at temperatures between 445 and 455°C and time in the range of 3 to 6 min. The time of immersion is used to control the thickness of the coating, which consists of iron-zinc alloy phases at the interface along with a top coat of pure zinc. Good cooling control is necessary because the zinc can continue to react with the substrate to produce further alloying and detrimentally affect the properties of the coating such as the grain size.

In continuous hot dip processing, welded coils of steel are coated at speeds of 200 m/min. The hot-processed continuous line is more complex in that the steel sheet is first cleaned at temperature in a reducing environment, annealed above the recrystallization temperature of about 700°C and then immersed in the molten bath. As the strip exits the bath, the thickness of the molten metal film is controlled by gas wiping dies that remove excess coating metal. After coating, the sheet is either cooled by forced air or subjected to an in-line heat treatment, called galvannealing, before being rewound into coil or sheared into cut lengths at the exit of the line.

Coating Microstructure

Generally the coating microstructure consists of

- the substrate,

- the interfacial alloy layer, and

- the overlay cast structure.

Depending on the type of coating, the microstructure and composition of these constituents changes. The substrate plays a major role in the type of coating obtained, and substrate composition can affect growth kinetics of the phases formed.

Substrate grain size greatly affects the nucleation of the iron-zinc phases. In aluminium-containing baths, the structure formed first is an inhibition layer that is dependent on bath composition and prevents further alloying for a certain short time before the inhibition layer becomes unstable.

When the zinc galvanizing bath contains only a trace of aluminium, zinc attack of the substrate is uniform and the phases that form are governed by the iron-zinc binary phase diagram. In Zn bath containing Al, the stability of the inhibition layer governs the amount of iron-zinc phases formed. Once the inhibition layer is no longer stable, outbursts or rapid growth of iron-zinc phases occur during hot dipping.

During the thermal cycle of the galvannealed process, the inhibition layer dissolves and iron-zinc phase layer growth occurs in a controlled manner until the entire coating is made up of iron-zinc phases.

8.3.1.2.2 Metal Spraying

It uses consumable in the form of a spray of finely divided molten or semimolten droplets to produce a coating.

Spray coatings (sprayed coatings) are obtained by spraying the surfaces of different objects (metallic or non-metallic), depositing a layer of substance which is generated by dispersion (usually with the aid of a spray gun) into tiny particles of powdered material or already powdered material, applied with high kinetic energy. Owing to this energy, the particles, upon making contact with the sprayed surface, exert pressure which assures good adhesion of the coating to the substrate. Dispersion of particles is usually accomplished by pneumatically, rather than by hydraulic means.

Material particles may fall on the substrate as

- cold (e.g. particles of paints, varnishes and plastics) and adhere to the substrate either by forces of viscosity or electrostatic forces (powdered coating materials), or both (liquids).

- hot (semi-plastic or plastic state or even heated to a temperature above melting point).

The first method is used for spraying paint materials and is counted among painting methods, while the second method is termed thermal spraying.

Paint Coatings

Three basic types of sprayed paint coatings are distinguished : those applied pneumatically, hydrostatically and electrostatically.

Smeared Coatings

These are applied by a brush, roller or sponge. Application of coatings by a brush is the most traditional painting technique, later improved by the use of the roller and, more recently, by a sponge. It is most frequently applied in repair and field jobs, in places with difficult access, in small projects involving different places, in small plants, especially for priming where the paint must be strongly rubbed into the substrate.

Flow Coatings

These are obtained by pouring paint, flowing from many nozzles (so-called multi-stream flow) under low pressure, covering the contours of the painted object. A modification of this method is gravitational flow of flat objects by paint flowing out of a slit nozzle, and roller painting, used for painting long and thin metal sheet. Flow coatings are smoother than immersion coatings; their thickness is in the range of 12 to 32 μm.

Pneumatically Sprayed Coatings

These are obtained with the use of compressed air, dispersing the coating material. The pressure of the compressed air depends on material viscosity and on nozzle diameter. The paint material is sprayed cold or hot (heated to several tens of degrees Celsius).

The thickness of a single deposition is 10 to 30 μm. The pneumatic method may be used for spraying all types of coating materials, although some limitations exist, mainly with respect to spraying of heated materials. This concerns mainly temperature of ignition.

Hydrodynamically Sprayed Coatings (without Air, under Pressure)

These are obtained by dispersion of the paint material without contact with a stream of air, but as the result of sudden decompression of a stream of paint material, fed under high pressure (up to 25 MPa) and flowing at high velocity (even exceeding 100 m/s) through a small diameter nozzle. Hydrodynamic spraying is used for the same paint materials as in the pneumatic method, applied hot and cold, the condition being very thorough refinement of the pigment. The only materials not suitable for this method are those with fibrous fillers and some chemo-setting substances. The hydrodynamic method is used for coatings on big, flat surfaces.

Electrostatically Sprayed Coatings

These are obtained by cladding the object with liquid or powdered paint materials after their prior electrical charging.

Spraying may be either pneumatic or centrifugal. Between the nozzle of the electrostatic spray gun and the coated object an appropriately strong electrostatic field is created. For this type of painting, materials with special dielectric properties are used. Coatings obtained by this method are characterized by high quality. This method is used for painting small objects in mass production.

Thermal Spray Coatings

Depending on the method of generating heat to melt or plastify the coating material, to be simultaneously or subsequently sprayed with a pneumatic drive, the following types of coatings are distinguished :

- **Flame :** When the particles are heated by passing through a gasoxygen flame.

- **Resistance :** When the coating material is melted in a resistance heated pot (in arc plasma) or when the material is passed through such a zone.

- **Induction :** When the powdered coating material is passed through a zone of induction plasma.

- **Plasma :** When the coating material is melted in an electric arc strongly extended by the flow of plasmogenic gas or when the coating material is passed through the arc zone.

The most often applied is arc spraying; less often are flame and plasma which allow the obtaining of highest plasma temperatures - more than 10,000 K. To the group of thermal spray coatings also belong **detonation (explosive) coatings (high energy rate coatings)**. Their deposition requires giving particles of coating material very high kinetic energy (highest of all achieved in thermal spraying). During the process, particles of powdered coating material heat up to a temperature lower than that of particles heated by plasma.

Because of the possibility of attaining temperatures within the range from several hundred to approx. fifteen hundred degrees, thermally sprayed coatings are predominantly ceramic and metal ceramic, with high hardness, heat and erosion resistance, and with controlled thermophysical properties.

The characteristics of thermal spray processes are indicated as follows :

- Substrate adhesion, or bond strength, is dependent on the materials and their properties and generally is characterized as a mechanical bond between the coating and the substrate, unlike the metallurgical bond found in weld-overlay coatings.

- Spray deposits can be applied in thinner layers than welded coating, but thick deposits are also possible.

- Almost all material compositions can be deposited, including metals, cermets, ceramics, and plastics, provided there is a stable phase.

- Thermal spray processes are usually used on cold substrates, preventing distortion, dilution, or metallurgical degradation of the substrate.

- Thermal spray processes are line-of-sight limited, but the spray plume often can be manipulated for complete coverage of the substrate.

Thermal Spray Processes can be classified into two categories, arc processes and gas combustion processes, depending on the means of achieving the heat for melting of the consumable material during the spraying operation.

In the lower-energy electric arc (wire arc) spray process, heating and melting occur when two electrically opposed charged wires, comprising the spray material, are fed together to produce a controlled arc at the intersection. The molten material on the wire tips is atomized and propelled onto the substrate by a stream of gas (usually air) from a high-pressure gas jet. The highest spray rates are obtained with this process, allowing for cost-effective spraying of aluminium and zinc for the marine industry. In the higher-energy plasma arc spray process, injected gas is heated in an electric arc and converted into a high-temperature plasma that propels the coating powder onto the substrate at very high velocities. This process can take place in air with air plasma spraying (APS), or in a vacuum with vacuum plasma spray (VPS) or low-pressure plasma spraying (LPPS).

In the lower-energy processes, electric arc (wire arc) spray and flame spray processes, adhesion to the substrate is predominantly mechanical and is dependent on the workpiece being perfectly clean and suitable rough.

For gas combustion processes, the lower-energy flame spray process uses oxyfuel combustible gas as a heat source to melt the coating material, which may be in the form of rod, wire, or powder. In the higher-energy, high-velocity oxyfuel combustion spray (HVOF) technique, internal combustion of oxygen and fuel gas occurs to produce a high-velocity plumecapable of accelerating powders at supersonic speeds and lower temperatures than the plasma processes.

Some porosity is always present in these coatings, which may present problems in both corrosion and erosion. The higher-energy processes – APS, VPS, LPPS, and HVOF processes – were developed to reduce porosity and improve adhesion to the substrate. In addition, these processes are capable of spraying materials with higher melting points, thus widening the range of applications to include high-temperature coatings and thermal and mechanical shock-resistant coatings.

Properties of Thermal Spray Coatings

The variations in oxide content and porosity, as well as the chemical composition of the coating, greatly affect the properties of the deposit and, in the case of corrosion, the underlying substrate. The splat morphology and, more importantly, the splat/splat and splat/substrate interface are critical to properties such as bond strength, wear, erosion, and corrosion. The mechanical properties of thermal spray coatings are not well documented except for their hardness and bond strength.

- One of the most extensive uses for thermal spray coatings is in wear applications.

- Generally, the wear resistance of coatings increases with their density and cohesive strength, so that HVOF coatings provide the best wear resistance in contrast to plasma spray coatings

- Thermal spray zinc, aluminium, and zinc-aluminium alloys are used for sacrificial galvanic protection for corrosion resistance on bridges, ships, and other large structures.

- Other corrosion-resistant applications for thermal spray coatings include oxidation and sulfidation resistance in power boilers and other high-temperature uses.

8.3.1.2.3 Cladded Coating

Clad metals are bonded metal-to-metal laminar composite systems that can be fabricated by a number of processes. The principal cladding techniques include :

- Hot-roll bonding,

- Cold-roll bonding,

- Explosive bonding, and

- Weld cladding (including laser cladding), although centrifugal casting, adhesive bonding, extrusion, and hot isostatic pressing have also been used to produce clad metals. Clad metals can be provided in plate, sheet, tube, rod, and wire forms. Most engineering metals and alloys can be clad.

The cladding of steel with stainless steel, copper, nickel alloys, titanium, and tantalum has become increasingly popular in the chemical processing industries. Applications include pressure vessels, reactors, heat exchangers, and storage tanks.

Clad metals provide a means of designing into a composite material specific properties that cannot be obtained in a single material. These material systems are currently being used for electrical and electronics applications, such as contacts and connectors with selectively clad (inlay) precious metals for low contact resistance and high reliability.

Corrosion Control through Cladding

Clad metal systems designed for corrosion control can be categorized as follows :

- Noble metal clad systems
- Corrosion barrier systems
- Sacrificial metal systems
- Transition metal systems

Proper design is essential for providing maximum corrosion resistance with clad metals.

- **Noble Metal Clad Systems :**

These are materials having a relatively inexpensive base metal covered with a corrosion-resistant metal. A typical example is carbon steel clad with a stainless steel or nickel-base alloy. Another group of commonly used noble metal clad metals uses aluminium as a substrate. e.g., in stainless-steel-clad aluminium truck bumpers, the stainless steel provides corrosion resistance, and the aluminium provides a high strength-to-weight ratio.

- **Corrosion-Barrier Systems :**

The combination of two or more metals to form a corrosion-barrier system is most widely used where perforation caused by corrosion must be avoided. Low-carbon steel and stainless steel are susceptible to localized corrosion in chloride-containing environments and can perforate rapidly.

When steel is clad with a stainless steel layer, the corrosion-barrier mechanism prevents perforation. Localized corrosion of the stainless steel is prevented; the stainless steel is protected galvanically by the sacrificial corrosion of the carbon steel in the metal laminate. Therefore, only a thin pore-free layer is required.

- **Sacrificial Metals :**

The metals such as magnesium, zinc, and aluminium, are in the active region of the galvanic series and are extensively used for corrosion protection. The single largest application for cold-roll-bonded materials is stainless-steel-clad aluminium for automotive trim. The stainless steel exterior surface provides corrosion resistance, high luster, and abrasion and dent resistance, and the aluminium on the inside provides sacrificial protection for the painted auto body steel and for the stainless steel.

- **Clad Transition Metal Systems :**

These systems provide an interface between two incompatible metals. They not only reduce galvanic corrosion where dissimilar metals are joined, but they also allow welding techniques to be used when direct joining is not possible. Clad metals provide an ideal solution to the materials problem of dual environments. For example, in the application of small battery cans and caps, copper-clad, stainless steelclad nickel (Cu/SS/Ni) is used where the external nickel layer provides atmospheric corrosion resistance and low contact resistance. The copper layer on the inside provides the electrode contact surface as well as compatible cell chemistry. The stainless steel layer provides strength and resistance to perforation corrosion.

The concept of cladded coatings has been significantly broadened. They comprise two groups : pressure and overlay coatings.

Pressure Coatings are obtained by joining the cladding material with the cladded material by exerting pressure, usually at appropriately elevated temperatures, in order to weld them. Most often, plating is accomplished by :

- **Mechanical Means**, by one-sided or two-sided hot rolling of sheet or strip from both metals, after prior cleaning of surface, mainly of oxides.

- **Detonation Action** - by generating very high pressure (even upto millions of atmospheres) as the result of detonation of explosive material and generating extremely high velocities of particles at the moment of contact with the substrate.

Overlay coatings are obtained by **pad welding** i.e., melting the plating material on the substrate surface, using various sources of heat : welding torches, plasma burners and lasers – **braze welding** - by melting, with the aid of flux (e.g. mixture, comprising 70% borax, 20% kitchen salt, 10% boric acid), of coating material, which is mainly common brass or nickel-brass, without melting the substrate material. The latter is usually a high melting point material, e.g., cast iron, bronze, steel coated with zinc or tin.

- **Electro-Spark Discharge :** by deposition of material of an eroding electrode on the substrate, due to electric discharges (spark discharge) between electrode and substrate. Plated overlay coatings require machining; in some cases prior heating is essential. Applications are mostly anti-corrosion and anti-wear. These coatings may also be used for corrective purposes, e.g., repair of streetcar and railroad tracks, worn journals, road wheels, excavator teeth, cutting tools, dies, punches, etc.

Cladding, also known as laser **plating** or **hardfacing**, is accomplished with process parameters similar to those in alloying and consists of melting a thick layer of the plating material and surface melting of a very thin layer of the substrate material. The aim of hardfacing is not the mixing of the plating material with that of the substrate but melting of the deposited coating material or its deposition and remelting in order to obtain better resistance to erosion, corrosion, abrasion and to other service hazards than that of the substrate material. The coating material may be soluble or insoluble in the substrate. The intermediate layer formed between the substrate and the plating is usually of a metallurgical character, in which case it causes strong bonding of the latter to the substrate.

Hardfacing processes have found application in two chief groups of materials :

- corrosion resistant, including those resistant at high temperatures, and heavy duty, wear resistant, mainly tooling alloys.

The unique properties of plating materials make them predestined to applications in conditions of heavy loads and high temperatures, as well as erosion and corrosion hazards, e.g. plating of sealing surfaces of valve seats and valves in combustion engines, water, gas and vapor separators, as well as components of metallurgical tooling.

8.3.1.2.4 Crystallizing Coating

- Crystallizing coatings are obtained in conditions of technical vacuum, as the result of crystallization of usually ionized metal vapours on a cold substrate or one preheated to 200 to 500°C. The metal vapours form compounds with ionized elements of gases which constitute the plasma (i.e. nitrides, oxides) or with elements from the substrate (i.e. carbides).

- Crystallizing coatings are mainly compounds of non-metals with metals (i.e. nitrides, carbides, oxides, borides, silicides, carbonitrides and aluminonitrides) or pure metals (e.g. aluminium).

- Coatings formed by compounds of metals with non-metals have thicknesses of the order of several micrometers, are very hard, wear resistant, with an attractive golden or gray color. They are bound to the substrate by adhesion, very rarely by adhesion and diffusion. Depending on the method of deposition of the metal vapour, these coatings are divided into

  (a) **Electroless Vapour Deposition :** These are usually metal coatings, obtained by thermal vaporization of the coating material and its electroless deposition in the non-ionized state, e.g. silver, aluminium. They are used as reflectors in optical and thermal devices.

  (b) **Ion Vapour Deposition :** Deposition of metal vapours from a gas which is electrically ionized; these are mainly composed of carbides, nitrides or borides, applied as technical coatings with high wear resistance, but also sometimes as decorative and optical.

8.3.2 Selection of Coating for Wear and Corrosion Resistance

(a) For Gears, where the Motion is Combined Rolling and Sliding, the Main Options are :

- Case hardening, that is, carburizing or carbonitriding, of low-carbon steels to give high hardness and wear resistance.
- Local surface hardening of medium-carbon steels to give maximum load capacity.
- Nitriding of alloy steels for lower loads.

(b) Oxidative Wear

If there is a small, slow-speed relative sliding between the parts, this may also lead to a fretting-type wear condition, with the oxidized wear debris trapped in the contact. It is common on chain links and wire ropes and sometimes occurs on pulleys.

The only viable solution for wire ropes is regular oil or grease soaking.

For parts under high loading, and that are traditionally made of highstrength engineering steels, there is usually no easy way to reduce the corrosive contribution to the wear process. The best approach is to increase the surface hardness so that it can resist the abrasion by the oxide debris.

For Example, Consider :

- Local surface hardening, for example, flame, induction, or laser for medium-carbon steels.

- Case hardening, for example, carburizing, carbonitriding for low carbon steels.
- Nitriding or nitrocarburizing if the loads are not too high and the steel has some alloying elements such as chromium or molybdenum.

(c) Corrosive Wear :

If there is concern about corrosion, then both the corrosive medium and the temperature are important. Also, if the part is in contact with another metallic component of a dissimilar material, then galvanically assisted corrosion, which accelerates failure, is very possible.

For Outdoor, Normal Atmospheric Corrosion, Consider :

- Hot dip galvanizing, which can provide prolonged protection even in polluted environments.
- Thermally sprayed zinc or aluminium.
- Electrolytic zinc.
- Painting or powder coatings with appropriate surface preparation and priming.
- Heavy electrolytic nickel provided there are no defects in the coating.
- Electroless nickel-phosphorus coating.
- Aluminium ion plating.
- Phosphating for moderate protection.
- Anodizing, preferably sealed, for aluminium alloys.

For More Hostile Environments, including marine and aerospace where galvanic corrosion will be a major concern, consider :

- Hot dip galvanizing, which will provide moderate protection.
- Thermally sprayed zinc or aluminium for moderate protection.
- Electrolytic zinc or zinc-nickel alloy (10-14% Ni) coating followed by chromate passivation and an organic topcoat.
- Painting, with appropriate preparation and priming, perhaps zinc or aluminium loaded.
- Cadmium plate, preferably chromate passivated for maximum protection.

(d) High-Temperature Oxidation and Corrosion

- The substrates for high-temperature corrosion applications are often superalloys, stainless steels, or titanium alloys. Protective coatings to be considered include :
- Diffusion chromizing for oxidation resistance upto 750 to 800°C.
- Diffusion aluminizing for protection against oxidation, carburizing, and sulfur and vanadium corrosion in chemical plants and gas turbines; can be effective above 800°C.

- Slurry/sinter formed ceramics (chromium oxide based) at temperatures upto 600°C.
- Thermally sprayed coatings, for example, MCrAlY corrosion protection layers and ceramic-based thermal barriers.

For Caustic Environments, consider :

- Slurry/sinter-formed ceramics (chromium oxide based).
- Thermally sprayed ceramics, for example, chromium oxide, alumina, preferably sealed.
- Cadmium plate, preferably chromate passivated for moderate protection.
- Electroless nickel.
- Heavy electrolytic nickel plating.

For Acidic Environments, consider :

- Slurry/sinter-formed ceramics (chromium oxide based).
- Thermally sprayed ceramics, for example, chromium oxide, alumina, preferably sealed.

8.3.3 Properties and Parameters of Coating

8.3.3.1 Geometrical Parameters of Coatings

Geometrical parameters of coatings include thickness, three-dimensional structure of the surface, unevenness and coating defects.

- **Thickness :**

Coating thickness is the basic parameter on which protective properties, decorative and technical properties significantly depend. Porosity, tightness, corrosion resistance and mechanical strength all depend on the appropriate coating thickness. Besides, for different types of coatings, this thickness has a different effect on usable properties. For example, protective properties of coatings increase with the rise of thickness, similarly to wear resistance.

- **Three-Dimensional Structure of the Surface :**

The three-dimensional structure of the coating surface is the result of the coating process, dependent on the method or technique used, on defects formed during the deposition and on substrate roughness.

- **Surface Unevenness :**

Surface unevenness of the coating is described by the same parameters as those used in the description of surface layers.

- **Defects of the Three-Dimensional Structure :**

Defects of the three-dimensional structure, which are simply coating defects, all have the same character as those of the surface layer The most frequent defects, common to both surface layers and coatings, are blemishes, scratches, cracks and porosity.

8.3.3.2 Geometric and Physico-Chemical Parameters of Coatings

Among the most important geometric and physico-chemical parameters are those which describe coating properties, such as :

- Relating to energy, mainly surface energy,
- Relating to radiation, mainly reflection and emissivity, and significantly less often (only for selected types of coatings) : radiation transmittance,
- Catalytic (dependent on degree of surface development and coating components which accelerate or retard chemical reactions),
- Thermophysical, mainly thermal conductivity and solderability.

8.3.3.3 Physico-chemical Parameters of Coatings

- **General Characteristic :**

Physico-chemical properties of coatings differ from those of coating materials from which they are made. Properties of metallic materials in the bulk state, i.e. as obtained in metallurgical processes, are usually different from the properties of coatings manufactured from them.

- **Structure of Metallic Coatings :**

Metallic coatings may be generated by crystallization of coating materials from solutions or, in vacuum, from metal vapors, by crystallization of a metallic bath or of a drop of coating material on the substrate surface, by chemical deposition or by spraying earlier formed ductile particles on the substrate surface. In each case, the structure of the coating - even when depositing always the same coating material on the same substrate material - will differ, depending on method used and deposition parameters.

- **Residual Stresses :**

These stresses are formed in coatings as the result of differences in thermal expansion coefficients of substrate and coating materials, as well as significant defects in the structure of the coating material. Residual stresses may play a positive or a negative role, depending on their character. Usually, compressive stresses are favorable, while tensile stresses are unfavorable. In order to reduce residual stresses of the first kind, multi-layered coatings are deposited, comprising a composition of layers with successively changing thermal expansion coefficients, relative to the substrate material. Residual stresses may be reduced by the selection of appropriate materials and process parameters.

- **Adhesion :**

Adherence of coatings to the substrate or of layers of multi-layer coatings to each other, described by the force necessary to detach the coating from the substrate or layers from each other, reflects the character of the dominating bond.

- **Hardness :**

Hardness of coatings is one of the most often determined parameters. For different coatings, it obviously differs and depends on the coating material and its structure. It varies within a very broad range, from the hardness of soft rubber to that of diamond Hardnesses of electroplated coatings are usually higher than those of same metals obtained by metallurgical means.

- **Ductility :**

The **ductility** of metal coatings, the equivalent of which in painted coatings is **elasticity**, is understood as the susceptibility of the coating material to plastic deformations without loss of cohesion (cracks, delaminations, etc.).

- **Electrical Properties :**

Electrical properties of coatings may vary and may pertain to conduction of electric current (electrical conductivity) or the ability to resist its flow (electrical resistivity), properties which insulate the object from the environment (electrical insulating power), resistance to electrical breakthrough and others. Metallic coatings are conductors or resistors, while non-metallic coatings are insulators.

- **Magnetic Properties :**

Magnetic properties are exhibited by some metallic coatings containing ferromagnetics, mainly iron, cobalt, nickel and their alloys with phosphorus.

8.3.3.4 Service Properties of Coatings

The most important properties of coatings directly related to service are anticorrosion, decorative and tribological. They are described by the same parameters as corresponding properties of the surface layer.

8.3.3.4.1 Anti-Corrosion Properties

- **Types of Corrosion :**

Besides static and dynamic loads from extraneous forces, and the effect of friction, corrosion is one of the main hazards to which all structural materials are exposed during service.

- **Corrosion Resistance :**

Ensuring protection against corrosion, i.e. imparting corrosion resistance, is the fundamental function of the majority of coatings. By corrosion resistance we understand it to be the ability of coatings to withstand the effects of different types of corrosion.

- **Porosity :**

Porosity is a characteristic of coatings, manifest by the existence in them of pores. It is usually determined by the ratio of joint volume of pores to the total volume of the coating.

- **Bulging :**

Bulging is the rise of volume of the paint coating due to absorption of liquids, most frequently of water. It will depend on the surface tension and the dielectric constant of the bulging liquid if dissolution, bulging, or solvation will take place or not.

- **Permeability :**

Permeability is the ability to allow fluids to pass through a paint coating, due to porosity. It is closely connected with the ability of an organic coating to bulge. In the case of paint coatings, the focus is mainly on permeability of water vapour. Permeability of a coating by water vapor depends on air humidity and temperature and rises with their increase

8.3.3.4.2 Decorative Properties

- **External Appearance :**

All coatings, to a greater or lesser extent, feature decorative values, but special decorative properties are required of decorative coatings, as well as protective-decorative paint, electroplated and vacuum deposited coatings. The basic criterion of a coating's decorative value is its external appearance.

- **Color :**

The concept of color has two meanings :
  - That of a physical property of light from a coating illuminated by electromagnetic radiation in the visible range (of 0.36 to 0.76 µm),
  - That of a psychological property of a visual sensation which allows the observer to distinguish differences in light stimuli caused by differences in the spectral distribution of the stimulus; visible radiation reflected by the coating surface (or its external layer) enters the eye and stimulates photosensitive elements of the macula, giving a sensation of color.

- **Luster :**

Luster is a property of the surface of a smooth coating (or surface layer) consisting of oriented reflection of radiation falling on it in such a way that clear images of bright objects are formed in the field of vision of the observer.

- **Coverability :**

Coverability describes the degree of coverage of the substrate by the coating material.

- **Specific Decorative Properties :**

Among specific decorative properties of coatings, pertaining primarily to paint coatings.

8.4 OTHER BEARINGS

  - Porous Bearing
  - Foil Bearing
  - Lobe Bearing
  - Hybrid Bearing

8.4.1 Porous Bearing

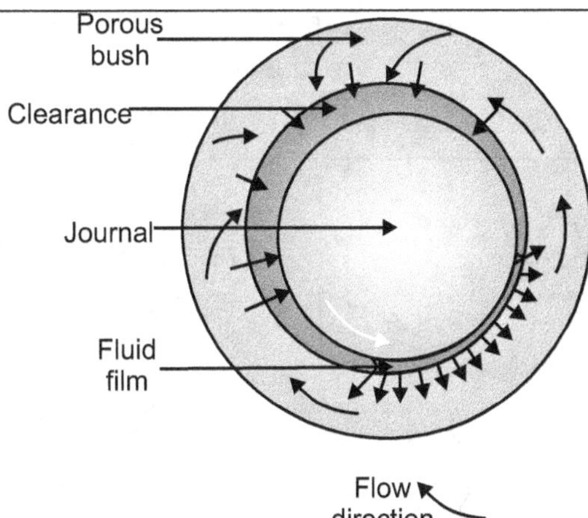

Fig. 8.12 : Structure of porous bearing

(Source : Report by Sietze van Buuren, KIT scientific publishing 2013)

The first hydrodynamic model for a porous journal bearing was presented by Morgan and Cameron. The distinguishing property of a porous bearing is its porous bush. This bush usually is made from sintered bronze or iron, Porous bearings are maintenance free, offer high precision, produce low noise levels and possess low friction values, all for relatively low production costs. They do not need continuous lubrication therefore their structure is simple and they also reduce costs. Despite these good properties porous bearings are not able to carry high loads and here solid journal bearings or ball bearings are the preferred alternative.

Due to its porosity the porous bush can absorb lubricant and sustain a lubricant flow as shown in Fig. 8.12 above. Typically fluid is pressed into the bush where a fluid film has formed and exits into the clearance outside the fluid film extent. Pressure formation still is very similar to classical journal bearings : due to an eccentric displacement and/or motion of the journal pressure will typically build up where the clearance converges and it will rapidly decrease in the diverging part of the clearance where pressure is for the most part atmospheric or depends on the surrounding pressure. However, lubricant circulation in the clearance and the bush as well as fluid exchange through the porous-fluid interface have an important impact on the fluid film extent and influence porous bearing characteristics significantly.

An important parameter of the porous material is permeability, which is the ability of the material to transmit fluid. For low Reynolds numbers flow through a porous material can be described with Darcy's law. Darcy's law relates the fluid's flow velocity to its pressure and will simplify to the Laplace equation of pressure, when the permeability of the porous material and viscosity of the fluid are assumed isotropic and constant.

The hydrodynamic load capacity and the equilibrium position of a solid journal bearing and three porous journal bearings are presented in the Fig. 8.13 below. The stiffness and damping coefficients of three types of porous journal bearings in comparison with a solid journal bearing are also shown in Fig. 8.13 below.

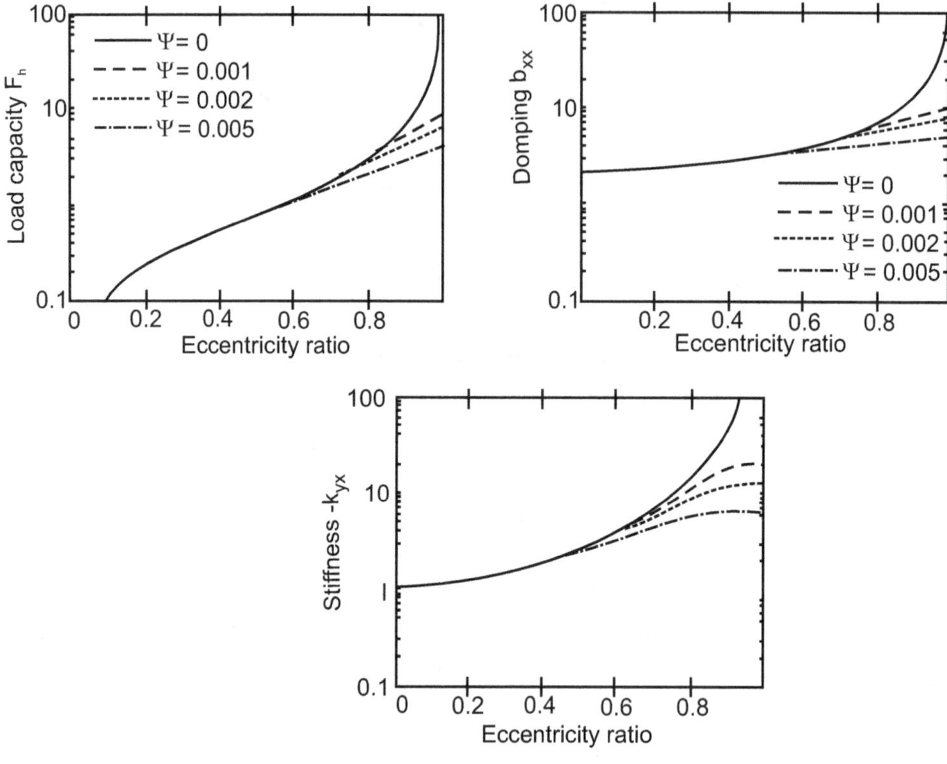

Fig. 8.13

It is clear that for higher eccentricity ratios (about $\varepsilon > 0.5$) the behavior of the porous journal bearing model differs significantly to that from the solid journal bearing. Not only the load capacity but also the damping and stiffness coefficients are lower compared to the solid journal bearing.

Due to oil seepage into the porous material pressure build-up is significantly lower for higher eccentricity ratios, which influences the stiffness and damping properties of the fluid film.

When the eccentricity ratio tends to one, the load capacity, the stiffness and the damping coefficients tend to infinity for the solid journal bearing, but approach a finite value for the porous bearings.

The surface roughness will start to noticeably influence the hydrodynamic pressure and that asperity contacts will generate additional contact pressure for porous journal bearings.

Porous-Fluid Interface :

To capture the essential behavior in a porous journal bearing, it is crucial that flow between the porous bush and the fluid film is incorporated adequately. The most important interactions are continuity of pressure and flow in radial direction. Additionally, continuity of flow in axial and circumferential direction can be demanded at the interface.

8.4.2 Foil Bearing

A foil bearing comprises a foil element which overlays the internal surface of the bearing sleeve as shown in Fig. 8.14 below. The viscoelastic foil overlay is fitted in the bearing sleeve at a single point along the sleeve's circumference. During normal operation, the bearing's functional behavior is similar to that of a traditional gas bearing. During overload, the journal hits the foil surface. Owing to its viscoelastic properties, the foil absorbs the energy displaced in the radial direction.

This simple solution does not differ significantly from traditional journal bearings. Various structural improvements have been developed, one of which is shown in Fig. 8.15 below. One layer of viscoelastic foil has been replaced with a second foil level which is fitted in a similar manner, but the foil element is long enough to wrap the internal diameter of the sleeve several times, creating a foil spiral inside the bearing. The foil is made of beryl bronze (in both cases). Spiral layers are separated with numerous copper wires. The resulting bearing can operate at the speed of around 220 000 rpm. The structure comprising several foil elements is presented on the right side of Fig. 8.15 below.

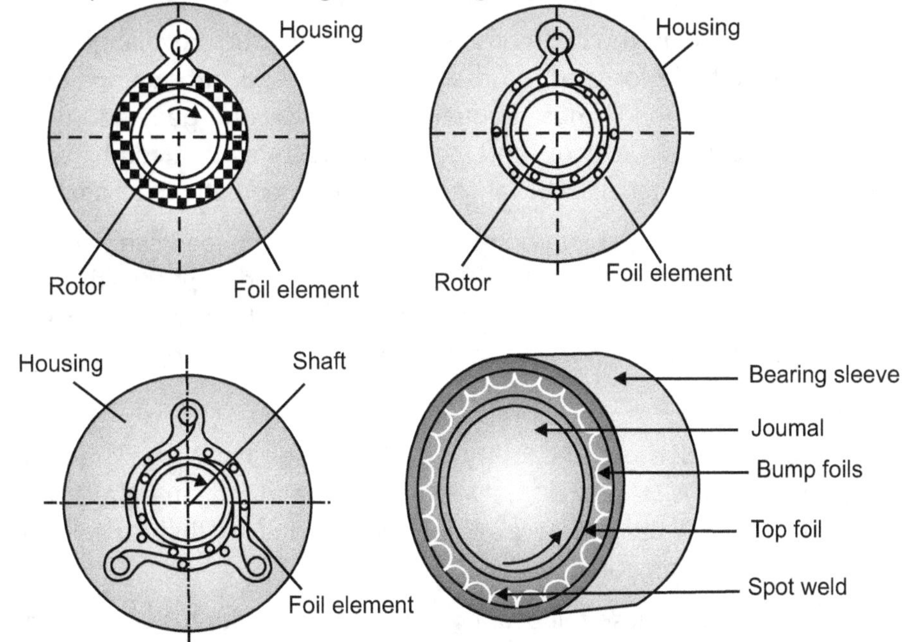

Fig. 8.14 : Structure of foil bearing
(Source : On the basis of XIONG et al. 1997)

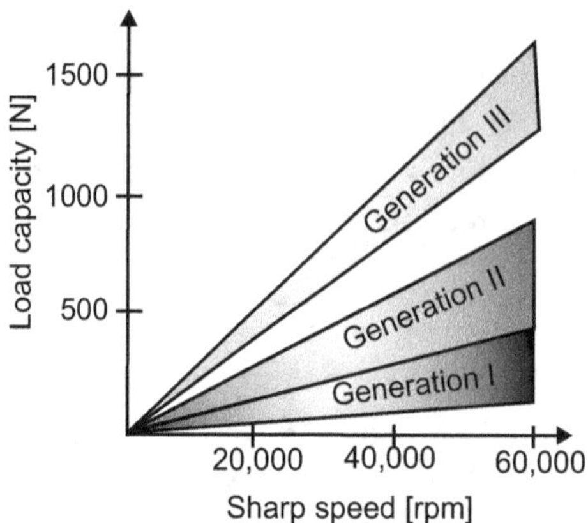

Fig. 8.15 : Load capacity of three generations of foil bearings
(Source : Report of DELLACORTE 2003)

First generation foil bearings are bearings whose load-carrying structure comprises only viscoelastic foil or a foil set whose properties are fixed in all directions. Such bearings are fit for use only in very small devices that are subject to small load, such as fans. The use of first generation foil bearings is limited by, among others, the properties of materials applied in foil production. In addition to delivering a high level of elasticity, foil elements have to be resistant to friction wear at high loads and speeds as well as to extreme temperatures. There are practically no materials that meet all of the above requirements.

In second generation bearings, the geometry of the support structure changes in one of the directions, which are suitable for use in turbocompressors and turbopumps during 1980s. Variability in the axial direction is most frequently noted. Second generation foil bearings paved the way to the development of more complex structures that combine the physical properties of the available materials with variable bump foil geometry in all directions.

In third generation foil bearings, changes in the properties of the load carrying structure are observed in minimum two directions. Due to their high load capacity, third generation bearings are used in micro-power plants, microturbines and devices in which first and second generation bearings could not be applied due to heavy load constraints.

Advantages of Foil Bearing :

- **Low Maintenance and High Reliability :** Foil bearings have an extremely long life because there is no physical contact between the foils and the journal/disc at operating speed. Additionally, foil bearings are highly reliable due to their simple design and minimal number of moving parts.

- **Zero Contamination :** Because foil bearings are lubricated with the process gas in which they operate, no petroleum based lubricants are required which could contaminate the process gas.

- **Wide Temperature Range :** Many petroleum based lubricants breakdown at extremely high temperatures and become too viscous at extremely low temperature. Because foil bearings are lubricated with the process gas in which they operate, they can be effectively used at temperature extremes.

- **High Speed Operation :** Because there is no physical contact between the foils and the journal/disc at operating speed, foil bearings do not limit the operating speed of the machine in which they operate. Greater operating speeds improve aerodynamic efficiency and do not adversely affect bearing life. Additionally, greater operating speeds increase the bearing's load capacity, stability, and vibration/shock load capacity.

Disadvantages :

- **Development Effort :** Foil bearings are not a commercially available product that can simply be ordered from a catalog. Each bearing is designed for a specific application which required development time and expense. However due to their simple design and limited number of moving parts, foil bearings can be very economical at production quantities.

- **Low Speed Operation :** Because foil bearings depends on sufficient hydrodynamic pressure for proper operation, machines that spend time operating at low speed are poor candidates for foil bearings. Low speeds, as related to foil bearings, are typically less than 40,000 rpm or a Sommerfeld number that is less than 6.

- **Start/Stop Wear :** Because foil bearings experience wear during start-up and shut-down, machines with frequent start/stop cycles are potentially poor candidates for foil bearings.

8.4.3 Lobe Bearing

Multilobe journal bearings are applied mainly in high speed rotating machinery, e.g. turbo compressors, turbines or in grinding machines. Hydrodynamic journal bearings can properly operate in the strictly determined range of rotational speeds upper boundary of which is determined by the permissible temperature of operation and the possibilities of heat conduction, but the lower determines the occurrence of fluid friction. It is convenient to apply such bearings in the grinding machines. However, to operate the grinding machine spindle bearing system at proper temperature it is important to apply the bearings assuring comparatively low temperatures of oil film. Using multilobe journal bearings with 3, 4 or 6 lobes of continuous can fulfill such condition of operation or non-continuous bore profile.

8.4.4 Lobe Bearing Geometry

The fixed lobe bearing is made up of a number of fixed circular arc segments called **lobes** or **pads**. The lobes are separated by axial lubricant supply grooves. A three-lobe bearing is sketched to illustrate the parameters used to describe the bearing geometry. Clearances are exaggerated in the Fig. 8.16 for illustrative purposes.

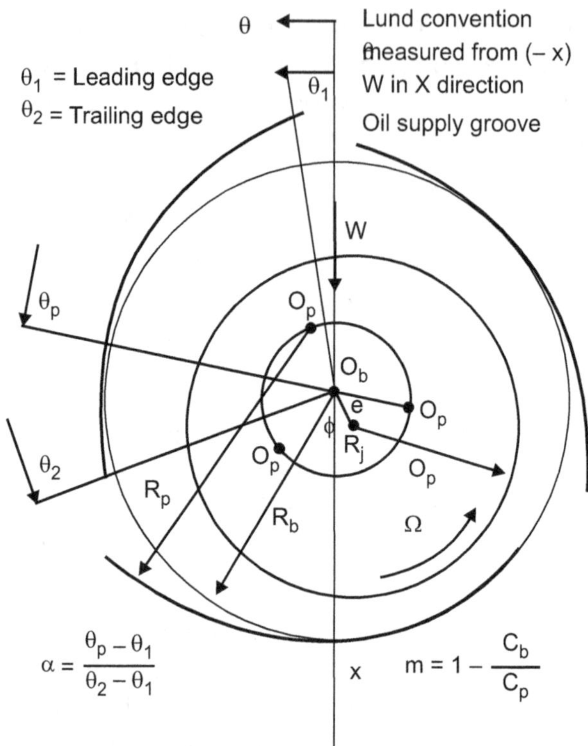

Fig. 8.16

The journal static equilibrium position is defined by the journal eccentricity (e) and attitude angle (ϕ). Under dynamic conditions, the journal is oscillating with small amplitudes around this equilibrium position. However, the bearing dynamic coefficients (stiffness and damping coefficients) can be calculated in any coordinate system (x,y,z) by specifying a Coefficient Coordinate Angle in the bearing input data. The Coordinate Angle is measured from the X-axis (used to describe the bearing geometry and the load vector) to x-axis (used to describe the bearing coefficients). The bearing radius at minimum clearance (R_b) for a centered shaft can be described as the radius of the largest shaft that could be inserted into the bearing. A circle drawn based on R_b is referred to as a bearing base circle.

For a positive preloaded bearing, pad radius (R_p) is greater than bearing radius (R_b) and the circular pads are moved inward the bearing center. Thus, when the journal is centered in the bearing, the pads are loaded by geometry effect. The fraction of the distance between pad center of curvature and bearing center to pad radial clearance is called **Preload** :

$$m = \frac{(C_p - C_b)}{C_p} = 1 - \frac{C_b}{C_p}$$

When the preload is zero, the pad centers of curvature coincide with the bearing center and the bearing is cylindrical. When the preload has a value of 1, the shaft touches all the pads and the bearing minimum radial clearance is zero. Typical preload value for a fixed lobe bearing ranges from 0.4 to 0.75.

Another key parameter used to describe the preloaded bearing geometry is the fraction of converging pad length to the full arc length. This parameter is called **Offset** or **Tilt** and is given by the following expression :

$$\alpha = \frac{(\theta_p - \theta_1)}{(\theta_2 - \theta_1)} = \frac{X_b}{X}$$

The value of offset is meaningful only when the bearing is preloaded. At θ_p, the bearing has a minimum clearance for a centered shaft and the lobe arc intersects with bearing base circle. A lobe which is symmetrically located with respect to the centered journal, i.e. offset = 0.5, is defined as having no **lobe tilt** and the clearance space has equal convergent and divergent arcs. An offset of 0.5 is commonly used to accommodate the reversal rotation of the shaft and also to avoid the problem of the bearing being installed backwards. An offset less than 0.5 increases the diverging film thickness and is not desirable. Typical offset ranges from 0.5 to 1.0. For an offset halves bearing, the offset could be larger than 1, depending on the position of pad center of curvature.

8.4.5 Hybrid Bearing

Hybrid bearings have rings made of bearing steel and rolling elements made of bearing grade silicon nitride (Si_3N_4). Because the silicon nitride ceramic material is such an excellent electrical insulator, hybrid bearings can be used to effectively insulate the housing from the shaft in both AC and DC motors as well as in generators.

In addition to being an excellent insulator, hybrid bearings have higher speed capabilities and provide longer bearing service life under the same operating conditions than same sized bearings with steel rolling elements. Hybrid bearings also perform extremely well under vibrating or oscillating conditions. Often, it is not necessary to preload the bearing or apply a special grease under these conditions.

As Hybrid Bearings have steel rings and ceramic balls, Si_3N_4 Ball is the most popular for the balls as it has only 40 percent of the density of bearing steel but is much harder giving greater wear resistance. Zirconia is heavier with 75 percent of the density of steel so is less suitable for hybrid bearings. Hybrid bearings are also capable of higher speeds. Sometimes, excessive claims are made about the high speed capabilities of hybrid bearings. They can run faster than all steel bearings due to the lower centrifugal force generated by the ceramic balls but this is partially counteracted by the lower elasticity of the balls. As the balls are harder, the contact area between the balls and the raceway is smaller which causes a higher contact pressure. Under load, this can cause the raceways to wear faster than they would with steel balls. The speed increase for hybrid bearings is approximately 30 percent with adequate lubrication. Hybrid bearings can also operate better with limited lubrication as the lower friction material generates less heat but running speed should be reduced. Hybrid bearings are also less subject to ball skidding under inital acceleration due to the lower ball density.

Factors that Influence Hybrid Bearing Performance

- **Insulating Properties**

As a non-conductive material, silicon nitride protects the rings from electric current damage and, therefore, can extend bearing service life in applications like AC and DC motors and generators, where there are electric currents that could damage the bearing.

- **Lower Density**

The density of a bearing grade silicon nitride rolling element is 60% lower than a same-sized rolling element made of bearing steel. Lower weight means lower inertia – and that translates into superior behaviour during rapid starts and stops, as well as higher speed capabilities.

- **Lower Friction**

The lower density of a silicon nitride rolling element, combined with its low coefficient of friction, significantly reduces bearing temperature at high speeds. Cooler running extends the service life of both the bearing and the lubricant.

Hybrid Bearings have Advantages Relative to Steel Bearings

- **High Speed**

Hybrid bearings can reach 3,500,000 DN in the condition of oil-mist lubrication, and can reach 1,200,000 DN in the condition of grease lubrication, this owes to the greatly reduction of relative slip, wear extent and heat productivity.

- **Long Service Life**

The service life of hybrid bearings is 3 to 5 times of that of steel bearings in suitable working conditions.

- **Self Lubricating**

Even in the condition of bad lubricating or no lubrication, hybrid bearings can ensure the bearings work regularly owe to its self lubricating.

- **Corrosion Resistant**

Hybrid bearings have good corrosion resistance, and can work regularly in the condition of corrosion.

- **High Rigidness**

The elastic ration of ceramics is 1.5 times of that of bearing steel, this highly increases the rigidity of bearing.

Low Friction Moment

Ceramics materials have low friction force, even in the condition of boundary lubrication, the surfaces are still very smooth, so its friction force is low and the rotation friction moment is low, also.

- **Wear Resistant**

The microhardness of ceramics can reach HV1700 kg/mm^2, this highly increases the wear-resistance of bearings.

- **Light in Weight**

The weight of ceramics is lower 60% than that of steel, this decreases highly the centrifugal force and the whole bearing's weight.

- **Special Performance**

All ceramic parts are non-magnetic and insulated.

EXERCISE

1. Explain lubrication in metal working.   **[P.U. Dec. 2010, 6 Marks]**
2. Give considerations while selecting a lubricant for metal working.
                                                                  [P.U. June 2009, 4 Marks]
3. Explain lubrication requirements in case of :
   (i) Rolling operation
   (ii) Forging operation
   (iii) Drawing operation
   (iv) Extrusion   **[P.U. Dec. 2008, 4 Marks; June 2011, 10 Marks]**
4. State various lubricants required for :
   (i) Rolling of steels (low carbon) and stainless steel
   (ii) Forging of aluminium, lead, magnesium and titanium
   (iii) Drawing of aluminium, steels, copper
   (iv) Extrusion operation on aluminium, nickel, titanium.
5. Why lubrication is required in metal working ? Explain the type of lubrication in metal working.   **[P.U. Dec. 2009, 4 Marks]**
6. State desirable properties of bearing materials. List few suitable bearing materials.
                                                                  [P.U. Dec. 2010, 6 Marks]
7. Explain in brief standard requirements for selection of a bearing material.
8. Write short notes on :
   (i) Score resistance   (ii) Deformability
   (iii) Structure   (iv) Corrosive resistance
9. List various bearing materials.
10. Explain various materials for bearings with their advantages, disadvantages and give atleast two applications of each material.
11. Write short notes on :
    (i) Babbitts   (ii) Trimetal bearings
    (iii) Sintered-metal bearings   **[P.U. June 2010, 8 Marks]**
    (iv) Carbon-graphite as bearing material
    (v) Ceramics and cermets as bearing material
    (vi) Teflon and rubber as bearing material   **[P.U. June 2010, 8 Marks]**
    (vii) Bi and Ti metal bearings   **[P.U. June 2010, 8 Marks]**
12. Explain bearing constructions with different oil groove patterns.
13. Give brief classification of seals.
14. Explain static seals and dynamic seals.   **[P.U. June 2009, 8 Marks]**
15. Discuss requirements of oil seals.
16. Explain oil seals used in lubrication practice.

---

17. Explain in brief :
(i)   Lip seals   (ii) Circumferential split-ring seals
(iii) O-rings   (iv) Labyrinth seal
(v)   Felt seals
18. Write short notes on :   **[P.U. Dec. 2008, 10 Marks; June 2011, 9 Marks]**
(i)   Oil seals   **[P.U. Dec. 2010, 8 Marks]**
(ii) Gaskets
(iii) Bearing materials
19. Explain different types of gaskets in brief.
20. Discuss in brief mechanics of tyre-road interaction.
21. Define the term 'Surface Engineering'. Discuss basic requirements of surface engineering with reference to growth industry.
22. State the significance and applications of Surface Engineering.
23. Explain the concept and scope of 'Surface Engineering'.
24. Explain in brief :
    (a)   Diffusion
    (b)   Coating- Eletroplating and Electroless coatings
    (c)   Hot dip coating
    (d)   Metal spraying
    (e)   Cladded coating
    (f)   Crystallizing coating
25. Discuss relative advantages and limitations of above coatings.
26. Discuss on selection of coating for wear and corrosion resistance.
27. Explain geometrical parameters of coatings.
28. Explain geometric and physico-chemical parameters of coatings.
29. Give service properties of coatings.
30. Discuss service properties of coatings with reference to anti-corrosion and decoration.
31. Discuss the following bearing with their working principle, advantages, disadvantages and applications of
    (a)   Porous bearing
    (b)   Foil bearing
    (c)   Lobe bearing
    (d)   Hybrid bearing
32. Define the term 'road-grip' and discuss rolling friction model.
33. Explain the concept of 'wheel on rail-rod'. Discuss the term 'shakedown limit' in brief.

✠ ✠ ✠

Marks: 30   **Time: 1 Hour**

---

1. (a) Explain the importance of 'Tribology' in the design of machine elements.

An oil of viscosity of 62 cP and relative density of 0.75 is used for lubrication. Convert the viscosity into centistokes, SUS and Pascal second units.

[5 M]

(b) Explain the basic modes of thick-film lubrication. Explain different types of lubricants.

[5 M]

OR

2. (a) Compare sliding contact bearings with rolling contact bearings.   **[5 M]**

(b) State the desirable properties of lubricants.

What are the additives ? Explain the different types of additives used in lubricating oils.   **[5 M]**

3. (a) State laws of friction. Enlist kinds of friction.   **[5 M]**

(b) Define wear. State assumptions made, prove Archard's equation of adhesive wear.

$$Q = k \cdot \frac{W}{3P_0}$$

and comment about magnitude of factor 'k'.

Comment on the range of values of cofactor 'k'.   **[5 M]**

OR

4. (a) Discuss 'Adhesion theory' of friction.   **[5 M]**

(b) Discuss methods of measuring wear. Enlist the factors affecting wear of metals. **[5 M]**

5. (a) Derive from basic principles two-dimensional Reynold's equation taking usual notations.   **[5 M]**

(b) The following data refers to a 360° hydrodynamic bearing :

    (i)   Radial load   =   3.5 kN

    (ii) Journal diameter   =   70 mm

    (iii) Bearing length   =   70 mm

    (iv) Journal speed   =   1450 rpm

    (v) Radial clearance   =   50 μm

    (vi) Viscosity of lubricant =   25 cP

    (vii) Density of lubricant   = 860 kg/m^3

    (viii) Specific heat of lubricant =   1.76 kJ/kg·°C

Assuming that the total heat generated in the bearing is carried by the total oil flow in the bearing, calculate :

(i) The minimum oil-film thickness.

(ii) The coefficient of friction.   **[5 M]**

OR

6. (a) Draw radial pressure distribution and axial pressure distribution for hydrodynamic journal bearing.

   Derive :
$$H = C (1 + \epsilon \cos \theta)$$

   where, h =   Oil-film thickness

                        =   Radial clearance

                  ϵ =   Eccentricity ratio

                  θ =   Angle measured from maximum oil-film thickness   **[5 M]**

(b) Write short notes on :

   (i) Sommerfeld Number

   (ii) Design considerations in hydrodynamic journal bearing   **[5 M]**

Sample Question Paper for
End-Semester Examination

Marks: 70   **Time: 2.30 Hours**

1. (a) What are causes of friction? What are laws of dry friction?

Explain the tribological design of seals and gaskets. Determine the viscosity of the lubricant in centipoise having viscosity 160 SUS and specific gravity 0.86.   **[5 M]**

(b) Explain in brief the following : (Any 5)

   (i)   Hydrodynamic lubrication

   (ii) Bearing materials

   (iii) Recycling of used oil

   (iv) Fatigue wear

   (v) Rabinowicz Quantitative Theory for abrasive wear

   (vi) Raimondi and Boyd method   **[5 M]**

2. (a) Discuss desirable properties of bearing materials.   **[5 M]**

(b) Explain working principle of hydrodynamic thrust bearing.

Derive an equation for maximum pressure and load-carrying capacity for Rayleigh step bearing.   **[5 M]**

3. (a) Explain principle of operation of hydrostatic bearing. State it's applications and advantages.

The following data refers to a hydrostatic thrust bearing :

(i)	Shaft diameter = 400 mm,	(ii)	Recess diameter = 250 mm
(iii)	Shaft speed = 720 r.p.m.,	(iv)	Supply pressure = 5 N/mm^2
(v)	Film thickness = 0.15 mm,	(vi)	Viscosity of lubricant = 30 cP
(vii)	Specific heat of lubricant = 1.76 kJ/kg°C		
(viii)	Specific gravity of lubricant = 0.86		

Calculate :

(i)	Load-carrying capacity of the bearing	(ii)	Oil flow rate
(iii)	Total power loss	(iv)	Temperature rise

Assume that total power loss in the bearing is converted into frictional heat.   **[10 M]**

(b) Derive an equation for load-carrying capacity for given instantaneous velocity of approach and film thickness in case of circular plate approaching a plane.   **[6 M]**

OR

4. (a) Derive expression for flow rate through rectangular slot. What are assumptions made while deriving the equation? **[8 M]**

   (b) Give practical situations where hydrostatic squeeze-film lubrication can be observed.

   A rectangular plate having length to width ratio of 0.25 is approaching towards a fixed plane with an initial oil-film thickness between the plate and plane as 0.05 mm. Load supported by plate is 12 kN for 4 seconds. The viscosity of oil is 35 cP. Calculate bearing length and width for final oil-film thickness as 0.01 mm. Also find maximum pressure value. **[8 M]**

5. (a) Explain the phenomenon of elastohydrodynamic lubrication. State the applications where elastohydrodynamic lubrication is observed. **[6 M]**

   (b) Derive governing differential equation for gas-lubricated bearings. Explain merits and demerits of gas bearings. **[10 M]**

OR

6. (a) Discuss the term 'Width of contact of two cylinders under radial load', with reference to elastohydrodynamic lubrication. **[5 M]**

   (b) Explain principles of air bearings. State its merit and applications. **[6 M]**

   (c) Explain working principle of Active Magnetic bearing. State its advantages **[5 M]**

7. (a) Explain lubrication requirements in case of :

(i)	Rolling operation	(ii)	Forging operation
(iii)	Drawing operation	(iv)	Extrusion **[8 M]**

   (b) Discuss the terms

      i.   Mechanics of tyre –road interaction.
      ii.   Wheel on rail-road **[5 M]**

   (c) What is surface Engineering? Explain Hot-dip coating. **[5 M]**

OR

8. (a) Give considerations while selecting a lubricant for metal working. **[5 M]**

   (b) Discuss potential properties and parameters of coating. **[5 M]**

   (c) Discuss in brief (Any 2)

      i.   Porous bearings
      ii.   Hybrid bearings
      iii.   Lobe bearings **[8 M]**

✠ ✠ ✠